Eating Hillary's Brain…

Eating Hillary's Brain…

Or, how a courageous, astute, kind and driven statesman acquired a taste for conscience-challenged hyper-capitalist basal ganglia & amygdala

ROB ETHINGTON

ISBN: 0996626824
ISBN 13: 9780996626828

To the late (?) Franklin Delano Roosevelt and his beloved visionary bride...

To Bill Moyers, Michael Moore, Tim DeChristopher, Bill McKibben, Matt Taibbi, William Greider, Josh Fox, Thomas Frank, Jim Hightower, Tavis Smiley, the late Edward Abbey, the late Howard Zinn, the late Martin Luther King Jr., Adam Veale and everyone else with the courage to speak truth to power, even when doing so risks unjust imprisonment (or worse)...

And to the long-suffering, kind-hearted, benefit-of-the-doubt-giving, hard-working woman who brought me into this world (who's also a huge fan of Bill Moyers) and, along with my father, taught me the meaning of true devotion to principles and to persons of principle...

And to my beloved son and daughter, who continue to inspire my earnest hope for the future...

And to my co-worker Sylvia, who always has something nice to say about my writing, my co-worker Vicki Jo, whose ability to almost always see the bright side in everything should be a required personality component for everyone and my co-worker Pag ("padge"), who deserves so much more from life than she usually gets...

And to the Love of My Life – who someday may <u>yet</u> "friend" me on Facebook...

Characters

- Percival (Percy) "Scruples" Van Mullder, nee Franklin Delano Roosevelt, returned from the dead ex-President
- Perry Ishmael "Pongo" Podrowski, holder of multiple jobs, including fast food, National Park Service interpretive tour guide/security officer and dog walker; also community college student; son of
- Melanie O'Leary Podrowski, deceased, and
- Phil Podrowski, health department inspector and shop steward
- Melanie's parents include Orvis O'Leary, a retired high school band director and
- Karin Engebritstian O'Leary, a retired high school journalism and English teacher.
- Phil's parents include Tom Podrowski, a retired grocer and former farmer and
- Annie Wilson Podrowski, a retired neurologist.
- Harry Peterson, holder of multiple jobs, including fast food and electronics store clerk; best friend of Pongo Podrowski and son of
- Mel Peterson, county roads department supervisor, and
- Dr. Cherisse Peterson, involuntarily-retired neurosurgeon now volunteering for U.S. Public Health Service.
- Gordon Sancho Graham, laid off Wall Street investment analyst and his buddy,
- Denny D'Amato, also a laid off Wall Street investment analyst.
- Heather Griffin, social work graduate student and part-time welfare eligibility worker; she's Pongo's long-time girlfriend. Her parents include
- Penelope Mitsuhama Duarte, confidential secretary to H. Fenster Rupphauser, of Whittmyer Industries, New York City, granddaughter of

now-deceased Japanese-American U.S. citizens detained in a concentration camp in Idaho during World War II; her second husband is

- Mitch Duarte, semi-retired Homeland Security Air Marshal.
- Pablo Justicia, Pongo's FDR Presidential Library and Museum supervisor; a naturalized citizen who grew up in El Salvador.
- Dr. Bianca Swanson, long-time girlfriend of Harry Peterson; she's a full-time medical student; her parents are
- Dr. Sam Swanson, semi-retired neurosurgeon/pathologist and
- Lucinda Rodriguez Swanson, FDR Center's National Archives director.
- Mark Tomkinson, History Department professor, Dutchess Community College.
- Idris M'Benga, full-time job development counselor and welfare eligibility worker for Dutchess County; close friend of Pongo Podrowski and Harry Peterson; son of
- Eugene M'Benga, Poughkeepsie, NY Sanitation Department manager and
- Estelle Suzuki M'Benga, family law attorney
- Holly Van Arsdale, Franklin's potential love interest at Poughkeepsie H.S. (daughter of Bud & Elinore)
- Nancy Perez, Holly Van Arsdale's best friend.
- Chester H. "Chet" Dale, Franklin's supervisor at Adams Landscaping.
- Marcia Dirkenstack, USA-SBR project manager.
- Sally Rose Cummings, Mormon pro-women priesthood activist.
- Billie Sue Wheeler, Sally Cumming's sister.
- Barry Menetto, NYC MTA subway supervisor.

Introduction

When Franklin Delano Roosevelt died on April 12, 1945 as the light at the end of the World War II tunnel was becoming fairly bright, he left undone a goal he had hoped his party and his country would embrace in the same way they had embraced his New Deal as he strove to lift up out of the Great Depression a country battered to a pulp by laissez faire capitalism. He proposed in his January 1944 State of the Union a Second Bill of Rights. That Second Bill of Rights would have ensured:

- The right to a useful and remunerative job in the industries or shops or farms or mines of the nation.
- The right to earn enough to provide adequate food and clothing and recreation.
- The right of every farmer to raise and sell his products at a return which will give him and his family a decent living.
- The right of every businessman, large and small, to trade in an atmosphere of freedom from unfair competition and domination by monopolies at home or abroad.
- The right of every family to a decent home.
- The right to adequate medical care and the opportunity to achieve and enjoy good health.
- The right to adequate protection from the economic fears of old age, sickness, accident, and unemployment.
- The right to a good education.

Unfortunately, FDR didn't survive long enough to shepherd his Second Bill of Rights through the byzantine process of amending the Constitution. In fact, as economic prosperity blossomed – for whites, at least – and anti-communist 'commie under every bed' paranoia poisoned minds in the 20-plus years after World War II, FDR's vision of "assuring equality in the pursuit of happiness" mostly faded into obscurity. Lyndon B. Johnson's War on Poverty and push for civil rights in the mid-'60s, though becoming monumental achievements, fell far short of what FDR had envisioned. Just two years ago, the U.S. Supreme Court proved how vulnerable a relatively straightforward law like the Voting Rights Act of 1965 could be to judicial review as it gutted voting rights protections in nine states which had long histories of erecting racist barriers to African-Americans' and Hispanics' access to the ballot box. (Remember: the State of Texas' Attorney General *proudly* announced **the _same day_ the U.S. Supreme Court struck down those protections** that he would **immediately** begin enforcing the former slave state's toughest-in-the-nation voter-ID requirement law – despite *not a single instance of voter fraud* being documented in the state.)

Worse yet, with each passing decade, the leaders of FDR's party, the Democratic Party, decided again and again that the best strategy to entice "independent" voters was to emulate the party of Big Business, the Republicans (apologies for redundancy). Jimmy Carter began the trend, with his close alliance with uber-pragmatist-slash-closet Republican Al From, founder of the right-wing Democratic Leadership Council (DLC), characterized by the Rev. Jesse Jackson in 1991 as "Democrats for the Leisure Class."

But that trend went on steroids during the presidencies of Bill Clinton and Barack Obama – with some exceptions, of course, such as Clinton's increase in taxes on the wealthy in 1992 and Obama's semi-heroic economic stimulus programs in 2009-2010 necessitated by "W" Bush's Great Recession. Nevertheless, President Clinton gave unions and the rest of the middle class a royal ass-whipping with passage of NAFTA and the repeal of FDR's Glass-Steagall protections against banking and investment excesses (eventually facilitating the 2008 meltdown under "W" Bush). And President Obama expanded on "W" Bush's unconstitutional domestic spying, approved extra-judicial assassinations of U.S. citizens overseas (for alleged terrorist involvement) and has been pushing **hard** (despite strong resistance from his own party) for a semi-secret foreign trade agreement (the Trans-Pacific Partnership) *which would send even more decent-paying U.S. jobs overseas.* In addition, Obama has deported even more struggling Mexican and other Latino immigrants than "W" Bush did.

Bottom line: Wall Street and the U.S. Chamber of Commerce, with complicity from **both** major political parties (but mostly Republicans), have exacerbated our government's transition into a corporatocracy steered by plutocrats and oligarchs. There are only a relatively tiny number of true FDR-style progressives and liberals left in each chamber of Congress and they are all Democrats or independents.

The only thing keeping the radical right from shutting down hyper-popular programs like FDR's Social Security Administration is the sheer fear of backlash. If Wall Street had its way, Social Security would be permanently privatized out of existence and converted into a for-profit multi-tiered scheme manipulated daily by 'too-big-to-fail' finance brokerages. Wall Street already has gotten its way, more or less, with dooming the U.S. Postal Service via the 2006 Postal Accountability and Enhancement Act signed by "W" Bush, which requires retirement benefits to be funded *75 years in advance.* (To put that ludicrously punitive mandate into perspective, ask yourself how many homeowners can fund their house payments *even seven weeks* in advance.) In the eyes of Wall Street, and all Ayn Randians out there, if something **doesn't generate a profit** for someone, **it's an evil communist-slash-socialist plot** and must be stamped out.

The cancer of money in politics, furthermore, has wiped out the concept of a Congress made up of average folks and small farm agrarians. There is virtually **no one** in Congress now who isn't part of the top 1 percent in income. And from the day a new member of Congress takes office, her or his top priority is daily 'dialing for dollars' fundraising for the next campaign.

So, as one of the most closeted of Republicans who's passed herself off as a Democrat since her marriage – former Goldwater Girl Hillary Rodham Clinton – has been preparing these past several years to run for the Presidency, some simple thoughts occurred to me as I looked in August 2014 at a FDR Presidential Library and Museum Henry A. Wallace Visitor Center photo of Hillary on display (she was pictured appearing as a guest speaker in 2009 as she accepted a Four Freedoms Award there from the Roosevelt Institute during the Institute's Campus Networks Leadership Summit):

- *How would FDR feel about a committed corporatist and Wall Street crony like Ms. Rodham Clinton not only being an honored guest speaker at his Presidential Library and Museum, but also being the likely standard bearer of his party for the 2016 election?*
- *What if he could come back to life as Hillary was having the red carpet tacked down for her dynastic coronation as the Democrats' Presidential nominee?*
- *What would a resurrected FDR do to try and make a Second Bill of Rights a reality? And would a new understanding for him of post-World War II historical developments compel him to make that Second Bill of Rights more comprehensive?*
- *And how would he react if the likely 2016 Democratic standard bearer were to actively support **virtually none** of the provisions of his updated Second Bill of Rights?*

This book attempts to bring FDR back to life **and** breathe life back into his love of the hard-working poor and middle class folks whose kind-heartedness helped our nation overcome its darkest economic days. It's set in a sort of parallel universe in which most (but not all) facts of recent history are the same as what Americans have experienced over the past couple hundred years. It's an alternative reality featuring appearances by real-life persons from our *current* reality expressing themselves in ways that correspond with *that* alternative reality, self-expressions which they could reasonably be expected to provide in that alternative reality.

None of the real-life *non*-politician persons featured in the alternative reality displayed here have endorsed this book or expressed direct or indirect support for it (so far). Which is not to say that their support wouldn't be welcomed. But one of the author's principle hopes is that those real-life *non*-politician persons will find their portrayals in that alternative reality **not** conscience-shocking in any way. In fact, it's hoped that they will find their alternative-reality portrayals to be reasonably plausible, if not actually fairly sympathetic.

Make no mistake, though: the real-life **political** and **quasi-political** figures in this book's alternative reality have received no special considerations whatsoever. They are portrayed from the perspective of your average garden-variety progressive-slash-liberal observer who has been viscerally disgusted for decades at the Democratic Party's lack of leadership and unwillingness to hold the oligarchs and plutocrats accountable for playing their golden fiddles while the rest of the nation burns to its foundations – and, especially, for being all too willing to *join in* on the fiddle playing, even when their Orwellian opposition describes their efforts to emulate the 'R's' as "socialistic" (i.e., the evolution of Romneycare into the virtually identical health care industry-friendly, but supposedly 'socialistic,' Obamacare).

Think massive 2007-2008 Wall Street fraud combined with "W" Bush's admission to felony violations of FISA court domestic surveillance requirements followed by President Obama's **_insistence_** – when pressed by core supporters and independents to pursue criminal charges against "W" Bush & cronies – that it was crucial to "look forward instead of backward." Right. Remember, all you marijuana-possession convicts stuck in prison: your President says seeking criminal convictions *against rich white-collar offenders* is the same as "looking backward."

Characters in this book which do not bear the names of real-life public figures are *in no way intended* to be based on any real-life persons. Off the top of my head, I can't think of a single person in this book who's *exactly* like anyone I know in real life.

If there are any shortcomings in this book I'm more than willing to admit to, it's probably that I haven't featured the far right's efforts to make jokes. The reason I haven't done that is that their attempts to show humor – while hard-wrought and sometimes almost clever – are almost never actually funny, as Michael Moore has observed. And they themselves almost always are the ones who laugh the hardest at their own jokes. As though their forced laughter can intimidate others into laughing too. Which, sometimes, unfortunately, it does.

In any event, this **is** fiction. Through and through – well, *except for all the actual indisputable historical facts from our own current reality.*

Hope you find some enjoyment and mental stimulation in the following pages.

Rob Ethington photo, August 2014, Hyde Park, NY

Final resting place of Franklin and Eleanor Roosevelt on the grounds of their Springwood estate in Hyde Park, NY (See full color version of image on www.eatinghillarysbrain.com & www.eatinghillarysbrain.net)

Sprite: 1.a. A small or elusive supernatural being. b. An elflike person. 2.a. A ghost. b. Archaic. A soul. 3.a. *Powerful rare electrical discharge usually involving strong earthbound lightning during thunderstorms, with sprite discharge spreading upward 50 miles or more into space as photographed 7/6/89 by University of Minnesota scientists.* 4.a. A brand name of lemon-lime soft drink. (Emphasis added)

∗ ∗ ∗

Amygdala and basal ganglia, i.e., so-called "reptilian brain" in humans: speculation suggests these may be the most savory morsels of brain tissue for humans involuntarily brought back to life.

∗ ∗ ∗

Worst, most undesired posting for Secret Service agents: being posted to the detail protecting Hillary Clinton (*"The First Family Detail,"* Ronald Kessler, 2014, Crown Forum)

∗ ∗ ∗

EDA gene: Gene which provides instructions for making a protein called ectodysplasin-A. That protein in certain cell layers forms the basis for many of the body's organs and tissues. Ectoderm-mesoderm interactions are essential for the formation of several structures that arise from the ectoderm, including the skin, hair, nails, teeth, and sweat glands. (Genetics Home Reference, 9/1/14)

Contents

Part One

GETTING OFF (AND OUT OF) THE GROUND...
BUT FIRST, A GLIMPSE INTO 2016

PONGO'S GETAWAY, PART I

April 25, 2016
10:21 pm
B Train, NYC MTA Subway

Perry Ishmael "Pongo" Podrowski was rapidly discovering a painfully should've-been-obvious truth of 21st century American life, a fact any Iraqi war refugee **or** any 18-year-old African-American male targeted by (usually) white cops for the dastardly capital offense otherwise known as breathing-while-black would've shared gratis:

Fleeing for your life from armed-to-the-teeth predators, whether they're religious fanatics or certified law enforcers (or both), is neither thrilling nor Hollywood-glamorous.

No matter how cool Steve McQueen, Tom Cruise or Ryan Gosling can make it seem.

It's. Just. Terror.

Twenty-five minutes earlier, when Penny Mitsuhama Duarte – mother of Pongo's girlfriend Heather Griffin - signaled the crew with the time-to-bail code at Whittmyer Industries, everyone followed the plan without hesitation or questions. But every last one of them was convinced that at any moment a swarm of Secret Service Agents would burst through the nearest doors with cold steel maws of high-caliber automatic weaponry laser-sighted at their vital organs.

After all, it's one thing to threaten the slightest bruise to the planetary-sized ego of a genuine modern oligarch-slash-corporatarch or one of their high-profile political doppelgangers, but Pongo and his friends had been hoping to sample the actual organic operating system – as in gray matter – of not just one but a half-dozen or so of American plutocracy's most shame-immune and powerful shills and cronies.

That's a recipe for a shitstorm of major fecal fecundity from the proud and undeniably brave agents of the Department of Homeland Security.

The exit plan's success hinged on all 17 of the group getting out unrecognized, if not unnoticed. When the dark-haired 5'11" Pongo sprinted out of the small banquet room where the procedures were done, the obvious question nudged him toward panic: now that we were forced to make a rapid exit, *did* someone get recognized?

Which tempted Pongo to indulge in some existential gloom:

"Will the lives of my family and friends be ruined by this? What happens if I lose my National Park Service job? Will I lose both my other part-time jobs too? Will everyone I know see me on TV doing a perp walk? What if the famously weak Podrowski family sphincter decides to unbutton its collar, relax and cut loose a tropical deluge during that perp walk?" He could almost hear his old grade school bullies mocking, *"Panty pisser, panty pisser!"*

But first and foremost beyond Pongo's narcissistic worries about himself was his fear for his most admired friend and mentor of the past six years:

"Did Franklin (the former President, now known as Percival "Scruples" Van Mullder, thanks to the re-appropriated identity of a deceased infant) *get away from the Whittmyer Building without being ID-ed? Has his aging finally been stabilized?"*

Pongo, who soon would be clad in a long-sleeved NY Mets jersey (bearing the number "69"), had secretly agreed with Penny to volunteer for the riskiest escape route of the seven in the Whittmyer Building. It required him to sling the weighted end of a zip line across a 60-foot gap between the 24th floor of the Whittmyer and the 22nd floor of the historic Gallatin Heights Apartments across the way, where a steel net had been secured in advance to catch the hook on the end of the line.

Getting the hooked end of the line secured was the easiest part. As Pongo was sliding halfway down the line, he looked back and saw the shadowy shape of a hulking man clothed in black approaching the window he'd just slid out of. The man in black was reaching inside his suit coat for something.

When Pongo was about five feet from the apartment window, the man he assumed to be a Secret Service agent yanked out what appeared to be a long-bladed serrated bayonet. The agent raised his hand high and, with a Roger Federer-style smash swoop, gashed the knotted edge of the zip line which Pongo had just minutes earlier pulled extra taught to support his weight. Just as the line snapped apart, Pongo bounced off the apartment windowsill and into the unoccupied room.

Pongo needed only another 4-3/4 minutes to get to the nearest subway boarding platform, thanks to a serendipitously opened elevator door.

He had his pre-paid subway fare card ready to go, with just enough time to duck into a restroom toilet stall for the impaired (he felt guilty using a stall for the impaired, but he needed plenty of room). He whipped off the royal blue hoodie he'd been wearing over a hotel-issue sous chef uniform, unbuttoned the uniform and tossed both, along with his fake moustache, into the large covered waste container sporting a "Fuck Censorship" bumper sticker.

Four times during his quick change, though, different persons banged on the stall door. The first of them, after pounding hard twice on the door, yelled, "How long you and your limp dick gonna be in there, Juanito?" (clearly confused about the actual occupant). The second gave one loud slam against the door, adding, "You prick, you got the only throne with any TP! Either hurry your white ass up or toss me a roll!!" Always a believer in good anal hygiene, he tossed the stranger a roll.

The third guy tapped gently on the door a couple of times and asked Pongo if he could use any company. The would-be visitor sounded _way_ too friendly to Pongo.

The final toilet inquirer, a middle-aged woman, knocked hard on the door five times, advising, "Necessito a limpiar tan pronto como posible, mielito. Da te prisa, por favor, o tengo telefonear la oficina de seguridad!"

Pongo's Spanish comprehension was almost as good as his Mandarin Chinese fluency. Which is to say non-existent. But he could understand that the woman wanted him out of there faster than flatus. And he was happy to comply, because each time someone pounded on the stall door, he came close to crawling under the stall divide like a panicked rodent, not to mention coming even closer to evacuating his bowels into his pants, involuntarily.

Thirty seconds later, Pongo was queued up with another dozen or so riders as he casually wiped off beads of sweat from his slightly acne-infested brow.

But the outwardly-calm 29-year-old's casual steps into the subway car moments later simply led to more imagined horrors:

> *"Did the agent in the window see my face?"* he thought to himself. *"Will there be some kind of person-by-person passenger screening at Penn Station? Will they know enough to screen passengers heading north to Poughkeepsie? Will they drag each of us straight from the Amtrak car to a waterboarding room in Homeland Security headquarters?"* He envisioned actors Richard Attenborough and Gordon Jackson in "*The Great Escape*" trying to evade Nazi SS officers on a train. Didn't turn out too well for their characters on screen **or** in real life.

By now, Pongo's skivvies felt like the sweat-stained boxers of a hygiene-averse piano mover who's been hauling baby grands up and down stairs by hand all day long in 98F/99% humidity heat. His hands were so greasy with flop sweat that perspiration was raining on the subway floor from his fingertips and starting to puddle next to his feet.

He'd had a death grip on a hanging subway sling for maybe 10 minutes when he realized he was on the receiving end of a not-even-close-to-gruntled stare from a barrel-chested olive-complexioned man just across the subway aisle.

"Buddy, if you keep sweating on my shoes, you're going to need some new dental work," the man carrying what appeared to be plumbers' equipment told Pongo. "And your breath smells like the crapper I just unclogged on 83rd Street."

Pongo tried not to make eye contact. He couldn't care less about some drain jockey's well-worn Nikes.

But he could – and did – care whether the plumber noticed how badly he was shaking. (The plumber was wearing a bright red T-shirt on which it read above the left breast, "Pete Renalus, Pete's Problem Plumbing Pipe Porter: Unclogging Pee Pots Since You Were Too Small To Reach One.")

"I'm sorry, Sir," Pongo said. "I just got word from my doctor that the test results showed Africanized-M.S. I'm not dealing with it very well yet." He hated lying about something as deadly serious as M.S., much less making up a fictional version of it guaranteed to scare any KKK-ers within earshot, but surely that tall tale would embarrass the pusillanimous Pipe Porter into silence. Surely.

"Hay-zoos H. Kee-reist, kiddo! If only I'd known you were sick, I'd have worn my shit-stained Sketchers just for *you*! Listen, piss-ant, just do your best to stay the frack away from my person, OK? I don't feel like catching your funky-ass bug."

As discreetly and rapidly as a 320-pound 59-year-old plumber can move, Mr. Renalus then made his way, along with a dozen or so other Ebola-terrified passengers, toward the front of the train. He looked back only once, just to make sure the 'bug-laden' Mets jersey guy wasn't following him to hock a loogie in his direction. Which is probably what he would be doing if the roles were reversed, Pete the Plumber realized.

Except for a 28-year-old Puerto Rican mother nursing her baby three rows away, that left Pongo all alone in the butt-end of the subway car. "*Africanized MS?!* You are *some* bullshit artist," she said, eyes rolling.

"Yeah, well, **his** IQ score (pointing at the belligerent plumber) is just slightly higher than the E Coli bacteria doing the breaststroke inside my intestine."

But for all Pongo knew, a swarm of Homeland Security Agents would be lined up at the next subway stop to introduce him to the unique pleasures of 24-hour tag-team interrogation under blinding sodium arc lamps. There had been talk of each member of the team pulling their subway cars' emergency stop levers so they could jump off and climb through a service access exit to the surface. But that would almost surely result in someone getting a good look at the face of at least one of their crew. Not to mention how hard it would be to know when to pull the lever to be less than a half-mile from the service exit.

"*Wouldn't it be nice right now just to be back home walking in the shade of the tall maples and oaks along the Hudson with Heather…or even just out walking the dogs?*" he thought to himself. He and the others had made a conscious choice to attempt this thing, though, knowing all the life-ending risks that went along with it. The risks were worthwhile simply because of the potential to bring positive change not just to Franklin, but to everyone in the country tired of a culture of permanent war.

Meanwhile, it was a question of which Pongo would lose first: his nerves or the contents of his stomach, his bladder or his colon. If it'd been a fantasy draft, he'd have chosen colon contents in the first round, with the hope of picking up some Pepto on waivers – provided his equipment manager had plenty of Depends.

Before any colon squirts could commence, though, he noticed on the overhead LED scrolling message screen that the Penn Station stop was 500 feet ahead. He had just enough time to make the 10:45 p.m. train, the final one of the day to Poughkeepsie. What would he see when the inertia of the steel carriage was exhausted at the subway platform?

He was about to be surprised...

MEET THE LUGBUCH-ERS

Aug. 15, 2010
10:02 am
Long Island, NY

Gordon "Sancho" Graham usually didn't bother to set his alarm clock these days. He and his roommate and long-time buddy, Denny D'Amato, both had been laid off from their jobs 2-1/2 months earlier as Wall Street investment analysts with Mendenoff family-owned Conscientious Securities Amalgamated, along with 4,400 fellow analysts and brokers.

On this particular day, though, Sancho, now hangover-free from his 33rd birthday celebration two days earlier with Denny (who'd spent the last of their severance pay to rent a couple of 20-something call girls for a few hours of drunken sex), had set the clock to go off at 10 a.m. It was set, as usual, to his favorite AM Radio station, which on this day was re-playing an earlier live show of the talk-radio idol for both Sancho and Denny: reactionary far-right political bomb-thrower Slash Lugbuch (pronounced "lugg buck").

Slash of late had temporarily dropped his diatribes about "slutty college co-eds" (who were lobbying lawmakers to require employers to provide free contraceptives coverage) in favor of exercising his fixation on a historical figure he'd personally designated the all-time American socialist demon of the 20th century. Not Big Bill Heywood. Not Eugene Debs. Not Mary Harris "Mother" Jones. Not Upton Sinclair. Not Pete Seeger. Not John Reed. Not Emma Goldman.

None other than Franklin Delano Roosevelt, great-grandson of the co-founder (along with that socialist radical – yeah, sure - Alexander Hamilton) of the Bank of New York.

Slash wailed his belief that, if Giuseppe Zangara had simply succeeded in his attempt to assassinate President-elect FDR in Miami, FL on Feb. 15, 1933 (Zangara *did* succeed in fatally wounding Chicago Mayor Anton Cermak, FDR's close friend who was accompanying him in an open car, but left FDR physically unscathed), the U.S.A. could've been spared almost 80 years of "creeping socialism," leaving far more $$ for the richest 1 percent to trickle down on everyone else.

Slash even went so far as to announce a contest to award a guest appearance on his show for the person or persons who could come up with the best way to humiliate the U.S.A.'s "socialist king" by Labor Day.

This was an instant inspiration for both Sancho, 33, a tow-headed 6'2" Zach Efron look-alike, and Denny, 32, a 5'7" Danny DeVito look-alike, both of whom had had little to be inspired by for most of their lives.

Sancho's parents died about a week apart when he was 7; both had contracted AIDS from blood transfusions three years earlier. The transfusions were needed as they went through surgeries to recover from injuries suffered in a tour bus collision with a train in upstate New York. Their tour bus driver, one of 11,345 air traffic controllers fired by Ronnie Reagan in August 1981 for having the audacity to go on strike for better working conditions and increased pay (only 1,500 or so, all scabs, were spared the ax), had been drunk at the time of the crash after receiving an eviction notice, divorce papers and a car repossession letter earlier in the day.

Sancho buttressed much of the remainder of his life, thanks to his final foster parents, with the belief that it was worthwhile for Ronnie Reagan to risk the safety of all air travelers to make the political point that unions represent the evil greed of the (supposedly) overpaid middle class. His deceased parents were simply an unavoidable casualty in the culture war against uppity commie unionists (the commie sympathizers were fixated on calling it a "class war," his foster father would often insist).

Denny's parents had died a month later when their VW Cabriolet convertible was T-boned on their way back from a wedding anniversary dinner near New Castle, NY by a police cruiser during the officer's high speed chase in pursuit of a teenage speeder. The 16-year-old, a straight-A student who didn't have permission to drive his father's Corvette, had been going 43 mph in a 35 mph zone when the officer turned on his flashing bright-colored strobe rotating beacons for the teen to pull over.

A series of byzantine twists and turns in each of their lives led to them being in the same East Elmhurst foster home, operated by Mike and Enid Johnsen, from the time Sancho was 15 and Denny was 14 until they each aged out of the Foster Care system. Their foster parents, unlike many (if not most) Foster Care parents, were hard-core lower-middle-class conservatives who despised the government for all the regulations their home had to meet. It wasn't uncommon for Mike to verbally pummel (in front of his favorite JP Morgan Chase Bank teller) "all the commie bureaucrat" Foster Care home inspectors as he was cashing – with his conscience unblemished - their $750 per month per child Foster Care subsidy checks. Checks signed by the treasurer of the government they hated (which, in this instance, was the Empire State government).

The Johnsens never missed an opportunity to remind Sancho, Denny and their other three foster children (ages 9, 10 and 12) how much better everyone's lives would be if there were no such things as Social Security taxes, income taxes and business license fees. In the Johnsens' world, as in Slash Lugbuch's, if the "free market" were simply left alone, the general public would eventually get all the roads, schools, parks, airports, libraries, police and armies it would ever need, all run by for-profit corporations answerable to (supposedly) assertive shareholders. Shareholders who could *surely* afford to keep up on the latest corporate machinations and travel cross-country just to attend corporate shareholder meetings. Shareholders who keep the likes of Monsanto (i.e., the new Cancer Inc.) in touch with their corporate conscience.

As long as almost all citizens fulfilled their duties by occasionally kicking their lazier neighbors in the buttocks from time to time and reporting unpatriotic behavior to police empowered to punish dissent, no one would ever need to fear hunger or homelessness. In *their* Ayn Randian world, at least.

Based on Mike's and Enid's reassurances about the private sector, Sancho and Denny took out *unsubsidized **private*** student loans to complete their college educations, both majoring in economics and finance at Bob Jones University. In May 2005, when they finished their bachelor's degrees (each in debt to the tune of more than $225,000 with 6.5% interest accruing), they started jobs as paid interns with family-run Conscientious Securities.

Seven months later, on a warm fall afternoon while they were laughing themselves silly over how hilarious Enron traders' jokes were about jacking up "Grandma Millie's" electric bills in California, they got the call from their internship supervisor offering them permanent full-time salaried analyst positions.

They could barely contain their joy, spending the next two days calling everyone they'd ever shared a bar bet with to boast about their career liftoff. Between calls, they spent almost half of their modest hiring bonuses on every kind of flammable alcoholic drink they could order at all the taverns within walking distance from their midtown Manhattan office. They used the remainder of the bonuses a week later on the deposit and first and last months' rent for a tiny bare bones two-bedroom apartment in the Washington Heights area.

And there they stayed. Until, that is, when Conscientious Securities was rocked in the spring of 2010 by news that the Mendenoff family's patriarch Yakov had not-so-conscientiously been secretly draining top clients' major investment funds which in reality were little more than propped-up pyramid schemes he'd used to support a hyper-posh jet-setting international lifestyle.

The Securities and Exchange Commission (SEC) takeover of Conscientious Securities' assets and mass layoffs two months later came as no surprise to Conscientious Securities analysts and brokers. Most of those same analysts and brokers, including Sancho and Denny, were convinced, however, that the SEC's move was purely punitive. They felt **only** Yakov Mendenoff ("YM") deserved sanctions – and mild sanctions at that, because there were *some* indications that, had he been left alone, he could've turned around the values of the top clients' investment funds in another **10 to 15 years**, embezzlements notwithstanding.

Investors weren't so sanguine about YM's intentions. Nor were SEC investigators. Yakov Mendenoff got life in the Bureau of Federal Prisons. All thanks to the assholes in that FDR-created SEC, Sancho reminded Denny repeatedly. The same kind of assholes who couldn't be bothered to jail much of anyone over the 2007-2010 financial meltdown fueled by Wall Street's bundling of securities backed by worthless mortgage derivatives **and** by Wall Streeters betting *against their own investment products* **without** their own investors' knowledge. One man gets shipped off to prison for life because he screwed over a couple hundred of his rich Jewish friends, Sancho bleated, while thousands of Wall Streeters remain free and untouched despite causing millions of middle class folks to lose everything they owned, not to mention lots of marriages. (Sancho neglected to mention there were a couple thousand non-Jewish YM victims who also lost virtually all of their life savings.)

All thanks to that walking, talking phallus Bill Clinton and his 1999 Glass-Steagall repeal bill, Sancho thought. Slick Willie probably signed the bill while Monica Lewinski was giving him successive blow jobs, Sancho had suggested to Denny when news of the layoffs broke. (Of course, Sancho forgot to remind Denny that they probably owed their original hiring to the financial free-for-all unleashed by that repeal.)

So, listening to Slash's description of the "Neuter the New Dealer Contest" rules on their alarm clock radio, the bleary-eyed Sancho perked up quickly.

"My wake-up-hard dick is telling me it's going to be you and me on airwaves pissing all over those pussy liberals in September, Den," Sancho shouted to Denny in the next bedroom over.

"You've still got that video disc camera with the HDMI connection and lighting attachment, right?"

"Your hard dick couldn't tell a pussy from a tailpipe, Sanchito. Jesus, do I HAVE to wake up now, you PRICK?! It's not even noon yet, shithead!"

"C'mon, buttwipe, do you still have it or not?"

"Yes, I do, but it needs a charge, maybe even a new battery."

Walking into Denny's bedroom still in his Angry Birds pajama pants, Sancho displayed his best shit-eating grin.

"You're gonna **love** this idea. Listen up."

And Denny listened, barely interrupting except to drain his dragon into the porcelain throne down the hallway. He was so distracted by all the weird black stuff growing at the waterline inside the toilet he almost missed some of the most important details Sancho was sharing.

Twenty minutes later, when Sancho was done, Denny, still in just his usual sleepwear (a jock strap), asked plaintively, "Exactly how are we going to avoid going to Federal or State Prison, bud? When they see the video, they're going to see us and him and it's lights out for five or ten years. We can't wear disguises or they won't believe it's us in the video."

"We're going to leave the place just like we found it, that's how. To have evidence that we actually did what the video *seems* to show, they'd have to literally dig it up. They'll NEVER do that, out of respect to their sacred New Dealer dude.

"And we can always say we faked the video if they're dumb enough to charge us. By that time, we'll already have won the contest and have been on Slash's show. Remember, this is just about winning that contest.

"What's more, once this is over and done with, we're gonna be like gods to the Tea Party and all those Fox Newsy bloggers. We won't be able to pull up a chair at any restaurant or coffee shop in the whole goddam country without some fanboy or groupie offering us free meals and blow jobs and who knows what other kind of shit. Hell, that goofy guy who does car commercials in front of live elephants probably will give us free SUV's for life."

"I always wondered if those SUV's smell like elephant crap; it'd be cool to find out. Y'know, Bunkie, this actually doesn't sound all that nuts," Denny said. "It sure as hell would be a nice break from pounding the pavement every other day or so. Maybe it'll get us a job as Fox News celebrities or something like that.

"I'd love to find out which brand of donuts is that Huckabee dude's favorite – he looks like he must shovel down a dozen a day. I'll bet his favorite Simpson's episode is the one where Homer's in hell and the devil punishes Homie by forcing him to eat an unending stack of donuts – and Homie **still** exhausts the supply, begging for more."

"Naw, I think Huckabee's some kind of preacher guy, so I bet he'd be pissed off at anyone trying to make the devil look like more of a dumbass than Homer Simpson."

"You just might be correct, there, Sanch-gut...Anyway, we've gotta find SOME kind of dinero before our unemployment runs out in a month or two – so I'm all in."

"OK, here's what we do first thing tomorrow morning..."

A GOOD DREAM COME TRUE

March 19, 2010
10:30 am
Poughkeepsie, NY

Pongo Podrowski was pleasantly shocked when he opened the letter he'd just removed from the mail lockbox at the end of the short driveway in front of his home. He started reading it while unlocking the door to his teal 1998 Honda Civic coupe as he was about to leave for his late-morning four-hour shift at one of the Poughkeepsie Dunkin' Donuts stores. It was from the National Park Service (NPS). When he'd applied for the NPS FDR Center interpretive ranger/tour guide position three months earlier, he'd gotten lots of help submitting his data on line from Mitch Duarte, the stepfather of his long-time girlfriend Heather Griffin.

Expert help notwithstanding, Pongo still thought he'd have to be pretty damned lucky for an HR person to agree that he met the minimum require-ments. Pongo had only 30 or so of community college credits (because he could only afford to take one or two classes at a time). But he did have lots of part-time work experience since he'd graduated from Poughkeepsie High. And his grades had always been exemplary.

Mitch Duarte, a 6'5" 56-year-old semi-retired Homeland Security Air Marshal (whom everyone agrees looks 15 years younger than his age), heard from Heather that Pongo had always dreamed of wearing the flat-brimmed NPS campaign hat as an interpretive ranger in nearby Hyde Park. Mitch had helped lots of young people with tips on how to apply for Federal jobs and was only too happy to volun-teer to shepherd Pongo through the on-line process. He'd known several of the young men Heather had dated during and since high school and as far as he was concerned, Pongo was hands-down far and away the finest of the lot.

Heather did not disagree. Not even a little.

Pongo's Dad Phil, 51, a Health Department inspector and union shop stew-ard, had drilled U.S. history details into Pongo's head since he was in kindergar-ten. When other kids were arguing over who was the best Ninja Turtle, Pongo was known to interrupt to ask insightful questions. Like whether the turtles might've been "downwinders" who could qualify for compensation based on their mutations because they grew up near a Department of Defense contrac-tor's nuclear fuel processing facility. His insights were occasionally rewarded with non-downwinder nuclear wedgies, but Pongo eventually learned to give as good as he got.

The job interview panel – composed of three middle-aged women and a 60-something man (who, unknown to Pongo, had worked with Pongo's father in the '80s before taking his current Federal job) – had done their best to put the interviewees, including Pongo, at ease. Pongo felt like he'd done sort-of OK with their questions, but he was most hopeful he'd outshined the competition during the portion of the interview when he was given the opportunity to use his own words to express why he'd be likely to succeed with the NPS.

He spoke eloquently of his long admiration for FDR and the facility in Hyde Park bearing his name. Pongo contrasted the differences between FDR's approach to the presidency and the governing styles of his predecessor and of each subsequent President. He spoke with near reverence on the courage FDR demonstrated in confronting not just his own infirmities but also the behind-the-scenes challenges of countering corporate callousness toward the unprecedented suffering of the Great Depression. He recounted the oral histories of that period often shared with him during evening meals by his father Phil and his paternal grandfather.

FDR was one of Phil's greatest heroes thanks to depression-era stories from his own father Tom, 78, a retired grocer and part-time farmer living near Fishkill. Phil had spoken often over many family dinners about how Grandpa Tom had pointed out to him during cross-country road trips each of the iconic structures that owed their development, if not actual existence, to the Works Progress Administration (WPA), Civilian Conservation Corps (CCC) and other New Deal-era agencies. Like Timberline Lodge at the foot of Mount Hood, Oregon. Like Grand Coulee Dam in central Washington state. Like Jewel Cave National Monument in South Dakota. Pongo lost count of all the FDR-related tourist attractions his Dad had pointed out along the highways.

Pongo had come to share Phil's admiration after reading about the excruciating pain FDR had endured during well-meaning but completely ineffective early treatments for his polio, and about the heartfelt empathy for fellow polio sufferers which motivated FDR to spend two-thirds of his inheritance – against Eleanor's advice – to purchase and shepherd re-development of the rehabilitation facility and hotel at Warm Springs, Georgia. From the time he was a toddler, Pongo also had made lots of visits to the FDR Center, which was just 15 miles or so from their 40-year-old split-level Van Wyck Drive home in Poughkeepsie. It was there that he'd seen old movies of FDR's earnest smiles and enjoyment while swimming and cavorting with fellow polio survivors at Warm Springs.

It left an impression.

And not the kind left by watching videos of other Presidents playing golf with billionaires and sports celebrities.

So it was a bit of a dream come true for Pongo to actually see in print that he was being offered the interpretive ranger position at the FDR Center. In addition, the letter confirmed that Pongo would be enrolled for a 90-day law enforcement certification program – which was mandatory due to certain part-time security duties associated with the position requiring the ability to use a sidearm - starting April 1, 2010. Pongo would work only weekend shifts not involving security duties (for overtime pay) at the FDR Center effective May 15 while participating in his Monday-through-Friday law enforcement academy training.

He rushed straight home from his donut shift at 3:30 that afternoon, composed his acceptance letter on his laptop, printed it, signed it and delivered it in his Honda Civic to the USPS branch on Raymond Avenue in time for their final pick-up of the day, using the next-to-last "Forever" stamp in his Dad's knick-knack drawer.

"Maybe," he thought as he dropped the letter into the slot on the blue mailbox, *"I can <u>think</u> about giving up my dog-walking business and just focus on the NPS job, the donut job and college, not necessarily in that order."*

But Pongo quickly realized he had come to love his adventures in canine ambulation. The dogs each felt like his own little Special Education students: there was Puny, the 150-pound Saint Bernard male who always seemed to slobber more saliva on the sidewalk than the water he drank; Huffy, the snobby little poodle-chihuahua mix who always held her head up high in the air, but was actually the most affectionate of the bunch; Spot, the black and white springer spaniel-fox terrier mix who always tried to drag the entourage to the closest playground so he could be petted by as many schoolchildren as possible; Dr. Ayn Strangelove, the schnauzer who liked to bark fiercely (but not bite) each time she saw another dog get a treat from Pongo; Barbara Boxer, a sweet but occasionally pugnacious boxer-border collie mix; Joe Cocker, a droopy-eyed purebred Cocker Spaniel who always wanted to stop in front of the electronics store whenever there was a nature program playing on display TV's in the window, and Victoria Jackson, a sort of half-witted Afghan-Yorkshire Terrier mix who, when she wasn't trying to lead the group off precipices overlooking the Hudson River, was constantly presenting her backside for Puny to pleasure himself.

Every once in a while, Pongo would include his own dog, Mr. Peabody, a 7-year-old hyperactive pug-Boston Terrier mix, in the group – but, frankly, he thought, Mr. Peabody could be kind of a poor influence on the group. Mr. Peabody liked to urinate on strangers' legs sometimes – but it always seemed to Pongo like the urin-ees' pre-leg-wetted personalities sort of justified Mr. Peabody's actions. He always seemed to choose first-rate assholes to piss on.

As much as he loved his canine charges, lately it seemed like the time it took to parade them around the Poughkeepsie neighborhoods and parks was just too much of a chunk out of his day.

But then he remembered how many more credits he would need for his B.A. His Dad had convinced him it was nuts to go deep into debt for college when it could take decades to pay off the debt. Like many others of their generation, Pongo and Heather each lived with their parents to stave off the debt tsunami which credit card companies and payday lenders were itching for them to surf.

"Nope, had best keep all three jobs at least 'til I have the B.A. and maybe even 'til I have a master's. I can handle it, as long as Heather and my Dad are OK with not seeing me a whole lot during the week. And every other weekend," he thought. The NPS job meant he'd be working **at least** every other weekend, maybe even every weekend for the first year. The letter said his _ONLY_ shifts at the NPS job during the winter probably would be on weekends.

Nevertheless, the job offer was news Heather would be thrilled to hear. It merited some celebration, maybe even some special alone time for the two of them, he hoped. It had been weeks since they'd gone to their "special place" in the rural Dutchess County woods. It was a place – beneath a dense canopy of maple and ash trees - they considered a perfect spot to make out and, more often than not, make love. If they didn't feel like driving all the way to their special spot, they'd sometimes settle for doing the teenage date cliché parked at the back row of the Hyde Park Drive In Theatre, which to this day still shows first-run movies alongside Albany Post Road. They'd never had a soul try to interrupt one of their intense saliva exchange sessions there. Though there were, unknown to them, the occasional discreet observers.

Pongo and Heather had met three years earlier while both were working on a seasonal U.S. Forest Service firefighting crew loaned out from their inland Maine headquarters to USFS managers near a central Washington state wildfire. Pongo knew as soon as he saw the curvy auburn-haired, green-eyed, 5'7" lass' beaming smile that he wanted to convince her he was the guy she'd always find it hard not to have nearby. Heather's interest was piqued when she heard how Pongo's Mom, Melanie O'Leary Podrowski, had died when Pongo was 9 after her health insurer had refused to authorize a visit to a pulmonary specialist.

Unknown to Melanie Podrowski at the time, she'd inhaled virus microbes from fresh deer mice urine infected with Hantavirus; she'd died about 72 hours after her first symptoms. In the ensuing litigation over Melanie's death, widower Phil's attorney convinced Phil – under lots of pressure – to accept the health insurer's $300,000 settlement offer. The attorney, whom Phil chose out of the Yellow Pages (and had graduated next-to-last in his class at Munchausen State), pointed out that the insurer *probably* could successfully argue there was no way to know a disease limited almost exclusively to the Southwest would suddenly show up in New York.

(Unknown to the Podrowskis, a newly-infected deer mouse had hitched a ride in a plastic soap container inside the suitcase of their next-door neighbor's son Denton Rifeswear when Denton returned from an Americorps job on the Navajo Reservation in Arizona. On its way to being gobbled up by a stray cat – which dropped dead a day later alongside Albany Post Road and was incinerated with roadkill a day after that – the mightily infected mouse stopped long enough in the Podrowskis' garage to urinate on the side of the rose food container Melanie used every week.)

After the attorney took his cut, Phil had $200,000 left, $150,000 of which went to pay off Melanie's medical and funeral expenses. He used every last penny of the remaining $50,000 for the down payment on their current home, which was the only way Phil could afford to keep a roof over Pongo's head with just one full-time income. Even with the monthly Social Security Survivor's Benefits coming for Pongo for the following nine years.

The Podrowskis had been ardently faithful members of the Holy Comforter Episcopal Church congregation in the 1990's prior to Melanie's death, rarely missing a Sunday service, even when their issues with respiratory infections, digestive tract issues and excessive imbibing during recreation from the previous night would've kept most other followers home. Melanie always felt strongly that anything which didn't require hospitalization or risk the spread of deadly disease shouldn't impede a truly faithful believer from the respectful, devoted worship Christ their savior deserved.

"Do you really think Jesus would've skipped the Sermon on the Mount if he'd had bronchitis?" she'd asked Pongo once a few months before her death when he tried to use his cough as an excuse to stay home. "Jesus didn't have Mucinex to dry up the green globs like you do, either!"

(Pongo had often asked while involuntarily accompanying Melanie on shopping trips to Bed, Bath and Beyond if the comforters they sold were the fabled holy ones their church was named after; Melanie was stunned to realize her third-grader was sophisticated enough to be making a religious joke.)

With only minimal prodding from their bishop, every congregant who knew Melanie – and dozens more who _didn't_ - showered Phil and Pongo with heartfelt sympathies and countless casseroles, beef briskets and homemade pies for months after her death. There were countless unsolicited offers from Holy Comforter members to babysit Pongo – which Pongo, about to turn 10, resented because, he groused, "anyone going into fourth grade doesn't need a babysitter!" – so Phil could make time for his own therapeutic recreation.

There had even been the occasional transparent attempt by this and that attractive single woman congregant to make inroads into the romantic void left in Phil's life by Melanie's passing. Phil always found tactful, respectful ways to decline the women's attempts at companionship without causing them to feel spurned.

But at least _one_ woman decided she **had** been spurned, despite Phil's earnest efforts to express his continued devotion to memories of his late wife, even going so far as to say he doubted he'd ever re-marry. The woman, a 38-year-old dentist with a daughter from a previous marriage, began spreading rumors about Phil being a misogynist and online porn addict. Phil didn't take the rumors seriously – he was convinced those who knew him would recognize the rumors as nothing more than a vindictive reaction from someone who was obsessed with rejection.

Unfortunately, churches of all denominations tend to be profoundly efficient growth mediums for gossip, and Phil's was little different, despite his bishop's best efforts to quash the backbiting. Soon the expressions of support and understanding for Phil's and Pongo's loss dropped off a cliff.

Church friends who regularly invited Pongo to their homes for sleepovers with his same-age friends within weeks stopped calling altogether. Those same-age friends – except for Pongo's buddies Harry and Idris – told Pongo at school they'd been told by their parents they couldn't go to Pongo's home any more and couldn't invite Pongo to theirs.

Phil was furious. He explained to Pongo in detail why it would be wrong for Pongo to take personally what his friends' parents had done. But the explanation barely jostled the knife Pongo felt in his heart.

They never attended another church service together at any church, anywhere. But Phil maintained his friendships with church members whom he knew hadn't participated in the gossip. They pleaded with him to find forgiveness for those who'd spread the lies. He said he'd already forgiven them, but _that_ wasn't the issue.

He explained that, when he confronted one of his union members about spreading lies about a fellow union member, he could almost always get the target of the lies to forgive the liar when the liar asked for forgiveness – but the relationship between the two members would never be the same. Likewise, he couldn't **trust** the church gossipers any longer: no amount of forgiveness would change the fact that seemingly pious people had caused lasting hurt to his only son's heart.

Heather had a wealth of sympathy for Pongo about his Mother's death – during an estrangement from her own mother, her father had sustained traumatic brain injuries when she was 15 after he walked in front of a city bus while he was inebriated. But what actually made her fall hopelessly in love with Pongo was watching how selflessly he labored on the fire line and, even more so, seeing how constantly upbeat he was as a volunteer later in the fall that year at a senior outreach center which specialized in home visits to living-alone elderly men with severe physical and/or mental impairments.

And Pongo, while nearly mesmerized by Heather's heartfelt smiles and spontaneous shoulder caresses (which he first mistook for simple unamorous flirtation), was just as taken by the courage Heather could show. Like when she stood up to their fire line boss. The 30-something male supervisor thought they could simply outrun an oncoming 40 mph wind blowing burning embers and dense smoke rather than hunkering as low as they could and curling up inside their protective individual portable aluminized cloth tent collapsible fire shelters. She prevailed; they survived. When it mattered most, Heather could speak truth to power with respect, assertion and fearlessness. It was a trait she'd learned from her biological father – who'd been a social worker and community organizer - before he'd had the stroke in his late 30's which sent him on a downward spiral with alcohol addiction and the ensuing divorce action by her mother.

Plus, Heather was no slouch herself when it came to hard work. She'd held down a 40-hour per week job at the local Stop 'n Shop and managed to maintain a 3.9 GPA with a full courseload both at Dutchess Community College and, later, at Marist College. Pongo's respect for Heather had grown exponentially when she introduced him the previous month to Cecilia McIntosh, her supervisor at Dutchess County Social Services, where Heather was finishing her first year as a welfare eligibility interviewer.

Ms. McIntosh spontaneously praised Heather for her non-judgmental demeanor. A significant number of Heather's older fellow eligibility evaluators who'd come of age during the 1980s, when Ronnie Reagan and pliant corporate media perpetuated and expanded the myth that welfare recipients were able to live a life of leisure (the lasting image of one lone impoverished single mother driving an older model Cadillac enraged the easily enraged). Most of them seemed to enjoy looking down their noses at clients, even occasionally lecturing them about laziness.

Heather, on the other hand, Ms. McIntosh said proudly, seemed to understand from Day One that life on welfare consists of constantly being on the verge of eviction, borderline malnutrition, losing transportation and being unable to purchase items required for children's elementary and high school classes.

Moreover, Heather had recognized right away that welfare recipients – usually single parents going through the end of relationships, often abusive ones, or parents with learning disabilities exacerbated by poverty – **never** look forward to applying for benefits. The welfare abuser, contrary to corporate media, Ms. McIntosh said, is almost as rare as the mythical species of human who commits voter fraud – and Heather gets that. "She's the best hire I've made in a long, long time," Ms. McIntosh said, almost under her breath, so Heather's co-workers wouldn't hear. "Not to mention that she told me she's now a third of the way through her Masters of Social Work program at Marist."

What truly hooked Pongo's heart, though, was the compassionate loving, playful care Heather showed her 5- and 7-year-old siblings every chance she got. It was easy for him to picture her as a pretty wonderful mother in the future – *distant* future, that is.

Pongo drove about 15 mph over the posted 35 mph speed limit to the Dutchess County Social Services office in Poughkeepsie to break the good news to her. A phone call was too impersonal for this announcement; besides, Pongo was the only under-60 person in the county (as far as he knew) who saved money by not having a cell phone.

"Hey, handsome!" Heather, 23, smiled as Pongo walked down the aisle of the cubicle farm which was Heather's daytime home. As she leaned out of her cubicle, he could see she was wearing *that* purple satin top – his favorite of her entire daytime wardrobe - and a tight beige just-over-the-knee-length skirt. "I get off in another 45 minutes – something urgent come up that couldn't wait 'til then?"

Pongo whispered provocatively, leaning to a foot or so from Heather's welcoming grin, "I'd like to help you get off sooner than that, Beautiful, but I can wait 'til then. It just so happens we have something to celebrate: I'm one of the newest members of the National Park Service, Sweetheart!"

"NO SHIT!" Heather inadvertently shouted, immediately blushing at her verbal faux pas that echoed over several rows of interview cubicles.

"If it weren't technically against our personnel code, I'd love to celebrate right here in this cubicle with a quick BJ for my favorite history nerd," she almost inaudibly breathed right into his ear, punctuated with a quick flick of her tongue. (Sch-wingggg!)

They agreed to meet at 5:30 pm outside her office. At the appointed time, Heather all but leapt into Pongo's Civic, smothering his face in kisses for a couple of minutes. Then, both as moist as they could be, off into the woods they headed to their primo parking spot 19 miles away. Collisions with *roadside* hardwoods were barely avoided a couple of times, owing to mutual manual explorations while driving. Collisions with hardwood *in the back seat* were soon to commence.

* * *

SHARING GOOD NEWS WITH FRIENDS

March 20, 2010
10 am to end of day
Poughkeepsie, NY

Pongo had barely gotten out of bed when he heard his Dad raise his voice at the other end of their house.

"Hope you don't mind I read your letter from the NPS, Pongo. I figured you were so busy having a blast with Heather that you probably forgot to tell anyone else. You need to let me know how you and I can celebrate this milestone, Kiddo!

"Did you let Harry know yet?? How about Idris?"

Harry Peterson, Pongo's all-time best friend, shared most of the same classes with Pongo since they were in first grade at Violet Avenue Elementary School. Harry, a 6'3" 160-pound Irish-/German-American beanpole, was on the verge of completing his Associate of Arts degree in Information Technology at Dutchess Community College. He was living with his father Mel, 57, a County Roads Department supervisor, and his mother Cherisse Colbert Peterson, M.D., 55, a somewhat-involuntarily semi-retired pediatric neurosurgeon who was volunteering for the Public Health Service. Reading between the lines, Pongo inferred lately that Cherisse had been trying to fend off her demons with the demon rum. With decidedly mixed results. The *best* results occurred when the mixture included fermented vine fruits, or so Cherisse had convinced herself.

Cherisse had taken an early retirement buy-out offer – not so much taken as chose instead of being sacked – from her county hospital job the previous year after showing up for work hung over four times in two weeks. Her fellow physicians and their nursing staff had concluded it had something to do with operating on the fifth pre-school child with malignant tumors from the same EPA Superfund site-bordering neighborhood in as many weeks – as well as realizing that the families of three-fifths of the patients she'd served in the previous year were going through medical bankruptcies because their out-of-pocket billing liabilities were so high, even with insurance coverage. Her husband Mel always was telling her she needed an 'off switch' for her conscience if she wanted to maintain her sanity. She would always reply that the **_real_** problem was most people needed an 'on switch.' Mel's job – building and maintaining county roads – was one for which the conscience switch could pretty much be left in neutral 40 hours a week, unless he inadvertently became aware of roadwork being done for political favors. He did his best to remain ignorant of such sordidity.

Harry himself had occasionally battled – maybe battled is the wrong word; it was more like pinkie-wrestled – a predilection for overuse of Jack Daniels Tennessee Honey Whiskey. Most recently while under its influence, he'd just heard about DirecTV being owned by Rupert Murdoch (of Fox News fame) and had made it a point to erratically cruise around low-income Poughkeepsie neighborhoods on his mo-ped and urinate on the electronics in DirecTV dish feed horns (the part of the satellite dish that points toward the center of the dish). His drunken urination didn't accomplish his goal (short-circuiting profits of News Corp. satellite feeds; the feed horns are, in fact, waterproof and, apparently, urineproof), but it did eliminate the chance any DirecTV dishes in those neighborhoods might be involved in the transmission of athlete's foot fungus along with the usual brain fungus associated with watching Bill O'Reilly.

Idris M'Benga, 23, a 6'1", 260-pound linebacker-shaped African-Japanese-American hulk, had been buddies with both Pongo and Harry since the start of second grade. He'd completed his B.A. degree at Marist the previous year and was hired soon after as a job development counselor/welfare eligibility worker with Dutchess County Social Services. The son of Eugene M'Benga, 54, Dutchess County Solid Waste Disposal Manager, and Estelle Suzuki M'Benga, 50, a family law attorney, Idris was the radical of the three longtime school chums.

To him, the culture of respect for FDR in his home county was not unlike heaping praise upon a President for hiring an Exxon Oil CEO as EPA director. Pongo thought that was loony-level ludicrous. But Idris thought the idea of praising the 32nd President for saving capitalism from itself was like honoring a neurosurgeon for carving up a shrinking cancerous tumor so it could be transplanted into a dozen new victims. Plus, Idris' maternal grandparents – coincidentally, just like Heather's – had been forcibly re-located with their parents into internment camps for Japanese-Americans (almost entirely U.S. citizens) upon FDR signing the infamous Feb. 19, 1942 Executive Order 9066 (Idris' maternal grandparents and great-grandparents were placed in the Minidoka, Idaho internment camp; Heather's maternal grandparents and great-grandparents were placed in the Jerome, Arkansas camp) – so there was **that** bone to pick too whenever Pongo started heaping adulation upon FDR's legacy.

Despite his distaste for certain particulars about FDR's lasting social footprint, Idris had learned to admire most of what FDR had attempted to accomplish for a nation of Great Depression have-nots through New Deal employment and agriculture programs. Years and years of listening to his mother's stories of positive results achieved through many hours of pro bono legal representation – including low income tenants protection from wrongful evictions, recovering property unlawfully repossessed, winning large judgments for victims of police brutality – had helped Idris acquire a deep-seeded heartfelt appreciation for public service. He simply couldn't imagine the kind of career many of his fellow high school classmates ended up pursuing as financial analysts: *"How could anyone receive any visceral satisfaction from working day in and day out to make rich people richer?"* he often thought to himself.

Harry was just as goofy-crazy about his sweetheart, Bianca Swanson, a second-year med student, as Pongo was about Heather. Bianca had been living with her father Sam, 57, a neurosurgeon and pathologist flirting with the idea of retirement, and her mother Lucinda Rodriguez Swanson, 54, FDR Center National Archives Presidential Library Director. Harry and Bianca spent almost every spare minute of their time together, often at their *own* "special place" outside of Poughkeepsie. Bianca, a 5'5" 115-pound strawberry blonde, in addition to being phenomenally comforting for one's eyesight, had been a teenage prodigy, a 4.0 college student receiving a summa cum laude undergraduate degree from Vassar at the age of 19. She was mid-way through her studies at the Albany School of Medicine. She had at first bridled at the idea of following in her father's footsteps when she completed high school at 16, but a summer spent working at mundane part-time retail jobs and watching her high school classmates do the same changed her mind. She meant to make a lasting difference with her life – medicine seemed to be the most productive way to do that. On numerous occasions, her mother had suggested to her that the world might have ended up a much better place had FDR been compelled by his health care confidants to overcome his nicotine addiction, as well as other less-than-healthy habits, potentially giving him a longer life in which to do more good – like pursue his Second Bill of Rights. Bianca knew of few careers other than medicine where an individual could have a greater direct impact on undoing harms inflicted by the environment, ignorance and poverty.

Idris hadn't yet met the love of his life, but occasionally would date women he met while volunteering or while making a knucklehead of himself at a local karaoke tavern.

Pongo, Harry and Idris had been spending less and less time together as their 20's progressed mostly because there simply weren't enough hours in the day. In addition to the time Pongo spent on his three jobs, attending classes and enjoying Heather's company, Harry had been holding down a nearly full-time job at a Kentucky Fried Chicken restaurant and a part-time job at a Best Buy since their high school graduation. Idris had recently added a part-time every-other-Saturday position as a county paralegal volunteer to his social services job duties. Still, the three of them tried to make time to get together at least once every six weeks or so at the Juliet Billiards Café on Raymond Avenue in Poughkeepsie to shoot some poker pool.

"Oh, CRAP!" Pongo yelled down the hall to his Dad. "I meant to call Harry and Idris before I hit the sack last night. I'll get right on the line to 'em as soon as I'm a little more sentient. I hope neither one of 'em heard about the new job from Heather or her family already.

"Whatdya say we head up to the Eveready Diner when you get off work this evening, Pop? I've got an itch for blueberry cheesecake..."

"Well, seeing as you probably got all your other itches scratched last night, I guess taking care of one more will be OK, Pongo-Mongo." (Phil had finally gotten around to telling Pongo the origin of his name the year before: it had nothing to do with the Disney movie about Dalmations; turned out Pongo had been conceived during one of many intimate breaks in a weekend-long binge of Pong competition between Phil and Melanie, who had considered herself the all-time

Pong champion of the universe. She actually *really was **that** good* at the prototypical video game, Phil had told Pongo. Especially at high speed.)

"No need to get graphic, Weird Parent." Phil was known for a frequently warped sense of humor. "I'll meet you here at home at 6 in the P.M., OK?"

"Works for me, Favorite Son."

Pongo liked being called that. Even though he was Phil's *ONLY* son.

Three hours later, while on his break at Dunkin', Pongo dialed up Harry, and then Idris, to share the good employment news.

"I TOLD you they'd want you, Padawan," Harry said. "If there's a more knowledgeable FDR geek lurking in the Hudson Valley woods someplace, he's probably nowhere near as good a lurker as you, Perv!"

"Thanks for that vote of supreme confidence, Your Exalted Hairiness." (Harry actually had a small, incipient follicle-challenged spot on the back of his head and was missing even the slightest hint of hair growth everywhere on his body *except* on his cabeza. Thus, his best friend's nearly-favorite choice of ironic nicknames was starting to stick like a cheap toupee.)

"They tell me I may be assigned some odd hours during my first few years on the job. May even have to cover for night security staff when they're taking vacation time during the winter holidays and in late summer. Think you might want to come and let me show you around in the middle of the night sometime? Surely you and Bianca aren't exploring each other's nether regions 24/7..."

"You call me a day in advance and I will be honored to get the 50-cent tour from my all-time favorite Star Trek-slash-political nerd, even in the middle of the night. Who else can say they've been the featured guest of honor for a tour of FDR's last resting place under the glow of the Milky Way?"

"Well, it won't be you if you can't show a modicum of respect for the greatest President of the 20th century, maybe even of all time. I'll never forget that time you showed up for my junior-year history presenta-"

"Oh, Christ save us, here we go again..."

"-tion. Yeah, _you_ know, when you were supposed to be the Lincoln to my Douglas in the re-creation of their debate? You know, when you showed up in a Chewbacca outfit wearing a stovepipe hat? And did that gargling voice every time you didn't like something I said about slavery?"

"Yeah, best damn high school debate in the history of debates."

"Yeah, OK, I did get an A on it. But that's only because you knew Mr. Mitchell was a Star Wars fanatic." History teacher Bill Mitchell actually WAS a Star Wars **and** Star Trek fanatic (more so the latter). Not only did he own every last movie of each franchise, he had a special room in his basement studded with the movies' action figures, posters, standees, plush toys, light sabers, phaser pistols, autographed photos and even licensed attire, including Star Trek undies. The prevailing school rumor was that Mr. Mitchell's wife tolerated his obsessive basement frolicking so she could frolic in her own spare time in the basement of the girls' basketball coach, Ms. Terry "Nipples" Whipple.

"Well, I HAD thought about showing up as Cletus the Slack-Jawed Yokel Lincoln. So, count yourself lucky."

"Listen, I don't know when it'll be OK to have you come along during my NPS shift. It might be several months. But I promise I'll try to call you at least a day in advance."

"No sweat. Believe it or not, I've been waiting all this time to go to the FDR Center just so I could get the cook's tour from my best buddy."

"No, I believe it not."

"Catch you later, Ishmael."

"Not if I see you first...or second, for that matter..."

"You thillypoo!"

"If you keep that faux-gay shit up, I won't take you anywhere – except maybe Taco Hell."

"OK, _thith_ter, I be a good little boy juthht for you!"

"You dick...I'm hanging up, bud."

And Pongo did.

The parrying during his donut break call to Idris was not too dissimilar. Idris picked up just as the call was about to go to voice mail.

"How hangeth thee, my intrepid dog-walking commando?" Idris asked without waiting for Pongo to identify himself; he would never, ever answer a call without a glance at the caller ID readout.

"Practically scraping the sidewalk," Pongo said. "No, seriously, this is some hot-damn fine news, Brother from Another Planet! *(They were both fans of the movie by the same name.)* I got the National Park Service job, believe it or not. And they're actually going to trust me to carry a firearm."

"Dear Lord and Master, was there a nuclear holocaust I didn't hear about or is there some other reason they couldn't find another human being who could actually hit a target more than three feet away? Did the hiring panel all suffer brain damage from seizures while listening to that Mary Hart chic? All I can say is they'd better start making Kevlar vests standard issue for the Visitor Center guests..."

"Yeah, well, I think I'll start my target practice on your massive black butt, compadre. You'd better just be glad I didn't go for one of the openings where you work. Everyone there would be overwhelmed from the additional case work just from all the people who'd be applying for benefits just on the slim chance they might be assigned to me for an interview. Can't keep 'em away from a handsome face, y'know."

"Yeah, drawn like flies to a rotting corpse...Naw, white boy, I know you'll be a fine doo-bee in that post. With all those Delano-philes swarming around Hyde Park, they just can't get a better Franklin fan-boy than my best bud. I give it 10 years before you've got all those tourists convinced FDR could walk on water without his toesies even getting pruny.

"Really, man, I'm absolutely, crazy-funky happy for my best bro. Seriously, dude, you will excel at that. You were **_MADE_** for that job, m'man."

"That means a lot coming from you, Id-dude…When are you going to let me show you around the grounds? I know you're just itching to learn all you can about the President who was the closest to being a pinko commie, right?"

"Yeah, well, actually, I probably should make time for that. I think I'm the last person in Poughkeepsie who hasn't set foot on those grounds. It'd be nice to see what every last non-Repulsivecan is so freakin' ga-ga about once and for all."

"Eeetsa deal, buddy o' mine. All going well for you with Social Services?"

"Could NOT be better. I'm up for a promotion."

"Anyone new for you to be hot and bothered about?"

"*COULD* beeee…but I'm going to keep it on the down-low 'til we have a couple more dates. Don't want to jinx it…" (That was a deep inside joke; Idris was about as superstitious as your average astrophysicist.)

"I trust you to let me know when there's a real-life significant other – you know, besides the inflatables you keep in your closet."

"Shit, those are just to keep the closet monsters from beating off under my bed."

"Keep it cool, OK, Iddy-o? I'll call you sometime after I finish the law enforcement certification program in August to nail you down on when you want my official tour."

"I'll be sitting by the phone like a teenage girl slathering on zit cream between gossip sessions. Just for you, daahhling."

"You'd better be, you Pussy!"

It was the last time they would talk until Pongo had a sobering discovery to share with Idris.

Barrels O' Fun

April 1, 2010-Aug. 15, 2010
Temple University, Philadelphia, PA and Hyde Park, NY

Pongo found his day-to-day experiences at the Temple University seasonal ranger law enforcement academy to be riveting stuff. Not so much for the content itself, most of which Pongo considered fairly predictable – he'd shown an uncanny intuition for interpersonal understanding in his undergraduate psychology classes – but mainly because of the, well, uniqueness of some of his classmates and instructors.

He'd found it especially hard to bite his tongue when not one, but two different 30-something hulking male instructors told their prospective law enforcer students that they would be "perfectly justified" to use deadly firearms force against someone who simply picked up a landline phone handset in anger, as though they were poised to hammer it at someone. The threat of a nightstick, mace, pepper spray or taser simply was not enough to deter possible injury from a phone handset wielded in anger, the instructors each insisted.

"Does it make any difference," Pongo asked the first time the issue arose, "if it's a princess phone, or a wireless handset, or a realistic toy phone?"

"Each certified law enforcer has to make his own decision in a split second," the instructor barked back, moderately pissed, with spit droplets flying out several feet in front of his face. "I'm just saying, my conscience would be completely clear if I put a .44 slug in that hophead's brain. You have to look out for yourself."

Pongo vowed to himself never to point a telephone handset again at anyone in a uniform, even at a Boy Scout troop leader. You just can't be too safe. And he promised himself to do everything in his power to transfer into or to promote into, eventually, an NPS position which didn't require, even part-time, carrying a sidearm.

He did not ask Heather, his father or anyone else to come to the law enforcement academy graduation ceremony scheduled at the end of June. He was a little bit afraid of what might happen if they inadvertently pointed a cell phone at some of the new graduates. Plus, he was having a hard time thinking of himself as someone who was authorized to use deadly force against others.

*"Christ, I must **REALLY** want this NPS job,"* he thought to himself on numerous occasions while he was on the Temple campus. Wielding weapons against strangers was the *last* thing he wanted as a career.

But Pongo surprised himself: he turned out to be an expert marksman after the first week of practice on the gun range. Just in case the FDR Presidential Library and Museum ever *were* invaded by space aliens, the archivists could rely on him to get a couple of truly accurate shots off before the aliens' disintegrator weapons turned him into vapor.

When Pongo showed up for his first day at the new NPS job at 1 pm on May 15, 2010 (after completing his mid-day dog-walking duties in Poughkeepsie and re-filling Mr. Peabody's food and water bowls), he met for about an hour with his supervisor Pablo Justicia, 42, a balding 5'8" slightly-overweight bespectacled man of El Salvadoran ancestry. Pablo had been at the job interview, where he'd checked each the ID's of each applicant and introduced them to the interview panel. He'd observed the interviews, but hadn't taken part in the interview process, though he had the equivalent of two votes on whom to choose.

"I was impressed with the way you conversed with the interview panel, almost from the start, Pongo," Pablo recalled. "You weren't even remotely pedantic or full of yourself in any kind of off-putting way. And yet you didn't seem to be embarrassed about sharing the knowledge you've accumulated in your life in a way that was occasionally funny and endearing and even enlightening. Pretty impressive stuff for a 23-year-old who doesn't even have a four-year degree yet.

"You seem to be – what's the best way to put this? - surprisingly well-grounded. I usually like to wait six or eight months before assigning a new interpretive guide ranger to the occasional overnight fill-in security shift, but, in your case, I think we'll be just fine to give you those shifts once you've finished your 90 days at the academy.

"Assuming you don't turn out to be part of a terrorist cell or something like that," Pablo chuckled.

"Geez, I'm sure glad I cut off all my contacts with Al Qaeda last year," Pongo laughed back. "Those guys just can't take a joke."

Both men laughed heartily. Then right back to business.

"Would you feel comfortable shadowing a couple of our tour leaders for the first week to get a feel for how they handle the different tour scripts and how they deal with the visitors' questions? Or would you like to dive right in?"

"I'd like to shadow for maybe a couple of *days*, but after that I'm pretty sure I'll be OK to lead my own tour groups. I've been going on tours here since I was, like, 7 or 8. I'd like to think I've got a pretty good feel for this work.

"I'm curious about a couple of other things, though…I was wondering how often it is that security staff has to actually take law enforcement actions. Y'know, like arresting someone or ticketing someone."

"Pongo, it's so rare I can't barely remember the last time we had a serious problem. Most of the time, it's an issue of illegal overnight parking, teenagers making out in the parking lot or in some remote location or… "

"Geez," Pongo thought, his face suddenly turning a bright pinkish-red, *"there was that time in my senior year when Celeste Singh and I were caught making out in the parking lot about 100 feet from here and the officer asked us to take it somewhere else! Did the ranger take down my license plate number? I can't remember!!"*

"…some inebriated local ne'er-do-well has to be shoo-ed away or driven home. I honestly can't remember the last time we actually had to do something which required someone to make a court appearance. Ninety-nine-point-nine-nine-nine percent of the people who set foot on these grounds have a special place in their hearts for the most famous Hyde Park native son. I suppose there's always a first time for a serious offense, though.

"The main thing is to keep your emergency protocols handbook with you or nearby at all times. It lists the steps to take in lots of different situations: floods, power outages, fires, burglaries, heavy snow – even earthquakes. You'll do just fine if you have that to fall back on – **and** if you remember to stay calm and level-headed.

"People respect the NPS uniform – always have. If you haven't seen it lately, check out the video of the "I Have a Dream" Martin Luther King Jr. speech; you'll see one of our most respected NPS rangers standing within an arm's length of MLK. We're the Forrest Gumps of America's most beloved places – with some-what higher IQ's, I hope.

"So, we'll plan for you to work two *shadowing* half-shifts **this** weekend and then two weekend *regular* daytime half-day shifts per week 'til you're done with the academy at the end of June. Then, we'll adjust your schedule to 40 hours per week, with full-day weekend shifts, 'til the off-season staff cutbacks in the fall.

By then, you'll probably have two full-day weekend shifts and one full-day non-weekend shift; by January, that will go to just full-day weekend shifts. I know you have other outside work which should bring you up to full-time earnings, so I'm hoping you'll stick with NPS throughout the year."

"That's my plan, Mr. Justicia. I just hope I end up being worthy of the responsibility you and the NPS are honoring me with."

"Don't think any of us need to worry about that, Pongo. You'll do just fine. Just remember to leave me a voice mail at work or at my home phone if you're ever sick or something unforeseen comes up that forces you to miss a shift, OK?"

"I only missed maybe a dozen days of school from the time I was in first grade 'til I got my high school diploma. I think I'll be here so much, you'll probably get tired of my face."

"Only if you start wearing Gene Simmons' *Kiss* make-up, compadre."

Twenty minutes later, Pongo put on his NPS Ranger uniform for the first time and accompanied Pablo on a tour of the facility, meeting all the on-duty co-workers there that day, including even the gift shop workers in the Henry A. Wallace Visitor Center. Pongo was viscerally pleased to see that several of the employees, like FDR, were succeeding in their positions despite obvious physical challenges.

Pongo felt like he and the NPS were a match made in heaven. Or, at least, in Springwood (FDR's home and birthplace).

Pongo's next three months flew by. He was always at least 15 minutes early for his NPS shifts – even when he had to leave a Dunkin' Donuts shift less than an hour before his NPS shift started. And he always volunteered to stay late if a co-worker needed to be covered – unless it might make him late to one of his Dutchess Community College classes.

The only time Phil could be assured of actually seeing Pongo was Sunday evenings, when Pongo would be in his room doing college homework or coming back from finishing his homework in the college library at Hudson Hall. Phil usually would be in bed by the time Pongo got home from his jobs and college classes during Phil's Monday through Friday workweek.

Still worse for Pongo, though, was that the only time Heather could be guaranteed of seeing him was during the break between community college terms. But the two of them did their best to make up for lost time. Judging from the number of their trips to the woods and the number of drive-in movies (sort-of) viewed.

Pongo had convinced Harry to pick up Pongo's dog walking duties from April through June while Pongo completed his law enforcement academy classes, with the understanding that Harry got to keep 100% of the income from that job. If he hadn't missed all the doggies so much, not to mention the extra dough, Pongo would've been tempted to let Harry keep that enterprise all to himself. At least he still got to see Mr. Peabody every day.

When July 1 rolled around Pablo formally designated Pongo as the back-up ranger for night security fill-in duties. The usual black blazer-wearing security officers took most of their paid leave from late June through mid-September and during the November and late December-early January holidays, meaning their shifts needed to be covered.

Pongo found himself scheduled for an average of three graveyard security shifts each week. Which made for a lot of semi-conscious work baking and selling donuts, cookies, bagels, coffee and sandwiches to Dunkin' customers during daylight hours. On more than one occasion, he almost fell head-first unconscious into vats of donut dough, but, with one exception, always snapped awake, barely, just in time.

He looked forward to getting back to a more consciousness-friendly schedule in mid-September. But Harry had been pestering him to go on a graveyard shift tour for weeks by the time mid-August rolled around. As much as he'd have preferred to wait 'til the college term break to have Harry go along with him on a graveyard shift, he decided to just go ahead and invite him the night of Aug. 16-17. Besides, he thought to himself, the glowing 90-day review he'd just received from Pablo left him sure there was little that could go wrong with having Harry along for the night. He even predicted to Harry that Harry probably would want to head home after just a couple of hours into the shift.

Harry ended up staying the full shift, though. It was a night they both would remember for the rest of their lives.

THE RE-BOOTING AND BRAIN BUFFET, A LA CARTE

Aug. 16, 2010
12:30 pm to 5:30 p.m.
Penn Station, New York City and Poughkeepsie, NY

Sancho Graham's plan required some clear thinking for them to be completely prepared by the time the Amtrak train for Poughkeepsie left at 12:45 p.m., so he and Denny D'Amato had agreed to forsake all spirits and brewed alcoholic beverages for the previous 48 hours.

[It caused them great distress. They actually had a brief fistfight the previous afternoon over whether to tune their cable channel to American Pickers or Storage Wars. The fight ended when Denny reminded Sancho, in mid-punch, that they were about to miss a re-run of Bill O'Reilly interviewing Sarah Palin. "Hot tits, she has," Sancho agreed. "Plus, her jokes are SOOO dumb, they're actually fart-blastin' funny." When the O'Reilly show was over, Sancho went back to trying to convince Denny that American Pickers actually was a Monty Python-inspired contest about nose-mining efficiency among traumatically brain-injured proctologists.

"You idiot," Denny said. "Don't you think I can read the show summaries on the cable menu?"]

Their mental acuity was at its highest point since each got 98% on their 8th grade finals spelling test. They'd both missed only the words sphincter (Sancho wrote "sfinkstur," which Denny copied over his shoulder) and puncture (Sancho wrote "punksure," which Denny copied as "pukesure," because Sancho kept waving him off and getting in his line of sight). And they both had copies of the test in advance, bought for $10 each from a classmate who would go on to be elected as a Republican to a Board of County Commissioners position in the Pacific inland northwest 30 years later.

They caught the Poughkeepsie-bound train with plenty of time to spare. On the way, Sancho reminded Denny of each detail of their plan, reading from a master list of notes:

- First, they would rent the car from the local Heaps are Cheap franchise, making sure one last time that they didn't have to drop it off only when the facility actually was open. They probably would want to get outta Dodge in a hurry when the time came, without having to wait 'til the mid-morning train.

- Second, they would need to purchase the required tools at local merchant Meuller's Hardware, plus an additional surprise buy which Denny agreed would be sure to cover their tracks even better than their original plan. Sancho had checked in advance – by calling the store manager and posing as a security camera salesman - and confirmed that, unlike The Home Depot, there were no high-def video cameras at Meuller's – now, if only they didn't go out of business between now and the end of the day. Home Depot, Lowe's and Wal-Mart had that effect on the local shopkeepers. Denny had made sure that morning that they had enough left on their credit limit on each of their credit card accounts.

- Third, they reviewed their script, line by line, for the video they would be making. Even though their aptitude as actors or news anchors (Sancho said those both were the same, actually) was pretty marginal, they wanted to come off as at least somewhat professional in the video. After all, this could – and should – end up a big hit on YouTube, Lugbuch's TV version of his radio show and maybe even on Fox News itself.

- Fourth, they discussed what they would do in the event things didn't turn out right: what to do if security showed up, what to do if they had to recharge the battery in mid-take, what to do if it started raining, what to do if the ladder collapsed, what to do if the shovel or pick-ax broke, what to do if they got lost on the grounds and what to do if there already was someone there when they arrived at the fenced entrance.

It seemed to Sancho and Denny that they'd covered all their bases. By the time they were approaching the Poughkeepsie station, they felt confident that they just might be on their way to stardom in the world of Rupert Murdoch and Roger Ailes.

Aug. 16, 2010
Podrowski home
9:45 pm

Harry was a good 15 minutes late showing up at Pongo's house for their ride to Hyde Park. He pulled up Phil and Pongo's driveway in a 2005 Chevy Suburban which Pongo didn't recognize.

"You realize we've gotta break all land speed records now for me to be on time, muchaco," the ticked-off NPS ranger told his best friend.

"Couldn't help it, bud. My Fiesta wouldn't start and, by the time I gave up on figuring out what was wrong with it, I had to track down my sister to borrow her guzzler. Let's just take *it*, OK?"

"Shit, that Fiesta of yours is about as dependable as those Adobe cars in the old Saturday Night Live fake commercials. WTF - we've just gotta go – NOW! So, make it so, Number One!"

They managed to get to the FDR Center complex just in time for Pongo to check out one of the two green and white NPS cruisers assigned to the facility that week. Harry had blown through three yellow lights, but had avoided any speeding citations.

"I'm going to start the shift patrolling the grounds of the Top Cottage and the Val-Kill estate – that's where Eleanor lived after FDR died. We'll drive over there – it's about six or seven miles – and then get out and walk around. I've got the keys to each of the buildings, so we'll go inside to make sure nothing unusual's going on, like a raccoon invasion or porcupines mating on FDR's couch."

"That's something I've always wanted to see: porcupines screwing. You'd think they'd go extinct just from the guy-'pines worrying about their pricks getting skewered by quills."

"I don't think you're going to get to see that – there's pretty much no way any wildlife can get into those buildings, except for a few bats sneaking in through gaps in the fieldstone masonry."

As they were about to get into the NPS cruiser, both Pongo and Harry noticed the wind, uncomfortably warm for 10 p.m., had suddenly picked up dramatically. Likewise, the humidity clearly had just shot way up.

"We may have to come back here to the main grounds to sit out the storm if this gets much worse," Pongo said.

"Bring it on," Harry responded. "This storm can French kiss my ass!"

Aug. 16, 2010
5:45 pm

The Heaps are Cheap car rental process was smooth as silk. Sancho noticed there didn't seem to be any security cameras inside the rental office, but he was sure that even this kind of penny-pinching business had security cameras in the lot where the cars were kept overnight. Sancho had reserved a large SUV and, sure enough, there was one in the parking lot waiting for them near the front door. The rental agent re-assured Sancho and Denny that there would be no problem with dropping the car and the car keys off after business hours, pointing to the after-hours key drop slot in the front door. From the inside, Sancho could see the secured lock box into which the dropped keys would fall.

By 5:55 pm, they'd made it to Mueller's Hardware and were starting down their to-be-purchased list. Sancho had assumed they'd be open 'til at least 7 pm, but he assumed incorrectly – it closed in another five minutes. The store manager, however, seemed so happy to have their business he told them simply to take their time getting what they needed as long as they could finish within 20 minutes or so. Sancho couldn't believe how dumb he'd been not to check Mueller's business hours – their entire plan could've been screwed.

Each of them grabbed large shopping carts and started filling them up. By the time they were finished, the carts were overflowing with two super-heavy-duty shovels, two heavy duty push-brooms, two five-gallon watering cans, a 10-foot folding ladder, heavy duty full-length rubber rainslickers and matching pants, a first-aid kit, two pick-axes, a rope-pulley-hook set, a couple of cheap folding chairs, a hardened-steel crowbar, battery-powered spotlights, a heavy-duty bolt cutter, long wood-handled steel garden rakes, several bags of Quikrete (if repairs to the concrete coffin vault were needed), four 5-gallon plastic containers of water and seven or eight-dozen containers of small plastic-potted annual flowers. They then went over the to the customer service desk and filled out the rental paperwork for the store's lone backhoe. The customer service clerk assured them that, like the car rental agency, they were OK with after-hours rental drop-offs. As long as they realized they'd still be paying for a full-day rental.

"Do you have a towing hitch for the backhoe trailer on your Expedition out there?" asked the clerk, a 22-year-old brunette still battling acne explosions, the latest currently on her slightly-pointy chin.

"Does a duck shit in the woods?" Denny asked.

"I think it's a bear," the clerk said.

"Yeah, running a backhoe for a few hours overnight isn't my idea of fun," Denny said, not realizing his malapropism.

"What are you working on overnight with the backhoe, anyway?" the clerk asked.

"It's a wedding anniversary surprise for his wife," Sancho said. "It's for their summer home site near Millbrook."

"Must really love her," the clerk said, admiringly.

"Shit, if you want married pussy, you gotta treat 'em right," Denny said, thinking how clever he was being.

"Uh, oookay," the clerk said. "Just make sure you get this back no later than this time tomorrow."

Sancho and Denny then visited the nearby Taco Hell to enjoy some wholesome, surprisingly edible fast food and wait for the last sparkles of sunlight to vanish from the sky. As they waited, they noticed there seemed to be an abrupt change in the weather.

"What if there's some big storm, Sancho? Do we still follow our plan to the letter?"

"You bet your fat ass, Nimrod. We didn't come all this way just to turn around and lose all the money on supplies and rentals. You've seen people on TV videos taken during big storms – as long as they speak loud enough, you can still see everything through the falling rain. It'll turn out just fine. Besides, when do you recall the last time – hurricanes excluded – that heavy rain lasted more than 20 or 30 minutes?"

"Let's head over there. Now."

As they got into their SUV rental, rain promptly began pouring down in sheets. Lightning flashes began as they pulled onto Albany Post Road, followed just a handful of seconds later by loud, booming thunder.

The last glow of twilight was fading ahead of the storm in the distance as they drove into the deserted FDR Visitor Center parking lot. Sancho kept on driving past the lot and parked along the footpath between the enclosed gravesite and the stables just to the west.

As he was about to turn off the engine a massive, blindingly white bolt which seemed to be as wide as a house (but actually was much narrower where it struck the earth) went off with an immediate eardrum-shattering boom just a dozen yards or so to their east, inside the gravesite enclosure. A second-and-a-half later, all the electric lighting within 25 miles winked out.

Unknown to everyone in Dutchess County (not counting an astrophysicist observing above the county in the orbiting International Space Station), the FDR Center had just experienced one of the rarest of lightning occurrences, a strike virtually never fully viewed in real time by anyone on the ground, but a type of lightning which had been happening with regularity on our planet for the previous three-and-a-half billion years. There was speculation that such strikes, which produce colored electrical explosions going 60 or more miles into space known as *sprites*, might have been the original catalyst for life when the planet had only the basic elemental building blocks of life-forming amino acids and other pre-organic molecules stewing around in roiling, nearly-boiling waters.

Eyes almost as wide as surprised Tex Avery cartoon characters, Sancho and Denny looked at each other, mouths agape.

"What the FUCK?!!" Sancho shouted, his ears ringing. Denny seemed to be dumbstruck. Their SUV still was shaking from the booming lightning strike.

The rain continued to come down in sheets, like a torrential tropical deluge.

"Let's just sit here for a while longer and see if the rain lets up, OK, Denny?"

"Christ, you couldn't pay me enough to get out there while there's still lighting flashing. What in the Wide, Wide World of Sports was that fucking flash-boom?"

"Beats the piss out of me, friend. I saw on TV somewhere, though, that being inside a car with fully-inflated rubber tires is the best place to be in a lightning storm. So, shit, you bet your anus we're going to stay in here a little while."

"You can bet Saturn and Neptune and Pluto too, 'cuz I frackin' can't stand to feel soaked, Sanchito."

About another 25 minutes passed before the rain dwindled to just a light occasional sprinkle. Sancho and Denny hopped out of their SUV and began unloading tools and supplies. They flipped the ladder over the fence and began tossing the supplies over into the enclosed gravesite area standing three rungs below the top step. It was then that they saw that someone had left a backhoe parked alongside the back edge of the fence enclosure. It appeared that a grounds-keeper had been trying to dig up a burrow of some kind of wild animal, like a porcupine. Denny ran over to the backhoe like an excited schoolgirl, visions of copulating porcupines in his head. Sure enough, in the bottom of the five-foot vertical trench, there were two porcupines screwing their brains out.

But, more importantly, the keys actually were sitting on the seat of the back-hoe. They wouldn't need to find a way to break the lock on the gate to the gravesite enclosure after all.

"You gotta see these fucking porcupines, bro!" Denny yelled.

"Shut UP, you prick! There might be someone from security staff wandering around in the dark. We've gotta be as quiet as we can be.

"What's the deal with that backhoe?"

"Believe it or not, Sanchito, the keys are in it. Guess we didn't need to rent one, eh?"

"What a fracking stroke of luck, penis-breath!" Sancho whispered. "If we'd had to break the lock on the gravesite gate to get our backhoe in, they might have found us right away."

"Look over there, Sancho. What's that between the headstone and the clos-est grave?"

Glancing in the direction Denny was pointing, Sancho saw a circular-shaped three-and-a-half foot wide hole which seemed to be steaming. He walked over and shined his battery-powered spotlight into the hole. Jutting just past the side of FDR's grave nearest the headstone, the hole appeared to be conically shaped, extending a full six feet down through a cement burial vault to the top of what looked like an actual bronze coffin, cracked open just enough for the mahogany casket to be visible.

"We must be living right, friend-o. Looks like that fracking bolty blast thing just did a big hunk of our digging for us. At least we know just how far down to dig with their backhoe."

In another 40 minutes, Sancho, a former summertime/college break construction worker, had excavated all the way down to FDR's coffin. Sancho and Denny used shovels to dig around the edge of the bottom of the hole so they'd have room to pry the coffin open. Five minutes later, it was popped.

Aug. 16, 2010
10:18 pm
FDR Center
Elevation: two meters beneath ground level

The jolt he felt seemed like a dream. It reminded him of the time he'd had some serious dental work done when the endodontist didn't wait long enough for the injected anesthetic to do its magic.

The last thing he remembered seemed to have happened just a few seconds ago. He'd been in Warm Springs, sitting in his wheelchair, reading while posing for a picture, when the massive blast of pain went through the back of his head. He remembered being taken half-conscious to bed and then, before this jolt, nothing.

*And now, just the tiniest sliver of light in the darkness - enough light to fog photographic paper, but no more than that. He was trying to breathe – though not much happening. So much darkness. And he felt like he could eat an entire baked chicken. Why did it feel like he really wanted **something else** to eat, though? And why did his arms and legs feel like they were coming ever-so-slowly out of numbness, like they were sealed in concrete?*

What the hell is this hard thing above my head and arms? he wondered. Could it be an iron lung? Maybe I just need to get back to sleep for a little while. That's all I need, he thought.

FDR Center
Aug. 16, 2010
10:40 pm
Ground level, gravesite enclosure

As Sancho and Denny propped the casket open, they'd prepared themselves for the sight of some "Tales from the Crypt" desiccated corpse, maybe even with worms crawling out of the eyes. They were pleasantly surprised to see a corpse which looked like it had only been embalmed a few weeks earlier, in an amazingly well-preserved state.

"Geez, Denny, I thought we might have to stitch his arm to his shoulder or something when we carry him out of there, but this guy looks like he's completely intact. Looks like we've lucked out all the way around here."

"Reminds me of the funeral for Maria's grandpa we went to a couple of months ago – you know, Maria, that bleached blond chick in H.R. with the huge mangoes," Denny said.

"You might wanna remember," Sancho said, almost sternly. "This dude actually was the President for more than 12 years."

"So, what you're saying is, we have to work extra hard to make sure everyone sees what a nitwit do-gooder he was, right?"

"Ex-ACT-ly, pal o' mine," Sancho laughed so hard he farted.

They carefully hauled the corpse out of the grave using the hook and pulley, making sure there really were no loose body parts ready to fall off. They'd already set up the video camera and auxiliary lighting about 25 feet in front of the headstone.

Sancho and Denny carefully dragged the body to the folding chairs, tying it by the waist to the chair on the right, as viewed through the tripod-mounted camcorder. They were surprised at the quality of the muscle tone and skin, especially his legs, which they'd assumed would be almost stick-thin because of the effects of decades of polio when he'd been alive.

Sancho sat in the folding chair next to the corpse, reviewing the script one last time while Denny finished prepping the camera and the portable lights.

"I'll give you the three-two-one hand signal when I'm ready for you to flip the light switches and turn on the camera," Sancho said softly.

Denny fixed the focus and reached for the light switches taped to the camera tripod.

FDR Center
Aug. 16, 2010
10:43 pm
Ground level, gravesite enclosure

The feeling of strength in legs that had been not much more than dead weight for 34 straight years was almost alien to Franklin. The feeling stirred comforting visions of youth, of standing on the prows of sailboats, of pulling on oars in crew boats, of hiking to hillcrests east of Springwood. Why were these feelings happening now?

And why did his armpits feel like he was being yanked up a flight of stairs, just the same way his attendants sometimes would carry him in the early 1920s not long after the polio did its worst?

Sensations he hadn't felt for decades were flying back, wrapping his torso and his lower body with the kind of prickly tingling that an amputee feels from phantom pain. Only he was positive he'd never had an amputation.

He felt as though, if he could just bring himself to open his eyes, he could spring to his feet and run a high hurdle race. "Why is this happening?" he thought to himself.

All of a sudden, the sensation of bright, blinding light. Reflexively, he couldn't help but gradually, haltingly open the eyes which had been shut far longer than he could begin to grasp.

10:45 pm
Ground level, gravesite enclosure

The moment Sancho's last finger, his index finger, went down from his three-two-one count, Denny flipped on the lights and started the camcorder.

Sancho managed to get out the first few words of his script ("My fellow Americans, the only thing we have to fear is queers themselves...") before he noticed Denny struggling to say something, with wide-as-saucer eyes screaming in horror without the slightest sound coming from his mouth. Gasping as though in the midst of a severe asthma attack, Denny managed to point to the chair to Sancho's left.

Sancho, confident Denny was doing his best lead-up to a phenomenal "gotcha" joke, laughed at his best buddy. "You dork, I haven't fallen for your 'gotcha' crap for at least a couple of months. We don't have time for that shit."

But Denny kept pointing, finally choking out the word, "EEEEYEES!" – which Sancho briefly mistook for "ICE."

Ready for the inevitable "Got yo' ass!" from Denny, Sancho turned his head toward the corpse. What he saw was a blinking, wheezing human being trying to lift what had been limp arms and legs, struggling to reach out to Sancho, with streams of clear saliva dripping down both sides of his chin.

The sheer terror of the sight of the former President coming to life was more than Sancho could take. His urethral sphincter immediately drained the contents of his bladder as he reflexively jumped backwards onto his folding chair. He seemed to be trying to climb up it backwards, as though it were a ladder. When that didn't work, Sancho jumped backwards off the seat of the chair, launching himself at least three feet higher into the air perpendicular to the direction of the extended arms of the reanimated President.

Once airborne, Sancho was unable to control his landing. The back of his head took most of the weight of his Fosbury-flopping body as his skull was more or less impaled on the front top corner of FDR's headstone. At the same time, the pick-ax which Sancho had propped head-up alongside the headstone shifted just enough for Sancho's torso to fall squarely onto the pointed edge. As the ax tip erupted through Sancho's chest with shreds of his heart wrapped around it, Denny thought he was going to pass out and vomit at the same time.

Rallying from semi-consciousness to a full panic, Denny moved his legs as fast as he could in the direction of the ladder hanging over the fence. Unfortunately for him, he forgot about the floodlight cords lying near the camera tripod, as well as the gardening equipment. Three steps into his sprint, his size 11 shoes tangled in the wiring. Gravity then took over as Denny launched head-first toward a pile of tools. With the floodlights pointing in the opposite direction, Denny could only make out grayish shapes stacked on the ground. Too late, he started to put his hands out to cushion his fall, forgetting the pile of tools was sitting a foot or so higher than the ground itself. By the time he realized his mistake, the 3-1/2 inch hardened steel tines of a garden rake had penetrated 3-3/8 inches into his forehead. Excedrin Headache #298 quickly graduated into daisy-pushing.

10:46 pm
Gravesite enclosure

Bright light...Have to see where that's coming from. Stomach's grumbling – Mama's apple pie would be so fine right now. Why's it so hard to open my eyes?? There, now I can seeee... What is that device next to those lights? It's way, way too small to be a newsreel camera.

No, no, NO! What is this?!! I don't know those men. Dear God, they can't be friends of ours – their furry coats, for God's sake! THIS IS NOT WARM SPRINGS!! How did I get back to Springwood?? Where's Lucy?? I don't know why we're here in Mama's rose garden near the stables. Why am I tied to this chair? I've got to stand up. But **WHY** are my legs moving?? If I can reach that man, I can show him what needs to be untied.*

Why is he jumping back? Why is he acting horrified of me? Dear Lord Jesus – he's accidentally impaled himself!!...He must be DEAD!

I've got to get over to him. There, now I can shake this chair off while I'm standing up. It's just a few steps over to that poor soul. This is astounding – I'm able to walk, WITHOUT MY BRACES!!!

He doesn't move when I touch him...that's not surprising. What can I do? Wait, that smell – ohhhh, what a tantalizing aroma...it's not the same as the Sunday roast beef dinners we have, but it's doing the same thing to my appetite...I wish I had a mouthful right now!

I wonder what will happen if I lift his head off the corner of this – this thing, is it a <u>cemetery</u> *headstone? Unnnffhh, there, it's off now, that wasn't so hard. This poor, pathetic man is beyond all pain. What will happen if I pull up these broken bones on his head to look at the inside of his wound? My legs are starting to feel weak again – this walking, it must be too good to be true. Maybe a weird dream.*

What will happen if I peel away these outer parts of the wound to get to the inner parts of his head? It's just like breaking open a walnut. God almighty, I am SO hungry. What could those little parts deep inside taste like? I really, TRULY want to know. But that's insanity – ISN'T it??

*Oh. My. God. WHY AM I TASTING THAT – WHY AM I **EATING** THAT? Why does it taste do damnably good? What have I BECOME? Why can't I **stop** myself???!! Why does it seem like the innards of this man's head on the ends of my fingertips are 20 feet away? Am I having some kind of seizure? (Slow, deliberate munching continues.) This CANNOT be real. But it must be – I am tasting his brains, for Jesus' sake!*

(He barely noticed he was dripping – no, drooling, baby-like – saliva into Sancho's deep head wound.)

Wait, the other man is lying over there like he's badly hurt...Let's see if I can make it over there so I can turn him over and help him. Legs are feeling slightly stronger now.

[As Franklin staggers over into the darkness where Denny lies dead, the last electrical impulses to Denny's limbs are giving his muscles a final twitching; Franklin sees what's happened.]

My Lord, what could make two young men so hopelessly awkward that they got themselves killed?! I've got to get the tines of this rake out of this man's forehead. I'll just pull up as hard as I can – no, is that what I really wanted to do? – his scalp and the skull underneath are cracking loose and coming off!!...Why are my hands pulling the lobes of his brain apart? Wait, there are those small pieces of the thing deep inside...why can't I stop myself from putting those into my mouth??! But it tastes so blasted delightful. This can NOT be anything but a terrible, sickening dream. Why am I not waking up? Is this what happens to me because I sent hundreds and hundreds of thousands of men to war, to their deaths?

What will these two boys' families think if they learn that I've actually swallowed parts of the insides of their heads? It surely won't matter to them that the young men already were dead when it happened. Could they **possibly** understand the feeling of starvation I had before this happened? Doubt it very much...

What were they doing here next to a cemetery headstone? Why did they have me tied to a chair here? What's that printed on the headstone?

[Some of the pieces of the puzzle begin to come together as Franklin looks closely at the headstone engravings, still illuminated by the battery-powered floodlights. He sees his date of death, then Eleanor's, finally realizing he's burst ahead in time by at least 17 years. He sees his own excavated gravesite with the scorched north-edge fringe and feels the horrifying reality of his return to the living. He picks up Sancho's blood- and mud-stained script and glances through it.]

Eleanor's GONE, for God's sake. Can Lucy still survive? And the children, what of them? What happened with the war? What sort of hatred could've compelled those two healthy-looking young men to desecrate this place? Does anyone still live in Springwood?

What is the point of this living damnation? Why am I alive again? How can I make this stop? How can anyone forgive me for what I've done to those boys?? How could anyone in their right mind understand it?

10:58 pm

At first still staggering but soon walking with an almost-normal gait, Franklin climbed on the ladder hung over the fence of the flower garden enclosure, making his way to the pathway between the enclosure and the stables.

He was beginning to feel overwhelmed with grief for the two young men whose bodies he'd just violated unspeakably. It was all too much to grasp. Several weeks earlier, on Franklin's timeline, he might've been shaking the hands of their parents or grandparents and soliciting their ideas about how their lives could be made better.

Franklin was horribly thirsty. He reluctantly took a long drink from a half-full Thirstbuster soda cup left on a toolbox by Denny. The sensation of liquid going down his throat was tremendously refreshing, although it felt like everything he was taking in would soon be on its way right out again.

Afraid to disturb anyone who might be living in Springwood, he trudged over to a finely-constructed building he didn't recognize (the Henry A. Wallace Visitors' Center, finished seven years earlier) and sat against the wood and glass door at the rear entrance. He saw the nearby shapes of the seated bronze sculptures of himself and Eleanor, but the darkness kept him from recognizing the figures as himself and his wife. As he sat down, he realized his entire crotch area was damp with the same liquid he'd just swallowed minutes earlier.

He didn't know it, but there were tears streaming down his face, mixing with streaks of blood-infused saliva on his chin.

10:18 pm

Pongo and Harry were just finishing a tour of the Top Cottage interior when the bright light and explosive thunder caused them to jolt their heads to the west in the direction of the sound. Pongo hurriedly ordered Harry into the NPS cruiser as soon as it was clear there was a widespread power outage. They waited 15 minutes to be sure the power wasn't coming back on. Pongo's agency protocol required him to return to the main FDR Center facility as soon as a major outage was confirmed. Pongo drove as fast as the slick two-lane road would allow without risking a deer through the windshield or a tree trunk protruding into the radiator.

As he drove into the empty visitor center parking lot – normally dark even when the power was on – he noticed a white glow from behind the building in the direction of FDR's gravesite.

"We need to make sure the buildings are securely locked first, Harry – then I want to check out that lighting. Something's not right about that. It shouldn't be there."

"Wow, Pongbong – I'm getting a new perspective on my best bud. Don't think I've ever seen you this serious before. Power never go out while you've been on duty?"

"Not 'til now, muchacho...If the lightning flash hadn't been so flipping bright and the thunder so damned loud, I wouldn't be so concerned. There's really nothing that'd be in danger of being damaged at the entire facility as long as the power comes back on within a couple of hours.

"That light by the gravesite is driving me nuts, though."

As Pongo and Harry circled around to the back of the visitor center building, they saw the slouching figure sitting against the rear entrance. Pongo's first thoughts were that it must be either a homeless person or one of the Hyde Park townsfolk who had one too many bottles of vino and wandered onto the grounds. It'd happened before, more than once, but not while Pongo had been on duty.

He pulled out his heavy duty 4-cell MagLite and shined it in the direction of the sloucher, careful at first not to shine it directly into his eyes.

When he saw the man was wearing a dirt- and blood-stained double-breasted blue business suit, he reflexively flipped the light toward the man's face. What he and Harry saw stopped them dead, so to speak, in their tracks.

"I'm **NOT** dead, dear gentlemen," Franklin said, trying to smile his kindest smile. His words at first were slightly raspy, as though the heavy humidity in the air were the only moisture he'd known for a long time. Which, except for 10 ounces of flat soda, was exactly right. "Honestly, I'm not dead, I promise…

"Do you have any idea what's happened to me?"

"Holy…" Pongo started…

"Freaking…" Harry continued.

"Shit," they both said, half-whispering, in unison.

Pongo recognized the face right away, because it looked exactly like all the late winter 1945 photos he'd seen of FDR. Harry recognized him a split second later. If you were from Dutchess County, his was not a face you'd consider foreign.

"Mr. President (Pongo found himself taking a deeeeep breath, stunned by the sound of those two words)…, my name is Pongo Podrowski and this is my best friend Harry Peter- "

"Hi, there, Your Honorness," Harry interrupted clumsily.

"-son. I'm a National Park Service interpretive ranger and security patrol officer. I was on duty here, on patrol at Top Cottage, when whatever happened happened.

"Mr. President, if this really is you, we need to see what's going on in your mother's flower garden," Pongo said, barely believing his own eyes. "Were you caught in the lightning and rain?"

"I don't remember much more than some light sprinkles. I do know that there were two young men who must have dug me out of the ground. The grass next to where they were digging looks scorched. It would appear everything they were doing was part of a grand plan to make me look foolish," Franklin said, looking down at the partly-rotted leather of his shoes. He paused, still overwhelmed with grief and shock, but refusing to frown.

"Would you kind Samaritans please tell me what year this is? I know it's at least 1962, because the headstone says that's when my dear Eleanor passed. And would you please tell me what happened with our war against the fascists? Surely, it can't still be continuing, can it? I don't see any swastikas on your uniform - at least there's that."

"Mr. President, would you please excuse us for a few minutes?" Pongo asked nearly reverently. "I promise we won't go far – just back around the corner of the building behind us. We just need to take a few deep breaths, OK?"

"Please take the time you need, friends. It would appear I have more than I ever thought I'd need.

"Before you step away, gentlemen, I must tell you that you're going to find a horrific sight when you venture over to the rose garden. The two young furry men who brought me out of my interment were so terrified at the sight of me waking from whatever state I was in, they managed to impale themselves on garden implements and such while they were trying to get away from me.

"I have no idea what happened to me when they split their heads open, but it felt like I was overcome with the smell of the insides of their ruptured skulls. I'm afraid I did some unspeakable things to the insides of their brains. I watched my hands pluck out the cores of their heads and I could not control what my fingers put into my mouth. It was like watching some perverse movie from the back row of an empty theater. I had nothing to do with their deaths, but that simply does not mitigate what these strange new reflexes of mine did. I will surely be imprisoned for such acts, I imagine – and rightfully so.

"I hope you can show a bit of compassion here, my good men. I did not choose for this to happen to me. I trust you'll understand that."

"We'll do our best to sort everything out, Sir. The last thing in the world we want is for there to be any more unpleasantness for you," Pongo said quietly as he kneeled down and grasped Franklin lightly by the left shoulder. Pongo was flabbergasted to feel what seemed like layers of firm muscle underneath Franklin's coat.

"Please try to relax for a few minutes while we step around the corner, OK?" Franklin nodded in the affirmative and waved them away.

As they started to walk away, Pongo thought there was something strange about the age lines on Franklin's face. They seemed to be growing ever-so-slightly fainter. He whispered in Harry's ear as they walked, at first backward, for Harry to check out FDR's face. "It looks like he's getting a little younger, Dude! Do you see that?"

Harry did.

When they rounded the southeast corner of the building, Pongo and Harry tried to shake loose their shock and come as quickly as they could to grips with the bizarre reality they'd been forced to confront.

"Pongo, this can't be happening. I mean, SHIT! I swear to Jesus, if this turns out to be one of your weird revenge pranks, I'm gonna stick a pole so far up your ass you'll be able to take a crap by blowing that pecker-shaped snout of yours. I am so friggin' fed up with your wussiness when it comes to being a prankee. When I put one over on you, you just need **to let it go**, Dude."

"When in hell have I had time to set up something like this? You must think I'm some kind of Greek god or something – you think I control **lightning** now? You saw his face, for Chrissake! If this is a prank, man, it's unlike any *I've* ever seen.

"Just in case you're not up on current events, Peterson, this thing's got me shaken up, big time. You know I don't like being expected to wield deadly firearms – not my bag, man. I'll tell you what: right now, I wish I had some kind of ray gun, you know, a phaser set on red-hot disintegrate. I am scared shitless to the max about what we're going to see at the rose garden.

"I think we need to bring our Dads in on this, maybe a few others too. We're going to need some people who actually *know* shit to make sure we don't end up doing anything that either causes the President to end up in a sideshow, or in a CIA dungeon or with us in jail someplace.

"Until they get here, I think I oughtta have Heather come and sit with him to comfort him while we check out what happened at the gravesite. She's got a helluva bedside manner for a welfare worker – and I think the sight of a pretty face would be comforting to him."

"I guess you'd know all about Heather's bedside manner, Pongerbonger... actually, though, that sounds pretty reasonable to me.

"But. W. ... T. ... F. ...!!! This is just too weird, too fuckin' Twilight Zonie, Pongpussy. I need some seriously distilled liquids, Homeboy. Whaddaya think fuckin' happened here?"

"We need to check out the grave in the rose garden before we speculate too much about that. It could be something as Mary Shelley-ish as re-animation from electricity of the heavens. You know, Fraaahnken-steen?"

"If he gets up and starts singin' *Puttin' on the Ritz*, I'm calling J. Edgar Hoover's gun-totin' cross-dressers, dickwad. This is just too much to for my sphincters."

"I'm serious, pinhead. There's the old saying that the greatest fiction – whether it's Frankenstein or A Space Odyssey – has roots in reality. Who the fuck knows what brought lifeless compounds to life all those billions of years ago?"

"Christ, who knows what brought your dead brain to life, Pongman?

"Just one more thing: how many people do we REALLY want to let in on this? Do you really think more than a couple of people can keep a huge ass secret like this? Human nature bein' what it be, this is the kind of thing that keeps the National Enquirer and TMZ in business. If there are bucks to be had, people's definition of the word *discreet* suddenly morphs into spilling everything to *merely* **one** TV network. AFTER getting high-def-friendly make-up applied."

"H-Pee, I think we know a handful of people close to us we can trust with our lives. And with Franklin's. Remember: once they're involved with us, they're as vulnerable to the horrible things that could happen to us as we are."

"Until a Man In Black threatens one of them convincingly enough, Pong."

"Enough kibitzing, Bro', there's a fine human being over there who needs our help, pronto – I need your cell phone."

"Are you *EVER* going to get your own, moocher?...Here, take it."

Heather picked up on the second ring.

"Hi, Honey – I'm sorry to call you so la – "

"No worries, Sweetie, I'm still up working on my master's courses. Probably won't be nodding off for another couple of hours. To what do I owe the pleasure of your voice in the middle of your shift, Darling?"

"That's the thing, Heth...I need to ask a massive favor of you. This is pretty 'out there' – I don't even want to try to explain it to you 'til you get here. But let's just say it's so weird you may decide to turn around and head home once you understand what's happening. Maybe even head to Brazil.

"I'll tell you this much: there's someone here we need for you to provide some tender loving care while Harry and I check out something nearby. It's someone you'll recognize, probably someone you've looked up to in the past. But it's bizarre. I'm hoping this guy brings out the best in you, Heth..."

"Wow. You've got my curiosity piqued, that's for sure, Pongie. How could I *NOT* come along for whatever this is? I'll be there as soon as I can get dressed and on the road."

"Can't tell you how relieved I am to here that, Sweetheart. I'll see you in 30?"

"Maybe sooner, Pongo."

"Love you, Heth."

Pongo called his Dad next. Phil picked up after four rings, sounding a little groggy.

"I know you're probably already in bed, Dad, so let me apologize up front for calling so late. I wouldn't be doing this if it weren't something fairly earth-shaking."

"Mmmphff, blort late runff ding...lightning wuzza mazing, no?"

"Hey, Pop, I need you to wake up pronto, OK? We've got a pretty amazing X-Files-type thing happening here and I need your worldly expertise. Just as soon as you can get here, OK?

"I don't want to go into too much de- "

"I'll be there in 30 minutes, Son," Phil said clearly, suddenly brought to full consciousness by the TV reference. He could remember virtually every X-Files episode.

Phil's end of the phone line clicked.

Pongo looked at Harry, shrugged his shoulders and said, "He's probably already pushing 80 mph on Albany Post Road."

Harry then called his Dad, Mel, who promised to be there as quickly as his purple 2009 Tesla Roadster would carry him. Mel wasn't especially curious about the reasons he was needed; he'd had several late-night calls from Harry in the past which turned out to be clever ruses to get a ride home without having to pay cab fare. Harry was thinking this might be one of the times Mel brought along his Mom, Cherisse. He knew she didn't need to be up early the next day because it was one of her days off from duties as a Public Health Service volunteer physician.

With great trepidation, Harry mentioned to Pongo the likelihood of Cherisse's unannounced arrival. To Harry's great relief, *Pongo* actually looked kind of relieved. Pongo hadn't wanted just to come out and ask Harry to have his Mom drag herself to Hyde Park in the middle of the night, but she was exactly the person who could be of greatest help to Franklin right now.

"I think it couldn't hurt for you to call Bianca too, Harry. With the kind of fresh medical eyes she has, she and your Mom both might have some pretty helpful insights about what to do next with our friend the President."

"You're not worried about what she might share with her mother, Pongo?"

(Bianca's mother, Lucinda Rodriguez Swanson, 60, was the FDR Presidential Library and Museum Archives Director. There was no way Pongo was going to let her become aware of this night's developments. He knew Lucinda wouldn't be able to keep her mouth shut about it.)

"You're **not** going to invite Lucinda. Period. If Bianca can get her father Sam to promise not to gab to Lucinda, he's welcome to come.

(Sam Swanson, 61, was a semi-retired neurologist and pathologist.)

"But I'd want both of us to face him eye-to-eye to know for sure if he truly intends to keep that kind of promise. Some husbands find it pretty difficult to keep secrets from the women they sleep with – I mean, their wives."

"If Lucinda finds out about this, everything probably goes belly-up – and Franklin either becomes a reality freak show star or the new Prisoner of Zenda. A prisoner who probably *NEVER* gets rescued. A library director with the world's best library specimen simply won't be able to keep her yap shut."

Harry's call to Bianca went much better than expected. She'd been dating Harry long enough to know his addiction to pranks, so she simply assumed she'd be in for some silly 'gotcha,' maybe followed by a brief booty call. She felt like she could use the latter even if the former probably was going to be an affront to the rational, intelligent boroughs of her brain. The non-rational, horny neighborhoods of her gray matter right then were conducting block parties with podcasted invitations to Harry's hairy member.

She promised Harry she'd call her Dad to join them if she felt comfortable with this Bizarro World situation Harry had alluded to.

Twenty-five minutes later, Pongo was in the parking lot to greet Heather as she drove up. Barely a minute later, they walked up to Harry and Franklin at the back of the Visitors' Center.

"This has GOT to be one of your pranks, Harry, you dipshit!" she said reflexively. But then she looked closer at Franklin: no hints of make-up, spirit gum, latex masking, fake blood or any other tell-tale signs that the person sitting against the door was anything other than the iconic figure he appeared to be.

"Oh….My….God."

"This is the thirty-second President of these United States, Sweetheart," Pongo said. "Mr. President, this is Heather Ann Griffin, a very dear friend of mine. She's going to be staying with you here for a few minutes while Harry and I go over to your Mother's flower garden to try and sort all of this out.

"Are you comfortable with that?" (Heather was glaring in Pongo's direction the entire time he spoke to Franklin.)

"I am if this lovely young woman is."

"Urrrr, uhh, Ooooo-k-k-k-ay," she replied, stuttering, on the edge of shock.

"Pongo, we need to talk for a moment."

"Please excuse us, Sir," Pongo said.

Around the corner of the building, as Harry crouched next to Franklin, the two sweethearts did their best imitation of a bickering old married couple - at first, anyway.

"Just what am I supposed to do, DEARest one? This feels like you've dumped me into a bad dream. What do I say to the re-animated soul of the finest President the country's ever had? I'm just a rookie welfare worker – what do I know about comforting the ex-dead?"

"You're a welfare worker who owes her job to the Social Security Act this man dreamed up and personally pushed through Congress with virtually no Republican votes. And you're the most compassionate person I know. Just think about what he must be going through right now!

"He has no idea yet what year this is. He has no idea what's happened to his loved ones. No idea what happened from April 12, 1945 forward. For all he knows, swastikas are *passe couture* now and what I'm wearing actually *is* the latest Nazi fashion.

"Maybe you can help ease him into this life just a little bit. I trust you to use your good judgment, Darling."

"Do I have a choice?"

"Sure you do, but if you choose to walk out on us, please just take the time to tell him why, OK?"

"Like I'm going to bail on Fala's Daddy..." (Fala was Franklin's black Scottish terrier; Fala was featured prominently in at least one of Franklin's most popular speeches.)

Heather was kneeling down next to Franklin as Pongo and Harry started off in the direction of the gravesite enclosure/flower garden.

Pongo and Harry saw exactly what Franklin said they'd see. Pongo read through the script composed by Gordon "Sancho" Graham. When he finished, all he could think was how much he wished that slob Slash Lugbuch could be there for him to rub Slash's bulging face into Sancho's and Denny D'Amato's remaining brain goo – which was surprisingly intact.

He read through Sancho's step-by-step plan of action and soon felt a plan gelling in his own noggin.

"Harry, here's what we need to do once our Pops show up...We can't waste any time – we've got to clean this place up before my 6 a.m. shift relief shows up. We've got to do it so well that no one'll even realize any of this happened."

Pongo listed the next steps to be taken before they could re-locate the all-time most-admired son of Dutchess County to the safety of the Podrowski home. Harry mostly just nodded in agreement. Paranormal events and Harry were about as good a match as brown (diarrhea-colored) mustard and blueberries. Which, ironically, would be discovered by neuropsychiatrists in the year 2092 as an effective treatment (in the proper precise proportions) for post-traumatic stress among torture victims who were forced to watch countless uninterrupted hours of Donald Trump re-runs of "The Apprentice."

* * *

While Pongo and Harry were starting to undo the physical damage to the flower garden by Slash Lugbuch's Loyal Luggers, Heather was doing her best to re-assure Franklin that he was among friends. Devoted friends.

"What can I do to help you feel better right now, Mr. President?" Heather asked as she crouched down next to Franklin; she had retrieved a re-chargeable hand-held mini-spotlight from her car trunk so they wouldn't have to sit in the dark. "Is there anything I can get for you?"

"It would mean a lot to me, Dear, if you would just speak with me for a while. I feel like I've been shot through a cannon. It would be nice to understand exactly where I've landed."

"Harry was saying the last thing you remembered before seeing those men in the flower garden was being in Warm Springs in April 1945. And that you know it's at least 1962, based on the dates on the headstone, right?"

"That's correct – it's Heather, right?"

"Yes, Sir. So, you understand that this isn't some sort of Rip Van Winkle-type situation, right?"

"I do not know *what* I understand, my Dear girl. Until this evening, did you believe it was possible for a person to come back from the dead?"

"No, Sir. A big part of me still thinks this could be some kind of weird dream."

"Exactly."

"But it's not, Sir. And it's not 1962. It's August 2010, almost August 17, 2010. You've missed out on a few things, like us landing men on the moon in 1969."

"What did they find there?"

"Lots of interesting rocks, lots of moon dust, lots of spectacular views of our little blue planet. No green cheese, no little green men."

"Would you be so kind as to tell me what happened to Eleanor?"

"She grew old and died, but not until she'd done a wealth of work for lots and lots of wonderful causes. She was close to your presidential successors and to world leaders from all over the globe. What seemed to make her the most proud, though, was her leadership in getting the United Nations to pass a Universal Declaration of Human Rights. At least, that's what I learned in high school and college."

"I'm not at all surprised. She had a huge heart and a brilliant mind. She made me a much better President.

"What about my children?"

"Mr. President, I have this device you can use to look up almost anything you want, whether it's what happened to your kids or grandkids or what happened with World War II after you collapsed in Warm Springs.

"It's called a smart phone. It's a portable version of a computer combined with a cell phone."

"Huh? Pewter cells?"

"Wireless telephones have been used by lots and lots of people for the past 20 years or so. They're called cellular phones, or cell phones for short. There's been a thing called the internet – it used to be called the World Wide Web – for almost twenty-five years. It's an electronic system literally everyone everyplace uses to look up information. It's like an electronic encyclopedia combined with a library reference desk, news reports, movies, just about anything. You can use the internet with a smart phone or with a computer. Computers originally were massive, the size of a house – now some can fit in your pocket.

"Let me show you how to use this so you can track down all the information you need, OK?"

"Sure, Heather - I appreciate your patience with this old poser."

Heather showed Franklin how to access MSN, Google and Wikipedia. Within a couple of minutes, Franklin read when each of his children had died and discovered that all his grandchildren still survived, as well as 29 great-grandchildren. He went on to read that Adolf Hitler survived only another 18 days after Franklin suffered his cerebral hemorrhage. He started to read about the end of the war in Japan, but decided to hold off 'til he could better absorb what he'd already learned.

"Do they still make phones you can just speak into?" he asked Heather out of curiosity.

"Sure. There are enough Luddites and cheapskates like my dear Pongo to guarantee that the phone companies will keep making land-line phones and simple flip phones way into the future. There are a fair number of others who refuse to use cell phones because they're afraid the microwave radiation might give them cancer someday.

"Most of the experts seem to feel that risk is remote, but some folks, like Pongo, think even a remote risk is too much."

"I probably won't be needing one of those, so I'm not too worried about it," Franklin said.

"Heather, my curiosity is driving me nuts. Is there any one thing that people seem to remember my presidency for – besides things involving the Second Great War?"

"You'll be happy to hear you're considered responsible for the most successful – and most popular - social program in our country's history. Your Social Security Act has helped keep many, many millions of elderly folks out of poverty. Not to mention keeping millions of disabled people from becoming homeless.

"Democratic Presidents who followed you were inspired to expand the number of programs created by the act. President Johnson signed Medicare into law in the mid-1960's. And programs like child support enforcement have been mostly funded under that act for decades. Our current President has just signed a law that eventually will provide private health care insurance to virtually every U.S. citizen. By the way, he's half African-American, the first black man to hold the presidency."

Visibly surprised, the President's jaw dropped open. "If the voters elected a Negro, then this country must have changed dramatically in the past 65 years. I *so* wanted to do more for the Negroes, but the racist hatreds back then were thick and impermeable, especially in the South."

"I wish I could tell you that's true, but we still have a long way to go. By the way, Sir, it's considered bad taste to refer to African-Americans as Negroes – just an FYI there. I know you don't mean anything by that.

"I'm a welfare worker myself. Pongo just reminded me that I wouldn't be getting a paycheck right now, but for you signing the Social Security Act into law. I've seen evidence first-hand how members of your party helped make the lives of lower-income folks survivable, if not actually enjoyable at times.

"From what I've read in school, most scholars agree your legacy inspired a Democratically-controlled Congress to pass laws creating the Food Stamps program. It's now called Supplemental Nutrition Assistance. It's the main reason hunger among the poor no longer is an uncontrolled epidemic. Of course, the other major party has done all it can to undercut and try to privatize those programs."

"Did you really say **private-tize**? As in for *PROFIT*?"

"That's correct, Sir."

"How in the name of God could the Republicans pull that off? Wouldn't they literally have to **steal** from the programs themselves or steal from the workers who administer those programs to generate profits?"

"You've answered your own question, sir."

"Blackguards, scoundrels and well-dressed hooligans. That's really all the Republicans are when they know people aren't watching."

"Well, sir, I don't know a lot about that. I mean, those are words no one uses any more...and nowadays, with television, everyone's watching everyone else all the time."

"Television? That silly box? I don't see how anyone could watch something that fuzzy and distorted. I'll take a calm, friendly talk on the radio any day over that."

"Well, actually, sir, we now have a thing called 'high-definition' TV with stereo sound. It's actually pretty easy to watch. I think you'll like it, whether you choose to watch scoundrels or anything else.

"I do apologize, though – I honestly didn't mean to delve into the nitty gritty of government policy with you just minutes after you've experienced the shock of a lifetime, Sir. I just thought it might be a comfort to you to know the lasting positive effects your life has had on so many millions of people."

"It means the world to me, Heather, Dear. You are far too kind. Almost anyone who wasn't wealthy in my time agreed it was just common sense for the government to do whatever it could to help people get back on their feet. Businesses can't prosper if their customers have no money to buy their products. But it *is* truly comforting to know we helped prevent some misery.

"It would be almost as comforting to understand now why I am back on this side of the ground, Heather. Do you have any ideas?"

"I don't know if you being here again is divinely-inspired or simply one of those strange occurrences nature summons up every now and then. I hope it's the former, but there's no way to know for sure, is there?"

"I suppose not, Dear...

"**But**, *based on everything you know about what's happened since 1945*, what would you surmise, young lady?"

"All I can tell you is, well, our government since 1945 has been run by two political parties: your party, which has been mostly controlled by for-profit corporations along with the other party, the Republicans, which is ***super-hyper-completely*** controlled by the greediest of greedy for-profit corporations.

"And, probably because of that fixation on profits, we've been in a nearly constant state of war with some other country, large or small, **or** with some nebulous organization of nefarious so-called evil-doers ever since World War II ended. For the *past nine years*, we've been at worldwide war against a noun: terrorism. It's turned our country into the most militarized democracy on the planet."

"It surely can't be as bad as all that, Heather. My experience is that the average person doesn't want anything whatsoever to do with war unless the threat is virtually at his own doorstep. Likewise, my experience always was that the monied interests - "

"You called them 'malefactors of great wealth' if memory serves."

"I did. As I was saying, my experience was that the wealthy always try to exert influence over both parties, *but* it's the *officeholder* who is in the position of greatest strength. Simply because the officeholder answers to **all** voters. As an officeholder, if the interests of the average hard-working person mean the most to you, it gives you genuine strength to face down the super-wealthy who would try to corrupt the process."

"But **you** were always ready to call big business' bluff. I remember reports of you saying you welcomed their hatred. Your successors - well, not so much. Modern Democratic Party leadership compulsively bends over backwards to try to please business interests, both large and small – that's a constituency that's pretty doggedly determined to never, **ever** vote Democratic. It's like the entire party has become an adult child of an alcoholic.

"You're right about one thing though: the average person hasn't changed that much, Mr. President. Most people still understand the horrible effects of wartime. But the influence of the profit-makers **has** changed. Like the worst kind of cancer. And don't get me started about for-profit health care corporations and corrupt banks."

"OK, I won't. Not just yet, Dear."

(*"Holy God,"* Heather thought to herself, *"I have just been speaking face-to-face to the <u>disinterred</u> Thirty-Second President of These United States, the man who got our country through the hell of the Great Depression and World War Two. Will my grandchildren ever believe this? Oh, who gives a shit!"*)

✳   ✳   ✳

The Petersons (Mel and a slightly whisky-fragrant Cherisse), Bianca Swanson and Phil Podrowski all arrived at the Visitor Center at almost the same time. They exchanged pleasantries. Phil and the Petersons laughed about what it's like to be parents of children with extended adolescences, thinking their sons must've screwed up and now needed to be bailed out in some way to avoid nasty consequences.

Then they saw Heather and Franklin.

Heather introduced each of them to Franklin and vice versa. The whites of their eyes would've illuminated the rear entrance to the visitor center quite nicely, thank you, even if Heather's flashlight hadn't been turned on. Mel and Phil echo-stuttered, almost like a comedy sketch, too stunned to know what to say. Bianca looked all zombie-eyed at Heather and mouthed at her, "What. The. Fuck!" Cherisse, ironically, grabbed a shred of sober mental acuity first.

"How on earth could **you** be alive?" Cherisse asked.

"I haven't the foggiest notion, Ma'am," Franklin smiled smartly, not unlike the way he used to react to reporters who asked questions about war strategies which they knew security protocols would prevent him from answering.

"Pongo and Harry are over in the flower garden at the gravesite," Heather explained. "They're trying to decide what to do next. The three of you – or at least Phil and Mel – probably should check to see if they need any help."

"I'm down with that," Phil said. "The truth isn't just *out there*," he said, pointing skyward, "it's right over there in the garden. Please excuse me, if you would, Mr. President. I can't wait to ask you about a thousand questions – but only if you feel up to it, of course."

"Of course – Phil, right?"

"Ohhh, **yes**, it's Phil," Phil said, inadvertently doing his best Justin Bieber teen fangirl imitation.

"Let's make tracks, Phil," Mel said, pointing west. "Cherisse, would you like to stick around here and give our 32nd Pres a check-up?"

"Try and stop me," Cherisse only half-joked. "I'm a physician, Mr. President. I would love to make sure you're going to continue to share our company for as long as possible. Do you mind if I examine you?"

"Not at all, Madam, as long as you're gentle."

"OK," Mel said. "If you don't mind, we'll take our leave, Mr. President."

"It would appear I'm in the excellent hands of three lovely young ladies. So, please make your way to the flower garden. Your young men seemed rather shaken, understandably so."

Mel and Phil started walking west toward the gravesite enclosure, rubbernecking back at Franklin off and on 'til they got around the southeast corner of Mrs. Nesbitt's Fireside Cafe in the Visitor Center (the café was named after Franklin and Eleanor's longtime devoted housekeeper, Henrietta Nesbitt; the café name changed to "Uncle Sam's Canteen" on April 1, 2013).

* * *

As Phil and Mel walked through the front gate to the graveyard enclosure, they could see Pongo and Harry speaking in what seemed to be frantic but hushed tones to each other. Each of them seemed to be taking turns pointing toward the heads of two clearly unconscious or deceased young men near their feet.

As soon as Pongo and Harry saw their Dads approaching, they motioned rapidly for Phil and Mel to come closer. Pongo gave a quick run-down of what they'd discovered by going through Sancho Graham's script for the Slash Lugbuch competition. He added what they'd found among Sancho and Denny D'Amato's personal effects, including their wallets plus their vehicle and equipment rental agreements on which Sancho had listed "No Family" as next-of-kin contact for both Sancho and Denny. Pongo explained that they were about to start down the impromptu list Pongo had made of what needed to be done to restore the appearance of Franklin's grave when Harry noticed something odd about Sancho Graham's and Denny D'Amato's heads.

The gashes in their exposed brains had started knitting themselves shut – the process was clearly visible in the rented floodlights. Pongo's guesstimate was that the deep head wounds and brain damage would be completely gone (healed?) within an hour. He'd even checked for a pulse: the first two checks 15 minutes earlier revealed no pulse whatsoever with skin cool to the touch. The third and final time he checked (which was, by then, about 45 minutes after both men had died), there actually was a faint pulse and the skin suddenly felt slightly warm.

"Just what the flying cock do we do with these jackass grave defilers if they're coming back to life as God-knows-what?" Pongo asked, sweat streaming down his brow, with his hand on his service revolver.

"This is way too damn much for me to absorb and stay continent, Pong-wad," Harry said, at the edge that precipice known as hysteria. "The first time one of their arms or legs twitches, I am fucking running for the hills. I did **NOT** sign up for this."

"Son, we're all experiencing the same bizarre shit and you are the only one who is grappling with whether it's OK to be a pussy," Mel said to Harry. "If this is that terrifying to you, please just head back to our car in the parking lot, OK?

"Just to clarify, sir," Pongo said. "You're looking at someone who's *constantly* struggling with whether it's OK to be a pussy. I'm in this uniform only because I enjoy taking people on historical tours and talking about my favorite President."

"Pongo, there's nothing to be terrified about," Phil said. "We're apparently not being invaded by outer space aliens armed to the teeth (there was a slight wrinkle of disappointment on Phil's face). Right? I mean, I hope not. Anyway, I just don't see either of these two buttwipes on the ground as an existential threat, as long as they're not walking and talking.

"Here's what I propose – please back me up on this, Mel, if you're of like mind, OK? I propose that we take that pick-ax you pulled out of that Sancho guy's chest and use it to pulverize the holy fucking shit out of each of those two ratfuckers' brains. Then we cram them into FDR's casket, try to seal the coffin and vault, fill that hole in, even out the borders where that scorched spot is and plant all those potted flowers on top of both FDR's and Eleanor's graves to mask what's actually happened. Then we load up all that rental shit into the SUV over there, return everything to the night drop-off spots and get our shit-streamin' asses outta this place and back to Poughkeepsie, along with our new houseguest…Except for you, Son, obviously. You've gotta be here when your relief arrives."

"Couldn't have said it better myself, Phil," Mel assented.

"Except for the brain pulverization thingie, that's exactly what my to-do list says, Pop," Pongo said sheepishly, gently waving the list.

"Oh, fuck this shit," Mel said, promptly grabbing the pick ax and sending Sancho's and Denny's rapidly re-animating brains smack-dab to Downtown Smithereens City.

"Smashing," Phil said, in his best faux British accent.

* * *

As soon as Phil and Mel headed for the flower garden, Cherisse quickly retrieved her physician's black bag from her car. She began her exam of the former President by checking his vital signs. She remembered that Franklin had chronic hypertension during his final years before his cerebral hemorrhage. Amazingly, his blood pressure was borderline low. His respiration was clear. His pupils were reactive to light. His sclera wasn't bloodshot at all. His reflexes were sharp. Lungs were clear. The dark spot on his cheek (visible in many historical photos), which some physicians had suspected might be a melanoma that could hemorrhage if he had a stroke, had actually disappeared. Completely.

His muscle tone was surprisingly good, especially the calves on his legs, which had, pre-mortem, been wasted almost completely away due to his polio myelitis. All symptoms of polio had disappeared.

Likewise, any traces of nicotine addiction appeared to have been lost to time.

"Doctor, it feels like I should be doing something with my hands – I'm so accustomed to having my cigarette holder either in my mouth or in my hands,"

Franklin said to Cherisse. "I definitely don't feel the urge for a cigarette, but it surely would be nice to have something to hold on to. Like a candy bar or toy, or maybe some marbles..."

"Cherisse, I don't think we should get him all Qweeg-ed up," Bianca said, referring to Capt. Qweeg of *The Caine Mutiny*. "Rolling around steelie marbles in his hands is one sure way to get noticed. In a not-so-great way."

"Next chance I get, I'll find a stress-relieving squeeze ball or one of those little rubber nun figures with the boxing gloves that punch out at you when they're squeezed," Cherisse said. "That's the best I can do for now. In the meantime, you two young ladies need to step over to the side of the building over there to give us a little privacy, OK?"

Heather and Bianca shuffled sheepishly away, about 30 feet to the east. They didn't want to miss anything, but they certainly didn't want to seem disrespectful to Franklin.

As Cherisse leaned across Franklin's body to examine the insides of his ears with her handy-dandy otoscope, her somewhat large breasts brushed against the top of Franklin's chest and his chin. As she sat back down to write some notes ("Ears: minimal wax accumulation"), she noticed some tenting in Franklin's crotch area. Which soon became a full-fledged erection.

(*"Dear Lord,"* Franklin thought to himself, *"my private parts are working again! But did it have to happen in front of these nice ladies? They're going to think I'm some sort of deviant. How can anyone respect someone they think is a deviant?"*)

Out of respect for Franklin, Cherisse made no remarks about his sudden apparent involuntary reflex of virility. But she made a mental note to have the Peterson and Podrowski men have a private talk with Franklin – to encourage him to give self-stimulation a try if he felt the need to take his sex drive out for a spin around the block. Then, she suddenly thought better of it – after all, she thought, males of all ages have been exercising that reflex for as long as they've been standing upright. On to more pressing health issues.

"Mr. President, the non-profit March of Dimes program you founded in 1938 led to a successful polio vaccine. It went into wide use just 10 years after your collapse in Warm Springs. I think our top medical priority needs to be for you to get that injection. Post haste, Sir...What do you think?"

"That would be deee-lightful," Franklin said, doing his best imitation of his late uncle-in-law, Teddy. "I never, ever want to lose my leg strength again. When you can't stand on your own two feet without help, it's just about impossible to set the boom vang tension during a sail."

Cherisse then resumed her examination, palpitating Franklin's stomach and abdomen, then examining his chest and back with his shirt off. She took copious notes as Heather and Bianca whispered to each other out of earshot of Cherisse and Franklin; Bianca and Heather were surprised at what a fine figure of a man Franklin actually was.

Cherisse wrote to herself that Franklin needed to get a full battery of cognitive and vision tests – plus other immunizations - as promptly as possible. She also was trying to figure out in advance how that could be done without leaving behind a paper trail – or, at least, a paper trail showing any traceable personal data.

∗ ∗ ∗

B y the time Harry, Phil and Mel were ready to decamp from the FDR Center, with Harry driving the rental SUV and rented equipment back to the rental agency and hardware store, it was 2:40 a.m. Before driving off, they walked briskly back to the rear of the Visitor Center where Heather, Bianca, Cherisse and Franklin were sitting.

Cherisse reported that her cursory exam of the 32nd President showed him to be somewhat malnourished, but otherwise remarkably healthy, if mostly bladder-incontinent. She said he had the teeth of a much younger man. And most stunningly, all of the effects of his polio myelitis had been completely reversed, with newly-grown leg muscle.

She delicately pointed out that Franklin likely would be needing adult diapers for some time. "For whatever reason, his digestive system – like much of the rest of him – seems to have re-booted. It seems almost like that of an infant, as far as continence and nutritional needs go. I would recommend easily digested fruits and fibers, probably baby food, until we can tell how his system is adapting."

Perhaps most bizarrely, she said, he seemed to be physically regressing in age. She estimated his current appearance to be that of a virile man in his mid-50s, rather than of a 63-year-old frail man on the verge of death. "At that rate," she said, with an expression of real (motherly?) concern on her face, "24 hours from now, the President's appearance might be as young as that of a 14- or 15-year-old."

She left it for the others to infer the logical progression from there.

"So, we have to hope we can find some way to slow down this age regression," she said. "Fast."

"We all need to talk about this together, pronto," Phil said. "But away from here."

Phil suggested they all meet at his home, as he and Pongo had the most space in their residence to accommodate Franklin. Franklin would ride with Phil. Pongo would join them as soon as his graveyard shift ended. He would be calling in sick for his Dunkin Donuts shift scheduled to start at mid-day.

Everyone, including Franklin, nodded in agreement. Barely a minute later, their little caravan was rolling out of the Visitor Center parking lot, with Pongo's NPS cruiser the only car remaining. They all followed Harry to make sure nothing went wrong with the rental drop-offs. Harry then joined Phil and Franklin as they led the caravan to the Podrowski home in Poughkeepsie.

In the FDR center parking lot, Pongo sat alone in his cruiser. He was exhausted enough to sleep for a week, but his heart was pumping as though he'd had a gallon of the strongest coffee, adrenalized by the thought of Franklin actually living in Pongo's own home. Never mind that his life was about to be complicated beyond his wildest imaginings.

"What was that thing he said about furry men?" Pongo suddenly thought to himself. *"Fur coats in August? Didn't find any of those in the rose garden. Probably a just-back-from-the-dead senior moment. Like Grandpa Tom gets after his volcanic farts on the toilet make him slur his speech for a few hours."*

* * *

Grandpa Tom Podrowski, a currently volcanic flatus-free retired grocer and part-time small farm operator, was waiting for Phil when their caravan pulled into the 25-foot driveway at Phil's home. He'd tried to call Phil's landline repeatedly starting shortly before 11 p.m. the previous evening to discuss a Jeopardy re-run which had just finished on the cable channel he'd been watching. When Phil didn't answer, Tom got worried. He tried again at midnight; still no answer. Grandma Annie Podrowski, 74, a retired internist/neurological surgeon, told her husband to chill the hell out and come back to bed. Unless he liked not being touched by her for a few days. Not even slightly daunted, Tom decided to drive from Fishkill to Phil's home in Poughkeepsie to make sure all was well. He'd seen too many "Dateline NBC" shows about home invasions and people being murdered in their sleep to know he wouldn't get a smidgen of shut-eye until he knew his son and grandson were safe, sound and somnolent.

When the caravan transporting Franklin pulled up to Phil's home, the first thing Phil saw was his Dad Tom standing inside the partly-opened front door. Phil felt semi-panicked, thinking, *"This is how this will spiral out of control. There will simply be more and more people who will find out about Franklin – and then we'll all end up in some CIA black ops site in Berzerkistan someplace. Waterboarding concierge services comped, naturally."*

Phil waved off the other two drivers, signaling them to stay in their cars. He needed to speak with his dad one-on-one, face to face, to impress upon him the gravity of having a formerly deceased President in their home – and to help Tom understand this was neither a prank nor some strange Slash Lugbuch-style publicity stunt. But without even looking at the other two drivers and their passengers, Phil could sense their collective desperation over dependence on yet another person's ability to keep a secret. Phil had his own near-panic issue to deal with, though: he was more than a little worried that the shock of seeing the 32nd President in person might bring on a stroke for his Dad.

But it didn't. Tom had watched enough *X-Files* and *Fringe* episodes with Phil to believe those in corporate control of the government could keep almost anything secret if they wanted to badly enough. Including contacts with aliens ***and*** bringing people back from the dead. He also believed those same secret-keepers could cause anyone they wanted to be squashed and forever-disappeared. So, Tom was no hard-sell on the concept of keeping confidences.

As the group walked into Phil's and Pongo's home, Tom slathered on admiration for Franklin. Tom recalled for Franklin how, from 1933 through 1944, Tom's father Pavel – whose first and second cousins lived in occupied Poland after the German invasion there - had required the family to calmly and quietly sit alongside their parlor room radio each time Franklin gave a fireside chat.

"It was like having another even wiser parent or grandparent speaking to us, re-assuring us. It made the reality of the Depression easier to live with when we could hear the earnest hope in your voice, Mr. President. You didn't sugar-coat things, but you always found the positive."

"That's what I was hoping to convey," Franklin smiled back. "I wish I'd had time to do more of those chats over the years."

"We kept hoping after Hitler invaded Poland that you'd find an excuse to get us over there to kick those bastards' asses to hell," Tom said. "My Dad kept telling us you'd do what you could do when public opinion would let you. But, from September 1939 to December 7, 1941 seemed like an eternity. We were so sad to hear about the Japanese sneak attack, but we knew it meant you might be able to save our cousins and aunts and uncles in Poland.

"My Dad Pavel was hacked off at you over the Soviets getting to Poland first. If he'd lived long enough to see the Polish re-gain their independence from the Soviets in '89, I know he'd have forgiven you.

"Bottom line is our family in Poland, almost entirely, survived World War II intact. That wouldn't have happened if you hadn't been so creative about finding ways to help the Brits and Soviets between '39 and '41. You and your advisors were brilliant."

"You know what they say about necessity being the mother of invention," Franklin said. "That's all it was."

"You're way too modest, sir," Tom said. "If it weren't for your eye for the future, your view of what the world could be after W-W II, I doubt I'd have been able to get the loan I got to open my grocery store in Fishkill. I doubt I'd have been able to convince my beautiful bride to marry me just on the prospect of having ten acres of produce growing next to my home."

"I think you give me far too much credit, Tom. I just wanted to leave behind a world where life meant something more than the richest people always having all the say about everything."

Phil sent Mel and Cherisse to the nearest Stop 'n Shop to pick up baby food (especially pureed carrots and other anti-oxidant-rich fruits and vegetables), blueberries, adult diapers, toothbrushes and other basic items for Franklin's use – plus, at Franklin's request, some hot dogs and sliced cheese for grilled cheese sandwiches. He suggested they all lie down for a few hours of shut-eye after Mel and Cherisse returned so they could discuss Franklin's situation with clearer heads when Pongo arrived home from his shift at about 6:30 a.m. They all agreed *at least* four hours of rest was a good idea. Tom called Annie to let her know he was staying the rest of the night at Phil's because, he sort of fibbed to her, he was just too sleepy to drive back home. He *was* sleepy, but not **that** sleepy.

For most of the 20-something minutes Mel and Cherisse were gone, Franklin asked the rest of the group about the outcome of WW II.

"From what I read on Heather's smart telephone, we didn't need to use on the Germans the super-weapon General Groves' group was building in New Mexico. Is that right?"

"That's right, Mr. President," Phil answered. "It wasn't ready to use before the Germans surrendered. The Army and Marines were planning a full-scale invasion of the main Japanese islands when the bomb finally was ready to test.

"There were scientists who thought the bomb shouldn't even be tested. A few at the test site near White Sands, New Mexico even had bets between themselves about whether the explosion would ignite the world's atmosphere, incinerating the entire planet."

"Christ in a cup! I never was told that was even a remote possibility!"

"Once the test succeeded, it was just a question of whether to use it and, if it were to be used, how to use it. After the generals told President Truman it likely would take maybe a half-million soldiers fighting house to house in Japan for months or years, the President decided to demand an unconditional surrender. He and the other allied leaders warned Japan about 'prompt and utter destruction' which would come if they didn't surrender."

"Did they surrender?"

"No. The first bomb was dropped on Hiroshima on Aug. 6, 1945," Phil recalled. "When the Japanese still refused to surrender unconditionally, the second bomb was dropped on Nagasaki three days later. The destruction was horrific. I don't recommend you watch any newsreels of the bombing victims on a full stomach. It was estimated that maybe as many people died of radiation exposure as from blast effects.

"Almost all of the bombing victims within a mile or two of ground zero were simply vaporized. In many instances, all that was left of them was a shadow burnt into concrete next to where they were standing.

"Most historians consider the dropping of those bombs to have been the beginning of the Cold War between us and the Soviet Union."

"Was there some kind of freeze weapon used in that war?" Franklin asked, puzzled.

"No, Sir," Heather said. "The Cold War was a war of intimidation and propaganda, based entirely on what was called 'mutual assured destruction,' or M.A.D. for short. It *was* sheer madness. At one point, the two sides had enough nuclear weapons to incinerate the entire planet maybe 50 times over.

"The world _was_ almost incinerated in October 1962 during the Cuban missile crisis. High-altitude U-2 spy cameras caught the Soviets sneaking nuclear missiles onto Cuba and President Kennedy set up a naval blockade encircling the island. The Russians disclosed decades later that one of the four submarines they had there came horrifically close to shooting a nuclear tipped torpedo at U.S. warships in the blockade which were dogging the sub.

"The torpedo was _as powerful as the bomb dropped on Hiroshima._

"As U.S. warships were harassing that sub with non-lethal depth charges – explosions the submariners thought _might_ be deadly - the Soviet submarine fleet commander _overruled_ both the captain of the ship he happened to be on **and** the Communist Party official on the sub who _already had the nuke torpedo loaded and ready to fire._

"The fleet commander – his name was Vasili Arkhipov - he finally ordered his sub to surface after many hours of stifling 120-degree heat inside and the confrontation was de-fused. Commander Arkhipov, **all by _himself_,** under heavy opposition from that sub's captain, almost certainly prevented a full-scale planet-wide conflagration.*

"And President Kennedy was pressured during that same Cuban Missile Crisis by some members of the Joint Chiefs of Staff, like Gen. Curtis LeMay, to _actually launch a pre-emptive nuclear attack_ on Moscow. Thank God he stood his ground against those warmongers. It would've been game over for every human being on the planet."

"So, do you think we should've used those bombs on Japan, Tom?" Franklin asked.

"All I know is I might not be here right now if we hadn't," Tom said. "But was it worth almost 45 years of being on the edge of global destruction? Who can say? All we know for sure is that, without those bombs, the Japanese probably would've fought to the last man – maybe even to the last pre-teen – to preserve their empire."

"I'm glad that decision wasn't mine," Franklin said somberly.

"I have to wonder what the true tally would be of all the persons who died prematurely from being exposed to radiation from nuclear bomb testing over all those decades," Tom said. "I have a sneaking suspicion it might be about the same as the number of soldiers who would've died in an invasion of the main Japanese islands.

"And who can tally the true cost of the terror experienced by every single person growing up in an age when the single push of a button could end up igniting the entire planet in fire along with centuries of deadly radiation?

"My son has an amazing book you'd be well-advised to read to bring you up to speed on the effects of nuclear testing just in this country," Tom said, reaching a volume on a nearby bookshelf. "Here it is: "_American Ground Zero_."" Tom handed it to Franklin. "It may give you some pretty wild nightmares, though, especially

---

* PBS' "_Secrets of the Dead: The Man Who Saved the World_," 10/23/12

after you read how multiple soldier witnesses saw at least one incinerated human body *chained* inside a steel cage as they were walking through a just-nuked landscape in Nevada.

"And take time to watch these videos," Tom said, handing Franklin DVD's one-at-a-time of "*On the Beach*," "*Fail Safe*," "*Mulholland Falls*," "*Blue Sky*," "*Atomic Café*" and "*Dr. Strangelove*," "once you're done reading the book."

Once Mel and Cherisse returned, Franklin scarfed down three containers of Gerbers, a bowl of fresh blueberries and a microwaved hot dog (Franklin had watched the microwaving the way a smart dog watches TV, not really taking in Phil's quick explanation about how microwave radiation could cook things from the inside out). He then washed it all down with a pint of cold apple juice, apologizing for eating in front of everyone else. Almost all of his meal ended up in his newly-fitted Depends a dozen minutes later, but Franklin said he felt much better. By now he appeared to be another five years or so younger.

Phil and Tom assigned each of the guests to beds, sleeping bags and couches around the house and, less than a half-hour later, all of them – including Franklin - were sound asleep. Phil put a note on the door for Pongo asking him to be quiet and to feel free to head to his own bed for as long as he could sleep, adding that they'd all be discussing their situation once he was rested.

Franklin dreamt of the last sunset he'd shared with Lucy Mercer near Warm Springs, GA on what seemed like just two-and-a-half days earlier to him. It was a very comforting, calming dream, until just as he turned his eyes from the waning western light to Lucy, ready to kiss her (no paparazzi to worry about then in rural Georgia), only to see her skin suddenly turned pale grayish-white, the skin of someone near death from leukemia – then he saw her eyes sinking deeply into gray sockets. He promptly woke up, remembered his new surroundings and, relieved it was all a dream, quickly fell back asleep.

Pongo saw his Dad's note when he got home from his graveyard shift. He brushed his teeth and crawled under his bedcovers. He woke up shortly after noon, hearing the sound of his grandfather and grandmother speaking outside his door. It turned out Grandpa Tom had gotten permission to bring Grandma Annie into the group an hour earlier.

Grandma Annie, whose parents Josh Wilson and Rosemary Turquisian Wilson had raised her in an apartment above their small Manchester, NH grocery store, knew first hand what the New Deal had meant to her parents. Her father had been able to keep the mortgage on their store paid with the Civilian Conservation Corps stipends he sent home to Annie's mother every month while he worked in Maine. And most of their grocery customers were able to keep their accounts up to date because a group of local businessmen who found FDR's economic optimism contagious were able to buy up the failing local textile mill and save the hundreds of jobs it provided. Rosemary, whose own mother had blazed an early feminist trail as her Montenegro town's equivalent of the only nurse practicioner in mid-1920's, had prodded Annie from an early age to excel in her science and mathematics courses, leading directly to Annie receiving a full-ride pre-med scholarship at Princeton.

So, once Annie recovered from the shock of the news about her revered childhood President being brought back to life, Annie was only too eager to find a way to be a productive member of their exclusive but secretive group.

And, to Pongo's surprise, Harry and Heather had convinced the others to welcome Idris into the gathering despite Idris' well-known far less-than-feverish admiration for certain select parts of FDR's legacy.   Harry and the others had concluded that Idris was such an integral part of their everyday life, it would've been crazy to try to keep him out of the loop, on a pragmatic basis, if nothing else. Much to everyone's relief, they soon discovered Idris actually was a much more devoted fan of FDR's than they'd ever suspected. Turned out Idris was keenly aware of how much FDR resented the racism and bigotry within his own party's southern wing well before his passing.

Even though everyone had been sworn to strict secrecy, it certainly seemed to Pongo the group had pretty much abandoned any commitment to circumscribe access to developments about their favorite, now un-dead, President.

After draining his bladder, Pongo wandered into the family dining room and found the entire group gathered at the table. Franklin was sitting, appropriately, halfway along the long side of the table in front of the window overlooking the back yard. It looked weirdly similar to a modern-day White House Presidential Cabinet meeting (minus the White House adornments). There were decidedly non-White House submarine sandwiches and sodas for everyone; someone had set the table with leftover old "Gore/Lieberman" napkins. The Lieberman part had been crossed out on every single napkin, with the words "Infected Anus" written above it (Pongo was sure that was the work of Grandpa Tom).   Franklin now appeared to be in his late 30's or early 40's. Pongo noticed one of the new arrivals: Bianca's father Sam was seated next to her. He looked like he wasn't sure if he really belonged at the table.

It appeared that Phil was leading the discussion, but everyone was contributing their two cents' worth.

* * *

CARING FOR THE COMMANDER IN CHIEF

12:55 pm, Tuesday, Aug. 17, 2010
Podrowski home, Poughkeepsie, NY

The Plan

Phil had taped a 3' by 5' piece of white posterboard on the wall next to the dining room table. It displayed an outline, which Pongo later learned had been composed a couple of hours earlier by Heather, Bianca, Phil, Mel, Cherisse and a surprise guest.

(I) Preserving and protecting Franklin's privacy.
- *(A)*   *Finding a new identity*
- *(B)*   *Disguise?*
- *(C)*   *Will dead nutjobs be missed?*
- *(D)*   *What to do 'til a new identity is finalized*
- *(E)*   *What are Franklin's preferences?*

(II) Franklin's health issues
- *(A)*   *Vaccinations*
- *(B)*   *Nutrition*
- *(C)*   *Stabilizing age regression/progression*
- *(D)*   *Digestive issues*
- *(E)*   *Preventing loss of impulse control*

(III) Personal day-to-day issues
- *(A)*   *Housing choice (eventual re-location?)*
- *(B)*   *Transportation*
- *(C)*   *Self-support choice*
- *(D)*   *Paying the bills (fair share)*
- *(E)*   *Contact with others/recreation*

(IV) Getting up to speed
- *(A)*   *Education enrollment (long-term plan?)*
- *(B)*   *Acculturation*
- *(C)*   *Socialization*
- *(D)*   *Technology*
- *(E)*   *Media*

Pongo thought this level of organization on such short notice had the fingerprints of Heather's Mom, Penelope Mitsuhama Duarte, all over it. Penny, 50, currently was confidential secretary to H. Fenster Rupphauser, of Whittmyer Industries, at Whittmyer's New York City headquarters. She previously had retired with honors after 25 years as a schoolteacher. She was the granddaughter of Japanese-American U.S. citizens detained with thousands of other Japanese-Americans in a concentration camp in Idaho during World War II. Those grandparents had lost all their financial assets during their imprisonment. Penny's husband (Heather's stepfather), Mitch Duarte, was on a cross-country Homeland Security air marshal flight assignment that day.

Sure enough, as Pongo looked around the room, there was Penny, sitting behind Heather, looking like the cat that swallowed the canary. Pongo was beginning to think it might be smarter simply to rent a local convention center and advertise the gathering as Jekyll&HydeParkComicCon; Pongo would come dressed as a pack of Camel cigarettes in honor of FDR's favorite brain hemorrhage-inducing brand (carton caption: "Our humps are made of the finest subdural hematomas"). Satire aside, Pongo was more than a little pissed that Penny's outline wasn't focused more on Franklin's wishes. *"All that education expertise,"* Pongo thought, *"and Penny only manages to list 'Franklin's Preferences' one lousy time. That should have been the top priority for every category."*

Phil and Cherisse ended up leading the discussion about Franklin's immediate and long-term future. They each, in turn, patted Franklin on the shoulder and arm and urged him to speak out whenever he felt the slightest need to express himself. Among all Presidents, he had proved himself to be perhaps the greatest listener, especially to the destitute, Phil said, but this was a time to speak out as much as listen.

* * *

PRIVACY

With Phil's encouragement, Heather and Idris began the discussion on Franklin's privacy issues on a positive note.

"I have good news about the possibility of a new identity for the President," Heather said.

"There is a files-purging at the county social services office scheduled for next weekend. It's a fairly big deal: it's been put off by management for more than 20 years simply because they didn't want to pay for overtime. But they have no choice now simply because all the old paper files are taking up precious space.

"Idris and I will be among a crew of about a half-dozen people going through old files to identify whether participants still have open cases. If they don't, the files get tossed into a large bin for shredding. I'm pretty confident we'll be able to find at least a handful of files with documents we can use to establish a new identity for the President."

"What'll you be looking for, Heather?" Franklin asked.

"Specifically, we'll have an eye out for thin files, files of women who applied for Medicaid just before giving birth, only to have the child die when just a few days old. I'm thinking the best files to find would be those where both the newborn and the mother died within a few days of the birth.

"We would be discreetly pocketing the child's birth certificate. The birth certificate would be crucial in obtaining a Social Security number under Franklin's new name. We'll probably want to find at least two or three files like that, because there's always a chance that a social services worker might've been able to get the mother to sign an application for the child's Social Security number before the child and mom passed. We don't want to submit a Social Security card application if a number already was issued for the dead baby.

"Of course, we want to find a file for a child with a birthdate which would give us as plausible an age for the President as possible."

(At this point, every eye in the room turned to Franklin, mainly to see how much more his appearance had regressed in age; he now appeared to be in his mid-20s.)

"Ideally, we'll be looking for a birthdate from the late '70s to the early '90s," Idris said.

"Aren't you worried about getting caught?" Bianca asked.

"Heather and I will be partnering the entire day," Idris explained. "If anyone wanders by while we have a likely candidate's file in hand, we'll just set the file aside 'til they're out of sight. I'm really not worried about it at all."

"I'm thinking it might be a good idea to go through old archived newspapers in the public library between now and next weekend to look through death notices from those years," Mel Peterson said. "If you know the names you're looking for going in, it could make your search lots simpler – you don't want to risk someone else in the purging group finding the file before you do, right?"

"Great idea, Mel," Phil said. "Let's plan on the Heather and Idris spending an hour or two doing just that on the day of their choice between now and next Saturday.

"Once they have the best birth records, I'll take the President to our local Social Security office early next week to apply for the card. We'll get him a library card and whatever other documentation is needed before we go. If need be, I'll explain that I'm the maternal uncle he grew up with after his mother died and that he was home-schooled for all these years. I'll do my best to sound like someone who's so constantly suspicious of the government that I just didn't want my nephew enumerated. Big Brother, you know.

"I'm sorry, Mr. President – that "Big Brother" remark is a reference you wouldn't know. I'll loan you my copy of the book "1984" as soon as possible. I imagine you're going to be doing a lot of that kind of reading in the next few years.

"Next thing on the list is a disguise. How do you feel about that, Mr. President? I mean, if there's anyone in this county, if not the entire state, who's a lock to be recognized, it's you, Sir.

"What do you think about facial hair?"

"I like it on bull moose, lumberjacks and sideshow carnival folk," Franklin responded. "And on my uncle by law." (He always thought T.R.'s moustache was dapper.)

"Well, here's the thing, Sir," Cherisse said. "We need for your face to be as unrecognizable as possible. And we need for the disguise you use to be as natural-looking as possible. I know a few accomplished plastic surgeons who could make you look like anyone from Claude Rains to Peter Lorre. (*Cherisse decided to use cultural references from the 1940's whenever possible 'til Franklin was more attuned to the present.)* But I'm thinking you probably don't want a permanent, irreversible facial remodel like that.

"A beard or moustache – or both – really make the most sense. Unless you want hordes of paparazzi and lunatics camped outside the front door here 24/7… not to mention Homeland Security agents breaking in through the roof to put you in full-body restraints for transport to God-knows-where. But, as always, the final decision is yours. Only you can decide what's best for you."

"Let me think it over, Dear. I may get to your way of thinking – I just need a little time. I'm somewhat more used to making short-notice decisions with considerably more potential for grave consequences. Like whether to invade Germany or the Netherlands. Deciding whether to grow a moustache just doesn't have the same kind of heart-stopping immediacy."

"In the meantime," Cherisse said, "we need to get some hair dye this evening for the President. His gray and white hair doesn't come close to matching the age he looks. Based on everything else that's happened, I suspect he'll only need the dye one time because his hair's probably going to grow out the color it was in his late teens.

"Heather and Bianca, would you help him with that after our meeting is done here?"

Heather and Bianca both nodded vigorously. "We'll pick up some dye from the Stop 'n Shop and bring it back here right after this meeting," Bianca said.

"It's time to talk about the pinheads who actually helped make this man's revival possible: Gary "Sancho" Graham and…Denny D'Amato," Sam Swanson said, reading from the dead men's driver's licenses.

"I'm thinking there's a very real possibility someone close to either or both of them is going to file a missing person's report. Meaning it's just a matter of time before some Detective Sipowicz shows up here asking questions none of us wants to answer."

"Well, it's right to be concer-…" Phil started.

"I don't think you need to be worried, Mr. Swanson," Pongo interrupted.

"We found a copy of an eviction notice in Mr. D'Amato's wallet showing both men as apartment lessees. We found copies of unemployment compensation expiration notices in both of their pockets. The car rental agreement they both signed stated that neither of them has any family for emergency notifications.

"I'm thinking their landlord's going to think they simply abandoned their apartment. I think we just might have gotten mighty lucky on this."

"Maybe the only thing we need to worry about is if some smarty-assed archaeologist in the distant future digs up the gravesite and wonders why there are two men with pulverized brains in the coffin of one President," Idris said, eyes rolling. "It's *just remotely possible* we might all not be around for that eventuality."

"My feeling is that, if the worst were to happen, if someone really did come looking for them, we can always fall back on the truth," Franklin suggested. "Their deaths *were* accidental, after all."

"You really are from a different time, Mr. President," Heather said. "No one would expect a politician of any persuasion nowadays to suggest relying on the truth. You can't imagine how refreshing that is – even if it would never work in a thousand years."

"Let's just agree to get together for an emergency meeting of this group if the worst ever does come to pass about those two dead wing-nuts, OK?" Mel suggested.

No one objected to that.

"So, what do we do 'til we have a new identity for the President?" asked Annie, Pongo's paternal Grandma. "Cherisse and I feel it's imperative that he receive all available immunizations right away. We don't want even the slightest risk of re-exposure to polio. But we don't know if it's possible to get those immunizations without presenting some kind of ID.

"Heather, they have those free immunization clinics at your office sometimes. Do you know what they require for ID?"

"Just a driver's license or state-issued non-driver ID card – or a combination of something like a library card combined with a utility bill sent to the person's current address," Heather responded. "But it's next to impossible to get a state-issued ID without a valid birth record. Do we want to risk trying to buy a phony ID to use 'til Idris and I can come up with a real birth certificate? Do any of us even know where to go to do that?"

"Hell, I guess it'd be me who knows that," Harry said, embarrassed. "But the guy I used to use when I was in high school isn't someone I'd trust not to black-mail an actual grown-up adult if he thought there might be major moolah to be had."

"So, that's a big '**no**' to buying a phony ID, right?" Bianca asked.

"So it would seem," Mel, Harry's Dad, said in a snarky tone.

"If Heather and Idris can come up with the documents we need to get a real Social Security card and a real driver's license by this weekend, I'm confident we'll be fine for the additional few weeks it takes for the card and license to be issued. I don't know about you, but I'm not currently in demand for summit meetings on foreign soil," Franklin said. "We will just have to be as discreet as possible until then.

"I just want to settle in, to get acclimated to this century, to all the changes I've seen. If you try to imagine what it would be like for yourselves to suddenly wake up 70 years in the past, without all your smarty phones, computers, televisions and fast cars, maybe you can begin to understand what the past day has been like for me.

"Let's just allow the next week or two to play out as naturally as possible, good people. That would be my wish."

"That certainly doesn't sound unreasonable to me, Mr. President," Phil said. "Is there anyone among us here who disagrees?"

Lots of heads shook side to side. No nodders – though Tom seemed to want to nod off.

*　*　*

Health Issues

"I certainly don't want to disagree with the President about how he adjusts to being thrust ahead 65 years all of a sudden," Sam Swanson interjected. "But I don't see what all the crap is about getting this man the shots he needs. I've been working at the County Health Department the past 30 years. If I walk in there and tell them I've come across a public health situation with an exigent need, they'll hand over to me whatever vaccines I need. And they won't give me bullshit about it.

"And even if they did – probably all they'd do is ask me why not wait for a public health nurse to take care of it – I'd just tell 'em it's for a down-and-out wetback family living in a ramshackle rental not far from my neighborhood…some salt o' the earth folks I don't want terrified about some stranger's car coming up their driveway.

"And if they didn't like that, I'd tell 'em to go fuck themselves. Pardon my French, Mr. Pres."

"No pardon necessary, sir," Franklin said.

"By the way, Mr. President, 'wetback' is **_NOT_** a word anyone other than someone with a blind spot about racism uses any longer to describe someone who's Hispanic," Phil said. "You'd never say that word within earshot of someone who's Latino, would you, Sam?"

"Shit, I guess not, Phil. I'll do my best to set a more politically correct example for Mr. Roosevelt here. You know me: my mouth gets ahead of my brain a lot."

"What we know about you, Sam," Phil said, "is that you throw around racist asshole words like _taco munchers_ and _burrito builders_ in front of your friends who know you can be a real dick sometimes when you're pissed off at Lucinda.

"Your friends know you and Lucinda have some weird dynamics in your marriage, what with the Swedish-Latino culture clash - "

"Christ, she calls me her slobbering _albondigas de salchicha Sueco_ (Swedish sausage meatballs) and I call her my curvy chili choker, **all** the time."

"Yeah, well, people who don't know you that well don't realize you'd never excrete that oral diarrhea in front of anyone who might interpret it just as hateful crap," Phil said. "So why not try to just permanently delete that shit altogether from your lexicon, OK?"

"You know what, friends?" Franklin asked. "If Sam agrees to dispense with the invective, I'm fine with him getting the vaccines you think I need. If need be, I'd even be willing to pose as one of those industrious immigrant laborers. I'm pretty proud of my background getting my hands in the soil. You might not know, but I did plant more than a thousand trees around Springwood."

"Mr. President, I don't expect we'll need you to disguise yourself as a Mexican farm laborer," Phil said. "It's good to know you're willing, though. We'll tuck that one into the utility belt maybe for future use.

"So, if the President is agreeable to Sam's suggestion, does anyone have any reservations?"

"Sounds like Sam has established a reputation for doing that kind of thing. I guess it couldn't hurt for him to try," Mel said. "Who's the best shot-giver in the group? We don't want the President ending up looking like some kind of addict with needle tracks all over his arms."

"S'pose that might be me," Bianca volunteered. "On our rotation with the hospital nursing director, I was the one in our group whose hands shook the least. In, squeeze 'n out, fast as a hummingbird, that is I."

"OK, then, it's set," Phil said. "Sam gets the vaccines today or tomorrow, gives them to Bianca and she comes here to shoot 'im up."

"Phil, my curiosity's been itching me like crabs in a crotch," Grandpa Tom said. "Does anyone here have any sliver of an inkling what made it possible for the son of Sara Ann Delano and James Roosevelt The First to be back in our midst?"

"Well, what about it, all you medical experts out there?" Phil asked. "Whatd'ya think Cherisse?"

"I suppose it's possible that the EDA gene throughout the President's body could've been stimulated in such a way as to re-energize all of his stem cells. Obviously, it's __pure__ speculation, but *some*thing clearly created the rejuvenation of almost every organ in his body.

"I'm not sure what could've caused that kind of massive change without any obvious superficial damage."

"Those of us who were at the gravesite last night saw what looked like scorching on the ground alongside the grave," Mel Peterson said. "It looked like something actually had stirred up the ground alongside the grave, extending out a few inches. We had to even out the grave border closest to the headstone because of it."

"I know it sounds a little Frankenstein-y," Pongo said, "but there was that massive lightning strike that caused the blackout not too long before we found Franklin at the Visitors' Center. It was kind of a strange flash."

"Yeah – I was watching the rain outside my bedroom window when it struck," Heather said. "There was a bright pink glow that seemed to go all the way up into the sky, as far as you could see.

"Before we got together for this lunch-meeting, I checked lightning entries on Wikipedia and found this thing about sprite lightning. They've been seen since at least the 18th century, but they're fairly rare. They extend 50 or 60 miles up into space with shapes like jellyfish or carrots.

"There's really not a lot known about them. Except that they're very, very powerful."

"So, it's just possible," Tom said, "that one of those things could've been the catalyst that re-energized all of the EDA genes and stem cells in Franklin's body."

"I wouldn't stake my professional career on it," Cherisse said, "but, as I mentioned before, he's here, he's got more or less normal vital signs and he's not turning into some kind of fiendish monster. Again, *some*thing did this – and it wasn't the tooth fairy."

"What about his loss of control when he said he was overcome by the smell that was coming from those two nimrods' fractured skulls?" Harry asked. "And what about what was happening to the insides of their skulls before we buried 'em? You know, where the President had kind of drooled into their heads."

"I wondered about that a lot before we went to sleep last night," Bianca said. "So, I took the liberty of asking the President for a saliva sample on a petri dish that was in Cherisse's medical bag – he was kind enough to co-operate. I noticed Pongo had an old biology class display of pinned moths and butterflies in his bedroom. I took a half-dozen of them off the display, placed them in a mason jar and poured the saliva sample onto them.

"Here's the jar," she said, reaching into her large purse.

As the jar emerged, there was a collective gasp of "Oh, shit"'s, "Holy shit"'s, "No fuckin' shit"'s, "Shit a brick!"'s, "Hayzoos Christ"'s, "Mother Fucker"'s and "Piss my pants!"'s from the group. And a "Merciful Minerva" from Franklin. Every single one of the insects was flying around inside the jar, pissed off and looking like they wanted out NOW.

"So, Mr. President, I'm thinking we might want to be prudent about the way you disperse your bodily fluids, especially your saliva. And we might want to take extra-special steps to keep this tidbit of information to ourselves," Bianca warned. "If you think paparazzi and Men in Black would be thick around a re-animated President, I expect they'd be downright smothering around a re-animated President who inadvertently brings other things back to life.

"Plus, we have no idea whether these things that come back to life are normal or if they're some sort of 'killer bee' version of themselves. No, offense, Mr. President. Or it could just work like that '*Pushing Daisies*' show. But just how far do we risk this?"

"OK, Bianca, I think we're all in agreement on the need for confidentiality and discretion, on every level," Phil said, looking profoundly pale. "But I don't think we can base our decisions on whether something might or might not conform to a fictionalized TV show."

"Wooooowwww," Pongo muttered under his breath, in Harry's direction. Harry and just about everyone else in the room were almost comically wide-eyed, still staring at the jar of zombie bugs.

"Let's get back to more urgent matters," Phil said.

"I think everyone – including our guest of honor – has noticed there's something not quite right about the way his age is reversing. I know there's speculation that it's from what he took and consumed out of those two pinheads' heads.

"Whether that's the cause or not, I'm thinking it's beyond urgent to come up with some ideas about how to experiment to find a way to stabilize Mr. Roosevelt's reverse aging. Any ideas out there?"

"If he continues to do well with the anti-oxidant fruits and vegetables we've been giving him – and I have no reason to think he won't – I think it would be interesting to have him start consuming the very worst of the worst kinds of horrible fast foods and junk foods. Plus foods with lots of MSG," Grandma Annie Podrowski offered.

"From what Cherisse told me, his incontinence situation probably will stabilize in a few weeks or months, so my gut – no pun intended – tells me that's probably not related to the age stabilization issue.

"Whatever we do, we want to be cautious. We don't want to accidentally reverse the reversal."

"Here's what I propose," Bianca started. "Let's see if we can balance off the potential aging effects of junk food and fast food with the potential anti-aging effects of the same kinds of things we suspect are causing the uncontrolled Benjamin Buttoning.

"Like, well, we can't just go out and find him human brain innards if he starts aging 10 years in a day. But we can find the amygdala and basal ganglia of the smartest unendangered creatures in nature. I saw on PBS not long ago that cuttlefish and crows have the most advanced non-mammalian brains, way smarter than dogs, supposedly – they can solve puzzles a human pre-schooler can't figure out.

"Cuttlefish probably would be too expensive, but there are plenty of farmers in upstate New York who probably would be only too happy to sell us culled crows' remains. We'd just have to have a believable cover story."

"I like Bianca's idea," Cherisse said. "Well thought-out, kiddo."

"Makes a shitload of sense to me," Sam Swanson said.

"If you can mix those things in with hot dogs or grilled cheese sandwiches, I'm all in," Franklin said with a big smile. "What I wouldn't give for hot dogs and ketchup right now."

"Sounds like a plan to me," Mel said. "Let's move on."

"Next on our list is, what do we do to prevent the President from having another episode like he did after those two pricks cracked their skulls open?" Phil said.

"He's made it clear it was the smell, or at least what _HE_ perceives as the smell from an open skull fracture, that caused him to lose complete control," Heather said.

"It seems pretty simple to me: we do our best to steer the President clear of Urgent Care centers, hospital emergency rooms and the scenes of major car accidents. Anyplace where peoples' brains could be leaking out of their heads."

"Can anyone think of a time when we might not be able to avoid that kind of situation?" Sam Swanson asked. "Besides the obvious, like if some asswipe t-bones the car the President's riding in at an intersection and the dickwad goes through his own windshield."

"Probably, we'd want to avoid roadkill," Harry suggested. "We don't know if animals' brain goo has the same effect on him as the homo sapiens version."

"What if, whenever we're going from one place to another with the President, we simply give him earplugs to stuff up into each of his nostrils?" Penny Duarte asked.

"The good ol' Occam's razor principle – simplest solution usually works the best. I like it," Phil said. "What do you think, Sir?"

"Don't know if I like the earplugs-in-the-nose idea all that much. But I would do almost anything to keep from having that loss of control again. I would _give_ almost anything to get out of my mind the sight of those boys' head injuries. I suppose you can count me in."

∗ ∗ ∗

PERSONAL DAY-TO-DAY MATTERS

"Mr. President, how do you feel about staying here in our home in our guest room for the foreseeable future?" Phil asked.

"How could I not feel like I am an enormous imposition upon you? Your hospitality aside, you know what they say about houseguests and fish, how they both start to smell horribly after three days.

"But since I am unable to stay in my own home, yours would be a wonderful place to sojourn. Provided you agree to allow me to pay for my own keep as soon as I'm able. I believe I'll be finding my own place once I'm better able to support myself."

Phil and Pongo at that moment both were relieved to hear the President's recognition of the financial realities of being back in the real world; the prospect of having to pay for Franklin's food, clothing, transportation and, probably, education had them thinking of huge high-interest credit card bills.

"Mr. President, stabilizing your health and your personal situation is our primary concern for now," Phil said. "Whenever you're able to contribute to the month-to-month costs here, it's OK. Please don't ever feel pressured about that.

"As far as you getting around, once we have a driver's license and such for you, we'll have you added to our car insurance policies so you can drive either of our vehicles. We've still got Melanie's – that's Pongo's late mother – we've still got her old Honda Civic in the garage out back. The battery's probably dead, but other than that, it should still be in good running order. I'm sure you'll be able to drive an automatic transmission.

"I imagine you'll want to establish education credentials for a new career for yourself once we have the new identity for you. But, like you already said, you'll be needing a way to support yourself until that time comes. Does anyone have any suggestions about a job for Mr. Roosevelt?"

Silence...which turned into nervous silence after a few seconds.

"Obviously, we're not talking about elective office or rocket science or computer programming," Mel added.

"What about working at the greenhouses with Adams Farm or Corn Crib?" Idris asked. "He said how much he enjoyed getting his hands dirty planting trees. Sure sounds like that could be a good match."

"Or how about the Poughkeepsie Yacht Club?" Annie Podrowski said. "I remember reading how much you loved sailing, Mr. President. I'm sure finding a good job match for someone like yourself won't be that difficult. You always were known as a hard-working soul, especially after you contracted polio. If that hasn't changed, you'll do fine, Sir."

"I'm not worried about it if no one else is. There is dignity in **any** honest line of work," Franklin said, with his signature warm glance.

"We're still coming out of the worst economic recession since the Great Depression, Mr. President, so finding work might not be all that simple," Mel explained. "The economy began collapsing at the end of 2008 because of financial crimes committed by the largest Wall Street firms.

"Almost a trillion taxpayer dollars were needed to bail out the worst offenders. Virtually none of them was prosecuted. It all went back to the repeal of Glass-Steagall, passed by Republicans in Congress and signed by one of your Democratic successors, Bill Clinton, in 1999.

"Now, this very summer, we've got self-described 'Tea Party' activists all over the country making loud, threatening disruptions at Congressional town hall meetings all over the country. They're mostly semi-literate and mostly racists, pretty much none of whom is aware the funding for their activities is coming from corporate interests – like the Koch brothers – whose main goal is to preserve huge tax loopholes for big business.

"The Tea Partiers are blaming the country's economic troubles on our current President and his efforts to provide health insurance to everyone.

Instead of placing blame where it belongs: on his Republican predecessor who facilitated the Wall Street collapse by encouraging questionable home loans even for low-wage workers. The *same pinhead* who started our country's **first** *pre-emptive* war seven years ago because he wanted revenge against a foreign leader – a man earlier used by our CIA as an *ally* - who once wanted to kill his Daddy.

"Our country has conducted two wars during the past decade and, for the first time in human history, actually *cut* wartime taxes – almost entirely on the rich. Meaning our nation's economy now is screwed six ways to Sunday.

"So, whatever job you end up finding, it probably won't pay all your bills, Sir, because employers have discovered it costs them less to avoid hiring people full time. Because they can legally cheat part-timers out of benefits. And if you thought you were going to find a well-paid non-government union job, dream on. Unions are just a slight shadow of what they were in your time, Sir."

"I do not understand how a Democratic President could allow Glass-Steagall to be repealed, especially if he were a student of history," Franklin said, as close to visibly angry as he was ever known to be. "In 1933, we considered Glass-Steagall among our **top** priorities specifically to *prevent* another Great Depression. How could he not understand the risks of allowing banks to manage people's deposits while engaging in both stock speculation and investment advising?"

"He was not just a student of history, Sir," Idris said, "he was a **Rhodes scholar**. As near as I can figure, the willful ignorance must've come from his roots as a lower-middle-class Arkansas kid who never knew his dead birth father and had an abusive drunk of a stepfather. It all seemed to give him some kind of default deference to people of great means. But you'd never know it to hear his convention speeches: lots of passionate populism weighted against the wealthy.

"He also had a real knack for developing friendships and respect among African-Americans. Millions of people of *my own race* considered him their first 'black' President. His wife tried to use that to her advantage when she ran against a bona fide African-American for President two years ago. Didn't work so well."

"OK, Idris and Mel, thanks for the brief recent history capsule there," Phil said. "So, Mr. President, it sounds like you feel comfortable with the kinds of job opportunities you're likely to find out there, even if it means maybe working a couple of jobs for a while."

"I know of one he can start right away," Harry said with a shit-eating grin. "I'm more than happy to let him take over Pongo's dog-walking duties I've been covering. I'll pay him $100 a week starting tomorrow. It's just an hour-and-a-half every weekday at about noon." (Pongo's former clients actually now were paying Harry $125 a week.)

"Whatdya' say, Mr. Pres?"

"I'm agreeable, Harry, if Pongo trusts me." (Pongo nodded vigorously.)

"And I'll pay you an extra $25 a week to walk my dog Mr. Peabody," Pongo said.

"Have you given any thought yet to how you might want to spend any spare time you have?" Phil asked. "All work and no play, you know..."

"I'm still trying to grasp the reality of being 65 years ahead of where I was a few days ago, from my perspective," Franklin said, smiling and wide-eyed. "Let's just let those kinds of things develop on their own, alright?"

"Sure, you'll call all the shots there, Sir," Phil responded. "There's certainly no rush."

∗ ∗ ∗

GETTING UP TO SPEED

"Does anyone have any strategy suggestions about the best way to help the President become caught up with all the developments of the past 65 years while he's getting an education for the new career he chooses?" Phil asked.

"Maybe the real question should be whether the President actually wants a new career, Phil," Heather suggested. "He was awfully good at politics and even better at steering lawmakers toward the changes which benefitted the most people.

"Would you disagree, Sir?"

"My Mother always told me a person should never be shy about tooting his own horn," Franklin said, "but I'm happy to let you do the tooting for me."

"Mr. Pres, most of the country now thinks tooting means farting, but we understand you don't wanna sound like you're bragging," Harry said, as his mother Cherisse's face quickly turned red.

"Thank you, Harry. It sounds like I have a lot to learn about the way people speak and behave in 2010," Franklin admitted. "Heather, my dream always was to reach for the job my favorite cousin Teddy had. I was fortunate to receive that opportunity. It would seem that I can't have that opportunity again.

"There may come a time when I might want to try to make a positive difference again in the lives of those who aren't as fortunate as my ancestors were. If that time comes, I promise I will let everyone know.

"For now, I would just like to get a better feel for where I am at in life and in this community in particular."

"How do you feel about one or two of us coming here to the Podrowskis' home in the evenings on weekdays and maybe on Saturdays to help you learn about historical and cultural changes since 1945?" Grandpa Tom asked. "Pongo's other grandparents were career teachers – we might be able to convince them to come over during the daytime on some weekdays to pitch in."

"Still MORE people into the mix?" Pongo thought to himself. *"When does it freakin' stop??"* Pongo's maternal grandparents were Orvis O'Leary, 73, a retired high school band director, and Karin Engebritstian O'Leary, 69, a retired high school journalism and English teacher. They were living in nearby Beekman.

"I'm just fine with that, if they won't be disturbed just at the thought of being in close proximity to someone who's just gone through what I've gone through," Franklin said. "I have always loved to meet new people. Especially people who weren't born with a silver spoon in their mouth."

"You should probably understand," Pongo interrupted, "Grandpa Orvis and Grandma Karin will force you to do things. Lots of things, if you let them. Like bowling, ping-pong, horseback rides, hiking, traveling, movies – ESPECIALLY movies - the list keeps going and going. They'll probably insist that *YOU* take them on a tour of Campobello. They are activity freaks. And they'll make you wash your own dishes and make your own lunches."

"I think I already like them," Franklin smiled. "Especially if they like grilled cheese."

"They do. You'll get sick of it," Pongo predicted.

"Once the President feels like the O'Leary's have him up to speed, he probably should consider enrolling for an adult education G.E.D. program through Poughkeepsie High to test out of the final couple of years of high school courses," Penny Duarte said. "Unless he'd just prefer to attend classes with a bunch of 16- and 17-year-old kids for a year or two. He's going to need those high school credentials to get into a college program for whatever career he ends up deciding on. The sooner the better."

"Well, there's plenty of time for Orvis and Karin to discuss that with the President," Phil said. "I'm sure they'll all know when the time is right."

"Harry, do you mind setting up some time with the President to show him things like computer basics, how to use TV remote controls, Netflix, DVD players, how to operate iPods and smart phones and such?" Phil asked.

"Eye Pods?" Franklin asked, his lips squirming in disgust. He envisioned, for a second, pods of cow eyes in a jar like what he'd seen as a student at Groton more than 110 years earlier.

"It's just modern technology for music and so forth, Sir," Phil said, waving his hands like a miniature safe-at-home plate signal. "Like what radios were when you were a young man."

"I'm down with that, Phil," Harry said. I'll let the Pres know when I'll be dropping by during the next week."

"Pongo, I think you, Heather and Bianca should get together and compile a list of important media productions – movies, plays, PBS documentaries, TV dramas and comedies – things the President not only might enjoy, but which would help him have the best feel for current culture and how we got here.

"Once you've compiled all those, we can set up a timetable for the President to see those, in chronological order. By the time we're all done, Mr. President, hopefully, you'll feel like you're truly back at home. And among friends, people of like minds.

"Now, let's find some ear-slash-nose plugs and a hoodie – plus some low-power reading glasses for a modest disguise so Pongo and I can take the Pres to look for some clothes at the Goodwill store in Wappingers Falls. He needs to get out of that old suit, as soon as possible. No one's going to recognize him with modern glasses and wearing a hoodie. 'Til he can decide on his preferred disguise, this one trip won't hurt."

"I'm definitely ready for a drive in the daylight," Franklin said.

"OK, let's all agree to meet back here this Sunday to see if Heather and Idris have had any luck with the new identity and to discuss ongoing plans in general," Phil said. "And let's all agree – just for safety's sake – not to discuss any of this on the phone unless there's an absolute emergency, OK? As our most recent mentally-challenged President taught us, you never know when the government is listening."

Everyone nodded in agreement.

As everyone but Franklin, Pongo, Phil, Tom and Annie headed away, they all noticed Franklin now appeared to be in his early 20's. He looked very little like the man who had the cerebral hemorrhage in April 1945.

* * *

THE CLOTHES MAKE THE MAN?

4:30 p.m., Aug. 17, 2010
Wappingers Falls, NY

The trip to Goodwill was an eye-opener for the 32nd President. He saw dozens of T-shirts and fleece sweatshirts, hoodies, sweatpants and the like with logos of pro and college sports teams from all over the northeast. Plus many T-shirts with the logos of soft drinks, restaurants, car companies, sci-fi movie franchises (Star Wars, etc.) and TV series (Breaking Bad, etc).

"So, does the average 21st century person supplement their income by wearing advertising?" Franklin asked Pongo.

"That's what it looks like, Sir," he said. "But, no, it just became stylish somehow. I think, mostly, it's just people trying to make a statement about some product or team or entertainment they personally like. You know, like wearing a campaign button."

"Are there elections for best soft drink?" Franklin asked.

"No, not really. Maybe, at some level, people are afraid something they like might be taken away from them if they don't 'support' it enough."

"Franklin," Phil said, barely above a whisper, "please try on these pants." Phil handed him a stack of blue denims and khaki trousers and pointed him to the fitting room. "I'll see what kinds of logo-free shirts they have in your size. We'll stop at Target on the way home and get you some boxer shorts and socks, plus some comfortable shoes – size 12, right? You can wait in the car for those…"

Franklin nodded. This was weird. The last time he'd had people help him pick out clothes was when his nanny did it at age 11.

Pongo walked with Franklin back to the fitting rooms. As Franklin was entering the middle fitting stall, he saw a twenty-something young man wearing a t-shirt and shorts coming out of an adjoining stall. The man had tattoos all over his arms and legs.

"Are you with a carnival somewhere close by?" Franklin asked. "I haven't been to one of those since my cousin's parents were gone and we sneaked away for a few hours when I was about 9."

The young man looked at the former President like Franklin was mentally challenged and then patted Pongo on the shoulder, saying, "God bless ya', what a good brother."

As the young man walked away, Pongo whispered into Franklin's left ear, "Sir, tattoos aren't just popular among carny workers these days. Maybe half of all young people get some kind of tattoo somewhere on their bodies. It's in style now."

"Good God. That's just strange – why would people deface their own bodies when it has nothing to do with their line of work? That must make for some fairly strange-looking older folk," Franklin chuckled.

"C'mon, step in there - you need to get these pants on. Let me know if you need a different size, OK?"

"Will do, Pongo."

By the time Franklin was done trying on pants and shirts, they had eight pairs of pants (two denim and six khaki) plus nine dress shirts, (two short-sleeve and seven long-sleeve). The total bill was just over $100.00.

On his way out, Franklin stopped to look at young men's popular culture T-shirts. Looking like a perplexed Cocker Spaniel, turning his head one way and then another, he held up a T-shirt showing Ralph Wiggum (from the Simpsons) picking his nose with a balloon caption above his head saying, "If I go deep enough, I can see Jesus!" He did the same with a T-shirt showing Family Guy's Stewie Griffin saying, "I come bearing a gift. I'll give you a hint. It's in my diaper and it's not a toaster."

"I feel kind of appropriately compelled to buy that Stewie shirt," Franklin told Pongo. "But I guess just about anyone wearing an adult diaper would, right?"

"I guess, Sir. I think you're entitled to at least one indulgence today. But don't feel like you have to share the adult diaper thing with the check-out clerk, OK?"

He finally put all the shirts down and left with Pongo. He asked Pongo later if all TV characters were as twisted as the ones on the shirts.

"On an imaginary scale from Mother Goose to Adolph Hitler, those TV characters are probably somewhere in Mr. Roger's Neighborhood."

"Huh?"

It's OK, sir," Phil said. "You'll get used to it."

Eventually, he did.

The stop at Target took only 15 minutes. Among the 10 pairs of boxer shorts and 10 pairs of socks, Phil threw in a pair of Simpsons boxers and a pair of Angry Birds socks. Just for a little levity. Franklin soon came to enjoy both of those bits of American popular culture. (A few months later, his favorite phrase just before breakfast was Homer Simpson's "*But what of donuts*??!!!"*")

On the way back to the Podrowski's four-bedroom chateau, Phil noticed that Franklin now looked barely 17 years old.

"We can't put this off any longer," Phil said, pulling into the McDonalds drive-thru.

Phil ordered two Big Macs, two Quarter Pounders and an extra large order of McDonalds indestructible (part-cardboard?) French fries, along with an extra-large strawberry shake and extra-large Dr. Pepper. All for Franklin.

Only two-and-a-half minutes later, the drive-thru operator handed Phil a cardboard tray holding the entire order, plus a half-dozen napkins and two straws.

"Sir, this is for you," Phil said, handing Franklin the tray. "If you don't want to end up looking like a two-year-old toddler by breakfast tomorrow, I recommend you pound all of that down now – or as much of it as you can stand. If you want me to pull over to a picnic table on the way back, I can do that."

"No, it's alright, Phil. I'd prefer not having to run into any more carny ride operator look-alikes until at least tomorrow. I'll be OK eating in the back seat. Next time, let's find a hot dog place, OK?"

"Can do, Sir," Phil said.

Franklin started methodically scarfing down the burgers. He clearly wasn't enjoying them, judging from his silly-strange facial expessions, but he appeared to be keenly aware of the risks of continually getting younger. The main drawback to this emergency diet: they had to stop twice between Target and home for Franklin to put on dump-free Depends. Phil was beginning to think that, 'til Franklin's digestive system matured a little more, it might be a good idea just to have him eat while sitting on the toilet. Or at least within a couple of steps of it. *"Depends can be pricey, y'know,"* Phil thought.

As someone who routinely cleaned bathrooms for pay, Pongo had a different thought: *"Presidential doody smells remarkably like Dunkin' Donuts customer doody."*

By the time they all were ready for bed that evening, Franklin's age seemed to have stabilized at about 17 or 18. Phil and Pongo both went to sleep that night greatly relieved, confident that Franklin would be with them for a good while to come.

---

* *"Treehouse of Horror V: Time and Punishment,"* The Simpsons Season 6, Episode 6

After Franklin went to bed in the guest room, he had some difficulty getting to sleep. He had noticed that, every time he saw a buxom woman on the TV set in his bedroom or in a photo in the magazines stacked near the toilet in his bathroom, he couldn't help getting an erection. Then, he remembered: *"You've got a 17- or 18-year-old's body now...frequent erections are just a fact of life."* So, he went into the bathroom and took quick care of his latest hard-charger. He soon would discover that, to avoid embarrassment in public, he would be needing to repeat that procedure at least every other day – sometimes twice a day.

"Everyone has their burden to bear," he thought to himself, laughing under his breath. Sweet thoughts of Lucy quickly followed.

Shootin' Up and Hygiene Issues

Aug. 18, 2010
1 pm
Podrowski residence, Poughkeepsie, NY

Bianca called to say she'd be dropping by a half-hour later to give Franklin the inoculations with the vaccines Sam had delivered to her that morning. She asked Pongo if they had any 91 percent alcohol to sterilize the injection sites on Franklin's arms and buttocks. Pongo put the receiver down, checked his the medicine chest in the master bathroom and came back to say yes.

Bianca arrived as promised. The injections went smoothly, with the President barely flinching at each needle stick. Bianca not only wore latex gloves, but also a gauze mask and plastic goggles. She didn't have to explain: she wanted no risk of Franklin's bodily fluids accidentally mixing with her own.

Seeing Bianca's precautions, Pongo started wondering if the hot water in their automatic dishwasher was sufficient sterilization for the family dinner plates, glasses and utensils. He started to ask Phil if maybe they should keep a separate set of plates and such just for Franklin and wash them separately, but decided there was such a thing as worrying too much.

Phil decided to take the rest of the week off so he could stay with Franklin, who was filling the first few full days in the Podrowski palace by binging, nearly mesmerized, on *Star Wars*, *Star Trek*, *Band of Brothers*, *Schindler's List*, *Saving Private Ryan* and *The Pianist* videos. Anyone stopping by would've taken him to be just another kid in his late teens fixated on videos. The main difference was the empty containers of baby food and blueberries scattered on the dinner table and on the coffee table in front of the 60-inch flat screen luminous electronic diode TV.

Transformed into Percival, aka Scruples

Aug. 22, 2010
3 p.m.
Podrowski residence, Poughkeepsie, NY

The entire group that had met at the Podrowskis' five days earlier was present for their planned meeting, plus Pongo's Grandma and Grandpa O'Leary. Phil had prepared the O'Learys for what to expect, but they still were fairly mouth-agape and stunned to get to meet the 32nd President.

Heather and Idris had good news.

"Thanks to the advance work we did with the archived newspaper microfilm at the library Thursday and Friday, we were able to find case files of about two dozen different newborns who'd died within a few days of birth during the appropriate time frame. But only three of them also had Moms who had passed away during child birth," Heather said.

"Welfare workers had been able to get Social Security numbers for two of the three because they were able to find extended family members to help with Social Security card applications," Idris added. "This was the only one who'd never received a Social Security number – his mother named him shortly before she died."

Idris passed around the plastic-bagged birth certificate of Percival Montgomery Van Mullder. The date of birth would make the child 19, almost 20.

"Judging from the President's current appearance, this age should be close enough to work," Idris said. "We may need to have you consume a few more fast food burgers and fries to get you closer to a 19-year-old's appearance, but even if there's no change, I think this age will work OK."

"What I would like to do, friends, is continue with the home-schooling, so to speak, here at the Podrowskis' for the next couple of weeks, get my Social Security card and driver's license and then enroll for the senior year at Poughkeepsie High School," Franklin said to a decidedly surprised group.

"We'll support your decisions any way we can, Sir," Mel Peterson said. "But are you absolutely sure you're ready for the dynamics of a classroom full of peers in their late teens? Kids can be pretty brutal to anyone they see as not fitting in with their group."

(Most members of the group were aware that Franklin's last experience with secondary education – at Groton – was not the most socially rewarding experience for him, what with him being seen as something of a Mama's boy.)

"Dad, there have got to be at least a hundred movies the Pres can watch about what it's like to be in high school since W-W Two," Harry interrupted. "Phil and Pongo have most of 'em: *Easy A, American Graffiti, Fast Times, Dazed and Confused, Election, Ferris Bueller, Back to the Future, The Breakfast Club, The Last Picture Show.*

Pongman and I can get him ready in the next two weeks if you and Phil can get him enrolled."

"If the President is agreeable, it sounds like this just might work," Phil said. "It's imperative that he get a high school diploma or GED. If the school setting doesn't work out, we can always fall back on GED classes over the internet."

"I think high school's the way to go, Sir," Harry said. "By the time we're done with you, you're going to be the coolest ex-President teen the planet's ever seen."

Eyes rolled and sighs were exhaled all over the room.

"I'm not sure cool or warm or anywhere in between is what I'm aiming for, Son," Franklin said. "It _would_ be nice to fit in as well as possible, though."

"Orvis and Karin, have you finalized your schedule for the next two weeks to cover post-World War II history with the President?" Phil asked.

"Geez, Phil, you don't really expect us to cover 65 years of U.S. history in barely two weeks, do you?" Orvis asked.

"Hell, Orvis, of course not. How far do you think you can get?"

"Well," Karin started, nervously, "I, uh, I was thinking, using Howard Zinn's _A Peoples' History of the United States_ plus the best films for the period – when he's not watching _High School Confidential!_ movie crap – we probably could cover through the mid- to late-'70s. Does that sound about right, Orvis?"

"You're the bookworm, Dear. I defer to you," Orvis said.

Although Orvis always had taken pride in keeping up to speed on current events, politically and otherwise, his focus as an educator had been on music, mathematics and sciences rather than literature – but every time Karin told him about a book he should read, he humored her and read each one, as long as he could make it through the first 50 pages without losing consciousness. His own father, a hard-drinking hard-rock miner from north Idaho, had practically worshipped FDR during the Great Depression and had made sure each of his children developed an appreciation for good newspaper journalism.

"OK, then, we'll be over here six hours a day, except for Sundays, over the next two weeks," Karin said. "Mr. President, we intend to fill your brain to the brim."

"That's fine with me, Karin. I hope you don't mind a lot of none-too-bright inquiries from a slow student. You may not know, but I was barely a B student at Groton."

"It's alright, Sir, we grade on a very generous curve – in that, well, we don't grade at all," Karin said. "We just want you to retain as much as you can."

Karin still was struggling with the complete surrealism of their situation. She'd grown up being told by her parents – themselves both teachers of high school English and civics classes – that it was the duty of every good citizen to be prepared to take on whatever task their country asked of them with little advance notice.

But this was beyond the pale: Karin's expertise was in the realm of inspiring slacker 17- and 18-year-olds not to drop out of high school for a challenging career cleaning toilets at Taco Hell. She counted it as a major moral victory when she could convince a senior majoring in skateboarding to register to vote. It was not what she'd had in mind decades earlier as she studied hard to graduate summa cum laude as a secondary education major at Vassar.

Now this former Girl Scout and college debate team captain was being expected to be responsible for the re-education of her most-admired – and long-deceased – former President. What if she forgot to mention something crucial, like the 1969 moon landing or the Mars rovers or the bullshit about how 'important' for the country it was that the corporate news media discovered Presidential candidate Sen. Gary Hart's mistress in 1987?

There definitely would be some sleepless nights for Ms. O'Leary in the weeks ahead.

Before the group broke up that day, they all took turns exchanging small talk with the teenage-appearing President, who now appeared to be in the pink of health, if slightly underweight. He graciously listened to every single one of them, thanking them profusely for keeping in confidence his sheer existence.

Each person promised to bring food and what money they could spare to the Podrowski home to help defray the costs of putting another "child" through high school. And, with the exception of Harry and Idris, every last one of them followed through.

* * *

The Edgy-u-cation of Our Favorite Hyde Parkian

Aug. 23, 2010
Podrowski home and elsewhere, Poughkeepsie, NY

Heather and Pongo's trip with Franklin to the New York DMV office on Monday morning in Poughkeepsie went surprisingly well, thanks to the certified copy of Percival Van Mullder's birth certificate. Franklin passed his written test and road test on the first try and left the building with a temporary photo ID. Franklin even used the motor-voter law to register to vote, giving him yet another ID card. On their way back to the Podrowski home, they stopped at the Poughkeepsie Public Library; 15 minutes later, Franklin left with a library ID card in Percival Van Mullder's name.

Their next stop was the local Social Security Administration office. Franklin submitted his application for a Social Security number along with photocopies of his three ID cards in less than 10 minutes. The customer service specialist told him he'd receive a Social Security card within about 15 days.

They returned Franklin to Pongo's home just in time for Franklin's day session with the O'Learys, who were just pulling into the Podrowski's driveway as Pongo and Heather pulled up. Pongo and Heather dropped Franklin off and headed off to their respective jobs.

The high school-themed videos Harry and Pongo had shown to Franklin over the weekend were well-received, especially "Election," although Franklin cringed a little every time F-bombs were dropped, especially when Heather or Bianca or some other woman happened to be in the room when that happened on screen. Use of coarse language, especially in mixed company, was not among Franklin's favorite pastimes. The least well-received of the scenes for Franklin were those which were poignantly sad – especially in "The Last Picture Show." Franklin clearly preferred movies which left the viewer certain of brighter tomorrows.

Fortunately, among the high school movies Harry and Pongo chose, genuinely morose scenes were relatively few and far between. Because Franklin had so many questions about the movies, he and Pongo decided to have a regular weekly late night movie review 'shoot the shit session,' as Pongo put it, every Saturday (barring important hot dates with Heather).

On the other hand, the O'Learys' presentations – using a state-of-the-art powerpoint projector with slides professionally prepared by Orvis - were sucked up by Franklin in their entirety like a vacuum cleaner. (Orvis referred a couple of times to Franklin "Hoovering" up knowledge. Franklin asked him not to do that. He still considered Herbert Hoover a prick of the highest order for Hoover's behavior on Franklin's first inauguration day.) Reality, even brutally sad reality, he could cope with – because he continued to have an almost indestructible optimism about the fate of humanity. It was an optimism that would grow more and more tested over the next six years.

* * *

That morning, the O'Learys started off with the Marshall Plan, which Franklin had strongly supported before his death. The last thing he'd wanted the Allies to do after WW II was punish the losing nations. He'd known all along that the Entente Powers' economic punishment of Germany and Austria-Hungary plus the mass deprivation which resulted there after the Great War (World War I) were what gave rise to Hitler and fascism.

He hadn't anticipated the reaction by the communist nations to the U.S.'s use of the atomic bomb on Japan, as well as the rampant red scare tactics of Republicans and southern Democrats. Franklin explained to the O'Learys that he'd read *American Ground Zero* cover to cover and watched Phil's video of the documentary "*Why We Fight*." He added that he'd gained a new appreciation for just how much sway the arms industry held over Congress and the Presidency.

He told them he could understand perfectly well why the Russians and Chinese might be terrified of just one country possessing the potential to inflict such horrifying destruction. Had he lived during the years immediately after the use of the

A-bomb, he said, he would've tried to make a case to American voters for sharing nuclear technology with all developed countries which were willing to submit to permanent on-the-ground arms control inspections conducted by impartial U.N. teams.

"What would you have done if most Americans had been repelled by the idea of voluntarily surrendering war technology?" Karin asked.

"I'm not sure, but I'd like to think that most Americans would see the foolishness in thinking nuclear might makes right, in thinking intimidation of potential allies during peacetime can _ever_ be a good thing. And if they couldn't see that, then I hope I would've stuck to my principles.

"I suppose they always could've thrown me in jail, couldn't they?"

"Well, sir, the government actually _executed_ a married couple, parents of two young boys, who shared your feelings," Orvis O'Leary explained. "Based on disputed testimony by the wife's brother, they were convicted of providing atomic secrets to the Soviets and sent to the electric chair in 1953. The brother was testifying in a plea deal for his own reduced prison time."

"Yes, I suppose sharing nuclear technology would've been a tough sell...but, obviously, I never would've shared bomb secrets without the authorization of Congress."

"Mr. President, I think hell would've turned into an ice skating rink before the Congress would've authorized that," Orvis said. "The Soviets forcibly took control of all of eastern Europe shortly after the war. They built the Berlin Wall and established what most people called an "Iron Curtain." It was a system of strict control over travel from Soviet-controlled territories to western Europe. People trying to leave without permission were shot. The Soviets systematically spied on the citizens of those countries, not to mention our own country, and censored all forms of their own citizens' mass media. They installed their own puppet governments and ran sham elections. It was truly totalitarian rule."

"We had anticipated Soviet control over much of eastern Europe," the President said. "Soviet soldier and civilian deaths were in the tens of millions, far more than we in the U.S. suffered. There's a long historical tradition that countries which liberate other countries from unwelcome invaders receive a level of control over the liberated lands.

"I always believed that, if a communist system was unwelcome in those liberated countries, as well as in Russia, the people themselves would demand a change."

"Well, hell, the Berlin Wall didn't come down 'til November 1989 and the Soviet Union didn't dissolve 'til two years after that. That was a damn long time for people to tolerate totalitarianism," Orvis said.

"Still just a smidgen better than worldwide nuclear annihilation, though, I hope you would agree," Franklin said. "In the end, the Soviets must've realized communism couldn't compete with a democratic marketplace of both ideas and products."

"Shit," Orvis said, "it was the friggin' satellite TV's that finally got the truth through to the average Joe over there. That and their Gorbachev guy finally realizing people getting to *buy* and *read* and *watch* the things **they REALLY wanted** was more important than trying to control every little detail of their private lives."

"That's actually pretty close to the truth," Karin said. "This evening, I want you to watch the video *The Lives of Others* to give you a grasp of what life under Soviet rule was like for people in East Germany."

✳ ✳ ✳

THE WORLD'S MOST TWISTED AND HATEFUL ANTI-COMMUNISTS: A TRULY AMERICAN BUMPER CROP

Aug. 24, 2010
Podrowski home

On Tuesday, Karin and Orvis covered the Sen. Joseph McCarthy red-baiting communist witch hunt era. Karin started by having the President watch the movie *Good Night and Good Luck*. She then assigned the President to read sections of Zinn's *A Peoples' History* about blacklisting and redbaiting. She also discussed the history of what happened to persons who were blacklisted, including Dalton Trumbo, Carl Foreman and others. She had Franklin watch a PBS documentary about Trumbo right after their lunch break. Afterward, she strongly recommended Franklin watch movies with scripts by blacklisted writers such as Trumbo's *Lonely are the Brave* and Foreman's *High Noon* - just to check for any supposed "commie" influences. She also assigned Franklin to watch the PBS docudrama *Oppenheimer*, starring Sam Waterston, as well as another PBS documentary, *The Trials of J. Robert Oppenheimer,* and the movie video *Fat Man and Little Boy,* all of which touched on FBI spying on American citizens, especially Oppenheimer, suspected of being sympathetic to communists.

Pongo, who was listening at the time of her recommendations, chimed in from down the hall: "Dad's got all five of those movies. *(Phil had almost as many videos in his personal library as the city library did.)* While you're at it, you oughtta read everything you can by the author who wrote the book that the movie *Lonely are the Brave* was based on (*"The Brave Cowboy"*), Edward Abbey. His writing more or less inspired an entire environmental movement called Earth First!."

"Thanks, Pongo, but you're getting way ahead of where we're at right now," Karin said. "I promise we'll get there, though, eventually."

Karin also led a discussion on then-FBI Director J. Edgar Hoover's rabid anti-communism, which fueled the FBI's spying on American citizens perceived as political liberals.

"Your successor, President Truman, accused Hoover of turning the FBI into his own private Gestapo-like secret police, regularly blackmailing members of Congress over their personal indiscretions. Hoover wanted Truman to arrest 12,000 people at the start of the Korean War because he suspected them of disloyalty. Truman refused. Both Truman and, later, President Kennedy considered firing Hoover, but neither did.

"He remained in his post 'til he died in 1972. And that's **despite** subsequent documentation that his agents spied on prominent civil rights movement leaders, including Martin Luther King Jr., even bugging hotel rooms and conducting warrantless audio recordings of MLK's extramarital trysts. One of his agents even sent MLK a letter pressuring him to commit suicide in exchange for the FBI not releasing those tapes. All because they thought there was a _chance_ a friend of MLK's could be a communist.

"His agents also had a long-standing practice of infiltrating anti-war protest organizations, even when the only organization members were elderly retirees. That's because he equated being opposed to war with being a communist or an anarchist or, just as bad, being unpatriotic. There were police organizations all around the country which continued that proud tradition of spying on private citizens all the way up through the Iraq War.

"Was there a reason you put up with Hoover's extremism?" Karin asked.

"There were a couple of reasons," Franklin said, sheepishly. "He had evidence of Eleanor's involvement with women lovers and he knew about my on-and-off-and-on again relationship with Lucy. Plus, it's always a risky political choice to discharge someone widely known for being tough on crime.

"In 20-20 hindsight, I wish I had sacked him as soon as his communist paranoia became clear. He was a truly dangerous man who damaged or destroyed the lives of many good people."

"You'd have fired him even if it had ended your political career?" Orvis asked. "Remember: the John Birch Society wasn't yet seen by then as the bunch of clusterfucker paranoid assholes they truly were."

"Well, we'll never know, now, will we?" Franklin said, smiling.

"Let's get back on topic, for now, Mr. President," Orvis said.

"Franklin, I'd also like for you to compare and contrast the post-World War II lives of Mr. Oppenheimer – the man who led the Los Alamos, NM, team that gave us the atomic bomb – and Edward Teller, one of the most rabidly anti-communists on his team. Mr. Oppenheimer always regretted his role in letting the nuclear genie out of its bottle.

"Mr. Teller was the inspiration for the _Dr. Strangelove_ movie character. He decided the atomic bomb just wasn't big enough. His creation of the hydrogen bomb – which scared the Russians into creating massive H-bombs potentially capable of 100 or more megatons - was part of his fixation on building more bombs and bigger bombs. He also spurred the government to keep testing bombs above ground, until the test ban treaty was passed, moving the tests underground. He once advocated for **using nukes to help extract tar sands oil in Canada**. Christ, the Koch brothers would've worshipped the excrement streaming out of his buttocks. Teller ended up a respected professor at Stanford University's Hoover Institute until his death when he was 95.

"Mr. Teller had testified at an Atomic Energy Commission hearing in 1954 that Mr. Oppenheimer's security clearance shouldn't be approved. The implication being that he might share secrets with communists.

"Remember: Mr. Oppenheimer, essentially, was the man who enabled us to end World War II in one fell swoop. But he was forever suspect simply because he **wasn't enough** of an anti-communist."

"And because he'd been screwing a communist sympathizer on the side," Karin said. "Until she committed suicide."

Karin and Orvis then ended their session early that afternoon to allow Franklin time to start binge-watching the assigned videos.

* * *

Concentration: The Camps, Not the Hugh Downs-Hosted Game Show; Raw Emotions Unlocked

Aug. 25, 2010
Podrowski home

Karin and Orvis dedicated the entire morning for Franklin to finish up watching his assigned videos. Then it was on to a discussion of post-WW II issues.

Like the Russians' reaction to U.S. use of the atomic bomb on Japan, Franklin also hadn't anticipated the shame visited upon him posthumously for his order to imprison Japanese-American citizens and permanent legal resident aliens in internment camps from February 1942 'til October 1946. Orvis had planned in advance that day to make sure Heather and Idris "just happened" to be visiting the Podrowskis' home – the O'Learys were keenly aware of the internment history of the maternal grandparents of both Heather and Idris.

Franklin admitted to Orvis, Karin, Heather and Idris that he was fully aware of the valiant combat records of virtually all members of the almost entirely Japanese-American "Go For Broke" U.S. Army 442nd Infantry Regiment who served in Italy, southern France and Germany. He acknowledged that most members of that regiment enlisted to prove Japanese-Americans were just as patriotic as caucasians. (The regiment produced **twenty-one** winners of the Congressional Medal of Honor, most of which were awarded posthumously.)

"I honestly felt that the internments were necessary to protect them. People in 2010 seem to feel there is serious prejudice against African-Americans, Hispanics and Muslims. But racism in my past life was epidemic. The number of whites who did **not** hold *some* sort of racist beliefs was a shockingly, embarrassingly small minority.

"We could've done our best to protect Japanese-Americans from racist attacks without imprisoning them. It would've taken lots of law enforcement resources. It would've resulted in many, many otherwise patriotic young white men likely ending up getting prison terms or long jail sentences.

"From my perspective, entering a new worldwide war against fascism – including the very worst, most dangerous kinds of foreign racists – a war which we **absolutely** could've lost if Great Britain had fallen, we needed *every warm body* we could get to contribute to the war effort. Including Japanese-hating racists. To me, it was that simple.

"To choose between potentially thousands of young men going to prison for their hatred of Japanese-Americans and having thousands of Japanese-Americans families locked safely away in well-stocked internment camps – well, it was never a comfortable choice, but it was a logical choice for a country that needed millions of able-bodied soldiers and sailors.

"If my apology would make a difference, I would give it. But it's hard to feel abject shame for a decision I still believe was, arguably, justified *at that time.*"

"The apology already has been given, Mr. President," Orvis explained. "A Democratically-controlled Congress passed a financial reparations law in 1988 and a key Republican senator (Alan Simpson of Wyoming) convinced President Reagan to sign the bill. The government paid out $1.6 billion, $20,000 each, to more than 82,000 persons who still survived as of 1988 – out of 120,000 or so total who originally were unconstitutionally imprisoned."

"Mr. President, Heather and I both had maternal grandparents whose families were interned for years," Idris said. "I guarantee you that **none** of them would've agreed in advance to losing all their freedoms for four years in exchange for $20,000 each *forty-three years later*. *Especially* just to keep racists out of prison."

"Please don't misunderstand me: I still feel that their internment was tragic, an inexcusable embarrassment for any democratic republic," Franklin said. "Yes, they were punished for their fellow citizens' racism. It could never have been fair or just. At the very least, we now know it can never happen again, correct?"

"For everyone's sake," Heather said, "we hope you're right, Sir. It would be easier to accept your sincerity if you'd taken a more active role back then to put down racist rantings in newspapers and movies.

"When the movie "*Air Force*" came out in 1943 – I think it went on to win an Oscar – it depicted a scene where Japanese-American snipers on Maui were shooting at a B-17 bomber crew that had made an emergency landing there just after the Dec. 7 attack.

"It was a scene intended to make everyone suspect **any** Japanese-American as a potential soldier-killer. It was also complete, unadulterated fiction. Those shootings never, EVER happened anywhere in the Hawaiian Islands at any time during the war. And neither you nor anyone in your administration ever said **word one** to try and dispel that kind of blatant race-baiting."

"I'm going to have to plead a poor memory on this count, Heather," Franklin said. "On the whole, we wanted to encourage patriotic movies during wartime. I imagine, if that movie won an Academy Award, there was more going for it than just that race-baiting scene."

"I don't know, Sir," Idris said. "I can only wonder if that lack of respect for individuals' rights back then maybe paved the way for the waterboarding and other kinds of torture our government inflicted on suspected terrorists during the past decade. Our own government used it routinely, at first in secret, while "W" Bush was our President.

"And the leaders of our government who signed off on that torture remain uncharged and unscathed by our justice system. Does that make you feel any differently, Mr. President?"

"I think it's a giant leap to suggest that carefully interning non-violent civilians for their own safety is on a par with torturing suspected terrorists," Franklin said. "I don't think it's fair to impose on me responsibility for criminal choices made by one of my successors. This "W" Bush should've spent time in prison for each person whose torture he allowed.

"It is **unfathomable to me** that this "W" varlet wasn't prosecuted for the torture he authorized."

"He and his Justice Department in 2002 and 2003 sought out from Justice attorneys John Yoo and Jay Bybee some ridiculously idiotic, convoluted and incompetent legal opinion memos which claimed it was an unconstitutional infringement on Presidential power for Congress to ban interrogation-related torture in times of war, especially when the torture took place overseas," Orvis recalled.

"Essentially, the opinion eliminated a major difference between us and the Nazis. And, for that matter, between us and terrorists too."

"Maybe, just maybe, someday, you'll get a chance to convince a President or U.S. Attorney General to indict "W" and his Justice Department leaders for torture," Idris said. "If you ever do have that kind of opportunity, Heather, Pongo and I would love to be there to watch you exercise your considerable powers of persuasion."

"Us too," Orvis and Karin chimed in, in unison.

"Maybe you can even convince private citizens to bring their own charges forward against "W"," Orvis said. "I remember reading somewhere in college that at least one or two states have an arcane constitutional method for individual citizens to submit true bills of indictment to county grand juries. I believe Arizona is one of those states.

"Of course, a Republican County Attorney could simply disband the grand jury if it looked like it was about to indict "W" or someone else needing political protection. But, if enough private citizens did that often enough in enough counties, just maybe an indictment might finally sneak through."

"Or, more likely," Karin said, "it might result in their legislatures amending the state constitutions to prevent that kind of citizen activism."

"I suppose, when it comes to going after social justice, it makes sense to use every tool in your toolbelt," Franklin said.

Orvis assigned Franklin to watch the movie video "*Snow Falling on Cedars*" that evening to get a better feel for life in internment camps.

* * *

A WALK DOWN FIFTIES LANE: TRUMAN AND IKE & WHAT IT WAS LIKE

Aug. 26, 2010
Podrowski home

The O'Learys went on to cover the Korean War combat between U.N.-authorized forces and forces from North Korea and China. They explained how Gen. Douglas MacArthur lobbied hard with President Truman for a blank check to send U.N. forces (mostly American soldiers) as far into China as needed and how MacArthur extended that lobbying into the mass media when Truman refused to go along.

They explained how Truman didn't trust MacArthur to avoid using tactical nuclear weapons (MacArthur wanted to use nuclear waste materials to seal off the North Korean border) and how Truman felt MacArthur was trying to implement a de facto overthrow of civilian control of the military, leading Truman to fire MacArthur.

"I never completely trusted Douglas," Franklin confided to Karin and Orvis. "Such a self-promoter, such a narcissist. But a helluva strategist."

Karin covered President Truman's de-segregation of the military, the Truman Doctrine, Truman's support of nuclear ICBM development and Truman's tepid support of the U.S. trade union movement.

Karin then assigned Franklin reading materials on the Eisenhower presidency, including details about the construction of the interstate highway system, ongoing cold war nuclear weapons buildups and Eisenhower's outgoing warning about undue influence of the U.S. military-industrial complex. She also focused on Eisenhower-era subversive actions by agents of the CIA and NSA to undermine governments in Iran, Central America and South America.

She assigned Franklin to read "*Confessions of an Economic Hit Man*" and to watch the movie *Argo*, to underscore the eventual effects of the CIA- and NSA-sanctioned 1953 overthrow of the freely-elected Iranian Prime Minister Mohammad Mossadegh in response to his nationalization of the Iranian oil industry. She pointed out that Teddy Roosevelt's grandson, Kermit Roosevelt Jr., was the CIA's Director of Plans who was directly involved in that coup d'etat, code-named Operation Ajax.

"How does it make you feel that your favorite cousin's grandson quarter-backed an illegal government overthrow which eventually led to the deaths of thousands under the Shah of Iran's dictatorship?" Orvis asked. "Not to mention an eventual revolution in 1979 which involved American hostages being held for more than a year?"

"That branch of my family had a different perspective on the best way to preserve capitalism," Franklin said. "Remember: they were Republicans. Corporations, for them, were the all-trusted vessels of American goodness, the lubrication of democracy.

"Teddy *eventually* reached a **much different** conclusion, but his children – not so. From my perspective, corporations can be trusted only to make profits. And they can be trusted to stretch the law to its most extreme limits to make those profits.

"**That's** how that makes me feel...And I trust that you won't find any of _my_ descendants involved in that kind of despicable subversion."

"No, not a single one of them," Karin said, cracking a smile. "So far."

Karin then covered Fidel Castro and Che Guevara and their involvement in the overthrow of the CIA-backed corrupt dictator Fulgencio Batista's regime during the Cuban Revolution. She assigned Franklin to read Guevara's "*Motorcycle Diaries*"and to watch the 2004 film based on the book. She explained that Guevara eventually was tracked down in Bolivia with the assistance of both the CIA and, apparently, Nazi war criminal Klaus Barbie, and executed by an alcoholic Bolivian sergeant after days of brutal but unsuccessful interrogation. The sergeant had tried to make it look like Guevara was killed in combat.

Karin also covered in detail the U.S. trade and travel embargo against Cuba (under the 1917 Trade With The Enemy Act) which continued to that time despite frequent lobbying by U.S. agricultural and other business interests to open up trade with the Tennessee-sized country of 11 million persons.

She assigned Franklin other reading on CIA-orchestrated South American and Central American uprisings during the latter half of the 1950's.

Needless to say, Franklin's video watching and reading continued through the evening and into the wee hours of the following morning.

* * *

JFK Wins and Anti-Communist Fervor Puts Planetary Incineration/Irradiation on the Front Burner – So to Speak

Aug. 27, 2010
Podrowski home

At the end of the first full week of daily sessions, Karin and Orvis covered the 1960 Presidential elections through the 1962 Cuban Missile Crisis.

Karin brought along a video showing clips of the first televised Nixon-Kennedy debate, and discussed the public's perception that Nixon's five-o'clock shadow caused most viewers to feel Kennedy won the debate. Marking the first mass recognition of television's power to enable appearance to influence perceptions.

She mentioned the Republicans' never-ending resentment over apparent ballot stuffing in two tiny counties in Vice President Johnson's home state which could never have kept that state from going to Kennedy, with the statewide Texas race being won by Kennedy by a popular vote margin of 46,000 votes - a margin far too large to have been the result of a conspiracy in a time of paper ballots. In addition, she said, Republicans had suspicions of ballot shenanigans in Illinois, which Kennedy won by 9,000 votes (0.2 percent), despite no actual hard evidence. Those supposed incidents, she said, continue to fuel Republicans' obsession with voting fraud to this very day, 50 years later, complete and utter absence of fraud evidence notwithstanding.

"But everything I've read suggests their obsession with voter fraud nowadays is phony and has nothing to do with actual fraud," Orvis said. "Their goal simply is to make it harder to vote for minorities and lower-income folks, because those are people who consistently vote *against* Republicans."

Karin assigned Franklin to read about JFK's authorization of the Bay of Pigs fiasco shortly after taking office, JFK's support of the Civil Rights movement, his Cold War-inspired declaration of NASA's goal to place a man on the moon by 1970, his willingness to send U.S. combat advisors to South Vietnam and his leadership during the Cuban Missile Crisis.

Franklin mentioned his previous discussions of that crisis with Heather. He said he couldn't begin to imagine what it must've been like for people living through that crisis to wonder whether they would be incinerated at any moment in a nuclear holocaust.

Karin instructed Franklin to watch the movie videos "*13 Days*" and "*Matinee,*" as well as to read about James Meredith's enrollment as the first African-American at the University of Mississippi in September 1962.

The O'Learys reminded Franklin that they'd continue to be coming to the Podrowskis' home for a half-day every Saturday for more instruction 'til they were all the way to 2010. She gave him a preview of the agenda for their next visit: President Kennedy's assassination, passage of the Civil Rights Act and the Vietnam War.

∗ ∗ ∗

Vietnam: Next in the Long Line of Phony Pretexts for War Profiteering

Aug. 28, 2010
Podrowski home

On Saturday morning, the O'Learys zeroed in on the Vietnam era with Franklin. After a relatively brief discussion on JFK's assassination (they emphasized that scientific studies – as shown in the PBS Nova "*Cold Case JFK*" documentary - now supported the "magic bullet" single-assassin theory), Karin went into detail about the way LBJ cajoled Democrats from both the north and south, as well as moderate Republicans, to support the Civil Rights Act passed in July 1964. Orvis recalled how LBJ presciently predicted the act's passage would cause Democrats to "lose the south" for at least a generation, but that LBJ felt it was the right thing to do for the country.

Karin then took a figurative magnifying glass to the start of the Vietnam conflict, which started barely a month after the Civil Rights Act was passed. She began with the phony "Gulf of Tonkin" incident, which led to a resolution supported by every member of Congress, except for two Democratic U.S. Senators, which allowed LBJ, essentially, a blank check to conduct an undeclared war against North Vietnam.

She reminded Franklin of the parallels between that phony gunboat attack and the U.S. government – at the behest of 'yellow journalists' Joseph Pulitzer's and William Randolph Heart's newspapers - blaming of the U.S.S. Maine's sinking in Feb. 1898 on Spain to start the Spanish-American War. Several subsequent studies showed an accidental uncontrolled coal fire caused the sinking, not the explosion of a floating Spanish mine (all studies noted that Spain consistently denied responsibility for the sinking).

Plus, as noted in Zinn's "*A Peoples' History,*" historians' consensus was that war was nothing more than a phony pretext for the U.S. to acquire the Philippines from Spain and Philippine resistance fighters. The Philippines would remain a U.S. possession (except for Japanese WW II occupation) 'til

1946. That war with Spain, she reminded Franklin, just happened to be the war that propelled "Uncle" TR to hero status. Three-hundred-thirty-two soldiers and sailors killed in combat and another 3,000 killed by tropical diseases, all for the flexing of U.S. imperialist muscle and glorification of heroes like TR.

So, Karin said, there was precedence for U.S. leaders' time-honored tradition of lying the country into war in Vietnam – with no criminal consequences for their lies. In fact, the most shocking incident of the Vietnam War – the March 16, 1968 My Lai massacre of approximately 500 non-combatants – resulted in only **one criminal conviction** among the 26 officers charged, she explained. That was of lowly 2nd Lt. William L. Calley Jr., charged with 22 murders. He ended up serving only three years house arrest of his life sentence, thanks to a pardon by Richard Nixon.

Orvis and Karin took Franklin through the eighth year of the Vietnam war, the MLK and RFK assassinations, Watergate, the 1972 U.S. Presidential election and the C.I.A.-supported overthrow of Chile's democratically-elected socialist President Salvador Allende in 1973. They went into detail about the installation of fascist Chilean General/President Augusto Pinochet and his responsibility for "disappearing" thousands of Chilean liberals.

"By the time Pinochet died in 2006, there were 300 criminal charges against him for human rights violations, tax evasion and embezzlement," Orvis recalled. "Exactly the type of puppet political leader our C.I.A. has a long tradition of putting into power."

In addition to assigning Franklin to read *"A Bright Shining Lie," "The Girl in the Picture," "Vietnam: A History"* and *"The Pentagon Papers,"* they assigned him to watch video movies *"Mississippi Burning," "Malcolm X," "Blazing Saddles," "All the President's Men," "Platoon," "Full Metal Jacket," "The Deer Hunter," "Apocalypse Now," "Born on the Fourth of July," "Forrest Gump," "The Killing Fields," "Casualties of War," "Missing"* and *"No,"* plus the PBS documentaries *"Two Days in October," "The Chicago 10"* and *"Vietnam: A Television History."*

When the O'Leary's weren't looking, Phil added *"The Magnificent Seven," "Shane," "The Ox-Bow Incident," "Little Big Man," "Dances with Wolves"* and *"Unforgiven"* to the viewing list. Phil figured no study of the ways cinema influenced and was influenced by popular culture would be complete without the very best of the Westerns genre – not to mention the need to demonstrate the *American cultural popularity of the theme that might **almost never** makes right.* The O'Learys appeared to agree, leaving Phil's additions unchanged.

The O'Learys set aside the entire mornings of each weekday of the following week for Franklin to get caught up on videos and reading.

* * *

DOGGEDLY HOT HEALTH ISSUES

Aug. 29, 2010
Podrowski home

Pongo and Franklin decided to spend the first half of their Sunday blowing off steam. It had been a fairly smooth work week for Pongo at his two jobs, but there were always his worries about Franklin:

- Was he still adapting well to being rocketed 65 years into the future? (His sessions with the O'Learys seemed to be going well and he'd been pestering Pongo to watch assigned videos with him.)
- Was his health still holding up? (It seemed to be, for now.)
- Were there any indications the Roosevelt family's problems with depression were cropping up with Franklin? (Not so far, at least.)

Those concerns stressed Pongo, not to mention his Dad and the circle of friends aware of Franklin's re-appearance.

So, a Sunday at the Mardi-Bob bowling alley and playing pool at the Juliet Billiards Cafe – with Harry and Idris joining them – seemed like a good diversion from Franklin's studies with the O'Learys.

They found out just what a good sport Franklin was when it came to bowling. For some reason, it hadn't occurred to Pongo that Franklin might not be particularly skilled at a blue collar sport like bowling, especially considering Franklin couldn't have bowled after the onset of his polio at age 39. Franklin's light 12-pound ball was a gutter magnet the first six times he tried to throw it. Pongo was about to suggest kiddie gutter bumpers, but thought that was unwise.

By the time they'd reached the fourth frame of the first game, Franklin had figured out how to throw a straight ball *("Teaching him the hook ball throw can wait 'til next time,"* Pongo thought to himself) well enough to take down at least six or seven pins a frame. By the eighth frame, Franklin earned a spare.

Pongo's favorite part of the competition was watching Franklin doodle on the score pad, with the doodles projected onto the overhead screen in front of them. One of his doodles was a picture of an angry-faced Hitler throwing a tantrum in front of a muscled-up bowling pin with a laughing face, with a balloon caption coming out of the bowling pin's mouth saying, "Shoulda invaded a different lane, turd!"

Franklin noticed that the thirty-something couple using the lane next to theirs were becoming well-lubricated with a local microbrew – they kept feeling each other up as one would pass the other between frames. Franklin told Harry he was going to grab a brew for himself, prompting Harry to remind him that, as "Percy Van Mullder," he was only just turning 18, still three years too young to buy brews and spirits. Which made Pongo wonder what it might be like in another three years to be around the former President if he got himself snookered.

Franklin then noticed the smell of hot dogs cooking at the concession stand inside the bowling alley. Five minutes later he returned with a half-dozen foot-long Coney Island-style dogs. He gave one each to his bowling buddies and kept the others, all of which were loaded down with ketchup, two kinds of mustard and relish.

"You're really going to try to shovel down four of those big dogs, Sir?" Idris asked. "Hope you realize what kind of mystery meats they use to make those babies."

"If you had to wait as long as I have for this kind of fine cuisine, you'd understand, Idris."

"I hear ya', Sir."

They bowled six games before deciding they'd had enough for the day; by the end of the sixth game, Franklin had thrown a half-dozen strikes. "A quick study, you are," Idris said, Yoda-style. Franklin grinned back, waving his hand Jedi mind control-style across his body and said with faux seriousness to Idris, "You will want to bowl with me again."

Franklin was considerably more skilled at pool. He even suggested they wager 50 cents each per game. He ended up winning all but four of the more than 20 games they played. What had been planned as a half-day's worth of recreation ended up filling all of their daytime hours. They would've kept playing into the night, but for having to meet with the group of 'confidants' at Pongo's home for the usual 6 p.m. Sunday status gathering.

At the Podrowskis' home, Franklin went into brief detail about the subjects covered by the O'Learys over the previous week. The meeting only lasted about 30 minutes. To a person, everyone there was hugely relieved to see the President in fine physical and, apparently, mental shape. Some indicated they were so pleased to see his level of progress that they might start coming to the Sunday status meetings at the Podrowski home only if there were something out-of-the-ordinary for Franklin to report.

* * *

AGING NOT-SO-GRACEFULLY – SO, EATING CROW...PLUS, BREAKING NEWS: MONGO LIKE CANDY!

Aug. 30, 2010
Podrowski home

The relief shared by everyone at the meeting the previous evening was short-lived.

When Franklin wandered into the kitchen for breakfast, the color promptly drained from both Pongo's and Phil's shocked faces. Franklin's face appeared to have aged more than 30 years overnight – his beard stubble was salt and pepper.

"Have you looked in a mirror yet this morning, Sir?" Phil asked.

"No – what's wrong?" Franklin asked.

"Just step into the bathroom and take a look in the mirror, Mr. President," Pongo said.

Franklin complied, quickly.

"Oh, crap!" his voice echoed from the bathroom down the hall. "It must've been all those hot dogs."

"Looks like we're going to have to implement the plan for the crow brains, Son," Phil said to Pongo. "Please call Bianca and have her jump right on this. Tell her it's a DefCon Four-type situation, OK? We have to get Franklin back to his 18-year-old appearance, or close to it, A-SAP! Attending high school as a middle-aged 18-year-old senior just isn't going to fly."

"Consider it a done deal, Dad."

During the ensuing 7:20 a.m. phone call, Bianca promised Pongo to have several pounds of crow craniums at the Podrowski home by the end of the day so Franklin could consume them as quickly as possible. She volunteered to extract the amygdala and basal ganglia, one birdbrain at a time, and blend them into an anti-oxidant fruit smoothie to kill the taste.

But Bianca had lots of trepidation about how convincing she could be approaching area farmers as a college researcher for a phony drug trial program.

When she approached the first Fishkill orchard owner an hour later about culling crows, all kinds of worst case scenarios jumped into her head.

"What if someone in some farmer's family knew me from high school or college?" she thought to herself. She'd purposely chosen Fishkill to avoid possible contact with acquaintances in Poughkeepsie, but, after all, it still wasn't that far away from her home base.

"What if the orchard owner asks for my credentials and calls my med school advisor? What if they'll help only if I promise to send copies of the finished research paper from the phony project?" So many things to go wrong...

But, after meeting the first two orchard owners, Bianca realized she hadn't needed to worry at all, thanks to one of the oldest-of-all biological truisms: males of almost any species will bend over backward to please a pretty female of the same species.

In addition, the orchard owners all were impressed with Bianca's marksmanship skills: although the only weapon she brought was an old Crosman .22-caliber pellet gun (she wanted as little damage to the culled crows as possible), her aim was dead-on. (She'd learned her shooting skills at the age of 12 from her paternal grandfather on his own small farm.) At the end of the day, she'd used only 78 pellets to bring down 75 crows.

Bianca had Idris consult with his father, Eugene M'Benga, a Poughkeepsie Sanitation Department manager, to find out the best way to dispose of the crows' remains without attracting unwanted attention. Eugene, who loved his son unconditionally, had volunteered to take care of it himself after Idris explained that the crows were part of one of his best friend's scientific experiments for a class project.

Eugene wondered why the 'class' involved in the project hadn't already arranged for such disposal, but he didn't want to ask any unwelcome questions. He'd gotten into the habit of avoiding alienating Idris' friends as Idris grew up in Pougkeepsie. Lots of white folks in Dutchess County, you see, and Idris needed every reliable, non-bigoted friend he could find growing up.

By 9:30 p.m., Bianca had dissected the undamaged brains of all 75 crows, extracting the amygdalas and basal ganglias from each. She blended those with the contents of an extra-large blueberry smoothie purchased at a 31 Flavors store in Poughkeepsie. By 10:30 p.m., Franklin drank the entire concoction. By 7 a.m. the following morning, to everyone's relief, he once again appeared to be in his late teens.

Phil made sure Franklin knew to thank Bianca profusely for giving up her day to save his bacon, so to speak. Franklin hardly needed to be told: as Phil was starting to speak, Franklin was sealing the envelope containing a full-page letter to Bianca he'd just completed expressing his deep gratitude for everything Bianca had done for him over the previous two weeks.

Decades later, the letter would become a family heirloom handed down to her only child and, eventually, to her great-great-great-great grandson.

While Bianca was out culling crows Monday morning, Franklin and Pongo had been discussing movie videos. Franklin had been so impressed with the songs from the *"Forrest Gump"* soundtrack, he'd asked Pongo to order the soundtrack for him over the internet.

"There was lots of killer music from the '60s and early '70s, like from Zeppelin, Cream, CSN&Y, Credence and such," Pongo said. "But once you get your fill of that, we'll start pumping you full of slightly more recent stuff, like the B-52's, Barenaked Ladies, Pearl Jam, Nirvana, The Roots, Rage Against the Machine, 30 Seconds to Mars, The Strokes, Anti-Flag, Steve Earle, R.E.M. – recording artists and performers your high school classmates won't make *quite* so much fun of you for liking.

"Hell, we need to get you out to a dance club sometime in the next couple of weekends so you can get your feet wet a little bit with the ladies. Can't have you experiencing a state of shock from culture clash when you start mixing in with other high school seniors."

"I suppose I'm OK with that," Franklin said. "Can't have the young people suspecting something is amiss, right?"

"Hopefully, you'll start to get a feel for the fact that 18-year-olds don't use words like amiss or varlet or scoundrel very often...Hey, don't worry too much about it – there's no one better than you at connecting with people," Pongo said, gently slapping Franklin on the shoulder.

The *Mississippi Burning* and *Malcolm X* videos Franklin and Pongo had watched the previous Saturday evening had left Franklin glum. Franklin was keenly aware of the reality of man's capacity for inhumanity to man and was sad to see that capacity had continued more or less unabated. However, watching *Blazing Saddles* the previous evening with Pongo (after the gathering of confidants) had left Franklin laughing so hard there had been tears running off his cheeks and onto his shirt.

As they continued their movie talk, they spontaneously starting exchanging lines from the video viewed the night before.

"Excuse me while I whip this out," Franklin said with a Sheriff Bart accent, pretending to reach into his pants, laughing, doubling over.

"Of course you'll have the good taste not to mention that I spoke to you," Pongo laughed to Franklin, doing his best elderly lady voice.

"Mongo *like* candy," Franklin laughed back. (Franklin recognized the Looney Tunes references in the movie from the mid-1940's cartoons.)

"Now is a time of great decision/Are we to stay or up and quit?/There's no avoiding this conclusion/...Our town is turning into shit," Pongo and Franklin sang together, laughing so hard the "shit" sounded like "sh-sh-sh-hi-hi-hi-it."

"How could anyone see that and still think it would be 'cool' to be racist?" Franklin said, wiping the tears off his face.

"You'd be amazed," Pongo said. "For one thing, *Blazing Saddles* was R-rated by the Motion Picture Association of America. Which meant that religious fundamentalists and Mormons all over the country wouldn't pay to see it _or_ let their kids see it."

"Oh, OK, yes, that explains a lot. We had lots more censorship during the '30's and '40's."

They then watched *All the President's Men* to fill out the rest of the morning. Afterward, Franklin said he was appalled at the corruption of the Richard Nixon Presidency and was both angered and surprised Nixon didn't end up in prison.

"You're not the only one who's still pissed off about Nixon getting off scot-free. I suppose Nixon's treatment paved the way for "W" Bush to avoid prison too. No one even felt the need for "W" to be pardoned. The O'Learys will get to that later, though."

✱ ✱ ✱

That Seventies Glow – 'Urp,' 1974 Model Ford Coup(é) de Pardon

That afternoon, the O'Learys discussed President Nixon's Watergate hearings, Nixon's decision to resign Aug. 9, 1974 after his U.S. House impeachment, with likely U.S. Senate conviction looming, and President Ford's September 8, 1974 pardon of Nixon. Karin showed the classic press conference video of Nixon insisting, jowls jiggling, "I'm not a crook."

Karin and Orvis also discussed the economic time bomb Nixon planted during his Presidency that went on to mortally damage the Presidency of Jimmy Carter.

"In 1971, facing an inflation rate of 4.6 percent, Nixon imposed a wage and price freeze program which lasted well into 1974," Karin recalled. "The OPEC nations in the middle east, including the Saudis, implemented an oil embargo against the U.S.A. in 1973, causing oil and gas prices to almost double overnight despite the price freeze on other items. After the Nixon freezes were removed, businesses everywhere did the completely predictable: they implemented price hikes to make up for lost time – with **far smaller** wage increases – price hikes which continued throughout the '70s. By the end of the Carter Presidency, inflation was at 14 percent per year, wiping out consumers' purchasing power.

"Of course, American voters' collective amnesia being what it is, everyone blamed Carter for having to pay more for everything."

"Which isn't to say that Carter didn't bring on his own problems," Orvis said. "He was the first Democratic President to welcome in anti-New Dealers like Mr. Al From for advice on how to deal with inflation. HOW'D THAT WORK OUT FOR YOU, JIMMY?" Orvis yelled in the general direction of Georgia as he cupped his hands around his mouth for amplification.

(Although Al From's Republican-Lite philosophy – combined with the Iranian Revolution/ U.S. hostage crisis and double-digit inflation – led to President Carter's 1980 loss to Ronnie Reagan followed by 12 years of Republican domination of the Executive Branch and the eventual Republican takeover of the U.S. House, Carter's personal future pathway actually turned out not so badly. He led what bi-partisan observers considered to be arguably the most exemplary post-Presidential life in U.S. history, devoting almost all of his waking hours volunteering with Habitat for Humanity, monitoring Third World elections for irregularities, embarking on occasional diplomatic forays and supervising philanthrophic projects through the Carter Center.)

"Mr. From went on to urge President Bill Clinton to abandon your commitment to guaranteed financial assistance to the poor with the 1996 welfare reform act. He had been the moving force behind creation of the DLC (Democratic Leadership Council) after Walter Mondale's landslide 1984 loss to Reagan. His entire philosophy was for Democrats to emulate Republicans whenever possible. He convinced so-called moderate Democrats – actually closet Republicans – that Reagan's wins weren't just a witty ex-actor's fluke of emotional manipulation, but a sign that voters despised most traditional liberal Democratic policies.

"Whenever possible, he encouraged Democrats to abandon traditional New Deal principles and switch to corporate-friendly positions, like de-regulation, as a short cut to deal with inflation. Some of the de-regulation eventually worked out *sort-of* OK, like with airlines and telephones. Others, like the Glass-Steagall repeal, were destined for disaster.

"But here's the kicker: in a May 2000 speech *at your own memorial library* in Hyde Park, President Clinton heaped praise upon Mr. From, the consummate faux Democrat anti-New Dealer, anti-social programs, pro-Charter Schools insider. Clinton said there was no single American private citizen who had a more positive impact on the progress of American life in the previous 25 years. **AT YOUR LIBRARY**, Sir.

"All of that praise for a slick political insider-slash-rich guy admirer whose sole educational background was that of a glad-hander with a journalism master's degree whose only journalism experience was editing Northwestern University's college paper.

"And that's not all: President Clinton in 1993 thoroughly greased the skids for FDA approval of rBGH – bovine growth hormone, a Monsanto-owned product designed to hormonally stimulate cows to put on more weight and produce lots more milk per day – despite studies which showed the hormone could cause breast cancer.

"So, why would a Democratic President do such a huge favor for a massive corporation like Monsanto, you might ask?"

"I would, I *would* ask," Franklin said, all *Blazing Saddles-ey.*

"Well," Orvis said, "my thinking is it just might have something to do with the fact that the law firm where his wife Hillary has worked off and on from the mid-'80s-forward – the Rose Law Firm in Arkansas – **had Monsanto as a client**. They also represent Wal-Mart and Tyson Foods, by the way.

"Sorry to get off on a tangent, but I thought you needed to get a better feel for how the Democratic Party got to the sorry state it's in today."

"It's really pretty Machiavellian when you look at it that way – pretty damned subversive how de facto closet Republicans wormed their way into the party leadership," Franklin said. "And, more importantly, *how they duped masses of voters into voting for candidates who stood against those voters' own economic self-interest, backing issues favored by the super-wealthy.*

"I wish I'd had a chance to be on the dais when Mr. Clinton was making his remarks at my memorial library. It would've given me great pleasure to take him down a rung or two – *after* giving him fair credit for his 1993 support of tax hikes on the rich, that is."

Orvis then went back to Nixon, listing the many criminal counts on which he likely would've been convicted, based on his presidential tape recordings and witness testimony. Orvis also reminded Franklin of the illegal bombings of Cambodia and Laos ordered by Nixon during the Vietnam era, bombings which likely exacerbated the subsequent genocide of as many as *2.5 million* by Pol Pot's Khmer Rouge regime, a regime which despised those linked in any way with foreigners.

They broke off the discussions early so Franklin could watch *The Killing Fields, Platoon, Full Metal Jacket* and *Casualties of War* with Pongo before sack time; they would be watching the PBS documentary *Two Days in October* before their noon session the following day. Karin also assigned Franklin to read online accounts about the My Lai massacre, napalm bombings of civilians and other Vietnam era war crimes by members of the U.S. military before they started their next session. Pongo and Franklin were done with those movies – including breaks for dinner and for Bianca's smoothie concoction – by midnight. Franklin took detailed notes in the dark during each movie and finished his online reading by 1 a.m.

* * *

SOMNOLENT VISIONS, PART I

*A*t first he thought he was hearing the sound of hundreds of sheets of sandpaper rubbing across the hardest of hardwoods as he was fighting the weight of his steel leg braces to make it from Springwood to Albany Post Road on a partly sunny morning. The sweat was pouring off his brow and onto his cheeks. He was completely focused on completing the full quarter-mile distance this time – he'd barely made it a hundred yards down the driveway on each of his previous efforts. But the sandpaper sound was becoming too distracting. Probably just the tree branches rubbing together in the wind, he thought. But just then, he noticed there was a dead calm. Nothing to make friction between the branches.

He was within maybe 150 yards from the edge of the road when the sandpaper sound became so loud he could no longer ignore it. As he turned his head around to see the source of the noise, he looked down to see he was dragging his lower torso inside what looked like a steel coffin riveted to his waist. He looked at his arms as his grip on his crutches tightened: his forearm muscles were shriveling before his eyes.

When he finally got his head turned back toward Springwood, instead of seeing a tree-covered landscape and green hills in the distance, he saw perhaps a hundred thousand human shapes dragging and shuffling their feet along the ground. When he looked closer, he saw not a horde of bloodthirsty zombies, but masses of ill-nourished, severely sleep-deprived, raggedly-clothed men, women and – mostly – children, all following him as though he could lead them to some sort of promised land. Some were carrying construction tools, others farm implements; some were carrying old laptops; a very few were carrying books. There were no smiles anywhere to be seen.

As he struggled to get nearer and nearer the highway, he noticed some shadows flitting around on the ground, apparently from something flying overhead. He looked down briefly – the steel coffin now had transformed into a set of cartoonish-looking oversized (size 30?) heavy boots made of some sort of semi-molten leaden metal, each weighing perhaps 250 pounds. Getting the rest of the way to the highway was going to take a lot longer than he'd first thought.

As he looked skyward, he saw the source of the shadows: a half-dozen large square-jawed heavily muscled – and strikingly handsome – 30-something men and physically perfect taut-muscle-toned women of similar ages, all propelled by feathery wings growing out of their shoulders, were flying above the masses of people following him. They flew up and down the irregular rows of foot-draggers (families?). They took turns stopping at about every thousandth family and dropped a huge, overflowing trash bag full of cash and jewels. The lucky families then immediately broke away from the throngs, but each time one family broke away, a thousand souls followed along, fighting among themselves to pluck up the one-hundred and five-hundred-dollar bills falling out of the fortunate family's cash sack.

As he approached the edge of Albany Post Road, he could see just beyond it gleaming, sparkling-new college, business and industrial campuses scattered among the dense, pristinely forested hills. Digital electronic signs in the distance were blinking off and on rapidly the words, "Now Hiring!!! On-the-Job Training Available!" Others blinked off and on the words, "Enrollment Open – Free Tuition!"

He turned around just in time to see each of the fortunate cash and jewel bag-carrying families coalescing atop a hill overlooking the Hudson River, banding together in a tight circle; every fourth or fifth person was holding a rifle or sidearm, ready to shoot if the less fortunate families approached.

But there was no need for the weapon-wielder worries: the tens of thousands of less fortunate families were using their construction tools, farm implements and assorted firearms to break open **each other's** skulls, impale torsos and sever limbs and heads as they fought viciously over the scattered handfuls of currency from the overflowing cash sacks.

He turned toward the road again. He was just a few yards from the highway. He looked down to see he had his feet back, but he was barefooted, with gangrened toes and black toenails. As he looked across the road, the gleaming, sparkling-new college, business and industrial campuses began cracking apart and disintegrating, as though they were sustaining damage from a massive earth-quake. As he looked closer, he could see his daughter's young children being crushed in the wreckage.

Turning to the scene behind him one last time, throngs of tearful children and hopeful-but-desperate weaponless adults were queuing up behind him, apparently wishing for some-thing better than battles over scraps. Most of the adults were sharing scraps of food and bottles of water with the children near them. In the distance behind them, the more fortunate families already had the lower walls of a massive fortress under construction.

Approaching swiftly in the sky above the partially-completed fortress, however, were huge ships – apparently interstellar spacecraft – from which cobalt-blue energy beams were being shot toward all the scattered groups of humans, turning each stricken body into lumps of sand and dust. The most intense of the destructive beams were levelling the partially-completed fortress.

That was when Franklin sat up in his bed in the Podrowski home, awake from the nightmare, stifling a scream. The digital clock on the nearby chest of drawers beamed reddish light showing 6:07 a.m. Realizing his return to reality, Franklin decided to get up and help Phil make breakfast before resuming his video-watching.

∗ ∗ ∗

Lubricating the Perpetual War Machine (After a Hearty Breakfast) and Perpetual Law Enforcement Abuses

Aug. 31, 2010
Podrowski home

Breakfast that morning was far more relaxed than the previous day's as soon as everyone saw the wrinkles of a 50-year-old man had vanished from Franklin's late-teen's face.

"Sure you don't want an Oscar Meyer's weiner blended in with your pancake?" Pongo ribbed.

"I'll stick with pancakes and fresh fruit, if you don't mind, Pongo," the President chuckled. "Maybe we can track down some leftover crow brains and intestines for you, though. You look a little piqued for a Federal law enforcement officer, I'd say!"

"Hey, maybe you've inspired me to go vegan...NOT!" Pongo said, stuffing a syrup-drenched bacon strip into his mouth.

✳ ✳ ✳

Franklin's noon session with the O'Learys started with his list of questions from watching the four movies the previous evening and the documentary earlier that morning.

"After the experiences of French armed forces in the Fifties in Vietnam, didn't anyone have even a sneaking suspicion it would be next-to-impossible to fight indigenous forces there?" Franklin asked. "Especially after we and the South Koreans were fortunate simply to achieve a stalemate against Korean communist fighters in the Fifties?"

"When it comes to flexing American military might, hubris has the memory of the dementia-afflicted," Orvis said. "Every new opportunity to face down 'godless commies' seems to give Americans a collective attack of amnesia.

"And it doesn't seem to hinder the amnesiacs when the arms industry comes with hands out to Congress. Our elected representatives have a long history of generosity to the armed services. They're always voting to fund weapons programs the generals don't even want. Just Google 'unwanted weapons programs approved by Congress'."

"Making matters worse," Karin added, "if some altruistic politically-disinterested person tries to make an issue of Congress voting for unwanted weapons programs as a form of corporate welfare for members' own districts – otherwise known as pork – corporate news media either will completely ignore the person or they'll go through every detail of her private life to crucify her in the court of public opinion."

"And if that doesn't work," Orvis said, "the altruistic person will be slammed in the press as being grossly unpatriotic for 'not supporting the troops.' There's no greater sin in this perpetual war culture than not supporting the troops. Even if the generals of those very same troops don't want a lot of the weapons programs boosted by Congress."

"All those lives lost, all those lives ruined by war crimes," Franklin said. "All because those malefactors of great wealth were afraid communism might spread from a small country in Southeast Asia across the Pacific?

"Did anyone bother to conduct any scientific sampling among the populations of Southeast Asian countries to see whether there actually _was_ any support for communistic economics compared to regulated socialistic and capitalistic economics? That Gallup organization in the 1930's and '40's seemed to be sort of reliable. Did anyone bother to do any real research before heading off to war?"

"That's easy, Sir," Orvis said. "No."

"If they had, maybe they'd have been able to foresee Vietnam, China and Russia embracing various levels of capitalism," Karin said. "But they didn't."

"It seems like those who controlled the government in the Sixties and Seventies purposefully ignored that possibility," Franklin said.

"You're catching on, Sir," Orvis said. "And not just in the Sixties and Seventies. The simple fact is: there's virtually no short-term corporate profit in diplomacy for conflict-prevention while there's lots of short-term corporate profit in manufacturing weapons of war."

"Because they know Uncle Sam always will pay the Pentagon's bills," Franklin said.

"BINGO!" Orvis said, pointing to his nose.

"What I don't understand is how all those dozens and dozens – hundreds? – of local law enforcement officers who beat the stuffing out of all those college men and women, professors included, in Madison, Wisconsin – and I guess in Chicago and other places too – how they avoided being charged with assault and battery. They pummelled people simply for protesting peacefully," Franklin said.

"And a lot of the beatings were captured on film and in still photos," Karin said.

"OK, so, please tell me, Karin," the President said. "How were they shielded from accountability?"

"On the relatively rare occasions when prosecutors charge police or soldiers, judges tend to defer to claims of self-defense by uniformed personnel, like with the Kent State massacre," Karin said. "Even when there's **no evidence** of a need for self-defense. Remember, none of the four students murdered and nine others wounded was armed. Sixty-seven rounds fired by soldiers versus zero by the victims.

"Much more common was the attitude after the police riots at the 1968 Democratic National Convention in Chicago: even though the pre-Nixon Justice Department could find no evidence for charges against the activists, the Nixon Justice Department attempted to convict protestors who were beaten and manhandled by police thugs, charging the Chicago Eight with conspiracy to incite riots. Essentially, a blame the victims strategy. There were – and still **are** - *two standards* of justice: one for the average non-law enforcement person and another for persons empowered to use deadly force."

"The most famous videotaped incident of brutality by law enforcement was the March 1991 arrest of Rodney King, an African-American construction worker who surrendered after a high speed chase in Los Angeles – he'd been speeding because he knew he'd had too much to drink and was afraid of a probation violation," Orvis recalled.

"Videotaped evidence of the incident showed five officers surrounding King – with others nearby watching passively – as several beat the shit out of him with nightsticks while he lay on the ground trying to cover his head with his hands. He ended up with multiple broken bones, skull fractures, broken teeth and kidney damage.

"Four of the officers actually were charged in Ventura County Superior Court over the incident, but they all were found not guilty by a jury which didn't include even a single African-American.

"Their acquittal on state charges in April 1992 resulted in massive riots, leaving 53 persons dead. It took another year before Federal prosecutors could win a guilty verdict against two of the original police officers for violating King's civil rights. They were sentenced to 30 months in Federal prison.

"That delayed justice for King actually was one of the few incidents where justice eventually won out. The double standard for criminal justice continues to exist all across the country, not just in political hot spots like L.A. or during the Vietnam War.

"On July 4 just three years ago, there were 18 people arrested and brutally assaulted in Spokane, Washington simply for peacefully protesting against war and police brutality in a public park. A year earlier, another person in the same city was wrongfully beaten and arrested by police *on video* while he was trying to buy a two-liter soda. He died a day or two later, with the death ruled a police homicide.

"The local county bobblehead Republican prosecutor there refused to charge any police officers in either incident despite photographed and videotaped evidence. It's *four and a half years* later and it looks like there's only a slim chance Federal prosecutors might file charges for the homicide."

"It is almost impossible to keep a tally over the years of the incidents involving police brutality across the country where local prosecutors have declined to prosecute law enforcement officers," Orvis said. "The majority of it involves people of color – and virtually all of it involves people who aren't wealthy, usually far from it.

"The added tragedy of it all is that it gives honest, conscientious cops a black eye and makes it more likely that random violence could be perpetrated against *any* officer. I'm hopeful that, someday, all armed law enforcers will be required, as a deterrent both for criminals and bad cops, to wear miniature digital video cameras."

"Maybe more importantly," Karin said, "let's hope that someday law enforcement officers' career culture will shift to one that's more circumspect. A culture that's more conscious of the socio-economic reasons why people make bad choices, that's more conscious of the fact that stiff jail and prison terms _alone_ rarely rehabilitate offenders who almost always are likely to be back in the community. A culture that's more aware of the fact that jails and prisons are never cost-efficient sites to place offenders who are mentally ill or mentally challenged.

"As long as there are law enforcement leaders like the sheriff in Maricopa County, Arizona, who believe the best bang for the buck is simply to make jail life as miserable as possible, there will continue to be generational offenders and random crimes against law enforcers."

"How does that sheriff make jail life as miserable as possible?" Franklin asked. "I would think that being behind bars in and of itself is a pretty miserable thing – how and why would someone want to make it worse?"

"He serves prisoners only two meals a day, usually without meat, using the lowest-quality foods he can find," Karin said. He makes them stay outdoors in tent cities – described as concentration camps – when the temperature is as high as 120 Fahrenheit. He forces prisoners to wear pink underwear. He routinely uses demeaning language with them and encourages his deputies to racially profile Hispanics, to see all brown-skinned persons as possible non-citizens to be arrested for deportation.

"The organization Amnesty International first took up the cause of Maricopa County prisoner abuse in 1997. I should emphasize that most of their work involves third world nations which torture and otherwise abuse political prisoners.

"That sheriff has had multiple prisoners die from mistreatment – including beatings - by Corrections Officers. A news report two years ago stated Maricopa County had to pay families of those victims $43 million during the sheriff's tenure.

"*Why* does he do all this? Well, he seems to genuinely despise those who break the law. But, over and above that, he appears to have learned that there's a guaranteed constituency among Maricopa County voters for immediate gratification when it comes to punishing people. He's been re-elected four times to four-year terms since his first election. Not a single opponent has succeeded in trying to remind voters that virtually every last one of his abused prisoners will end up back on the streets, without a shred of exposure to compassion during their incarceration.

"His voters only seem to care about how much money he saves them *right now*, **not** how much is saved by helping prisoners make better lives for themselves later on.

"Short-sightedness has become a popular personality trait in our culture. It's such a horrifically tragic thing."

"If you were an attorney," Franklin said to Karin, "I would've been honored to choose you as Attorney General. It sounds like **you** already have a nicely circumspect understanding of the strengths and shortcomings of the law enforcement system.

"Here's what I would do about feckless bloviating demagogues like him if I still were in office:

"I would bring up each and every one of those slimy bastards in my regular press conferences – one of them per session – and call them out for the phony manipulators they are. I would ask their local constituents to confront them at every public appearance and pepper them with questions about the hypocrisies and cruelties they support until they either admit the errors of their misjudgments or resign from office. I would urge their constituents to begin petition drives to recall them from office. I would plead with constituents to publicly pressure local prosecutors to seek grand jury indictments against the likes of him for malicious and abusive actions under the law. And if their pleas to prosecutors fell on deaf ears, I would insist that they take those same steps against each unresponsive elected prosecutor."

"But conservative establishment-types and members of corporate media would quickly dismiss your pressure as simple political manipulation," Orvis said.

"Is that not what political office holders are required to do if they honor their oaths of office?" Franklin asked. "For a democratic society to stay healthy, must not the office holder summon all his powers of eloquence to aim the most potent screed at the office holders who are the most incompetent, the most malicious and the most deserving of removal?

"If we censor ourselves simply because we fear the other side will try to impugn our motives, are we not surrendering the strongest part of the foundation of our moral imperative without a fight? Is it not how the average citizen actually perceives our motives more important than how minions of the monied elites want them to perceive those motives?

"If it *is*, then the officeholder who values his integrity **must persist** with those efforts to shed light on the reptilian, craven motives of the tools of greed. I would continue to rail at the likes of that sheriff week after week until his own constituents began to take pride in their own righteous indignation.

"It speaks volumes about the failures of the local news media in Maricopa County that a majority of their readers, viewers and listeners there would perpetually support an officeholder as embarrassing as he is. I would hope that, eventually, the Phoenix newspapers and other media would be shamed into shedding more disinfecting sunlight on their county's top law enforcer.

"I just read online that the New York Times labeled him the worst sheriff in the entire nation. Surely the local media can summon that same kind of courage at some point."

"What do _you_ think keeps the current President and other national Democratic leaders from making those kinds of assertive calls to action?" Karin asked. "And not just about 'Sheriff Joe,' but about all kinds of embarrassing officeholders around the country – there are perhaps a dozen GOP U.S. House members – like Texas' Louie Gohmert - who say something appallingly stupid on the record almost every week who continue to get re-elected time after time."

"I honestly have no idea. It seems almost like they're afraid someone will make them stay after school – you know, get detention or something. It's like they don't understand their own abilities to make a difference for their constituents. What do **you** think?" Franklin asked, brow furrowed.

"Maybe it's that they all get their largest campaign donations from the same places: Wall Streeters," Orvis said. "They're worried about getting detention from some Vice Principal on Wall Street. That's the kind of detention that can cut your number of TV ads aired in a home district from several dozen per day to one or two lonely spots a day."

"It probably would be useful to remember that the last time *you* plunged ahead trying to convince voters from your own party to throw out knucklehead members of Congress – mostly southerners - who were blocking your reforms, Mr. President, it didn't turn out so well," Orvis said.

"You mean before the '38 elections?" Franklin asked.

"Yes."

"Well, they did throw out one of them."

"Out of, what, several dozen?"

"Alright – point taken. It's important to be circumspect when going after officeholders who have a history of popular local support."

"You spoke about demagogues," Karin said to Franklin. "As an educator, I can tell you first-hand that part of the problem is the fact that maybe only one in twenty U.S. high school graduates can even tell you what a demagogue is.

"Since the so-called Reagan revolution in the early '80's, lots of school boards around the country have been taken over by ultra-conservative stealth candidates. It's not like those school boards were bastions of radical progressivism to start with. But the Reaganite-controlled school boards around the country have marched in lockstep.

"Their goals have been to suppress any and all textbook content which might shed historical, factual light on the flaws behind the leaders and those leaders' decisions which have shaped our country.

"And they've perpetuated – for the most part – the long-standing tradition among principals of assigning male high school sports coaches, especially football coaches, the task of teaching U.S. history and civics courses. What you end up with – with some exceptions, obviously – is macho men who believe might makes right on the playing field teaching impressionable teenagers the same thing about life off the playing field. Macho men who believe questioning authority is heresy, something contrary to 'solid team play' – macho men who find creative ways to convince young people that same might-makes-right philosophy makes for a healthy society outside of sports.

"Plus, for a lot of administrators, they're more concerned that their coaches can teach what they see as a 'simple' subject: a class where the teacher can just test students on major historical events and dates without delving into subtexts and the ulterior motives of history-makers and their corporate puppet-masters. Something where the teacher can work on offensive and defensive team play strategies while students watch corporate-biased videos and take tests.

"So, it shouldn't be any huge surprise that, as time has progressed, we have multiple generations who equate military might with patriotism, who see unquestioning allegiance to people in positions of authority, even to abusive bosses, as a way to have successful careers and happy families.

"Along the way, that mindset was helped by those same corporate-purchased politicians around the country figuring out after the Vietnam debacle that filling the armed forces with 18- to 29-year-old draftees from all walks of life wasn't the best way to build support for wars. In July 1973, they switched over to an all-volunteer military and re-inforced G.I. Bill educational and retirement benefits with huge enlistment bonuses, not to mention government-sector post-enlistment hiring preferences **for life**. It suddenly became not only the macho thing to do to be in the military, but also the smart economic thing to do – provided you weren't too worried about coming home in a body bag from some undeclared war overseas."

"As a not-all-*that*-macho man, I don't disagree with Karin," Orvis said. "But I don't know how much of it is attributable to Reaganites and their mutated offspring like W's Karl "Turdblossom" Rove and how much of it is simply the vicious circle of pressure from stingy voters on politicians to constantly cut taxes for schools and infrastructure, consequences be damned.

"Schools using 25-year-old textbooks are just as crippled as schools using textbooks censored by wacko right wingnuts in Texas."

"What do wacko right wingnuts in Texas have to do with textbooks being censored?" Franklin asked.

"Major national textbook publishers wait every year to see when the Texas State School Board decides what kind of textbook subject matter it will demand to be included and to be suppressed," Karin said. "It's not uncommon for that board to demand that references to the theory of evolution as settled science be suppressed."

"So, if I understand you correctly, the Texas School Board gets to decide what reality is **for almost every student in the U.S.A.**," Franklin said.

"Their purchasing power translates into power to control minds," Orvis said, nodding.

"That's so damnably disturbing," Franklin said. "It certainly sounds like the Republicans continue to be aliens to the spirit of American democracy. How does that get changed? It's just profoundly dangerous."

"The state's rights nuts out there – you know, the ones who wrap themselves in the flag and claim state's rights equal patriotism when they're mostly really just racists – they've managed to conflate local control of schools with patriotism," Karin said.

"The only way we'll overcome insane anti-science and anti-equality themes in school curricula is if there is a constitutional amendment ensuring a national right to a free education through college graduation, an education based on national standards of empirical reality."

"Which won't happen as long as the Citizen United Supreme Court ruling stands."

"Why is it bad for citizens to be united?" Franklin asked.

"Citizens United is the name of the U.S. Supreme Court decision early this year which essentially killed off campaign finance reform," Orvis said. "It was named after a far-right-wing Republican group which fought being designated as a campaign contributor because it wanted to air a virulently fact-challenged movie about Hillary Clinton during the 2008 Presidential primary campaign. The decision essentially removed virtually all limits on corporate and union campaign contributions and allows candidates' supporters to conceal the source of contributions.

"It reinforced the sick 1886 legal interpretation by a Supreme Court law clerk that corporations have 14th Amendment rights of persons, even though they're artificial limited-liability entities created by and regulated by state governments.

"Because huge corporations and their directors have virtually unlimited financial resources, it's a monstrous advantage for the party of big business, the Republicans. The last thing the 'R's want is a free empirical reality-based education through college for everyone."

"All the studies have shown those with B.A. degrees and advanced degrees are far more likely to vote against Republicans," Karin said.

"As I said in 1936, government by organized money is just as dangerous as government by organized mob," Franklin recalled. "If the party of the corporate kings of organized money, the Republicans, is still unanimous in their hatred for progressives, why don't the progressives show they're unashamed to welcome that hatred?

"When I said those words 74 years ago, it made it clear to victims of the Great Depression whose side we were on.

"It's why one of my biographers has flatteringly labeled me a traitor to my class. I couldn't be prouder of that description."

"The Democratic Party of the 21st century has been partly co-opted by corporate money," Orvis said. "Their leadership, from the top down, made the pragmatic decision that the only way they can buy enough media advertising to compete with business-bought candidates is to take money from big business too. You remember our talk about the DLC.

"Their strategy seems to be that they're willing to sell a little bit less of their souls to corporate fascists than Republicans are, so they're the more virtuous candidates. I just can't see that as a winning campaign slogan. Besides, once they get a taste for that corporate celery, the appetite for it just seems to keep growing."

"Here's what I'm thinking, Mr. and Mrs. O'Leary: it's time for a new constitutional convention," Franklin said.

"The convention should, once and for all, permanently rescind the idiotic doctrine of corporate personhood. And it should enshrine forever the doctrine of equal rights for women, equal pay for equal work.

"And while they're at it, the convention should implement the Second Bill of Rights I proposed in 1944: the right to a useful and remunerative job which pays enough to provide adequate food, clothing and recreation for a family; the right of every non-corporate farmer to raise and sell his products at a return which will give him and his family a decent living; the right of every businessman, large and small, to trade in an atmosphere of freedom from unfair competition and domination by monopolies at home or abroad; the right of every family to a decent home; the right to adequate medical care and the opportunity to achieve and enjoy good health; the right to adequate protection from the economic fears of old age, sickness, accident, and unemployment plus the right to a good education, including up to four years of college or trade school."

"Do you have any ideas about how to orchestrate nationwide support for a constitutional convention?" Orvis asked, trying to stifle a laugh. "Keeping in mind the national news media are controlled by fairly monolithic ultra-conservative corporate interests. You know, the kind of forward-thinking geniuses who've given us bubble-headed bleach blondes on news programs gushing about the latest trends in fashion for cats and dogs."

"You know, Orvis, if highly-motivated people like yourself think a constitutional convention is so unlikely as to be a laughing matter, isn't that giving up before the first pitch is thrown?" Franklin asked. "Republicans don't think that way. They set high soul-crushing goals and then fight hard and dirty to achieve them, even if those goals seem wildly unattainable. From everything I've been reading in the past few days, they're probably going to win control of enough state legislatures this year to gerrymander Congressional districts all over the country to guarantee a U.S. House majority for at least another ten years.

"If some Republican strategist in some smoke-filled room someplace hadn't had the audacity to suggest that was possible right after President Obama was elected two years ago, they wouldn't be about to succeed now. Sure, it meant they had to demonize the President from his first day in office forward, even at the risk of appearing unpatriotic during wartime. But they knew there were enough racist hatemongers to make that strategy feasible.

"What if progressives had the same kind of audacity to bet on the character of the majority of voters around the country who support both social justice and economic justice? I'm talking about the descendants of all those good men who fought fascism – they're called Boomers, right? Surely their memories can be refreshed about what happens when too much money is in too few hands."

"*If* they can be torn away from their smart phones, video games and cable TV – **and** torn away from the effects of their shrinking incomes," Karin said. "Numbing the minds of the average person is a mega-billion dollar industry. Microsoft, Apple, Time-Warner Cable, Comcast, Dish Network, DirecTV, Netflix, Verizon, AT & T, Sprint – 'information technology' is all the rage. It might as well be called electronic lobotomization. Huge volumes of enlightenment available on the internet are more than offset by hundreds of YouTube kitten and puppy videos.

"I'd like to share your optimism about people supporting social and economic justice. But the first time you try to organize a **real** movement for that, TV news directors will be putting on camera all kinds of Republicans and closet

Republicans – like Hillary Clinton – who'll predict failure for the movement and claim those behind it simply want to raise taxes on _every_one, not just the rich, truth be damned."

"Middle income tax-raisers are the 21st century's version of commies-behind-every-corner," Orvis said. "Something the corporate media equates with terror."

"There doesn't have to be any truth behind it – even when an initiative says in _bold black and white print_ that a new tax will **only** be on the wealthy, massive TV advertising funded by fat cats can still convince lower-income people _they'll be next,_" Karin said, making a faux dramatic face. "There's an initiative exactly like that on the ballot in the State of Washington in two months and polls say it's going down in flames for exactly that reason."

"Never mind that continually cutting taxes means school classrooms get more and more crowded with students, that more and more bridges are falling apart occasionally killing people, that more and more diseases are becoming harder to cure," Orvis said.

"The Republicans' answer to the problems caused _by them continually under-funding government_ is to _privatize_ everything," Karin explained. "Unfortunately, making a profit on privatized government services usually means having to cheat, having to find a way to illegally or unsafely cut corners – as well as cutting employees' wages and benefits.

"They've even found a way to privatize public schools: the so-called charter school program. It's designed to draw the brighter students away from regular public schools – cherry-picking. The schools make a profit by paying teachers less and providing poor employee benefits with little or no retirement pay. All while sucking taxpayer dollars away from traditional public schools.

"That's how they've managed to keep alive myths like trickle-down economics. They can control curricula in the charter schools, so they can keep teaching high school juniors and seniors phony stuff like the Laffer Curve, ridiculous theories with absolutely no real-world supporting evidence. You'll learn more about that when we cover the Ronnie Reagan era. Trickle down was a theory that, if we just let rich people keep getting richer – _at everyone else's expense,_ their blessed munificence would lead to more and more manna trickling down to the hoi polloi. Reagan's **own Vice President** called it voodoo economics. But compulsive Republican liars keep repeating its supposed wondrous effects and cramming it into charter school students' brains, not to mention using corporate news media talking heads to perpetuate the fantasy.

"We thought the 2008 financial meltdown drove a stake into the heart of that theory once and for all, but the "R's" keep bringing it back. Their latest most favorite version is the one about how rich peoples' largesse creates jobs. Despite the fact that virtually every economist agrees it's healthy consumer demand – middle-class and working poor folks _actually having money **to spend**_ on non-essentials – which motivates business to create jobs."

"I'm convinced that's the reason corporate news media fixates on the British royal family so much," Karin said. "They keep showing those cherubic smiling royal faces, as though they want to drill it into all their viewers' brains that the royals' sheer inherently opulent souls radiate goodness – it's as though every time the latest royal baby takes a diaper dump, some talking head wants to mine it for magic diamonds.

"In other words, the very wealthiest of white folks always are equated with kind wishes for their lessers. Almost never, **ever** mentioned are the Brits who object to the massive taxpayer subsidies for those same royals. In fact, quite the opposite: the British antithesis of the New Dealer, 1980s Prime Minister Margaret Thatcher, was mostly lionized – like Ronnie Reagan – for trying to crush labor unions, slash government benefits for the non-wealthy, cut industrial wages for the British middle class, decimate taxes on the rich and jack up taxes on the non-rich."

"We digress a bit there, Dear," Orvis said. "Back to privatization in the USA. There are the privatized so-called niche success stories, like Gilead," Orvis said. Gilead is a for-profit company doing what the likes of Jonas Salk and Albert Sabin did in the 1950's completely out of altruism. Except the Hepatitis C cure they're working to perfect won't be given out at clinics free like the polio vaccine was: they're planning to charge $84,000 - $1,000 per pill in the U.S.A.

"*Despite* charging $10 per pill *for the same drug* in Egypt. The so-called free market at work."

"And corporate news media have managed to keep the story of obscene medical profits pretty well suppressed," Karin said.

"Another growth industry for privatization since the early 1980s has been privatized prisons," Orvis added.

"You've got to be joking," Franklin said. "How can a privatized prison possibly succeed?"

"Depends on your definition of success," Orvis said. "If success is measured by profits, then privatized prisons are right up there. Corrections Corporation of America is a major Wall Street player. They've been getting contracts from state governments to run prisons since early 1983 and even got a contract to run a Federal prison in 1992.

"They've got critics - LOTS of 'em," Karin said. "They allege that prison privateers routinely understaff detention centers, lobby for laws and contract provisions which are designed to keep prisons full of non-violent offenders, undercut availability of rehabilitation programs, skimp on medical supervision, mistreat prisoners, falsify records, obstruct unionization efforts and mismanage prisons so badly that prisoners are more prone to violence. All in the name of profit.

"*Even children* have been victimized by for-profit detention centers. Two Pennsylvania judges actually pleaded guilty last year for taking kickbacks to help PA Child Care keep its juvenile detention centers full by improperly sentencing children to serve detention terms. Children taken into police custody for common adolescent violations – like shoplifting and defying parental discipline by running away – were placed in detention alongside teenage rapists and violent gang members. It was called the Kids for Cash scandal. When we're done today, you can watch the "*Capitalism: A Love Story*" video for more details."

"Monetizing peoples' miseries. It's now the American way," Orvis said.

"Dear God…," Franklin said, pausing, his face turning redder and redder.

"OK, I grant you good people that this all sounds pretty depressing. But I refuse to give up on the belief that Americans want to be optimistic about the future. Optimistic enough to want to fight for social and economic justice.

"I am going to make it my goal to figure out a strategy to get Americans to demand a new constitutional convention. To get the constitution right once and for all. To get rid once and for all of the defects that those slave-holding, greedy bastard economic royalists insisted on including in the 18th century. The defects designed to preserve massive wealth of huge land-holders."

"Karin and I both hope you'll come up with a brilliant strategy, Mr. President. If anyone can, it's you."

Orvis was pretty sure he could already see the wheels turning in Franklin's mind on that very strategy. In fact, Franklin would be demonstrating that strategy as early as his spring 2011 school break.

The Orvises assigned Franklin to watch videos from the President Jimmy Carter era that afternoon and evening and before their noon session was to start the following day, including "The China Syndrome," "Taxi Driver," "Close Encounters of the Third Kind" and "Norma Rae." Once again, Franklin prevailed upon Pongo to join him for the parade of videos.

∗ ∗ ∗

Sept. 1, 2010
Podrowski home

The first topic of discussion between the Orvises and Franklin on the first morning of the new month was about nuclear power. Franklin was dumbfounded that an industry with so many risks had managed to gain a foothold in the 1970s.

"How in the world did profit-making utilities convince the public to allow nuclear plants to be built **_anywhere_**?" Franklin asked. "What sort of sentient person with even a sixth grade education would want to be in the same **hemisphere** as one of those toxic behemoths?"

"There was a culture of pro-nuclear propaganda which had been scattered hither and yon in the public consciousness for decades," Orvis explained. "As far back as 1950, rich white business people in the film drama "*Destination Moon*" were touting the use nukes to power space exploration and industrial activity on Earth.

"Pro-nuke industrialists wanted people to associate nukes with something other than horrific death by irradiation and incineration. They claimed nuclear power would be so cheap it wouldn't even be worth metering by utilities. They wanted to use nuclear weapons to excavate for dams and drill for oil. It was absolute insanity."

"President Carter had been an officer on board a nuclear submarine. He was a nuclear energy supporter – he even went in person in April 1979 to Three Mile Island in Harrisburg, Pennsylvania shortly after the nuclear meltdown there to re-assure the American public," Karin recalled.

"But I think most people these days associate nuclear power with evil power plant owner C. Montgomery Burns and the mutated three-eyed fish Blinky on "*The Simpsons*" TV show. The only country in the world which produces a significant share of its power from nuke plants is France. That doesn't seem likely to change."

"At least, not until someone can figure out a way to transform deadly nuclear waste into yummy cookie dough or sweet-smelling fairy farts or some such thing," Orvis quipped.

"I still don't understand why taxpayers tolerate picking up the tab for safe disposal – if there even *is* such a thing as safe disposal, that is – of the nuclear wastes. Especially when the waste is coming **from *for-profit* utilities**. Doesn't anyone have the guts to speak out about that kind of corporate welfare?" Franklin asked, red-faced.

"Utilities are fabulously wealthy organizations," Orvis explained. "Their front groups air phony TV and radio ads touting nuke energy as clean energy, as global warming-friendly energy. Never mind that the nuclear wastes will be the deadliest substances on the planet for hundreds of thousands of years.

"They managed to buy the allegiance of our current president with massive campaign contributions leading up to the 2008 election. They're not stupid – they know how to spread money around to officeholders in both major parties."

"Jesus Henry Christ," Franklin said. "How in God's name could the Supreme Court rationalize that massive concentrations of corporate money are the same thing as a lone individual taking out a newspaper ad or making a $100 contribution to a candidate? How does the public not see that for the blatant corruption it bespeaks? How does the public not take to the streets with torches and pitchforks demanding the removal of those corrupt judges and justices?"

"It's really sadly simple," Karin said. "The middle class these days focuses virtually all of its attention on surviving, on not losing their homes and their meager, if any, life savings. Thirty years of intense anti-union propaganda, Republican union busting and corporate wage stagnation will do that."

"That's right," Orvis said. "Once the Republicans' mid-'50s skull-fucking of the Iranian government eventually spawned the 1979 Iranian revolution which led to Jimmy Carter's re-election loss to Ronnie Reagan, the anti-union propaganda took off like a cast of crabs up a cheap whore's cu-, uh, country home. Pardon my French, by the say, Sir.

"Reagan flexed every bit of his testosterone-fueled dickishness when he proudly fired striking PATCO air traffic controllers who refused to return to work in August 1981. For wanting better, safer working conditions and a guaranteed middle-class income, the union members were labeled as greedy law-breakers by Reagan. He summoned every bit of his Hollywood charisma to portray the strikers as selfish lazy government workers. And he put the entire flying public at risk of major accidents by replacing strikers with 5,000 less-than-qualified scab controllers.

"All to bring about the death of the union movement. And, for the most part, he succeeded far beyond his wildest dreams. The only remaining relatively healthy unions left in the country represent government workers, teachers and, ironically, airplane manufacturing employees. And every year, even with the 2008 financial crash, there are more and more billionaires."

"So, it's no wonder the middle class has no time to take to the streets with pitchforks and torches," Franklin said. "They're too busy working two and three jobs apiece."

"You're learning fast, Sir," Orvis said.

"As if sucking the life out of unions weren't enough, the corporatists have taken on a new challenge in the last decade: trying to *gradually wipe out requirements for overtime pay* under your 1938 Fair Labor Standards Act," Karin explained.

"In 2004, "W" Bush's Labor Department revised the definition of which employees were considered management – and, therefore, not entitled to being paid time-and-a-half for overtime hours – causing as many as SIX MILLION hard-working folks to lose their right to overtime pay.

"We're talking about fast food franchise assistant managers who make less than $22,000 a year in some situations. Can you imagine being expected to work 65 hours or more a week for the equivalent of $6 or so an hour? Could the Republicans' contempt for working class families be any more transparent?"

"When I signed that Act into law in '38, $6 would buy quite a bit," Franklin said. "It would've been a decent day's pay."

"That was more than 70 years ago, though, Sir," Karin said. "Six dollars today will buy a couple of pounds of high-fat hamburger meat if it's on sale. That's it. And it's more than a dollar an hour less than the shamefully-low Federal minimum wage.

"It's guaranteed poverty.

"The corporatists of both political parties are fixated on the cold bottom-line perspective most hard-core capitalist employers have toward their workers: they see employees the way an oncologist sees cancer. In their view, each employee is a parasitic tumor which grows from unavoidable exposure to consumers. They want to figure out how many tumor-employees they can permanently scalpel out and still be able to prosper."

"And it's *not just* both union **and** non-union hourly workers, along with newly-privatized government services, that have been screwed over while the middle class has been decimated," Orvis said. "The corporatists even figured out how to profit off Workers' Compensation.

"They set up different systems from state to state all over the country. For instance, a woman who loses a hand on the job in Alabama might be paid $37,000 and a woman with the same injury in Nevada might be paid $740,000. There's neither rhyme nor reason to it. It's all about insurance profit and keeping employers' insurance premiums as low as possible.*

"Ronnie Reagan was the first post-New Deal, post-Great Society President to blame government for everyone's problems," Orvis continued. "He famously lambasted wasteful spending, especially on social programs, but he went on to be responsible for the most massive amounts of deficit spending in the history of the country at the time. Mostly throwing our tax bucks at weapons systems – Pentagon spending.

"By the time he left office, the national debt under his watch had more than doubled from the time President Carter left office. Think about it: all the debt accrued by our country over 204 years doubled by Reagan in eight years. A coalition of Republicans and so-called conservative Democrats – actually closet Republicans mostly from the South – gave the military whatever it wanted *and then some* during those years.

"Reagan wanted the Soviets to know we had plenty of weapons to destroy them and that we were willing to use them. It was a profoundly scary time."

"And amazingly ironic in that the party which considers him the most revered figure in Republican history probably would kick him out if he came back today and tried to get away with all that deficit spending," Karin said. "Not to mention his tacit support of women's control over their bodies, pro-choice, whatever you want to call it.

"But what's most important to today's Tea Partier "R's" **isn't** the dark, stealth corporate money funneled by corporate toady-slash-ex-Republican House Whip Dick Armey from the likes of the Kochs that's fueling their activities.

"What's most important to them **is** that big lie Reagan kept telling throughout his presidency that keeps getting repeated again and again and again: demonizing "*the government*" as what's out to make the average person's life harder.

"When, in fact, government of the people, by the people and for the people – elected **by the _people_** and **_not_** by *corporate boards* – is the **_only_** mechanism in _any_ country that can keep the playing field level for the average worker and consumer. The unspoken implication in Reagan's big lie is that, if we just kept the government's nose out of businesses and let them do their business without all that "awful" regulation, everything would constantly be coming up roses from the lowliest toilet scrubber up to the richest C.E.O.

"Never mind all that pesky U.S. history, what with child labor abuses, mandatory seven-day workweeks, no sick pay, no paid holidays, lots of deadly working conditions, lots of deadly products – all those things that were commonplace *before* laws were passed *and* enforced by the **evil ol' government** to protect workers

---

* 3/8/15 *Spokesman-Review* "Smart Bombs" column, Gary Crooks

and consumers nationwide. Things that *still* get duplicitous corporations into trouble with the government – like exploding coal mines, exploding Ford Pinto gas tanks, GM vehicles with ignition switches that kill occupants by turning engines off without warning, food container linings which reduce men's sperm counts, Monsanto's genetically-modified organism (GMO) frankenfoods – the list goes on and on.

"So rich person suck-ups like Reagan notwithstanding, with all the crap corporations already try to sneak past us, can you imagine what corporations would do to us if we didn't have government oversight agencies looking out for us?

"Reagan also was the first President to use the strategy of appointing to cabinet posts cravenly political hacks dedicated to destroying the departments they supervised," Karin explained. "People like Anne Gorsuch Burford at the EPA – who, ironically, or *justifiably*, died of cancer after working hard to gut regulations on environmental carcinogens – and James G. Watt at the Interior Department, the most anti-environment public servant in U.S. history. He worked hard to open up government-owned lands to exploitation by energy and timber industries, environmental consequences be damned. "W" Bush followed Reagan's and Watt's lead during his eight years in office.

"Watt, by the way, was charged with 25 felonies in 1995 related to his Housing and Urban Development lobbying later in the 1980s, but he was only convicted of *one misdemeanor* – he got no jail time. Like most rich white people charged with crimes.

"Not to mention all the ways Reagan's appointees found to look the other way when it came to enforcing laws against unfair labor practices, wage and hour violations, workplace safety rules – you name it.

"The newly-elected Reagan even appointed an FDA commissioner - at the documented behest of his campaign crony Donald Rumsfeld, who was then the Searle Corporation chairman – with the intent that the new FDA commissioner would manipulate approval of Searle's artificial sweetener aspartame, later marketed as Nutrasweet. That product wasn't even originally intended to be a food additive – a researcher in 1965 was testing it as an anti-ulcer drug when he accidentally discovered it had a weirdly sweet taste by licking his finger to turn a page.

"FDA regulators previously had repeatedly refused to approve the additive due to studies showing it screwed up brain chemistry and contributed to autoimmune disease, cancers, seizures, memory and vision losses, methanol poisoning leading to addiction and comas - not to mention killing lots of lab animals. Nevertheless, Searle still got aspartame's approval on a silver platter from **their hand-picked FDA commissioner**.

"That FDA commissioner who approved its use in soft drinks and food products went on to leave office under allegations of accepting gifts for political favors. And Donald Rumsfeld went on to get a previously-promised $12 million bonus in mid-1985 when – *wait for it* – Monsanto purchased the Searle Corporation."

"Yet, even with all that corporate cronyism crap, Reagan was re-elected in 1984 in a huge landslide," Orvis said. "The corporate mass media were in love with his folksy, humorous personality. He became known as the Teflon president for the way scandals seemed to slide right off of him. (Teflon, by the way, Sir, is a non-stick coating used on pots and pans to keep food from permanently burning into the pan surface.)

"Even after it became clear some of Reagan's closest associates were involved in an illegal arms for hostages deal – called "Iran-Contra" – he was never in any real danger of prosecution.

"Gary Webb, a San Jose, California newspaper journalist, in 1996 exposed a link between Reagan's CIA protecting crack cocaine dealers in California and proceeds from those dealers' illegal sales of crack cocaine being used to illegally fund Contra revolutionaries in Nicaragua during the Reagan years," Karin said.

"Even after that, Reagan's reputation as a genial, good-humored ex-B movie actor remained almost completely untarnished among corporate news media.

"In fact, corporate media took it upon themselves to attack Webb's expose. Gary's own employer backed away from supporting his work. He eventually committed suicide. But his expose has withstood the test of time."

"And, once again, even though there were felony convictions related to the Iran-Contra scandal, every last one of those persons indicted or convicted – all rich white people, as I recall, including then-headed-for-felony-trial former Secretary of Defense Caspar Weinberger – were pardoned by President George H. W. Bush at the end of his presidency," Orvis said. "There would've been far more convictions had huge volumes of evidence not been withheld or destroyed by Reagan administration officials."

"I am absolutely flabbergasted that the millions of people sitting in prisons across this great country for minor drug offenses, petty theft and such don't rise up once they're released and organize a revolution," Franklin said, again red-faced. "How is it that the foul depths of such injustice continue to remain unplumbed and uncleansed? These are the kinds of travesties which would've driven thousands to violence if they'd been allowed to continue during the Great Depression."

"Maybe the answer is that our society now manages to spread *just barely* enough financial help, *just barely* enough housing help, *just barely* enough food assistance to those who might otherwise be moved to revolt to keep them pacified *just barely* enough to figure that continued peaceful survival outweighs the risks of forcefully fighting for lasting change," Karin said.

"The government <u>mostly</u> doesn't let enough people get truly desperate. So far, at least. If they do reach that level of desperation, they have a vast system of prisons – largely privately-managed and for-profit - to contain the angriest. Our country now has the highest percentage of its population in prison of any country in the entire world, including Russia, totalitarian China and North Korea."

"Along with a military – just like the military during the violence against Bonus Marchers in 1932 and the National Guard Kent State massacre in 1970 – which would blindly follow orders to kill anyone trying to revolt without so much as a millisecond of doubt about injustice," Orvis added.

For the first time in all of their sessions so far, Franklin's eyes appeared to be moist.

"God help us all. It certainly sounds like our country has become, or is on the verge of becoming, everything we fought against in the 1940's. Nothing less than fascist," Franklin said. "How could so many good people let this happen?"

"It's the old frog on a skillet analogy," Orvis said. "Toss the frog onto a skillet that's already boiling hot and it'll hop right off. Toss a frog onto a cold skillet and then heat it up gradually – and before long, it's cooked through and through. We've become slow-cooked-inured to fascist features of our culture just a tiny bit at a time over the past 65 years.

"So **much** so that, now, when huge financial corporations like HSBC are charged with laundering massive amounts of drug cartel terrorists' money and they escape actual prosecution simply by paying off a nominal sum to the government, the average person just chalks it up to rich people's privilege. A fact of life, like an icy cold rainy day.

"Something no one can do anything about."

"As long as I'm still drawing a breath, I'm going to try to figure out a way to do something about it," Franklin said. "Curling up in a fetal position should not be the new default pose for social and economic justice.

"You know, this discussion today has left me the angriest I've been in a long, long time. If it's alright with you two, I'm going to take the rest of the day off to catch up on my reading and go for a swim at the Y. I'm way behind on reading the Vietnam era assignments you've given me – and I still haven't quite finished Zinn's *People's History* book, as well as "*The Motorcycle Diaries.*"

"You don't need our permission to take time off from this, Franklin," Karin said. "I suspect Pongo and his friends would enjoy getting to spend some time with you anyway. You've been so busy – and they've been so busy – well, we've kind of been monopolizing most of your time."

"OK, I'll plan to see both of you at noon tomorrow. After a day like today, though, I'm wishing I had an I.D. card that would allow me to engage in some hangover-inducing activities."

"That's fairly understandable, Sir," Orvis said. "Please just try to avoid hot dogs, OK?"

"Will do my best."

* * *

While Franklin was swimming laps in the Poughkeepsie YMCA pool, he day-dreamed about the privileges he'd taken for granted in his previous life and how much he'd been tempted to feel sorry for himself when the harsh reality of polio set in. He remembered feeling ashamed of himself for those feelings the first time he shared the swimming pool at the Warm Springs, GA resort with other polio victims.

He remembered seeing the struggling families of those polio victims routinely extending kindnesses to other victims' families they barely knew, offering homegrown fruits and vegetables and homemade clothing to each other with no expectation or desire to be re-paid in-kind or otherwise, even though they could barely afford their own basic needs...or offering transportation or child care to people they barely knew – or didn't know at all.

He recalled thinking at the time what a remarkable thing that was: for people who had so little – especially compared to his own family – to share with others when they had no guarantee that their own fundamental material necessities would continue to be met. He remembered how it occurred to him that families of his friends within his own social class would rarely make those kinds of offers, especially offers of something as simple as friendly companionship during a time of illness.

"Those folks living in poverty weren't people coming from a place of hatred in their hearts," he thought. *"Those were people who understood at the most visceral level what it means to put themselves in the shoes of others even less fortunate. They lived the New Testament's Golden Rule every day of their lives, even when living that way put their own lives at risk.*

"I still have to believe in the inherent good will of the vast majority of people in this world. Even with the passage of 65 years, I cannot accept that most people have come to believe cold, hateful disregard of their fellow man is a wise long-term strategy for their own survival."

As those thoughts coursed through his mind, somewhere in some alternative cosmological existence, the not-so-angelic spirit of Ayn Rand listening to those same musings was having a hysterical, spitting nails-fierce ear-splitting-screaming rage-filled meltdown. Such a shame that Franklin couldn't hear it.

By the time he finished his laps in the pool, the heaviness in his heart was largely gone. He was still convinced there has to be a true majority of compassionate and sincere people who share a priority for social and economic justice and equality for everyone.

When he returned to the Podrowskis' home for the evening, he asked Pongo to come along with him for an evening walk after dinner. For an hour and a half as they strode parallel to the Hudson River's east shoreline they talked about girls, sports, movies and their dreams for the future. Strictly guy stuff. By the time Franklin was reading himself to sleep with his copy of "*The Motorcycle Diaries,*" he felt truly lucky to have another chance at life, especially with folks as kind as the Podrowskis. Royally screwed up country notwithstanding.

* * *

Taking the Twisted Turnpike
to 'Repubican Lite'

Sept. 2, 2010
Podrowski residence

K arin and Orvis wasted little time wading through the details of the election of George H. W. Bush. They pointed out how Bush's opponent Michael Dukakis lost mainly because of negative TV ads which painted him as a criminal-loving liberal who approved a furlough program which allowed an African-American murderer in prison for life without parole (William R. "Willie" Horton) to commit a rape and armed robbery while on furlough. Dukakis also lost, Orvis emphasized, because he looked like an idiot when he was filmed driving a huge tank as he tried to pander to pro-military voters.

They discussed how Bush, a former CIA director, successfully convinced the Democratically-controlled Congress to support a war against Iraq after the country led by Saddam Hussein – a man whom Bush had once met with as an ally - invaded tiny Kuwait. How Bush got his way with Congress even though most Democrats and independents – and even many Republicans - across the U.S. saw the war as nothing more than a "blood for oil" conflict.

Then they explained how Bush's wealthy Ivy League patrician lineage left him so far out of touch with working people that Bill Clinton – the 'man from Hope (Ark.)' - was able to oust the incumbent in the 1992 election with an appeal to both middle class populism and fundamental traditional family values. Despite opponents bringing up his Arkansas reputation as a "Slick Willie" wheeler-dealer and womanizer.

Little-noticed by corporate media two days before "tough on crime" George H. W. Bush left office was Bush's pardon of then-32-year-old Pakistani drug trafficker Aslam P. Adam, Orvis recalled. Adam had been convicted of conspiracy to possess and distribute $1 million (1992 dollars) worth of heroin and had been sentenced to 55 years in Federal prison. Bush refused to explain why he pardoned Adam. A *Rolling Stone* report in October 1994 characterized Adam as a drug pusher with apparent ties to high-ranking Pakistani government officials, adding that **only** the *Charlotte (NC) Observer* bothered to ask the Justice Department about the pardon shortly after it happened; there was no White House news release or Justice Department announcement when the pardon was issued, unlike with the Christmas Eve 1992 pardons of Caspar Weinberger and five other Iran-Contra offenders.

Karin speculated that corporate news media "would've repeated that story *ad infinitum*" had it been a Democratic President who did the pardoning. (She elicited a promise from Franklin to study up as much as possible on the shifting ownership trends and mergers among corporate media outlets around the country – and he would do exactly that less than a year later when it became evident he would be appearing with fellow Poughkeepsians at regular news conferences.)

"No Democratic President ever would've been allowed to refuse to explain a pardon for a Pakistani heroin trafficker. News media would've dogged a Democrat to his deathbed for being soft on crime over that one," she said.

Orvis reminded Franklin of President Bill Clinton's role with the so-called moderate, Al From-founded organization known as the Democratic Leadership Council (DLC), which actually was composed almost entirely of conservative closet-Republican corporate-shill Democrats, almost entirely from the Sun Belt. Thanks to Clinton, Orvis said, the Democratic Party took a hard right shift toward Wall Street insiders on the theory that voters would support national Democratic candidates only if they adopted more Republican-like policies. The fact that Wall Street corporations would turn on the campaign donations tap also was not insignificant.

Thus continued the Democratic Party's slide toward its current "Republican Lite" status, Karin said.

Orvis again echoed Franklin's earlier praise for Bill Clinton's success in convincing the Congress to vote to increase taxes on the wealthy in 1993. It was a masterful example of leadership which paved the way to annual Federal revenue surpluses by the end of Clinton's presidency (surpluses which eventually would've *paid off the national debt* had President George W. Bush not signed a repeal of the tax increases in 2001), he said. Unfortunately, Republicans systematically demagogued the tax issue, along with Clinton's failed 1993 health care reform attempt (spearheaded by his wife Hillary), during the 1994 campaign, he explained. They convinced voters nationwide to turn the U.S. House of Representatives over to a Republican majority for the *first time in 40 years*, not to mention giving Republicans a majority in the U.S. Senate.

Clinton's other main accomplishment of his two terms – besides avoiding conviction after his impeachment over his affair with Monica Lewinsky – was the repeal of welfare laws guaranteeing a financial stipend to the poor, laws which had been in place since being signed by Franklin, Karin said. Clinton's welfare reform required states to implement a lifetime benefit limit of no more than five years for most cash welfare recipients. Some states would go on to limit lifetime welfare benefits to as little as two years. Other states, she said, would go on to use the new law to shame the poor by prohibiting them from using their welfare money to pay for their children's trips to swimming pools or discount movie theaters – *while still allowing recipients to spend the funds on guns.* The law's passage also meant wide disparities in benefit amounts from state to state: a classic race to the bottom to motivate the poor to stay out of the stingiest states.

One state would even go on to limit recipients to $25-per-day withdrawals of their welfare benefits, forcing them to incur lots of additional ATM fees to pay their bills. Ironically, it means more corporate welfare for rich bankers at the expense of financially terrified families, Karin said. *The New Deal turned upside down.*

"The Republicans <u>still</u> can't seem to shake their obsessive delusion that people go on welfare to live 'the good life,' " Karin said. "As though $454 per month for a family of four is 'the good life.' There's nothing good about that. It's an economic horror story for any family desperate enough to apply for those benefits. They're almost always families where one of the spouses has abandoned his kids and the other spouse – **_NOT_** 'crafty scheming grifters' looking to game the system like the super-rich corporate shills want people to believe.

"Classic blame-the-victim strategy – it's always good politics for demagogues who like to stir up hate because the poor don't have the energy, the time, the power or the self-esteem to speak out and fight back. They're too busy working two or three jobs just trying to survive."

The Clinton-signed 1996 Personal Responsibility and Work Opportunity Act passed with support from only about half of Congressional Democrats, she added, though almost all Democrats praised provisions in the bill providing for job training, job search assistance and aid for child care related to employment.

Orvis added that Clinton's 1996 re-election likely had little to do with his compulsion to shame the poor, a bizarre perspective considering he was raised in a relatively poor family. It was much more likely that his win was propelled in no small part by his calm, compassionate leadership in the aftermath of Timothy McVeigh's and Terry Nichols' April 1995 Oklahoma City bombing of the Murrah Federal Building which killed 167 and injured more than 600, including 19 fatally-injured children. (The bombing was the far right-wing pro-militia ex-Army buddies' response to FBI-involved deaths at a Waco, Texas religious fanatic's compound in 1993 and at the family cabin of an alleged gun law-violating white supremacist in Ruby Ridge, Idaho in 1992.)

By the time Clinton left office, his tax increases on the wealthy plus middle class-friendly economic policies had resulted in a strong rebound of the economy, Orvis recalled. When he stepped down in 2001, his popularity was at an all-time high despite his affair with Ms. Lewinsky. It appeared the general public felt that the President's missteps in his private life shouldn't diminish the positive economic leadership he demonstrated at times, Orvis said.

Unfortunately, Karin said, the positives didn't include Clinton's signing of the Glass-Steagall repeal passed by the Republican Congress in 1999, which led directly to the 2008 financial meltdown, the worst economic crisis since the Great Depression (though *only very slightly worse* than the 1981-1983 Reagan Recession).

"But we already discussed Glass-Steagall a couple of weeks ago," Karin reminded Franklin, "so, we're not going to go into more detail at this point."

"So, essentially, you've told me again that the most popular Democratic President since I held office was pretty much a closet Republican who happened to have a taste for progressive income tax policies," Franklin said. "Not to mention being a guy who liked having sex with lots of different women other than his wife."

"Well, he's since pretty much insisted it was 'only' oral copulation," Karin said. "But there apparently are multiple Secret Service agents who've overheard lots of intense screaming matches between him and his wife over his repeated serial dalliances."

"My Lord, I can't imagine why Democrats have struggled to maintain credibility," Franklin said sarcastically. "Let's see: they try to emulate Republicans about some social and economic policies, they take tons of money from Wall Street corporations (OK, just a fraction of what the Republicans take, I grant you), they support wars over oil and their most popular modern President was a serial philanderer.

"What is it going to take to clear out the corruption among the party leadership? What's it going to take to get them to re-focus on the hard-working people who've always been the core of their support?"

"A complete re-boot?" Orvis asked. "I don't know. I wish I did. It gets pretty depressing at times. Politicians have developed such a horrible reputation in general since the 1940s and 50s, it seems like a lot of the people with the best character traits don't want to associate with the low-life officeholders they see in Congress."

"We hope maybe someone like yourself can figure out a solution," Karin said with a plaintive smile. "You do now have time for that in the years ahead, Sir."

"We'll see, I suppose," Franklin said, non-committally.

∗　∗　∗

Tripping the Light Fantastic

That evening, Pongo decided to take Franklin out to a DJ dance club to blow off steam; as the sessions with the O'Learys progressed, there seemed to be more and more steam to blow off. It was past time for the President to dip his toes into the pool of eligible young maidens – or at least get a feel for what it was like to socialize with people in their late teens and 20s.

They decided to drive to the Fusions Night Club in Fishkill. Pongo invited Heather to come along, but Heather politely declined. The club scene wasn't really her thing, she said.

Pongo was pretty sure his grandparents wouldn't see him going in there – the club was several miles from their home. Just in case things didn't go well, he thought Fishkill would be a safer place than a local Poughkeepsie nightclub for Franklin to test his social skills in his new century. He wasn't as likely to see fellow Poughkeepsie High classmates at that venue.

It could've gone better.

Seeing less than fully-clad dancers who wanted to give lap dances was a huge culture shock for Franklin. When Pongo first told him they'd be going to a dance club, Franklin had ballroom dancing – or at least semi-formal lounge club dancing – in mind.

Asked by Pongo if he wanted a lap dance, Franklin first blushed bright red and then an odd greenish color which made Pongo wonder if Franklin might be about to vomit.

A few minutes after that, one of the lap dancers – a smiling, attractively buxom bleached blonde with gleaming white teeth - walked up from behind Franklin and placed a gentle hand on his shoulder. When he looked around and saw the 30-ish woman with heaving breasts bulging a foot away from his face, almost the entire contents of Franklin's stomach spewed all over her chest.

"I amsh shooow shorry," Franklin whizzled in the woman's direction, completely embarrassed, his mouth still half full of partly digested grilled cheese on wheat bread. When he tried to reach over and help the woman – her nametag read, "*My Name is GINGER / May I Pitch a Tent on YOUR Lap, Honey?*" – by wiping food chunks off her chest, she gave him a roundhouse slug to the nuts. Which only made him spray on her everything left in his mouth.

"Christ, Lady, this is his first time at a club," Pongo said. "He was just trying to apologize for having a nervous stomach. This can't be the first time that's happened to you."

"It's the LAST time *that* geek is going to hurl in my direction," "Ginger" said. "You need to fork over $20 for my dry cleaning right now or get your tight little buttocks out of this establishment. Immediately."

[When she threw her soiled cotton peek-a-boo top into her laundry basket that night – a top which, actually, did NOT require dry cleaning – she had no idea that the next morning the fibers in the stained area all would be growing tiny new roots. As the pukee, she figured the puker simply had some sort of awful mold growing in his stomach. She tossed the top in the trash as soon as she saw the "moldy" growths and thought no more of it. A few months later, a clump of highly frost-resistant cotton plants were seen growing out of a nearby landfill; but they soon were covered up by tons of new trash.]

"Consider us gone, bitch," Pongo replied, clearly pissed.

Pongo helped Franklin limp out to his car. Pongo apologized profusely for his choice of dancing venues; Franklin graciously told him not to worry.

"There was no way you could've known how uncomfortable all of that would make me feel, Pongo," he said, massaging his testicles gently. "Next time, we need to go someplace a little more traditional, a little more formal, if we're going to try dancing.

"By the way, please don't take this the wrong way – I'm not some kind of sex-crazed pervert – but just what *is* it with all of these women with the huge teats??

"Did some sort of new disease start spreading in the past fifty years that causes ladies' bosoms to grow freakishly large?"

"It's kind of complicated, Sir," Pongo explained.

"It's not a disease – well, not a biological thing, anyway. It didn't happen all of a sudden, not overnight-like or anything. What happened was, well, back in the early to mid-1950s, a publisher – his name was Hefner – decided to put out magazines with 'tasteful' color photos of naked women – mostly women with larger-than-normal boobs.

"It was called 'Playboy.' It was wildly popular with men. As it became part of popular culture, female nudity in movies became more and more accepted. Women with large breasts – Jayne Mansfield and Marilyn Monroe, for example – they took up a special place in popular culture.

"Eventually, there were popular movements in favor or gender equality, movements supporting women's rights not to be harassed or discriminated against or harmed by their husbands. Those movements made it socially unacceptable for men to openly objectify women. The magazines glorifying big breasts started losing subscribers, big time.

"The culture had changed, though: what used to be called smut in your time had become known as pornography, or porn, whether it was hard-core or soft-core. There was a consistent demand for it – probably mainly by adolescents and lonely middle-aged singles, or married persons whose spouses lost their sex drive. Private do-it-yourself sex became socially acceptable – lots more so than seeking out sex for pay. When the internet started offering free access to hard-core porn about a decade ago, anyone could press a few buttons and see big knockers in action in a matter of seconds.

"But don't get me wrong: it still would be a matter of deep embarrassment for a supporter of women's rights to be caught using on-line porn. Most women still see porn as inherently demeaning to women, objectification in action.

"But a lot of women saw the attention given to ladies with large boobs as a sign of the power that physical attractiveness gives to women. A lot of women wanted the sheer sexual allure that goes along with having a huge chest.

"A program I saw on TV said the trend among women to have their breasts surgically enlarged started in the early '60s. They used silicone implants for quite a while, but those would leak and make women sick. They've been using saline implants for breast augmentation for a few decades now.

"The procedure is so common that pretty much any middle class woman with a few thousand dollars to spare can afford to have the surgery. For women who feel insecure about being flat-chested, it's probably more common than getting a nose job. I think for a lot of women, they feel like a big chest is a sign of power.

"Personally, I don't know if I'd want to be with a woman who was so insecure about her own body that she had to have it surgically altered. If she's got that kind of major insecurity, she's probably got lots of other insecurities that would make a lasting relationship hard to sustain."

"I suppose there must still be quite a few women who *aren't* insecure about their bodies, or virtually every woman we see would have bosoms out to here," Franklin said, stretching his hands out two feet in front of his chest.

"I guess," Pongo said. "I'd be surprised if more than one in three women gets her boobs augmented. It's probably less than that. But it's still pretty amazing when you look at old pictures of women in a crowd alongside pictures of women today. Quite a contrast."

"You're telling me. It's got to be distracting for men at work. Not to mention hard on the women's backs."

"If it were my sweetheart and they gave her back pain, I'd encourage her to have breast reduction – no one wants a loved one to be in pain," Pongo said. "As for the power of distraction, it's like anything: if you see enough of it often enough, you get de-sensitized to it."

"Well, it might take me a while to get used to – being this young again, well, it's invigorating for me all over, including the nether regions, as they say."

"What works for me is thinking about Donald Trump's combover." (Pongo held out his index finger starting in a straight position and then moving in a slow limp-listing motion; he whistled in a downward tonal arc as his finger relaxed.)

They were back at the Podrowski home and going down for the night 45 minutes later. Franklin's thoughts once again floated back to Lucy, to a time when superficiality meant far less, as he drifted off to sleep. In the darkness, moisture trailed out from the corners of his eyes.

Two rooms away, Pongo reflected on how his 21st-century popular culture must appear through the prism of someone who just stepped out of the mid-20th century. Lessons were learned today, he thought, by both him and his newest best friend.

* * *

PUSSIES. PUDNOCKERS. AND SHILLS. YOUR DEMOCRATIC PARTY FOR THE OUGHTS

Sept. 3, 2010
Podrowski home

Vice President Al Gore's popular vote win in the 2000 election over his folksy opponent George Walker "W" Bush and the U.S. Supreme Court's 5-4 decision to award the election to "W" by ordering the State of Florida to stop re-counting ballots – which most studies subsequently showed would've given Gore Florida's Electoral College votes had the re-count been completed – was at the top of the O'Learys' agenda for the final Friday before Labor Day. There was a lot of emphasis on the fact that the five clearly partisan Republican-appointed Supreme Court Justices all voted to stop the ballot counting.

"Two things:" Orvis began. "First, Gore had no business having the election that close to begin with. His DLC ties left him looking like Republican Lite, just like Slick Willie. Why would an independent voter go for a faux Republican when they could vote for the real thing (Bush)? If he had emphasized the progressive issues on which he agreed with the independent candidate Ralph Nader, he might've neutralized Nader's support. But, no, he kept again and again trying to come across as the kinder, gentler version of Republicanism. Even though "W" already had upstaged him with his phony claim to 'compassionate conservatism.'

"Second, he turned down Clinton's offers to campaign for him, even in Clinton's home state of Arkansas. If he'd let Clinton cover Arkansas for him from border to border with his populist stump speech, he just might've won that state. If he'd won Arkansas, the Florida vote-counting chicanery wouldn't have mattered in the Electoral College; Gore would've won by three electoral votes. Or maybe even more likely: if Clinton had campaigned hard in New Hampshire, a state where he'd been wildly popular, Gore probably could've made up the 7,000-vote margin "W" won with there, which would've given Gore just enough electoral votes for the Presidency. And Gore barely even bothered to campaign *in his own home state* of Tennessee.

"So, there are plenty of reasons why Gore should've been able to overcome the vote counting funny business in Florida.

"It's important to keep in mind that, while all of the 2000 election mess was sorting itself out, the mostly-Saudi Arabian terrorists behind the September 2001 World Trade Center and Pentagon attacks were deep into planning their hijackings after first coming up with the idea five years earlier.

"Osama Bin Laden's Al Qaeda organization was bent on revenge for U.S. attacks against Somalian Muslims, U.S. military bases in Saudi Arabia, U.S. 'plundering' of Saudi oil reserves, U.S. support of Israel after Israeli attacks against Lebanese Muslims and U.S. sanctions against Iraqi Muslims over the 1990-1991 Gulf War.

"'W' Bush was on vacation in Texas when he received a daily briefing on Aug. 6, 2001, more than five weeks before the 9/11 attacks, stating that Bin Laden was determined to launch a major attack against the U.S., but no special alerts were ordered.

"The CIA director, George Tenet, later testified to Congress that he found out on August 23 or 24 – almost three weeks before the attacks – that Zacarias Moussaoui, an Islamic jihadist, had been taking lessons on how to fly a jet airliner, but Tenet didn't pass the information on to 'W,' because 'W,' like Tenet, still was on vacation.[*]

"It was disclosed later that the FBI had been monitoring at least one of the 9/11 hijackers who was taking flying lessons in Arizona during the months before the attacks.

---

[*] 4/14/04 *Slate*, Fred Kaplan

"Lots of clues and no one connected the dots. So, then we fast forward to the day of the attacks and 'W' Bush is reading "*My Pet Goat*" with second graders in Florida when he hears about the attacks. And he simply sits there for seven full minutes after being told about the attacks.

"And here's the really golden frosting on the cake to show you just how charmed Mr. Henry Kissinger is - you know, they guy who won the 1973 Nobel Peace Prize for negotiating a Vietnam ceasefire which actually never happened:

"Kissinger picks the day before the 9/11 attacks to admit to a national television audience on '*60 Minutes*' his and the Nixon administration's complete and unambiguous complicity in the violent military coup against the democratically-elected President of Chile, socialist Salvador Allende, on Sept. 11, 1973. He 'fessed up that the CIA and U.S. military were deeply involved in the coup, which left Allende dead.

"They had been pissed off at Allende's nationalization of partly U.S.-owned copper mines and ITT Corporation facilities there. You remember from watching the movie "*Missing*" what happened when the U.S. puppet-fascist Gen. Augusto Pinochet succeeded Allende: thousands of 'disappeared' political liberals.

"Of course, the headlines in the Sept. 11, 2001 newspapers about Kissinger's admissions were quickly forgotten as all of us were overwhelmed by the 9/11 tragedies."

"We're going to stop right now so you can watch the movie "*Fahrenheit 9/11*," Karin said. "It'll give you a feel for just how screwed our country was, and continues to be, thanks to the Supreme Court's election of "W."

Two hours and three minutes later...

"Holy. Jesus. Christ," Franklin said as the credits rolled.

"When you consider that a more competent President might've been able to stop the 9/11 attacks, that a more competent President probably could've avoided going to war in **both** Afghanistan and, ESPECIALLY, Iraq – and that a more competent President might've been able to make finding Osama Bin Laden a higher priority..." Orvis said.

"Just look at the cost in lives and the cost to our treasury," he continued. "It could be a century before our country recovers from the unfunded deficit spending on those wars. Maybe almost as sad: if "W" hadn't cut taxes on the rich early in his presidency to stimulate the economy, the national debt could've been nearly paid off by now. Think about it."

"Instead of spending billions and billions just on the interest on the debt, think of all the things we could've done with the extra revenues," Karin said. "Free college tuition for everyone, free health care from cradle to grave, subsidized first-time homebuyers' down payments, huge increases in funding for research to cure diseases – I mean, Jesus, just think about it."

"But what we got was more endless war," Franklin said. "Thousands of soldiers dead in far-away places where the local non-combatants don't even want us to be."

"And that doesn't even scratch the surface of what "W" did to undermine traditional governmental institutions," Orvis said.

"For example, "W" signed the Postal Accountability and Enhancement Act passed on a simple voice vote by both chambers of the lame duck Republican Congress in December 2006. The Act required the Postal Service to fund employee retirements *75 years in advance*," Orvis explained. "To this day, most Americans don't realize the Republicans have turned the USPS into a government version of "The Walking Dead.""

"In the entire history of humankind, no institution ever before has been required to fund retirement accounts for employees *not even born yet!* And that's for an institution that's been around since 1775 when Benjamin Franklin was the first Postmaster."

"Can you guess why the Postal Service became a target for the Republicans?" Karin asked.

"I can't begin to imagine why," Franklin said. "Despite the rare instance of this or that misrouted letter, it was always a highly dependable institution in my day. People complained about it, but they knew it was reliable _and_ inexpensive."

"The Republicans knew they could convince corporate media that the Postal Service was on its last legs because people were sending correspondence electronically instead of through the mails," Karin explained. "While their letter volume had dropped off significantly, management had made the adjustments to stay in the black.

"The real reason they sneaked in a poison pill law to try to kill the USPS was simple: it doesn't make a profit for Wall Street. The for-profit delivery companies – FedEx, UPS, et cetera – **they can't compete** with the USPS for delivery of letters and magazines.

"If they can force the USPS out of business, it's a gold mine for the for-profit delivery companies. Instead of paying 44 cents to mail a letter or a bill payment, the average person would end up paying, say, $5 for cross-country delivery of a one-ounce envelope. First-class mail postage has been *one of the best deals there's ever been* for U.S. consumers – all because the USPS is _not for profit_.

"The projection for pieces of mail to be delivered by the USPS this year is 171,000,000,000. One-hundred-seventy-one billion times a Wall Street profit of, say, $4.50 per item delivered. You do the math."

Taking Karin literally, Franklin grabbed a piece of paper and a pencil. Thirty seconds later, he said, "That's an annual profit of $769.5 billion. Dear Jesus, no wonder they sneaked that through."

"They had to rush it through under the radar simply because the 2006 elections gave the Democrats majorities in both the U.S. Senate and U.S. House effective January 2007," Karin said.

"Wanna know something else truly maddening?" Orvis asked.

"I suppose," Franklin said, rolling his eyes.

"After Nancy Pelosi, the first woman ever elected Speaker of the U.S. House of Representatives, took her post in 2007, among the first things she did was refuse to attempt impeachment of "W" – despite **his own public admission** in December 2005 to breaking surveillance laws against warrantless wiretapping. We're talking *Federal felonies **plus** <u>overwhelming</u> <u>evidence</u>* he and his minions lied to Congress before the vote to allow the Iraq invasion. And she refused to hold a vote to end funding for the undeclared war. ***And*** she refused to hold a vote to repeal the kill-the-Post Office Act.

"Those actions sparked a serious primary campaign in 2008 against Pelosi by a genuine anti-war activist, Cindy Sheehan, whose son was a soldier killed in Iraq in 2004. The Democratic Party's response was to try to crush Sheehan's campaign. There were allegations of dirty tricks, including tapped phones and repeated campaign office vandalism. Sheehan went on to get about 16 percent of the vote in a seven-way race, after insider factions of the party refused to endorse her. She eventually gave up on Democrats altogether, along with who-knows-how-many others."

"How in God's name did "W" ever get re-elected in '04?"

"He had a profoundly weak opponent. A candidate who not only was *even richer* than "W," but who could take the text of the most stirring speech ever written and make it sound like reading pages out of the phone book with cotton stuffed up his schnozz.

"And it's largely fate that an even weaker candidate didn't get nominated – that being the truly charismatic Sen. John Edwards, who went on to cheat on his dying cancer-afflicted wife and father a baby out of wedlock in 2007. **And** lie about it repeatedly, on TV, no less.

"If there were stronger candidates, they simply didn't want to take on challenging an incumbent President, even one as grotesquely inept as "W." Which, once again, says so very much about how far the Democratic Party has sunk."

"And yet the DLC corporate-types continue to hold sway with the party leadership," Franklin mused morosely.

"That's the addiction to organized money," Orvis said. "They simply don't want to give it up. The current President's protestations notwithstanding. He was the first Democratic Presidential candidate to drop out of the campaign public financing system two years ago. He did manage to raise lots of small donations. But he dropped out of public financing so he could accept huge packaged donations, like the ones he got from the nuclear power industry.

"It would certainly seem that no Presidential candidate's hands – except maybe for Rep. Dennis Kucinich in '08 – have been clean when it comes to the filthy lucre of big money. Sen. Hillary Clinton's certainly weren't."

"And popular media ridiculed Kucinich **_not_** for his positions on the issues - all of which were **spot on** for progressives, unlike Obama's. He was the butt of jokes – including Saturday Night Live skits - about his five foot-seven inch stature," Karin said. "Which was especially obvious when he stood next to his beautiful six foot tall wife on TV."

"So television would seem to have the final say on who gets to be President," Franklin observed.

"Amazing how our democratic republic made it through 150-plus years without the idiot box, isn't it?" Karin asked.

"So, just how was it that Mrs. Clinton was unable to beat out Mr. Obama in 2008?" Franklin asked.

"From what I could tell, most voters saw Mr. Obama to be the more genuine candidate, the one who came across as the most sincere," Orvis said. "Hillary seemed to set off the buzzers on a lot of folks' phoniness detection meters. She didn't help herself with some of the things she said, either.

"Like when she actually came out and made remarks to the effect that she'd be the President far less likely to be assassinated – because of then-Senator Obama's African-American appearance, what with all the racists around the country.

"Plus, a lot of folks remembered her absolute fiasco as the person in charge of health care reform in the early '90s."

"Surprisingly, though, not many people – besides Bill Moyers and Elizabeth Warren – pointed out her hypocrisy on personal bankruptcies and other corporate-biased policies," Karin said. "When she was First Lady in the '90s, she opposed credit card industry efforts to pass a law making it harder for private citizens to shield certain assets, like primary residences, during bankruptcies. She said back then the proposed law would be cruel, penalizing mostly those who were going deep into debt over out-of-pocket medical bills.

"But when she was a U.S. Senator in 2004, she actually voted *for* virtually the very same bill she'd opposed ten years earlier."

"It would seem like to me, the best way to offset the manipulative effects of those televised images of the chronically hypocritical would be to get back to grass roots organizing," Franklin said.

"That's what President Obama's organization did in 2008," Orvis said. "They had on-the-ground local organizers in multiple locations in every state – lots of knocking on doors. Phenomenally-edited video clips of hypocritical pols saying one thing and then obliviously reversing themselves on Jon Stewart's Daily Show on Comedy Central helped a lot too. But Comedy Central viewership just isn't as widespread as it would need to be to really make a difference between Presidential elections.

"Likewise, grassroots organizing didn't seem to make enough of a difference when it came to health care reform passed last March. President Obama bent over and spread his cheeks for pretty much every level of the health insurance industry. He gave away the farm to Big Pharma, no pun intended. Pharmaceutical companies aren't even required to negotiate lower prices for large groups of states or local organizations, like they already are required to do for V.A. hospitals and clinics."

"But, to be fair, there are lots of folks who are convinced he couldn't have corralled the votes in the Senate to pass reform if he hadn't been so generous to the health care industry," Karin pointed out. "Remember, dozens and dozens of Senators have taken massive sums of money from the health insurance industry and Big Pharma."

"On that note," Orvis said, "let's stop now and watch the movie, "*Sicko*."

Two hours and four minutes later...

"How in the hell do U.S. citizens tolerate having crappier health care than Canada, Britain, France and pretty much the rest of Europe?" a clearly agitated Franklin asked. "Once again, why aren't the victims of medical bankruptcies storming the Congress in protest?"

"Probably because they can't afford to get there, much less organize effectively all across the country," Orvis said.

"I know, I know – but Dear God, don't people understand how they're being screwed just so their doctors and pharmaceutical executives can afford multiple mansions and lots of high-end cars?"

"No," Orvis said. "Telegenic public relations flacks for the A.M.A., Big Pharma and the health insurance industry made the rounds of all the corporate news organizations around the country trying to discredit "Sicko" because – as *they claimed* on camera – the movie's director supposedly is a big business-despising commie USA-hater.'

"Not once were they able to actually discredit any of the situations shown in the film, though. But they knew they could rely on corporate news media, especially Fox News, to use their remarks to smear Mr. Moore.

"Even a *Public Broadcasting Service* **news anchor** – Gwen Ifill, who holds a bachelor's degree from a small women's liberal arts college – in June 2004 **smeared** Mr. Moore on NBC's Meet the Press as a compulsive "America-basher" and faux documentarian, all because she didn't like '*Fahrenheit 9/11.*' But she failed to cite any specific misrepresentations in the movie, other than to allege it was a supposedly quote-unquote cheap shot."

"At least there's some genuine hope that President Obama's Patient Protection and Affordable Care Act (ACA) will dramatically reduce the number of bankruptcies related to uninsured medical expenses," Karin emphasized, with a wan smile.

"But haven't the Republicans already vowed to keep trying to repeal it until they succeed, no matter how long it takes them?" Franklin asked.

"Well, they can try 'til the cows come home, but it isn't going to work as long as the man who signed the bill is the one who can veto the attempts to repeal it," Orvis said. "But you already know that. It certainly doesn't look like the Republicans will be having a veto-proof majority any time soon – even if they have a big win in November."

"Preserving working people's huge medical debts by trying to kill health care reform: that's what Republicans have come to. Just amazing," Franklin said. "If there were real justice in this life, there would be some kind of Biblical plague on the houses of every last person who begrudges help for persons less fortunate than themselves.

"I suspect there would be only a very tiny fraction of Republicans left on the face of the Earth if that came about."

"OK – I think we're done for today, Sir," Orvis said. "When we have our noon session tomorrow, please give us a list of where you're at with your reading, OK? We'll keep tomorrow's session short so you can enjoy the holiday weekend. We won't meet again 'til Tuesday and that'll be our last session before your classes start on Wednesday."

"Short sounds good...I think we all could use a break," Franklin said.

* * *

HE'S GOT A TICKET TO RIDE

As the O'Learys were driving away, Franklin checked the Podrowski mailbox at the end of the driveway. He was pleasantly surprised to find both his new driver's license and his Social Security card had arrived.

He made Pongo promise to let him drive Pongo and Heather someplace that evening in Pongo's mother's old Civic.

An hour-and-a-half later, Franklin, Pongo and Heather went to see "Scott Pilgrim vs. the World" at the mall cinema. A good time was had by all, especially when Franklin approached a mall food court Italian eatery and asked for a large malt.

The young man running the cash register rang up the purchase and was about to hand Franklin a large malt liquor bottle when he asked Franklin for his photo I.D.

"Photo I.D. to buy a malt? But I didn't even tell you what flavor I want," Franklin said. "And how can a real malt – I assume it's vanilla – be in a sealed bottle?"

"Listen, buddy, I just sells 'em ta punks likes yous," the olive-complected 20-something guy said. "I doesn't watch how dey's made and I doesn't taste 'em to see if it's da flavor yer Mama told ya' t'get. Now, eeda fork over yer photo I.D. or let yer big sistah over dere make da' buy."

Pongo and Heather gently escorted Franklin away from the dispenser of haute cuisine and explained to him that very, very few places still sell actual malt-ed milk drinks. Milk_shakes_ have supplanted malted milk concoctions, Heather advised. And in lots and lots of flavors. They made it a point to promise to buy Franklin a blueberry shake at the Eveready Diner in Hyde Park that weekend.

On their way out of the mall, Franklin wandered into the Target store connected to the mall lower level. He wandered through the store, marveling at the variety of clothing and consumer electronics available. But he was absolutely mesmerized by the women's negligee and swimsuit section, staring intently at multi-colored scant brassieres and panties until Heather finally had to tug him away when a 60-something woman clerk started giving Franklin the stink eye – unknown to them, she was wondering what sort of perverse style Franklin was wearing under his khakis.

"Guess we need to take you on a Victoria's Secret reconnaissance mission one of these days when you're bored, Sir," she said.

Franklin barely heard her as he quickly pulled his hand out of a stack of thong underwear, embarrassed. "I really don't want to press Victoria about her secret – I mean, she's entitled to her privacy," Franklin said earnestly.

It wouldn't be the last embarrassment he would experience in his new life, not by a long shot.

Franklin dropped off Pongo and Heather at the Podrowski home after they had burgers and ice cream at the mall. The young lovers then hopped into Pongo's Civic and retreated to their special place in the woods while Franklin retired for the night.

* * *

SOMNOLENT VISIONS, PART II

*F*ranklin saw lots of beautiful vistas outside of his train window. He noticed he had a laptop computer and lists of university student leaders on top of the laptop. Some of the university names he recognized, others he did not. One moment, he looked up and saw what looked like Glacier National Park. A minute later, he looked up again and saw what looked like Lake Michigan near Chicago, but the skyline was much different from what he remembered. But all the scenes outside his window nevertheless looked familiar as they kept changing each time he put his head down and then up again. How many cross-country train trips had he taken over the decades? They were almost beyond counting.

He suddenly awoke to a call from Phil to come to breakfast. The dream quickly faded from his memory.

* * *

BANKING SEEDS OF IMAGINATION, WITH COMPOUNDED INTEREST

Sept. 4, 2010
Podrowski home

After Franklin composed his reading status list for the O'Learys, he and Pongo spent half of the remainder of the morning driving down to the Hudson to hike across the old Poughkeepsie-Highland river-spanning railroad bridge and back. The other half of the morning they spent walking the local mall, observing the socializing of local teens. People-watching, as Pongo's mother used to call it.

Pongo sat in on the noon session at the Podrowski home with the O'Learys. Pongo was a little surprised by Orvis' first question to Franklin.

"So, are you still thinking a Biblical plague on the greediest Republicans might be a good thing for everyone?" Orvis asked.

"Well, I don't know, I suppose it might work if the children were spared. At least the ones whose hearts weren't already permanently hardened by exposure to their parents' mean-spiritedness," Franklin said.

"Sometimes I wonder if maybe a large meteor strike on the southeastern corner of the U.S. might work better, but then I remember the good people of Warm Springs. Obviously, we're joking around – it would be nice if there were a simple, relatively quick answer to prejudice against the poor and minorities, but the fact is, there isn't.

"It will take generations for hatred against minorities and poor folks to die out. Unless there's better leadership across the board in Congress, it could take centuries."

"So, this would be a good time for you to ask us any questions you feel like we haven't covered in our material," Karin said. "We haven't talked a lot about the Tea Party. Is there anything you feel like we should've covered in more detail?"

"I guess it seems like there hasn't been a lot of discussion about how the country has prepared itself for things hard to predict precisely," Franklin said.

"From reading *Rolling Stone* and other sources, I know one of the things the scientists have been able to predict with reasonable certainty has been continued human-caused global warming," Franklin said. "The predictions have been that it's going to cause the sea level to rise anywhere from 50 to 70 feet by the end of the century, turning maybe a billion people living along coastlines into refugees. And it's supposed to cause widespread crop failures just as the worldwide demand for food is peaking. It's even going to make places like Glacier National Park glacier-free within the next couple of decades, if not sooner.

"What is it going to take for the Congress to take global warming seriously?"

"Well, once again, the Republicans adamantly refuse to lend any credence to global warming – even if lending credence at 40 percent annual interest could make them fistfuls of money, they wouldn't do it," Orvis said. "Their key Senate Environment and Public Works Committee member – an ignorant pinhead named Imhofe from Oklahoma – he still contends global warming is a hoax.

"Not only do they refuse to set limits on carbon pollution, they actually are working hard to expand hydraulic fracturing for natural gas – it's called fracking. Even though fracking is reported to release far more greenhouse gases than any other kind of fossil fuels extraction – **and** cause earthquakes, to boot. All they care about is preserving massive profits for the fossil fuels industry. Those profits will continue to be massive as long as the industry doesn't have to pay for cleaning up its industrial wastes – which are the invisible carbon dioxide and methane it spews into the atmosphere."

"If only people could actually see CO2 and methane the way they can see gunky oil spills in the ocean, maybe it'd be different," Karin said.

"I bet they'd just add an artificial fragrance and call it free air freshener," Pongo joked.

"Before I forget, Franklin, make sure you watch Josh Fox's documentaries *"Gasland"* and *"Gasland Part II"* between now and Saturday," Karin said. "Pay special attention to what happens when he tries to perform actual journalism before a House Congressional committee."

"My prediction is that our staunch defenders of capitalism won't decide global warming is a danger meriting actual action until it's so hot that people are having to live underground," Orvis said.

"I suppose the Republicans could legislate that it's illegal to experience hoax-caused perspiration," Franklin said. "They could assess fines for unauthorized sweating which could go toward offsetting increased air conditioning costs for Republicans living in McMansions of more than 5,000 square feet.

"The global warming crisis isn't the only potential disaster somewhere on the horizon I've been checking out. I was reading a National Geographic article with an amazing three-dimensional drawing showing the huge volume of molten rock below the Yellowstone caldera.

"The article said the caldera has had major eruptions about every 600,000 years, give or take, with the most recent one 640,000 years ago. It said that kind of major eruption probably would bring our species to extinction, because of the planet being shrouded by clouds of erupted rock dust for a couple of years, causing crops everywhere to fail in an ongoing deep freeze.

"It would be re-assuring to know governments around the world are trying to prepare for that, that they're spending at least as much on disaster preparation as they are to prepare for war.

"And I read in another National Geographic how the impact of a large asteroid or comet could cause the same kind of extinction of our species. Are people taking these threats seriously?"

"There's a lot of talk, Franklin, but only a teensy-tiny portion of the U.S. budget exists for detection of large threatening space objects," Orvis said. "There are professional observers looking for those objects all the time, but right now, the general consensus is that, if a species-threatening object is detected, we'll probably only have six months to two years to prepare for its arrival.

"And I'm not aware of any preparations for a major volcanic eruption, except that there are secure seed banks in Norway, Great Britain and New South Wales. No major facilities like that exist in the U.S., as far as I know. In any event, the seed banks exist for farming by catastrophe survivors – which assumes there will be survivors. To my knowledge, there are no long-term storage sites with canned foodstuffs saved for the general public."

"But, if I understand you correctly, we still have a nuclear arsenal to use against patchwork groups of terrorists who have no air force or navy," Franklin said.

"We've never really had a sanity-based program for survival," Karin responded.

"Hey, Gramma, don't forget: we can always call upon the Avengers to save us," Pongo said, chuckling.

"Your grandson is absolutely right, Dear," Orvis said. "The U.S.A. has the very best of the best fictional superheroes. And we make the very best movies in the world about them. Gotta wonder how many movie-goers actually believe they really exist out there somewhere…"

"Would that they did…stacks of comic books probably aren't all that good to protect yourself from two full years of winter after a volcanic blast or comet impact," Franklin said.

"Let's make this your assignment for our next session next Saturday," Karin said. "You come up with a plan to save the human race from mass extinction following a comet impact, Yellowstone caldera explosion or invasion by ray-gun blasting aliens."

"I know you're joking, Dear Lady," Franklin said.

"No, I'm barely half-joking. I'd be truly interested to see what a man of your historic vision can come up with. I'm just talking about a general outline, not a 500-page step by step plan."

"Hey, I think we can do this, bro'," Pongo said.

"OK, we'll give it our best effort, Karin," Franklin agreed. "At least the pressure's off, assuming there are no explosions or invasions in the next seven days."

"We'll all keep our fingers crossed, Sir," Orvis said.

∗   ∗   ∗

That evening, Franklin decided to take a long walk by himself in the direction of Hyde Park. His walks had come to be his favorite solo activity. To have legs and feet which worked again – how could anyone remotely understand what that's like after decades of struggling with heavy steel braces?

Before he knew it, walking the five miles-plus parallel to the Hudson River, he was approaching Springwood, just as the sun in the west was touching the tips of the tallest pines and ash trees. He wanted so much to hear his mother ring the large dinner bell. To walk up to the front door and sit down at the long dining table for a hot bowl of Fairhaven fish chowder. To enjoy the company of his children again at that table. To comfort his sons over being ridiculed by horrifically mean-spirited Republicans who belittled their combat records, despite James, a Marine combat officer, being awarded the Navy Cross and Silver Star for separate incidents of bravery under fire, including saving three men from drowning. To see the warmth of his mother's smile again.

He circled around Springwood, marveled at the growth of the many hundreds of trees he planted and headed back to Poughkeepsie. He stopped for donuts along the way and, serendipitously, ran into Pongo behind the Dunkin' Donuts counter.

Pongo asked him to wait another half-hour for his shift to end so he could give him a ride home. Franklin politely declined and headed south to Poughkeepsie, munching on his doughnut as he walked out the front door. Pongo was a little worried about the wistful look on Franklin's young face, but soon forgot about it.

That evening, they spent their last three hours before bedtime watching the "*Gasland*" documentaries. Franklin was visibly moved by Josh Fox's courage to try and film the Congressional committee meeting – and even more moved by Josh's assertive poise as the Congressional security staff forcibly removed him from the hearing room. Simply for asserting his First Amendment rights as a journalist.

"Why would anyone knowingly sell fracking rights to one of those fossil fuels extraction companies when they know it's going to ruin the very groundwater they drink and use to water their crops and livestock?" Franklin asked. "Why is that even legal?"

"As the movie briefly mentioned," Pongo reminded Franklin, "the Republican-controlled Congress passed and "W" signed in 2005 the Halliburton Loophole law amending the Federal Safe Water Act to **exempt fracking companies** like Halliburton from having to *disclose the chemicals they inject into groundwater* while they're fracking.

"The profoundly infuriating thing is that the fossil fuels industry held such lobbying sway that even the Democratically-controlled Congress has been unable to repeal that loophole from January 2009 up to now."

"Just astonishing," Franklin said. "How could so many members of the party of the working class sell their political souls for a few thousand dollars each?"

"Beats the shit out of me, Sir. It happened, that's all I know," Pongo said. "If you get a chance, please feel free to ask Nancy Pelosi. I keep waiting for Jon Stewart to – she's on his show a lot."

"I'm going to go take a Tylenol PM and try to sleep through the night – hopefully, dream-free," Franklin said.

"Nightily-night, Franklin," Pongo said.

And neither of them could recall a single dream from that night. With the exception of one by each of them featuring flames coming out of a spigot. The documentary had left an incendiary impression.

* * *

Sept. 5, 2010
Podrowski home

B oth Pongo and Franklin slept in 'til almost noon. Pongo awoke just in time to prepare for his 1 p.m. donut shop shift.

Franklin and Phil decided to make a day of it together exploring the Taconic State Parkway route, driving north from Poughkeepsie and into Massachusetts as far as they could get before having to turn around to get back to Pougkeepsie by 7 p.m. for dinner with Pongo.

Franklin enjoyed the drive through Albany and on to the Green Mountain National Forest. He borrowed Phil's digital camera to take lots of pictures, having Phil stop at every roadside historical marker. The sights brought many memories rushing back of travels with Eleanor and the children from home to the state capitol. If nostalgia were a drug, Franklin would've had a fatal overdose that afternoon.

Phil convinced Franklin to join him on the tour of the U.S.S. Slater World War II destroyer escort on their way back at Albany. As they walked around the ship, Franklin couldn't help but think of all the thousands of smiling sailor's faces he'd seen, all the vigorous handshakes he'd shared with the modestly heroic sailors and soldiers he'd met in his lifetime. He still retained a great deal of pride for his love of all things Navy. He hoped to himself that the day would never come when the Navy could be considered obsolete, even if its sole missions were for exploration and law enforcement.

On the prow of a fine ship on a blustery, sunny day – a day like today – all could seem right with the world, at least for a day.

That evening, only the Orvises, Podrowskis, Harry, Idris, Heather and Bianca showed up for the regular weekly update session on Franklin's status. They decided it was time to switch from regular Sunday get-togethers to scheduling a status meeting only if there was something significant or unusual to discuss about Franklin's progress.

* * *

Recreating with the Driver

Sept. 6, 2010
Labor Day
Podrowski home

P ongo, Idris and Harry all had Labor Day off from their respective jobs this year. They decided to take Franklin to the local driving range to see if the powerful golf swing he was reputed to have had pre-polio had returned.

Franklin was a little hesitant at first. He'd done a lot of walking these past several weeks, but he didn't know if his legs were back to the strength they had in his 20's and 30's.

His first three or four swings were a little embarrassing.

"Hey, Commander in Chief, there's bound to be some rust after – well, what is it, 89 years since you last swung a club?" Harry asked.

"More like 90, Harry, but it only seems like a couple dozen or so. Still a long time," Franklin said. "But I bet I could arm-wrestle any one of you whippersnappers left handed and win. I'm willing to take actual bets, by the way."

"Not gonna snap my whip, Mr. Pres," Harry said. "Maybe Idris's, though. I understand he's game for that kind of thing."

"Go piss up a rope, dork," Idris said to Harry. "Sir, I'll bet you're going to get that swing back in the next 15 minutes. I've never seen the kind of arm muscles you've got."

"At the risk of sounding like that "W" guy, now watch this drive," Franklin said.

His swing barely touched the ball, which dribbled off the side of the tee.

His next swing, however, sent the ball soaring high and far, landing close to three hundred yards downrange.

"Did you say 15 minutes, Idris?" Franklin smiled cagily.

"Well, shit fire and spit in it – pardon my Francais, your honor," Idris said.

"Where'd you learn how to do that?" Pongo asked.

"Let me put it this way: when you're Assistant Secretary of the Navy for seven years, you get invited to golf a lot. By people who actually know what they're doing," Franklin laughed.

"I think we've found a possible future career for our favorite ex-President," Harry said under his breath to Pongo.

"I heard that, Harry – and hanging around with golfers is probably the next to last thing I'd ever want to do regularly," Franklin said.

"What's the last thing you'd wanna do, Sir?" Pongo asked.

"Clean toilets at the offices of the Republican National Committee. I don't think I could stand all the sweet fragrances," he said. "From what they used to tell me, their shit's always smelled like fresh roses."

All three of the Poughkeepsie natives laughed hard.

They ended up going through four buckets of balls each. By the time they were done, Franklin's Titleists were grouped together at the far edge of the range; Idris' balls were grouped about three-fourths of the way down the range and both Pongo's and Harry's were grouped fifty to a hundred yards from their tee spots.

"If I were you, Sir, I'd find a way to make money from those kinds of skills," Idris said.

"If Pongo and I don't find me a decent job in the next few days, I might just have to do that, Mr. M'Benga," Franklin smiled.

The four of them spent that evening binge watching Jim Carrey movies. Franklin became an instant fan. "Uh like him uh-LOT," Franklin cracked after "*Dumb and Dumber*." Franklin didn't hit the sack 'til after 1 a.m.

* * *

Fretting the Fractiously Frightening Frenzied Phony Fur-Frackers

Sept. 7, 2010
Podrowski home and elsewhere in Poughkeepsie

Franklin and Pongo spent the final day before high school classes started by checking out job openings at the Dutchess County One Stop Workforce Connection office in Poughkeepsie.

Pongo found a part-time weekend evenings city library assistant position which seemed to fit Franklin's schedule. Franklin wondered if it would be smart to be in a facility where there were pictures of him at every stage of his life posted on the walls.

Pongo said, with a sardonic smile, "Let me just give you one word, friend: beard."

"You won't let go of that, will you?" Franklin said.

"Let go of your beard? Never...C'mon get real. It's a safety issue. You – and the rest of us – none of us can risk you being recognized."

"What's it going to take to convince you that facial hair and I are a bad match?"

"I don't understand, Franklin. I can picture you looking damn good with a beard, whether it's short or long like a sailor who's been at sea for months. Always thought you liked the sailor look."

"There's something that just rankles me about facial hair. I don't think you would understand."

"Help me understand, my good man. I'm a good listener."

"Do you remember me telling you about the furry coats I saw that night you found me at the Visitor Center last month?"

"Sure – it sounded like you were a little delirious. Completely understandable."

"It wasn't delirium."

"I don't follow, Sir."

"What I'm telling you is something I've shared only with my own mother, my wife and a few of my children who have the same sensitivity I have.

"I can see this thing almost no one else can see. It's this light, platinum-colored, shiny, delicate, ultra-fine sensillum-like furry coating of hair only some people have on their bodies. Maybe five percent of the general public had it back in the 1940's. I can see it. My mother could see it. Two of my sons and my daughter could see it. One of my cousins could see it. But I never met anyone else outside my own family who could see it.

"It's easiest to see in the daytime. Usually, it's visible only within ninety to a hundred feet of the person who has it. The thicker it is, the further away you can see it.

"It's really not the furry coats that's the thing – even though they do look kind of funny on women, especially on their faces.

"The thing that's most striking about the coats of fur is what they signify about the people who have them: without exception, every single person I ever saw with that delicate furry coat was obsessed with greed. With accumulating money. With financial selfishness – sometimes on behalf of their family, sometimes without the slightest care for their own family. Selfishness at all costs. At the cost of shredding their conscience. They usually were law abiding people, but not always. And the very thickest fur coats of all were on people who weren't just greedy, but were as phony as a Republican social worker.

"It was a valuable perception to have. It helped me to know who to appoint to the Vice Presidency, to my cabinet and to sub-cabinet positions. It helped me to know who to place in political positions where avarice was a helpful characteristic. It helped me to know who was likely to be loyal and who wasn't. When I was younger – once my Mother explained to me what this ability actually meant when I was about 12 – it helped me decide who the best people would be to work for.

"But it always did and always will make me uneasy about growing my own fur on my own face. It may sound nuts, but I simply don't want even the slightest risk of being confused for one of those furry-coated people. Just in case there are people out there besides my own family members who have this ability."

"Christ, how many more surprises are we going to learn about you, Franklin?" Pongo said, goosebumps on his arms. "I probably should have you watch the movie "*They Live*" with me.

"Are any of my friends sporting those furry coats?"

"Well," Franklin said, "Harry has kind of a very, very light mangy-patchy looking coat. But it's the kind I used to see on people who, at most, would tell 'little white lies' to further their own agendas. I probably would trust him for serious matters – not so much when it comes to stealing the picnic lunch sandwich you packed for yourself."

"But everyone else we know is fur-less?"

"As far as I know. I've never seen anyone try to groom or shave that furry matter. I suppose most of the people with it can't actually sense it."

"You'd tell me if you saw someone who actually has this thing, wouldn't you, Sir?"

"Probably. As a rule of thumb, the most common places to find people with the fur is at car dealerships and Republican gatherings. I would say maybe three in four persons at Republican rallies look, to me, like furry creatures. And one in two car salesmen. Maybe one in three building contractors.

"It's really not the kind of thing we would need to worry about unless the person with the furry coat is involved with us in some way."

"Geez, I'm glad you shared this with me," Pongo said. "I'm going to rely on you to have my back – and my family's back – when it comes to dealing with these furry people. God, I can't get over how full of surprises you are, Mr. President."

"Anyone who's lived the kind of life I've lived is bound to know things the average person wouldn't. It doesn't make me better than anyone else."

"I think there probably are millions of folks who would disagree with that, Sir.

"So, what does your gut tell you about which of these job listings you'd like to go after?"

"I'd like to work for one of the companies advertising for landscaping crew members to work five-hour shifts Fridays, Saturdays, Sundays and Mondays. I'd like nothing better than to get back to planting trees when I'm not in school."

"Let's make that happen, Sir."

By the end of the day, Franklin had signed on to work for Adams Landscaping, starting Sept. 16, 2010: starting pay=$10 per hour, paid bi-weekly, with his first partial payday on Sept. 24. For a man who had faced down a worldwide threat of fascism, Franklin felt surprisingly proud over this employment accomplishment. He'd been awarded this job not for his family name or reputation, but for a bare-bones resume and a stellar interview performance by Percy Van Mullder. A performance during which his dogged work ethic came shining through like his winning smile.

* * *

FAST TIMES AT POUGHKEEPSIE HIGH –
ALLURE IN THE AISLES

Sept. 8-Oct. 31, 2010
Podrowski home, Poughkeepsie High School & various Poughkeepsie locales

Franklin's enrollment that day at Poughkeepsie High School as senior Percival Van Mullder for 2010-2011 was not without its hurdles. Phil had to attest to a curriculum completed by Franklin while being home-schooled. Phil simply checked on the courses covered at Groton when Franklin attended there more than a century earlier (using Groton's archives) and adapted that list to the requirements set forth by the New York State Education Department. Phil also had to produce home testing results from each of those years of schooling; in the three days before school started, he printed out copies of all the required Freshman through Junior year tests, had Franklin take the tests in the evenings and scored them. Franklin passed them all, but only by the skin of his teeth on the required math sections.

By this time, Franklin's digestive system and sphincters had more or less stabilized. He no longer needed to wear Depends, especially during the daytime. Just as relieving to Franklin, he now appeared to be *consistently* able to keep down nutrients more complex than baby food. He hadn't relished the prospect of having to bring jars of baby food to high school in a lunchbag. At the recommendation of Bianca and Cherisse, though, he continued to eat anti-oxidant fruits and vegetables as much as possible and had started taking multi-vitamins and fish oil capsules every morning before breakfast.

Franklin's senior class list included English 7-8, Social Studies 7-8, French 3-4, Environmental Science 1-2, Government 3-4, U.S. History 7-8 and Bowling 1-2.

He found himself struggling to stay awake at times even from Day 1 during the Social Studies, Government and History classes, simply because he was well-prepared for each, having actually witnessed most of the first-half 20th century subject matter first-hand. When he wasn't struggling to stay awake, he was nervously trying to hide frequent erections. He found it astonishing the kind of revealing clothing that young women routinely wore in public.

Two weeks into the semester, one remarkably attractive 18-year-old classmate in his Environmental Science class, Holly Ann Van Arsdale, couldn't help noticing first the embarrassed expression on the face of this "Percival" – then she noticed the little mountain in his crotch area and put 2 + 2 together.

She had noticed Percival almost always had the correct answer whenever their teacher, Ms. Watkins (a 50-something stout plain-faced woman of eastern European descent with an assortment of warts on her forehead), called on him in class. She also noticed that Franklin usually looked away, sort of shyly, whenever Holly caught him looking at her out of the corner of her eye. He didn't seem to want her to know he thought she was pretty.

And think *that*, he did.

He was drawn to her the first time he saw her auburn-blond hair, round hazel eyes set off by stylish glasses and her shapely 5' 9" frame. What sealed the attraction was her unambiguous intellect. When he listened to Holly and the teacher discuss the day's lesson, it was like hearing two professorial colleagues speaking instead of a teacher and student.

Franklin/Percival wanted to know Holly better. *Lots* better. And although he didn't know it yet, the feeling was reciprocal.

＊　＊　＊

THE PRICE OF DOMINOES

Catching up on the O'Learys' reading assignments would keep Franklin busy in his spare time for the next two months. Their Saturday sessions during that time mainly involved Franklin's questions about the material.

During that first post-start of high school Saturday (Sept. 11) session, the O'Learys decided to go over the Vietnam era with a fine tooth comb. Franklin's primary question was about the news media.

"When I was leading the country, the newspapers and radio reporters questioned almost every detail of the war. We might not have answered every question we were asked, but reporters did their best to leave no stone unturned when it came to the need to put lives at risk.

"Why didn't that happen at the start of the Vietnam War? How did the newspapers let President Johnson foist that phony gunboat attack on the public as an excuse for war? Was there really a panicky kind of fear about communists taking over countries one at a time across the Pacific? That Domino thing you mentioned, right?

"Or was it all just a cynical ruse, a catalyst to enrich that military industrial complex mentioned by General – I mean, *President* Eisenhower? And, if that complex was such a threat to prosperity, why didn't Ike do something about it *while he was President* instead of waiting 'til just before he left office to warn everyone?"

"Perhaps someday, you'll decide to pursue a Master's Degree based on research into that question, Franklin," Karin said. "From what I understand, there's plenty of evidence on both sides of that 'fear of Communism vs. corporate enrichment issue.'"

"Christ, either way, I don't understand how they could be that cavalier about sending hundreds of thousands of soldiers into battle whether they were scared of capitalism being compromised or they wanted lucrative contracts for corporate military spending. Either way, it just does not sound like the kind of **existential threat** we faced from the fascists," Franklin said, looking dismayed.

"That's because it wasn't – the North Vietnamese had no Navy, no real Air Force," Karin said. "That's why hundreds of thousands of young men fled to Canada to avoid being forced to fight. It was a monumental tragedy that it took the rest of the country so long to see the reality those young men saw early on.

"As someone who was young back then, I will never, ever forgive the likes of religious leaders like Billy Graham for wrapping themselves in the flag with their unquestioning support for the war, in front of thousands of young people at religious rallies.

"The first huge crack in the dam of public opinion happened when "Uncle Walter," Walter Cronkite, the CBS Evening News anchor, pronounced in February 1968 that continued escalation of the war risked 'cosmic disaster.'

"It took tens of thousands of soldiers' lost lives, a chaotic 1968 Democratic National Convention in Chicago with many hundreds of protesters brutally beaten by police and, finally, the May 1970 murders of four unarmed peacefully protesting Kent State students – and wounding of another nine - by the Ohio National Guard to permanently turn the tide of public opinion against the war.

"The abandonment of the war was a fait accompli after the Kent State shootings – shootings which have gone unprosecuted to this day. And **yet** the war dragged on another five years, 'til April 30, 1975, mostly thanks to President Nixon and Henry Kissinger, before the last American soldiers were brought home to safety. It was another 21 months later, the day Jimmy Carter took office, when Carter implemented an unconditional amnesty for Vietnam era draft evaders who had fled to Canada.

"More than 50,000 American lives lost and millions of Vietnamese lives lost simply to try to protect capitalism from irrational fears. Irrationality on full public display day in and day out in modern Vietnam – which now is a full-fledged trading partner with the U.S.A."

"I noticed this morning that the underwear I have on was made in Vietnam," Franklin said. "All those deaths to keep underwear from being made by communists there. And the Vietnamese figured out their version of capitalism *all on their own*. No. Bombs. Required."

Karin and Orvis soon ended the session early so Franklin could start work on his assigned reading.

* * *

NANCY THE CUPID NOT STUPID – NO FOLLY THIS HOLLY, SHOWS MERCY TO PERCY: SMART FOR HIS HEART

The following Monday couldn't come soon enough for Franklin – he couldn't wait to see Holly again.

As he was shaving and showering before school that morning, Franklin kept thinking just how grateful he was Pongo and Heather had insisted he watch those movie videos about being in high school. The last thing he wanted was to come across to Holly as some sort of bashful dork.

Bashful dork, however, was exactly what Holly was thinking the first time she approached Franklin to talk with him, at the beginning of that third week of classes, as she sat down across from him in the school cafeteria, where he was sitting by himself.

Holly had no idea what she was getting into with this young man who clearly was smitten with her.

"So, I hear you're living with the Podrowski's. I'm Holly Van Arsdale – I sit across from you in Environmental Science. This," Holly said pointing her open hand to a borderline-emaciated, shabbily-dressed 17-year-old whom Franklin/Percy had noticed sitting next to Holly in class, "is my best friend, Nancy Perez."

"I know – I'm Percy Van Mullder. It's great to meet you both. The Podrowski's took me in after my parents passed away. They were distant relatives of Pongo's Mom. What brings you two to this corner of our fine dining establishment?"

"Well, I just wanted to try to get to know this handsome young man I occasionally notice staring at me when he thinks I'm not looking. And Nancy told me to stop being a wuss and just come over. OK, Nancy, you can go now – you don't have to nag me anymore."

"See," Nancy said, "it wasn't that difficult, was it? It's really nice to finally meet you, Percy. You be nice to my BFF, OK?"

"Looks to me like you both have good taste in BFF's," Franklin/Percy smiled. "Thanks for encouraging her, Nancy. You know you don't _really_ have to go, right?"

"Actually, I really DO have to do some last minute finishing touches on an assignment that's due today, so can't linger. You two need to get to know each other anyway. See you both later!"

"'Bye, Nance – watch out for that Pfeffernan horndog next to your locker!" Holly said as Nancy walked out of the cafeteria. Jim Pfeffernan was the varsity basketball co-captain who'd developed a reputation for pursuing only the very thinnest girls on campus.

"So, what's it like to be new to Poughkeepsie?" Holly asked Franklin/Percy. "I certainly wouldn't know, 'cuz I've been here my entire life!"

"It's different. We used to live in Manhattan. It's much more beautiful **here.** I can't wait for all the leaves to change in another couple of weeks."

"I know. People who live in a desert, like in Arizona or New Mexico – I don't know how they can stand all that brown when there are places with the kinds of glorious colors like we get."

"I've been hoping I'd get a chance to speak with you, Holly. I love listening to the sound of your voice when you're talking with Ms. Watkins. You sound a lot older and wiser than you look. That's pretty enticing to a fellow like me."

"Well...uh, that's nice to hear. What kinds of things do you do in your spare time, Percy? Any hobbies or pastimes?"

"I like walking in the woods just before and after sunset, especially in the fall. I can never get enough walking. To me, this seems like just about the most beautiful, walkable place on earth.

"Would you maybe like to come with me for a walk during lunch tomorrow? I have to use most of my lunch hour each day for my dog-walking job..."

"That sounds just fine, Percy."

"OK, I'll look for you in the lunchroom tomorrow and we'll take off as soon as we're done eating. If you're not busy after school, I'd be honored to walk with you along the river 'til sunset." He wondered what the sunset would be like with her beautiful head and delicate rosy lips pistoning between his legs.

"That sounds great to me, Percy. I'll bring my walking shoes tomorrow," she said, getting up to go to her next class. As she walked away, she wondered what it would be like to have *his* head, a sublimely sensuous study in symmetry atop supremely-sculpted shoulders, rocking up and down between her legs.

"Fantastic," Percy/Franklin said. "I'll see you then." He stayed seated for a while, legs crossed, needing his hormones to take a breather.

In Franklin's mind, all he could think of was what it might be like kissing Holly and holding her in his arms. In Holly's mind, the same kind of fantasizing was in progress.

But Franklin's fantasy was interrupted by a sober realization: *"Doesn't she have the right to know that sharing any kind of bodily fluid with me – even saliva – might mean she could never go anywhere near anyone with a head injury again, ever? What if she wants to become a doctor or nurse? And doesn't she have the right to know who I really am?"*

His crotch mountain promptly plummeted, not to be resurrected for more than an hour…which is probably the longest such hiatus on record for any healthy teenage male.

Holly's and Franklin's walks together the next day were as enjoyable as they both imagined they'd be. Franklin/Percy was enrapt by Holly's description of her family and her life experiences; Holly was mesmerized by Franklin/Percy's descriptions of travels he'd had around the world and his passion for sailing and fishing, though she always sensed there was something a little mysterious about certain omitted details. But she felt it would be rude to press about the personal details of someone who'd lost both his parents.

Franklin was fascinated by Holly's telling of the history of her friendship with Nancy. Turned out Holly took Nancy under her wing after Nancy's mother Rosita moved Nancy and Nancy's older brother Paul to Poughkeepsie from Brooklyn when Nancy was just 6 years old. The move happened shortly after Nancy's father Mark, a drywall hanger, abandoned the family in the wake of a huge argument with Rosita over finances and Rosita's insistence that Mark help out around the house.

For a week there had been no word from Mark. Then Rosita got a call from Mark: he told her he'd found a county in south Texas well known for its lack of effective child support enforcement services. He promised that it'd be a cold day in hell before she's see him voluntarily pay a single red cent of child support. ("You can suck my boner for a week, or 'til that icy cunt of yours thaws out, whichever comes first, if you think you're going to get child support from me," were Mark's actual touchingly sensitive words.)

So, since the move to Poughkeepsie three years earlier, Rosita had been unable to afford to buy any new clothes for any of them and could barely keep food on the table, despite holding down two minimum wage jobs. Money from *Nancy's* 30-hour per week job the past two years at a local thrift store was the main reason the Perezes weren't evicted from their two-bedroom apartment.

As the late-afternoon sun was setting behind the hills west of the Hudson River, the cloud-filtered rays shining through Holly's fine tresses, Franklin leaned in close to Holly, his hand gently caressing her shoulder. Holly leaned back in toward him, starting to kiss him, when Franklin slowly held her back.

"You need to know something right now, something that you won't believe but something you deserve to know for your health and long-term sanity, Holly."

"What, do you have some kind of fatal STD?" she asked, on the verge of laughing. "Christ, you're not gay are you?!"

"I wish it were something as simple as an esty-dee, whatever that is," Franklin said. "And I'm not any more carefree or cheery than anyone else – but I'm not sure why that would matter. Let's talk about it tomorrow evening – if you still want to walk with me then, that is."

"Of course I'd like to walk with you again. My curiosity is killing me – I know you wanted to kiss me just now, as much as I wanted to kiss you right back...I can wait a day to find out what it is I've done to put you off or what it is that's scaring you about me."

"It's not what you think, Holly, I swear to God. You haven't done anything wrong, I promise."

"OK, I believe you, Sweetie."

Franklin decided not to share his potential romantic developments with Pongo and Phil that evening. They spent part of their evening watching The Daily Show, The Colbert Report and pro football.

When it came time to knock off for the night, it took Franklin almost an hour to nod off. He was especially nervous about what might happen the next day with Holly.

$$* \quad * \quad *$$

Somnolent Visions, Part III

*T*en minutes into their walk as the sun sank into the western treetops, Franklin first took Holly's left hand and then her right, and looked directly into her eyes. It was the most earnest, sensitive gaze he had summoned since that last evening he'd spent with Lucy near Warm Springs.

*"What I'm about to tell you can**not** be shared with anyone. Not your parents, not your confessor, not your school counselor, not even your dog. I'm serious – well, maybe not about the dog. I **mean** this, though – there are people who could be killed or tortured or, literally, thrown into a dungeon at some undisclosed location if you repeat what I'm about to tell you."*

"I know how to keep things to myself, Percy. You can count on me."

"I'll just say it: my name isn't really Percy. It's Franklin. As in Franklin Delano Roosevelt. I. Am. He. A bizarre series of events brought me back, apparently starting with a rare kind of lightning. It caused my age to regress to, well, about 18 now. My real age is about 128.

(Holly listened, speechless, her eyes reflecting a combination of shock and subdued terror.)

*"The worst part is, thanks to the way I was brought back, if you share **any** bodily fluids with me, you might be infected with this thing which could turn you into an uncontrolled brain-eating crazy person anytime you're anywhere near someone with a bad head injury.*

"At least that's what it did to me about a month or so ago.

*"So, as much as I'd like to kiss you and hold you in my arms until I am a really old person again – if I ever **am** going to get old again – I can't do that in good conscience. Unless you are convinced it's worth the risk.*

"I can see by your expression that you don't believe what you're hearing. If you want to check photos of me on your smarty phone from when I was 18, back in 1900, you're welcome to. I know it's crazy. You probably want to run away as fast as you can right now. I am stunned – and grateful – that you're not screaming at this very instant."

"My. Dear. God." Holly said, gasping slowly. *"OK, let me look on my smart phone."* About a minute and a half passed.

"Dear Jesus. It IS you."

A long, silent pause ensued. Holly looked at her phone, at Franklin, back down at her phone, at Franklin again. Another pause.

"So, you're saying the worst that could happen to me is that I couldn't have a career in health care services and I would have to avoid urgent care and emergency room facilities the rest of my life, right?"

"As far as I know. This isn't something there's much medical literature about."

"Well, Mr. Roosevelt, I am all in. I never wanted to be a doctor or anything remotely like that. Come here, Dear," she said, clutching his shoulders and pulling Franklin in slowly for a long, soft, tongue in mouth kiss.

Before Franklin knew it, they were lying on the grass in a dense tree thicket, engaging in side-to-side oral sex with each other, in that unique shape like the weather map icon for a hurricane. It <u>could</u> be, he thought, the first of many, many trysts they would share the rest of their high school and college years. It took about 10 minutes before the both of them were overcome by orgasms, almost simultaneously.

But as they were walking back, Franklin had second thoughts. He was terrified that Holly might share details of his real identity with someone else, especially members of her family or church. By the time they approached his car, he summoned the courage to tell her what had just happened was a mistake, that he'd decided it would be best to wait to fully consummate their relationship 'til they were out of college.

What happened next was something Franklin might've seen coming, if he'd understood adolescent women better. But he didn't.

Holly flew into a rage. With flecks of spittle flying out of her mouth, she dressed down Franklin, calling him a sexual predator freak. She told him she was going to have her brothers come and set him straight. Then she said she'd be calling the National Enquirer to make sure every grocery store shopper in the country knew this freak was claiming to be FDR re-incarnated. Finally, she said, *"Here's MY New Deal for YOU!"* as she reared back her raised fist and slugged as hard as she could right between Franklin's legs.

At that point, Franklin woke up. Dripping with sweat. Worst. Wet. Dream. EVER.

* * *

Teenage Gossip: Mind-Fucking - with All Refills Free...But Candor, Vulnerability and Credibility Empirically Strike Back

The next day's classes passed at a glacial pace. Holly sat with Franklin at lunch, but their conversation was awkward and stilted. After she left to spend time with her friends, a fellow Environmental Sciences classmate walked over and sat across from Franklin.

"Hi – I don't know if you remember me from Envai Sci, Percy – I'm Ralph, Ralph Pearson," he said.

"Yes – I've seen you in class. I apologize for not introducing myself sooner," Franklin/Percy said.

"No problem, Percy," Ralph said. "Listen, I've seen you spending some time with Holly. I just thought you probably would want to know a little bit about her modus operandi."

"Are you saying she's a criminal?" Franklin/Percy asked anxiously.

"No, no, no, not at all," Ralph said. "It's just that she rode a little roughshod on the feelings of a friend of a friend. She dated this guy – you wouldn't know him, his name's Rory Richardson – for a couple of years.

"Not to tell tales out of school, so to speak," Ralph whispered, "but she and Rory probably gave each other head five times a week over the past year. I don't think they ever actually did _IT_, but they did almost everything else.

"Anyway, she'd been discussing this church she goes to – it's one of those where the people are supposed to share all their sins with their spiritual leader, their bishop or pastor or whatever – and he told her he simply couldn't see himself being a part of it.

"So, what does she do? She goes home and tells her Daddy all about all her oral sex with Rory and then tells her church bishop and then tells her best friends and then tells her brothers. Daddy orders her to stop seeing Rory. And she simply follows Daddy's orders.

"It broke the living shit out of Rory's heart. His folks thought for a while they'd might have to put him in one of those fancy mental hospitals for a while, but it didn't get quite that bad.

"Anyway, I thought you might want to be aware of what you might be stepping into. I know I've only heard Rory's side of what happened, so there's every chance that she might not be as cold and heartless and obsessed with making her Daddy happy as he's made her out to be.

"Still, I just thought, what with you being new here, you deserve to know about potential hazards with Holly. I'm not ashamed to tell you, though: she is _so_ goddam hot, I'd almost be willing to risk a little mind-fucking myself to get a taste of that particular vixen."

"I appreciate your concern, Ralph," Franklin said. "But this really sounds like some pretty standard high school gossip. It would mean a lot more coming direct-ly from this Rory guy. I can understand, though, why he might not feel comfort-able sharing those details himself – picking at the scab on a wound and what-not.

"I promise I'll tread carefully with her."

"Excellent – keep it prudent, Dude," Ralph said, unsuccessfully attempting a fist-bump with Franklin as he got up from the table and left.

Minutes later, as Franklin walked the dogs by himself, all he could think about was how he would explain his situation when he and Holly met for their walk near the river that evening. His mind that afternoon couldn't have been further from classwork. All of the things that were crises for the entire world 65 years earlier seemed like just so much ethereal mist. Adolescent hormones manufacture their own kaleidoscope for the teenage perspective on reality – but that sort of circum-spection was far outside Franklin's grasp on this day, with a brief exception.

His libido paused long enough for him to consider that, on his timeline, it was only about six weeks earlier that he was in a different reality. A reality in which his first serious love interest almost 100 years earlier, Alice Sohier, had rejected him because she was repulsed by Franklin's remarks that he wanted as many as six children; the rejection pushed him into the arms of the niece of his idolized cousin-President – a rebound relationship which changed the course of his life forever. (*"Was this leap forward in time just another type of rebound?"* he wondered.)

That earlier reality also featured a devoted former secret lover who repeat-edly crossed the country simply to spend time with him – as well as a reality with a quasi-estranged wife who, nevertheless, admired much about him. Along with the reality of five beloved children who loved him back, not to mention almost an en-tire nation which saw him as a father figure. But those magnificent realities were 65 years lost to time and space. This new reality featured a beautiful 18-year-old girl who *seemed* to have nothing but unconditional love and honesty in her eyes.

As they started their walk together that afternoon, Franklin was about to share some of his most personal details with Holly when she surprised him by breaking the awkward silence first.

"Franklin, I think you deserve to know something that could someday keep us apart," she said. "I'm in a church which strongly discourages its members from marrying outside of their faith. And if I have conventional intimacy with you, I am required to share every detail of it with my local church leader, someone you'd consider a pastor or priest – if I don't want to be excommunicated, that is.

"There's even a commonly-used saying among unmarried members my age: stay moral, go oral. (By the way, Dear, I assume you're astute enough not to have oral intimacy with anyone when you have a cold sore in your mouth – don't know if I could forgive you if you gave me genital herpes for the rest of my life, not to mention maybe invasive cervical cancer.)

"If my father finds out about us, and my church leader will make sure of that, he'll demand that you stop seeing me unless you join my church. And if I keep seeing you after that, he and my mother probably will disown me. Worse than that, he'll have my church leader and others in local church leadership pressure both of us to end our relationship."

"What in the hell kind of church is this?" Franklin asked. "Mormon? Fundamentalist Baptist? Some strange middle-ages Catholic throwback?"

"It doesn't even matter. You may think of me as some bright, modern, assertive woman, but when it comes to the church I've known since I was a toddler, and the church community I've been a part of since then, I know I'm not strong enough to abandon it. Not now. Maybe someday, maybe never. But not now. I just don't want to be without it, for now, maybe always.

"I'll understand if you don't want to see me again this way."

Franklin had started the walk with Holly determined not to be prejudiced by Ralph's second-hand account of Holly's previous relationship with Rory. But Holly's own candor had buttressed most of the details shared by Ralph. And there was that strange dream he'd had the night before, one of those weird dreams that sticks with you, even long after you wake up.

"Here's the thing, Holly," Franklin said. "I **_DO_** want to see you that way. I want to be as emotionally and physically intimate with you as you want to be with me.

"But there are things you deserve to know **about me** which I'm uncomfortable sharing with you as long as your church and your parents are the primary focus of your life. I can see myself someday **maybe** being _convinced,_ _under_ _pressure,_ out of loyalty to you to try and make your church and family the focus of my life, but that's really not where I want my life to go.

"I would want you in my life only if each of us makes our own relationship the main focus of our personal lives. It doesn't sound like you're at that point in your life yet – and it sounds like there a chance you might not ever reach that point.

"What do you think?"

By this time, tears were starting to precipitate out of the corners of Holly's eyes.

"I think you might hate my church. And my church and my family are what make me most of who I am," she said.

"I said nothing about hating anything. But it sounds like you're not ready for what we might be able to share together some day. If that time comes, if you are ready someday to try a relationship which isn't _dependent_ on church and parents being the primary focus of your life, I hope you'll seek me out.

"I feel like there's an untapped vein of devotion and fidelity in there for what we could have together someday."

"Let me think all of this over, OK?" she said. "But don't hold your breath about me. I am who I am, what my life has made me. I s'pose it's always *possible* I might take my life in a different direction someday. Who can tell?"

"But, for now, let's just finish our walk and go back to being good school friends, OK?"

"That sounds just fine to me, for now," Franklin said.

And they finished their two-mile walk together. The last quarter-mile coming back to Franklin's car, Franklin tentatively reached over and held Holly's left hand in his right hand. Holly thought it seemed like a gesture of genuine caring on Franklin's/Percy's part. When he dropped her off at her house, they embraced for a good half-minute before she left the car; Franklin kissed her gently on the cheek as the embrace ended, forcing himself at the last second to pull back from the kiss he wanted to place on her lovely lips. Franklin was convinced Holly was *not*, in fact, the kind of cold, heartless person described by Ralph. He truly hoped there would be more for them to share in the future – even if that future were years away.

* * *

DEAD PEASANTS AND DECEPTION, CORPORATE AMERICAN-STYLE

The following Saturday's session (Sept. 18) with the O'Learys covered the transition from the nuclear inferno politics of the Cold War to the emerging spread of capitalism among former Cold War adversaries – and the effects of all those dynamics on capitalism in the U.S.A.

The discussion began with Franklin's notes on the documentary *"Capitalism: A Love Story."*

"If there were only one thing among all the outrages this movie brought to light that I could make sure every American knew about, it would be dead peasant insurance," Franklin said. "How can Americans ever look at corporations the same way again after realizing a lot of companies take out life insurance on their employees with the benefits payable *only to the employer*?

"Why is that even legal?"

"Because no Federal law prohibits it," Karin said.

"Is that what China and Vietnam and Russia are learning from us master Capitalists?" Franklin asked. "That it's smart economics to profit off your employees' deaths while those same employees' families can't even afford a decent funeral?"

"I hear you," Orvis said. "It's a slimy practice. Its original version was intended only for highly-paid employees who'd be hard to replace. It first involved *low-level* employees when low-wage employers started taking out policies en masse in the 1980's. Wal-Mart took out policies on 350,000 of its employees back then. I'm not aware of businesses in any other countries taking out those kinds of policies on that kind of scale."

"Probably because ours is the only country which encourages its employer class to behave like craven sociopaths," Franklin speculated. "Once again, I don't understand what's kept the average working person from taking to the streets with torches and pitchforks to protest that kind of economic injustice."

"In this situation," Karin said, "it's probably because dead peasant insurance policies are mostly taken out in secret. Only a handful of states require employers to notify their employees when they take out those kinds of policies.

"Plus, not that many people saw that movie – in theaters, anyway. It only took in $14 or $15 million at the box office."

"And, of course, if educators tried to teach from it in public schools, they'd face the wrath of extremist local school board scolds," Franklin remembered. "Being factual alone just isn't good enough to be included in school curricula, right?"

"Sadly, that's been a fact of life for a while now," Orvis said.

"People have struggled mightily with their finances since the 2007-2008 meltdown, as you already know," he continued. "Millions of homeowners have lost their homes – as was so eloquently pointed out in this movie – while $700 billion-plus was forked over in taxpayer dollars as corporate welfare to huge financial institutions simply because they were declared 'too big to fail.'

"The struggle for affordable home payments has become so bad, people actually are buying up deeply-discounted decommissioned nuclear missile silos around the country and moving into them to live.

"Can you imagine anything more disturbing, more horrifically symbolic of what our country's hyper-capitalism has done to Americans' consciences?

"I mean, can you picture some missile silo condo owner posting a sign at his driveway entrance reading something like, 'Duck and Cover Acres'? Can you imagine the kinds of dreams a young kid would have growing up sleeping in a bedroom near where a mass-incineration nuclear warhead once stood?"

"After reading "*American Ground Zero*," and watching "*Atomic Café*," I can only worry about their very souls," Franklin said, uncharacteristically grimly.

"If there are any bright spots, it's got to be the kind of feistiness and candor bright people like Elizabeth Warren bring into public consciousness. I will keep hoping people like her will continue to find the courage to confront the kind of soulless Ayn Randian greed the Republicans as a party have embraced as their official standard."

"Unfortunately," Orvis said, "the actions of religious-extremist terrorists from many thousands of miles away have become existential threats in the minds of many – if not most – Americans. Even though those terrorists have no navies or air forces which could reach our shores, not to mention only having soldiers who are organized on a shoestring budget. We can thank our corporate media for continuing to gin up that constant fear, for keeping alive the concept that permanent war is plausible.

"That perceived threat has greatly overshadowed the middle class-friendly, consumer-friendly voices of smart people like Ms. Warren. People simply no longer buy the idea that fear itself is the worst thing we have to fear, I'm sad to say."

"Just maybe, someday we'll have a national leader again who has the courage and strength of will to bring that kind of circumspection back to people," Karin said.

"Why are you looking at me that way, Karin?" Franklin asked. "Surely you don't think I could magically become President again, do you?"

"No, Sir," she said. "But I think you might just figure out a way for people to discover someone who could. Maybe figure out a way for circumstances to make that discovery more likely."

"Right now, I just want to find a healthy slice of normality," Franklin said.

✳ ✳ ✳

Bushy Brown Roots

Franklin's part-time work at Adams Landscaping that started that week turned out to be a pleasantly surprising diversion from his high school classes and history sessions with the O'Learys.

And it tapped an aptitude and passion for all things arboreal which Franklin had been unable to exercise since polio nearly destroyed the use of his legs in August 1921.

His primary assignment was providing customer service in the tree sales department and traveling to customers' homes and businesses to plant the trees they purchased. Chester H. "Chet" Dale, the 45-year-old supervisor who hired Franklin/Percy, went along with Franklin on his first two landscaping site assignments. Chet was impressed immediately with Franklin's non-allergic reaction to hard work.

Franklin made it clear that he and garden implements had been on a first-name basis for a long, long time. When Franklin/Percy completed the transplantation of six 50-gallon Red Sunset maples into dense rocky clay soil in front of a local Episcopal church in two and a half hours – and promptly asked what else he could do – Chet decided this Van Mullder kid was just the kind of go-getter who not only would make Chet's work life a little easier, but also would make Chet look like a pretty smart H.R. person.

"Percy, I tell ya' what," Chet said. "I like your attitude so much, from now on, I'm callin' ya' Scruples. That OK with you?"

"Call me anything but late to dinner," Franklin said, laughing under his breath.

"I like the cut of your jib, kiddo," Chet said. "If ya' ever want any extra hours, just let me know at least a day in advance, OK?"

"Works for me," Franklin said. But he still found it hard to get used to being called Percy, Scruples, late to dinner or anything other than Franklin or Mr. President. As long as his legs and heart kept working, though, he *really was* happy to answer to anything at all.

The next day, he had a surprise on-the-job visit from Pongo, Harry and Idris. Harry kept asking him for advice on the best way to plow the bushy brown roots of a 23-year-old peach.

"Well," Franklin began after it became clear Harry really wanted a response, "I suppose you'd start with one of these Garden Weasel tools to break up the soil, unless it's already moist and warm – if the soil's extra firm or super frigid, I'd try to penetrate using the Garden Weasel claw tool."

Each time Franklin used the words moist, warm, penetrate and frigid, Harry and Idris let out loud horselaughs, while Pongo literally had to bite the back of his hand to keep from laughing in Franklin's direction.

As soon as Idris' and Harry's hysterical snickering subsided, Pongo discreetly whispered to Franklin what Harry's question actually meant.

"I believe the cultural term of art to describe the likes of you two is 'dickheads,'" Franklin laughed (mostly at himself), looking at Harry and Idris.

"Shit, Sir – pardon my French - if we don't educate you in the ways of the world, who will?" Idris asked, still laughing.

"As long as the tuition for your teaching services isn't unreasonable, please kindly accept my earnest gratitude, uh, um, 'dickwads,'" Franklin said, pausing for effect before finding that final word of choice and raising his middle finger at Harry and Idris.

"You're right, Pongo, this gent is one quick study," Harry said.

"Now, just to demonstrate what superb customer service you provide, Sir, if you'll please direct us to your vegetable seeds section, we'd like to take advantage of your clearance items," Pongo said.

Franklin escorted them to the Northrop King seeds display, where they each selected approximately $10 worth of clearance-priced seed packets.

"My supervisor Chet told me I could use my employee discount for my closest friends once a month, so you'll save another ten percent," Franklin said proudly.

"You are just too good to us, Sir," Pongo said.

"I'll be even better to you if you get your wide load buttocks on your way so I can get back to what I was working on," Franklin said with a large grin.

"It's a deal," Harry said.

As they left, each of them patted Franklin on the shoulder and thanked him for being a good sport. Idris told him to keep his right arm flexible for bowling with them later that evening.

The rest of his shift, Franklin thought about how lucky he was to have found such fine friends in his 65-year jump ahead in time.

* * *

A Red Under Every Bed=Twice the Lunch, Twice the Fun

His third full week at Poughkeepsie High went as well as could be expected. The French class was surprisingly enjoyable, especially because the teacher, Joy Dupree, a 35-year-old 5'9" blonde, was achingly beautiful, with a personality to match.

But the class was so packed full of horny 17- and 18-year-old young men, there was barely room to walk between the rows of desks. There was a standing list for her 8th-hour (after-school) study hall/tutoring posted next to the door which was always full of male names. Franklin noticed that his French 3-4 classmates tended to head straight for Ms. Dupree's classroom as soon as school doors were unlocked at 7:30 a.m. each day to sign their names onto that list.

Franklin was thinking it would be more convenient for the participants if there were a boy's bathroom adjoining the classroom so they could take turns going in there and engaging in some DIY orgasms stimulated by Ms. Dupree's nearby salivation-inducing visage.

English, Social Studies, U.S. History and bowling were just barely challenging enough to keep Franklin awake for 50 minutes each.

Environmental Science was a mighty challenge simply because it took all of Franklin's focus to keep his mind off the lovely Ms. Van Arsdale. Every time he'd be tempted to strike up an open-ended conversation with her, he would force himself to think of the limitless possibilities of being on the wrong end of a woman scorned – or one who might see herself as such, reality notwithstanding.

She would still join him at lunch from time to time in the far back corner of the school cafeteria – each time she did, it took all of his self-control to keep from putting his hand inside hers under the table. He knew if he did that, he would want even more to put his hand between her perfectly shaped thighs – if she allowed it, that is.

He succeeded – for the most part – in keeping their lunchtime conversations on a purely friendly basis, discussing mostly mundane topics, while at the same time trying to politely ferret out additional details about Holly's family life and life plans. She did likewise.

The Government class, however, was Franklin's Jolt Cola for his otherwise skim milk schedule. The instructor there, an ex-fundamentalist Christian pastor named Glenn Spadnik, took every opportunity to rail against supposedly socialist features of post-New Deal U.S.A. history.

He emphasized that, "to this day," there still was no way to know how many Federal and state government agencies had been infiltrated by communist-sympathizing radicals. He regaled the class with tales of his ancestors' harrowing journey from Siberia through eastern Europe and on to the U.S.A. in the mid-1920's. They had been Russian patriots, he proudly recalled, who fought against the Leninist revolutionaries until they had to run for their lives into hiding.

"So, they fought hard for the rights of the super-wealthy to keep the working class folks mired in abject poverty, right?" Franklin asked, jabbing the sharp stick into the side of the pit bull.

"I see you're one of those who believe the rich among us deserve to be punished," Spadnik, wearing a moth-eaten patched up old puke-green sweater, asserted blithely, looking out the window toward the soccer field.

"You mean, like when they're forced to pay a couple percent of their annual income to avoid going to jail over multiple felonies after being caught red-handed?" Franklin asked.

"No, I mean like when they're made to pay more than everyone else in the progressive income tax system," Spadnik shot back.

"Like when Mitt Romney has to pay 13 percent of his earnings in taxes while the waitress at Denny's has to pay 20 percent?" Franklin asked.

Spadnik's face was almost beet red by this point.

"Mr. Van Mullder, you and I need to speak briefly after class," he said.

"I believe I can squeeze you into my schedule, sir," Franklin replied, admiring the thick-but-invisible-to-others light-brown furry sensillum-type fine hair coating all over Spadnik's face and arms.

Ten minutes later, shortly after the class emptied, Spadnik motioned Van Mullder over by pointing his index finger and curling it back at himself.

"Here's how this is going to work, Sparky," Spadnik, a short, stout man of 50, said.

"I'm going to get a signed authorization from the Principal for you to test out of this class. My envelope from Carnac the Magnificent (holding a business envelope to his forehead) tells me you're going to get a 98% score on the test.

"Once your score is certified by my department head, you'll get an "A" for this course and get to spend the rest of the semester in study hall for this hour – or, with authorization from Phil Podrowski, you'll get to spend the hour at home or at an off-campus job if you prefer.

"How does that work for you?"

"What would you say if I said no?" Franklin asked.

"I'd say you were a self-abusive idiot, because I would make your life a living hell in this class," Spadnik said in a barely audible whisper, so as not to be heard by anyone monitoring the class over the intercom system. "And if you tell anyone else I said that, I will deny it in the most convincing way and accuse you of feeling spurned after I declined your offer of a blow job."

"Not bad, psycho-Spad, sir. I think that's an offer too good to be refused. Just tell me when and where to take the test."

"Plan on it during zero hour two days from now. You can spend tomorrow in study hall during this hour."

And that was how Franklin aced his fall semester Government class – and managed to have a two-hour lunch the rest of the semester.

* * *

Post-Secondary Plans with a Lovely Van Arsdale Tweak

The main topic of discussion with Phil and Pongo lately was Franklin's post-high school plans. Phil and Pongo encouraged Franklin to shoot for the stars, applying to every Ivy League college that interested him, as well as Stanford University, the so-called Ivy League of the West.

Franklin explained that a university like Stanford founded by a railroad baron which sucked up to warmongers like Condoleezza Rice, Edwin Meese and Edward Teller didn't particularly appeal to him, not to mention its historic association with Herbert "Hooverville" Hoover through the Hoover Institute.

"I'd be interested, though, to see if Herbert's institute there or his Presidential Library gift shop sell any miniature burned-out shanties to commemorate his use of the Army to crush the Bonus Marchers' movement by World War I veterans in 1932. Compassionate guy, he was," Franklin said sarcastically.

But, more importantly, Franklin said, he didn't want to end up being deep in debt from the huge student loans which likely would be needed to get through four years of an Ivy League education.

His plan was to attend Dutchess Community College for two full years and then apply to Marist College in Poughkeepsie, with a double major in social work and pre-med/pre-health. That would give him the option of pursuing a doctoral degree in physical therapy upstate at Sage Colleges School of Health Sciences in Troy, 8 miles north of Albany. He hoped to save significant sums from his current part-time jobs to minimize his need for student loans. He would apply for scholarships, but with just one year at Poughkeepsie High and minimal extra-curricular activities, he doubted that kind of financial aid would be forthcoming.

He was correct.

Phil and Pongo supported Franklin's strategy, especially because it would mean he'd still be nearby, in case he had any health issues crop up needing assistance from his extended Podrowski and O'Leary support team. Not to mention the reduced costs that went along with getting to continue to live at the Podrowski estate – such as it was.

Chet Dale at Adams Landscaping was just as supportive when Franklin/Percy shared his college plans with him. It would be hard indeed to find a replacement as fit and responsible as 'Scruples,' Chet told Franklin/Percy. "Now, don't you get such a big head that you think you can come to me for a raise every other month, Scruples," he jokingly warned.

When Franklin shared his post-high school plans at lunch with Holly – who was maintaining a 4.0 GPA and a list of extracurricular activities as long as her waist-length hair – she surprised him with a sobering announcement.

"If it won't offend you, I'd like to make the same plans for college – obviously, not the same majors as you, Percy, but the same strategy for junior college, then two years at Marist and then graduate school," she said. "I'm thinking of going into pre-pharmacy and then on to the Albany College of Pharmacy and Health Sciences, in the Albany University Heights area not all that far away from Troy.

"And, yes, those plans have a lot to do with you. Does that bother you?"

Franklin was at a loss for words.

"I don't know what to say. I'm tempted to say I'm flattered – I certainly don't want you to think I'm dismissing your plans. I'm actually kind of excited about the possibilities. As long as we both understand each other clearly. *I mean*, when it comes to your ties to your church and your parents. You do understand that I'm not even remotely likely to become affiliated with your church, right?"

"I do," she said, eyes moistening slightly. "But I am quite taken with you, in case you weren't already aware – and I think the reverse is true too, from the look I'm seeing on your face. Except for that yucca-poo sleep-gunk stuck in the corner of your eye."

They both laughed as she dabbed at Franklin's left eye with her cafeteria napkin.

"OK, I just wanted to make sure we're both on the same page. Of course, I'd be happy to be at the same college as you. It will be interesting to see where all of this will take us, Holly Ann."

"Please just be patient with me, OK?" she said.

"Can do. As long as you can do likewise, Dear. I'm frankly pretty shocked you haven't been swept off your feet in these past several weeks by some tall, dashing football quarterback."

"A girl never knows what the future holds," she whispered, "but it certainly feels like there's no quarterback or halfback or leatherback who'd be able to pick the lock you have on my heart."

As she got up to leave the cafeteria, she planted a long, soft, moist kiss on Franklin's cheek. He didn't mind that one little bit.

Later that day, he invited Holly to meet him, Pongo, Heather, Harry, Bianca and Idris for some Frisbee golf the following Sunday at Mansion Square Park. She accepted. The five of them ended up having a blast. Much ice was broken, to Franklin's and Holly's lasting relief.

* * *

Pongo convinced Franklin, reluctantly, to go to high school made up as a back-from-the-dead Ronald Reagan for the Halloween observance on Oct. 29th. Franklin/Percy eventually took to it with ease, mockingly moaning of his hunger for welfare moms' brains as he walked the school halls. Pongo even made an ersatz nuclear warhead for zombie Ronnie to carry around school that day.

Franklin was tempted to go around trick-or-treating that Sunday night, but finally decided there were little kids who deserved free candy lots more than his 128-year-old soul.

* * *

Part Two

USA-SBR:
FRANKLIN'S PURPOSE
RE-DISCOVERED

Patriotic Evictions and Other
Musings on the Golden Rule

Nov. 1-Dec. 31, 2010
Poughkeepsie, NY

The Nov. 2, 2010 Tea Party-fueled mid-term election wins for Republicans – taking back the U.S. House of Representatives after only four years in Democratic hands – was the topic du jour in Franklin's Social Studies and U.S. History classes most of that week.

Those classes, both still taught by Pongo's good ol' Star Wars/Star Trek-obsessive Bill Mitchell, had become Franklkin's favorites.

Mr. Mitchell showed his Social Studies class the video clip of the ranting CNBC reporter Rick Santelli making fun of "losers" who couldn't pay their mortgages after the 2008 economic meltdown and arguing that they should lose their homes so more worthy people could buy them.

"How many of you in here have ever heard of the Golden Rule?" he asked.

Every hand went up.

"Who can give me a definition?" he asked.

Daryl Youngblood's hand rocketed up.

"OK, Daryl, what's the Golden Rule mean?"

"It means those who have the most gold get to rule," Daryl said, snickering, with the class echoing in mock hilarity – like they hadn't heard THAT one before.

"OK, Daryl, I grant you that's the reality of power in government most of the time," Mr. Mitchell said. "Anyone want to share the more traditional meaning of the Golden Rule?"

Alicia Montgomery, sitting in one of the front row seats, spontaneously answered before any other class clown could chime in: "It means treating others the way *you* would want to be treated, even when the others don't always treat you that way. It means doing the right thing even when it's hard to do it."

"That's spot on, Alicia," Mr. Mitchell said. "Thanks for that!"

"How many of you think the Golden Rule shouldn't apply to people who've lost their jobs or lost their savings or have had to file a medical bankruptcy?" he asked.

One person raised his hand.

"OK, Mike," he said to Mike Marshalton near the back of the classroom. "Please share with us why you think there are some people who don't deserve for the Golden Rule to be applied to them."

"It's all about accountability, sir," Mike said. "If we go easy on some people, then anyone's going to feel like they can be irresponsible."

"Have you ever lost a job or had a boss treat you unfairly, Mike?" Mr. Mitchell asked.

"Yes – and I sucked it up and moved on."

"But you had parents – a home, a guaranteed meal, a warm bed, all those things you could rely on, right?" Mr. Mitchell said.

"So, are you saying my parents shoulda kicked me out?"

"Of course not. I'm just saying, your situation wasn't the same as a family where one or both of the parents lost their job and they had to worry about keeping a roof over their children's heads.

"Would you really want the children of the person who lost his job or who had a medical bankruptcy to suffer?"

"Naw, guess not," Mike admitted.

"So, you *do* believe the Golden Rule really should work for them too, is that right?" Mr. Mitchell asked.

"Yeah."

"So, how do you feel about Mr. Santelli's remarks about the U.S. needing a new Tea Party so everyone wouldn't have to pay for "losers" who can't pay their mortgages?" Mr. Mitchell asked.

"It's pretty dickish," Wendy Walters said from the third seat back in the fourth row, to many laughs.

"If it were his own sister who'd lost her job and couldn't pay her mortgage, I bet he wouldn't be saying that to her," she said. "Unless he's an even bigger asshole than he seems to be on that video."

"That's what it's all about, isn't it, fellow future mortgage-payors?" Mr. Mitchell asked. "De-personalizing real people as "losers" and "shirkers" and such without any close examination of peoples' actual circumstances.

"That's how the German government in the '30s and '40s succeeded in demonizing Jews, homosexuals, gypsies and so forth.

"Here's an extra-credit assignment: a minimum 25 extra points for anyone who puts together a cogent 500-word-minimum essay on circumstances which might motivate people who've suffered social and/or economic injustice to depersonalize and de-humanize their fellow victims of social and/or economic injustice. When writing about those people, try to remember the Golden Rule for them too.

"And I will grade down for misspellings, unlike the Tea Party."

Franklin's extra credit essay two days later earned him 100 bonus points.

✳ ✳ ✳

Franklin went on to have a spirited discussion with Mr. Mitchell in his U.S. History class later that day about how the mid-term election losses by the Democrats to Tea Party Republicans might have been due to President Obama doing his best with the Affordable Care Act to emulate Republican Gov. Mitt Romney's Romneycare program in Massachusetts instead of pushing hard for the kind of single-payor (Medicare for All) health care system Obama had praised as a U.S. Senator.

"Why do you think the President sold single-payor care down the river, Percy?" Mr. Mitchell asked Franklin.

"If I had to guess, I suppose it would have something to do with health insurance industry donations to both major political parties through Wall Street," Franklin/Percy said.

"There you go," Mr. Mitchell said. "The same reason Obama didn't do the socially just thing and nationalize the financial institutions which almost destroyed our country's economy two years ago.

"Of course, there was a precedent for that: after the 1929 stock market crash and start of the Great Depression, the first thing President Franklin Roosevelt did after taking office was declare a bank holiday. He could've nationalized the banks in a heartbeat and virtually none of the voters who'd given him a landslide victory the previous November would've begrudged him that decision.

"But, FDR, our most socialistic-leaning President, decided the priority needed to be saving capitalism, not converting it into a hybrid of capitalistic socialism. And his legacy worked fairly well 'til our country got back into a boom and bust-slash-permanent war-slash-stock market obsession.

"You seem to be squirming in your seat, Percy," Mr. Mitchell said. "Anything you want to add to that?"

"I guess just that, just *maybe*, FDR's decisions had a lot to do with the personal family history which was his perspective at the time. His family had had great success with capitalism – and he was convinced capitalism **combined with** institutionalized compassion could lead to lasting prosperity in the U.S.A."

"Fair enough," Mr. Mitchell said. "But would you agree, in light of what's happened in the past 100 years, that our constitutional system is pretty much stacked **against** institutionalized compassion co-existing with capitalism?"

"I guess I would have to agree with that," Franklin/Percy said. "There would have to be some massive constitutional changes for those two contradictory items to co-exist."

"Class, I'm offering an extra-credit assignment worth at least 50 points for anyone who submits a 500-word-minimum essay on what kinds of constitutional changes would be needed to make capitalism and compassion compatible. The assignment's due a week from today."

Franklin's essay a week later earned him not 50, but **200** extra-credit bonus points from Mr. Mitchell.

* * *

THE UN-SCREWING OF AMERICA-SECOND BILL OF RIGHTS (USA-SBR)

Franklin's essay proposed a constitutional amendment which would establish a new Bill of Rights. Franklin titled his essay, "The Un-Screwing of America-Second Bill of Rights" (USA-SBR). Its provisions included:

I.   PROTECTION FROM MANIPULATION BY WEALTHY CAPITALISTS

Recognizing once and for all that **the influence of wealth on the political system is directly associated with the likelihood of corruption**, this Second Bill of Rights establishes, among other rights, **the right to be protected from manipulation of the political process by monied interests**, including:

> # **A permanent ban on corporate personhood**, forever undoing the Supreme Court's Citizen United ruling that the use of un-limited amounts of campaign contributions is free speech pro-tected by the First Amendment and forever banning the legal fiction that corporations have the same rights as human beings. In addition, businesses (incorporated or otherwise) now have the same criminal law accountability and civil damage liabilities for negligence and intentional harm as human beings; likewise, business owners, corporate officers and CEOs shall **not** be im-mune from liability for actions or inactions which cause harm to any person, business or other entity.

> # **A permanent ban on <u>at-large</u> elections** involving commis-sions, councils and other government entities with two or more voting members where the population being represented is 1,000 or more based on the latest U.S. Census data. Recognizing that at-large elections for such entities are designed to protect the influence of monied interests and non-ethnic minority vot-ers, the ban requires that those entities be divided into equally-proportional districts (if not already so divided) and requires election-by-district voting and representation for **<u>both</u>** primaries **<u>and</u>** general elections.

A permanent ban on the use of caucuses to determine parties' candidates for general elections, recognizing that caucuses are subject to disproportionate influences of the wealthiest individuals and organizations able to hire organizers to pay persons to show up at caucus meetings and to pay those same persons to promise to cast their non-secret votes as instructed by the organizers. The permanent ban is enacted recognizing that caucus gatherings to nominate candidates involve only a tiny fraction of all eligible voters and, as such, by definition are an undemocratic and ineffective method of determining the will of the majority of voters. All political parties now are required to nominate all candidates for all elections through primary elections conducted by election officials of counties and states throughout the nation. In addition, recognizing that states' individual Presidential primaries serve primarily to allow candidates to dupe residents of each state into believing that their needs somehow supersede the needs of residents of other regions, all individual states' primary elections now are replaced with a single nationwide primary election conducted every Presidential election year on the Tuesday closest to 100 days in advance of Election Day. Barring the death or voluntary withdrawal of a candidate or a lawful court order, political parties now are bound by results of all primary elections.

Recognizing that monied interests have a history of paying witnesses, expert or otherwise, to mislead congressional panels, legislative committees, county boards, city councils, etc. in order to achieve their lawmaking goals, there is **a permanent ban on testimony and other remarks _not_ taken under oath** before all levels of government – Federal, states, counties, cities, towns, etc. Persons participating in any and all such gatherings before any and all levels of government who are alleged to have knowingly spoken untruths during their participation shall be subject to Class C Federal felony perjury charges.

Recognizing that political parties holding majorities have a history of gerrymandering districts to gain ballot advantages, there is **a permanent ban on gerrymandered districts** of _all_ political entities; the ban would require districts to have **regular** rectangular shapes with 1x1, 1x2, 2x3, 3x5, 4x6, 5x7, 8x10 & 11x13 proportions, with voters in any overlapping areas getting to choose on their own the district in which they would be voting. Overlapping areas shall be the smallest possible size.

 # Expanded representation by elected officials: Recognizing that continued population growth without matching expansion of representational membership both dilutes the power of voters and increases the likelihood of manipulation by monied interests, membership of the U.S. Supreme Court, U.S. Senate and U.S. House of Representatives shall immediately be expanded proportionally based on the increase in U.S. population since 1911 (93.9 million to current 308.7 million), when Federal law set U.S. House membership at 435; future membership adjustments shall be based on population changes every 10 years using U.S. Census data. The same expansions of representation shall be required immediately of all state legislatures, county commissions, city councils, school boards and all other government entities with voting members nationwide in jurisdictions with populations of at least 1,000 persons, with subsequent adjustments every 10 years based on the latest U.S. Census data. Should U.S. population ever shrink (for example, due to catastrophic events related to disease epidemics or natural disasters or dramatic declines in birth rates), representation shall be adjusted downward on the same proportional basis using data from the U.S. Census.

Recognizing that the current system of Supreme Court justice selection traditionally results in disproportional representation by corporate-biased justices, **there shall be national popular-vote elections of no more than one-half of the justices of the newly-expanded U.S. Supreme Court**, with the remaining half selected by U.S. President under the previously-existing system; under this new Bill of Rights, **all** U.S. Supreme Court justices are subject to *national retention votes* every four years, running against jurist candidates who collect signatures of at least 1 percent of the voting-age population in each and every state.

 # A more representational U.S. Senate. By reducing the mandated number of U.S. Senators guaranteed for each state from two to one, representation of voters in more populous states will be less diluted. The remaining U.S. Senators shall be apportioned among the states by districts according to the most recent U.S. Census in the same manner as membership of the U.S. House of Representatives.

 # A guarantee that the majority of voters shall always be the deciding factor in Presidential elections. Recognizing that the Electoral College is an anachronism long overdue for elimination, an outmoded vestige from the time when the only a small handful of states in the eastern half of the country were densely settled, it now is immediately and permanently dropped. All Presidential elections shall be decided based on the votes of the majority of persons casting ballots. When the top Presidential vote-getter receives only a plurality of votes, a national runoff election shall be held on the Tuesday before Thanksgiving featuring the top two vote-getters.

Publicly financed Federal, state and local elections. This new Bill of Rights shall implement a hybrid of the public election financing systems set forth by Maine and Arizona, but using Arizona's original system for permanent removal of elected lawmakers and judges who knowingly violate rules of the financing system. In addition, there shall be a $10 Federal income tax credit for each tax filer ($20 for jointly filing parties) who provides proof that she or he voted in the most recent general (even-numbered-year) election to stimulate voter participation. Each county in each state shall issue by U.S. Mail a Federal uniformly-designed numbered national proof of voting card to each voter within 30 days after each of those general elections.

A national right to vote for all persons 18 and older, including even ex-felons who have completed their sentences and have been complying with court-ordered restitution and fine payment plans. As with Canada and some European countries, national right-to-vote cards shall be issued to each voter just prior to their 18th birthdays. Only those convicted of voter fraud shall be permanently barred from voting. The definition of voter fraud shall include actions to intimidate and otherwise suppress lawful voting, including conspiracy to suppress and attempted suppression. No voter photo identification shall EVER be required - just the voter's signature. Persons convicted of felonies shall have their voting rights restored once they are released from prison and have started making regular installment payments on fines and restitution. Voters shall be entitled to vote up to 21 days early in person or by mail and at *any* in-county polling site (*regardless* of the voter's residential voting precinct) on election days. Election days shall be defined as a 25-hour period for in-person voting starting at noon on the first Tuesday of November and ending at 1 p.m. the following day; mailed ballots postmarked by the second day of voting shall be honored. Recognizing that electronically-tallied ballots are subject to computer programming manipulation, voters now have the right to cast secret paper ballots on which simple "X" marks designate the voters' choices; photocopies shall be made of each ballot for purposes of quality control during the

tabulation process. Citizens also have the right to register to vote as late as election day at **any** polling site **regardless** of the location of their residential voting precinct. The voter registration process also shall include a declaration on registration forms specifying that voters have the right not to participate in exit polls and discouraging participation in exit polls unless the Congressionally- or court-authorized organization conducting the exit poll is attempting to document whether there is fraud in the vote tallying process. In addition, all registered voters now are entitled to at least four hours of paid leave time from employers during the 25-hour voting period.

Strict limits on campaign contributions: $200 per person, per union and per business (incorporated or otherwise) for national campaigns; $100 per person, per union and per business (incorporated or otherwise) for statewide campaigns and $50 per person, per union and per business (incorporated or otherwise) for countywide and citywide elections; those limits shall be inflation-adjusted annually. Contributions by political action committees and their equivalents are permanently banned. Those convicted of intentionally violating contribution limits and/or conspiring to violate those limits shall have their voting rights permanently forfeited. In addition, campaign contributions at all levels shall be banned during the 31 days immediately prior to each election. Each candidate and ballot initiative organization shall be required to disclose to the Attorney General of the appropriate jurisdiction no later than 24 days prior to each election reports which fully detail total amounts received from each, separate campaign donor during the entire campaign period. Failure to timely submit those reports disqualifies the candidate/initiative from the election (whether or not the candidate's name or initiative can be physically removed from ballots before the election). Failure to submit any such reports at all, even untimely, shall result in the candidate/initiative organization director being subject to Class C Federal felony charges.

There is **the right of all citizens to be exposed to print and broadcast media which are _not_ the products of concentrated ownership**. Therefore, the same individual or business (incorporated or otherwise) is permanently banned from having an ownership interest in more than one newspaper plus one broadcast station or pay-television station (radio or television) anywhere in the U.S.A. Individuals or businesses which own both a newspaper **and** a broadcast station or pay-television station are

permanently prohibited from owning both the newspaper and the broadcast station based within the same state. In addition, all broadcast stations **and** pay-television stations are subject to Federal Communications Commission (FCC) licensing requirements. Once each station's seven-year license is due to expire or be renewed, the license shall be rewarded to the applicant for the license who has the **most investors** who have invested at least $50 apiece; the total amount of money invested shall be irrelevant. Any license applicants who knowingly submit applications listing fraudulent or sham investors shall be subject to Class B Federal felony charges. Likewise, pay-television service providers also shall be subject to FCC licensing rules. Those service providers also shall have seven-year licenses. Once each pay-television service provider's seven-year license is due to expire or be renewed, the license shall be rewarded to the applicant for the license who has **the most investors** who have invested at least $50 apiece; the total amount of money invested shall be irrelevant. Any pay-television license applicants who knowingly submit applications listing fraudulent or sham investors shall be subject to Class B Federal felony charges. Investor groups shall be permanently prohibited from holding more than one pay-television service provider license per county at a time. The number of pay-television service provider licenses shall be limited to seven per county (there are 3,144 counties or county-equivalents in the U.S.A.); no service provider shall have more than one license per county. A primary condition to qualify for a license is an indemnified agreement to make dependable services available to each and every home in the county covered by each license. The FCC shall be responsible for setting new license, re-licensing and annual operation fees county by county based on fixed percentages of full market value as determined by the FCC. The total annual fees assessed by the FCC against each license holder shall not exceed 5 percent of each broadcast station's/pay-television provider's full market value. One-fifth of all FCC-collected fees shall go to a fund dedicated to providing free general election campaign advertising for candidates who win their parties' primaries and who have signed a binding contract to abide by clean election rules set forth under the USA-SBR's provisions.

Recognizing that existing sales taxes, property taxes and small business fees and taxes inflict a disproportionately unfair economic burden on the non-wealthy **and** recognizing that the nation's most prosperous economy occurred when Federal income tax rates on the wealthy were as high as 90 percent (thus providing sufficient revenues for massive infrastructure projects including the interstate freeway system), this new Bill of Rights **permanently bans _all_ sales, property and non-income-related taxes nationwide and requires that they be replaced with truly progressive income taxes** on individuals and business entities (whether incorporated or not), with the exception of the temporary stock purchase transaction tax (see Section L. below). So-called "sin taxes" designed to discourage otherwise legal activities or consumption of items determined to be less than healthful also are exempt from that requirement. Likewise, tax cuts for wealthy individuals and corporations are permanently banned for as long as government entities at **any** level have a deficit balance.

All tax loopholes for wealthy individuals and for-profit businesses (incorporated or otherwise) are permanently banned, while existing mortgage interest deductions for each homeowner's primary residence (including deductions for points fees) are permanently protected; never again shall a wealthy person or wealthy family or for-profit corporation end up paying zero taxes or end up with an effective tax rate of less than 39 percent on gross income or, for businesses, on net profits. The sole exception to the ban on loopholes is a 5 percent tax credit for businesses with 50 or more employees which can prove beyond a reasonable doubt that the tax credit caused them to schedule at least 98 percent of their workforce for 40-hour work weeks. Wealthy individuals are defined as anyone whose gross income is more than $150,000 per year; wealthy families are defined as any family with gross income of more than $200,000 per year. Wealthy corporations are defined as any corporation with more than $250,000 per year pre-tax net profits. Those graduated amounts shall be inflation-adjusted annually.

High-income limits on F.I.C.A. Social Security payroll taxes (which prevent the wealthy individuals, unlike non-wealthy individuals, from having to pay a progressively increased share of their incomes) are permanently removed.

Recognizing that employers are motivated to pressure Congress to make as many employees as possible exempt from wage laws requiring overtime pay, **there are now no employees whatsoever** – regardless of pay rate, pay scale, pay frequency or job description – **who are ineligible for at least time-and-a-half overtime pay** once their work hours exceed 40 hours during any seven-day

period. Likewise, there is **no right for employers to implement mandatory overtime** hours. In addition, **all employees now have the right to at least double-time overtime pay** once their work hours exceed 50 hours during any seven-day period – and **all employees now have the right to at least triple-time overtime pay** once their work hours exceed 60 hours during any seven-day period. All employees also have the right to at least two full unpaid days off consecutively every week in addition to all other forms of paid and unpaid leave time; employees on five-day weekly work schedules have the right to overtime pay on each day they work more than eight hours. **All employees have the right to decline compensatory time in favor of overtime pay; all employees also have the right to decline overtime work, with employers permanently banned from implementing both direct and indirect sanctions, penalties and other punishments against employees who assert any and all rights under this and other provisions of the USA-SBR.** Employers formally alleged to have violated any of *these* provisions of the USA-SBR are subject to Class C Federal felony charges.

Recognizing that the **General Mining Act of 1872** constitutes nothing less than government welfare for the mining industry, that act **is permanently repealed. U.S.A. taxpayers have the right to be properly compensated for private mining companies' activity on public lands** through royalties based on **FULL actual market value** of the minerals, gases and oils extracted from those public lands as determined by the Secretary of the Interior. Failure to accurately set actual market values of such items shall result in the Secretary of Interior being charged with a Class B Federal felony. Whenever practicable, extraction of minerals, oil and gases from **public lands** shall be conducted by **Federally-employed resource extractors (including miners, oil drillers, etc.) and resource extraction administrators** through a new branch of the Department of the Interior known as the **Federal and Private Lands Mining Administration (FPLMA)**, *recognizing that privatized mining results in lower profits for the Federal government, less safety, fewer benefits for employees and less accountability for environmental damages.* **Mining on private lands** is subject to strict safety and environmental inspections conducted on a surprise basis at least weekly by the FPLMA. Failure to comply with Federal safety and environmental regulations shall result in Class B Federal felony charges against mining managers and owners, as appropriate. Managers and owners of mines in which fatal incidents have occurred are subject to Class A Federal felony charges if there is evidence of gross or willful

negligence and to Class B felony charges for simple negligence. Those same managers and owners of mines are subject to Class B Federal felony charges for each formally alleged instance of environmental contamination.

\# Recognizing that for-profit utilities and for-profit energy extraction companies have built vast empires upon huge profits as the result of extracting natural resources from public lands for more than a century at artificially low prices **and** as the result of being able to expel invisible pollutants (including CO2) into the air without paying for the damage caused to the atmosphere (primarily due to those exhausts being invisible), all due to the influence of their paid lobbyists, **there shall be a national binding referendum vote** in the first Presidential general election after passage and ratification of the USA-SBR. That referendum shall determine whether those for-profit utilities and energy extraction businesses shall be permanently nationalized as promptly as possible for conversion to not-for-profit entities operated by the Federal government, never again to be privatized.

\# Recognizing that contracting out not-for-profit government services to for-profit business entities (incorporated or otherwise) means profits can be achieved only through private entities cutting types of services and hours of services, hiring persons who are less-than-fully qualified, cutting staff pay and benefits (leading to low morale and reduced employee retention), using cheap infrastructure and amenities (often designed to last only for the duration of the contract), cutting corners on safety and lobbying for more mandatory prison sentences as well as mandatory lengthened prison terms, there is the **right of all citizens to not-for-profit government services which are untainted by private sector profit motive.** Thus, _all_ for-profit contracts for not-for-profit government services through private corporations are banned, including – **but not limited to** - for-profit prisons, for-profit government hospitals, for-profit toll roads and highways, for-profit waste collection, for-profit parks management, for-profit law enforcement services for both criminal _and_ civil laws, for-profit child support enforcement services, for-profit welfare eligibility determination services, for-profit fire departments, for-profit security services, and all other for-profit public safety services. Likewise, recognizing that monied interests from Wall Street and elsewhere will attempt to find ways for the Congress and Legislatures to privatize institutions which provide government services by taking steps _causing those institutions to fail,_

such backdoor privatization – including, but not limited to, re-quiring retirement accounts of future employees to be funded far into the future (causing agencies to be unable to perform their statutorily prescribed responsibilities by under-funding them or by refusing to fund them altogether) and agencies' management failing to require enforcement of agencies' laws, rules and regulations – **is permanently banned**. Therefore, ex-isting such laws - like the Orwellian-named *Postal Accountability and Enhancement Act of 2006*, which was designed to cause the U.S. Postal Service *to fail* by requiring pre-funding of employee retirement accounts 75 years in advance – are immediately ren-dered unconstitutional and unenforceable. In addition, direct privatization of government-provided services – including, but not limited to, public schools, the U.S. Postal Service, wel-fare services, food and safety inspection services, law enforce-ment, military services and so forth – is permanently banned. Recognizing that they deplete funding for conventional public schools and "cherry pick" students, charter schools shall be disbanded or converted into conventional public schools ef-fective with the upcoming school year.

There is the **right of all citizens and permanent residents to protection from all types of fraud,** including but not limited to schemes such as the credit default swap scams which led to the 2008 national financial meltdown. Financial institutions which perpetrate such frauds are subject to immediate and per-manent nationalization by the executive branch.

Recognizing that Federal, State and local governments may at times be tempted or pressured by monied interests to sell off or lease off government-owned infrastructure – including, but not limited to, parks, wilderness areas, senate and house buildings, historical landmarks, school and university buildings, bridges, airports, railway stations, scientific research facilities, etc. - for short-term profit at long-term loss to taxpayers simply to balance a short-term budget, **citizens have the right for all government commons to be protected from liquidation and/ or leasing.** Therefore, all levels of government **are forever banned** from selling off and/or leasing off government com-mons unless a ¾ majority of the legislative body votes to place a referendum on the sale of such an item on a Presidential elec-tion ballot and voters approve each such proposed sale by a ¾ majority. Previous agreements to sell off or lease off such com-mons are immediately rendered retroactively null and void and unconstitutional. Buyers and lessees are entitled to reasonably

negotiated compensation for returning the purchased and/or leased properties to the government under the doctrine of estoppel.

Recognizing that the financial influence of the military-industrial complex has led the U.S.A. into unnecessary wars and prevented the U.S.A. from entering into treaties which would deter armed conflicts and improve other international relationships, Congressional *rejections* of Executive Branch-negotiated treaties with foreign nations for peace and other armed conflict prevention issues now require a ¾-majority in both chambers of Congress, while declarations of war and other authorizations of armed conflicts in foreign lands now require approval of a ¾-majority in both chambers of Congress.

Recognizing that wealthy individuals, sole proprietorships and corporations have used their lobbying prowess to limit access to the courts by parties alleged to have been damaged, injured or harmed by their abuses and/or negligence, those who seek to pursue class action lawsuits against individuals, sole proprietorships and corporations now have **the right to pursue such lawsuits in any state in which any plaintiff has resided, in any state where the defendant does business and/or in any state in which any plaintiff is alleged to have been damaged, injured or harmed** by abuses and/or negligence of the defendant individual(s), sole proprietorships, corporations or any other business entities.

Economic treason: There is the right of consumers, taxpayers and other members of the general public to know which corporations and sole proprietorships are undermining national, regional and local economies by outsourcing jobs to foreign nations where employees will earn less than U.S.A. residents who had been filling those positions: those businesses which outsource 5 percent or more of their full-time equivalent positions to other nations are deemed to have committed economic treason and are required to label all items they produce in the U.S.A. as "Made By Economically Traitorous Company"; likewise, they are required to include in all business logotypes for their U.S.A. operations the designation "Economically Traitorous Company" in bold-faced type visible to anyone with 20/20 vision from 100 feet away when placed on outdoor signage and in at least a 16-point bold typeface on pre-printed materials. Such businesses shall be removed from that designation once they prove beyond reasonable doubt that at least 99 percent of their full-time equivalent staff positions are located

in the U.S.A. The U.S. Department of Labor is responsible for enforcing these provisions. Corporate and/or sole proprietorship officials formally alleged to have evaded or attempted to evade responsibility for such outsourcing shall be prosecuted for Class B Federal felonies.

Commissioner of the Food and Drug Administration (FDA) shall be selected by popular vote in national elections held at the same time as Presidential elections. That commissioner has the authority to permanently ban all food additives and medicines which have been demonstrated to have harmful side-effects. Producers of food additives and medicines with harmful side-effects are no longer permitted to escape liability for damage caused by their products and by consumer items containing their products simply by listing side effects on those products. FDA requirements for listing harmful side effects of products shall continue, however. Persons formally alleged to have suppressed or omitted such information shall be charged with Class B Federal felonies. That commissioner has the authority to enforce all FDA laws, including the authority to charge individuals, businesses (incorporated or otherwise) and business officials with felony crimes.

Administrator of the Environmental Protection Agency shall be selected by popular vote in national elections held at the same time as Presidential elections. That administrator has the authority to enforce all environmental laws, including the authority to charge individuals, businesses (incorporated or otherwise) and business officials with felony crimes.

Secretary of the Treasury shall be selected by popular vote in national elections held at the same time as Presidential elections. The Secretary is barred from declaring any financial institution as "too big to fail." A declaration of failure of any financial institution shall be followed immediately by the institution being permanently nationalized by the Federal government to function as a not-for-profit Federal government-operated entity.

Secretary of Transportation shall be selected by popular vote in national elections at the same time as Presidential elections. The Secretary's title is changed to **Secretary of Transportation Safety and Efficiency.** In addition to existing responsibilities, the Secretary's primary priority is to facilitate the public's transition off of using fossil fuels in favor of renewable energy not related to food production and promoting use of mass transit and other alternatives to freeways such as

one-way surface streets and Commute Trip Reduction (CTR) program incentives (such as reimbursing employees for 100 percent of the cost of monthly bus passes). Recognizing that *freeway systems within metropolitan areas contribute to urban sprawl, traffic fatalities and gridlock during heavy volume commuting periods (failing at the most crucial times)*, contrary to what freeway promoters claim, the Secretary is required to enforce a ban on Federally-funded new projects which facilitate continued use of single-occupancy vehicles by commuters (such as new freeways) *within* metropolitan areas. Completion of such projects which are already approved and already fully-funded shall be allowed; however, expansion of those in-progress roadways and already-existing freeways in the future shall be funded only to the extent that the expansion encourages use of mass transportation and high-occupancy vehicles (HOV's); for example, widening of freeways is allowed only for lanes permanently designated as HOV lanes, with HOV usage defined as three or more occupants during high-traffic hours and two or more occupants at all other times. Funding for new non-HOV freeway construction is restricted only to interstates between metropolitan areas, not within metropolitan areas, recognizing that the interstate highway system originally was intended to facilitate transportation between metropolitan areas rather than within metropolitan areas as a strategy to facilitate evacuations of metropolitan areas during emergencies. Highest funding priority is granted to construction of subway systems within metropolitan areas.

Secretary of Agriculture shall be selected by popular vote in national elections held at the same time as Presidential elections. The Secretary is responsible for enforcing mandatory nationwide labeling of all items for sale containing laboratory-produced genetically modified organisms (GMOs), as well as all items for sale which were produced from animals fed with products containing GMOs. Likewise, the Secretary is responsible for ensuring animals used for agricultural purposes are raised under cruelty-free conditions. In addition, the Secretary is responsible for ensuring that all animal processing facilities are subject to surprise safety and health inspections conducted at least weekly by inspectors who are fully funded by the Federal government and unlinked in any way to the facilities they are inspecting.

Secretary of Energy shall be selected by popular vote in national elections held at the same time as Presidential elections. The Secretary's title is changed to **Secretary of Renewable**

Energy. The Secretary's top priority is to transition all energy uses from fossil fuels and food-related renewable energy to solar energy, wind energy, hydropower which doesn't interfere with or endanger fish migration/spawning and non-food-related renewable energy (such as from sawgrass and waste biomass), provided the non-food renewable energy isn't derived from acreage historically used for food production. The Secretary is required to enforce a ban on all taxes and fees against solar energy and wind energy generated by private homeowners. Entities (and their agents) attempting to create and/or collect such taxes and fees from private homeowners shall be charged with a Class B Federal felony.

Chairperson of the Consumer Product Safety Commission shall be selected by popular vote in national elections held at the same time as Presidential elections. That chairperson is responsible for enforcing all consumer protection laws, including the authority to charge individuals, businesses (incorporated or otherwise) and business officials with felony crimes.

Secretary of the Department of the Interior shall be selected by popular vote in national elections held at the same time as Presidential elections. The Secretary's title is changed to **Secretary of Interior Lands Protection.** The Secretary is responsible for enforcing all laws related to lands administered by the Federal government, including the authority to charge individuals, businesses (incorporated or otherwise) and business officials with felony crimes. The Secretary has a fiduciary duty to bring all accounts receivable collections for the Department – including but not limited to lease payments, grazing fee payments, etc. – up to date and is responsible for ensuring that lease fees are set at full market value; formal allegations of willful failure to perform due diligence on collections and fee-setting shall result in Class B Federal felony charges against the Secretary followed by automatic removal if found guilty.

Secretary of Labor shall be selected by popular vote in national elections held at the same time as Presidential elections. A primary responsibility of the Secretary of Labor is to remove barriers to union representation elections in the workplace and to enforce penalties for employer retaliation against pro-union employees.

Secretary of Health and Human Services shall be selected by popular vote in national elections held at the same time as Presidential elections. Primary responsibilities for the Secretary of Health and Human Services are enforcement of

requirements for food safety, requirements for out-of-pocket cost-free health care services and requirements for accessibility to low-cost prescription medicines from the least expensive FDA-certified-safe sources worldwide.

Consumer Financial Protection Bureau Director shall be selected by popular vote in national elections held at the same time as Presidential elections. That director has the responsibility to enforce all laws related to protection of consumers' financial interests, including the authority to charge individuals, businesses (incorporated or otherwise) and business officials with felony crimes.

U.S. Attorney General shall be selected by popular vote in national elections held at the same time as Presidential elections. The Attorney General, in addition to historical law enforcement responsibilities, shall make as his top priority enforcement of anti-trust laws and anti-corruption laws related to Wall Street and banking interests; the Attorney General is permanently banned from substituting civil sanctions for criminal charges. The Attorney General's office shall review all corporate mergers approved during the previous 30 years for possible rescissions. Future mergers shall not be approved if it can be proved in court by a preponderance of evidence that the merger would result in more than five persons being laid off. Another top priority for the Attorney General is prosecution of any individual and/or business entity (incorporated or otherwise) charged with fixing prices or conspiring to fix prices; those formally alleged to be involved with price fixing are subject to Class B Federal felony charges. De facto evidence of price fixing sufficient to constitute probable cause for search warrants, criminal charges and/ or criminal indictments shall include print or broadcast advertising from the same day by multiple (more than two) competing businesses showing the exact same prices for the exact same products and/or services.

Recognizing a long history of political manipulations of grand juries by both elected and appointed prosecutors, **all citizens have the right to present to grand juries at all levels of government – including, but not limited to, Federal, state, county and city – true bills of indictment.** This provision enables citizens to pursue prosecutions of persons and corporations often considered "too powerful to prosecute," such as when prosecutors declined to charge President George W. Bush with felonies after he admitted in 2005 to violating the Foreign Intelligence Surveillance Act prohibiting warrantless

wiretaps. Likewise, all prosecutors – whether elected or appointed – at all levels of government are permanently barred from dismissing grand juries before their terms expire because grand jury jurors aren't voting as the prosecutor prefers or because grand jury jurors are presenting questions not endorsed by the prosecutor to grand jury witnesses. Any prosecutor formally alleged to have impeded or refused any citizen's right to present a true bill of indictment or to have improperly dismissed any grand jury before its term was to expire is subject to Class B Federal felony charges. In addition, all grand jury jurors (as well as all other juries' jurors) shall be selected truly at random from databases including all registered voters. To encourage the best work by jurors, all jurors are guaranteed full-time daily pay equivalent to at least the median net income (converted to gross income) for their age group based on U.S. Bureau of the Census data. Jurors whose incomes are greater than the median net income (converted to gross income) shall be compensated based on their verified actual gross income from current employment.

#Recognizing that powerful corporations and sole proprietorships have demonstrated a history of infringing upon patents of private party inventors, any plaintiff inventor(s) alleging patent infringement by a corporation or sole proprietorship is (are) entitled at government expense to representation in litigation by a well-qualified attorney specializing in patent law. If the plaintiff's/plaintiffs' litigation is successful, the defendant is responsible for paying attorney fees incurred by the government on the behalf of the plaintiff(s). This shall be known as the **Robert W. Kearns/Philo T. Farnsworth Provision** of the USA-SBR.

Recognizing that all citizens of the United States are entitled to reasonably equal physical access to the halls of government to minimize disproportionate accessibility by corporate interests based on the east coast, **the national U.S. Capital - including the Congress, U.S. Supreme Court, Presidential and Vice Presidential residences, Executive Branch agencies, etc. – shall be re-located to the demographic center of the 50 states**, which is near Plato, Missouri, approximately a 1,000-mile drive west from Washington, D.C. (Plato, Missouri is approximately 782 miles southeast of the geographic center of the 50 states at Belle Fourche, South Dakota.) The re-location of the U.S. Capitol shall begin the month after ratification of the USA-SBR and shall be completed within

10 years after ratification. The re-location shall not affect the continued operation of government museums and other tourist facilities in Washington, D.C.

II. *PROTECTED RIGHT TO PRIVACY*

Recognizing that all levels of government in the U.S.A. at times have violated private citizens' right to privacy - also known as the right of protection against unlawful search and seizure - there is a sacred right to privacy for all U.S. citizens and lawful resident aliens for whom there is neither probable cause nor reasonable suspicion for government authorities to believe they are involved in a criminal offense. Bulk collection of private citizens' phone, E-Mail and other electronic data by government is forever banned. Government authorities are required in all instances to obtain search warrants from a judge sitting on a newly-established Federal Civil Liberties Court in advance of any surveillance or search activity – except for expedited instances when a F.I.S.A. court judge rules *on the record* that there is, in fact, probable cause to believe a terrorist act or act of mass murder would occur if a warrant had to be sought in open court. Government employees at all levels of government – including all elected and appointed officeholders – formally alleged to have knowingly violated this right of privacy are subject to Class B Federal felony charges.

III. *RIGHT TO PROTECTION FROM TOXINS AND CARCINOGENS*

Recognizing the proliferation of toxic and/or carcinogenic substances (such as butylated hydroxyanisole (BHA) and butylated hydroxytoluene (BHT), which are found in almost all U.S. packaged foods despite being banned for human consumption in more than 160 countries[*]) used by various domestic and international industries and the tendency of those substances to find their way into persons' bodies, there is the right of all persons not to be subjected to either intentional or negligent exposure by individuals, businesses and governments to toxins and carcinogens in air, water, food, clothing, building materials, bedding, furniture and any other potential source of consumer exposure to those harmful materials. Members of Boards of Directors, CEO's and owners of corporations, sole proprietorships and partnerships and any other business entities which continue to include those substances in the items they sell, grow or otherwise produce shall be subject to Class B Federal felony charges as well as Federal felony charges for violations of civil rights.

---

[*] Microsoft News 5/8/15

IV. RIGHT TO PROTECTION FROM BIOLOGICAL CONTAMINANTS IN FOODS

There is a right of all persons to be protected from biological contaminants in foods presented for sale throughout the country. The U.S. Department of Health and Human Services (DHHS) and its Centers for Disease Control and Prevention (CDC) shall take over operations of the U.S. Department of Agriculture's (USDA's) Food Safety and Inspection Service (FSIS). Under that new management, the FSIS, in co-operation with states' food safety agencies, is obligated to promptly identify potentially deadly strains of foodborne bacteria and viruses (including, but not limited to, E Coli O157:H7 and Heidelberg salmonella) and declaring each of those potentially deadly strains to be adulterants, effectively banning the sale of all foods containing those potentially deadly bacteria and viruses. The DHHS, CDC, FSIS and USDA shall immediately implement the farm to market protocols used by Denmark to rid the food chain of salmonella; those protocols include compensation to farmers for destruction of their flocks when salmonella (such as Heidelberg salmonella) is found to contaminate their flocks (Denmark has had no salmonella outbreaks since 2011 under its new protocols[*]). The Congress also is obligated to adequately budgeting the DHHS, CDC and FSIS so that at least 1 percent of foods potentially carrying foodborne bacteria and viruses implicated in serious health risks are inspected daily by FSIS inspectors using the most advanced microbiology testing kits available; testing by merely visually examining, smelling and touching food products shall be immediately discontinued. Furthermore, DHHS, CDC and FSIS have the obligation to issue mandatory immediate recalls against food producers whose products, based upon a preponderance of evidence (potentially including DNA evidence), have been determined to be probable carriers of such deadly adulterants. Persons working for the DHHS, CDC and FSIS who are formally alleged to have failed to meet their obligations under this provision of the USA-SBR are subject to Class B Federal felony charges. Businesses and individuals formally alleged to have failed to comply with immediate recalls of suspected contaminated food products are subject to Class B Federal felony charges.

V. RIGHT TO LIVABLE WAGE EMPLOYMENT

There is the right for all persons who have reached their majority to a useful and good-paying job, paying enough to provide adequate food, clothing and recreation; that pay rate is defined as $15 per hour in 2012 dollars or 275 percent of the latest Federal poverty guideline income level for a single-person household, whichever is greater; that minimum

---

[*] PBS Frontline, "The Trouble with Chicken," 5/12/15

hourly wage shall automatically be indexed to the rate of inflation annually. There shall be **no exceptions**, including businesses with employees who receive tips, to that minimum wage. In addition, governments at all levels are banned from reducing wages (with the exception shown below) paid through prevailing wage requirements, requirements which shall be adjusted annually based on the rate of inflation. Those prevailing wage requirements shall remain the law of the land, except during times of deflation, when they may be adjusted downward annually based on the rate of deflation.

VI. *RIGHT TO PROTECTION FROM EXTREME INCOME INEQUALITY*

Recognizing that income disparity among working persons is a primary cause of poverty, bankruptcies, homelessness, ill health, family separations and divorces, foreclosures, child abandonment, unfulfilled education goals, etc., **all workers have the right to be paid no less than 1/25th of the earnings of the highest-paid persons** affiliated with their employer regardless of whether the employer is a corporation, a sole proprietorship or any other entity; calculations of the highest paid persons' incomes shall include all forms of compensation including – but not limited to – deferred compensation, stock options, vehicle allowances, retirement contributions, etc. Likewise, **all employers** – whether those are corporations, sole proprietorships or other entities – are permanently barred from paying the highest-earning persons affiliated with their organization more than 25 times the earnings of the lowest-paid persons affiliated with their organization. Due to the nature of employment in the entertainment and professional sports fields, where career durations are unpredictable and often short, pay for those employed in those areas are exempt from the 25 times lowest pay rate cap.

VII. *RIGHT TO EFFECTIVE INVESTIGATIVE JOURNALISM FROM INDEPENDENT ENTITIES NOT PART OF MULTI-STATE CORPORATE MEDIA EMPIRES*

Recognizing that predatory capitalists have rendered print, broadcast and on-line journalism virtually toothless in its traditional role of 'afflicting the comfortable and comforting the afflicted,' there shall be created upon USA-SBR ratification a permanent investigative journalism subsidy account funded out of general Federal tax revenues which shall be distributed proportionately – based on certified circulation and viewership data – among all daily and weekly newspapers, weekly, monthly and semi-monthly magazines, radio stations and television stations throughout the nation which are **NOT** part of multi-state corporate media empires. The fund balance shall be no less than .005 percent of the nation's gross domestic product annual equivalent at the beginning of each year and the entire amount of the fund shall be distributed each year. Any formal allegations by prosecutors or grand juries of misuse of the fund's proceeds shall result in Class C Federal felony charges. There shall be a permanent firewall created to protect those news outlets receiving the subsidies from interference by elected officeholders. It is the responsibility of Congress to authorize any additional funding for the account if the required set-aside from general tax revenues proves to be insufficient.

VIII. RIGHT TO PROTECTION FROM UNFAIR PROPERTY SEIZURES OF PERSONS ONLY PERIPHERALLY INVOLVED WITH CRIMINAL PERPETRATORS

Recognizing that asset forfeiture laws allowing seizure of property belonging to persons accused of and/or convicted of crimes have resulted in widespread abuses of authority and evasion of due process by prosecutors seeking to augment government budgets, such asset forfeiture proceedings are banned except in instances where law enforcement officers recover monies proved to have been received by the perpetrators convicted of sales of illegal substances. Even then, however, the asset forfeitures are limited only to the actual recovered monies and property proved to have been purchased with such monetary proceeds from the sale of illegal substances. Asset forfeiture laws banned include, but are not limited to, those laws allowing seizure of vehicles driven by intoxicated drivers and laws allowing seizure of long-held family farms on which relatively small tracts of illegal substances were being cultivated with or without the knowledge of the landowner.

IX. RIGHT TO VIEW UNEDITED VIDEO-RECORDED ACTIONS OF LAW ENFORCEMENT OFFICERS

Recognizing that disputes over interactions between law enforcement officers and the general public can often be resolved through video evidence, all government officers involved in enforcement of criminal laws are required to wear digital forward-facing head-mounted cameras at all times while they are on duty effective 30 days after ratification of the USA-SBR. Persons who are arrested and/or charged with criminal offenses have the right to have suppressed any of their remarks which are video-recorded before an arresting officer explains their Miranda rights to them. Copies of video recordings of persons suspected and/or arrested and/or charged with criminal offenses shall be made available to the attorney representing the person as promptly as possible. Any law enforcement officer formally alleged to have tampered with such video recordings shall be subject to Class C Federal felony charges.

X. *RIGHT TO GOVERNMENT NOT ENGAGING IN DEADLY ACTIONS AGAINST NON-COMBATANTS IN LOCALES NOT INCLUDED IN ANY DECLARATION OF WAR*

Recognizing the hatred toward the U.S.A. generated by killings of non-combatants through the use of drone aircraft and other deadly methods of assault used by the U.S.A., any non-combatant deaths stemming from drone use or other methods of assault **in locales for which there is no lawful declaration of war by the U.S.A.** shall result in Class B Federal voluntary manslaughter charges against *each and every person involved in such authorizations and executions of deadly force,* including even the President of the United States if the President's specific authorization was required for that drone action.

XI. *RIGHT TO EFFECTIVE ENFORCEMENT OF WORKPLACE SAFETY VIOLATIONS*

Recognizing the widely understood ineffectiveness of misdemeanor charges and negligible fine levels for enforcement currently in place with the Occupational Safety and Health Administration (OSHA), the right of employees to a safe workplace shall be enforced through minimum charges of Class C Federal felonies for simple negligence, Class B Federal felonies for gross negligence and Class A Federal felonies for willful negligence. Minimum OSHA fines shall be $500,000 for each partial loss of a limb or other body part, $1 million for each complete loss of limb or other body part and $10 million for each loss of life resulting from an employer's negligence. Fines for gross negligence shall be at least five times those amounts. Fines for willful negligence shall be at least ten times those amounts. Minimum fine amounts shall be adjusted annually for inflation.

XII. *RIGHT TO LAW ENFORCEMENT BY HUMAN BEINGS*

Recognizing that corporations such as Lockheed Martin have entered into for-profit contracts with local governments around the nation to provide technology for traffic and transportation enforcement which does not involve actual human beings issuing citations and recognizing that local governments often have implemented such technology without regard to actual risks involved with the such enforcement (using augmented revenues as their primary motivator), all motorists and other potential defendants have the right to be free from prosecution and persecution involving automated ticketing/citation systems such as red light cameras. Elected and appointed officeholders of such governments which continue to use that technology for ticketing and citations involving traffic and transportation enforcement are subject to Class C Federal felony charges.

XIII. *RIGHT TO NATIONWIDE UNIFORM FAIR COMPENSATION FOR ON-THE-JOB INJURIES*

There is the right to fair compensation for on-the-job injuries and illnesses including the right to compensation without discrimination based on the state in which the on-the-job injury or illness occurred. Never again shall the on-the-job loss of one person's body part(s) in one state result in compensation which is different from what is provided in a different state. There shall be a uniform system of compensation nationwide for on-the-job injuries and illnesses administered through the new Federal agency known as the Workers Compensation Administration (WCA), led by the Secretary of Workers Compensation, a Presidential Cabinet-level position. The Secretary of Workers Compensation shall be elected in national elections at the same time as Presidential elections. The Workers Compensation Administration shall be funded from general tax funds rather than employers' workers' compensation insurance fees; fees which employers previously paid for such coverage shall be incorporated into progressive income taxes levied against corporations. Federal lawmakers, Congressional staff, the Secretary of Workers' Compensation, lobbyists and immediate family members of all those previously-mentioned persons are barred from purchasing supplemental Workers Compensation coverage, as motivation for coverage through the WCA to be as generous as possible.

XIV. *RIGHT TO DECENT HOMES AND IN-HOME CARE*

There is the right of every family to a decent home, including residential care for the aged and terminally ill. Within 90 days after ratification, there shall be created a permanent family housing/terminally ill and aged residential care subsidy account funded out of general Federal tax revenues which shall be distributed proportionately among all states based on annually adjusted U.S. Bureau of the Census data. The fund balance shall be no less than .01 percent of the nation's gross domestic product annual equivalent at the beginning of each year and the entire amount of the fund shall be distributed each year. Any alleged misuse of the fund's proceeds shall result in Class C Federal felony charges. It is the responsibility of Congress to authorize any additional funding for that account if the required set-aside amount from general tax revenues proves to be insufficient.

XV. *RIGHT TO SINGLE-PAYER HEALTH CARE WITH NO OUT-OF-POCKET COSTS WHATSOEVER; BAN ON TOBACCO PRODUCTS*

There is the right to adequate medical, dental, vision and pharmaceutical care and to achieve and enjoy good health, including the right to single-payer Medicare For All with **no** out-of-pocket expenses for all medical, dental and vision care, as well as for all prescription drugs. There shall be a major emphasis on preventive health care due to the documented costs savings of prevention. Based on the philosophy of prevention, therefore, all tobacco and nicotine-containing products are permanently banned effective 30 days after ratification of the USA-SBR.

XVI. *RIGHT TO STABILIZED POPULATION GROWTH AND ASSOCIATED INCENTIVES*

Recognizing that continued unlimited population growth in the U.S.A. and the remainder of the world constitutes an existential threat to finite supplies of potable water and acreage on which crops can be farmed and homes can be built, the tax codes for all levels of government (Federal, State, County, City, etc.) shall no longer provide as a deduction from taxes the same amount for the 20th child in a family as for the first child. Effective for the tax year at the time of ratification, tax deductions for the third child in a family as well as each subsequent child shall be eliminated. Persons having more than three children are required to pay an annual surtax for the fourth and each additional minor child; the surtax for each of those children shall be the equivalent of 1 percent of the filer's adjusted gross income.

XVII. *RIGHT TO PAID TIME OFF FOR RECOVERY FROM HEALTH PROBLEMS AND FOR LEISURE ENJOYMENT*

Recognizing that virtually all industrialized nations guarantee rights of employees to paid vacation leave time, it is now the right of all employed persons upon completion of a full year of employment to at least four weeks of paid leave time (part-time workers are entitled to paid leave based on their average hours worked per week); upon completion of five years of employment, there is a right to at least six weeks of paid leave; upon completion of ten years of employment, there is a right to at least eight weeks of paid leave; upon completion of fifteen years of employment, there is a right to at least 12 weeks of paid leave. Likewise, recognizing that virtually all industrialized nations guarantee rights of employees to paid maternity leave and paid paternity leave as well as paid non-maternity/non-paternity sick leave, upon completion of one full year of employment, all employed women have the right to at least nine months of paid maternity leave and all employed men have the right to at least three months of paid paternity leave. Likewise, at least 90 days per year of non-maternity/non-paternity paid sick leave is guaranteed once the employee has completed a full year of employment (see above). Maternity, paternity and non-maternity/non-paternity paid sick leave times each shall be *in addition* to other earned paid leave times **and** *in addition* to any rights to paid and unpaid leave already required under the Family and Medical Leave Act. Employees have the right to use their non-maternity/non-paternity paid sick leave to care for members of their immediate families and extended families. Employers have the right to request documentation of the conditions prompting extended sick leave requests. Employers shall **not** have the right to discharge any employees who have documented personal health-related reasons or family/extended-family member health-related reasons for taking extended leave, whether paid leave or unpaid leave.

XVIII. *RIGHT TO DEPENDABLE RETIREMENT BENEFITS AND ECONOMIC SAFETY NET BENEFITS*

There is a right to adequate protection from the economic fears of old age, sickness, non-work-related accidents, on-the-job injuries, illnesses and unemployment: Workers' Compensation, Unemployment Compensation benefits, TANF benefits and Food Stamps/SNAP benefits nationwide shall be **indexed annually to inflation**. Likewise, private businesses and all levels of government which offer retirement plans for their employees are banned from offering anything other than defined retirement benefits plans which shall be **adjusted annually for inflation**; 401K accounts shall no longer be offered in place of defined retirement benefits. Furthermore, businesses and all levels of government are barred from reducing those promised retirement benefits – except that, in the event of deflation, they are allowed to adjust those benefits based on the Federal government-certified rate of deflation.

XIX. *RIGHT TO TUITION-FREE AND FEE-FREE PUBLIC EDUCATION THROUGH COMPLETION OF COLLEGE UNDERGRADUATE DEGREE*

There is the right for all to a good tuition-free and fee-free public education, including up to four years of undergraduate enrollment at any government-operated university or college or trade school, as well as completely free public education at government-operated schools from full-time pre-school and kindergarten through 12th grade. There shall be no use of government funds for privately-operated schools (including church-operated schools), either non-profit or for-profit.

XX. *RIGHT TO PROTECTION FOR BUSINESSES FROM UNFAIR COMPETITION AT HOME AND ABROAD AND RIGHT TO TRADE WITH OTHER COUNTRIES NOT INVOLVED IN OR PLANNING ARMED CONFLICTS*

There is the right of every businessman, large and small, to trade in an atmosphere of freedom from unfair competition with monopolies at home and abroad, including the right to trade with any and all nations who aren't involved in armed conflict with the U.S.A. or its allies, who aren't actively supporting armed conflict in other countries and who aren't actively planning an armed conflict with the U.S.A.

XXI. *RIGHT TO PRACTICE RELIGION AS LONG AS PRACTICE OF RELIGION DOESN'T IMPOSE ON OTHERS' RIGHTS AND RIGHT TO MAKE ONE'S OWN CHOICES ABOUT ONE'S OWN MEDICAL PROCEDURES*

There is the right of all persons to participate in the religion of their choice, provided that such religions comply with all civil and criminal laws. Likewise, those who don't wish to participate in a religion shall have the right to be free from proselytizing by persons outside their immediate families after an initial contact from the proselytizing organization. Religious organizations shall have the right to attract new members the traditional American way: by using their own revenues to do unconditional good works of charity and kindness for the needy in their local communities. In addition, there is the right of persons to be free from interference by any other persons or groups claiming to be acting on the basis of religious belief with their choice of any and all medical procedures done upon their own bodies or on the bodies of persons for whom they are the lawful guardians.

XXII. *SPECIFICALLY CIRCUMSRIBED LIMITED RIGHT TO BEAR ARMS*

To clarify ambiguity within the 2nd Amendment of the original Constitution, it shall be clear that prohibiting infringement of the rights of the people to keep and bear arms shall involve only those rights associated with being an officially-appointed member of a government-organized militia which is well-regulated, including (but not limited to) members of police departments, sheriff's departments and sheriff's posses, state police agencies and militias such as the National

Guard, federal armed services, executive branch law enforcement, etc. Non-law enforcement and non-military/militia firearm users shall have a qualified right to purchase, own and use firearms provided that those persons:

> # have no record whatsoever of any violence-related criminal convictions.
>
> # pass a formal Federal background check for such criminal convictions and for mental health issues.
>
> # pass a mental health screening by a mental health professional; in lieu of such a screening, the would-be purchaser may provide affidavits from three persons familiar with the person's personal history. However, persons providing false information on such affidavits are subject to Class B Federal felony charges.

These requirements apply to all sales and purchases, including licensed dealers, gun show participants and private parties. In addition, mechanisms of firearms manufactured for non-military/militia and non-law enforcement use are limited to bolt-action and lever action functions with tubular/cylindrical/magazine capacities of no more than six cartridges/shells. Within six months of ratification of the USA-SBR, there shall be ongoing Federally-funded gun buy-back programs administered through local criminal law enforcement agencies throughout the country focused primarily on incentivizing owners of semi-automatic weaponry to give up those guns, which are the weapons of choice of mass murderers. Recognizing that state and local governments around the country have a hodgepodge of rules and regulations governing where a person may lawfully carry a firearm openly - with the exception of certified law enforcement, military and state-sanctioned militia personnel - there is no right to openly carry firearms or to carry concealed firearms in any public gathering place (except licensed shooting ranges and designated hunting areas) or in any public park, including within storage areas in vehicles.

XXIII. _RIGHT TO RESIDE IN THE COMMUNITY OF ONE'S OWN CHOICE IN THE COUNTRY OF ONE'S OWN CHOICE_

There is the right of every human being to freely immigrate from a foreign country to the U.S.A. if that foreign country formally recognizes the right of every U.S.A. citizen without felony criminal convictions (including persons whose felony convictions were expunged and/or pardoned) to immigrate without restrictions into that country (regardless of whether the Congress formally recognizes reciprocal such rights in the U.S.A.). It is a primary duty of the Secretary of State to negotiate treaties with all other countries providing for a right to unrestricted immigration into those countries by U.S.A. citizens without felony criminal convictions (including persons whose felony convictions were expunged and/or pardoned). Likewise, there is the right of every human being without felony criminal convictions (including persons whose felony convictions were expunged and/or pardoned) to freely immigrate at any time from the U.S.A. to any other country with which the U.S.A. has a treaty recognizing the right of mutual immigration for citizens of the countries which are parties to the treaty. In addition, there is the right of every human being without felony criminal convictions (including persons whose convictions were expunged and/or pardoned) to freely immigrate at any time from the U.S.A. to any other English-speaking country and from any other English-speaking country to the U.S.A. provided both the U.S.A. and the other country(ies) have signed a treaty recognizing that right of mutual immigration for citizens of the country(ies) which are parties to the treaty. English-speaking countries are defined to include all countries in which a *plurality* of residents *speak English as a second language*. There also is the right of every human being brought into the U.S.A. by her or his parents, *legally or illegally*, when that human being was under the age of 16 to remain in the U.S.A. as a permanent legal resident, provided that person has no felony criminal convictions in that person's previous country of residence.

XXIV. *RIGHT OF CHILDREN TO BE TRIED AS MINORS*

There is the right of children under the age of 16 to be tried in all U.S.A. courts as minors.

XXV. *RIGHT TO A FRESH START*

Recognizing this country's tradition of providing persons with challenging backgrounds a fresh start, all persons whose criminal records include **only** non-violent felony and/or non-violent misdemeanor convictions who have completed twenty-four consecutive months without any offenses of any kind (including misdemeanors) and have maintained the obligation to make payments toward restitution and fines have a right to have their criminal records expunged by petitioning the county-level court in which their most recent felony conviction occurred. The records expungement for those non-violent offenders shall be automatic once the court has certified that the petitioner has met the minimum required offense-free and payment maintenance period. There shall be only two such opportunities for fresh starts during those persons' lifetimes. All persons with felony and/or misdemeanor convictions *involving violence* shall have the right to *petition* the court of their most recent conviction for expungement of their criminal records once they have completed a thirty-six month period *without* any offenses of any kind (including misdemeanors) and *with* required payments for restitution and fees, but expungement for persons with violence-related convictions – unlike for persons with non-violence-related convictions – shall not be automatic upon certification of completion of the required offense-free period. There shall be only one such opportunity for an offender with one or more violence-related convictions to successfully petition the court for a fresh start. If and when expungement is approved by the court, all of the petitioners' rights shall be restored, without exception, including voting rights. However, if the petitioner fails to maintain her or his obligations to make payments toward restitution and/ or fines, those rights shall be suspended until the court certifies that the petitioner has resumed maintaining those payment obligations.

XXVI. *JEAN VALJEAN/SCOTT SISTERS RIGHT TO REASONABLE PROSECUTION AND SENTENCING*

Recognizing that many states have sentencing provisions which fail to take into account certain key factors about offenders, this provision of the USA-SBR, which shall be known as the **Jean Valjean/Scott Sisters Provision**, requires that persons convicted of their first offense for any crime in which the victim(s) was (were) neither physically harmed nor both intentionally and severely psychologically tortured shall be automatically diverted into a first-offender program (involving **no** prison time) aimed at discouraging recidivism. Offenders who complete the diversion program and don't re-offend within 24 months after their conviction shall automatically have their conviction expunged and all their rights restored, provided they maintain any required restitution and fee payments once they are employed. In conjunction with this amendment, there shall be established a Sentencing Consistency Commission which shall keep statistics on sentences handed down against affluent offenders. When non-affluent offenders are being sentenced, they shall receive sentences which are no more severe than the average sentence handed down for the same offense committed by an affluent person. All courts throughout the U.S.A. and its territories are required to comply with statistics collection requests from that Commission. Judges or justices of any individual courts failing to comply shall be notified of intent for removal; if they still haven't complied within 60 days after receiving that notification, they shall be removed from office permanently. Offenders are considered affluent if their Federal adjusted gross income on their latest Form 1040 is $100,000 or greater on a person filing an individual return or $200,000 or greater on persons filing a joint return. Those amounts shall be adjusted annually for inflation once the USA-SBR is ratified. Judges or justices in individual courts found through the Sentencing Consistency Commission's statistical studies to have discriminated negatively against non-affluent offenders shall be permanently removed from the bench within 20 days of such a statistical determination. A judge's or justice's only basis for appeal of removal shall be a finding of tallying errors in the statistical study(ies) involved.

XXVII. *RIGHTS OF CONVICTED NON-VIOLENT SUBSTANCE ABUSERS*

All persons currently imprisoned or incarcerated only for non-violent substance abuse offenses with records of good behavior shall be reviewed for eligibility for early release into drug rehabilitation programs within 90 days of ratification of the USA-SBR. There is a presumption of qualification for release unless there are issues which overcome that presumption. Those who fail to comply with drug rehabilitation requirements after their release are subject to prompt re-imprisonment or re-incarceration.

XXVIII. *RIGHT TO CLEAN WATER AND AIR PLUS RIGHT TO PROTECTION FROM HUMAN-CAUSED EXACERBATION OF GLOBAL WARMING*

Recognizing the right to a clean environment without exacerbating global warming, including the right to clean water and air, activities known to contaminate water, including hydraulic fracturing (i.e., "fracking"), are permanently banned. Except for aircraft, watercraft and railway engines, combustion is allowed only for heating and for production of electricity by utilities, provided that all combustion wastes are neutralized or scrubbed. Purchases of **new** internal combustion engines are prospectively banned forever, except for aircraft, watercraft and railway engines – but purchases of new internal combustion aircraft, watercraft and railway engines also shall be permanently banned as soon as new technology enables reliable use of electric- or solar-powered aircraft, watercraft and railway propulsion. Meanwhile, conversions of existing aircraft, watercraft and railway internal combustion engines to non-food renewable biomass fuels such as sawgrass and waste product fuels such as used cooking oils and logging/sawmill wastes are required within four years of ratification of this Second Bill of Rights. In addition, all direct and indirect government subsidies for fossil fuels industries are forever banned. Likewise, **industries** which caused pollution at existing and future congressionally-designated Superfund sites are required to pay for clean-up of all such sites; the government is banned from using taxpayer dollars to clean up such sites except when the business responsible for the pollution is completely defunct. Furthermore, recognizing that wastes from nuclear power plants are the most long-lastingly toxic substances in the universe (deadly toxic for hundreds of thousands of years), construction of new nuclear power plants are permanently banned; existing nuclear power plants shall be decommissioned and permanently shuttered as soon as their current licenses to operate expire, with the exceptions of nuclear plants located within 10 miles of seacoasts to prevent risks of tsunami damage and nuclear plants located within 50 miles of fault lines with risks of 5.0 Richter Scale or higher quakes as designated by the U.S. Geological Survey. Coastal area and fault line area nuclear plants shall be decommissioned and permanently shuttered immediately. In addition, *all restrictions*, including aesthetic restrictions, on residential uses of rooftop and other solar energy generation devices are immediately and permanently banned. Likewise, sales of non-white colored roofing materials are immediately banned to improve solar heating reflectivity of rooftops. Finally, all new power transmission lines shall be buried at a safe depth (determined by the Secretary of Renewable Energy) and all existing above-ground power transmission lines shall be buried within 10 years from the date the USA-SBR is ratified. New above-ground power transmission lines are immediately banned forever. Utilities refusing to comply or failing to comply with USA-SBR requirements shall be permanently nationalized, to be owned and operated not-for-profit by the Federal government. Furthermore, all for-profit utilities are required to convert to hydropower (which is certified as not interfering with fish migrations and spawning), solar and wind energy technologies for 90 percent of energy generation and to non-food-related waste biomass technology for the remaining 10 percent of energy generation within 10 years of the passage and ratification of the USA-SBR. Those utilities are required to convert to hydropower (which is certified as not interfering with fish migrations and spawning), solar and wind energy technologies for 100 percent of energy generation within 15 years of passage and ratification of the USA-SBR. Any utilities which fail to comply with those requirements shall be immediately nationalized by the Federal government and operated by the Federal government as not-for-profit entities, never again to be privatized.

XXIX.   *RIGHT TO EQUAL COMPENSATION*

There is the right to equal pay for equal work, regardless of gender, gender preference, age or physical/mental barriers.

XXX.   *RIGHT TO PROTECTION FROM DISCRIMINATION*

There is the right to be free from discrimination based on gender, same-sex orientation, trans-gender orientation, physical disability, mental disability, age and race. There is no right for government or businesses of any kind to discriminate against any person on any such basis. There is no right to refuse to marry **any two persons, including persons of the same gender,** who have reached the age of majority and are no more closely related than 2nd cousins, provided neither party isn't already married to someone else. Persons formally alleged to have committed acts of discrimination are subject to Class D Federal felony charges, one charge for each act of discrimination.

XXXI. *RIGHT TO PROTECTION FROM WRONGFUL EXECUTION*

Recognizing that the criminal justice system in the U.S.A. has a long history of imposing wrongful convictions, *unless* a method is developed (with complete success and without permanent harm) to reverse the death penalty once it is imposed **and** *unless* the governor, judge, jury and prosecutor who authorize the death penalty on a *convicted serial/ mass murderer* are willing to promise to accept the imposition of that same death penalty on themselves were it to be demonstrated at a later date that the conviction was wrongful, there is the right of persons convicted of any crime **not** to be put to death. All juries have the right to sentence persons convicted of multiple pre-meditated murders to life in prison without the possibility of parole. Persons convicted of any crimes have the right to have their convictions reversed at any time post-conviction upon a hearing in which new evidence establishes to the court's satisfaction that the previous conviction was wrongful and/or unjust. Criminal law enforcers formally alleged to have knowingly used false or unsubstantiated evidence which led to a conviction are subject to Class A Federal felony charges.

XXXII. *RIGHT OF PRISONERS TO HUMANE TREATMENT AND EFFECTIVE REHABILITATION*

There are the following rights for prisoners: the right of incarcerated and imprisoned persons to humane treatment, including the right **not** to be placed in solitary confinement for more than one 48-hour period per month (with two hours per day spent outside during solitary confinement), the right to healthfully nutritious meals and hydration; the right to adequate clothing and bedding (including blankets during winter); the right to a quiet environment during rest periods; the right to competent medical, dental and psychiatric care; the right not to be subjected to involuntary labor without reasonable compensation (defined as at least minimum wage less no more than 50 percent deductions to offset costs of income taxes, FICA, food, shelter, child support, restitution and fines), the right to be sheltered indoors at a reasonable temperature no greater than 76F and no less than 68F plus the right to be protected from extreme outdoor weather elements, including outdoor temperatures above 86F and below 50F, with seasonally-appropriate clothing provided. Likewise, recognizing that the vast majority of prisoners eventually are released back into the general population, there is a right of incarcerated and imprisoned persons to participation in reasonable rehabilitation programs, including education programs, provided the inmate does not commit successive acts of violence during such rehabilitation programs.

XXXIII. RIGHT OF THE PUBLIC NOT TO BE REPRESENTED BY PERSONS WITH HISTORIES OF RACIAL BIGOTRY

Recognizing the especially long-lasting corrosive effects of racial bigotry, **persons determined, from the age of 21 forward, to have participated in or publicly encouraged any actions – either overt and implied – involving racial bigotry shall have no right whatsoever to hold any and all elective AND appointive offices at all levels of government, including – but not limited to – federal, state, county and city.** Such actions shall include actions which were previously legal but have since been made to be illegal, as well as actions which, while not considered illegal due to First Amendment free speech protections, are nonetheless racially bigoted. For example, U.S. Supreme Court Chief Justice William Rehnquist's aggressive participation during his late 30's in then-legal voter literacy testing in Phoenix, AZ African-American and Hispanic neighborhoods (as part of a co-ordinated Republican Party effort to disenfranchise minorities during the 1960s) would've precluded his nomination to the Supreme Court had this provision of the USA-SBR been in effect at the time of his original 1971 nomination by President Richard M. Nixon. Persons involved in such racial bigotry who already are in office at the time of the USA-SBR's ratification are allowed to complete their current terms – but they are barred from seeking re-election **or** being re-appointed.

XXXIV. ROY S. MOORE RIGHT TO PROTECTION FROM JUDGES WHO REFUSE TO ACCEPT ARTICLE 6, CLAUSE 2 (SUPREMACY CLAUSE) OF U.S. CONSTITUTION

Judges in state courts who refuse to comply in a timely fashion with orders from Federal courts shall be immediately and permanently disbarred from the practice of law nationwide and permanently removed from all judicial offices and permanently ineligible to hold such offices throughout the country – once they have exhausted their due process rights. This is referred to as the Roy S. Moore Provision of the USA-SBR.

XXXV. _RAY BRADBURY RIGHT TO PROTECTION FROM THOSE WHO WOULD BAN TEXTBOOKS AND OTHER LITERATURE DESPITE THE ACCURACY AND EMPIRICAL REALITY OF THEIR CONTENTS_

There is the national right to a free public education based on **empirical reality**. School boards for both public and private schools nationwide are prohibited from banning any textbook contents or other forms of literature unless those items don't comport with empirical reality or they contain material **intended** to be pruriently pornographic. Both public and private schools, likewise, shall have no right to discipline their students for making use of any forms of literature which comport with empirical reality and aren't **intended** to be pruriently pornographic, whether those sources are on "approved" reading lists or not.

XXXVI. _RIGHT TO PEACEABLY GATHER IN ALL PUBLIC COMMONS INCLUDING_ DE **FACTO** _PUBLIC COMMONS_

There is the right to _**non-violent assembly**_ in **any** government-owned or government-leased commons area, as well as in any _de facto_ public commons, such as shopping malls open to the general public. Only privately-owned areas with lawfully-restricted access would be exempt from that right. Law enforcement officers formally alleged to have violated this right or to have conspired to violate this right are subject to Class D Federal felony charges followed by prompt dismissal proceedings and a permanent ban nationwide from the law enforcement profession if convicted.

XXXVII. _RIGHT TO PEACEFUL RESIDENCES_

There is the right to peaceful residential neighborhoods, free of noise which disturbs or prevents sleep (except for use of emergency vehicles during actual emergencies). Commercial aircraft, general aviation airplanes, private business airplanes and military aircraft (except during declared wars or propulsion difficulties) are banned from flying lower than 5,000 feet above ground level over all residential neighborhoods. Neighborhoods already established within two miles of airports beneath lower-level takeoff and landing flight paths are exempt from this requirement; however, those neighborhoods shall be given highest preference for rezoning conversion to industrial uses.

XXXVIII. RIGHT TO LEGISLATIVE INITIATIVE PROCESS AT ALL LEVELS OF GOVERNMENT, INCLUDING FEDERAL; PAID SIGNATURE GATHERERS BANNED

There is the national right of legislative initiative for *all levels* of government, enabling citizens to circulate petitions nationwide, statewide, countywide and citywide in all jurisdictions to place national, state, county and city legislation on Federal, state and local election ballots every two years (odd-numbered years for many local elections) for approval or rejection by voters at all levels of government. There is no veto right for initiatives approved by voters. The minimum number of required signatures is the equivalent of 10 percent of the national voting-age population for national initiatives (including 10 percent in each state), 10 percent of state voting age population for statewide initiatives, 10 percent of county voting age population for countywide initiatives and 10 percent of municipal voting age population for citywide initiatives, based on the latest U.S. Bureau of the Census data; signatures shall be verified by each state's Secretary of State. The U.S. Attorney General is responsible for determining the constitutionality of each proposed national legislative initiative before petitions could be circulated; states' attorneys general shall determine the constitutionality of non-Federal initiatives. Gathering of signatures by paid signature gatherers is permanently banned, recognizing that the absence of such a ban would result in wealthy corporations and wealthy individuals dominating the initiative process. There also is a right of citizens to use the initiative process to amend both state and Federal constitutions using the same process described for legislative initiatives; no Attorney General vetting is required for the constitutional amendment initiative process.

XXXIX. VOTERS' RIGHT TO ENDORSE OR RESCIND DECLARATIONS OF WAR OR OTHER ARMED CONFLICTS WITH FOREIGN COUNTRIES OR ORGANIZED ENTITIES

There is the right of voters to participate in a binding national ballot referendum on whether or not to declare war or to authorize any other armed conflict against another country or organized entity. The referendum shall be conducted as promptly as is practicable. The right of voters to that prompt referendum shall not prevent the President from taking prompt action in response to military threats during emergency situations, provided the President obtains Congressional authorization for such actions as promptly as possible.

XL. *RIGHT TO OPEN GOVERNMENT AT ALL LEVELS*

Recognizing that secrecy in government is like a cancer which discourages and eventually kills effective grassroots participation in the legislative process, **all government proceedings** – including whenever **two or more** voting members of a government entity *meet or communicate* with each other – **shall be open to the public** – including all print and broadcast media, with no restrictions on pooled video and radio coverage – at all stages of the legislative and deliberative processes, including the executive, legislative and judicial branches of *all levels* of government from the smallest community and school district to the Federal government. This requirement includes, but is not limited to, all proceedings involving direct and indirect expenditures of government resources. The only exemptions for required open proceedings are for court juries and for when there has been a documented finding – through open government deliberations and proceedings – by an open vote of Congress that a foreign government is planning to wage war or already has recently (within the previous 12 months) committed acts of war against the U.S.A. Members of government entities who are determined through due process to have violated this provision of the USA-SBR shall be immediately and permanently removed from the entity on which they were a voting member and they shall not be eligible to be a voting member of that or any other government entity ever again.

XLI. *RIGHT TO PROTECTION FROM ALL FORMS OF TORTURE*

There is the right of **all parties** within and outside of our country to be protected from all forms of torture (including so-called "enhanced" or "harsh" interrogation techniques) committed by persons employed by the U.S. government or acting on behalf of the U.S. government. Persons formally alleged to have committed such acts or to have conspired to commit such acts are subject to Class A Federal felony charges. There shall be no Statute of Limitations on the crime of torture.

XLII. *RIGHT OF ALL WORKERS TO ORGANIZE FOR COLLECTIVE BARGAINING*

There is the right of all employees working for any employer with 10 or more employees to automatically be certified for labor union representation whenever more than 50 percent of employees sign National Labor Relations Board (NLRB) union authorization cards designating the union. The cards shall be available online through the NLRB website. When less than 50 percent but more than 30 percent of employees sign such cards the NLRB shall conduct a union representation election by secret ballot.

Persons formally accused of intimidating, attempting to intimidate or conspiring to intimidate employees trying to organize a union during a unionization campaign are subject to Federal Class C felony charges. Employers found by the NLRB to have demoted or fired an employee for trying to organize a union are subject to Federal Class B felony charges. Once union representation is certified by the NLRB, the union has the right to collect union dues from all employees (because the union is required to represent all employees); there is no right for employees represented by NLRB-certified unions to opt out of representation or opt out of paying union dues, because all such employees benefit from union representation whether or not they support union organizing efforts.

XLIII. RIGHT TO GROW, PRODUCE, POSSESS AND USE ANY NATURAL SUBSTANCE UNLESS THE FOOD AND DRUG ADMINISTRATION HAS DECLARED THE SUBSTANCE TO BE TOXIC AND/OR CARCINOGENIC

There is a right of all adult citizens at least 21 years old to grow and/or produce at home, possess and use – without being subject to either criminal or civil charges – any natural substances unless the Food and Drug Administration has declared the substance in question to be toxic and/or carcinogenic when used in moderation.

XLIV. RIGHT TO UNIFORM FEDERALIZED CHILD SUPPORT ENFORCEMENT ADMINISTRATION THROUGHOUT THE U.S.A. AND ITS TERRITORIAL POSSESSIONS

Recognizing that varied state-by-state laws governing child support enforcement have erected significant barriers to effective support collections, there shall be a nationalized Federal child support enforcement system which shall within nine months of ratification of the USA-SBR replace the hodgepodge of state and county child support enforcement agencies and their widely varying enforcement standards and limitations. Employees of existing non-privatized child support enforcement agencies shall have hiring preference for the new Federalized agency; all privatized support child support enforcement agencies shall be permanently closed. Establishment and enforcement provisions shall include:

#Federal administrative establishment of orders of enforcement (which would be superseded by orders established through county-level courts during divorce or other proceedings).
#Bi-annual reviewability for order modification of both administrative and court orders, with a right to a free

modification action if the proposed support amount is at least $100 per month greater or less than the existing monthly order amount.

#Free paternity testing at each child's birth hospital within a month after birth.

#Obligations to pay appropriate portions of out-of-pocket health care and child care expenses.

#Automatic seizure of both state and federal income tax refunds up to the full amount owed once debt is at least $250 past due as of Dec. 1st each year.

#Automatic suspension actions against **all** of a non-custodial parent's government-issued licenses once debt is the equivalent of six months past due.

#Automatic statewide liens in state of latest residence on both real estate and vehicles once debt is at least $250 past due.

#Automatic passport revocation once debt is at least $250 past due.

#Automatic referrals for Civil Contempt through local county-level courts once debt is at least $1,000 past due (with Federal Class C Felony prosecution against any county prosecutor who fails to pursue such actions).

#Enforcement officers' option to seize financial accounts balances if a parent goes more than 31 days without making a payment, with **_ALL_** U.S. city-, county-, state- and federally-chartered financial institutions required to honor administrative Orders to Withhold and Deliver.

#Enforcement officers' option to have non-custodial parents' vehicle(s) seized by the appropriate county prosecutor and auctioned once debt is at least $2,500 past due.

#Enforcement officers' option to withhold up to 50 percent from **any and all** monthly net earnings and benefits from Federal sources [including but not limited to all Department of Veterans' Affairs retirement **_AND_** disability benefits, Department of Defense net earnings, Social Security retirement **_AND_** disability benefits (but not SSI, except for 50 percent of lump-sum payments) **and** Federal payments to contractors].

#Requirement that employer payments to **all** employees on their regular payroll, contract workers, subcontractors and private parties are subject to withholding of up to 50 percent of net pay (net defined as gross pay less withholding which is **not** optional to the payee).

#Immediate wage withholding is **_ALWAYS_** required in both administrative and court orders.

#Paying parents are **always** required to make payments **_ONLY_** through the new Federal Support Registry (FRS) (with **each state** having a registry processing center to speed up payment processing). Paying parents **shall not** receive credits for payments not made through the Federal Support Registry because parents receiving child support **_and_** parents paying child support have the right to a permanent and indisputable record of all payments and the requirement to pay through the FRS shall be made clear in EVERY child support order, whether the order is administrative or filed through a court.

#After the paying parent is served with an order of support or a support order is signed by a county-level court judge, non-custodial parents have financial liability for cost of process service when an enforcement officer determines the paying parent has been avoiding service of process.

#Custodial parents have the right to have administrative and/or court orders established for the support of children under age 23 during periods of post-secondary education.

#There is the right to have **_all_** employers comply with child support wage-withholding requirements. Employers are required to begin and continue compliance with wage-withholding within 20 days of receiving a wage-withnolding notice. Employers which fail to comply shall be fined $250 for each violation and shall be subject to having funds seized from their financial accounts for both the fines and the unpaid child support (subject to the results of any due process appeals requested). Employers which pay any worker "off the books" to avoid having to comply with wage-withholding requirements are considered in violation and their fines shall be doubled.

#There is the right to have **_all_** employers comply with the mandatory Federal New Hire Reporting system, through which employers must electronically report all new hires within 24 hours (one business day) of each new employee formally accepting a job offer (whether in writing, in person, by phone or via electronic media). Employers which fail to comply are subject to a $1,000 fine for each violation; employers which pay workers "off the books" to avoid reporting are considered in violation and their fines shall be doubled.

#**All commercial trade is suspended** between all entities in the U.S.A. and all entities of all foreign nations the governments of which have not signed **_and_** complied with reciprocal treaties promising to honor all lawful child support enforcement orders created through government administrative agencies and/or government courts of each treaty signatory. Those trade suspensions shall be lifted country by country once each country has signed the reciprocal treaty with the U.S.A. and had begun complying with all treaty provisions, as certified by the U.S. Secretary of Health and Human Services.

XLV. *RIGHT TO FACILITATION OF PARENTING PLAN WITH DETAILED SPECIFIED VISITATION RIGHTS*

Recognizing that non-custodial parents who have regular visitation are more likely to co-operate with the financial support of their children, there shall be established within nine months after ratification a Federal system for administratively-determined Parenting Plans administered through administrative law judges in each county of each state. The parents of each child shall have a right for an administrative law judge to set forth specific rights to weekly visitation and visitation during holidays and school break periods, unless an administrative law judge determines visitation is inappropriate due to a non-custodial parent's personal circumstances, including (but not limited to) substance abuse, psychological and/or psychiatric disorders, records of criminal law violations, abusive behaviors and lack of a suitable residence. Non-custodial parents have the right to appeal administrative law judges' determinations to the county-level trial court in the county of the child's primary residence. Non-custodial parents are responsible for transportation costs associated with visitation when the non-custodial parent chooses to reside in a county which is different from the child's primary residence. Otherwise, such transportation costs shall be shared equally between the two parents. The non-custodial parent's share of costs associated with visitation is collectable through the Federal child support enforcement system if the custodial parent alleges non-payment.

XLVI. *RIGHT TO SIMPLE MAJORITY APPROVALS FOR REVENUE INCREASES*

Recognizing that adequate funding of government is crucial to providing essential government services, it is now unconstitutional to require more than a majority of voters (50 percent plus one vote) to approve any increases in taxes at all levels of government nationwide.

XLVII. *RIGHT TO GOVERNMENT WITHOUT GRIDLOCK*

Recognizing that government gridlock often prevents passage of crucial legislation, the U.S. Senate is permanently prohibited from requiring the votes of more than 55 percent of senators to cut off filibusters and is permanently required to allow filibusters only when senators participate in filibusters in person on the floor of the Senate; likewise the U.S.

Senate is permanently prohibited from allowing a single senator to block any Executive Branch nomination or other action.

XLVIII. RIGHT TO PROTECTION FOR NATIONAL PARK SERVICE-ADMINISTERED LANDS, WILDERNESS AREAS, NATIONAL MONUMENTS, NATIONAL RECREATIONAL AREAS, NATIONAL WILDLIFE REFUGES, NATIONAL FORESTS, ETC.

Resource extraction projects – including, but not limited to, oil, natural gas, precious metals, etc. – within 60 miles of any U.S. National Park Service facility and/or Federal wilderness area and/or Federal national monument and/or Federal wildlife refuge area are permanently banned prospectively; existing such projects shall be permanently closed no later than one year after this Second Bill of Rights takes effect. In addition, National Monuments and National Parks created through Executive Branch actions shall require a ¾-majority vote of both chambers of Congress to override those designations. The Congress shall have only a three-month period during which to override such designations; once that three-month period has passed, the designations are permanent and cannot be overridden, ever.

XLIX. RIGHT TO PURSUE AND COLLECT CIVIL CLAIMS FOR DAMAGES AGAINST GOVERNMENT AT ALL LEVELS; BANNING ALL REMAINING VESTIGES OF THE LEGAL DOCTRINE OF REX NON POTEST PECCARE (THE KING CAN DO NO WRONG)

There is an absolute right to submit civil claims for damages and to recover such claims for damages through due process actions against all levels of government throughout the U.S.A., including the Federal government. All remaining vestiges of the legal doctrine of "*rex non potest peccare*" (the king can do no wrong), also known as sovereign immunity, are forever considered null and void. In fact, all civil claims previously denied by any court in the U.S.A. under that doctrine for which the Statute of Limitations has not expired, may be filed or re-filed against all levels of governments. The principle in law that any level of government must give its consent to be sued on issues of liability under the doctrine of sovereign immunity is forever considered null and void. Surviving justices and judges who in the past voted to uphold that archaic legal doctrine are required within 30 days of ratification to issue formal apologies to plaintiffs whose claims were denied as the result of such actions by those officers of the court. Their apologies shall acknowledge that the archaic legal doctrine they voted to uphold is an un-American vestige of historical monarchies which never should have held sway since the success of the American Revolution, a doctrine designed to allow governments at all levels to avoid responsibility for incompetence, negligence, intentional wrongdoing and unwillingness to properly fund government oversight activity through increases in tax revenues, especially tax revenues against the wealthy. Officers of the court formally alleged to have failed to comply with that obligation to apologize are subject to Class D Federal felony charges.

L.   *NATIVE AMERICANS' AND AFRICAN-AMERICANS' RIGHT TO REPARATIONS*

Recognizing that all Native American tribes suffered inestimable losses of their inalienable rights to life, liberty and pursuit of happiness, as well as inestimable losses of property rights, during centuries of forced colonization with multiple deadly assaults and massacres of non-combatant men, women, children and the elderly by the armed forces of the United States of America – including an 1862 mass execution in Mankato, Minnesota ordered by none other than President Lincoln – each and every Native American who was born in the U.S.A., who still resides in the U.S.A., who can prove at least ½-blood Native American ancestry and who is at least 18 years old at the time of ratification shall receive a one-time reparations payment from the U.S. Treasury of $1 million within 120 days after ratification. Likewise, there shall be $1 million reparations payments set aside for each African-American who had been enslaved at any time during the Civil War. Those reparations payments shall be made to the surviving descendants who provide documentation proving they are, in fact, descended from at least one person who was a slave during the Civil War. The first descendant to make such a successfully-documented claim for each such slave ancestor shall be paid the $1 million for that ancestor, with the condition that the $1 million be paid into each claimant's account with the newly-created Federal Slave Descendants' Trust Administration pending claims from other possible descendant claimants (for the same enslaved person) whose claims, if approved, would result in proportional shares of each original claimant's $1 million. Those additional claimants shall have one year to submit their documentation of ancestry to the Federal Slave Descendants' Trust Administrator (appointed by the President with consent of the U.S. Senate). At the end of that year, the administrator shall have 120 days to determine the validity of claimants' claims on those reparations payments and to disburse proportional payments among claimants of each slave's descendants (claimants may make multiple claims if more than one ancestor was enslaved). The costs of all those reparations payments shall be funded through a 5 percent Federal transactions tax on all stock purchases. That transactions tax shall expire once the costs of all reparations payments are recovered, unless a simple majority of each chamber of Congress approves its extension. Those reparations payments are permanently exempt from taxation by Federal, state and local governments.

* * *

Franklin also drafted a document to be signed by each elected officeholder and prospective candidates for elected office which would put them on the record as supporting the Un-Screwing of America Second Bill of Rights:

Candidates' Contract of Support *for* the Un-Screwing of America Second Bill of Rights (USA-SBR) in Exchange for Support *by* USA-SBR Advocates

The undersigned promises to use all opportunities to advocate for and to vote for passage of the amendment of the U.S. Constitution known as the Un-Screwing of America Second Bill of Rights (USA-SBR). Likewise, the undersigned promises to actively advocate for ratification of that constitutional amendment once it is passed by the U.S. Congress. In exchange for that active support of the USA-SBR, the undersigned shall receive advocacy and votes of other USA-SBR backers during any campaign for elected office. If the undersigned breaks this promise of advocacy and support for the USA-SBR, then supporters of the USA-SBR shall campaign against and advocate against the promise-breaker.

Signed on this _____ day of _____, 2_____,

_____

Signature

State of _____

County of _____

The foregoing instrument was acknowledged before me this _____day of

_____,

2_____, at

_____(city), _____(state), by _____

to be his/her voluntary act and deed.

_____

Signature of Notary Public

_____

Printed Name of Notary Public   SEAL

Notary Public, State of _____

My commission expires: _____

∗   ∗   ∗

F ranklin's long-term plan was to circulate both documents as widely as possible, as soon as possible.

∗   ∗   ∗

M r. Mitchell took Franklin/Percy aside at the end of class the day after Franklin turned in his extra credit essay because he wanted to compliment him on his vision for what could make the U.S.A. a more just place to live. But he wanted to make sure his star pupil understood the likely obstacles to enacting a whole new supplemental Bill of Rights.

"You do understand, I'm sure, that any President who tried to implement this kind of Bill of Rights would immediately be scorned by the opposition for allegedly attempting a huge power grab, right?" Mr. Mitchell asked. "Especially with that Superior Court expansion.

"You do recall what happened when FDR tried to expand the Superior Court, don't you? I mean, even **he** admitted to his favorite cousin it was, basically, a way to improve his chances of flexing his political muscle with New Deal programs the court had rejected, right?"

"Yes sir, I do recall you covering that in class a few weeks ago," Franklin/Percy said quietly, with a straight face. "I believe, though, that if you re-read the provisions of *that part* of the new Bill of Rights, it gives far more power to the general public than to the President.

"I have a *strong feeling* that, if FDR still were around, he'd give this kind of proposal his hearty endorsement. When people lambasted his original proposal to enlarge the Supreme Court, I think they unfairly overlooked his genuine interest in making our version of democracy more representative, less beholden to the fattest wallets."

"Yes, the voting public would, once and for all, actually have some clout over the Supreme Court, especially after the fact, with those retention elections every four years," Mr. Mitchell said. "Accountability to voters is always a good thing. I'm just saying, it's an issue that wealthy pro-corporate types would be quick to raise when they try to stop this kind of thing in its tracks.

"It's a not-so-insignificant thing to remember when you realize all of the other hurdles to be met, like getting two-thirds of the U.S. Senate and U.S. House to pass this measure, followed by three-fourths of state legislatures ratifying it. How would you manage to achieve the election of just that many members of *Congress* alone when there probably are only a tiny handful – maybe just two or three in the Senate and maybe a dozen or two in the House – who currently would support this new Bill of Rights?"

"I grant you, sir, that this will be a monumental task. It will require an organizational effort of herculean proportions. But great achievement usually requires even greater labor, is that not true?"

"Well, I would be interested to know if you actually intend to begin such an organizational effort and how you'd go about that. If you ever have some time to kill, I'd love to discuss the details with you. My curiosity's killing me, though: how did you learn so much about child support? You're only 18, for God's sake!"

"The best friend of someone close to me struggles every day due to lack of support from her father. That spurred me to read about it. I seem to have developed some wicked good speed reading skills."

"I think you have an admirable vision here, but I don't want you to work yourself into an early grave tilting at windmills. At least, not without making sure you have a workable strategy."

"Next time I have a few hours between my jobs, my classes and what little recreation I manage to get, I'll let you know, OK, sir?"

"Fair enough, Percy. Don't give up on this, at least not right away, OK?"

"I won't if you won't."

And Franklin/Percy did not.

* * *

HEALING LASTING WOUNDS, MANO A MANO

The O'Learys decided that, after going into great detail over Howard Zinn's *"Peoples' History of the United States,"* the Vietnam War, the Grenada War, The Panama War, the Gulf War, the Afghanistan War, the Iraq War and the end of the Cold War during their previous five Saturday sessions – not to mention many movie videos from those periods, that Franklin's final Saturday session with them would be Dec. 18.

Franklin was just fine with that. He was exhausted from reading about wars, watching movies about wars and talking about wars. So much so, he wished he could dig up Charlton Heston and pry his gun out of his cold, dead hands and melt it into some kind of plowshare – or into some sort of fancy convertible coupe, like the convertible touring car in the basement of his memorial library.

The final Saturday session covered the wisdom of trying to eradicate terrorists and their extreme hatred of the "Great Satan" U.S.A. through war – Wall Street's preferred option – or by reaching out to the terrorists and their acolytes through humanitarian actions. Letting actions, not lofty words shouted from behind a gun barrel, speak for the intentions of the average American.

"There may always be some extremists whose hatred is so great that not even the most humanitarian, positive, unambiguously generous kindnesses will penetrate their callous hearts," Karin said. "The kinds of people who believe they're placed on earth to execute the so-called "will of God" or "will of Allah" are convinced God or Allah is communicating directly with them."

"You mean, like Texas Baptists," Franklin half-joked.

"Unfortunately," Karin said, "you're not too far off there.

"Those kinds of hyper-religious fundamentalists – whether 10,000 miles away or lurking in the Lone Star state hill country – might merit temporary control by armed force.

"But the vast majority of those foreigners who hate our country – those who remember how *our country* overthrew a democratically-elected President in *their own country*, as in Iran in 1953, so we could install a brutal dictator, the Shah, who was *our country's* buddy – those who hate us on political principles rather than religious principles, **those** people *can* be swayed by long-belated good deeds. By long-delayed earnest – shall we say, shit-eating – apologies."

"Earnest good deeds will win out in the end," Orvis said. "There may be a few of our valiant diplomatic souls whose first encounters with that hatred may end up sacrificing their own lives. But, eventually, if we persist in doing good for those who hate us, the hatred will erode. The erosion may be slow, but it will happen.

"History has shown us repeatedly that can happen. Just look at our progress with Vietnam. If ever there were a country which could understandably despise ours for a virtual eternity, Vietnam would be it. But as you noticed a while back, people now buy and wear undergarments made in Vietnam every day and think nothing of it.

"Time – and money…**and** face-to-face reconciliation – those three things heal almost all wounds."

"What do you believe would be the best way to help Americans understand that going to war with those who hate us is like trying to put out a fire with gasoline?" Karin asked.

"If I were President again, I would try to engage those who hate our country on a face-to-face basis whenever possible," Franklin suggested.

"You know, Karin, when you Google the visit by Soviet Premier Nikita Khrushchev to the U.S.A. in 1959, there are references to his earlier 'we will bury you' remarks and to him losing his temper when the Los Angeles mayor criticized him in public, as well as to his anger over Disneyland refusing to let him have a recreational visit.

"But what still comes through when you read **all** the accounts of his tour across the country, including his visits to northern California, to Iowa and to Pennsylvania, is his politeness, his almost sweet, casual admiration for things America had which his country did not have. Things like supermarkets, cafeterias, amusement parks, huge movie studios, middle-class labor-saving devices.

"In short, what came across was his humanity."

"Did you see where he got to meet Eleanor and actually laid a wreath on your grave?" Karin asked.

"Yes, I saw the photos on the Smithsonian website. It...touched my heart... to see those heartfelt smiles on Eleanor's face." Franklin had to pause briefly to wipe his eyes.

"That same Smithsonian website stated polls showed 30 percent of Americans were so hard-line anti-communist that they didn't even want Khrushchev on our soil," he said. "Despite those polls, the rest of the people were almost relieved at the man's humanity, his sense of humor, his occasionally cherubic countenance.

"Just his simple, natural, occasionally avuncular personality told people this was not some evil monster just itching to incinerate us capitalists with a white-hot nuclear holocaust.

"That couldn't have happened if he'd never set foot in our country, never walked among us. And the reverse surely happened for him: the hundreds of protesters holding hateful placards notwithstanding, the vast majority of regular folks Khrushchev encountered face-to-face were smiling, polite, welcoming people who wanted to find reasons to befriend him, not to hate him.

"If we can remind people – especially people too young to have lived through that time – of how simple face-to-face meetings with adversaries, even nuclear-armed adversaries, can change a dynamic from hate to eventual friendship, perhaps Americans can be convinced war is an obsolete way - not to mention a phenomenally ineffective, inhumane and astronomically expensive way - to de-fuse hatred. Especially when it's hatred which *is*, arguably, *deserved*, at least on some level."

"Franklin, I think we've taught you just about all we can," Orvis said. "And you've taught us more than we ever could've hoped to learn."

"Ditto," Karin said. "To call it a privilege to share these sessions with you is the understatement of the 21st century."

"Right back at you both," Franklin smiled.

$$* \quad * \quad *$$

First Christmas Since Being Reconstituted

The Christmas holidays Franklin shared with Phil, Pongo, Tom and Annie Podrowski, Heather Griffin and the others were a nice break from his usual routine, but they served mostly to make him miss past Christmases with Eleanor, their children and grandchildren.

He thought about asking the others if he could reprise his long tradition of reading half of "A Christmas Carol" before Christmas dinner and the rest after all the stomachs were full. But he quickly realized it simply wouldn't be the same as having all of his own progeny around to hear his different voice stylings for the characters, especially Mr. Scrooge.

Annie made his day, though, by looking up the old recipe for his mother's chestnut stuffing and replicating it to a 't'...Franklin was so touched at Annie's smiling recognition of his fond memories, his eyes moistened. He and she shared a brief embrace as the others around the dinner table looked on.

"One could do far worse than to be inserted into this kind of adoptive family," he thought to himself. *"No more feeling sorry for myself, ever."*

Annie also told him there would be no tolerating of one of his documented long-standing Christmas traditions: waiting for days or even weeks before getting around to opening his own presents. (He always enjoyed watching others open their own presents far more than he liked opening his.)

His favorite gift from his new replacement family turned out to be what Phil and Pongo got for him, concealed by wrapping paper embossed with cartoons of a hundred or more characters from "The Simpsons" TV show: an expensive pair of hiking boots from R.E.I. with an enclosed note which said,

"Every day we see you take a step with us, we count ourselves blessed by your return to this life. We enjoy every step you take, so we just wanted to make sure every step you take is as comfortable as it can be. Please enjoy your new-found mobility every single day as much as we enjoy seeing it! You're the best thing that's ever happened to us!"

It was the first of many subsequent Christmases which Franklin would enjoy with his serendipitously-discovered new friends. On the next Christmas, they even convinced him to read "A Christmas Carol."

And, notwithstanding his long-gone wife and children and now-elderly absent grandchildren, he loved it. Having a new love interest by then helped. A **lot**.

* * *

Birth of a Movement – Funded the Old-Fashioned Way... At First, Anyway

Within a month after turning in his extra credit assignment essay on the new Bill of Rights constitutional amendment to Mr. Mitchell, Franklin decided to map out a strategy for setting up a grass roots organization of activists with the goal of compelling members of Congress and state legislatures to support the amendment – and compelling qualified candidates to run against elected officials who refuse to support the amendment.

He set as his target date for implementing the nationwide election of members of Congress and state legislators supporting the USA-SBR the 2016 general election, giving him almost six years to rally backers across the country.

It quickly occurred to Franklin that there would be one significant hurdle to overcome for him to have any realistic chance of gathering support for the proposed Constitutional Amendment: how to pay for all the travel and lodging needed to reach prospective supporters in person all over the U.S.A.

Then he remembered "The Boxes."

"*How had I not remembered those sooner?!!*" he thought to himself. "*Guess some of the synapses are just now growing back together in this recycled brain.*"

When he was only 14 years old (in 1896), his mother had taken him aside late one Saturday evening as he was finishing his homework in advance of his travel back to Groton the following morning. She'd explained to him that, in the past, relying on financial institutions to protect significant sums of personal wealth had been a high-risk proposition.

"The country has just had another financial panic," Sara told Franklin at the time. "There was another *just three years ago* which caused many, many banks to fail. You have some extended family members – shall we say, 'shirttail relatives'? – who lost most of their money when two of those banks closed.

"Walk with me outside for a few minutes, Franklin," she said.

He followed her about a third of a mile north-northeast of their Springwood home. She showed Franklin a large pumpkin-shaped granite rock – weighing perhaps 750 pounds – resting a couple of feet from the base of a huge ash tree.

"If there ever is another stock market crash or financial panic of some sort, Franklin, this is where you will find the means to protect your family's home and belongings if neither your father nor I am around to help. There are sealed aluminum footlockers buried about four feet beneath that rock which contain about 1,000 pounds of solid gold bars and another 200 pounds of rare gold coins.

"If that isn't enough to resolve a financial crisis, then the world probably will have gone to hell in a handbasket anyway and money may be the last thing on your mind.

"I just wanted my only beloved child to know about this. I trust you not to share this information with anyone, Franklin, not even your own wife when you marry someday. These are assets that have been in your father's family for more than a hundred years."

"You can rely on me, Mama. If need be, this is a secret I will take to my grave."

And he did – although, truth be told, his pre-occupation with WW II and his health crises actually contributed to that secret stash completely skipping his mind in the final days of his life. Along with the fact that he actually hadn't truly believed he was about to die when he did that cool, breezy April of 1945.

But now the sight of that granite rock at the foot of the ash tree was as vivid in his mind as if he'd just been standing there with his mother minutes ago.

Time to do some shoveling, he thought.

So, later that night, with the assistance of Pongo, Harry and Idris – each of whom used heavy steel rods as levers to move the stone about three feet further away from the base of the tree – the footlockers were exhumed and their contents were discreetly re-located to the Podrowski household. Half of the gold bars and rare coins were transported in Pongo's Civic and the other half were transported in Franklin's adopted Civic.

Franklin explained to the three of them that he intended to use the proceeds from the sale of the bars and coins to travel around the country organizing support for his Un-Screwing of America Second Bill of Rights.

"How in the hell are you going to make time to do that?" Harry asked skeptically.

"Chet at Adams (Landscaping) already has given me permission to take a couple of weeks off in early January, plus the full week break we get from school in March," Franklin explained.

"So, who do you think is going to take an 18- or 19-year-old guy seriously when it comes to amending the U.S. Constitution?" Idris asked.

"Well, shit, *I* take him seriously," Pongo said. "In fact, I'm going to join him in January and March. I think he's got a helluvan idea here."

"My thinking," Franklin interrupted, "is that the first thing we'll do at each city we visit – probably just cities with universities - is to try to get a local activist of some repute on board. Once we find someone who already has the respect of local academia or local media who agrees to champion this project, we'll hold a news conference and pass leaflets around town asking interested folks to come to an organizing meeting.

"Our main organizing focus will be around repeal of the Citizens United decision. But we'll be quick to point out all the other provisions designed to un-fuh – I mean, un-screw the country."

"We should be doing a powerpoint slide presentation and screening "Capitalism: A Love Story" at each organizing meeting," Pongo added.

"If need be, we'll even hand out pre-packaged new clean underwear and ramen noodles to motivate college students to be involved, the way Michael Moore did during his 'Slacker Uprising' tour in '04," Franklin said. "I'm thinking we'll start with Missoula and Bozeman, Montana in early January, catching UM and MSU students just before spring semester classes start up."

"So it's Don Quixote and Sancho Panza going out to conquer the capitalist dragons," Harry laughed. "I hope you can come up with something better than one of those Saturday Night Live Adobe cars to get around in."

"Actually, my preference is travel by train," Franklin said, "so, if Pongo's willing, I'm planning to get us Amtrak tickets."

"I'm willing to give almost anything a try at least once," Pongo said. "As long as there's a way to get a shower now and then."

"So, why don't the two of you come along too?" Franklin asked Harry and Idris.

"You're comping travel, lodging and meals?" Harry asked.

"Sure, why not?" Franklin said.

"OK, I'm in," Harry said. "I've never been to Montana, so I'm stoked to see the scenery, if nothing else."

"Christ help me – count me in too – I've got at least a month of paid leave accrued," Idris said.

"You're sure we're not heading into the midst of some yahoo yokel bedsheet wearers still pissed off they didn't get in on the Freedom Rider killings of the '60s, right?"

"Pretty sure, Idris," Franklin said.

Actually, he _wasn't_. Not at all...

* * *

FINANCIAL STRATEGIES: PLANNING AHEAD TO OUTFOX THE FOXHEADS

Upon seeing via the internet that his 1,000-plus pounds of gold was valued at about $21.34 million and the rare coins likely were worth about $88 million, Franklin almost passed out. He made a mental note to make sure, in the event of his unexpected death, that he left a will designating the Podrowskis, his great-grandchildren and multiple charities as his estate's beneficiaries – and then he realized that it would be impossible to explain how the money was his. He promptly decided to have Phil liquidate only $100,000 of it right away, planning to place the remaining bars and coins – with Pongo's help – into a dozen large safe deposit boxes inside Marine Midland Bank and Upstate Bank in Poughkeepsie. He decided to pay the rent on the boxes six years in advance. Just in case something might happen to him to keep him from getting to the bank.

Pongo pointed out to Franklin that it was ironic he'd remembered all that wealth on virtually the same day the Congress voted to extend the "W" Bush era tax cuts for the wealthy and super-wealthy. The extension was supported and signed into law by President Obama after Republicans threatened to cut off extended Unemployment Compensation benefits for long-term out-of-work 2008 financial meltdown survivors. Even progressive U.S. Sen. Franken voted for it – much to the frustration of his supporters.

"Well I s'pose that will make this windfall last a little longer," Franklin said. "But I'd have been much more pleased to have seen the additional revenues from the expiration of those tax cuts go toward helping the non-wealthy."

"Christ," Pongo said, "those additional revenues probably would've just been popped into a pneumatic tube over to the Pentagon."

Franklin and Pongo planned to scatter the $100,000 of their windfall in multiple $9,990 accounts at Marine Midland and each of the other banks and credit unions in Poughkeepsie so as to avoid any pesky red flag reports to the IRS – not because Franklin didn't want to pay taxes on his windfall, but because he didn't want to risk any unnecessary examination of his Percy Van Mullder alter ego's background.

But then Phil came up with a better idea.

If people or organizations were to decide in the future to punish Franklin, the Podrowski's and others for their USA-SBR activism, the first thing they would do, Phil said, would be to follow their money trail.

Ironically, Phil said, the best way to aim at giving a dead end to those with ill will toward their efforts would be to do exactly what Franklin already had done: "dig up" the gold, _again_, so to speak.

A decade or so earlier, he explained, his Dad Tom had signed over to him two densely-wooded Hyde Park-area acres held by the Podrowski family more than 25 years which had long ago been owned by the Roosevelt family. The land, located less than a mile from the National Park Service's Roosevelt Top Cottage, was intended by Tom to be held as a long-term investment for Phil and Pongo.

If and when – and the 'if' part wasn't really in doubt – any hyper-capitalists wanting the USA-SBR to fail were to discover, or, were to be told the primary source of the organization's funding, not only would no one question someone discovering "buried treasure" on old Roosevelt property, but the Podrowski's could quietly settle all the income tax issues long before any public revelations about the "found" windfall.

Everyone agreed with Phil's strategy. The next morning Phil and Pongo drove to the Podrowski's Hyde Park property and dug and stirred up enough dirt to make it appear that 1,200 pounds of long-lost lucre had been discovered and excavated. Just in case anyone checked years later.

Then Phil contacted his Dad's accountant to report – on the condition of absolute confidentiality – the "discovered treasure" so all of the appropriate tax filings could take place. The accountant figured out that there would be a Federal tax liability of at least 35 percent plus another 7 percent liability for New York state income taxes. That left a net of more than $60 million for the group to use. All agreed Franklin should decide how the funds would be used. Phil had "Percy 'Scruples' Van Mullder" added as a joint tenant for each bank account and for all of the safe deposit boxes where the gold was stored.

* * *

TESTING THE BIG SKY WATERS – AND GRATEFUL FOR AN OLD MAN'S QUESTION

Franklin's plan for the trip to Montana was to travel with Pongo, Harry and Idris via Amtrak to Kalispell, MT, where Pongo would rent a car so they could drive south to the University of Montana in Missoula. Franklin had fond memories of his travels to Glacier National Park when he was President, so he looked forward to the views as the train traveled along the southern border of the snow-packed park.

After an internet search, Franklin decided to look up local Missoula activist Ellie Hill, who operated the state's largest shelter for the homeless. Ms. Hill agreed to help Franklin/Percy and the others to distribute fliers for an organizing meeting and connected them with other Missoula area activists. She even agreed to contact local news media to schedule a small press conference at which Franklin/Percy and Idris would be introduced as the primary spokespersons for the organizing effort.

The press gathering the next day with reporters from the Daily Missoulian, the Missoula Independent and the local NBC television affiliate was mostly an educational session, as Idris and Franklin/Percy spent the entire time explaining each of the USA-SBR provisions.

The reporters appeared to take most of the provisions in stride, at least until they reached the final clause about reparations for Native Americans and for African-Americans descended from persons who were slaves during the Civil War.

Reggie Royfontler of the Missoulian summed it up best for the entire group of journalists:

"Are you worried that non-Indians and non-blacks are going to be afraid of the economic power those reparations will create?"

"We're mostly concerned about one major thing: trying to make amends for shameful periods in our history," Franklin/Percy said.

"If our country can find it in our hearts to pay reparations to Japanese-Americans who were unconstitutionally shunted into concentration camps in World War Two for three and a half years, then we can surely find the will to try to make amends for even worse offenses against our own people.

"The way we see it, when it comes to slavery and the quasi-slavery of forced assignment to reservations after the theft of land and resources there should be no statute of limitations – just as with murder.

"To let the millions of victims of our country's injustices committed against African-Americans and Native Americans go another year without formal compensation is just asking for an attack of bad karma on our entire country.

"It is shamefully past time for that provision of the USA-SBR and don't let anyone tell you it's not."

* * *

Franklin also took out full-page display ads in the Daily Missoulian and the Missoula Independent weekly promoting the organizational meeting. Ms. Hill was kind enough to agree to emcee, though she couldn't guarantee her support for every last detail of the proposed Second Bill of Rights.

About 600 persons of all ages showed up for the gathering, two-thirds of them Native Americans from western Montana and northern Idaho reservations. Looking out into the crowd as he walked up the center aisle to the podium at the front of the University Center Theater, Franklin didn't see a single person with facial or arm sensillum-type fine fur (the kind *only he* could see) – which did not surprise him.

Many of the attendees remarked during the question-and-answer session at the end of the presentation that they were impressed at just how young Franklin and his entourage were to be undertaking such a daunting project.

"Well, heck, we figure, if we can start this young," Franklin/Percy told the crowd, "we *just might* finish this up by the time we're eligible for Social Security retirement. No, seriously, our goal is to have the first significant number of pro-USA-SBR state legislators and members of Congress elected during the 2016 general election.

"But it's going to take virtually every last one of yourselves prodding existing lawmakers and members of Congress while corralling good candidates to replace the sitting lawmakers who don't want to back this project. If we all work together, this can happen.

"Just remember, it took five years for the National Organization of Women to convince the Congress to pass the Equal Rights Amendment and another five years to get 35 of the required 38 states to ratify it. We've got almost six years before the 2016 general election. We intend to organize in virtually every state in the union between now and then.

"We came to Montana first because we admire the streak of grassroots democracy that exists in Montana. A streak which emboldened your state's legislators to ratify the Equal Rights Amendment in 1974. A streak which has propelled your brightest, most courageous, most dependable citizens to take to the streets from time to time when government and business actions threaten the precious scenic resources of this great state.

"This Second Bill of Rights **can** be achieved if enough people are willing to hold their representatives and senators accountable. Before you leave this evening, please make sure you each of you signs up at the back of the auditorium to contact at least three state legislators, your U.S. House representative and your U.S. Senators either by phone or by mail to support this.

"And please share with us on our Facebook page or on our website what kinds of responses you get from each elected official you contact. Please make sure you take with you enough copies of the proposed Second Bill of Rights to share with each elected official you contact."

To Franklin's surprise, every last one of the 1,500 copies of the proposed Constitutional Amendment were taken for distribution and all but a small handful of the persons attending signed up to contact their elected officials. There were volunteers' names in the spaces next to each and every elected Montana official on the master sign-up list; the spaces next to each of their U.S. Senators' names were filled with the names of six attendees each.

As they prepared to leave after chatting for more than an hour with the activists in attendance, Ms. Hill gave Franklin/Percy repeated pats on the back, both literally and figuratively, for his positive, optimistic attitude.

"I don't know that I ever remember meeting someone who seemed to have as much faith in the good will of the people as you do," she said. "There's something familiar about you, though, something I can't quite put my finger on."

"It's probably that upstate New York accent I'm burdened with," Franklin/Percy said. "Almost as bad as having a lisp."

"No, nothing like that, Percy. You acquit yourself quite nicely in public – truly something remarkable for someone just 19 or 20 years old. I predict you'll make a positive impression wherever you go."

All four of the traveling Poughkeepsie activists thanked Ms. Hill profusely for her hospitality as they left for their hotel rooms. They had an early wake-up call set for the following morning when they were to leave for Bozeman and Montana State University; Franklin set his alarm clock an hour early to give him time to get 2,000 more copies of the USA-SBR at the local Kinkos.

*　*　*

Franklin already had taken out display ads in the Bozeman Daily Chronicle and Billings Gazette promoting their organizing meetings in Bozeman two nights later and in Billings two nights after that. They were scheduled to meet briefly the following afternoon in Bozeman with actors Jeff Bridges and Peter Fonda, both of Livingston, plus members of the Bozeman chapter of the Citizens Climate Lobby.

Idris and Harry were curious about the backgrounds of Bridges and Fonda, so Franklin printed out and was about to share with them copies of IMDB filmographies for both actors, including their Academy award nominations and wins.

But, just as he was about to hand the printouts to Idris and Harry, Pongo said, simply, "Righteous Lebowski *Dude* and Easy Rider Captain America."

"No shit, man?!" Harry said. "We're actually going to meet **those** two dudes?!! That's just too tight!"

"Sounds like Harry and I better bring along autograph books for this meet-up," Idris added. "You think they'll be OK with us taking some selfies with them?"

"You idiots are going to embarrass us all, aren't you?" Pongo said.

"Let's try to remember why we're here, OK, gentlemen?" Franklin said. "Mr. Bridges and Mr. Fonda could help bring a fair amount of recognition to our campaign, but they're not wild-eyed radicals. We need to be able to convince them we're serious about **what we're doing**, _not_ that we're serious autograph hounds."

The meeting with Bridges, Fonda and the Citizens Climate Lobby representatives went surprisingly well. While the actors wouldn't necessarily commit to all provisions in the USA-SBR, they agreed to appear at the organizational meeting on the MSU campus. Both men promised to offer positive words of encouragement to those gathered. Citizens Climate Lobby leaders volunteered to introduce Franklin/Percy and Idris to the crowd at the Strand Union Building Ballroom A the following evening and to help hand out copies of the USA-SBR for distribution to elected officials and others.

One personable 30-something Citizens Climate Lobby member even volunteered to help Franklin/Percy and Idris answer reporters' questions during the press conference set for later that afternoon.

At the gathering the next day, almost 200 persons of all ages showed up ready to take on the world. There was lots of applause for remarks by Bridges, Fonda, the Citizens Climate Lobby speakers and even for both Franklin/Percy and Idris.

"We have to help potential supporters of this new Bill of Rights understand the connection between predatory capitalism and the destruction of the environment," Franklin/Percy said. "People understand the likes of Koch Industries are focal points of massive greed. People understand fossil fuels emissions – the spewing of invisible CO2 and methane – are destroying our atmosphere as they warm the planet exponentially.

"But people don't seem to understand that the likes of Koch Industries are knowingly poisoning the planet's atmosphere and knowingly contributing massively to global warming *simply to pad their own corporate profits*. And they don't seem to understand how the likes of Koch Industries have actively suppressed efforts to hold them accountable for what should be considered criminal acts against the environment.

"It's now our job to make sure people become aware of those connections. It is now our job to make sure people understand this proposed Un-Screwing of America Second Bill of Rights (USA-SBR) will short-circuit the conscience-shocking actions of obscene profit pimps like the Kochs.

"It is *our job* to make sure people everywhere understand that blame for Grinnell Glacier in Glacier National Park going from hundreds of feet thickness in 1900 to, basically, a lake with small icebergs today rightfully rests with CO2 spewing companies like Koch.

"It is *our job* to make sure that the public understands that responsibility for the **complete disappearance of glaciers** in Glacier National Park by 20 years from now rightfully rests with the likes of predatory fossil fuels capitalists like the Kochs.

"It is *our responsibility* to make sure the public understands that the trillions of pine bark beetles killing off massive swaths of pine forests from Mexico north to Canada are thriving because winters which used to kill them keep getting progressively warmer **thanks to fossil fuels pushers like the Kochs**. *(A before and after photo of a Spokane, WA county park with dozens of mature brown-needled Ponderosa pines which had to be logged due to beetle damage was projected as Franklin spoke that last sentence.)*

"We know we can't *rely* on corporate media to spread that understanding, the understanding that this Second Bill of Rights is required to neuter the fossil fuels bulls. We have to rely on the courage and hard work of grassroots sentinels like yourselves.

"You will be doing nothing less than helping to save our civilization from a terminal illness, from its *own...deadly...addiction* - **to dirty energy**."

Members of the audience scattered in multiple different spots stood to applaud before the word addiction was all the way out of Franklin's mouth. The remainder of the audience quickly joined in the standing applause, not stopping for more than two minutes.

By the end of the evening, once again all their copies of the USA-SBR had been handed out to those attending. And, as in Missoula, there were no empty sign-up spaces left on the pledge-to-contact-lawmakers sheet at the back of the ballroom.

Their pre-press conference meeting in Billings the next day with Northern Plains Resource Council (NPRC) leaders went much the same. The NPRC reps agreed to introduce them at the gathering in the MSU-Billings Student Union Petro Theater the next evening.

About 150 persons, mostly 20-something students, showed up. All appeared to be enthusiastic about the USA-SBR. There were plenty of questions for Franklin/Percy and Idris to answer, but none of the questioners appeared to be Fox News acolytes. By the end of the meeting, there appeared to be just as much enthusiasm for the cause as was evident at the gatherings in Missoula and Bozeman. All 1,500 new copies of the USA-SBR they'd picked up earlier from the Billings Kinkos were quickly distributed by Pongo and Harry during the gathering.

During the question and answer session following the *"Capitalism: A Love Story"* screening, one 50-something grandfatherly-looking man's question made Franklin stop and think.

"Just what is your motivation, what is it that stirred you up inside to start a project which might end up taking you 15 years or more to complete, if ever? A project that brings you no personal financial gain whatsoever?" the fair-complected mustachioed white-haired man asked.

"In my short life, I've traveled all around this fine country and to other nations around this planet," Franklin said softly and slowly. "No matter how different the landscape, no matter how different the demographics, no matter how different the climate, the people all have one thing in common, with rare exceptions: they try to treat others the way they would want to be treated.

"The two main exceptions to that rule involve religious extremists and predatory business practices. There always will be freedom of religion, so we'll always have to live with the risk of that kind of extremism.

"But the effects of predatory business practices – or, more simply put, **_greed_** – are visible everywhere there is poverty to be found, everywhere there is hunger, everywhere there is homelessness, everywhere there is a young person who can't afford college, everywhere there is a financially struggling person who's enticed by benefits to enlist in the military, everywhere there is an inmate in a for-profit prison. Unchecked greed does **not** need to be a fact of life in the richest country on the planet.

"The introduction of the Constitution states in the boldest print, 'We, The People' – **_not_** 'We, the Corporations' **nor** 'We, the Banking Interests.' The goals of a more perfect union, justice, tranquility and general welfare are **in no way** supported by unchecked greed.

"If people like you and me want our children, our grandchildren and our great-grandchildren not to be potential victims of the culture of predatory capitalism, not to be victims of the cultures of permanent war and fossil fuels addiction which benefit only Wall Street short-term investors – then, we must do what we can to ensure those cultures are prohibited by our Constitution or, at the very least, shamed into non-existence.

"This *"Un-Screwing of America Second Bill of Rights"* is what we decided would be our best effort to make that happen. We have no guarantee of success. But if we do nothing, we are guaranteed to fail. And our descendants are guaranteed to be victims.

"We may never be able to mandate that people and corporations *play nice* with their neighbors, but we can mandate that people and corporations not actively screw over their neighbors.

"That, after all, is the role of government: to protect people from social and economic predators, to work to achieve social and economic justice. Notwithstanding all the bullshit Ronald Reagan said about government being the problem.

"Government is the problem only if you're a predator who doesn't want to be caught. And that buttwipe Reagan knew that all along."

The middle-aged avuncular gentleman who asked the question about motivation promptly stood up and applauded; the rest of the audience joined him. The standing ovation lasted more than a minute.

The Poughkeepsie bunch were pleasantly surprised, nay stunned, to see that Franklin's response to the elderly man aired virtually verbatim in its entirety on the 10 p.m. news of the local CBS affiliate that night. It actually went viral on the internet within three days, with more than 10 million hits. It was even listed on the "Daily Kos Recommended" list sent each day to Daily Kos E-Mail subscribers for an unprecedented full calendar week.

Unfortunately, their brief claim to fame was pushed aside by national and local media outlets the next day when news broke of U.S. Rep. Gabby Giffords being critically wounded with severe brain damage, shot at point-blank range in an assassination attempt during a meet-the-constituents gathering outside a Tucson, AZ Safeway supermarket. An additional 18 persons were shot in the same incident, leaving six persons dead, including U.S. District Court Chief Judge John Roll. The shooter was a mentally ill 22-year-old Community College student who'd been suspended due to his bizarre behaviors. He had been allowed to buy a semi-automatic pistol at a Tucson Sportsman's Warehouse store because his mental health issues at Pima College had not become part of a court proceeding and, therefore, hadn't ended up in the government's mental health database.

"*Three cheers for the Second Amendment!*" Franklin thought to himself sarcastically.

* * *

NATURE'S LITTLE QUIRKY QUAKES

The following day, the group decided to take a side-trip rather than drive straight back to the Kalispell Amtrak station. They ventured into West Yellowstone, stopped for an hour or so at Old Faithful and then drove to Montana's Quake Lake State Park, where a 7.5 Richter Scale earthquake at Hebgen Lake on Aug. 17, 1959 caused the entire side of one mountain to collapse and bury 28 campers under 50 to 60 feet of rock and rubble, where they remain buried to this day. The group toured the visitor center and walked up the trail showing just how far the 80 million tons of rock and debris traveled from near the top of the mountain on the southwest side of the Madison River up the side of the mountain on the opposite side of the river.

"Mind-blowing," was all Pongo could say as he pondered the remains of the people permanently entombed far below his feet.

"What it must've been like to feel the hurricane-force wind from the rockslide and see that wall of debris coming at you knowing there was nothing you could do," Harry said. "I'll bet they still tried to run up the side of mountain to get away from it. They'd have needed the speed of a cheetah, though."

The group suddenly noticed Franklin solemnly bent on one knee, appearing to pray for the dead still buried there. They left him to himself.

* * *

During the 375-mile drive back from Quake Lake to the car rental agency near the Kalispell Amtrak station, the four Poughkeepsie compatriots mused about what they'd started during the previous week.

"Have any of you thought about the kind of corporate blowback this thing might aim in our direction?" Harry asked. "I mean, crap-on-a-biscuit, what if people actually start taking this seriously?"

"The more corporate blowback, the more publicity we get," Franklin said. "The more publicity we get, the more support we'll get."

"And, just maybe, the more intense the opposition will get," Idris said.

"We can't think that way," Franklin said. "We have to be confident that the truth, the righteousness of this cause, will filter through to people.

"The more heat we take from Slash Lugbuch and his semi-literate followers, the more sympathy we'll gain from good people who understand Slashers are nothing more than minions of conscienceless corporations which don't care if the middle class is crushed, as long as they can eke out a nice profit."

"You know we're all behind you on this, Franklin," Pongo said. "But at some point, don't we need to be concerned about you being recognized? Remember that nice lady – Ms. Hill, right? – the one who helped us so much in Missoula? It sure seemed like she was close to recognizing you.

"Would you _**please**_, for Christ's sake, re-consider some facial hair - or at least some red or black hair dye?"

"I guess a moustache could work," Franklin said. "And I wouldn't mind trying the black hair dye, at least for a few weeks. I just don't want my shirt collars ending up black. Let's see how it works when we get back, OK?"

* * *

In the back of his mind, Idris already was thinking the actors they got to know in Bozeman were pretty darned savvy to have found such a spectacularly beautiful place to live. He could easily picture himself someday residing among the beautiful peaks and valleys of the Yellowstone, Gallatin, Madison or Jefferson rivers.

As they drove west along Highway 2 skirting the snowy southern border of Glacier National Park en route to Kalispell, Idris asked the others, "How can people who own or operate for-profit corporations - people who depend on Wall Street's thirst for short-term profits – how can they ignore the reality that they're putting all of this – all of these sacred places – at risk of destruction? All for just a few years or a few decades of **super**-profits, rather than just being satisfied with modest profits."

"They can do it because the addiction to accumulation of great wealth is a form of sociopathy," Pongo said. "Their lust for lucre has digested and defecated their own consciences, their ability to see beyond next year's quarterly profit reporting. It's like, when they were kids, they played Monopoly a few hundred times too many and now they think real life is a game you win only by dying with the most money.

"Their usual claims to be strong religious fundamentalists notwithstanding, they have a congenitally difficult time grasping the scripture about it being harder for a rich man to get into heaven than for a camel to pass through the eye of a needle."

"They probably just all have these huge rich-guy 50-foot tall needles from way back in those days when Fred Flintstone was screwing around with dinosaurs," Harry laughed. The others winced at Harry's goofy anachronistic reference, but let it pass.

"All I know is, if we can ever actually get this country un-screwed, un-fucked, whatever the most palatably descriptive verb is, I wouldn't mind coming back to this place to stay. There is a real peace here," Idris said.

"Shit, you urine-brained dick," Harry said. "It's peaceful because _almost no one lives here._ Unless you count moose and wolves – and slack-jawed _Cletus Spuckler_ wilderness yokel unicorn-poachers who vote Republican."

* * *

The long train ride back to Poughkeepsie from Kalispell was a nice break from the constant interactions with strangers over the previous week-plus. At least six times during the trip, Franklin and Pongo saw passengers watching Franklin's/Percy's Billings speech on YouTube using their laptops, tablets, Kindles or smart phones. The last time they witnessed a passenger doing that, the two friends clasped each other's shoulders and simply looked at each other, smiling and nodding, saying wordlessly to each other, "This thing that we're trying to make happen, it is a fine thing, a blessed thing."

BACK HOME IN THE HUDSON VALLEY: MOVING AHEAD

Once back in Poughkeepsie, the four traveling buddies settled back into their respective work and school routines fairly seamlessly. Heather and Bianca – whom Pongo and Harry had frequently texted and Facebooked during the trip – each made sure their respective beaus promptly addressed their companionship needs the day after they returned. Heather practically dragged Pongo by his johnson into her bedroom when he came over to take her out for dinner.

Franklin brought Mr. Mitchell up to speed on their rail and road travel. Mr. Mitchell said he followed their appearances on YouTube, but that Holly actually brought her laptop to class to re-play his Billings, MT speech on YouTube for everyone to watch. He told Franklin/Percy his aptitude for public speaking belied his youth.

"You really seem to know how to work a crowd, how to tell a joke," Mr. Mitchell said. "You must've been bitten by the political bug when you were just out of diapers."

"Who said I was out of diapers?" Franklin/Percy joked, flashing that trademark FDR smile – minus the prominent cigarette holder clamped between his teeth.

"All I know is, you keep this up, and you're going to have to deal with groupies and such, young man!" Mr. Mitchell warned. "I think Ms. Cioffi (the principal's secretary) actually had a video paparazzi-type come to school yesterday asking for your schedule. Of course, she politely declined to share that."

"Oh, crap. Can't have that - at least, not if I'm not at an organizing function."

"My humble advice: get used to it."

* * *

Chet Dale made sure to greet Franklin/Percy as soon as Franklin walked in the door at Adams Landscaping – with an autograph book shoved into Franklin's face and a faux teenybopper squeal.

"Please, sir, will you sign my left tit?" Chet grinned.

"So even old farts like you know how to watch YouTube, eh?" Franklin said.

They joked around for a few minutes and Franklin regaled Chet with details of their travels in Big Sky country. Chet mentioned that one of his favorite uncles had lived in Livingston and Gardiner when Chet was growing up; Chet said some of his fondest memories were playing cowboys and Indians with his young cousins in the shadows of the Roosevelt Arch at the north entrance to Yellowstone.

"Guess I'd better think twice before giving you so much time off again, Scruples. You might decide the lovely lasses of Montana's Paradise Valley have the fertile grounds where you were intend to plant your seeds."

"You never know, Yoda. If living in Poughkeepsie could do to me what it's clearly done to you, I just might have to trot back to the Big Sky tomorrow," Franklin cracked.

"Just let me know first chance you get, trotter," Chet said. "'Cause it'll take me a good five minutes to find someone as competent as you to fill your spot on the schedule." Which was as bald-faced a lie as Chet had ever told.

But before they could spend too much time B.S.-ing, it was back to work for Franklin/Percy sorting bare root roses, seed packet shipments, hardware stock, etc. Franklin actually felt more at home than ever after the trip; Chet didn't need to worry about Scruples fleeing to greener pastures.

* * *

The next Sunday meeting of the Podrowskis, O'Learys, Swansons, Petersons and other keepers of the Franklin/Percy identity secrets brought questions of concern for Franklin. Several asked Franklin if abandoning a low profile once and for all really was the smartest thing to do. They also commented on his decision to dye his hair black.

"You must be having some concerns about people connecting your appearance and your accent and speech patterns," Mel Peterson said.

"Actually, not so much, Mel," Franklin said. "But I appreciate your concern. I've tried to adjust my speaking patterns a little bit, and I don't think very many people even remember what I looked like in my previous life when I was under 35 years old."

"Well, shit, something must be worrying you or you wouldn't have changed your hair," Sam Swanson said.

"There was some concern by my fellow travelers when a woman who helped us in Missoula seemed to sense something unusual about me. But, for all we know, I might've reminded her of her favorite childhood babysitter."

"We're not too worried about that kind of thing right now, Mr. President. I think, with the new hair shade and moustache you're sprouting, you'll probably be just fine," Phil Podrowski said. "We just hope you'll be prudent about how you handle yourself if the national media come calling down the road.

"If they pick up on the speech patterns and start suggesting you're actively trying as Percy to imitate FDR, well, it could suck the credibility out of what you're trying to do. You know, make it look like you're doing the entire thing just to put a spotlight on yourself."

"I understand completely. That's why I'm hoping Idris will take a more prominent role with the organizing effort. I don't see how we can be taken too seriously when I haven't even graduated from high school yet," Franklin said.

"Well, hell, I'm not even 30 years old," Idris said. "It's not like I have a mountain of life experience."

"If any of you haven't seen that Billings speech, you need to watch it," Bianca said. "And, if you've seen it and you still think Franklin will be seen as some kind of lightweight, you need to watch it again.

"If anyone can get this process going, if anyone has the energy and drive to do it, it's our former President here."

"The real test will be when those Fox News pricks decide he's actually making an impact," Harry said. "The shitstorm they would unleash if they perceive he's really making a difference will put us all under the microscope.

"So, if you have any bales of dope in your basement, now might be a good time to consume or dispose."

"You're probably the only one who needs to worry about his stash status, Hairyback," Pongo said. "As for that Lugbuch prick and his Rupert Murdoch affiliates, I'm pretty confidant Franklin can give as good as he gets.

"Don't know if you all recall – some of us weren't exactly born back then, y'know – but Franklin did pretty damned well with multiple migraine-inducing servings of rancid recycled ratshit on his plate. You know, a few little minor distractions like psycho Hitler, scrotuMussolini, Hirohito-sheet-o, the Great Depression, lots o' starving po' folk, the Dust Bowlerama – you know, little nuisances."

"I'm with Pongo on this," Heather said. "Let's not put the cart before the horse. Let's give Franklin and our guys the chance to get their Second Bill of Rights off the ground.

"The worst that can happen is people who don't want to show their true colors just might **have** to. And a lot of folks might finally take notice that the emperor's new clothes make for a really disgusting view."

"Teabags for the teabaggers – love it!" Harry said.

* * *

Once Franklin realized his minor celebrity status – thanks to Holly - among his fellow students in his spring semester Environmental Science class actually would be survivable, he was able to focus on trying to repeat his 4.0 GPA from the fall semester.

He was relieved he only had the distraction of Holly's stunning good looks for just the one class again. But he still couldn't help his physiological reactions to the sight of her – what might have been called in his earlier life an ache in the loins – so he made sure his seat in the Enviro Sci hour was two full rows in front of Holly.

The weeks mostly flew by, what with so much of his spare time taken up with classwork and his job at Adams Landscaping. Chet kept pestering him to consider three days a week off the schedule so Franklin/Percy could actually have a life, but he always politely declined. Franklin suspected more free time probably would simply enable his teenaged hormones to get him into trouble, along with everyone else who knew his real identity. Big trouble.

* * *

RISING SUN FORESIGHT: MAYBE WE'RE RIGHT ABOUT OTHER STUFF?

O n March 11, eight weeks after classes started, Mr. Mitchell was waiting for Franklin/Percy at the main Poughkeepsie High entrance when Franklin arrived at 8:15 a.m.

"How did you know?" Mr. Mitchell asked.

"How did I know what?!!" Franklin/Percy responded.

"So, you haven't seen TV news yet today." Mr. Mitchell said flatly. "You need to."

"Why?"

"Because there's been a monumental disaster in Fukushima, Japan. There was a 9.0 earthquake in the ocean east of there, followed by a massive tsunami which overwhelmed the nuclear power plant there.

"There were multiple meltdowns. Huge plumes of highly radioactive emissions exploded into the air. Enormous areas for miles in all directions have been contaminated, probably for decades, maybe even centuries. Not to mention, maybe 20,000 people being drowned in the tsunami – like the December 2004 tsunami that hit Thailand.

"So, how did you know to include a provision in the USA-SBR about that specific risk??!"

"Well, sir, I **had _no_ way** to know that would happen. I **_did_** know it was a real **risk**. Thanks to the O'Learys, I had read enough about nuclear power and nuclear wastes to know tsunamis can mean an existential disaster for anyone living near a coastal nuke plant."

"All I can tell you is, as far as I'm concerned, your credibility as a young adult just went up to 12 on a scale of 10 – at least, as far as I'm concerned. I wouldn't be surprised if you get some news media contacts from people in Montana who noticed your prescience with the USA-SBR copies you had distributed there."

"We'll deal with that when the time comes," Franklin said.

"It's always nice when you're told you were right about something. It would be even nicer to get the respect that goes along with having some foresight.

"Respect is hard to come by when you're barely 20 years old. My thoughts right now are mostly with the families of those poor souls in Fukushima whose lives are over because their government allowed them to live in areas that never should've been developed.

"I imagine there probably are quite a few areas in this country – floodplains, riverfront properties and such – places where there are lots of residences which local governments should never have allowed to be built."

"You would be imagining correctly, Percy," Mr. Mitchell said. "Maybe that kind of risk is something you should discuss at the next USA-SBR rally you have.

"For what it's worth, young man, I'm in there pitchin' for ya'."

"It is appreciated, Mr. M."

* * *

CINCY-TUCKY FUN

By the time high school spring break rolled around the second full week of April, Franklin was itching to get time off to get back on the road to drum up support for USA-SBR.

This time, Harry decided to keep the home fires burning while Pongo and Idris joined Franklin for an Amtrak trip to Cincinnati for a gathering at the Main Street Cinema in the University of Cincinnati Tangeman University Center followed by a jaunt to Lexington, KY for a session at the University of Kentucky Student Center.

Franklin/Percy E-Mailed Cincinnati frequenters George Clooney and Woody Harrelson copies of the USA-SBR plus the link to the YouTube video of Franklin's Billings speech. To his everlasting shock, both gentlemen accepted his invitation to speak at the event; Clooney even offered to introduce Franklin/Percy and Idris.

At least 500 people – mostly under 40 – packed one of the student union theaters for the Cincinnati presentation. Both Clooney and Harrelson offered enthusiastic encouragement for their efforts and encouraged voters to enlist strong candidates for primary challenges against incumbents of both parties who balk at backing this Second Bill of Rights.

Stepping out onto the stage to chants of "Munson, Munson, Munson" from fans of his *"Kingpin"* role, Harrelson was pelted lightly with packs of Twinkies, an homage to his recent *"Zombieland"* post-apocalyptic comedy.

As he munched on one of the tossed Twinkie packs, Harrelson explained with gusto that he was convinced passage of the new Bill of Rights would undercut continued efforts by some of the for-profit healthcare industry to block legalization of both medicinal and recreational marijuana nationwide. Anticipating that the states of Washington and Colorado might during the following year's general election approve recreational marijuana use, he praised the provision which would prohibit nationwide any criminal or civil charges against adults for growing at home natural substances which were not designated as toxic or carcinogenic by the FDA.

Harrelson even did his own stand-up comedy take for 10 minutes on what it means for the average working class stiff to "bend over and take one for the team" to keep the likes of Charles and David Koch able to buy up as many political hacks as it takes to keep Big Oil in control of the Permanent War culture.

Clooney, a Lexington, KY native, also agreed to introduce the Poughkeepsie guys at their University of Kentucky rally two days later. Franklin, Idris and Pongo also convinced Lexington native Michael O'Bannion - via E-Mail, phone calls and YouTube links - to appear briefly for their cause there. Idris and Pongo had long been huge fans of O'Bannion's work in the movie "*Responsibility Lane*" – for which he received a Best Supporting Actor Oscar nomination – as well as his work in "*Shelter Needs*" and "*Empire of the Corrupt.*"

The UK rally – which, like the University of Cincinnati rally, had been promoted in a news conference covered by at least two local TV news teams three days earlier – had a somewhat smaller-than-hoped-for turnout, but the crowd nevertheless was primed to pump up the volume. Clooney's and O'Bannion's presence alone ratcheted up the pulse of the attendees – there was a certain degree of swooning in the air among the distaff attendees.

By the time they'd completed both rallies, the attendees had scooped up a total of 9,700 copies of the USA-SBR, with more than 1,000 persons signed up to contact elected officials and share those copies.

✳ ✳ ✳

On their drive back to the Cincinnati car rental agency near the Amtrak Station, Pongo, Idris and Franklin discussed more long-term strategy.

"Do you maybe want to think about finding a way to hire a project manager who can co-ordinate responses to inquiries about this project? You know, so we have someone who can at least respond to inquiries on our website and react to contacts from elected officials," Pongo said.

"We're bound to have at least a few elected people reach out to us at some point if even a small fraction of the people who've signed up to contact their representatives follow through, after all."

"I do have enough resources now – from the gold we liquidated – that we could do that," Franklin said. "I've been answering inquiries on the web site every day, usually late in the evening once I'm home from work. We probably should've thought about a project manager as soon as we got back from Montana, though - but not a single Montana elected official reached out to us."

"Can't say as I'm shocked by that," Idris said. "It'll take a lot more than a few hundred or even a few thousand grass roots voter contacts in Montana for us to be taken seriously."

"Then, as soon as we have a chance once we're back in Poughkeepsie, I'll meet up with Pongo, Heather and Bianca to discuss the criteria we want to use for selecting this project manager and how we're going to go about recruiting the right person," Franklin said. "We need to make this a priority if we intend for this to succeed."

"Agreed," Idris and Pongo said almost simultaneously.

✳ ✳ ✳

Lovin' Liz and Winnin' the New Face Lottery

Two days after their return, Pongo, Heather, Bianca and Franklin met at the Podrowskis' to reach agreement on recruiting the USA-SBR project manager. They decided to hire a professional head-hunter for the position.

Franklin and Pongo traveled to New York City for an 8 a.m. meeting with their preferred head-hunter on April 26 (fortunately for Pongo, he didn't have to get special dispensation for a day off, because his work hours were still on an off-season schedule, with just 32 hours a week of work). The meeting went smoothly, with the head-hunter concurring with all of their criteria for the position. He promised to have at least six qualified candidates to interview with them for the position within 30 days. Franklin mentioned that that would give them just enough time to arrange to lease or purchase office space in Poughkeepsie for their new hire.

Their meeting finished up around 9:30 a.m., giving them just enough time to walk the six blocks to the site of the building where the Daily Show was taped for that night's broadcast. Both Franklin and Pongo were itching to see Elizabeth Warren in person there.

After the taping was completed, as Franklin and Pongo were walking the six blocks back to the parking facility to get Franklin's Civic, they did a Siskel and Ebert-type review of the program.

"She had me at 'word-barf'," Pongo said, referring to Warren's description of fine print language in credit card contracts.

"She actually, genuinely, earnestly wants to protect middle class families from unknowingly getting sucked into unwanted financial risks through sneaky fine-print financial services agreements," Franklin said. "Like Jon said, that makes her a 'draconian emperor of finance' to corporations thriving on the worst predatory features of capitalism."

"She didn't actually come out and say it, but it's clear she understands that opposition to the Consumer Financial Protection Bureau is entirely based on craven, heartless, Simon Legree-style greed," Pongo said. "When she quoted the financial industry's contention that 'those families will be just fine' despite being screwed over – how fucking cold-bloodedly sociopathic can that industry get?"

"God bless her soul," Franklin said. "If I were running against her in a Presidential primary, I would drop out and ask all my delegates to pledge themselves to her – and I'd beg her just for a chance to be in her cabinet, even as secretary of keeping the coffee hot, if that's all that were available. She is that good.

"Why in hell is **she** _not_ President?"

"Maybe someday, Sir, just maybe."

"And what about that piece on 9/11 first responders not having health insurance coverage?" Franklin asked. "Has this country fallen so far that it can't even afford to take care of its heroes?

"Why aren't people out in the streets with torches and pitchforks demanding that every member of Congress who voted against coverage for those heroes be expelled immediately?"

"Probably because there is so much bullshit committed by Congress these days, now that the House is back in Republican control, people are just de-sensitized to it, numbed by it," Pongo said.

"No wonder so many people are addicted to tranquilizers and painkillers," Franklin mused.

Both of them were so pissed off that, at first, when they started their drive back to Poughkeepsie, they just sat silently. Finally, Pongo popped the comedy CD "Robin Williams Live 2002" into the car stereo. Within 10 minutes, both of them were laughing so hard, tears were dripping off their chins.

* * *

Bin Laden's Excedrin Headache #42; No Vaccinations Against Unintended Consequences

L ess than a week later, on May 2, Franklin, Pongo and Phil were watching some TV over a late dinner after Pongo and Franklin got home from their respective shifts at work when President Obama broke the news that U.S. Navy Seal Team 6 had succeeded in tracking down Osama Bin Laden in his secret compound located less than a mile from the Pakistan national military academy complex. Shot dead in the head as he cowered in a corner, he was later buried at sea. What happened to the stash of porn videos found with Bin Laden wasn't really made clear by the U.S. military, which decided to keep the contents secret.

"Think he figured out a way to share the images with his 72 heavenly virgins?" Pongo asked.

"Maybe he's already hard at work with them making little baby terrorist angels," Franklin said. "I doubt they worry much about contraception in paradise, do you?"

Fox News-y angry uncles all over the country spent the next year and a half, in advance of the 2012 general election, finding countless different ways not to give President Obama credit for overseeing the successful hunt for the World's Most Wanted Man. And just in case that wasn't enough, there were rumors of private "forgetting counseling" sessions being provided in local GOP offices around the country, just to help any poor souls who simply could not get out of their heads the sight of President Obama 'accomplishing' Dub'ya Bush's special 'mission.'

As for the Poughkeepsians, to a person, they were massively disappointed that the Seal 6 attack team hadn't had the restraint to take Bin Laden alive. Seeing him tried for the murders of the 2,977 persons killed in the 9/11 attacks would've set a stellar example for the rule of law in the U.S.A., Franklin said. They all agreed that having Bin Laden summarily shot in the head as he sat cowering in a corner could only inspire more revenge killings around the world.

* * *

About five weeks after Bin Laden's death, the CIA disclosed that they found Bin Laden through a ruse involving a technician posing as a public health polio vaccine immunizer. Disclosure of that strategy led to anti-Western Islamic activists murdering dozens of polio immunization workers in Pakistan and other countries, prompting some groups to stop participating in the polio vaccination program.

[*In August 2013 (though not disclosed 'til the following May), the CIA decided to stop using vaccination worker ruses, but the murders of vaccination workers continued as late as November 2014 and polio viruses linked by DNA to Pakistan were found to have spread as far as the sewers of Egypt and Israel in the meantime.*]*

As he was sharing breakfast with Pongo and Phil on June 11, 2011, Franklin read in the New York Times about the CIA's polio vaccination ruse. The Podrowskis weren't surprised in the slightest that this was a big deal to him.

"Why couldn't they have had the technician pose as an athlete's foot fungus eradication specialist or something like that?" Franklin asked. "Or maybe a Publisher's Clearinghouse Prize Patrol?

"Surely they could've come up with *something* that wouldn't've had huge public health impacts later on."

* CNN, 5/20/14; LA Times, 11/26/14; NY Times, 9/9/13; Express Tribune, 1/22/13

"Do they have Avon ladies in Pakistan?" Pongo asked. (They still would have the occasional Avon solicitor ring their doorbell seeking out Melanie. Hard to find the right shade of foundation for someone who's as pale as a corpse, though.)

Phil promptly started punching in data on his smart phone.

"No *shit*! They actually **do**!!" he said.

"I guess we know now that Avon hasn't cracked the CIA operatives market," Franklin said. "The invisible hand must be too busy applying eye shadow to pass out samples in Langley."

$$* \quad * \quad *$$

FOUND: ONE COMPETENT EMPTY-NESTER, BARGAIN PRICE

Just as promised by their Manhattan head-hunter, the Poughkeepsians received a list of six highly-qualified candidates on May 25 for the project manager job. Bianca contacted each of them and scheduled the interviews to take place the day after Memorial Day in their newly-leased furnished office space near the Poughkeepsie Mall. They decided to use a temp agency to fill a half-time support staff position until there was enough work to justify a full-time hire.

Considering that they were offering $77,500 for the full-time position, they felt that most of the interviewees were somewhat over-qualified. Two had Ph.D.'s; three had Master's Degrees with more than 20 years of experience each; one had two Master's Degrees, one in political science and the other in journalism, a bachelor's degree in education plus six years of experience working at daily newspapers.

In the end, they all agreed that the candidate with multiple degrees and actual newspaper experience – a 43-year-old empty-nester mother of two from Manchester, NH named Marcia Dirkenstack – stood head and shoulders above the rest. Plus, her resume showed she'd been a full-time campaign volunteer for Minnesota Sen. Al Franken in 2008. Pongo and Bianca explained in detail to Franklin about Sen. Franken's successful progressive talk radio program and his involvement with Saturday Night Live as a comedy writer and performer.

Marcia, a 5'5" dishwater blond who looked 10 years younger than her age, was only too happy to agree to take on the responsibilities they'd laid out for responding to website inquiries, USPS mail correspondence and telephone contacts, as well as responsibilities for arranging all details for upcoming USA-SBR rallies, including press conferences, guest emcees, lodging, transportation and so forth. She even agreed to come along on each future rally trip to act as their road manager and liaison for the local press corps, not to mention setting up all the F.I.C.A, Federal and state tax wage-withholding and other red tape paperwork required of any new business.

Franklin, Pongo and the others felt like they'd just won a modest lottery prize.

* * *

GRADDYAYSHUN REDUX: MEETING HER MA AND PA

Franklin's final exams went considerably better than expected, taking into account all of his travel, part-time job responsibilities, USA-SBR organizational set-up efforts and limited time for homework. He ended up with a 3.9 GPA, surprising himself but no one else among his circle of friends.

The graduation ceremony in mid-June felt a little silly to Franklin, considering his personal history, but he participated with a smile on his face, wanting to be as good a sport as anyone else. As the proceedings wound down that Friday evening and the families were embracing their newly-graduated children, Holly walked over and introduced her mother and father to Franklin/ Percy.

Franklin was pleasantly surprised to find Bud and Elinore Van Arsdale both to be charmingly gregarious and pleasantly insightful, with self-effacingly positive attitudes. He could see how Holly came by her hard-not-to-like affectionate perkiness.

He was proud to introduce Phil and Pongo to the Van Arsdales; he was impressed at how well the Podrowski men had practiced his backstory and how they managed to weave details of "Percy's" earlier life into their getting-to-know each other conversation. Phil and Pongo both spoke at length about their high hopes for the USA-SBR project and how it was almost entirely Franklin/Percy's idea.

Just the same, though, when everyone dispersed into the night, Franklin was relieved that he'd never have to go through another high school graduation again. Two in one lifetime was more than enough. Especially when the latest one served mostly to remind him of the absence of his mother and father.

* * *

WESTWARD HO, SISTER WIFE

Three days after graduation, Franklin, Idris and Bianca headed off with Marcia via Amtrak for their latest USA-SBR rally tour, which was to last just over two full weeks. This one included stops at University of Nevada-Las Vegas, Utah Valley University in Orem, University of Utah in Salt Lake City, Weber State University in Ogden, Utah State University in Logan, Idaho State University in Pocatello, Boise State University and University of Nevada-Reno.

This time, they decided to follow through on their earlier idea to shamelessly rip off Michael Moore's underwear and ramen noodles gimmick. After all, it had worked pretty darned well for him, even attracting a nuisance lawsuit from the Michigan Republican Party accusing him of trying to "buy votes" with the free handouts. Not to mention playing a significant role in the under-30 crowd voting overwhelmingly against "W" Bush in 2004.

Needless to say, Marcia drew lots of strange glances as she pushed two shopping carts full to the brim with Fruit of the Loom tighty-whities and Top Ramen Noodles through the Las Vegas Maryland Parkway Target checkout counter.

Before the eyebrow-raised checker could say anything, Marcia said, simply, "Sister wife." She was thinking that line probably would work even better up north on I-15 in Utah County in another two days.

"You look _really_ good," the female teenage checker said, awkwardly. "I mean, that is, for anybody who's had all those kids." (The checker's mother used to see lots of sister wives in the store before the St. George, UT Target opened 12 years earlier.)

"Well, thank you, young lady," Marcia said. "You look really good for someone who _hasn't_ had all those kids."

"Uhm, uh, thank you. Do you need help out to your car?"

"Naaaww," Marcia said, "one of my husbands is waiting outside the front door."

"No _SHIT!_" the checker said, clearly in awe.

"No shit," Marcia said. "Do you know if Target carries any sex toys?"

Blushing almost as red as the Honeycrisp apples in the produce aisle, the checker just shook her head side-to-side, eyes wide.

As Marcia exited, she made sure to wave Idris in through the door to take one of the carts while the checker still was watching.

"Little teenage airhead's probably about to crap her shorts wondering what it's like for a horny middle-aged white woman to have multiple African-American husbands," she thought to herself, grinning, knowing she'd just provided Target break room discussion fodder for the next couple of days.

* * *

The UNLV crowd lapped up the underwear and ramen noodles shtick the next day, as lots of laughter and applause echoed through the Student Union Ballroom.

The Poughkeepsie organizers had decided to dedicate the gathering to Las Vegas progressive icon Ralph Denton, who was then battling terminal cancer.

Franklin reminded the attendees that Denton would be the first to support the provisions of the USA-SBR establishing the right of everyone to a clean environment and to carcinogen-free air and water, including in all workplaces, as the best way to prevent cancer.

"If Ralph could be here today, he would tell you the real meaning of the Golden Rule is to try to make your city, your state, your world a truly better place for those who come after you," Franklin said.

"This Un-Screwing of America Second Bill of Rights – USA-SBR - is the key to putting power back into the hands of working people and taking it away from the current corporate overlords. The power working people **have** to *have* to make this a far better place for the working people who come after us.

"The Declaration of Independence speaks of life, liberty and the pursuit of happiness, but the Constitution does not, at least not specifically. The Constitution preamble speaks of the general welfare of the people, a more perfect union, domestic tranquility and justice.

"This USA-SBR will enshrine forever the essentials, the foundation and building blocks upon which will forever **thrive** a **guarantee** of that right to pursue happiness.

"The foundation and building blocks which will **guarantee** that our government shall be a government of 'We, the People' and not of 'Corporations, our Overlords.'

"The foundation and building blocks which will **guarantee** that **justice** is _not_ simply a *lofty concept* which can be purchased only by those with the priciest legal representation and lobbyists, but a *hard and fast reality* for **everyone** from the hardest-working teenage fry cook to the middle-aged paper-pusher still struggling to pay off student loans.

"This Second Bill of Rights will be the tool each of us can use to turn the playing field of life from the **steepest mountain** with the super-rich perpetually defending the goal line at its summit into a *certifiably-balanced* **level flat surface** giving *every living soul* – not just the children of privilege - a fair chance to live long and **prosper**. *(Franklin held up his right hand with the fingers split in the middle, Star Trek-style, to sustained applause.)*

"But it can actually become reality only with years of work by many, many fair-minded individuals like yourselves who are dedicated to ideals of social and economic justice. Ideals which _are_**, in fact, attainable**, contrary to what Ronnie Reagan told everyone almost 30 years ago. Ideals which are, in fact, _achievable_, contrary to how Ronnie Reagan _and_ Ayn Rand **misled** everyone decades ago, BUT *only if we take government back from the bulging-billfold bulls of Wall Street and **make** it work for the middle class!*

"To paraphrase the late and senile corporate tool Reagan, government by corporate overlords is not the *solution*, it is the **problem**!"

As the last syllable of "problem" echoed in the ballroom, the crowd spontaneously rose in a standing ovation which lasted three minutes. During the final minute, there was a sustained chant of, "Fuck O-ver-**Lords**! Fuck O-ver-**Lords**! Fuck O-ver-**Lords**!"

Franklin, beaming with thumbs-up to the crowd, thought to himself, *"Don't think we'll be hearing that one from the Utah crowds."*

He actually had a surprise coming about that.

* * *

Franklin/Percy's UNLV oration had 10,000 hits on YouTube within an hour after the gathering was dispersed. Within a day, it had 1 million hits. There was a small handful of non-snarky positive comments remarking how "Percy" appeared to be channeling FDR with his similar speech patterns.

Bianca noticed Franklin's old habit from his previous life of emphatically punctuating his major speaking points with enthusiastic head-bobs had morphed into much more subtle head gestures. Even more noticeably, he now seemed frequently to be speaking *with his hands*. She quietly asked Idris if he'd noticed that too.

He had. Idris speculated that Franklin's rejuvenated muscular legs might have something to do with that.

"It's hard to make spontaneous hand gestures, especially dramatic ones, if you're worried that you might lose your balance and fall splat on your honker if you let go of the podium in front of you," he whispered.

The 900 persons who had attended the rally took with them 5,000 copies of the USA-SBR. So many persons signed the elected official contact sheets, Marcia had to use a photocopier down the hall in the Student Union to make another two dozen copies while Franklin, Idris and Bianca addressed the crowd.

For the first time on their rally tours, their website too was jammed with positive comments and links to laudatory blogs by the time midnight rolled around.

Local news media covering the event were terse in their reports, but, surprisingly, once again took pains to confirm the unbridled enthusiasm of the crowd. Two of the local network affiliates even included recordings of the "Fuck O-Ver-**Lords**!" chants, though both bleeped out the "F" part of the F-bomb. Not that anyone **wouldn't** know it *was* the F-bomb.

"Shit, if this keeps up, Percy, pretty soon those co-eds are going to be throwing their underwear in your face," Idris said as they headed to their hotel room. He used Franklin's alias because Marcia was within earshot.

"I suppose we all have our burdens to bear," Franklin said, straight-faced – for an entire two seconds, before completely cracking up.

* * *

UNTRAMMELLED BEAUTY: TAKING THE ORDER INTO ORDERVILLE (CANYON, THAT IS)

At 4:15 a.m. the next morning, they traveled in their rental car north on I-15 in the direction of Salt Lake City. Marcia had convinced them to take two days off for a side trip to Zion National Park. She'd read about an amazing day hike to Orderville Canyon via the Zion Narrows of the Virgin River's North Fork starting at the Temple of Sinawava, as well as a separate day hike to Hidden Canyon from the Weeping Rock Trailhead. Marcia had even finagled hiking permits from the National Park Service for all four of them.

After seeing reviews and photos of the hikes on-line, Franklin/Percy was itching to test the limits of his newly-found leg strength. Tested they were as he and the others waded against the 50F-degree waist-deep swift current of a Virgin River tributary in the "Wall Street" slot canyon before entering the mouth of Orderville Canyon. Franklin was more than a little red-faced after the strength of the current pulled his hiking shorts down to his ankles.

"Good thing I brought some clean underwear on **this** particular trip," he smiled.

Franklin's uncharacteristic slack-jawed, awestruck expression continued throughout most of the first day's hike as he marveled at the contrast between the cobalt blue sky and the reddish mountainsides in almost all directions.

The starkly steep slot canyon walls were a constant source of amazement for Franklin and the others.

"It's like nature created its own fortress," Franklin said, "and is defying the mightiest of conquerors to overcome it. Exactly how is it that this place isn't overrun by hordes of humanity drawn by all this beauty?"

"Aren't there pretty strict limits to the number of hiking permits the National Park Service issues each day, Marcia?" Idris asked.

"You are correct, sir," she said. "There was only one permit left for today and tomorrow after we got ours."

"Thank God this park is protected from energy companies," Franklin said. "This kind of spectacle should be preserved for our descendants for all millennia to come."

"Know how they got the name of Orderville Canyon?" Bianca asked Franklin.

"Does it have something to do with law and order?"

"No. It's named after the nearby community the Latter-Day Saint pioneers started based on their United Order. Kind of a Mormon version of a kibbutz: everyone was expected to share virtually all of the food, crafts and clothing they produced with the local church and church leaders were expected to fairly redistribute those items with everyone in the community," Bianca explained.

"It actually was fairly successful. The main reason the town shrank – there are only about 600 residents there now – was because the church abandoned the United Order and many of the polygamist family leaders in the late 1800's were jailed or driven underground after the church officially outlawed plural marriage."

"Suppose the church abandoned it because some of the '*items*' subject to redistribution were the multiple wives?" Idris asked.

"Just might be," Bianca said.

They continued on the trail, constantly gaping at the sheer, nearly 90-degree angle canyon walls and occasional waterfall sprays, until there **was** *no more trail.* After spending close to 30 minutes at the sprawling Orderville Canyon overlook, they had to practically pry Franklin away from his prized view as he sat at the edge of the trail.

"Percy, if we don't turn around now," Marcia told Franklin, "we're not going to make it back to our lodging 'til past midnight. Our dogs," she said, pointing to everyone's feet, "are going to be barking like Old Yeller with rabies on the hike to Hidden Canyon tomorrow if we don't get some serious sack time tonight."

"Rabid feet are than last thing I need," Franklin said, regretfully. "At least we've got gravity on our side for the rest of the afternoon and evening.

"Idris," he then whispered, out of range of Marcia's hearing, "is 'Old Yeller' some kind of elderly screamer? Or is it a racial thing, something about Asians?"

Whispering back, Idris explained, "It's a classic movie about a family's beloved dog. Next chance you get, you should watch, but make sure you have some Kleenex handy.

"You're gonna have a ton of gravity on your side if you slip off to the left there, sir," Idris said, back at full volume, pointing to a 1,000-foot high cliff just inches from the trail's edge.

At almost that exact same time Franklin glanced back at Idris and he did, in fact, slip, letting out a staccato "CRAP!" He went down to one knee, but avoided – by less than a foot – trundling over the side of the trail. FDR=1, Gravity=0…so far, at least.

By the time they reached the parked rental car, the group had taken perhaps 300 photos of the scenery among themselves, including shots of a pack of 20- and 30-something New Zealand tourists who seemed more sure-footed than even the bravest bighorn sheep.

That night the group checked in with Pongo and Phil by phone. Franklin spent almost a half-hour describing the Zion National Park grandeur he'd seen up close for the first time. *"He actually has the enthusiasm and verve of the 20-year-old man he's become,"* Phil thought as he and Pongo listened on speakerphone.

Once Marcia left the room for an expedition to buy supplies for the trail the next day, Idris brought up an issue on the phone that had been nagging at him every time the four of them had been together on the trail earlier in the day.

"I think it's time we brought Marcia in on who 'Percy' really is," he said. "I'm convinced it's just a matter of time before I forget to call Franklin by his assumed name in front of her. And if it's not me who forgets, it's going to be someone else in this group or back in Poughkeepsie.

"I'm not saying we tell her everything – I don't think it's good for any of us for her to know there are other people in Franklin's grave. But we can allow her to assume it's empty now.

"I feel really strongly about this."

"What do you think, Franklin?" Pongo asked, the speakerphone connection now punctuated by static interference.

"I am tired of the awkward feeling I get every time she calls me Percy. If any of you can think of a reason why we shouldn't trust her, please share it now. Otherwise, I think we should bring her completely into the fold."

"Anyone feel differently from the President?" Phil asked.

"Not on this end," Idris said after seeing Bianca shake her head side-to-side.

"OK," Pongo said. "Let's plan on Idris and Bianca introducing Marcia to the President using his true identity tomorrow – in the privacy of the trail out there in Zion. At least, if there are any screams or shrieks or some other form of apoplexy, there probably won't be any other people around to see it."

"I am comfortable with that," Franklin said.

"Us too," Bianca added.

"What if Marcia wants out once we've shared this?" Pongo asked.

"Let's just take it one day at a time," Phil said. "Again, like I've said before, even if someone leaves our group, it's fairly unlikely they'd be believed by anyone if they tried to spread the word that our favorite President is back among the living.

"We'll have to do our best to get Marcia to recognize that unmitigated confidentiality on this is an absolute requirement for her continued employment. But let's not make this into some sort of existential crisis just yet, OK? Marcia seems like the kind of person who takes the unexpected in stride."

"Agreed," Idris and Bianca said at almost the same time.

* * *

The next day's hike to the Hidden Canyon overlook was even steeper and more challenging than the previous day's – but not as wet. Idris and Bianca decided to wait 'til the group had scaled a particularly scary-steep stretch of trail, a portion requiring the hikers to grasp a long chain bolted into the side of the mountain face, to pause and introduce Marcia to Franklin as their revered former President instead of Percy Van Mullder.

Marcia's out-of-breath reaction to Idris' and Bianca's revelation, predictably, at first was that she was being pranked.

"When my older son Woody was a teenager, he used to think it was clever to prank me about every other week. The first time we had Al Franken over for dinner, he not only placed rubber vomit all over the dining room when I wasn't looking, but he also fed our dog Crocko Cocker so much peanut butter that Crocko spewed **real** vomit all over Al's shoes under the table *while we were eating*. And after Al took his shoes off for Woody to clean, Woody used Crocko's latest anal Tootsie Roll as shoe polish. Al seemed to think Woody was quite the comedian. But what you're telling me is dumber than anything Woody ever did," Marcia said. "Y'know, this actually is a pretty huge insult to my intelligence."

But Idris and Bianca persisted, explaining in detail the theory expounded by Grandpa Tom Podrowski that sprite lightning could've been the catalyst which revived President No. 32. They consciously avoided mentioning the suspected additional catalyst for Franklin's age reversal. Wouldn't do to have her see her favorite President as some sort of Zombie hybrid, especially if word got around that he'd involuntarily snacked on the brain cores of a couple of young reactionary political zealots. They simply suggested the sprite lightning must've catalyzed some sort of massive EDA gene replication which rejuvenated Franklin's entire body.

It was Franklin himself who finally convinced her he was the real deal.

"Look me in the eyes, my dear," he said to Marcia, less than an arm's length away. "It's more than fear to be feared here, isn't it? It's like a crime against nature, you're probably thinking.

"Please believe me, dear, when I say I had no say in this. One moment, I felt a horrible, excruciating pain in my head, then complete darkness, and then I was among people kind enough to take me in, kind enough to protect me from becoming a sideshow attraction and kind enough to let me try to make a positive difference in peoples' lives again with this USA-SBR.

"Please try to put yourself in our position, alright, Marcia?"

And then the reality of all the unreality sank in for her.

She plopped down, butt first, on the edge of the trail, seeming not to care that her legs were dangling above a 700-foot precipice as she stared straight ahead at the reddish-golden mountainsides a quarter-mile away, lost in thought.

"Hay-zeus saves at First Federal of Christ My Lord!! Why didn't you share this sooner??" Marcia asked, face pale as the parts of her white socks not yet dusted with red trail powder.

"We were afraid you might quit," Bianca said. "And, most importantly, we were afraid you might tell someone outside of our group. That just CANNOT happen, by the way."

"I certainly can't imagine quitting now. And I'm not stupid enough to try and convince anyone the resurrected finest President in all history has been co-signing my paychecks under a goofy alias.

"Mr. President, I hope you'll understand if I don't feel comfortable calling you Franklin just yet."

"I understand completely. I'm not especially comfortable with being known as 'Percy,' but it's not like I have a lot of choice, is it?"

"I guess this explains your obsession with grilled cheese sandwiches."

"I never get tired of them. Never will."

"Tell you what, if you'll indulge me by answering some questions while we finish our hike today, I promise I'll make you the best grilled cheese sandwiches whenever you like for as long as you like," Marcia said.

"That seems like a fair trade, Dear."

"Where to start? Jasper the Gasper, I have no idea where to begin."

But begin she did. And she didn't stop 'til they were back in the rental car and once again on the way north to Salt Lake City. Near the end of her questions, she asked Franklin how someone who fought as hard as he did to preserve and protect the banking industry, as well as employers with large payrolls, could author something as contentious for those interests as the USA-SBR.

"When we were trying to undo the damage of the Great Depression in the early '30s, the leaders of the most powerful corporations and banks seemed to understand that not taking care of the middle class could send the country spiraling into rebellion, perhaps even revolution," Franklin told her. "There were exceptions, but most wanted to co-operate with us to get folks back to work at living wages.

"They knew people who could barely afford to feed themselves weren't going to be able to buy their products. They knew a nation of struggling wage-earners with children near starvation would be vulnerable to the nation's enemies. They knew that the voting public recognized the difference between corporate shills and genuine populist political leaders. And they knew all but the most hyper-partisan newspaper publishers around the country would hold accountable all officeholders who told bald-faced lies.

"What I noticed not long after coming back into this life is that every one of those truisms has changed. Corporate heads now appear to care only about what's going to happen to their earnings in the next quarter on the calendar. They want to squeeze as much profit as possible out of the smallest target market as possible. Think of yacht builders and high-end sports car manufacturers. Corporate heads want to develop drugs that treat chronic conditions, not cure them, because cures aren't so profitable. When they do come up with a cure, they price it so that only the very wealthiest can afford it. Think Gilead Corporation and Hepatitis C - $84,000! Corporate heads want a significant demographic to be perpetually poor or nearly poor because that gives them a dependable pool of volunteers for the armed services to fight perpetual wars motivated by corporate profit, even if it leaves the country full of low-educated low-functioning, marginally-creative human drones who rarely question authority, especially if that authority wears a uniform. They want their corporate media 'news' purveyors to excrete corporate propaganda belched out by elected corporate shills about the myth of wealthy job creators and the myth of wealthy benefactors' 'trickle down' when they know *almost all jobs are created by the purchasing power of the middle class.* And they want their **_elected_** corporate shills to be able to lie all day long **with impunity** if the lies serve their short-term profit goals.

"Business leaders during the Great Depression may have had the same bottom-line mentality, but they knew we would summon the will of the backbone of America – its working class families – to hold them to account for unbridled greed. Everyone could connect the dots: corporate excesses CREATED the Great Depression.

"Corporate heads and their shills – both elected and unelected – have made it hard nowadays for the average person to connect their blatant misdeeds from the last decade to the worldwide meltdown of 2008. And when the average person has connected those dots – between, say, J. P. Morgan Chase and massive mortgage fraud, they *don't see a single high-profile soul in handcuffs* doing a...perf-, prep- what is it?"

"Perp walk?" Marcia said.

"Thank you, Dear – that's it, perp walk, that's what they call it now. Yes, it's like, if you dress stylishly enough, the prosecutors allow you to make a dignified entrance to be booked on criminal charges. It would seem that, these days, prestige will purchase a person almost anything. Including that "Get Out of Jail Free" card.

"If our USA-SBR becomes the law of the land, that will change. It HAS to change. Otherwise, working class families are doomed to a life of struggling – on every imaginable level. The alternative – a revolution – would damage the country as we know it beyond repair."

"Did Phil or Pongo show you any video from the mostly peaceful overthrow of the Soviet regime?" Marcia asked.

"They did."

"Do you think our military would turn over their tanks to the revolutionaries if something like that happened here?"

"If the average U.S. soldier still follows orders as unquestioningly as they did during the put-down of the Bonus Marchers in July of '32 in Washington, D.C., it would **_NOT_** bode well for any group hoping to forcibly throw out the most corrupt leaders of our country. The Soviet soldiers looked at the swarms of protestors and saw their neighbors and relatives. Our soldiers just might look at swarms of protestors and see enemies to be stopped *at all costs* – **if** that's what their orders were.

"Whether the American public would sit by and either actively or passively support the wholesale slaughter of protestors bent on taking down a corrupt government – that's an open question. I hope we never have to find out the answer."

"The American public certainly didn't support what happened to the Bonus Marchers," Marcia said.

"I know, I was there, Marcia," Franklin said. "But these are different times. There was no 'Fox News' back then. And no blank check for the military back then."

* * *

DANCING FOOLS

By the time they reached their rental car, the four hikers had taken more than 1,500 digital photos combined on their four cameras. But they were, to a person, so trail-worn that they could barely summon the energy to stay conscious 'til they reached their hotel room in Cedar City that evening. They were so wiped out, they decided to stay an extra day and night in the largest community in Iron County.

After sleeping 'til noon and spending a few sunny hours taking in the sights of Cedar Breaks National Monument and the nearby town of Brian Head (the highest-elevation community in Utah at 9,800 feet), the group decided to spend the evening at Toadz, a garden-variety bar and grill with live music in Cedar City. Marcia and Bianca took turns dancing with Franklin to covers of 80's and 90's rock songs while Idris nibbled on chicken wings and counted the number of under-50 men with beer bellies entering the establishment. Fortunately for Franklin, the results of his latest attempt to 'get down' were not as disastrous as Franklin's earlier attempt at contemporary rug-cutting in Fishkill. There was neither vomiting nor slurred speech – although Bianca noticed a slight hardened protrusion below the belt area as she danced with Franklin to a slow-paced cover of Roy Orbison's "You Got It." ("*You got wood!*" she sung to herself in her head.) She thought it best not to mention it to Franklin, wanting to avoid embarrassing him – though she did bring it up confidentially with Harry during a phone call two days later. (*Harry quickly laughed it off, joking that he must have the hottest girlfriend in the history of the country if she was, in fact, able to stimulate a hard-on for a 129-year-old dick with so little effort.*)

By the time the evening of dining and dancing was done, Franklin was feeling much more like the man in his early 20's whom he resembled than someone born in 1882. If someone as beautiful as Holly Van Arsdale were to walk into his hotel room that evening and remove her shirt and brassiere, he would've been hard-pressed – no pun intended – not to ravage her, not to do everything in his power to give her orgasm after orgasm until the sun protruded from behind Brian Head Peak to the east. Instead, he administered a DIY orgasm of his own and slept peacefully through the night – except for a brief dream in which a tall, muscular man in a black suit with the words "Hil's Wall Street Roadie" on the back pointed at him and then pointed at a nearby open casket, motioning with his hand and head for Franklin to get in it. "If you don't do it on your own, we'll do it for you," the gravelly-throated figure said, voice as serious as the radio reporter narrating "The War of the Worlds" in 1939. Startled, Franklin woke up, but quickly fell back to sleep.

* * *

Scruples Scrupulously Fixates on Pop Music, Repeat-Style

As agreed late the previous night, they all were up in time to get their continental breakfast the minute it was first ready at 6 a.m. and were on the road to Salt Lake City an hour later.

Franklin decided a little audio stimulation might make the hundreds of miles pass more quickly.

As they drove north on Interstate 15, Franklin pulled a handful of CD's out of his backpack. It was then that they all were first exposed to Franklin's new musical obsessions. First, inspired by all the travels the group had already undertaken, he popped in a B52's CD and played "*Roam*" – on repeat *FOR 20 MINUTES*.

About 10 minutes into the re-plays, Idris said while driving, "OK, who in the frack showed Franklin how to use the frigging repeat button on the stereo?"

So as not to offend further with *that* song, Franklin next popped in the soundtrack to "*The Magnificent Seven*," and turned it up to nearly maximum volume.

"Really gets the blood pumping, wouldn't you say?" he said to Bianca.

"Like a 747 jet on final landing approach as it passes over your bedroom at 3 a.m.," she said, bleary-eyed.

"Did you notice when you were watching that movie the small print in the credits about where they got the story from?" Idris asked.

"Must've missed it."

"It's a tale from our country's former mortal enemies," Idris said. "It's from a story called "*The Seven Samurai*," which was made into a movie in the mid-'50s by Akira Kurosawa."

"Just makes me like it that much more," Franklin said, "that two widely different cultures could have in common a love of rooting for the underdog, pulling together to overcome injustice inflicted by bullies.

"Hey, here's the very best part."

At which point Franklin again pressed the repeat button, for the "Strange Funeral/After the Brawl" part of the soundtrack. This time, he turned the volume up to maximum and played the selection for a full half-hour. Then he took the repeat button off and let the CD finish playing.

The next CD he put in was a Yardbirds album; when it got to the "*I'm Not Talkin'* " track, he repeated the repeat button, to a chorus of:

"*Oh, shit, not again!!?*" from Idris and Bianca. Marcia was still a little too mentally woozy from the revelation two days earlier to assert herself.

So, Franklin then inserted the original Led Zeppelin CD and, when it progressed to "*Communications Breakdown*," he waited 'til Idris wasn't looking and set it on repeat again.

"Really? *Reeeallly?*!!" Idris said during the second play of the hard-driving song.

Finally realizing he was flexing a little too much control over their audio choices, Franklin took the repeat button off.

"Who the frack got those CD's for you?" Idris asked, half-jokingly pissed off.

"Phil helped me get a credit-slash-debit card and showed me how to order on-line a couple of weeks before we left for this trip. I bought a portable CD player a few days before we left. Pongo tried to convince me to get an iPod, but I couldn't see spending a dollar per song, at least not yet. A dollar still seems as big as President Taft's butt to me most of the time."

"Well, we don't mind you playing your favorites, Sir, as long as you can try to avoid that constant repeat button, OK?" Bianca said.

"That seems fair. Don't want to overstep."

At that moment, both Idris and Bianca were thinking how much *some* of Franklin's behaviors seemed to have molded to his current biological age. But his biological age would become an issue again before they knew it.

They stopped for an early lunch at the Carl's Jr. in Fillmore and then headed north from Millard County straight to their hotel room at the Salt Lake City Red Lion Hotel. By this time Franklin had taken to using noise-cancelling headphones on his own CD player so he could use the repeat button on it as often as he liked. He listened to "Four Sticks" from Led Zeppelin's "Zoso" album about a dozen times and then went on to Rage Against the Machine, Audioslave, Bruce Springsteen, the Youngblood's "*Get Together*," Cat Stevens' "*Greatest Hits*" and collections of the Beatles' and Rolling Stones' greatest hits. It made the last 200 miles of Interstate 15 pass more quickly than he could've imagined. Marcia and Bianca, grateful for the silence, snoozed 'til Idris pulled into the hotel parking lot.

Before they hit the sack that night, the four of them discussed plans for their news conference scheduled in advance of the next day's gathering at Utah Valley University's Ragan Theater in Orem, as well as the rallies two days later at the University of Utah Huntsman Center, three days later at Weber State University's Browning Center and four days later at Utah State University's Dee Glen Smith Spectrum center.

* * *

ROCKIN' THE FOURTH ESTATE

The small handful of print and TV reporters who showed up for the 10:30 a.m. press conference at the Red Lion Hotel were, predictably, focused on the more potentially scandalous features of their rally rather than the substantive details of the USA-SBR.

"YouTube appears to be on fire with that obscene audience chant from Las Vegas several nights ago," Royal Pincus of the Salt Lake Tribune said to Franklin/Percy. "Just how to you expect to win over independent voters with that kind of offensive display?"

"That is an excellent question – Mr. Pincus, right?" Franklin/Percy said. "Let me just remind you that none of us encouraged that kind of chant. It happened spontaneously.

"We've had sociologists tell us that, when that kind of spontaneous expression comes from a large crowd, it suggests they feel, Number One, that what they're chanting is **important**, and Number Two, that what they're chanting is something most people have been ignoring up to then because the people doing the chanting have been **too passive**.

"They seemed to feel strongly that corporate overlords have replaced democratic representation in this country. Let's take your newspaper, for example. It's the Salt Lake Tribune, right?"

"That's right," Pincus said.

"Well, profit pressures have led to your paper being owned by a huge New York City hedge fund, Alden Global Capital, which contracts with Digital First Media to manage it, right?"

"That's correct," Pincus said, turning a little red-faced.

"Do you feel your journalistic independence is enhanced by your newspaper being one of dozens of media outlets owned by a massive corporation? Do you feel that the massive corporation has good journalism as its top priority, or profits?" Franklin asked.

"I don't think we're here for me to speak for my employer," Pincus said.

"You're absolutely correct," Franklin said. "But we're here to help people remember that many, many things which used to make this country great – like local ownership of media outlets by members of the community whose top priority was to make their community a better place – those things are evaporating in the heat wave of predatory profit-seeking.

"I suspect your employer – like so many other absentee media owners – doesn't believe for a second that local news consumers think those owners two thousand miles away give a tinker's damn about the day to day lives of those local consumers. Those consumers know exactly what your employer is all about: profit for bottom-line investors all over the world.

"As long as your employer can turn a profit for those investors, those absentee owners don't care whether the news hole is filled with astrological forecasts, lost dog bulletins or stories about next fall's designer hemlines.

"The people who attend our rallies are fed up with that craven perspective. They want 21st century culture to be all about the social and economic justice that no longer matters to corporate overlords. They want news media to educate news consumers about why the middle class is dying, not why the middle class won't be cool if they don't buy the latest Apple iPhone.

"Next question, please."

"Heber Pratt, KUTV News."

"Hi, Mr. Pratt – KUTV, part of Sinclair Broadcast Group of Hunt Valley, Maryland, one of 165 stations they own, right?"

"Sounds like you did some homework, sir. Just wondering why you folks felt like you had to copy that Michael Moore stunt with the clean underwear and ramen noodles."

"I think I speak for all of us campaigning for the USA-SBR when I say we thought Mr. Moore's strategy was hilarious – and popular as heck," Franklin/ Percy said, intentionally using the Utah-friendly 'heck' instead of 'hell.'

"Could any of you folks in the media here use some clean undies or noodles?" Franklin asked, holding up packages of both.

"Maybe Shumway in the back over there with Deseret News," Pratt said. "He and Loni are up to eleven children now, so they probably go through a lot of 'em."

"Crackerjack sense of humor, there Heber," Nephi Shumway said. "To tell you the truth, I'd love to take some free clean underwear for the little ones, but our ethics rules don't allow taking freebies from news sources."

"If they're going to make fun of you, Mr. Shumway, you should at least get to ask a question," Franklin said.

"Sure, happy to oblige," Shumway said. "My readers would be interested to know if your USA-SBR is just the first step toward a socialist takeover of the government, state-by-state?"

"By socialist, do you mean communist?" Franklin asked.

"I don't, but I imagine our readers do," Shumway said.

"Why do you think they would mistakenly think we're communist, Mr. Shumway?" Franklin asked. "Do you think it might have something to do with all the blog comments your employer allowed to be posted on your paper's website alleging that we're a bunch of antichrist commies?"

"I don't know," Shumway said. "There must be some reason they're afraid you organizers are a bunch of radicals. What do *you* think that is?"

"I would never presume to know why a handful of your readers think the way they think," Franklin said. "I do know that one of the responsibilities of news media is to help *all* their news consumers – not just bloggers - realize when their thinking is based on ignorance or prejudice rather than facts.

"Here are the facts: the Un-Screwing of America-Second Bill of Rights was created to make a permanent dent in systemic social and economic injustice.

"I challenge anyone in this room *and* anyone who consumes news from anyone in this room to present a specific piece of evidence to contradict the fact that every single provision in the USA-SBR will be better not just for virtually everyone in the middle class, but virtually *every* *non-wealthy* individual in this country *over the long term.*

"The only people who will be adversely affected by the USA-SBR will be millionaires and billionaires – and even they will be adversely affected *only in the short term.* That's because, once all the provisions of the USA-SBR take effect, the middle class is going to rebound to where it was in the 1950's, taking the billionaires along with them. We might even see the day again when frugal families can get by with just one full-time wage-earner instead of two.

"What's been lost with all of the corporate media coverage of these issues is **who the real job-creators are.** They're *not the millionaires and billionaires* out there. They're **_consumers_**. There's not a billionaire corporate C.E.O. out there who's willing to create *a single solitary job* if there's no consumer demand for what that job produces.

"If you don't believe me, just ask Nobel laureates Paul Krugman and Joseph Stiglitz.

"Once the provisions of the USA-SBR have resuscitated the middle class, consumer demand for non-essential products and for bigger-ticket items will go into the stratosphere. That consumer demand – **_not_** the mythical generous fairy godmother billionaire – will produce new jobs by the millions.

"What's *even more important* are the provisions of the USA-SBR which will help heal the environment by stemming global warming. If dramatic reductions of fossil fuel use, especially fossil fuels obtained through fracking, aren't treated as an existential emergency, then every member of humanity – **_including_** predatory capitalists – may be missing from the planet - its surface, at least - in another hundred and fifty years.

"The USA-SBR treats the continued human addiction to fossil fuels as the **existential emergency** it truly is. For anyone interested in facts, these are not liberal versus conservative issues. These are issues for the sheer survival of our species."

"We encourage you to share copies of the USA-SBR with your readers," Idris said, pointing to a large stack of USA-SBR copies at the back of the Red Lion conference room.

"And, just as importantly, we encourage you to ask your state's elected representatives in your Legislature and in your Congress to go on the record either in support of or in opposition to the USA-SBR.

"The people coming to our rallies deserve to know where their democratically-elected representatives stand on this amendment drive – so they know whether those representatives need to be replaced or not. Those people deserve to be able to depend on their news media to shine a light on what their elected representatives really think about this kind of crucial proposal.

"Last time I checked, *that* is how democracy is supposed to work. Democracy simply will **_NOT_** work without news media which are willing to go to bat for working stiffs who would otherwise be victims of manipulation by organized money."

The journalists filed out of the room mumbling to each other various comments about young naïve idealists. Each of them picked up small handfuls of USA-SBR copies, however. And each of them was thinking as they walked to their cars and vans how they could convince their respective cynical city editors and ratings-obsessed news directors to devote at least a token amount of coverage to the USA-SBR rallies.

* * *

A LITTLE FRICTION – BUT NOT THE GOOD KIND

Thanks to a few minutes of video coverage of their news conference during that evening's local news, Franklin and the others were showered with attention by approximately 25 local Tea Partiers at the rally in the Ragan Theater the following evening in Orem. Out of a total of 1,000 attendees.

However, they made up in volume for what they lacked in both numbers and literacy. Their hand-made signs included such standards as:

"The Bible say God helps them who's helps theirselves (sic) **– Poor Folk need to use them bootstarps** (sic)**"**
"These commies want the guvvermint (sic) **to give em free money"**
"These radicals want your taxes to pay for pollewshun (sic)**"**
"Them commies'll have to pry our guns from our old dead hans (sic)**"**
"Food Stamps is what makes lazy fokes (sic) **lazier"**
"Obama wants Mexican Nashunuls (sic) **to over take your jobs"**
"Give a man a welfare for a day and he cheats for a day – kick him in the ass and he <u>eats</u> with the rest of his wives"

Midway into his presentation – after their powerpoint presentation and before the screening of *"Capitalism: A Love Story"* – Franklin/Percy took time to address the Tea Partiers, who'd been fairly boisterous throughout the rally. As he started to speak, he noticed that at least three out of four of the Tea Partiers carrying the hand-made signs had the tell-tale visible-to-Franklin (only?) fine sensillum-type fur growths on their faces, arms, hands and necks.

"I see our Tea Party friends in the audience have taken the time to put together some impressive signage before sharing our rally this evening," he said.

"Let's take some time to address the issues each of their signs has brought up, OK?"

"First, that golden oldie about the Bible saying God helps those who help themselves: guess what? That's nowhere in the Bible. I checked. YOU should check before you make your next sign.

"That saying came from Benjamin Franklin and, earlier, from a 17th century English politician named Algernon Sidney. Mr. Sidney was an outspoken critic of the absolute monarchical actions of King Louie the Fourteenth. Mr. Sidney eventually was executed for treason. An interesting footnote: after his death, it was discovered he'd been dependent upon a pension from Louie the Fourteenth.

"Drawing any parallels between Mr. Sidney and modern-day bashing of the government safety net for the poor by recipients of **_corporate_** welfare is entirely up to you.

"Next, that sign about 'commies' wanting the government to give them free money: guess what? All studies show that virtually all of the monetary assistance distributed through the government's TANF program goes to single parents, mosty women, and their children who've been abandoned by the father in the family, often after subjecting them to abuse.

"So, the so-called free money – which has to be paid back to the government in the form of child support by the parent who's left the family – does **NOT** go to any wild-eyed commies. Or to crazed illegal aliens. Or to ray gun-toting green-skinned aliens.

"And – get this – the annual cost of **ALL** government social programs for the poor is about $59 billion, while the annual cost of government *corporate subsidies* – otherwise known as corporate welfare - is about $93 billion.

"That sign about welfare recipients supposedly being cheaters who need kicks in the butt to motivate them? That's a myth that Ronald Reagan followers have been spreading for the past thirty years. It couldn't *BE* further from the truth.

"All the studies show that less than five percent – *fewer than* one in 20 – of welfare recipients receive benefits when they actually had no eligibility whatsoever. Try asking someone who's been on welfare at one time in her or his life whether it was something they looked forward to getting.

"Here's what they'll tell you, folks:

"They'll tell you filling out paperwork listing their personal circumstances in painstaking detail was one of the most humiliating things they've ever done.

"They'll tell you that they did it NOT as a first choice, but as a last resort – to keep their children from being out on the streets.

"They'll tell you that having to go through the paperwork, having to come up with documentation required for eligibility, having to show up for multiple interviews, having to complete separate paperwork for child support enforcement, that they'd trade all of that hard work for a couple of things:

"*Not having* their child's other parent **abandon them** and, most importantly, _**HAVING**_ a *decent full-time job* so they wouldn't have to **depend** on the other parent who abandoned them.

"Another thing they'll tell you is that 'kicking them in the butt' to motivate them is nothing more than kicking someone when they're down. Americans don't do that. Americans cheer for the underdog.

"Figuratively kicking a poor mother of two when she's financially struggling and on the verge of homelessness, is like holding a drowning man's head under water. It's like trying to kill the underdog instead of cheering for them. That's not what we do, it's not what Americans have EVER done.

"That's why Americans threw Herbert Hoover out of office in a landslide after he had the Army systematically beat up and burn out World War I veterans, the Bonus Marchers, from their Washington, D.C. shantytown in 1932.

"Never again. Not if this Second Bill of Rights becomes law.

"Then there's that sign about us supposedly wanting the government to pay for cleaning up pollution: guess what? Our Un-Screwing of America Second Bill of Rights **bans the _sources_** of pollution and makes it far more likely that solar energy devices will become inexpensive enough for every household to use.

"What's even more important to understand is that this Second Bill of Rights prohibits the government from using taxpayer dollars to clean up industrial pollution. Instead, it requires the industries which **created** the pollution to pay up – or else.

"Under existing law, the taxes on industries which funded the Superfund clean-up programs _expired in 1995 and were never replaced,_ due to lobbying from the polluting industries subject to the tax.

"This Second Bill of Rights would _neuter_ the power of those lobbyists - I love the visual image of that: '_neutered lobbyists'_ – it would require Congress **to tax those industries once again** to pay for Superfund clean-ups. If this Second Bill of Rights does NOT come to fruition, **YOUR** **taxes** _will_ have to pay for those clean-ups.

"As for that sign about taking people's guns, well that's just nuts. There is **ABSOLUTELY NO MENTION** of seizing guns anywhere in this Second Bill of Rights. So, everyone worried about the Second Amendment, please take a chill pill. The Second Bill of Rights simply stops sales of semi-automatic weapons, the NUMBER ONE choice of serial killers, mass-shooting offenders and lunatics. And it imposes requirements designed to make it far less likely that guns are sold to criminals, persons prone to violence and the mentally unbalanced.

"When it comes to that sign about government food assistance supposedly making people lazier – well, that just couldn't be further from the truth. And, shame on all of you for implying that all poor people are lazy.

"Government food assistance does one thing and one thing only: it prevents people from starving. The party of business is always trying to force cuts to food assistance. That is just mean-spirited and hateful, pure and simple.

"Those of you waving those signs, please take the time to put them down and do a little research in your college libraries or on line. Here's what you'll find: before there were government food assistance programs, Republicans like Herbert Hoover were absolutely sure private charities could come up with enough food to keep the poor fed.

"But the actual history of those private charity efforts during the Great Depression showed those charities – including the Red Cross – failed miserably. Mostly because their financial resources were **dwarfed** by the huge size of the problem. It took a co-ordinated _government_ effort and the power of the Federal treasury to successfully prevent mass starvation in this country. Private enterprise and private charities simply **could not do it**. Check it out.

"And that sign about the President wanting Mexican nationals to take your jobs? That is just NONSENSE. President Obama has authorized _more deportations_ of illegal immigrants from this country **_than any President in U.S. History_**. Check it out.

"The President simply wants compassionate treatment of those who were brought to this country illegally by their parents when they were children – they're called 'dreamers' because all they want is the same shot at the American Dream as the other kids they grew up with. The vast majority of those 'dreamers' are highly-fluent in English and graduated from U.S. high schools. Many even have degrees from U.S. colleges.

"Once again, maybe we all need to remember: almost all of our original ancestors who came to this country were illegal immigrants – at least from the perspective of the Native Americans who shared the first Thanksgiving with them.

"There just doesn't seem to be a heckuva lot of good karma in bashing people who want to be in this country to have a better life. What we would like to see is **all** countries worldwide dropping restrictions on immigration. People should have at least as much freedom to settle in the country of their choice as the freedom a box of Idaho potatoes has to be shipped to New Zealand.

"People around this country have what I believe is an unfair image of this beautiful state in their minds.

"People around the U.S. tend to see this as a backwater state where every other household has a half-dozen wives.

"A state where people don't mind if the local industrial plant spews toxic chemicals into their air.

"A state where people don't mind if industrialists like the Huntsman family dump toxic and carcinogenic wastes into the Jordan River or into Utah Lake as long as they donate money to universities and get stadiums and cancer-treatment centers named after them.

"A state where people don't mind if there are military nerve gas depositories hither and yon as long as there are lots of military facilities providing jobs to local contractors.

"A state where people don't mind that the climate keeps getting warmer and warmer as long as there are plenty of poison-spraying exterminators to kill the extra bugs that survive the warmer winters and plenty of loggers to clear out the massive swaths of dead pine trees killed by the bark beetles that survived the warmer winters.

"Those of us supporting this Second Bill of Rights, the USA-SBR, believe all of those people around the country have it all wrong about this lovely state.

"We believe that the people of this state love a clean environment. We believe they love social justice and economic justice just as much as anyone else in this great country.

"Sure, this state's history includes the likes of 'W' Bush's buddy Karl "Turdblossom" Rove going to Olympus High School up the interstate and getting his far-right-wing career off the ground there.

"But Utah's history also includes the likes of the martyred Joe Hill, a proud union member who was wrongfully convicted and executed mainly because of his activities with the IWW, the Wobblies.

"Mr. Hill coined the term "pie in the sky" in a song he wrote. The song encouraged folks to focus on achieving lasting social and economic justice based on peoples' actual reality-based needs **in this life** instead of taking comfort in the promises of a glorious "pie-in-the-sky" after-life.

"We believe there are lots more Utah folks along the likes of Joe Hill than of the Turdblossom Rove ilk.

"We believe Utah folks simply haven't had a fair chance to pursue social and economic justice because the political game here – as in most of the rest of the country – has been rigged. Rigged to make sure your efforts to create positive change stay as stuck in the ground as dead brine shrimp stuck in a dried out patch of Great Salt Lake shoreline muck.

"This Un-Screwing of America Second Bill of Rights will punish the people who've been rigging that game. It will take a huge step toward making ours a true government of the people, by the people and for the people – instead of government of, by and for predatory corporations.

"Make no mistake: there **will be dire sky-is-falling predictions** of economic catastrophe from Wall Street's so-called experts.

"Remember this one thing: they're predicting catastrophe because they're worried that a handful of **bill**ionaires – heaven forfend! - will be transformed into merely mega-**mill**ionaires. Because they're worried that **obscene profits** those billionaires have been pocketing by manipulating business monopoly pricing and by manipulating our government and economy *will be transferred back into the wallets of the middle class.*

"Never, ever forget: Wall Street billionaires' definition of catastrophe equals long-overdue justice and prosperity for the rest of us. Remember _always_: those _billionaires_ don't create jobs – **OUR CONSUMER DEMAND** creates jobs. And our consumer demand can be strong _only_ if our middle class incomes are strong.

"After you consider all of those billionaires' sky-is-falling predictions compared to the middle class reality of shrinking paychecks over the past 30 years, if you still side with your poor, burdened billionaire corporate overlords, what we're doing probably isn't your cup of tea.

"But if you're not so worried about your corporate overlords being able to afford their seventh or eighth luxury vacation home or their ninth or tenth luxury Lamborghini sports car, then just how do you feel about them??"

"Fuck O-ver-LORDS! Fuck O-ver-LORDS! Fuck O-ver-LORDS!" the crowd answered, chanting.

The chanting continued for almost two minutes as Idris, Pongo and Bianca cheered the crowd on from each of the far ends of the stage. Franklin finally had to yell over their chanting, asking them to chill out, which they slowly did.

"As you leave here tonight, keep in mind that this USA-SBR *(holding up an oversized copy)* can become the law of the land **_ONLY_** if you make it a personal priority to hold accountable _each_ of your elected legislators and members of Congress – including your U.S. Senators.

"You're not likely to find corporate news media holding them to account for whether they support the USA-SBR or not. That's because the USA-SBR would force huge media corporations to divest ownership of almost all the media outlets they control. So, it's up to each of you to find out where your lawmakers stand.

"Once you do find out where your lawmakers stand on the USA-SBR, please post the results of your contacts with your lawmakers on our website and on our Facebook page. If you don't like using our website or our Facebook page, we'd love to get an E-Mail from you. Or you can send us a letter through the Postal Service.

"Bottom line: we want to hear from you. This nice lady here *(pointing to Marcia)* and her assistant are going to document everything we hear from you. We will be posting ongoing results of your contacts with lawmakers and contacts of people just like you with their lawmakers in other states.

"When we know of lawmakers who either oppose the USA-SBR or who decline to go on record as supporting it, we will share those lawmakers' names on our website and our Facebook page. And we will issue news releases to corporate media too, for what that's worth.

"Then, once we know who wants to stop us, it will be up to **each. of. _you_** *(Franklin slowly pointed once in each of three directions at the crowd)* to make sure a quality USA-SBR-friendly candidate goes forward in a primary challenge against the lawmakers who are unfriendly to our efforts.

"That's the only way this little brine shrimp of a document is going to rise from the muck and be transformed into a larger-than-life powerful sentinel for justice and equality.

"And for those of you who need a little extra motivation, here's my friend Pongo with clean, new underwear and ramen noodles to share with you.

"So, heads-up!"

* * *

Perhaps the most important result of the rally for Franklin was when one of the Tea Partiers approached him a half-hour after the rally was over and asked him to forgive her. A slight, 5'3-1/2" woman in her early 20's, she explained that she'd never actually read the USA-SBR before that evening, so she picked up a copy on her way out and examined it as she walked toward her car.

"I was stunned by the time I was halfway through it," she said. "It bore no resemblance to what the other Tea Partiers were telling me it said. It sounded nothing whatsoever like what Slash Lugbuch was saying about it on the radio yesterday.

"I feel like a real fool for yelling out at you along with the other Tea Partiers earlier this evening. I hope you can accept my apology, Mr. Van Mullder."

"You don't even need to apologize, Dear," Franklin/Percy said. "You were actively misled. Misled by people with an agenda to manipulate. You were just trusting what your friends told you.

"If you want to make a real difference, perhaps you can convince one of your fellow Tea Partiers to actually read the document before the next time they're thinking about carrying protest signs."

"That's not a bad idea, Mr. Van Mullder. I know some of them are planning to go to your University of Utah rally in a couple of days. I'll do my best to get them to be more open-minded."

"Don't feel discouraged if they aren't as open-minded as you," Franklin said. "Sometimes people who are already so angry that they're carrying a homemade sign are so invested in the perspective they've already got, their minds are impervious to empirical reality."

"I'm still going to try," she said.

"Well, hang in there – we need several million more people just like yourself," Franklin said, patting her gently on the shoulder. He didn't notice that, as he walked away, she put a sticky note with her name and phone number into his coat pocket.

* * *

Fun Correspondence

The coverage of the UVU rally that night among local media was spotty; there was nowhere near the media buzz that had been generated by the Michael Moore rally seven years earlier in opposition to "W" Bush's re-election. But, once again, every last copy of the USA-SBR – more than 7,000 in all – which they'd left for attendees to pick up were taken. And the lawmaker contact sign-up sheets showed all but about 50 of those in attendance had pledged to contact at least three lawmakers each to compel them to support the USA-SBR.

By the next morning, the USA-SBR website and Facebook page were filling quickly with comments from Utah County residents who'd attended the rally the previous evening. Several of the comments included names of potential primary challenge candidates the commenters intended to ask to run against incumbents reluctant to support the USA-SBR.

But the comments which Franklin enjoyed the most were the ones quoting the lawmakers contacted by the rally attendees (which he reviewed while they were driving from Orem to Salt Lake City for the next rally):

"My state rep told me on the phone we can play with our own dicks 'til we're blue in the face, but that he's not gonna touch the USA-SBR with a 10-foot pole," wrote a pharmacist from Orem.

"Our state senator told me when I called that I can take my USA-SBR and use it to funnel douche into my wife's private parts. He said we're tools of Chairman Mao," wrote a registered nurse from American Fork.

"Ms. Hansen, our congresswoman, told us we'd see her dancing topless in the Mormon Tabernacle before we'd see her vote for the USA-SBR," wrote a fast food manager from Payson, UT.

"Our U.S. Senator told us we must've been abducted by aliens and had part of our brains sucked out if we thought he would be sympathetic to anything that would require the government to break up the big corporations that've contributed to his campaigns," wrote a schoolteacher from Sandy.

"We had one state senator tell us he'd be happy to post an anonymous Facebook photo of his hand flipping the bird at us and we had a state representative promise to come post a yard sign in our front yard identifying us as the neighborhood communists if we ever called her again about supporting the USA-SBR," wrote a Utah Valley University history professor and his city planning director wife.

"A legislator who happens to live next door to us told us he would vote for the USA-SBR but that he couldn't actively support it in public because it supposedly would cost him every single campaign contributor he's ever had from the financial (Wall Street) sector," wrote a South Jordan social worker.

"The mayor of our community told us at a reception after a town hall meeting that he'd sooner have daily prostate exams for a month than admit he supports the USA-SBR, even though he thinks it's the smartest thing he's read in his entire life," a Bluffdale hydrologist wrote.

Franklin, Idris and the others could see that there would need to be a huge groundswell of support for the USA-SBR from grassroots activists before just about any already-elected lawmaker was going to go on record supporting their cause.

* * *

MAD MEN TO THE RESCUE?

While sitting in bed at their hotel, Idris pictured in his mind a possible TV advertising campaign for the USA-SBR – one that might, through humor, loosen up public figures inhibited by long sticks lodged in their rectums – provided they could agree on a way to fund those kinds of pricey ads.

His vision of the ads went something like:

(First shot of first ad: Man is shown standing in front of a strip mall next to a couple of signs posted alongside each other. One says, "Sign petition today supporting 'Un-Screwing of America Second Bill of Rights,'" pointing to the right; the other, pointing to the left says, "Free Prostate/Rectal Exams; No Health Insurance Necessary: Must Commit to Five Consecutive Daily Probes."

(Second shot: Close-up of same man, holding an Rx note, which shows him scratching his chin and looking upward, unable to decide which to choose, first looking to his left and then looking to his right.

(Third shot: Scene shows man shrugging his shoulders, starting to turn to the right and looking back at the camera, saying, "I heard they might be giving away free clean underwear. Might come in handy later."

(Final shot: Close-up of first page of USA-SBR with voiceover explaining, "If you're pretty anal about just how accountable your government is, you probably should give this baby your own probing exam. We think you'll be surprised at just how good it feels when you're done...")

(First shot of second ad: Woman is shown standing in front of a different strip mall next to a couple of signs posted alongside each other. One sign says, "Free Colonoscopies/No Waiting; Must Be Willing to Drink Strong Potion Causing Hours of Bowel Evacuations," pointing to the left; the other, pointing to the right, says, "Sign petition today supporting "Un-Screwing of America Second Bill of Rights."

(Second shot: Close-up of same woman, holding an Rx note, which shows her scratching her head and looking skyward, eyes shifting back and forth left and right, clearly undecided which way to turn.

(Third shot: Scene shows woman shrugging her shoulders, starting to walk to the right and looking back at the camera, saying, "My friend at work said they might have free clean underwear. There must be more to this than just serendipity."

(Final shot: Close-up of first page of USA-SBR with voiceover explaining, "If you're pretty sure it's way past time to clean out the bowels of government and make it truly accountable for smooth and efficient movements for the middle class, you probably should give this baby a close-up inspection. We think you'll feel greatly relieved when you realize how much waste and how many wasters this thing will excrete from Congress' rear exit."

(First shot of third ad: Young couple is shown standing, arm-in-arm in front of a strip mall with a pair of signposts posted alongside each other. On the left side of the screen, one sign says, "Free Test-Drives of Soon-To-Be-Recalled Obsolete High-Pollution Internal Combustion Cars with Engines Which Will Shut Down Without Warning While Traveling at High Speeds on the Freeway" and points to the left. The other signpost on the right has a sign at the top stating, "Sale on Fossil Fuel-Free Vehicles at PureGreen Motors" with a separate sign below on the same signpost saying "This Way to Sign Petition Supporting Un-Screwing of America Second Bill of Rights" and points to the right.

(Second shot: Shows same couple holding form for 7-year $45,000 car loan application at 15 percent APR plus the wife holding a paystub showing a $9.50 per hour pay rate and the husband holding a paystub showing a $9.75 per hour pay rate.

(Third shot: Shows same couple, with the husband scratching the side of his chin and looking upward and then looking left to right, clearly undecided, while the wife is dramatically tugging at her hair with both hands at the top of her head, looking frustrated, looking up and then left and right, also clearly undecided.

(Fourth shot: Both husband and wife are looking at each other and shrugging their shoulders as they start walking to the right, looking back at the camera, with the husband first saying, "Before we let the car dealer screw us, we thought we'd check out what it's going to take to get this **country** *un-screwed," followed by the wife saying, "Can't cost us more than what we're already paying to keep our corporate overlord billionaires rolling in dough."*

(Final shot: A close-up of the first page of the USA-SBR, with a voiceover explaining, "If you're tired of big business screwing you over for low-quality products at high-quality prices on one end while big banking institutions screw you over with predatory financing using money the Fed gave 'em for zero interest, maybe it's time to read how we propose to un-screw this country and give working people rights they should've had all along."

"It just might work," Idris thought to himself. *"We've got to have some way to prime the pump when people start feeling intimidated by all the discouraging bullshit coming from shills of entrenched corporate power."*

He made a mental note to talk over the advertising ideas with the others the next day on their way to Weber State University in Ogden.

✳ ✳ ✳

THUS SALLY-ED FORTH A SHINING EXAMPLE

The group decided that they would invite Sally Rose Cummings as their featured guest for the rally at the 15,000-seat Huntsman Center that evening. Sally had gained a modest level of prominence in at least northern Utah and southern Idaho for her public pressure of Latter-Day Saint (LDS) church leaders to grant priesthood to women, citing early church historical accounts of members praying to "Our Heavenly Father and Our Heavenly Mother." She also had become known for repeatedly reminding church leaders of the church's early attempts at achieving social and economic justice through the United Order, a quasi-communal organization in which the labors and assets of entire communities were shared among the residents fairly equally.

A raven-haired 35-year-old third-generation Swiss-American, Sally often publicly urged church leaders to return to those early themes of social and economic justice. She was repulsed by the predominant "God bless the child who gets his own and doesn't have to share" attitude among members – an attitude which she was convinced fuels political dominance in Utah by the "I've got mine, who cares how you get yours" party (i.e., Republicans).

For all her efforts, the single mother of a 14-year-old son and 6-year-old daughter was in the midst of an excommunication process in her Mormon ward; her local bishopric had tentatively determined that her activism constituted apostasy. Her temple recommend had been suspended months earlier, preventing her from participating in the most sacred of LDS rituals.

Sally made ends meet by operating her own youth vocal and dance performance training center while holding down a full-time job as an elementary school music teacher in one of the poorest school districts in the state. She had repeatedly described herself as a dyed-in-the-wool capitalist. So, when she met Franklin/Percy, Idris and Bianca that afternoon in the lobby at the downtown Red Lion, she took great pains to explain how a hard-core capitalist like herself could support the USA-SBR.

"It's pretty simple: the deck is stacked against anyone who's not wealthy," Sally said. "If I want to open up one or more small musical training centers in Salt Lake or in one of the suburbs, like Bountiful, and there's an existing national corporate chain of similar musical training centers, that chain can pay big money to have someone lobby the local planning commission to prohibit zoning for studios the size I can afford.

"If anyone tries to tell me that can't happen, I can vouch not only that it can, but that it's happened to me – more than once!

"Your Second Bill of Rights would make it at least a little harder for those kinds of corporations to throw their money around to squeeze out little businesses like mine."

"How did you find out about the USA-SBR?" Bianca asked.

"My son Royal was watching a YouTube video of your visit to UNLV a couple of days ago. I overheard the F-bomb chant about corporate overlords and was about to ground him for the weekend and lock his laptop away for a week. He and his school buds have been pretty supportive of me through all this church mess, so I felt like I owed it to him to hear him out when he begged me to watch the entire video.

"He's pretty persuasive for a 14-year-old. If he were, say, five years older, he probably could convince me it would be smart for him to join you on one of your rally tours."

"We just might need him in another five years," Franklin said. "So, please tell him to keep in touch."

✳ ✳ ✳

T he arena was, surprisingly, at least two-thirds full when the time came for the rally to begin. Franklin's quick eyeball survey of the crowd suggested that Royal and his network of high school buddies must have done some major-league social media promotion of their gathering: at least half of the crowd appeared to be of high school age.

"They probably just want a chance to mouth off the F-word with impunity, without their church bishop or their parents having to impose any discipline," Franklin thought to himself.

Sure enough, as Sally, Franklin and the others walked onto the dais, the chant started.

"Fuck O-ver-LORDS! Fuck O-ver-LORDS! Fuck O-ver-LORDS!..."

The chant went on for close to two minutes, 'til Franklin/Percy stepped over to the podium and waved his palms downward, asking for the crowd to chill.

During his introduction of Sally, Franklin lavished praise on her for the courage to go against the grain of the culture of conformity which is perceived by those outside of Utah as the *dominant* culture there. He called Sally the prototypical "anti-Stepford wife."

"She's someone who overcame a moderately abusive husband – a man who told her she'd start her own business over his own dead body, a man who literally shoved her to the ground a couple of times in front of her children – and she went on to establish a successful small business.

"A successful small business in a state where more than two-thirds of small businesses are owned by men.

"And she continues to grow her business despite – or maybe even because of – her willingness to speak her mind in public about issues which the dominant church culture and dominant business culture don't necessarily want to have spotlighted.

"If we had to choose between having a Utah corporate overlord share his version of reality with you and having Sally Rose Cummings share **_reality_** reality with you – well, as you can see, that was a no-brainer choice for us."

"Please show her the kind of well-deserved respect and admiration she doesn't get from the entrenched Utah power structure, OK?"

A sustained standing ovation for Sally followed, along with a much more restrained smattering of "Fuck O-ver-**LORDS**," apparently subdued out of deference to Sally's motherly composure.

"What we have here is a failure to communicate," Sally started, in a faux Florida accent, in homage to the character of actor Strother Martin in *"Cool Hand Luke."*

"But not for any lack of trying to communicate," she continued for one last sentence in the fake accent. "We tell our friends, our spouses and our church leaders every chance we get how difficult it is to be a working parent, how difficult it is to operate a small business enterprise, how difficult it is to be in a loveless marriage, how difficult it is to be overwhelmed by a corporate-controlled government which is rigged to nickel and dime to death everyone except the wealthy elite.

"What we get back in response is, typically, 'Pray for the Holy Spirit's guidance.'

'Be more frugal.'

'Work harder when you feel like giving up.'

'Concentrate on making your husband happier and you'll be happier.'

'Don't fret over problems out of your control.'

(A color copy of the Tom Tomorrow cartoon "Experts Agree: Nothing Can Be Done" was projected on the screen behind Sally at that moment.)

At that point, a group of approximately 100 persons in the crowd – mostly women, all sitting together – began repeatedly chanting, "Apostate Slut! Apostate Slut! Apostate Slut!" For the moment, Sally ignored them, continuing to speak from her prepared remarks.

"It's enough to make you want to give up, move to someplace else *far* away – maybe even to some other country - and go on welfare. But we don't. We keep getting out of bed every day and putting one foot in front of the other. We keep trying, because our culture teaches us it's always wrong to give up. Wrong to risk relying on someone else.

"But it also teaches us to *put up with feeling punished* every time we keep on trying and trying and trying.

"I'm tired of feeling punished by the kinds of corporate overlords who run our Federal, state and local governments. I'm tired of automatically thinking that the problems caused by all of that concentrated wealth, the problems caused by all that organized money, are problems *'out of our control.'*

"If the Founding Fathers and Mothers of our great country had adopted that perspective when they were considering moving here from England – if they'd thought that solutions to their grievances against King George were *'out of their control,'* we might all be laboring in Newcastle coal mines right now. Including our children.

"This Un-Screwing of America Second Bill of Rights would give us the chance to gain some control over those corporate overlords. Grassroots control that's been usurped by the sheer volume of billionaire dollars poured into Washington, D.C. lobbying for a hundred years.

"But what will it take to make this Second Bill of Rights the law of the land? Here's what: it has to be passed by both chambers of Congress with two-thirds of those voting supporting it. Then it must be ratified by three-fourths of the states' legislatures – 38 of the 50 states.

"That can happen only one way: with a groundswell of grassroots support from supporters all over the country. That means those of you right here in this arena tonight need to get commitments for support of the USA-SBR from your members of Congress in the U.S. House and in the U.S. Senate. Likewise, you need to get commitments for support from your legislative representatives and senators in your state legislature.

"If those people elected to represent us either refuse to support it or decline to take a position on it, they need to be replaced. They can only be replaced by you finding qualified candidates to run against them. We can't do that for you. You have to organize yourselves and make that happen.

"But here's the advantage you have: all those corporate overlords out there who've bought off most of the Congress don't think you're up to the challenge. They're going to ignore you, probably for a long time. They've ignored these good people from Poughkeepsie, NY who started this and their millions of YouTube hits for quite a while now.

"So, my message is: make hay while the sun shines. Get out there tomorrow and start sending E-Mails, mailing letters and making phone calls to your elected officeholders. Make them take a stand. If they ignore you, send letters to the editor documenting their failures to respond. If they support you, send letters to the editor praising them for taking a courageous, smart position.

"And then, for those who still blow you off, surprise them with a quality challenger in their next primary and general election. This CAN be done. But only if you grab them by the balls, figuratively speaking, and get them to see it's not business as usual any longer.

"Or, you can sit back, spend all your time eating the ramen noodles you've been tossed tonight, trying on the new underwear thrown to you this evening, watching football on TV all day long, goofing around on Facebook and planning your picks for your fantasy sports teams – *if* you **like** corporate overlords controlling lots of your life choices.

"It's up to each of you. Please choose wisely. And please take as many copies of the USA-SBR from the tables in the back as you think you can share with your friends, co-workers and families.

"Thanks for wanting to make a difference – please stay now for the movie… unless you want to get a head start on contacting your elected officeholders.

"And any of you corporate overlords who might be out there this evening, we hope you find a special joy in watching this movie. It's all about the wonderful ways in which you've enriched all our lives."

The crowd then gave Sally a two-minute standing ovation and added another minute of "**Fuck O-ver-LORDS!**" chants.

It was Franklin's turn to get up and thank Sally for her presentation, but his face was nearly beet-red. He was, uncharacteristically, furious over the insulting chants against Sally by the small group in the crowd.

After praising Sally's poise, courage and insights, Franklin patiently took verbal aim at the religious extremists in the audience.

"I have some advice for those of you who chose to disrupt Sally's presentation," he said. "It has nothing to do with the disruption itself – there are times with disruption is appropriate. Like times when the leaders of a government are about to take their country over a cliff. Like in 2003 before the Iraq War or in 1964 before Congress' Gulf of Tonkin resolution started the Vietnam War.

"But I want to ask those of you who decided this is an appropriate venue for disruption to consider some facts about whom you've chosen to target.

"Instead of trying to speak truth to power, instead of trying to challenge a person or organization which actually has real impact on your daily lives, you've chosen to verbally smear someone who's found the courage within herself to step beyond the day-to-day responsibilities of raising children on her own. Responsibilities which dwarf the responsibilities of most of the ambitious college students in this arena.

"She decided to take the risk of speaking out because she wants to make this world a better place for her children. Instead of assuming there was no impact she could make on corporate overlords, both near and distant, who adversely affect our lives, she invested her heart in the notion that every human being can make a difference.

"By simply speaking out to suggest that the all-male elderly hierarchy in her chosen faith just might not have the most perfect spiritual insights into the lives of women, she's brought down a world of intimidation upon herself. The institution which comforted her as a child now is deciding whether to shame and shun her.

"By smearing her with your words of contempt, you've chosen to debase not just your own dignity, but the dignity of all those who hail from this beautiful, blessed state. It's a state full of kind-hearted, hard-working, well-intentioned thoughtful people, people who would no sooner turn their backs on a neighbor in need than jump up and down barefooted on broken glass.

"But it's a state that can't shake the image of old-time religious fanatics marrying dozens of wives, some as young as 13. A state with a religious culture which, to this day, still holds as its official position that the most pious members will have multiple wives once they reach their place in the celestial kingdom.

"When the most fanatical of those among you out there publicly take to task an overwhelmingly endearing, lovely soul like Sally – and take her to task with such shamefully obtuse and disgusting words, you reinforce that image of this precious state as a fertile breeding ground of hard-hearted fanaticism.

"If that is your goal - to make your spectacular state as unattractive as possible to evenly-balanced persons from other regions, to forever brand this state as the home of the generic Stepford wife – just keep treating people of good will like Sally as though they're diseased human refuse.

"Compassionate stewards of the human condition like Sally deserve far better. *Every Utah resident* deserves far better. To paraphrase someone infinitely wiser than I, those of you who keep chanting about Sally should try removing the beams from your own eyes before you start picking at the motes in someone else's."

As the last of Franklin's words echoed in the arena, most of the women in the group of "Apostate Slut" chanters quieted, though the men in the group resumed their chanting and increased their volume.

As Franklin and the others on the dais took turns embracing Sally, the slut-chants were drowned out by a sustained standing ovation. There were what Franklin assumed to be tears of appreciation on Sally's face as she whispered her heartfelt thanks into Franklin/Percy's right ear. She called her children, Royal and Chloe Masterson, up from the audience to share in the embraces.

While the ovation continued, Franklin glanced more closely at Sally, Royal and Chloe and noticed there were nearly threadbare spots on Sally's dress. Likewise, he saw that Royal's pants ended almost two inches above his shoes and that the socks on Chloe's little feet were pock-marked with holes, whether from moths or lots of washing and wearing. It was clear to Franklin that Sally was trying to squeeze every last penny out of her budget.

Had he been able to visit Sally's rental house in Taylorsville, he'd have found lots more evidence of forced frugality: their only television was a 25-year-old 19-inch screen analog set with a rabbit ears antenna; their only car was a 1987 Plymouth Reliant with a failing valve, balding tires and one stuck window; their only couch was a tattered upholstered convertible sofa covered with a duvet and their only cooling system was an old ceiling fan – and windows which had been painted shut 'til Sally pried them open with kitchen knives.

Approximately 99 percent of the arena crowd remained for the movie. A few could be seen in semi-darkness trying on the underwear they'd been tossed as the lights went down.

As the lights went down for the movie, Sally, still crying, motioned Franklin/Percy to come backstage, where they began talking.

"Do you know why I can't stop crying?" she sobbed quietly.

"I imagine it has to do with the cruel things those lunatics were yelling out about you," Franklin said, now feeling worried. "Is there something else we should know about, Sally?"

"I don't think you get it," she said. "It's like you're stuck in the 1950s or something. If you're wondering if I've been some kind of 'loose woman' after I separated from Mike, well maybe I was, the way it's defined around here: I went on one date just before my divorce was final. I don't even remember the guy's name. We had dinner, went to a movie and he dropped me off at home. We didn't even hold hands.

"Here's the thing you don't seem to grasp: I'm a woman, not a child who needs to be protected. I can stand up for myself. I can decide when it's time to confront people – and I can decide who deserves to be confronted and when.

"Maybe there are some things about our culture you don't yet understand, but, in general, we see contentiousness as a last resort. Maybe it's because contentiousness rarely changes peoples' hearts and minds. Maybe it's because getting us to self-censor our inclinations to be contentious makes us less likely to openly question the things that keep old white men in power.

"Whatever it is, each of us feels like we have the right to decide for ourselves when the time is right to use that last tool in our toolbelt.

"You took that choice away from me when you dressed down those fanatics. You decided I needed rescuing. But you didn't ask me.

"The difference between women of my generation and women of my mothers' and grandmother's generations is we do _**not**_ want our lives to be defined by whether we're _'fortunate enough'_ to have a man around to rescue us. We don't want to become dependent on a man's imposing presence to ward off those who would try to intimidate us.

"When I was little, I saw what happens when little boys got into playground fights and the weaker of the fighters called out for help from the nearest grown-up recess monitor: the weaker boy was never again treated with respect by his little peers.

"When well-meaning men like yourself take up the cause of defending poor little Miss Put-Upon, it makes us women look like that weak child on the playground who needs the gym teacher to come and restrain the husky bully.

"We don't like that, Mr. Van Mullder. Personally, it doesn't just take away my own voice, it makes a little bit of me die inside.

"I know you didn't mean for me to feel that way. But I hope you can see now why I *do* feel that way. I hope you – and any other man in a similar situation in the future – will respect me enough to ask me beforehand if I want to be verbally defended.

"If you haven't already figured it out, this was not the time I wanted to confront the pro-Stepford Wives faction of women and men in this state. That time may come soon, maybe even next week, but if it does, please trust me to figure out when that time is right, OK?"

"This is a lot to take in, Sally," Franklin said, visibly embarrassed. "As you said, I had no intent to overstep. I had no intent to do anything other than demand that those people stop verbally abusing you."

"I'm perfectly capable of making that same kind of demand, Percy," she said. "Speaking directly to those orally flatulent nimrods simply took the emphasis off of why we're here – the USA-SBR – and put it on my personal life.

"I don't think **any** of us wanted that."

"In retrospect, I couldn't agree more. I hope you'll forgive me for acting on my emotions instead of on my insights about how to connect with people. Flies with honey, you know."

"What are you, 20? You'll get the hang of this pleasing-the-crowd thing. I can tell you have a real aptitude for getting people to grasp new perspectives on things. If *you* don't dwell on this mis-step, then *I* won't, OK, Percy?"

"Agreed, Sally. What do you say we try to get this right tomorrow in Ogden? Will you join us there? Please??"

"I don't know – let me sleep on it tonight. I'll let you three know first thing in the morning, if that's OK."

"That'll do nicely."

Once the movie was over and the crowd had left the arena, another 50,000 copies of the USA-SBR had been picked up by those attending the rally. More than 7,000 of the attendees had signed pledges to contact area elected officials to compel them to take a position on the USA-SBR.

✳ ✳ ✳

The phone rang at 8:30 a.m. the next morning in Franklin's room, a half-hour before the Poughkeepsie trio planned to travel up Interstate 15 to the Browning Center at Weber State University in Ogden. To Franklin's great relief, it was Sally: she'd decided to join them for the stops in Ogden and, the next day, at the Dee Glen Smith Spectrum arena in Logan at Utah State University.

One of Sally's longtime women church friends dropped her off at the Red Lion about 45 minutes later; her eyes still were red and her face still appeared slightly flushed, as though there had been ocular leakage off and on throughout the night. She explained that she'd left the children with her sister Billie Sue Wheeler in West Jordan for the next two days. She planned to take a bus back to Salt Lake City after the rally in Logan.

"Are you sure you're up for this?" Idris asked, looking intently into Sally's weary eyes. "I heard most of what you and Fra-, er, Percy were talking about off-stage last night. Sounded like you were none too pleased."

"It really wasn't meant for anyone's ears except Percy's," Sally said. "I think I made my point – and I think he understands now that if he goes off on a tangent about me in front of a crowd again, my special touch might change him from a baritone to a castrato – and provide me with some portable stress-relieving squeeze balls at the same time. One bird killing two stones, so to speak."

"Guess we'd better have Percy start wearing a cup around you," Idris said. "Seriously, though, you look either like someone who's got a hideous hangover or like someone who just did an all-nighter studying for a final exam. I'd offer you something not available at your average Walgreens for what's ailing you, but Percy's pretty adamant about us treating our bodies like we want 'em to last 200 years."

"A good nap in the back seat on the way to Ogden and I'll have as much vim and vigor as Van Mullder there." At the moment Sally said that, Franklin/Percy was sitting in the back seat yawning and inadvertently belching, barely conscious as he scratched the crotch of his pants, first from the outside and then reaching inside. He seemed unaware anyone was watching.

"Find anything interesting in there?" Bianca yelled.

"Mmmph," Franklin/Percy half-snored. "Time to go to Warm Springs?" He was disoriented, groggy from a catnap started while he was waiting for Sally to show.

"You mean the side trip to Lava Hot Springs in Idaho – no, that's the day after tomorrow, Percival," Bianca said, thinking on her feet. "You need to wake up if you're going to do the driving to Ogden."

"That's OK, I think I'll take a snooze 'til we get there – Marcia, would you please take the wheel?" Franklin asked.

"Only if you agree to stop the personal self-inspection of your factory-installed equipment, Mr. Van Mullder," Marcia said.

He did.

* * *

The rally at the Browning Center that evening once again filled about two-thirds of the arena. Franklin was relieved that there were no organized anti-Sally Cummings hecklers. But he and the others were peeved that there appeared to be Mormon missionary pairs scattered throughout the audience wielding phone cameras. Their mission that night appeared to be to photograph "Fuck O-ver-LORD!" chanters in mid-chant so their use of obscenity could be relayed to their ward bishops.

"It's a free country," Franklin/Percy whispered away from the microphone to Idris, Bianca and Sally. "If people feel strongly enough to use that kind of language, they need to be prepared to defend their right to do it and even accept any consequences their church might dispense.

"What do *you* think, Sally?"

"I've never been even remotely comfortable using obscenity or profanity," Sally said. "Using those words certainly displays the well-deserved contempt for their corporate abusers, but I don't know if it wins over people who don't understand the difference between mega-corporate overlords and much smaller companies.

"But, **unlike** Saint Reagan in the '60s at Berkeley, I'm all for free speech. Like you said, though, they just need to be prepared to defend their First Amendment rights and take the fecal-smelling consequences they had reason to know might be crawling out of the scriptural sewers where the proud pious pants-pooping patriarchal punishers self-perpetuate."

"Still, though," Idris said, "it seems *sooo* un-cool to try to intimidate people gathered in a large crowd for a completely legal event by taking random pictures. Seems like something that would've been done in 1930's Germany to keep the Hitler Youth in line."

"Tell you what: just to be fair to everyone here, in case they don't want to be surveilled by roving bands of LDS missionaries, let's make sure everyone's aware of what's happening, OK?" Franklin asked.

All heads, including Sally's, nodded in agreement.

Franklin/Percy stepped to the mic, introduced himself, explained the agenda for the rally that evening and then said:

"Please excuse the young ladies and gentlemen taking photos around the arena – I'm told that they're participants in an LDS program to train members with homosexual preferences to get straight by taking pictures of people they'd like to seduce for gay sex so they can easily remind themselves about the kinds of people they should NOT socialize with.

"So, if you see them pointing their phone cameras at you, for their own good, try to make the most suggestive poses possible so they'll get as much practice as possible to suppress their normal personalities. If they're going to stay in the church, they'll need to suppress 24/7. After all, if God gave them those desires, he must've known they'd have the strength to suppress them, right?"

The ensuing silliness that spread through the audience led to lots of goofy interactions between the crowd and the surreptitious missionary photographers –

including a smattering of private body parts exposed by the most enthusiastic attendees. Within five minutes, the photographers, frustrated by almost every last person in the crowd making over-the-top posing gestures, huddled together at the end of the arena opposite the dais and shortly afterward left the building.

Franklin/Percy noticed.

"It looks like our gay-challenged photojournalists have decided they have enough pics to practice not masturbating to," Franklin said. "Let's all give them a big hand for keeping those cold showers going. And for keeping those shake weights shaking!"

The crowd, laughing heartily, gave the exiting spy photographers a 30-second ovation. There were hundreds of air-masturbation gestures aimed in their direction as they left the arena.

The rally went on as planned: packages of underwear and ramen noodles were slung into the stands, Franklin/Percy and Sally gave inspiring speeches, "Capitalism: A Love Story" was screened and thousands more copies of the USA-SBR were carried away for distribution by the attendees. There were smatterings of hecklers during Sally's talk, but Franklin restrained himself from engaging them. Sally ignored them – outwardly, at least.

Shortly after the rally ended, Marcia advised Franklin and Sally that Terry Gross, National Public Radio "Fresh Air" host, had been in the audience and was hoping to interview them about the USA-SBR on audiotape for later airing. Franklin and Sally both agreed to the taping, Franklin more enthusiastically than Sally.

The focus of Ms. Gross' interview was, essentially, how the USA-SBR organizers planned to be taken seriously by the media and political establishment, especially considering how young they all appeared to be.

Franklin/Percy responded by saying their goal wasn't to be taken seriously by corporate media and corporate-shill politicians.

"Our goal is to be taken seriously by grassroots voter activists. Period," Franklin said. "The more our followers put pressure on elected officeholders and media, the more seriously we'll be taken by other voters. It has to come from the ground up if we're ever to get the numbers we need to actually amend the Constitution."

"The more we can spread the word that the USA-SBR will make real differences for those at the bottom of the earnings pyramid, the more seriously we will be taken," Sally said. "Reporting on grassroots organization efforts like ours leads to active public participation in social and economic justice movements. I believe that's actually part of the original NPR mission statement, as far as I know.

"I don't believe it states anywhere in that mission statement that there's a minimum age requirement for leaders of grassroots organization movements. From what I've seen, these people from Poughkeepsie are mature far beyond their years."

Franklin and Sally appeared to impress Ms. Gross; 10 days later, their interview was the lead feature on the national "Fresh Air" broadcast. She included excerpts from "man/woman on the street" interviews of about two dozen others whom she'd met in the audiences at the Ogden, Salt Lake City and Orem venues with their individual takes on the USA-SBR. Almost all of the persons she'd met were hopeful about the prospects for real change which could result from eventual ratification of the USA-SBR. Gross also included excerpts of a few interviews with Utah elected officeholders, each of whom was surprised at the level of support for what they'd thought the rally audiences would see as radical features of the USA-SBR.

In the meantime, Franklin pleaded with Sally to continue on with them to Idaho State University in Pocatello and Boise State University in Boise, ID. She listened to Franklin/Percy's impassioned reasons for her to accompany them at least two more times as their featured guest speaker.

"We're just a handful of good government advocates from upstate New York," Franklin said. "No one in Utah could care less what **we** think about making peoples' lives better.

"You're not just one of them. You're one of them who's had the fortitude to stand up to conventional thinking. You're one of them who's had the courage to publicly risk her standing in the church simply to do the right thing. You're one of them who's got almost every single parent church member in the state cheering you on. And a lot of the parents of those single parent church members too.

"We're way, _way_ stronger with you than without you. It's not even close."

"If I stay on for two more rallies, what do I tell you when you ask me to stay yet another day?" Sally asked.

"You tell us you promised to stay just thru Boise. If that's what you prefer."

"This is the longest I've been apart from my children since they were born. My daughter told me on the phone last night that she lost a tooth yesterday. I know that must seem like a silly thing to be concerned about for people who want to stop working people all over the country from being ripped off.

"The most important thing in my life is my family. I'm doing this **because** they're so important to me. But I don't want to become _so wrapped up_ in this USA-SBR campaign that I end up risking my relationships with my children.

"I will stay with you through the Boise rally, but I won't guarantee that I'll ever participate again. I _will_ guarantee that I'll always have good things to say about what you're trying to do."

Later that evening, Sally called her sister Billie Sue to confirm whether she would be OK with keeping her children a few days more. She was. Billie Sue was unabashedly proud of what Sally was doing; Billie Sue wished _she_ had the guts to speak out as forthrightly as her sister.

"Give 'em heck," Billie Sue told Sally. In Utah, people generally don't say hell. But they still mean it.

* * *

The rally in Logan surprised the Poughkeepsians because the *"Fuck O-ver-LORDS!"* chants were much more sparse than at any of the previous gatherings. Sally wasn't surprised, though. She told Franklin/Percy later that most of those attending USU were devout LDS members who weren't fortunate enough to be admitted to Brigham Young University, the LDS-owned institution about 125 miles away in Provo. Recreational use – or any other use, for that matter – of obscenities is strictly verboten among LDS faithful.

But Sally's talk seemed to resonate deeply with the crowd, which was perhaps two-thirds female. At times, it was so quiet as she spoke that Franklin thought he could almost hear his own heart beating. The attendees appeared most moved by Sally's first-hand account of what it was like to be an abused single mother of two whose own bishop's primary advice was to give her estranged abusive husband more chances to abuse her. While trying simultaneously to pay rent and keep the children well-fed and clothed despite receiving virtually no child support. Her descriptions of constantly mending worn out under- and outerwear and going without food for herself one in every three days from time to time seemed to hit home the hardest, as well as her descriptions of countless sweaty hours over steaming hot water while canning thousands of jars of home-grown vegetables and fruits for food storage for the always-around-the-corner 'second coming of Christ.' Likewise, she described uncounted times of being told it was her responsibility to take their sick or injured children to the doctor - even when injuries resulted from their father's negligence – and always being expected to pay doctors with her own money. The same money expected to be used for her husband's personal expenses if his earnings suddenly "came up short." And hundreds of times being reminded by her husband that it was "God's will" that she submit to *him* as the head of their household. All without once hearing a thank-you or seeing any other form of heartfelt appreciation from her then-cohabiting husband. Unless repeatedly being shoved to the ground counted. And always having to explain to the children why Daddy was angry at Mommy. And always having to explain to the children why Mommy's earnings weren't enough to buy the new clothes or new school supplies they needed. Idris and Bianca could see tears streaming down the faces of most of those in the audience as Sally spoke.

"When I read that executives at fossil fuels corporations, major airlines and other high-profit industries have hired lobbyists to work hard to block any attempts to enact meaningful minimum wage increases – like, say, to $15 per hour – while those same executives are drawing record-high pay, I was furious.

"These super-rich corporatists and their shills – they care exactly zero about how hard it is for working people like us to pay our bills on the poverty wages they pay. For all they care, we can all drop dead at our jobs. They probably already have 'dead peasant insurance' on you. Their only worry is how quickly they can substitute another warm body in your place.

"This USA-SBR would put in place some real protections for the financial security of every last one of us. Most important, it would make it hard – supremely hard – for the super-rich to pull those protections out from under us by making it **harder for them** to influence who's elected.

"The USA-SBR would force elected officeholders to be accountable to each and every voter by severely limiting the amount which can be donated to campaigns by individuals and organizations. And it would put real teeth into the prosecutions of those who try to game the system.

"If you like the way things work right now, leave here tonight and never think of the USA-SBR again. If you don't like the way things work right now, leave here tonight and make it a top priority to get commitments in writing from each of your elected office holders on whether they support the USA-SBR.

"And if they don't support it or won't say *whether* they support it, find a candidate who **does** to run against them. Even if it means running yourself.

"Never, EVER again let there be a worker who can't afford to purchase the product or service she or he labors hard to produce. Never, EVER again let there be a worker whose full-time earnings aren't enough to pay for a decent home. Never, EVER again let there be a worker whose hard-earned pay isn't sufficient to keep every family member well-fed and well-clothed. Never, EVER again let there be a worker whose children can't afford to go to four years of college.

"And never, EVER again let there be a worker who is too afraid to blow the whistle on an employer who's breaking the law or otherwise endangering the lives of employees and members of the general public.

"When you've left this gathering tonight, listen to your own heart, listen to that spirit inside you which you've learned to trust. Listen to everything that matters most and decide on your own whether the USA-SBR deserves your full and lasting support. Whether it deserves your honest, dedicated energy and efforts.

"That's how we un-screw America. Once and for all, for ourselves and for all of our descendants.

"Our future is in _your_ hands, depending on what each of you does and does not do. Our future does **NOT** have to be in the hands of our corporate overlords. Our future does **NOT** have to be a future in which our children are brainwashed to be content with poverty wages from multiple jobs.

"If anyone tells you otherwise, make no mistake: they. are. lying.

"I know that's true because I know that, for **each and every hard-working person in this nation**, _**this**_ (*holding up a copy of the USA-SBR, pointing it in the direction of each section of the audience and pausing for effect*)…is. **truth**."

The previously enrapt crowd immediately broke into a standing ovation which lasted for minutes. Franklin strode toward Sally, extending his right hand to hers and shook it firmly with his left hand clasped around her right wrist. He then immediately held up her right hand with his left in the gesture of a newly-crowned prizefight winner.

Once again, applause continued well into the opening credits of "Capitalism: A Love Story."

* * *

Loganites' enthusiasm notwithstanding, local media mostly ignored the rally. There were mentions on the local TV news broadcasts of remarks by "the controversial Mormon single mom" who dared to challenge several church traditions. But details broadcast about the USA-SBR were minimal. However, USA-SBR website activity continued to be brisk, as were almost-entirely supportive blog postings and YouTube hits.

Idris and Franklin discussed the prospect of airing national TV and radio ads about the USA-SBR. Franklin calculated the approximate costs and concluded one-fourth of the proceeds from his stash of gold bars and coins would be exhausted within two years if they advertised the way new movie releases are advertised. While they agreed that a month or so of ads might be fruitful to prime the publicity pump, there needed to be a strategy which would galvanize grassroots supporters in such a way as to mostly eliminate the need for advertising. Idris convinced Franklin that advertising money mainly needed to be reserved for quick responses to corporate smear campaigns. They found out many months later that he couldn't have been more correct.

* * *

Nostalgia and a Near-Miss Munching

The next day they were compelled as the result of Bianca's previous remarks to make their detour to Lava Hot Springs on their way to Idaho State University in Pocatello. It turned out to be a welcome day trip respite for the group, not to mention stirring up plenty of comforting nostalgia for Franklin. On the way there along Route 91, Idris made a point of stopping at the Preston, Idaho Post Office so Franklin could view the Works Progress Administration-funded mural in the lobby of the WPA-funded Post Office building there. Idris quietly reminded Franklin that it was just one of many hundreds of such artworks made possible by Franklin's vision of the mission for the WPA.

"I wish we had time to visit every last one of them," Franklin said as he viewed "The Battle of Bear River" mural, his eyes moist. "I wish I could shake the hand of every single artist who left her or his mark for this fine country, for such miniscule compensation."

An hour up the road at Lava Hot Springs, all five of them decided to test the therapeutic potential of the warm waters – and every last one of them came away completely de-stressed and relaxed. Franklin particularly enjoyed rubbing elbows with both the southeastern Idaho hoi polloi and the late spring tourists from assorted far-flung locales.

He remarked how wonderful the warm waters had been for severe muscle pain he'd suffered years earlier and asked a few tourists from the Midwest whether they'd ever had any ancestors who suffered from diseases of the spine. One, Porter Armstrong, a middle-aged construction contractor from Fort Wayne, Indiana, actually had a long-deceased grandparent who suffered from polio myelitis. Franklin enjoyed listening to the man describe his family history along with the man's own contemporary health struggles. It turned out that the man had been on the verge of filing for bankruptcy relief from his medical expenses when his wife suddenly won a $100,000 lottery prize.

Bianca and Idris noticed Franklin's friendly fixation on the Indiana family and began to worry that they might get a little weirded out over a previously-unknown 20-ish young man's efforts to socialize with them. Not to mention Franklin perhaps inadvertently making a remark that didn't synch with his youthful appearance. It probably didn't help that Franklin was wearing plaid old-man style swim trunks (chosen himself at the Poughkeepsie Goodwill store) and had a tan roughly equivalent to that of a recently-exhumed Transylvanian bloodsucker. It was time, they agreed, whispering to each other, to approach Franklin with some made-up situation which would enable him to excuse himself from his current conversation.

But then Bianca noticed something else that made the hair stand up on her neck as though lightning were about to strike just a few feet away. When she looked over her left shoulder in the direction of a water slide to the east, she saw a partly facially-disfigured young man in a wet suit with a recently re-bandaged severe head wound showing a slight dark-pinkish blood stain.

She yanked Idris' sleeve so hard, she thought his glasses were going to fly off as he swayed back toward her right side.

"It's Defcon 5, Idris," she whispered directly into his ear. "Check out the quasi-gomer at six o'clock – about 50 yards right behind us.

"We've got to get the President out of here. NOW!"

Idris didn't even need to respond verbally. He started half-sprinting toward Franklin and Franklin's new acquaintance, Mr. Armstrong. Bianca began walking slowly backwards toward Franklin, keeping a constant eye on the bandaged-head military veteran just in case she might need to improvise some sort of physical barrier to keep the head-injured man from getting closer to the President.

It simply would not do to have a healthy-looking 20-year-old tourist from Poughkeepsie start trying to extract the brain matter from another tourist.

As Idris briskly approached Franklin, he realized he was almost too late.

"What do you folks think of all this computer hi-teck-ery going on these days? Do you think they'll be able to do the Dick Tracy wrist TV-phone thing-a-ma-jig someday soon?" Franklin asked the vacationing contractor. "And what about all these new-fangled throw-away nappies for babies? Does anyone besides me think those have got to be way more expensive for young parents pinching pennies?" In addition to being unaware that Skype functioned the same way as the Dick Tracy device, **and** unaware that most people under 50 have no idea who Dick Tracy was, Franklin was managing to sound EXACTLY like an out-of-touch elderly man who mostly just wanted to talk to strangers about old times.

"Does your family still have a Victrola for playing your rec-"

At that moment, there was a twitch on Franklin's face and a reflexive jerk of his head in the air, with Franklin involuntarily sniffing the air like an alpha wolf who's sensed a nearby competitor's pheromones.

"Percy," Idris interrupted, grabbing Franklin's shoulders in a firm, friendly gesture, "we just got a call from Candace in Pocatello that they can fix the car this afternoon if we arrive there by 4 p.m."

Franklin's aroma-seeking proboscis was suddenly distracted from the faint scent of nearby brain leakage and the fixed yellowish glaze on his eyes quickly re-focused on Idris as his pupil dilation rapidly shrank back to normal. The visceral compulsion to consume cranial matter was nipped with milliseconds to spare.

"There's something wrong with the ca-," Franklin started to ask.

"You remember, the alternator's been acting up – we don't want to get strand-ed somewhere between Pocatello and Boise, right?"

"Oh, uh, yes – makes perfect sense. I hope you'll excuse me, Mr. Armstrong."

Mr. Armstrong, visibly relieved, did exactly that.

At that moment, Bianca was spilling – accidentally on purpose – the con-tents of her purse, including three dollars in change, directly alongside the head-injured veteran half a football field away. The veteran instinctively bent over to help her pick up the strewn items for the lovely damsel in minor distress as Idris signaled to Bianca to meet them ASAP at the car.

Franklin and Idris then made a beeline to the parking lot, with Sally join-ing them not far from the exit. Along the way, Franklin, noticing Idris' flushed perspiration-beaded face, asked if Idris had eaten some bad food.

"Nothing a few fresh hot *tacos de sesos* wouldn't fix, Sir," Idris said.

* * *

Disappointed their Lava Hot Springs stay was about to end, Franklin made a mental note to return to that lovely valley someday so he could hike the Portneuf Mountain Range nearby, a range which could compete nicely in a con-test for the most-underappreciated natural beauty in the country. The area east of the lavas around the cliffs on Snow Peak in the Bonneville Peak Roadless Area had a special appeal to Franklin, as did the North Pebble Roadless Area, with its reputation for blazing fall colors. As someone not especially inclined to pack tents in and out on hikes, he thought staying in one of the numerous rental yurts would be "a blast," as Pongo might put it. Plus, the idea of searching for undis-covered caves among the many thick limestone deposits in the range would be an enjoyable challenge. He suspected it would be the kind of outdoor adventure Pongo and Heather might love. The hospitality of the local folk had left a lasting impression on him; he wished he'd been able to spend time in the area during his presidency, but decided he liked it much better being unrecognized.

At that moment, he made a final decision that it was crucial to modify his appearance in any way reasonable. He decided to make an appointment with an orthodontist *and* optometrist as soon as he returned to Poughkeepsie. And to grow both a *thick* moustache and a goatee as quickly as his facial hair would co-operate. He wanted, as much as anything in his life, to be able to travel around the country by train, bus or on foot whenever he felt like it without ever again having to worry about being recognized.

* * *

On to Boise: Corporate-Adorned Arenas for Your Low-Wage Pleasure

Of course, there was nothing wrong with their rental car. Idris tried to explain the situation away by saying that the alternator appeared to have fixed itself. But Franklin, who knew a thing or two about motors, especially on watercraft, quickly deduced that he'd just been "handled" not unlike the way his political managers had shuffled him in and out of public gatherings long ago to keep him on schedule. *(It would be a few days before Bianca would have a chance to delicately explain to Franklin how he'd sounded like a lonely elderly man while he was speaking to the Armstrongs from Indiana – something he promptly agreed that he wanted to avoid whenever possible. She and Idris decided it would serve no purpose to mention to Franklin how close he'd come to possibly having his brain-gobbling compulsion overwhelm him again – but changed their minds a day later, concluding he deserved to know.)*

They checked into their hotel room at the Best Western in Pocatello before heading to nearby Holt Arena at Idaho State University. While the others took naps in advance of the rally scheduled for 7:30 p.m. that evening, Franklin found himself surfing the cable TV offerings. He seemed most fixated on previews of the Discovery Channel's upcoming series about the homesteading Kilcher family's efforts to survive in Alaska, plus an episode of HBO's *"Boardwalk Empire."* He actually watched a few minutes of Fox News, but switched channels when he thought he was experiencing the same sort of symptoms he had just before his fatal stroke. He wondered what sort of hyper-angry, hyper-paranoid, hyper-ignorant personalities could actually enjoy such a roiling paranoid departure from reality.

That evening's gathering, which they'd decided to dedicate to ISU progressive icon Charles E. "Chick" Bilyeu (who'd passed away four years earlier), drew the fewest attendees of any of the arena venues they'd visited to that point. Holt

Arena was slightly less than half-full. Marcia had made sure Franklin/Percy and Idris had participated in advance through phone interviews with local radio and print news organizations, in addition to placing a half-page advertisement in the local Idaho State Journal, but they'd not had a chance to do local TV news interviews.

But what the crowd lacked in numbers, they made up for in spirit, with *mucho gusto*. There were frequent standing ovations, proud brandishings of newly-distributed clean underwear and dozens of hand-made "We Love Sally Cummings" signs with drawings of encircled Mason jars with diagonal slash marks through the circles. Apparently, the Pocatello area was rife with people who didn't care if they survived a holocaust or the lunatics' highly-anticipated second coming of Christ.

Even a contingent of mostly white-shirted young folk wearing BYU-Rexburg-logoed sweatshirts and baseball caps in the nosebleed section of Holt Arena who'd traveled south for the event appeared to be having a genuinely good time – although that section of the arena was fairly quiet during the "Fuck O-ver-LORD!" chants at the beginning and end of the rally.

What encouraged the Poughkeepsian rally organizers the most, though, was the hearty spontaneous laughter during the showing of "*Capitalism: A Love Story.*" The part of the "*Capitalism*" movie with a scene lifted from the movie "*Jesus of Nazareth*" which has a capitalist-converted Jesus voice dubbed so Jesus says the poor shall "pay out of pocket" for their "pre-existing conditions" drew especially raucous guffaws.

By the time the night was over, they'd won over a half-arena-full of new Michael Moore fans.

On the way back to the hotel after the rally, Marcia provided the latest stats from their website and blogs along with another pleasant surprise: U.S. Rep. Alan Grayson had agreed to be a guest speaker at their gathering two nights later at Boise State University's Taco Bell Arena.

Of course, Franklin, who'd been exposed to relatively little *commercial* television and, surprisingly, no Mexican fast food outlets, had to ask:

"Just what is a tahcoe belle? Is that a Lake Tahoe company's female concierge?"

"Bless your heart, sir," Bianca said, "but women – outside of Alabama, Mississippi and Louisiana, at least – very rarely are referred to as belles. It's almost a sexist kind of thing. Very archaic.

"Taco Bell – spelled capital T-a-c-o capital B-e-l-l – is a major fast food chain selling cheap Mexican food like tacos, burritos and quesadillas. It's owned by a major conglomerate, Yum! Brands, which also owns Kentucky Fried Chicken and Pizza Hut. You've probably been driven past the Taco Bell restaurant on Main Street in Poughkeepsie a dozen times, so I don't know how you've missed it."

"I honestly don't go down Main Street that much – mostly Albany Post Road - and when someone else is driving, I'm usually reading something for school," Franklin said. "Is that the pinkish bell logo? I remember seeing that, but not the name that went with it. Anyway, what's a thing called Yum! Brands doing sponsoring a state university's athletic arena?"

"Like the Cracker Barrel Old Country Store Restaurants and Darden Inc.'s Red Lobster and Olive Garden restaurants, Yum! Brands lobbies hard against unions and minimum wage increases," Bianca said. "Their sponsoring things like state universities' athletic arenas is a huge public relations gesture designed to take peoples' minds off how little they care about working people being able to pay their bills. At last count, there were more than a hundred stadiums, arenas and raceways *just in the U.S.* named for their corporate sponsors. Toyota Corp. alone has at least 10 venues named for it. Taco Bell's not even the only taco restaurant with an arena name: Taco John's has one in Cheyenne, WY. And Taco Bell Arena isn't even the only Yum! Brands business with an arena named for it: Yum! also has KFC Yum! Center in Louisville. There's even a Whataburger Field for the Corpus Christi, Texas minor league baseball team."

"When I was dealing with business leaders one-on-one in 'olden times' 75 years ago, they would've been embarrassed to have their company's name splashed across a sporting arena or a racetrack," Franklin said. "It would've been seen as a patently undignified way to boast about what should've been private charitable activities.

"For the vast majority of business leaders back then, charitable activity for the public good was undertaken primarily because it was the right thing to do. But, back then, there were far more privately-held businesses and far fewer mega-corporations.

"Do you suppose, perhaps, that there's a significant portion of the population that confuses sponsorship with ownership? Yet another reason for all those corporations to attach their names to taxpayer-owned facilities on campuses and in high-traffic-volume city centers."

"I'm thinking, Mr. President, maybe you might not want to make a *habit* of eating at places like Yum! Brands fast food joints," Idris said. "Unless you're a really, really big tipper.

"They're the kinds of businesses that spend millions and millions of 'dark money' dollars on TV ads – mainly on Fox News-type shows – spreading the myth that minimum wage increases contribute to unemployment and inflation.

"It's a huge lie. All major studies over the past 30 years have shown annual minimum wages increases and higher-paying union-type jobs in general result in people spending more on basics and even non-basics. More spending equals more demand, which equals more jobs, which also equals less government spending on welfare, Food Stamps and health care. Which means fewer tax dollars required for the needy.

"And the obvious: inflation __not__ related to energy and health care costs over the past 25 years has been *almost non-existent.* __Despite__ numerous states regularly increasing minimum wages.

"Even so, if a big lie is repeated often enough – and without being refuted in similar proportions – the lie takes on a life of its own. So, those corporatist bastards who don't give a shit about their own employees manage to perpetuate the myth. Reality notwithstanding."

"Myth perpetuation…That seems to be the dog in the manger obsession for conservatives of the past 75 years," Franklin said. "Their compulsive mindset is that, even if they can be enormously rich, they'll never be rich enough as long as the working class can live comfortably on dollars that conceivably could go to those at the top. They pretty much view it as a cultural atrocity for hard-working middle class folks to live in financial comfort."

"That ties it up in a nice bow," Idris said. "If the middle class and working poor – *especially* folks of color – if they can live debt-free financially worry-free lives, then conservatives see the country as having defecated its Ayn Randian 'me-first' vital organs in favor of some sort of communist-slash-socialist cancer. Lots and lots of health care-related and education debt-related bankruptcies: those are prime indicators of the robust health of a predatory capitalist economy to the Randian conservatives.

"Without those bankruptcies, banks and credit card companies can't ratchet up high-interest so-called short-term debt on struggling working folk. Gotta keep 'em in a hole they'll never get out of if we want to keep those stock prices nice 'n high.

"Plus, the most massive corporations, including those restaurant corporations Bianca mentioned plus a host of other huge companies, all are lobbying largely in secret to support the Trans Pacific Partnership trade agreement.[*]

"If the TPP should somehow pass the Congress, it could lead to widespread setbacks in food safety standards, massive outsourcing to sweatshops, extensions of consumer-screwing drug patents, government job privatization at the expense of experienced employees' wages, benefits and professionalism, gaming the system in favor of industrial agriculture over family farmers even more than it's *already* fucked up – you name it, the TPP is a dream list for corporate greedheads.

"Any single one of those TPP elements would create a shitstorm if brought up one at a time, but the genius of the TPP is that, as a trade agreement, it could pass the Congress relatively scrutiny-free with all its toxic particulars intact. Unless people like Rep. Grayson drag those putrid details out into the sunlight for disinfection.

"And a little birdie told me Mr. Grayson just might be going to court to do exactly that."

"So why in God's name doesn't HE run for President one of these days?" Franklin asked.

"Well, as I understand it, Sir, he lost his latest election last year due to Republican gerrymandering," Bianca said. "But maybe he'll run again. Maybe in a different district."

---

[*] 8/19/14 *Counterpunch.org* interview with Alan Weissman by Mickey Z

"He sounds like my kind of Democrat," Franklin said. "A bona fide, real, dyed-in-the-wool scrapper. Someone who'd rather chew steel wool than mince words. We used to have a lot of those."

"And then came the big-money elections that go along with TV ads," Idris reminded Franklin. "It takes a lot of corporate sucking up for some people to raise the money they think they need."

"That's why we're doing this, remember? That's why I wrote the USA-SBR," Franklin said. "All that corporate brown-nosing can't continue. Not if the country as I used to know it is going to come back and thrive."

Protected from Invasion by Coloradans

The trip to Boise the next day began with a diversion to Mountain Home Air Force Base. Franklin wanted to see where all the stacks of taxpayer dollars had gone for this former Cold War-era nuclear missile and bomber base-turned-fighter jet base. As the result of a formal request to the base commander by Marcia shortly after she was hired, they took a brief driving tour of the base through the housing area for the 3,000-plus on-base residents and were then allowed to visit a hangar storing a handful of the base's F-15 fighter jets.

Franklin was impressed by the professionalism of the military staff he saw, but he was absolutely stunned at the level of technology and sheer air power evident during the tour.

"I remember when this base was opened at the beginning of the Second World War," Franklin recalled as Idris, Bianca, Sally and Marcia rode with him on the partly-cloudy breezy morning. "We wanted it far enough inland that it would be safe in the event of a surprise invasion. But now, as I understand it, they have lots of special radars and satellite detection which make it highly unlikely there would ever be any surprise on-the-ground invasion near any of our coasts or land borders.

"Just why do you think the base is here nowadays? I mean, instead of on the coast or near one of our international borders. Surely they don't think Montana or Wyoming are going to secede and declare war on the rest of the U.S. – there aren't any plans for a conflict with Canada, are there?"

"What a professor once told me," Idris said, "was that these bases are spread around the country to strategically distribute the Pentagon dollars and civilian Department of Defense jobs in such a way as to maximize local voter sympathy for people employed by the military.

"He said it had very, very little to do with actual strategy for military defense or offense. If it were on the basis of being as far as possible from potential enemies, all our bases would be in the handful of centrally-located Midwestern states. It's purely a political calculation. Same with defense contracts. It certainly makes sense from the perspective of the folks on Wall Street who stand to gain from that kind of corporate welfare.

"Makes it really hard for any given base to be closed or for any existing military contract to be completely terminated. Members of Congress routinely support each other's districts' bases and defense contracts. I'll scratch yours if you scratch mine, y'know."

"So, essentially, once again it's all about the concentration of profits for a select group," Franklin said, teeth gritted. "I've seen it before, but never at this level."

"That's pretty much now the American Way," Sally said, shrugging, eyes aimed at the ground. Today she was wearing repeatedly-patched overalls with a homemade blouse, plus canvas-topped deck shoes worn so thin that her little toes on both feet could be seen through the threads. "At least they have nice day care facilities on the bases, I guess. They certainly do at Hill Air Force Base in Davis County, Utah. I've visited friends there."

"No doubt, stationed there to protect us from the hordes invading westward from Colorado," Franklin joked, eyes rolling.

"I'm ready to leave," Franklin announced abruptly. "What's say let's take a drive to the Sawtooths? I'd like to get as far away from the instruments of war as I can for the rest of the day."

And that he did: they drove about 175 miles to Redfish Lake Lodge near Stanley, ID to stay the night on the north end of the lake there before going on to the downtown Boise Grove Hotel at mid-morning the next day. But not before stopping for an hour-long press conference at the hotel with local Boise print and broadcast journalists.

Idaho Statesman political reporter Stan Flopster, Idaho Press-Tribune reporter Juan Buncito, Boise Weekly reporter Elijah Grunge, local NBC affiliate's veteran reporter Stu Lincoln and a handful of bubbly-headed bleached blondes from other local broadcast TV stations showed up for the conference. Some of the reporters – such as Grunge and Flopster - were more conscious and sentient than others.

Lincoln led off the questioning by asking what was in it for the relatively youthful Poughkeepsie activists to push for the USA-SBR when the odds against success seemed so high.

"How can you know the odds against success are high when our organizing efforts aren't even old enough to be in pre-school?" Franklin/Percy asked.

"We're very optimistic. Every rally we've had has given us reasons to be hopeful. If we had another dozen like Sally Cummings, we'd have it made in the shade."

Flopster asked if Ms. Cummings' involvement might be seen as more of a detriment than an asset to the Poughkeepsians in areas where Mormon church activity was strong.

"This is an area where LDS women have begun to realize their concerns about gender equality aren't taken seriously by their church leaders," Franklin said. "As I understand it, Mormon women are organizing among themselves to break the tradition of feeling forced to wear dresses to church. It seems they're starting a 'Wear Pants to Church' movement.

"If Mormon women in Boise can embrace wearing pants to church as a form of protest, then they surely are primed to hear the compelling talks that Ms. Cummings has to share with them.

"That makes us especially optimistic."

The remaining questions involved strategies the Poughkeepsians intended to use to gain coverage from news media despite a major USA-SBR provision being designed to break up corporations with multiple media outlets.

"We don't intend to be dependent on corporate media," Idris said. "If need be, we're prepared to continue airing paid advertising.

"But we're not giving up hope on more traditional media, especially print media. We know the vast, vast majority of journalists out there are dedicated to peeling back the veils concealing the truth from their news consumers.

"So their job covering us should be fairly easy: we've already removed those veils. The USA-SBR is as open as open gets. No hidden agendas. Just the best interests of everyone from the pilot who keeps the commuter jet in the air to the minimum wage single mom who cleans hotel rooms for a living."

By the end of the press conference, the Boise-area journalists left the Grove Hotel surprised at just how credibly the young Poughkeepsians presented themselves. It came across in their news coverage, much to the Dutchess County residents' relief.

* * *

Laketime Leisure for Capt. Roosevelt

The Poughkeepsians arrived at the lodge in the Sawtooths Range by mid-afternoon to a stiff breeze blowing in thunderheads from the west. Once the threat of heavy rain subsided, Franklin persuaded Idris and Sally to join him in a small rented boat with an outboard motor to troll for cutthroat trout and grayling.

Catching fish wasn't really a priority for Franklin, though. He simply wanted to be out on the water, to feel the surges of the turgid whitecaps on the aluminum hull, to feel the boat's motor struggle against the sheer mass of the clear waters. When Sally broke into a shrieking smile as she felt the brisk tug of a six-pound brown trout on the end of her 4-lb test line, the rest of the lake cruise was all gravy for Capt. Roosevelt/Van Mullder.

He watched with unmitigated pleasure, standing firmly on his rejuvenated sea legs, as Sally's fiberglass rod arched from the struggling freshwater leviathan's power to almost kiss the water with its tip. Sally beamed with an experienced angler's pride as Idris netted the gleaming trout at the end of its unsuccessful 20-minute battle to stay submerged. But after cradling the slippery broad-shouldered eagle's cuisine for less than a minute, she handed it back to Idris, asking him to slip the lake dweller back into its moist roofless rent-free expanse.

They continued crossing back and forth across the acres and acres of royal blue former mountain peak snows as Bianca and Marcia watched from the lodge until shortly after the sun set behind orange and purple cumulonimbus clouds.

It was an afternoon Franklin and the others would remember long past the conclusion of their many visits to USA-SBR tour destinations. They all slept comfortably and dreamt peaceful dreams that night.

Little more than a day and a half later, though, Sally's life would be changed forever.

$$* \quad * \quad *$$

By 2 p.m. the next day, they'd arrived at the Boise Grove Hotel, after a spectacularly beautiful drive through the Sawtooth Range and Boise National Forest. At Franklin's request, they'd stopped for lunch on the way at Trudy's Kitchen in Idaho City. It was exactly what Franklin had hoped it would be: fine, old-fashioned American cooking. He had, among other things, one of his favorites: grilled cheese. Being in an adventuresome mood, he added a large slice of Trudy's famous mouthwatering huckleberry cheesecake – plus a huckleberry milkshake.

The rest of the group lunched on equally pedestrian main courses: cheeseburgers, hot turkey sandwiches and chicken-fried steak, with plenty of artery-plugging fries and onion rings.

Packed full of L-Tryptophan amino acids, they all were virtually nodding off by the time Marcia drove their rental car into the Grove Hotel parking facility, so it was nap time the rest of the afternoon for the entire group.

There was a message waiting for them from Rep. Grayson when they arrived confirming he would be meeting them at Taco Bell Arena at 6:45 p.m.

$$* \quad * \quad *$$

CEO's in Orange Jumpsuits on the Side of the Road

The rally was...well, it was. A rally. At least in the technical sense. Despite Rep. Grayson headlining at his rousing, zinger-slinging best along with plenty of underwear and ramen to toss to the eds and co-eds, the crowd barely filled one-fourth of Taco Bell Arena.

Rep. Grayson nevertheless gave the crowd his best burns, lambasting Republican Gov. Butch Otter for failing to try to block Canadian tar sands-involved corporations from transporting megaloads across state highways. The megaloads, besides forcing usual users of state highways to make huge detours, facilitate the Canadian corporations' clear-cutting, strip mining destruction of Canada's boreal forests, releasing vast amounts of global warming-inducing carbon into the atmosphere.

He went on to blast "one-party government" by Idaho Republicans for being among the most unquestioning supporters of the American Legislative Exchange Council (ALEC), specifically for their support of "Ag-Gag" laws which enable local authorities – arguably unconstitutionally – to arrest individuals and journalists for photographing or video-recording animal abuses at corporate farming facilities.

Corporate felons like Lockheed-Martin, Boeing, Northrup Grumman and Pfizer – which get to pay fines instead of going to jail – also took the brunt of Grayson's ire. Especially Lockheed-Martin.

Lockheed-Martin, known for its less than stellar performance at the Idaho National Engineering Laboratory (re-named Idaho National Laboratory in 2005) in Idaho Falls during the 1990s as the contractor responsible for nuclear waste clean-up, was convicted of multiple Federal felonies in the '90s.

"Here's what I'd like to see," Grayson told the crowd. "CEO's and Chairmen of the Board for companies like Lockheed-Martin should be out there in prison orange jumpsuits on the side of the road picking up trash with some shotgun-toting Strother Martin-type guy standing over them. If the Supreme Court can magically turn corporations into persons, then some of those corporation's flesh and blood human beings should have to answer for crimes their businesses commit.

"It just wouldn't be the same to have an animatronic anthropomorphic ledger book bearing the company's name out there in prison orange collecting trash. And the corporate officers **should** have to clean prison toilets and show up at corporate dinners serving tables in their prison orange outfits.

"'Course that's not gonna happen. This is America. We only let poor and middle class people go to prison in America. Especially if they have the bad taste to not be rich *in public*. Even on the rare occasion when someone like an Enron higher-up gets sent to the slammer, it's usually **many** years after the charges were first investigated. And they NEVER serve their full sentences.

"And the most wonderful, heart-warming thing: we consider corporations re-habilitated after just a handful of corporate heartbeats. Lockheed-Martin got its next huge government defense contracts the year after it paid $10.5 million to the government in 2008 to settle charges of submitting false invoices. In 2009, Lockheed received more in government contracts than ever before, $30.2 billion.*

---

* *U.S. Sen. Bernie Sanders' 10/20/11 report that hundreds of Department of Defense contractors which defrauded the U.S. military received more than $1.1 trillion in Pentagon contracts during the previous decade.*

Before its government-greased merger with Martin-Marietta, Lockheed was convicted of spreading bribes around the globe from the '50s through the mid-'70s. Lockheed's crimes were so egregious, they helped inspire the Foreign Corrupt Practices Act of 1977. And Lockheed and other corporate felons like it thrive on massive government contracts from the same government they previously took pains to defraud.

"When Lockheed-Martin decided military contracts alone weren't lucrative enough, they decided to pioneer the hated red-light cameras – you know, the ones that automatically generate massively expensive tickets if your car was seen entering an intersection a microsecond after the light went from yellow to red. Never mind that the one-second interval between the light turning red in your direction and the light turning green in the crossing direction would make a collision virtually impossible. It's about a corporation colluding with local governments nationwide to implement a scheme that enriches both the corporation and the government at the expense of the middle class. Never mind that the red light cameras actually have proven to cause far more collisions than they stop, by forcing drivers to slam on brakes so hard that drivers to the rear can't keep from ramming them from behind.

"The list of corporations that have paid eight-figure or larger fines or settlements to the government for fraud, waste and abuse in weapons systems and other contracting includes not just Lockheed, but also Northrop Grumman, Rockwell, Boeing, Hughes Aircraft, Raytheon Company, Teledyne, McDonnell Douglas, ITT Industries, United Technologies Corporation, BAE Systems, Bechtel Corporation, McKesson, Health Net Inc., Hewlett Packard Company, Humana, Fluor Corp., Kellogg Brown & Root (KBR), Honeywell International Inc., Textron Inc., General Electric and General Motors, to name a few.[*]

"And that doesn't even take into account *privatized* military mercenary war contractors like Blackwater – now known as Academi - and Greystone Limited. Blackwater's contracting rights for Iraq mercenary work were only *temporarily* suspended after one of their guards was convicted of murder, three others were convicted of manslaughter and another pleaded guilty to manslaughter after 17 Iraqi civilians were shot dead and another 20 were wounded in September 2007.

"Flesh and blood human beings convicted of substance abuse or drug possession, though – we keep 'em on a short leash. We pop 'em back in prison if they pee in a cup and it comes up cannabis. Gotta re-hab 'em to learn to defraud the Department of Defense, I guess.

"Ain't it wonderful?"

To which the crowd responded with a chorus of "*Fuck O-ver-LORDS!*" chants.

---

[*] *"Take the Rich Off Welfare,"* Zepezauer & Naiman, 1996; U.S. Department of Justice 3/27/07 bulletin regarding ITT Corp.'s $100 million fine; Project on Government Oversight (POGO) Federal Contractor Misconduct Database, 1/25/15

"And I see your governor, Mr. Otter, is happy to take lots of campaign dough from the for-profit private prison industry. Doesn't seem to mind too much when media report that CCA - Corrections Corporation of America - has been letting Idaho prison gangs run wild. Three times as many inmate-on-inmate assaults at the CCA-run prisons compared to the state-operated facilities.

"And CCA lied about filling guard positions it actually left vacant. Cuh-LASSY.

"So, you fine folks out there in the audience feeling the joy of all those corporate profits?"

To which the crowd responded with yet another chorus of "*Fuck O-ver-LORDS!*" chants.

"Hey, maybe those corporate overlords can find some love in those CCA prison showers? Y'think?"

Then Grayson himself started flinging the traditional clean underwear and ramen noodles into the crowd as a happy farewell gesture just before introducing Sally to the gathering.

What turned out to be Sally's final discussion of her struggles for women's respect from her church, her life as a single mom and ways the USA-SBR would raise the standard of living for every non-wealthy person in the U.S.A. was received by the crowd with warmth, respect and chanted murmurs of "*Rally for Sally.*"

Like the crowds at the previous USA-SBR venues, the audience appeared especially affected by her description of what it was like to juggle two jobs, child care expenses, a failing marriage, tone-deaf church leaders and her own health challenges plus dealing with bill collectors representing a half-dozen health care providers.

"To just have the free full-time public school kindergarten and pre-school the USA-SBR would guarantee – what a difference that would've made," Sally said. "There were so many times I would have to put off buying things like socks and shoes for the children – real necessities – so I could pay for their day care and keep food on the table.

"A lot of men – especially those we keep electing to public office – don't seem to understand that when you have to work to keep a roof over your head – even a leaky one, your three- and four-year-olds simply have to be in some sort of school or day care.

"Leaving them at the Governor Otter's mansion for day care while you're at Carl's Jr. flipping burgers probably isn't going to fly.

"Or maybe it would: let's call the Gov to see what he says!"

Taking a page from Michael Moore's playbook, Sally pulled out her cell phone and dialed up the direct line to Gov. Otter's top personal assistant which an "undisclosed source" had provided to Rep. Grayson earlier in the day.

Sally put the phone on speaker and held it up to the mic while she asked to be connected to the governor.

"We're just wondering whether the Governor has someone who can provide free day care services at his mansion for a few of the folks in our audience. We figured that, if he can afford to pay a rich corporation a premium to use kid gloves on prison gangs in Boise, he's probably got some legal tender locked away somewhere to pay for taking care of innocent pre-schoolers.

"We'll even agree to putting them through metal detectors, if need be."

The personal assistant on the other end of the line, Rufus McPinsulnack, was completely tongue-tied for most of a minute before he uttered anything intelligible.

"Surely you don't expect the governor to be responsible for a bunch of rugrats in his own home," McPinsulnack said. "This sounds like some kind of prank. The governor doesn't believe there's any connection between day care for children and taking care of adult felons in our prisons.

"We'll spend whatever it takes to keep the public safe from the offenders in our prisons. Children don't pose that kind of threat, would you agree?"

"Well, *actually*," Sally started, "children who aren't old enough to reach a light switch just might end up being a threat someday if they have to be left to their own resources while mom's working a full-time shift at the local minimum wage fast food joint. Not to mention an **immediate** threat to every other person in the apartment complex where they live if they start a fire while they're unsupervised."

"Well, missy, that's an example of an irresponsible, unsuitable parent," McPinsulnack said. "Who does that mom think she is going off and leaving a child unsupervised?"

"She probably thinks she's the backbone of the new middle class," Sally said. "You know, the ones you Republicans continue to refuse to give minimum wage raises to. Maybe she should go to work for Corrections Corporation of America and barter with prison gangs.

"Governor Butch doesn't seem to give a rat's ass that this state is ranked 52nd among all states PLUS the District of Columbia and the Department of Defense in licensing and oversight of both child care centers and in-home child care businesses.[*] What's it like, Rufus, to be a government flack for a state that's DEAD LAST in day care standards on top of being ranked 48th in K-12 public education?[**]

"See any dots to connect there, Rufus?

(Simultaneously, there was chanting from the crowd audible on McPinsulnack's end of the line: *"Rufus the doofus, Rufus the doofus..."*)

"I apologize for our frenzied radicals' candor, Rufus. You're welcome to give my number from your caller ID to Governor Butch just in case he's got a few slots

---

[*] Child Care Aware of America
[**] Education Week ranking, according to Don't Fail Idaho campaign

at the mansion for the pre-schoolers of parents in our crowd. His commercials always seem to have a lot of kids around him, so I'm sure he's familiar with the concept.

"Looking forward to hearing back –

"Click." McPinsulnack hung up.

" – from Butch.

"Prick," she said, bluntly, as the crowd booed McPinsulnack's lack of phone etiquette.

"Please, everyone feel free to call Mr. McPinsulnack at the number on the screen above. I'm told he has a huge voice mail account, so please take the time to leave a message about how you feel about Governor Butch's leadership, especially on child care and family support issues."

She went on to profusely thank the crowd for their support and introduced the screening of "Capitalism: A Love Story."

$$* \quad * \quad *$$

The attendees appeared to leave the arena with far more enthusiasm than they'd arrived with. An hour later, Franklin was still chuckling over Sally's impromptu phone call to McPinsulnack (he pictured in his mind a skinny pencil-necked 30-something nimrod on the other end of that call; he actually wasn't far off) when he saw Sally look up from her cell phone with a horrified expression, with tears starting to stream from the corners of her eyes.

"What's wrong, dear?" Franklin asked.

"Billie Sue, my sister, just told me my children's father – Mike – just got off the phone with her in a rage. She said he told her he's coming to pick up the kids for as long as he wants instead of waiting 'til Friday. He told her if she or her husband try to stop him, he'll splatter their brains all over the wall.

"He told Billie Sue he won't stand any longer for his kids' minds being warped by some radical feminist man-hating slut.

"She and Caleb, her husband, have taken their three kids along with Royal and Chloe to a hotel for the night. She says Caleb is furious at me for 'putting them' in this position because they can't afford an expensive hotel room for very long.

"I've got to get back there. NOW."

"Consider it done: Idris will drive you to the airport right now to get on the next available flight to Salt Lake, at our expense," Franklin/Percy told her as he gave a comforting squeeze of her hands.

"Is there anything else we can do to make this easier for you?"

"Can you wave some magic wand that makes Mike Masterson less of an impulsive, angry asshole? That's about all that would help here, Percy."

"I'm afraid we're fresh out of magic wands," Franklin/Percy said. "But if you want some company, we can send either Idris or Bianca along with you on the flight."

"I think the last thing Billie Sue and, especially, Caleb want to see is me getting off the plane in Salt Lake with a 'fellow commie.' No, I'll be OK once I'm back with the kids. Royal actually *sort of* understands what a wack-job his Dad is, but this is all beyond Chloe's understanding. She used to have night terrors after Mike and I would argue."

"Just please promise us you won't let anyone put you in jeopardy of Mike harming you, OK? In the short time we've been fortunate enough to get to know you, Sally, you've come to be like a sister to us – and not the kind we'd push into the mud or take Halloween candy from."

"Don't worry, Percy. The first thing I'm going to do tomorrow morning is go to the District Court and get my restraining order against Mike renewed. I'm going to try to convince Billie Sue and Caleb to get one too. But it sounds like Caleb blames me, so that probably won't work.

"Dear Jesus, I hope I didn't make a massive mistake by taking up your cause."

By this time, Idris and Bianca had overheard most of the discussion between Franklin and Sally and were standing alongside them.

"If that prick Mike lays a finger on you or either Royal or Chloe, I'll make sure he regrets it," Idris said.

"Won't Mike lose his Temple Recommend over threatening his estranged wife?" Bianca asked.

"I honestly don't think that's something he's thinking about right now," Sally said. "And, to answer your question, no, I don't think he will. If church members who organize themselves to chant "Apostate Slut" in public don't worry about that, then I don't think Mike will either."

"If you need for any of us to be there with you, all you have to do is call," Bianca said. "You've got each of our cell numbers, right?"

"Yes, but don't hold your breath waiting for a call. I still have church friends I can rely on – I *think*. And Billie Sue will always be there for me, dipshit Caleb notwithstanding."

"OK, let's stop deliberating here and get this fine lady to the airport," Idris said. "I'll get us all back to the hotel and take her to Boise International as soon as she has her bags ready to go."

Which he did. He and Sally only had to wait a little over an hour for the next Delta flight to Salt Lake City. The last-minute ticket purchase was astoundingly expensive for a 340-mile flight ($525), but that was literally the very least of worries for Franklin.

Sally called Franklin/Percy from her home as soon as she was re-united with Royal and Chloe there. She explained that she and Billie Sue had concluded that Mike Masterson was simply hysterically angry because of a combination of events: his favorite NBA team, the Utah Jazz, hadn't even made the playoffs, his vegetable garden sprouts had been entirely destroyed by rabbits, his elderly mother had told him she might be disinheriting him for marrying "such a floozie" and said "floozie" had turned into a feminist radical – by Utah standards, at least.

"As soon as he's had a couple of nights of sleep and watched a few of his favorite Sylvester Stallone videos, he'll be back to his usual mildly obnoxious self," Sally said. "But don't worry, I'm still going to get the restraining order re-instated."

✳ ✳ ✳

Only the Good Die Young

The next morning, Franklin, Idris, Bianca and Marcia drove their rental car to Salt Lake City and turned it in near the airport before boarding the California Zephyr Amtrak train for the long trip back to Poughkeepsie. There were mumblings from Idris and Bianca about how Franklin needed to step into the latter half of the 20th century and embrace domestic airline travel. Franklin said he'd consider it – especially if the sleeper cars continued to be mediocre.

By the time they arrived back in Poughkeepsie, it was June 30. Pongo, Harry, Phil and Heather already were at the Amtrak station to meet them when the train slowed to a stop. As Franklin, Bianca, Idris and Marcia were getting their bags, Franklin's cell phone rang with a caller ID readout showing the call was from Billie Sue Wheeler in Utah.

"Hi, this is Percy," Franklin answered. "How's the sister of our favorite Utah radical?"

Then he heard the sobs.

"She's gone," Billie Sue said. "And the kids with her."

"Please don't tell me it's what it sounds like, Billie Sue."

"Mike went to their home at about midnight last night. He knocked on the door loudly, according to the people in the next apartment. He said something to convince her to let him in and he pulled out a Glock 9-mm. He screamed at her long enough that the neighbors had time to call the police.

"But just as they got off their 9-1-1 call, they heard the blasts. Mike shot her once between the eyes, once in the heart and once between her legs. The kids had come running into their living room. He shot each of them once in the head and once in the heart. Then he shot himself in the head, barrel in his mouth.

"The whole thing took less than four minutes."

"Dear God. Did he tell anyone about what he was going to do beforehand?" Franklin/Percy asked.

"Doesn't look that way," Billie Sue said, choking on the words between sobs. "The neighbors said they heard him say he wished he could've taken me out too, for enabling her 'radical' feminist activism."

"I don't know what I can say to make any of this hurt less," Franklin/Percy said, himself by now sobbing heartily, "except that we're sorry for the loss – and that we loved her and the children dearly."

"We don't hold any of this against you," Billie Sue said. "Please don't take it so hard. Those last couple of weeks she was with you folks, she seemed the happiest she'd been in a long, long time. She told me just how much she enjoyed that day at the lake in Idaho.

"We all thought – especially Mom and Dad - that there was something pretty askew with Mike by the time she married him. If it hadn't happened last night, it probably would've happened in six months or a year. He was a freaking lunatic, a hyper-controlling women-hating fanatic who knew how to be smooth when he needed to be."

"Will you let us know when the services will be?"

"Don't think Mom and Dad want anyone from outside the family to be there. If you think I'm losing it, you should see them. They don't blame you either, but they don't want to be around anything or anyone that reminds them how Sally tried to set herself apart from the average Utah Stepford wife."

"I can understand that," Franklin/Percy said. "If you'll give us an address, we'll send flowers and cards, if that's OK."

"That would mean a lot, Percy. We know how much you and the others admired Sally. She was never happier than she was when she was with you New York folks. Maybe she should've just up and moved there…"

"I suspect Mike would've followed her there and done the same thing, eventually," Franklin/Percy said. "Wish I could understand how so much hate can go into one human being. If only there were an immunization people could take for hate, the way there is for polio."

"Maybe someday," Billie Sue said, her crying subsiding. "Maybe someday, what you're trying to do will help people to hate less, to be better people. To hold accountable the people who really are responsible for people's lives being under so much stress."

"Please come to see us in Poughkeepsie if you ever have the opportunity, Billie Sue. It would mean a lot."

[It was the next-to-last time Franklin and Billie Sue would talk to each other. The next time was years later when the Poughkeepsieans, in a ceremony on the Capitol steps, dedicated the U.S. Senate's passage of the USA-SBR to Sally and other victims of domestic violence and gun carnage, to keep memories of them alive.]

"What in God's name was that about?" Pongo asked, watching tears roll down Franklin's ashen face.

"Someone we came to know while we were touring through northern Utah and Idaho," Franklin said, gasping between every few words. "You surely saw her on our web posts. She was Sally Rose Cummings. She shared some heartfelt words at several of our gatherings. And her sister just told me she and her children were murdered last night by her ex-husband."

At that moment, Bianca and Marcia both reflexively grasped their midsections as they bent forward, as though the air had just been sucked out of their lungs, while Idris collapsed to the ground on his knees, his bowed face covered by his hands.

"Good Jesus," Phil said. "Had he threatened her before?"

"Not explicitly," Franklin said, still choked up. "Sounds like he resented Sally leaving the kids with her sister instead of him while she went with us. He certainly made sure he wouldn't have any more visitation disappointments. Did I mention he ate his gun when he was done murdering his wife and children? No? Well, the thought of him as worm food takes at least a tiny bit of the sting out of this horror.

"Her sister – she's Billie Sue Wheeler – she said it probably would be better for us to just send flowers and cards to Sally's family. They're not blaming us in any way, but they're worried people might see it as poor taste for a group like ours – one that's sought out publicity – to be seen trying to comfort Sally's parents in person.

"I wish I could disagree, but they're probably right."

"We should send her parents and Billie Sue an open-ended invitation to be our guests of honor at any time they choose in the future," Heather said, her arm by then around Pongo's shoulder. "We should make it clear we consider them to be like family. We should ask them what _they_ think is the best way to honor the memory of Sally and her kids."

By then, Bianca was crying on Harry's shoulder. Harry could be seen mouthing the words, "_What the Fuck?!! What the fuck?!!_" repeatedly as he looked over Bianca's slumping shoulder toward Pongo.

"That sounds like the most compassionate thing we could do, Heather," Marcia said. "I'll draft a letter for everyone to sign to go with a large bouquet. I'll have it for all of you by first thing in the morning.

"Franklin, I'll put together a news release expressing our group's sadness and sympathies for Sally's family – it'll be ready for approval by you, Phil and Pongo first thing tomorrow – I'll fax that to the AP and all the other news networks once the three of you OK it. I'll do my best to fend off any direct contacts from the media – whoever said any publicity is good publicity clearly never had to cope with the horror of a murder-suicide."

"If there's a way to use this tragedy to teach other single parents how to protect themselves from angry ex-es, I think that would be the most hopeful thing that could germinate from this terror," Franklin/Percy said. "Marcia, Let's put together a Powerpoint – that's what it's called, right? – a Powerpoint presentation with audio features showing ways to prevent unwanted home entry by angry boyfriends and ex-es, OK? Maybe 10 to 15 minutes long – something we can show at the beginning of each rally we have from now on.

"Let's make sure part of it shows the main thing that facilitated Sally's hateful killer: opening the door late at night to ANYONE who shows up uninvited."

"I'll have it for you within a week, Franklin, with all the bells and whistles," Marcia said.

And she did. The 21-minute, 49-second presentation was titled, "Sally's Legacy: Taking Meaning from Senseless Deaths." It would be seen by more than 100 million persons within a year on every pay TV channel, multiple YouTube links and every PBS station nationwide; it later would be translated into two-dozen languages and seen worldwide by 1.5 billion persons within five years.

* * *

A Bracing Summer

The remainder of the summer was spent with the USA-SBR organizers returning to their usual day jobs and occasionally helping Marcia with maintaining their website by responding to blogs entries, answering media inquiries and answering both electronic and U.S. Postal Service-delivered correspondence. They had started receiving about a half-dozen inquiries a week from members of state legislatures and the U.S. Congress, apparently the result of grassroots direct contacts by their constituents.

Within two days of returning to Poughkeepsie from Idaho, Franklin followed through on his plans for orthodontia as part of his strategy not to be recognized. He decided to go with special braces with brackets and wires colored to match the enamel of his teeth (he didn't want to deal with the responsibility of having to remove Invisalign aligner trays from his teeth at every meal and every time he drank anything other than water, so braces were the option of choice). He looked forward to the two years of monthly maintenance visits at the dentist about as much as he used to look forward to having excruciating therapy on his shriveled leg muscles 80 years earlier. But he looked forward to being recognized as a resurrected formerly dead President even less. Far, far less.

After his orthodontist visit, he went to the Podrowski family's optometrist, had his vision checked: surprisingly, his uncorrected vision now was 20-10, far better than it ever had been in his previous life. Nevertheless, he purchased two pairs of glasses, one with a Maui Jim's frame and the other with a Versace frame, with plain glass lenses. Asked by the optometrist why he wanted them despite having perfect vision, Franklin said it was simple vanity: he liked the way they looked on him. (He actually liked how differently they made him look – the good ol' Superman turns into Clark Kent theory come true.)

When he returned to the Podrowskis', both Pongo and Harry made the 'sizzle' gesture as they touched Franklin's shoulder, laughing hard over his efforts to look the cool 20-something. After Harry left, though, Pongo took Franklin aside and, under his breath, said, "Mr. President, all kidding aside, you rock those glasses. I didn't think you could pull that off, but damn if you haven't!"

"Well, ahem, eh, er, from the bottom of my heart, your re-tread President thanks you," Franklin said. "But, seriously – do you think these will appeal to the coeds?"

"Only if they have a pulse," Pongo said. "Geez, I'm sorry – I guess that maybe was in poor taste, Sir."

"Don't feel embarrassed, Pongo. I've had a pulse again for almost a year now. I try not to question it. I'm just grateful for another chance to make a positive difference. To be worthy of a second chance."

"I don't know if worthiness influenced what happened to you or if it was just a quirk of global warming. Whatever it was, there's no one I'd rather see getting a second chance to make a difference than you. Well, maybe that Marilyn Monroe chick – or that Jayne Mansfield babe. Naw – just joshin'…"

"I'm assuming those two women weren't astrophysicists."

"You'd be assuming correctly, Mr. President."

"OK, Pongo, I do believe you are a healthy American male. No need for you to stock up on those – what'd they call them? – boner pills?"

"You got that right, Sir – no need whatsoever!"

∗   ∗   ∗

PROFESSOR RABID RANDIAN

The rest of the summer, Franklin/Percy managed to find time to go to movies and dinners on a handful of double dates with Holly, her BFF Nancy and Nancy's latest boyfriend. He still couldn't quite bring himself to go on solo dates with Holly; he simply didn't think it would be smart to put himself in a position of having to share his true identity with her. But it didn't make it any easier for him to ignore the attraction he felt for her.

For her part, Holly couldn't help but be impressed and in no small way in awe of Franklin/Percy's ambitions for the USA-SBR. She still was convinced of his attraction to her and she knew he wasn't a same-sex preference guy, but she intuited that trying to press that issue would simply drive him away. She sensed that her patience just might eventually be rewarded.

Franklin started classes at Dutchess Community College on Aug. 29. He was looking forward most to his political science class with instructor Mark Tomkinson in Taconic Hall. He'd seen on-line that Mr. Tomkinson was of the Ayn Randian (anti-government, anti-regulation, anti-consumer protection) persuasion and he was licking his chops at the opportunity to open a few fissures in Mr. T's hardened presumptions.

The first few weeks of classes were fairly fundamental, covering details which most high school students should have known, but, sadly, did not. Schoolhouse Rock kinds of details, how a bill becomes law. Franklin made sure to consume liberal quantities of caffeine during those weeks.

However, by early October, what Mr. Tomkinson would later remember as 'the trying times' began with oral clashes over the USA-SBR's provisions for U.S. Supreme Court enlargement, re-apportioning U.S. Senate membership to be more representative and prohibiting at-large elections for multiple-member government bodies.

"What makes you think simply adding more warm bodies to the U.S. Supreme Court will make its decisions more just, Percy?" Mr. Tomkinson asked one unusually warm October afternoon. "You still would have half the justices placed on the court using the existing process. Wouldn't adding the other half by popular vote simply subject those justices to the same corrupting influences of campaign dollars as every other politician?"

"You're forgetting, Mr. T –,"

"I've asked you before, please STOP calling me Mr. T," Mr. T said.

"You're forgetting the other part of the USA-SBR which sets strict limits on campaign contributions. If any one person's $200 campaign contribution to a Supreme Court justice's campaign is going to corrupt that justice, then we're pretty much doomed as a culture, wouldn't you agree?"

"But getting back to my first point," Mr.Tomkinson said, "we'd still have half of the Supremes placed on the court using the traditional process. How is that going to change anything anytime soon?"

"It might take a few years," Franklin/Percy admitted. "But, eventually, with ALL of the Supremes subject to voter retention once every four years, they would HAVE to be more accountable to voters. If they knew they could be sacked each time they signed on to a decision as fundamentally retarded as Citizens United, we'd have far fewer Citizen Uniteds.

"Likewise, with the strict campaign donation limits for Presidential campaigns as well, I'm hopeful we'd soon see fewer hard-core corporatists nominated to the Supremes by our Presidents."

"Y'know, it sure sounds to me like you'd love to see this country completely free of corporations, Percy," Mr. Tomkinson said, with a snide, borderline-contemptuous expression on his face.

"Do you **REALLY** believe corporations are going to flee our country just because they've been required to stop cheating the system?" Franklin/Percy asked. "You seem to think that the impoverished, poorly-fed, ill-educated peoples of the Third World are more productive and more skilled than our own U.S. citizens… Do you _really_ believe most corporations prefer those kinds of workers to laborers from their own country?"

"I'm convinced they'd take the steps necessary in those Third World locations for their employees' most basic needs to be met – needs like nutrition, maybe even company-owned housing. If it would save those corporations' bottom line, I think they would risk using Third World workers. Look at Levi-Strauss. They moved their production offshore more than a decade ago. People still buy their jeans."

"Not this people," Franklin/Percy said.

"There don't seem to be enough people who think the way you do, though. There's currently no practical motivation for corporations to be loyal to their workers in the U.S.A. It's all about profit."

"That's why the USA-SBR is so crucial: as long as corporations control our Congress, our Legislatures, our County Boards of Commissioners and Supervisors, our City Councils, it **WILL** continue to be all about profit. Corporations are sociopathic. The USA-SBR would put the needs of real, pulse-pounding human beings ahead of corporations. The way it used to be. The way the New Deal meant for it always to be."

"Yeah, sure. Government gave birth to corporations. The Supreme Court decided those were live births, live corporate beings. So you can't put one class of live beings ahead of another. Just not going to happen. Citizens United is as definitive as it gets."

"OK, let's see Citizens United comfort you when a loved one has passed. Let's see Citizens United give you an honest bid knowing it would mean its favorite corporation gets less business. Let's see Citizens United pleasure you in bed," Franklin/Percy said.

"No matter how you gussy up a stack of ledger books, they're never going to be flesh and blood. They're never going to be able to comfort you with make-up sex after a draining argument about an in-law. They're never going to be able to give you a prostate exam with a human touch. They're never going to be able to caress the back of your head while you're throwing up over a commode. They're never going to kiss you for remembering the favorite part of an anniversary.

"They're dead. They're heartless. They're soulless. They're like Great White Sharks prowling endlessly for things to eat. But instead of defecating digested little fish, they defecate digested hard-working middle class mothers and fathers, devoted workers who float in the dung-filled seas of retirement with fewer and fewer benefits. Because enrichment of the corporatist god is this nation's de facto cult of worship.

"You worship corporatism or you work in a soup kitchen – or some other non-profit. That's this country's new concept of a choice, of free agency."

"Sure, that's what it's all boiled down to," Mr. Tomkinson said derisively. "Nothing like oversimplification to keep the rabble roused, right?"

"What's oversimplified about at-large elections diluting the power of voters? Surely you're *not* so mathematically challenged or delusional as to suggest that requiring candidates for <u>all</u> city council districts within a community to be elected by a majority of **ALL** of the city's voters gives voters more power than only requiring the voters from each individual district to elect each district's council member.

"Do you really, truly believe it's **not** easier for big business to influence elections when all majorities must be won citywide rather than district by district? C'mon Mr. Tomkinson, you're smarter than that."

"I'm sure there are those who would argue that requiring candidates for local city and county offices to win citywide or countywide majorities causes the voter to feel like he or she is part of the entire community than just an artificial politically contrived sliver," Mr. Tomkinson said. "There are a lot of people who would argue that it's important for voters to feel like they have a say in what happens throughout the community, not just the neighborhoods surrounding the voter's own home."

"Isn't that why we have at-large elections for Mayor?" Franklin/Percy asked.

"C'mon, sir, if *you* had a huge bankroll to influence elections in a city, would you feel more threatened by an upstart candidate you didn't like if she or he had to compete across the entire community or if she or he only had to convince a majority of people within a district a fraction of that size to throw your favored council member out of office? You and I both know the answer to that, Mr. Tomkinson.

"And you have to know that organizations like unions whose primary concerns are the welfare of middle class voters and the working poor get more bang for their campaign donation bucks when they can focus on individual local district races instead of at-large citywide contests. At-large elections are strategically set up primarily to suck the influence out of those kinds of worker advocacy organizations while further empowering the already powerful. You can't dispute basic arithmetic, sir.

"So, tell me how that's wrong, Mr. Professor, sir. I'm all ears. Maybe you haven't noticed, but unions are virtually extinct in the private sector and the ones that are left are constantly caving in to management demands for contract concessions.

"Corporations can bully their workers all day long, as long as they don't blatantly violate the law. And even if they do, they'll only have to pay an insignificant nuisance fine. Even if a corporate manager shot an employee in the face, they might not have to worry about actual jail time. So, tell me, Mr. T, how have corporatism and corporatism-preservation tools for *legally* cheating – things like at-large elections and voter suppression – how have those things enriched the middle class?"

"It's enriched the job creator class, Percy. Without a rich upper strata of job creators, none of us would have jobs. Without those enriched job creators, taxes wouldn't be paid because no one would have jobs," Tomkinson said.

"You corporate apologists will suckle from trickle-down economics 'til that dried-out shriveled teat is pulled from your cold, dead lips – reality notwithstanding," Franklin/Percy said. "What will it take for you folks to let go of that obsession? What will it take for you to admit that jobs are created by consumer demand and **_NOT_** by the unicorn-like munificence of the well-to-do?

"The simple fact is, that if your super-rich so-called job creators decided tomorrow to hire no more employees forever and simply sit on their vast buttocks of cash as they watched from afar waiting for the western hemisphere to sink into an abyss of jobless anarchy, they would be profoundly disappointed."

"And how is that, Mr. Van Mullder?"

"That's because those who were not as obsessed with obscene profits would fill in the void created by the super-rich obstinately refusing to hire staff to meet consumer demand. Not to mention the fact that the USA-SBR would foster greater competition between businesses by breaking up the vast monopolies of the super-rich. Meaning more hiring for more jobs."

"And what if financial institutions refused to loan to those who wanted to supplant the super-rich?" Tomkinson asked.

"If financial institutions combined and conspired to block loans to otherwise qualified business persons, they would place themselves in the position of being nationalized. Which is something President Obama should've done after the 2008 meltdown and something President Roosevelt should've done in 1933. But hindsight is always 20-20, right?"

"We probably would be speaking German right now if FDR had nationalized the banks in '33," Tomkinson said. "We needed healthy, functioning private financial institutions to help our industries come up with the capital needed to meet the demand for war production after the Dec. 7 attack on Pearl Harbor.

"Can you imagine the kind of government red tape there would've been for industries applying for loans through a government-owned bank?"

"Don't know if you've noticed, sir, but there's just a *teensy-tiny* bit of red tape when applying for loans through private bank corporations. You're implying that government is static, inflexible and unresponsive in times of national emergencies. If I live to be 200, I'll never understand how people can be so gullible as to swallow whole the business community's hagiographic narcissistic narrative that business is inherently more efficient than government.

"If your implication is true, how was it that private charities failed so miserably at the outset of the Great Depression while government was able to save millions and millions from starvation as businesses were laying off millions due to lack of demand for their products and services?"

"OK, there are some problems that become so massive that a massive organization – yes, like government - is the only thing that can prevent catastrophe," Tomkinson said. "But liberals seem to feel that the default answer to every problem is government."

"Maybe that's because history has taught us that the private sector excels first and foremost at making a profit – and that the most efficient way to address extreme human need is to take profit out of the equation, the same way you take a cancerous tumor out of an otherwise healthy child."

"The ability of entrepreneurs to make profits – whether obscene or barely marginal – is what motivates business persons to do great things – it's what makes this country great," Tomkinson said.

"You won't be shocked to know that I disagree: what makes this beautiful country great isn't the motive to profit off of our neighbors' needs. What makes it great is what motivates us to care about our neighbors down the street and our neighbors across state lines when the unforeseen happens. When Hurricane Katrina struck, we didn't ask the victims to wait six weeks for the Red Cross or Donald Trump to bring them a few loaves of bread and Bactine antiseptic. We had a social service safety net – underfunded as it was – in place to meet basic needs almost overnight. And we didn't expect for the government to profit off of the victims' dire needs. We didn't ask for their credit card numbers before offering help.

"You can find the profit motive *in every country on the planet*. It doesn't make one country better than another. The degree to which a country facilitates unfettered greed doesn't make that country better than others. The degree to which a country helps its people without forcing them to pad the coffers of for-profit mega-corporations - that's what makes a country stand head and shoulders above others."

"If you'll recall, though, Mr. Van Mullder, the Federal Emergency Management Agency fell flat on its face after Katrina. So much for the wonders of government."

"Mr. Tomkinson, virtually everyone inside government and outside of government now agrees FEMA failed during Katrina because the person selected by President "W" Bush to run FEMA was grotesquely unqualified to direct that agency. **And** because the agency was grotesquely under-funded by the very President and Republican-controlled Congress responsible for its management – because they hate government and want to prove it doesn't work.

"That's been the Republican game plan since Ronald Reagan was in office: select people who are unqualified or underqualified to be responsible for huge Federal agencies and their top priority – with a wink-wink, nod-nod – is to make sure those agencies fail to function as Congress intended when they were created.

"Think of James Watt at the Department of the Interior, Anne Gorsuch Burford at the EPA, Jeane Kirkpatrick – a super-hawk warmonger - at the United Nations, Gale Norton at Interior – the list goes on and on. There were more foxes guarding more Federal chicken coops during the Reagan administration than at any time in U.S. history before then. And later, when they couldn't plant poison-pill appointees to lead Federal agencies, they did their best to turn off the funding spigots for them – hoping those agencies would dry up and blow away. Anything to give them an excuse to come up with phony justifications to privatize government services.

"Do YOU think it's fair for Republicans to constantly bad-mouth government while they're consistently trying to make **_sure_** it doesn't succeed, Professor Tomkinson?"

"Is any of this going to be on the mid-terms or the finals, Mister Professor?" interrupted Dirk Mandible, a 21-year-old power forward for the DCC Falcons basketball squad, who was sitting, as usual, at the back of the classroom.

"Do you think it should be?" Tomkinson asked.

"Hell, no," Dirk said, to supportive laughter from the other 47 students in the room. "Unless it's a multiple choice test, I guess."

"Sorry to disappoint, Mr. Mandible, but it's **_ALL_** going to be on every exam," Tomkinson said, knowing perfectly well that almost NONE of it would be on those tests. "If you've been taking good notes, you'll do just fine.

"Back to the discussion, Mr. Van Mull-"

"My Dad owns an insurance franchise," interrupted Monique Walsh, a pert 20-something redhead in the second row. "He says it's not fair for the government to do things not-for-profit when it takes clients away from him. How does he make a profit if the government can undercut him on prices?"

"Ms. Walsh brings up a good point, Mr. Van Mullder," Tomkinson said. "What do you say to that?"

"I would say it's the government's duty to provide essential services which everyone needs regardless of their income. Otherwise, the private sector is going to do its best to drive up prices and profits every chance it gets, guaranteeing that a huge segment of the population can't afford those essential services.

"If your father were here right now, I would tell him he should focus on services which aren't seen as essential – like life insurance and pet health insurance. If he can't make a profit off of services like those, then maybe he should be considering a different career path.

"Would you want **_your_** children and grandchildren being stuck with health insurance premiums which go up ten or twenty percent a year when non-profit single-payer health insurance – Medicare for All – could guarantee premium stability by guaranteeing coverage for **everyone** from cradle to grave?"

"I just want my Papa to be able to make enough profits to help me get through Dutchess C.C. and then maybe Harvard," Monique said sheepishly. "And so he and Mama can retire to their second home in Nevada someday."

"But that's the kind of tunnel vision I've been trying to get people to give up for a long, long time," Franklin/Percy said, eyes rolling skyward and hands raised to the heavens like an evangelist. "We can't live our lives based on short-term me-first thinking and expect civility to flourish. That's what poisoned the culture in Germany after World War I – simple, unmitigated selfishness and vitriol from war winners who wanted to financially punish EVERYONE in Germany, not just the political hacks who ordered everyone to war. Punishment that paved the way for fascists' power grab and World War II.

"I hope you'll keep in mind that, while you're wanting your Dad to be able to rake in enormous health insurance premium profits, there are adult children of for-profit military-industrial contractors who want their Papas and Mamas to be able to make enough profits to put them through the finest colleges.

"Does that mean we should declare war on other countries or groups every time we get a chance? After all, it would mean big profits for *those* students' parents, right? By your logic, if it's OK to financially screw over the general population in one area to help businesses maintain profits, it should be OK to do almost anything at any time to screw over the general population if it leads to business profits.

"Are business profits really the top priority for our government to consider all the time?"

"If I may interrupt your harangue with Ms. Walsh, here's what I see, Mr. Van Mullder," Tomkinson said. "I see a country where maybe half the populace distrusts government and wants businesses to be free to do pretty much anything they want as long as they don't cheat customers, employees and taxpayers and as long as they don't ruin the environment.

"And I see a country where maybe half the populace distrusts businesses and wants the government to be able to do whatever it needs to do to keep businesses – especially those operated by the super-rich – from cheating customers, employees and taxpayers and from ruining the environment.

"So it seems like the major difference between the two sides is that one side distrusts the government more than businesses while the other side distrusts businesses more than government.

"This may surprise you, Mr. Van Mullder, but I am embarrassed at what's become of the Republican Party, the party I used to admire for decades. In the past, the Republican Party would've worked with the Democratic Party to make _both_ the government and businesses more worthy of peoples' trust. But, for much of the past 35 years – especially the past three years, the Republican Party has become fixated on destroying their political opposition instead of working toward constructive compromises. Its leadership has compulsively obstructed, obfuscated and disemboweled every significant attempt to legislate.

"Until 2009, the Congress may have had a handful of deeply mortifying moments of meaningless contentiousness over the centuries, but since then it's been just one manipulative ploy after another by the Republicans to try to make President Obama look powerless. It's no longer the libertarian-leaning, fiscally-responsible organization it was before Reagan was elected.

"It's become a radical organization which champions all the wrong things: gun rights for violent ex-felons, 'too-big-to-fail' protections for irresponsible financial institutions, silly barriers to peoples' right to vote, virtual blank checks for military contractors and perpetual armed conflicts with overseas countries and organizations.

"Its leadership has nothing but scorn and disdain for moderates like myself. Its leadership appears to value ignorance and hatred over post-secondary education and tolerance. It simply is not any longer the party that worked with Democrats to create the interstate highway system, family farm assistance and Food Stamps.

"It's become the party of mental midgets like Sarah Palin and Louie Gohmert. But their sprint toward the idiocy of irrelevance doesn't mean the USA-SBR you've been advocating is the cure for what ails the country.

"I don't know that there's any way to effectively pass laws to force people to be unselfish. I think that's the main reason you could be doomed to become a 21st Century Sisyphus if you continue on with your advocacy."

"I think you've missed the entire point of the USA-SBR," Franklin/Percy said. "It's designed to appeal to the *self-interests* of 95 percent of Americans, not the top 5 percent who compulsively object to paying any taxes at all because they're convinced they can never, EVER have enough money. The USA-SBR would construct permanent pillars of economic and social justice for every last person in the U.S.A.

"Of course, the corporatists whose profit margins might shrink by a small fraction when the systematic unfairness is excised will try to spin the USA-SBR as just the opposite of what it is. But, to paraphrase Shakespeare, I'm hopeful that, over time, truth will out.

"No doubt, it will take great effort to overcome tidal waves of false propaganda. I hope someday, you'll be able to look at the USA-SBR through an unbiased lens, Mr. Tomkinson – and maybe even come to support it."

"I wouldn't bet the family farm on it, Mr. Van Mullder," Tomkinson said. "You'll need to convince people like Ms. Walsh for that thing to have even a remote chance of success.

"How many others of you have family members who own small businesses or yourselves work for a small business?"

Nine persons in the room full of 48 students raised their hands. Two of them – both males – pointed their middle fingers at Franklin/Percy as their hands went down.

"You'll probably need to win at least some of them and their families over too, Mr. Van Mullder," Tomkinson said. "If there's a group that will fight tooth and nail to keep the government from having more power over businesses, it's the owners of small businesses. Even if you bend over backwards to make it clear your USA-SBR only will affect the largest of businesses, they won't hear that, I guarantee you. They'll only hear 'more government power over businesses.'"

"All I hear is a lot of bullshit about how life in the USA is unfair if you're not rich," piped up Kevin McCarthy, a 25-year-old first-year student seated next to Dirk Mandible wearing a soiled long-sleeved t-shirt with the logo "Battle Ax Construction" over its front pocket. "The rich always have had unfair advantages and always will. Jesus Christ, just man up and take responsibility for what *you* already **can** control, Percival. You sound like kind of a pussy sometimes, you know?"

"OK, you just lost points with me for the personal remarks, McCarthy," Tomkinson said. "If you can't keep the conversation civil, you can skip this class – I'll even see that you get at least part of your money back."

"Just keepin' it real, sir," Kevin said. "Please accept my apology, Percival. You're too tall and handsome to be a pussy." Kevin said the word pussy with a lisp and made a limp-wristed gesture as the word came out of his mouth. The rest of the class was evenly split between laughs, boos and Bronx cheers aimed at Kevin.

"OK, class time's up – remember to cover the chapters in your text on the New Deal's National Recovery Administration and the Works Progress Administration for our next class," Tomkinson said.

Tomkinson motioned Franklin/Percy to stick around briefly as the other students filed out of the classroom.

"Please don't get me wrong, Percy," he said, voice just above a whisper. "I look at what you're trying to do and I have nothing but admiration for your ambition. There definitely are parts of your USA-SBR I believe would make this country better, lots less contentious.

"If I had your energy and your youth, I just might be tempted to do something similar. Everything these days changes after you get a family and a mortgage, not to mention huge student loans."

"I appreciate you saying that, Mr. Tomkinson," Franklin/Percy said. "Your positive remarks mean a lot to me. I think you grasp that I'm not some kind of wild-eyed radical. If you knew the people working with me on the USA-SBR, you'd see they aren't either."

"Well, if your group ever needs this classroom for a meeting, just let me know – I'll grease the skids for you with the department head. Oh, wait, just remembered: *I'm* the department head, how about that!" They both laughed at Tomkinson's semi-lame attempt at humor.

"So, just let me know a day or two in advance if you need to use the classroom some evening. Shouldn't be a problem."

"That's really kind of you, sir. Wish everyone were as civic-minded as you."

"Well, once again, don't misunderstand: you might see members of the local Tea Party branch coming out of the classroom as you go in. I'm an equal-opportunity fan of just about anyone who likes tilting at windmills."

Franklin was convinced of Tomkinson's equal opportunity sincerity when his USA-SBR organizers encountered members of the local Mutual U.F.O. Network (MUFON) leaving Tomkinson's classroom as Franklin and the others entered it on a Saturday evening the following weekend. Idris was relieved to see none of the MUFON-ers were wearing tinfoil hats – until he noticed a couple of them sporting pointy Spock ears and using handheld metal detector wands to check each other for alien implants.

"We're not in their league, right?" Idris asked Heather as the MUFON-ers left the building.

"If you have to ask, then you'd better start checking for secret implants yourself," Harry said after overhearing Idris. "Unless you're talking about tit implants – always thought you could use a little augmentation there, Dude!"

Which prompted Idris to grab and twist Harry's right nipple.

* * *

The USA-SBR group – sometimes including Pongo's, Heather's, Harry's and Bianca's extended families, sometimes not – continued to meet at least weekly on weekends while Dutchess Community College was in session.

Most of what they discussed involved organizing strategies, correspondence with out-of-state organizers, contacts with elected officeholders and planning for upcoming rally tours. The next tour was scheduled during the Christmas and New Year's break, when they planned to leave for Arizona and Southern California on Jan. 2. Marcia was assigned to supervise production of 30-second TV ads to be aired locally in Arizona and Southern California.

Franklin went on to pass his final exams with flying colors, ending up with a 3.9 grade point average. He was looking forward to his next class with Professor Tomkinson during the spring session – he felt like there were still important USA-SBR issues to discuss during class. If nothing else, it would be excellent preparation for scrutiny by national news media and political pundits.

He also was pleasantly surprised to find that the previous USA-SBR classroom discussions with Tomkinson had inspired a handful of his classmates to become involved with their organizing efforts. He was hopeful more classroom back-and-forth on those issues would bring at least a few more new recruits to their cause.

* * *

DICKENS AND FOOTBALL FOLLOWED
BY A BOLD FLIGHT WEST

Christmas 2011 with the Podrowskis in Poughkeepsie, which included Christmas dinner with Grandpa Tom and Grandma Annie – as well as Orvis and Karin O'Leary plus Heather Griffin and Penelope and Mitch Duarte, featured the normal amount of fixation on televised football along with the traditional Christmas week movie viewing. That year they took time to watch the World War I drama "*War Horse*" and the Iranian-filmed drama "*A Separation*." Franklin enjoyed both movies, especially "*War Horse,*" because of its relatively happy ending and the way it humanized both British and German soldiers.

His most enjoyable moments came after the group prodded him to renew his tradition of reading "A Christmas Carol." He did a spot-on Mr. Scrooge impression as he read the classic Dickens text.

The next most enjoyable part of all for Franklin, though, was the time spent sharing dinner and watching televised sports with the Podrowskis, O'Learys and Duartes. He'd come to feel like a genuine member of a family. Like someone who always would be welcomed in the home there, no matter what else happened in his life for good or ill. Likewise, Pongo had come to feel as though Franklin was the younger but wise-to-the-ways-of-the-world brother he'd always wanted. It was one of those weeks everyone involved wished they could freeze in time forever.

∗ ∗ ∗

After an hour or so of gentle-but-persistent persuasion by Phil, Pongo and Tom in early December, Franklin had relented on his insistence that long-distance travel be by train only. So, when Jan. 2 rolled around and it was time to embark on their flight to Tucson via Atlanta on Delta Air Lines, the friendly persuasion had to be ratcheted up a notch or two. After the last time Phil had flown on Delta – a few years earlier – when bags were lost, departure times and flight numbers were changed less than 12 hours before departure and flight attendants had exhibited all the tact of Viking raiders – he'd sworn he'd never fly on Delta again. But this flight was the most economical and time-saving he could find for the cross-country trip – plus, they had a special promotion allowing one bag to be checked free. (*"I remember when airlines would no sooner charge you to check your bags than they'd charge you for not traveling naked,"* Phil thought to himself. Now, Southwest was the only airline still allowing two bags per person to be checked free.) Phil and Pongo kept re-assuring Franklin that flying on a jet would be far faster and safer than using Amtrak again.

But then they got on the plane.

Since the last time Phil had flown on Delta, the seats in coach had been narrowed by four inches each and the legroom had been shrunk by three inches per row. Or, at least, it surely felt that way. Both Phil and Franklin were 6-foot-2, so their seating was comfort-challenged, to put it mildly; Franklin was given the aisle seat so he could more easily stretch his longer legs.

Phil decided some instructions were in order.

"You'll notice, Sir, that most seats – like ours – can recline. If you can call an inch or so reclining. But if you want to avoid hammer and tong treatment by Nurse Ratched over there (*he pointed to the flight attendant, a 50-something woman who appeared to have spent every day from her 12th birthday forward sucking the skin off a fermented prune*), you'll want to make sure you listen for the announcement over the loudspeakers that you have *official permission* to recline.

"Likewise, you'll want to make sure you keep your seat belt fastened unless they announce you have official permission to unclick it. And don't assume that, just because your bursting bladder needs to piss up a storm, it's all peachy keen to get up and write a quart's worth of your name in the green toilet goo of their luxurious 2-foot-by-2-1/2-foot water closet, especially right after take-off and just before landing.

"Unless you're partial to skull fractures and lifetime brain damage, it's probably a good idea to keep your seatbelt fastened as much as you can. When they're flying around at 30,000 or 40,000 feet above sea level in cloudless, stormless skies, there is, from time to time, a little frequent flier bonus called clear air turbulence. If your seat belt is unbuckled when the plane hits that crap, you might end up with somebody's laptop trying to give you a colonoscopy.

"And because you tend to want to be friends with just about everyone, you should know: if you feel a compulsion to chat with the pilot while we're in flight - well, I just hope your soap bar gripping skills are up to snuff, 'cause you're gonna be locked up as tight as Chris Christie on a Twinkie – and no number of your glad-handing Harvard handshakes is gonna bail you out. Since 9/11, the only thing more serious than trying to approach a pilot in flight would be trying to install a screen door on a plane with a welding torch while soaring over the Grand Canyon.

"Oh, and if you were expecting something nutritious to assuage your empty stomach, keep an eye out for tiny little packets of cardboard-tasting hunks of salt with microscopic pieces of pretzel between the crystals. That's what passes for airline cuisine nowadays. You could always pay for one of their featured menu items – if you're OK with spending, say, $19.95 for a two-day-old six-ounce tray of GMO fruits under cellophane. And, of course, if you fall asleep while the flight attendants are serving, they might come back and drop off your food a minute-and-a-half before final trash collection.

"Let's see, am I missing anything? Oh, yeah – if you try turning on any electronics – especially a cell phone – during the first half hour and the last half hour of the flight, you're gonna find out whether that lemon-sucking flight attendant over there had anything with garlic and onions in it for lunch, 'cause she's going to be *ALL* in your face. Apparently, these massive jet-powered aircraft are at risk of crashing and burning if a transistor radio is operating in the cabin."

"Well, *silly me*, wanting to travel by train," Franklin said. "What a relief to know I was fortunate enough to be using the nation's most astute travel experts for this trip, the Podrowski Agency."

Franklin tried to relax, but his mind wasn't diverted from the less-than-stellar travel atmosphere 'til the in-flight movie started.

An hour and a half later, at the conclusion of "*Jack and Jill*" (which movie critics rated a 23 on a scale up to 100), Franklin briefly wondered if just maybe it wouldn't be better to be back under the ground at Springwood.

Phil told him to be grateful it wasn't a double-feature with "*Abraham Lincoln: Vampire Hunter.*"

"Forgot to mention to you: airlines assume everyone on their flights wants to see the cheapest, worst-reviewed maggot-infested pile of horse dung movies available," Phil said. "If it weren't for airlines, Adam Sandler probably would be working at Wetzel's Pretzels in the Poughkeepsie Mall. You'll notice a lot of people bring their own videos to watch."

By the time the flight was over, Franklin whispered to Phil that a submarine bunk felt like the size of a polo field compared to the seat he'd just been stuck in for hours. But, as Phil pointed out, flying did save a full 2-1/2 days of travel time, not to mention considerable money.

"For truthfuless in advertising, though, they really should change the name of the airline to Lilliputian Airways," Franklin said.

They went straight from the airport to check in at the Tucson Hampton Inn and Suites on North Oracle Road. While they were unpacking, they caught a broadcast of their TV ad which had been airing locally for the previous two days. They then went to the 5 p.m. news conference arranged by Marcia at the hotel's San Miguel Room to promote their rally the next day at the Tucson Convention Center arena. Representatives from the Arizona Daily Star, Tucson Weekly and each of the local NBC, CBS, ABC and Fox broadcasting affiliates plus the local NPR affiliate and KQTH News Radio were present.

Marcia distributed copies of the USA-SBR along with all the latest data on signed-up USA-SBR supporters nationwide to all reporters present and displayed a slick updated PowerPoint presentation which highlighted all of their proposal's provisions.

Anticipating questions about how their rally tours were being funded, Marcia explained briefly that the money came from personal funds of the families involved as well as from small donations by supporters all over the U.S.A.

She then introduced Franklin/Percy, Pongo, Idris, Heather and Bianca and welcomed the members of the local press to ask questions.

Most of the questions revolved around the issue of just how serious the group was, considering how dramatically different some of the USA-SBR provisions were compared to existing laws.

"Comparing the Un-Screwing of America-Second Bill of Rights to existing laws is a little bit like comparing the laws of King George in 1787 to the original Constitution," Franklin/Percy said. "Your perspective is ass-backwards if you fixate on existing laws.

"Existing laws stacking the deck in favor of huge corporations are what have created systematic injustice for everyone but the wealthy.

"If you think it's fair for low-income retired folks to pay the same property tax rates as mega-billionaires, then the USA-SBR is not for you.

"If you think it's fair for hard-working middle-class families to pay the same per-gallon rate of gasoline tax as mega-billionaires, then the USA-SBR is not for you.

"If you think it's fair that our prisons are full of 2.3 million low-income and mentally ill persons while billionaire Wall Street crooks never even miss a tee time, then the USA-SBR is not for you.

"If you're OK with all the dozens of gated neighborhoods of multi-million-aires - which didn't exist in Tucson 30 years ago - while non-millionaires' neigh-borhoods struggle with an epidemic of property crime here, then the USA-SBR is not for you.

"The USA-SBR is all about achieving and maintaining economic justice and social justice.

"Without the USA-SBR, a struggling middle-class wage-earner finding jus-tice is kind of like a starving Wile E. Coyote trying to make a meal out of the Roadrunner. In other words, lots of good people flailing around in the air flap-ping credit card wings after running off a cliff before they plummet a thousand feet into an economic abyss.

"And not knowing who to blame for chasing their dream off that cliff.

"If the USA-SBR someday is ratified, then, thirty years later, we guarantee that jails and prisons will no longer be de facto debtors' prisons. We guarantee poverty no longer will be the result of a lack of educational opportunity. We guarantee that the quality of public education no longer will be dependent upon living in communities with high property values.

"If you are so cynical that you don't believe this can be done simply because it's never been done before, then answer me this: why do we no longer have po-lio epidemics? Why do we no longer depend on natural gas flames for lighting? Why do we no longer have toxic smoke clouds over our cities from burning trash?

"Obviously, the answer is: people with optimism and vision of a better life decided it was worthwhile to risk their efforts to pursue the possible – even if the possible seemed highly unlikely."

"So, how long to you expect it to take for two-thirds of the U.S. House and U.S. Senate to approve the USA-SBR?" asked Brutus Shillstein of NBC local affili-ate KVOA-TV.

"Let me respond to that, if I may," Idris said. "We don't expect even a major-ity of either chamber of the Congress to support this effort until voters make it a priority to expel Republicans and corporatist Democrats from Congress at the ballot box.

"That cannot happen until the news media does its job to educate the public to demand an end to gerrymandering and to demand an end to corporate cam-paign contributions. Unfortunately, the news media - including local media and now even PBS and NPR - literally are controlled by corporatists and Wall Street."

"You tell us," Pongo said. "Do you really think more people want to watch Donald Trump bloviate than watch hard-hitting reporting about how their lives are being manipulated by the Koch brothers?"

"Right," Bianca said. "It's not about ratings – it's about corporate media pounding mind-numbing crap into viewers' heads night after night. Crap that diverts their attention from the essential truths being disclosed at massive personal risk by First Amendment whistleblower heroes.

"As long as corporate media suppress those essential truths, the democratic part of our democratic republic simply cannot function as the founders intended. Media simply must resume fulfilling their crucial role holding monied interests accountable unless we want the things that made this country great to disintegrate."

"So, it's going to be a long, slow, grinding, glacial process," Franklin/Percy said. "But, as any first-year geology student can tell you, glacial power may be slow, but it re-shapes entire continents for thousands of millennia."

"It goes without saying, we're in this for the long haul," Heather interjected.

"What do you say to those who may contend your group is trying to wipe out the country's top earners?" asked Amelie Bagelle of the Arizona Daily Star.

"If anyone truly believes there is any law or amendment to the Constitution which will cause wealthy people to become poor, we'd be happy to take your investments in our machine which turns lead into gold," Pongo said.

Crickets…

"Errr, in other words, I'm saying anyone who believes we're out to destroy the 1 percent is gullible. To a fault.

"We believe there is a role for wealthy folks to play in society. We just don't believe their wealth needs to depend on the rest of the country's families being in a permanent state of financial stress.

"Our country's financial history shows that prosperity is the greatest when _everyone_ *from the bottom up* - not just the top 1 percent – does well. Our country's history shows that middle class wages are the strongest when union membership has been the strongest. Only the negotiating power of organized labor can offset the ruthlessness of the corporate power.

"The USA-SBR will breathe new life into unions and union negotiating power will breathe new life into hourly workers' pay. Those higher wages will translate into more consumer demand, which will lead to higher employment.

"*Higher wages and higher consumer demand equals higher employment.* It's that simple. We dare you to produce a legitimate economist – other than some corporate shill or Republican Party crony – who says otherwise."

The remainder of the press conference covered much of the same ground as their previous conferences. But, surprisingly, there appeared to be little focus on how youthful the organizers were. "*Perhaps that's because Tucson is a college town,*" Franklin thought to himself. "*Or maybe it was because every single one of the reporters at the press conference was under 35.*"

Franklin and the others had fairly low expectations for attendance at the rally the following evening; after all, most of the under-40 target audience for the rally, especially University of Arizona students, were out of town for the holidays.

Nevertheless, around 6,500 persons appeared at the convention center arena – and almost a third of the crowd had at least some snowy white tones to their noggins. Well, after all, it was Arizona – magnet to elderly snowbirds. It appeared that the USA-SBR's provision to switch to a graduated progressive income tax to fund everything had a visceral appeal to retirees trying to balance meager fixed Social Security and private pension incomes with ever-increasing food, clothing and utility expenses.

Finally, mature people were starting to figure out the fundamental injustices of sales taxes and property taxes.

But, for the first time at any of their rallies, the organizers noticed a smattering of posterboard signs from a different constituency:

"Don't bankrupt our schools"
"Public schools will have to close"
"Property tax=Educators' lifeblood"
"Don't hate teachers"

Pongo took Franklin and the others aside just before they were about to begin the rally.

"Some group purporting to support public schools started running radio ads here yesterday decrying our group as trying to strangle funding for schools," Pongo explained. "I have a sneaking suspicion it's actually an astroturf group – probably Republicans, or maybe closet Republican Democrats, like Hillary."

"So let's address this thing up-front, right away," Franklin said.

The rest of the group nodded vigorously in unison. "Go for it," Idris said.

* * *

"We've seen some new signage out there tonight," Franklin said as soon as the introductory PowerPoint video presentation was completed.

"It looks like an astroturf group has been running radio ads here in Tucson the past few days trying to obscure a basic truth:

"First, tax funding not based on a progressive income tax will always – repeat, ALWAYS – be fundamentally unfair. Sales and property taxes will ALWAYS favor the rich. Sales and property taxes are to the rich like a gnat is to Moby Dick.

"Second, once the USA-SBR eliminates all sales and property taxes, state and local governments will be FORCED to replace school funding with revenues from progressive income taxes. IMMEDIATELY.

"State and local governments simply will **_NOT_** be allowed to leave public schools unfunded. The wealthy finally will be forced to pay their fair share toward school funding. And the quality of public schools will never, _EVER_ again depend on your children living in a school district which just happens to have high property values.

"Students living in the barrio FINALLY will be able to get public school educations of the same quality as students living in the Catalina Foothills School District.

"Anyone here have any objections to that?"

Franklin/Percy and the others were surprised to see the crowd rise - slowly at first, but finally the entire sea of attendees - to a loud, sustained standing ovation of approval.

The rest of the rally covered all the main issues of the USA-SBR, followed by the group's latest version of their recruiting message. By the time the crowd had left the premises, they had another 5,000 or so persons signed up to distribute copies of the USA-SBR and to contact their elected office-holders to urge their support of the project.

When they returned to their hotel room, Marcia confirmed that there was another surge of supportive entries on the USA-SBR website and Facebook page.

* * *

Peak Performance Followed by a Visitor

They all headed to bed relatively early; Marcia had planned for them to hike from Madera Canyon to the top of Mount Wrightson south of Tucson the following morning, returning to the hotel by late afternoon.

Because it was Arizona, the weather co-operated.

But, by the time their switchback trail was well into the steep alpine slopes below the mountain's summit, they all wished they'd brought two gallons of water each instead of one. Along with portable toilet seats (there were no bathrooms between the oak-surrounded Madera Canyon picnic area and the top of the peak).

Franklin thought he was going to drop from exhaustion as he navigated the steep tree-free switchbacks on the last half-mile below the mountaintop, but, along with the rest of the bunch, he survived the pain of his aching calves to reach the concrete slab at the top of the peak where a small building once had braved thousands of lightning strikes.

The 360-degree view of the surrounding mountains and valleys was nothing less than stunning. Franklin wondered if the huge telescopes at Whipple Observatory on Mount Hopkins to the south could be (a) trained in their direction or (b) just pointed skyward (answer: b). He also wondered what it would be like to be on the relatively tiny tip of this peak when there was a thunderstorm.

Then they saw the dark clouds on the western horizon.

"Time to go," Idris said.

They took the shorter, steeper trail down the western face of the mountain to get back to the picnic area parking lot. They all took a half-hour breather-slash-nap once they reached the parking area, just to be sure their driver wouldn't fall asleep on the drive back to Tucson via Green Valley. To a person, they'd all worked up a huge appetite – and had hearty helpings of some of the best Mexican food of their lives that evening at Molina's on East Speedway. Including the best cheese crisps on the planet.

There was enough log-like sleeping among the group that night to build a cabin on top of Mount Lemmon – and there would've been plenty of room, thanks to fallen pine bark beetle-infested Ponderosas.

However, Franklin was startled awake at 2:30 a.m. when his phone rang. It was an urgent lobby visitor. That's all the night clerk would say.

When he arrived in the lobby, he saw a tall man in plaid golf slacks and a fluorescent blue polo shirt near the breakfast area at the far end of the lobby. The night clerk was nowhere to be seen. The man roughly resembled the Ed McMahon-looking guy he'd seen months earlier in a dream, the dream when he'd been beckoned to return to his coffin.

Franklin held out his hand to introduce himself to his visitor.

The visitor's hands stayed at his sides.

"I'm here to warn you that what you're doing is dangerous," the man said. "I represent a Wall Street consortium. You do not need to know anything more specific than that. You do need to understand that my associates are powerful people.

"They are people used to getting what they want. They are people who *keep the wrong people from being elected President*. They already know who will be elected – I should say re-elected – as President later this year.

"They already know who they prefer for President in 2016. And she is not someone who will support what you are trying to do. **That** is why they will support her.

"What I am here to tell you is that if you continue to pursue what you've been doing up to now, you do it at your own risk. Do you remember Gary Hart?"

"Not really." (Franklin vaguely recalled something about an extramarital affair by a presidential candidate.)

"Let me just say, keeping him from reaching the ballot was too easy for us.

"Remember Slick Willie Clinton?"

"Uh, er, OK, yes." (Again, Franklin recalled extramarital affairs, but by the President who served during the 1990's.)

"Do you think we didn't know about his dalliances before he won in 1992?"

"I wouldn't know."

"Well, we did. But we could've convinced Joe Sixpack that Slick Willie was as virtuous as a 10-year-old altar boy if we needed to. We knew he was on board with us. He chose our boys for Treasury. He chose our people for Secretary of State. He chose that semi-socialist jew-boy Reich for Labor, but we really didn't give a shit. We knew his '93 tax hike would put our people in power in the House for the rest of the decade.

"The people I represent are confident his lovely long-suffering bride will make the choices which preserve their way of life after the 2016 election. Choices which will keep their corporate influence intact. We've already seen to it that the person from her own party most capable of overtaking her in '16 won't dare try.

"We had our little talk with *her* a few months ago.

"Bottom line: if you think Democratic Party leadership is going to have your back, you're back is going to look like a bayonet pincushion."

"We think Democratic voters and most moderate Republican working class folks will have our backs – eventually, at least."

"Good luck with that.

"We just want you to understand that we're going to turn over every stone and every pebble in your back yard to see what's growing under there. Gary Hart's going to look like a fucking eunuch compared to what we're going to do to you nice folks.

"Just don't say we didn't warn you. Keep acting like a bunch of pussy do-gooders all you want. Just know that there will be a price to pay. And for all the warning we're giving you here tonight, we guarantee you won't see it coming."

"I am not one to use foul language with abandon, Mr. Plaid Pants," Franklin said slowly in a calm and subdued but dead-serious voice.

"So, I hope you'll appreciate my well-thought-out choice of verbiage when I say to you, in all earnestness...please do feel free to GO FUCK YOURSELF."

Mr. Plaid Pants reached slowly into the breast pocket of his long coat. He suddenly and quickly pulled out – as Franklin reflexively jerked to attention – a plain white business card with a single pre-printed toll-free phone number on it.

"If you change your mind and want to negotiate a payout in exchange for dropping your efforts or providing information about your fellow operatives, just call that number.

"Otherwise, you'll probably never see me again. Even if I see you."

As Mr. Plaid Pants turned to walk out of the lobby, Franklin slowly-but-firmly raised the middle finger on his right hand in the direction of his visitor.

Franklin walked slowly back upstairs to his room and crawled into bed. He thought he'd have a difficult time getting back to sleep.

Surprisingly, he did not.

* * *

AIR POWER IN THE DESERT: PERPETUAL
THREATS=MILITARY PROFITS

The following morning, the Poughkeepsians spent a couple of hours at the Pima Air & Space Museum on Tucson's southeast side before heading north. Franklin and the others were stunned at the sheer size and variety of the display of historical civilian aircraft and warplanes dating from World War I-era biplanes through the Cold War, aircraft from both the U.S.A. and its World War II and Cold War opponents.

Walking around and underneath the massive aircraft both indoors and outdoors, Pongo remarked on the many hundreds of billions of dollars that went into producing the thousands of B-29's, B-36's, B-47's, B-52's, B-1's, F-18's and so forth during the Cold War.

"So much deficit spending on weapons of war simply to ensure the Russians wouldn't dare to try to force communism on us," he said. "While they did the same to ensure we wouldn't try to force capitalism on them. And what we're seeing here is only a scratch on the surface of one solitary branch of our armed services."

"Imagine what all that money could've done for advancement in science and health care and education," Franklin said. "Things that could've contributed to positive creativity rather than things which depended upon a need to inflict violence to be used. How many schools could've been built? How many college educations could've been funded?

"Didn't our spies know that the Russians were spending themselves into oblivion on their defense programs before communism fell? Didn't they know there was never any intent to go to war with us?"

"Those kinds of truths wouldn't have been conducive to continued military industrial complex profits," Phil explained. "Y'see, to keep the massive military engine going, there's got to be the perception of a continual existential threat coming from _**SOMEPLACE**_.

"Through the late '80s, it was Russia. In the '90s on through today, it's Middle East terrorists. Soon, it'll maybe go back to Russians. Or, maybe heathen athiests. Or, maybe radical anarchists – they're always a good go-to resource if unions try to make a comeback. You remember from the early 1900's, right?"

He did.

As much as anything, though, Franklin marveled at the sheer technological genius exemplified by vast sizes and impressive features of the warplanes. With all that knowledge, _surely_ the U.S.A. could send manned expeditions to any part of the solar system – or beyond – where curiosity compelled science to explore, he said.

"Not quite," Idris replied. "There's a popular astrophysicist – his name's Neil deGrasse Tyson – who's pointed out repeatedly that we've only sent humans on long-distance space expeditions, like the lunar landings, when we were competing with our Cold War enemies for space prominence.

"Once it was clear the Cold War was over, the budgets for long-distance manned space expeditions shrank to next-to-nothing. It was once thought we'd have humans on Mars by the end of the '80s. Now it's by MAYBE the 2030's."

"Shit, if they find liquid dead dinosaurs on Mars or some weird creature that eats dirt and shits gold, we'll be up there in a year or two," Harry said. "And they'd figure out a way for the Koch brothers to catch a ride there relaxing on satin pillows while munching on chocolate truffles the entire way. They'd probably even figure out a way for some space robot to wipe those oil boys' asses with super-soft extra-squeezable Charmin' after each defecation."

Just as the word "defecation" came out of Harry's mouth, a Harris hawk flying overhead squirted out some birdshit which missed Heather's head by about an inch and plopped onto her almost-new Sketchers.

"Crap-on-a-croissant!" she said. "What's say let's limit the rest of this visit to the inside of the hangars?"

"Done and done," Phil said, with nodded assents from the rest of the group.

∗ ∗ ∗

On to Maricrappa County via Best Pizza on the Planet

That afternoon, the Poughkeepsie crew drove their rental cars northwest to Tempe and Phoenix via Casa Grande, where they stopped for lunch at Dell's Pizza for the best pizza any of them had ever had in their lives. What a pleasant surprise, thought Marcia, who'd been told about the restaurant by an attendant at a nearby gas station. Pongo was just happy they served Dr. Pepper.

During the drive there, Franklin debated in his head whether and when he should discuss with the others his meeting with Mr. Plaid Pants from the previous night. He decided the best time would be after they finished their current rally tour. It was clear Mr. Plaid Pant's visit was intended to intimidate. The intimidation might or might not succeed, but Franklin thought it would be unfair to the thousands who were looking forward to their rallies to act as Mr. Plaid Pant's intimidation spreader before the latest rallies were completed. By the same token, he knew he had a responsibility to make the risks clear to the other organizers. Just not right away.

After checking in at the Tempe Best Western Plus by the Mall, they went downstairs to the hotel conference room for their press conference in advance of the rally the next day at Wells Fargo Arena.

They followed the same routine as three days earlier. There were reporters from the Arizona Republic (owned by Gannett Corp. of USAToday fame for decades after they purchased it from former Vice President Dan Quayle's grandfather's widow), the East Valley Tribune, the New Times weekly and each of the major broadcast networks' local affiliates, including PBS and NPR.

Their questions were surprisingly similar to those at previous press conferences, except that this time around, the Arizona Republic's political reporter, Stan Parcheesi, asked if the Poughkeepsians had an anarchist bent.

Franklin explained – in almost identical terms used during the Tucson rally – how the USA-SBR's plan to replace state and local sales and property taxes with progressive income taxes would simply mean more just and equitable funding of public schools nationwide.

"Arizona would have a leg up on some states, because it already has a state progressive income tax system," Franklin/Percy said. "Please feel free to check out the YouTube video of our Tucson rally if you need more detail.

"Beyond that, I'm not sure how you could conceivably consider us to be anarchistic. The last time I checked, anarchists didn't believe in amending constitutional law. Because they don't believe in having laws."

Pongo and the others got the impression that the Phoenix journalists – such as they were – were simply going through the motions. Idris later predicted that the Republic probably would place the coverage of their press conference on page D-18. It actually ended up on page E-12; seven paragraphs. Poor reporter didn't even get a byline. At least they got the date, time and location of the rally right.

But they were pleasantly surprised at the coverage by the local ABC affiliate. It was the second story on both of their evening broadcasts. They even did an on-camera interview of an Edward Abbey-ish poli-sci sociologist from the University of Arizona who gave the Poughkeepsians high marks for circumspection and long-term thinking.

"I just think their reporter enjoyed saying the word 'Poughkeepsie,'" Heather said.

* * *

The next evening's rally went off without a hitch. The arena was about two-thirds full, once again with a surprising number of older participants. And all the ralliers – including the older ones - appeared to have a much greater interest in the free top ramen and clean underwear than attendees at previous rally sites.

The most popular part of the evening was a riff by Pongo and Idris on Maricopa County's Sheriff Joe Arpaio. If there was anyone in the crowd before the rally who didn't understand Arpaio's McCarthy-esque anti-immigrant and anti-poor politics when they showed up, they most assuredly did by the end of the rally.

"We thought, in honor of Sheriff Joe," Pongo said, "we might toss out packs of moldy expired shelf date-bologna instead of ramen noodles as a tribute to

America's favorite Mexican-hater. But we figured it would be a waste 'cause good ol' Joe probably will figure out a way to get most of you into his jail and eating from his fetid menu offerings sooner or later."

Pongo and the others went on to conduct a skit with Pongo made up to look like Sheriff Joe wearing Nazi SS insignia on his collar and asking people lined up at a roadblock to "show your papers," with each person stopped – except one - found to lack appropriate documentation and hauled away in plastic hand-ties. People failing the ID test in the skit included Pope Francis (Harry), Justice Ruth Bader Ginsburg (Bianca), President Obama (Idris), Kate Upton (Heather) – whom Sheriff Joe told would fit in perfectly in her bikini in his tent city during the summer, Joe Biden (Harry again), Ann Romney (Marcia) – who "Sheriff Joe" sent on her way unfettered ("You can't get any whiter than that!"), Arizona Cardinals' receiver Larry Fitzgerald (Idris again) and U.S. Rep. Raul Grijalva (Harry again) – with a cameo appearance by the real Rep. Grijalva, who was standing in line behind the fake one. Pongo's goofy remarks as Sheriff Joe about why each person was being detained kept the crowd in stitches (for Biden: "Anyone whose teeth are that perfect must be getting cut-rate dental from a brown guy in Hermosillo!").

"So, what's the deal, can't you guys afford to find any REAL Hispanic bit players?" Rep. Grijalva deadpanned as he brought up the end of the line, to lots of laughter and applause.

"OK, take this one away too," Pongo/Sheriff Joe ordered. "They don't come any more Mexican than that!"

As "Sheriff Joe" turned to watch Grijalva being led away, two guys in dark windbreakers with big "FBI" letters on the back walked up behind the "sheriff." The first one (Harry) said, "OK, are you Joe Arpaio? Yes? OK, we've got some papers for **you**! And we DO need our stinking badges!" "Agent" Harry then handed the "sheriff" a large manila envelope labeled with the words "Arrest Warrant" in big letters.

The crowd roared with approval.

* * *

WILDERNESS SPECTACLE EN ROUTE TO FLAGSTAFF

By the end of the evening, approximately 6,000 more people had signed up to distribute copies of the USA-SBR and to lobby their elected officeholders to declare their support for it. For the remainder of the week, the USA-SBR website and Facebook page were inundated with thousands of positive comments from rally participants in the metro Phoenix and Tucson areas. Marcia once again had to enlist help from Heather, Bianca, Pongo and Franklin to keep up with responses. The proposed extinction of sales taxes and property taxes appeared to be especially popular with Arizonans. Even better, word appeared to have spread – partly due to the latest local TV ads placed by Marcia with Phoenix TV stations that week – that public school funding not only wouldn't be endangered by the USA-SBR, but would become truly fair from district to district for the first time in U.S. history.

The group decided to use their two days off between the Tempe rally and the upcoming Flagstaff rally at Northern Arizona University's Walkup Skydome to view the remote Pine Mountain Wilderness, Montezuma's Castle, Oak Creek Canyon and Walnut Creek National Monument.

The most challenging of the outdoor adventures turned out to be the hike to the crest of the Pine Mountain Wilderness in the brisk-but-sunny mid-winter Arizona air. Just getting to the trailhead proved to be a challenge; they all thanked Marcia for having the foresight to rent a high-riding extended-cab four-wheel-drive pick-up. After finding an oak leaf on the ground more than a foot wide, Franklin pledged to return someday during the fall so they could see the colorful foliage. At the crest of the trail, the group could see multiple sapphire-colored desert lakes in the distance to the south.

"Just how is it that more people aren't taking advantage of natural wonders like this?" Franklin asked.

"It's probably because the people who would enjoy this the most are busy working two and three jobs just to be able to pay their rent, mortgages and student loans," Idris said.

"Let's hope it won't always be that way, Idris," Franklin said. "Sights like this are what make life worth living."

"You got that right, Sir," Pongo said, laughing as he smashed a ball of snow – picked up from the shade at the base of a Ponderosa pine – on the back of Franklin's neck.

After completing their round-trip hike to the crest of the wilderness trail, they drove on to Montezuma's Castle, spending about a half-hour there (visitors aren't allowed to actually climb to the ruins) before driving through Oak Creek Canyon via Sedona on their way to Flagstaff.

They checked in to their rooms at the Drury Inn & Suites just as the orange-hued sun was setting behind the mountains to the west. They planned to visit Meteor Crater, Walnut Creek National Monument and Sunset Crater National Monument the next day, with their news conference for local media scheduled for 3:30 p.m. at the Drury Inn banquet room.

Not a single one of the Poughkeepsians needed any sleep aids that night after their wilderness hike and long drive. By the time they'd finished their hot breakfast the following morning, they were fully refreshed for their hikes at the two national monuments. Franklin couldn't have been happier to be hiking more than 15 miles in two days and getting to see pre-historic Native American ruins at two different well-preserved sites. He was somewhat less than impressed with Meteor Crater, though.

"Everything I've read says it's lots more impressive from the sky than from the rim of the crater," Pongo said. "Just kind of looks like a scooped out hole in the ground from here on the rim."

"Wouldn't have wanted to be standing right here 50,000 years ago when this happened," Franklin said. "Would've been like Quake Lake on steroids. I imagine anyone standing within 20 miles of this would've been vaporized."

* * *

They returned from their sightseeing day trip barely 30 minutes before the press conference. Reporters from the Arizona Daily Sun, the NAU Lumberjack newspaper, the NAU National Public Radio affiliate and the local NBC television affiliate were scheduled to participate.

They didn't disappoint: ironically, the local Flagstaff reporters appeared much better prepared than those the Poughkeepsians had encountered in Tucson and, especially, Phoenix. Although their questions covered many of the same areas as their fellow reporters to the south, their follow-up questions showed real perspective and acuity.

"*Must be the clean mountain air,*" Idris thought to himself.

The local PBS affiliate reporter, RuthAnn Simonson, seemed most interested in the group's strategy to win over reluctant elected officeholders without alienating them.

"We hope to appeal to their instincts to serve their constituents," Franklin/Percy said. "We only can do that if they hear from large numbers of their constituents that the USA-SBR's passage is important to them.

"We certainly don't want to encourage our supporters to threaten or try to intimidate their representatives into backing the USA-SBR. Our hope is that, if an existing elected officeholder is determined to oppose the USA-SBR, one of our supporters will run against that officeholder.

"But we would much rather use friendly, logical persuasion to convince an officeholder to support our proposal. So much of what we're ultimately able to do will depend on how the USA-SBR is received by individuals and corporations with the greatest financial assets. We hope to demonstrate to them that it's in their own long-term financial interests to support the USA-SBR simply because it will lead to their customers having more money to purchase their products and services."

"So, what happens if the wealthiest individuals and corporations decide it's in their best interests to actively oppose the USA-SBR?" Ms. Simonson asked.

"Our job gets tougher – and takes longer," Pongo said. "If that does happen – and we certainly hope it does **not** – we will try to persuade our supporters to patronize only the corporations and sole proprietorships which support the USA-SBR, or those which at least remain neutral."

"One of the primary goals of our group," Bianca said, "is to reduce the financial inequality which has turned most of the middle class and all of the working poor into little more than indentured serfs.

"Remember: 'serfs' is not an exaggeration. Many large corporations still, to this day, make use of dead peasant insurance for their employees, to profit off their employees' untimely deaths."

"Once again, though," Franklin/Percy said, "we need to emphasize that our primary goal with these rallies is education: if our rallies can simply wipe out one perpetual far-right myth – like the myth of wealthy so-called 'job creators' – we would count our efforts as a success."

"Are you saying there are lots of non-wealthy job creators?" asked Jessica Woodstein of the local NBC affiliate.

"That's *not* what we're trying to say," Franklin said. "We're trying to dispel the myth that the wealthy create jobs out of the goodness of their hearts. Except for the occasional nepotism hire, wealthy and non-wealthy job creators alike create jobs **only if consumer demand justifies it.**

"The more discretionary spending money the middle class has, the more likely that they'll be buying goods and services, creating that consumer demand – and causing businesses to create jobs. If they don't have discretionary spending money, the air is sucked right out of consumer demand – and job creation stays bogged down.

"It has ABSOLUTELY NOTHING to do with the magnanimity of well-to-do business owners. No amount of tax credit schemes and other government incentives will induce a business owner to create a job if there isn't the consumer demand to justify adding that job.

"So, if we can relegate that one myth to the dustbin of business propaganda history, we will count our rallies as a success."

"Good luck with that," said Henry Halsell of the Arizona Daily Sun. "You could make a career out of counting the number of times Fox News repeats the 'wealthy job creators' mantra every day.

"Y'know, it really sounds like a lot of your efforts depend on people under 40 disconnecting their video games, their smart phone games, their reality TV viewing and their obsessions with sports and replacing all those habits with education and activism about your USA-SBR.

"Is that actually realistic?"

"Time will tell, Henry," Franklin answered. "If enough middle class folks grow weary of super-rich employers turning them into wage drones who have too little legal tender to pay their medical bills, too little to take a no-frills vacation, too little to replace their banged-up old car – well, it could happen.

"It won't happen overnight, though. It will happen only if conscientious journalists like yourselves do the due diligence to educate your readers, listeners and viewers about the difference between what corporatists want and what the middle class wants.

"That's another myth we want to target: that corporatists just want 'what's best' for their employees. As I recall from my college history courses, that's very similar to what 19ᵗʰ century slaveholders said about their human property.

"Slaves never got to have unions. The business community has long aspired to keep 20ᵗʰ and 21ˢᵗ century workers from having union representation. It's far easier to keep workers from 'getting uppity' if it's just the worker versus the employer instead of an entire union versus the employer.

"'Uppity workers' have that unpleasant tendency to want decent pay and decent benefits. Take away union representation and it's way easier to keep the grumbling down on the plantation – I mean work campus.

"It's *no simple coincidence* that the massive, stunningly **huge** income gap between the middle class and the top 1 percent of earners in this country has grown at the highest-warp speed – to paraphrase Star Trek – during the same period that union membership has plummeted in the U.S.A."

"If employers get their way, unions will become as extinct as the passenger pigeon. And we will then have a strictly two-tiered society: the super-wealthy and the rest of us.

"*That's* what the USA-SBR is designed to remedy. But it can be the remedy only if we have elected officeholders who support it."

"What do you say to those who suggest your provision for reparations payments is just an attempt to pander to built-in constituencies of Native Americans and African-Americans?" Halsell asked. "There's word out that your rally is going to be overwhelmed with non-white participants."

"If we wanted to pander to constituencies, we would've proposed middle class reparations payments of a million dollars each," Franklin/Percy said. "Unfortunately, there isn't an infinite supply of money.

"The reparations payments are about a long-delayed attempt to correct issues of social justice which have left lasting scars on this nation's soul. We want it done because it's the right thing to do. It's deserved.

"Please let us know if you find any elected officeholders willing to go on record as saying reparations payments are not deserved. We have plenty of would-be candidates who want to be the first to vote in Congress to support the USA-SBR."

"Here's what we can tell you that you might find as a surprise," Halsell said. "It was just announced today that virtually every new car dealer organization across the country is supporting the provision for reparations payments. Seems they're speculating that one of the first things someone with a new financial windfall does – besides going to Disneyland, I guess – is to buy a new car."

"I suppose even pragmatic hyper-capitalists can be right now and then," Franklin/Percy said. "You know, like a broken clock, at least a couple of times a day."

* * *

The Skydome rally the next evening drew almost 15,000 souls – one of the largest non-athletic, non-concert crowds ever to assemble in Flagstaff. Perhaps 9,500 of the attendees were Native Americans from Navajo, Hopi and Apache reservations across Northern Arizona; another thousand or so appeared to be African-Americans.

The Poughkeepsians dedicated the rally to former longtime Flagstaff resident Clyde Tombaugh, who discovered Pluto while in Flagstaff, and to Percival Lowell, who studied the "canals" of Mars from his observatory in Flagstaff.

"Misters Lowell and Tombaugh both saw mysteries in the night sky and both were persistent in their searches for answers to those mysteries," Franklin/Percy told the crowd.

"They never gave up on their search for answers. Mr. Lowell discovered features on Mars which we now know were likely related to water and wind erosion on its surface. Mr. Tombaugh eventually discovered Pluto and countless asteroids. It took years of hard work and persistence by both of them.

"It is in that spirit of persistence that we present to you the Un-Screwing of America – Second Bill of Rights as a lasting and just remedy to atrocious social and financial inequalities which threaten to tear apart the fabric of our nearly 250-year-old society.

"We look to the power of the First Amendment, the massive power each and every one of you holds, to express yourselves to those who work FOR YOU. Those elected officeholders whose entire job is to REPRESENT YOU.

"Whether you express that power through the 20th century technology of a ballpoint pen or through the 21st century technology of electronic mail, Facebook petitions and blogging – or even through street demonstrations or – who knows? – even running for office against a Tea Party troglodyte, each and every one of you has far more power than you realize to make change.

"But it will take each of you turning off your Candy Crush games, your Silent Hill and Grand Theft Auto video games, your reality TV shows and your YouTube cat videos for you to make the time to actually express those First Amendment rights.

"And make no mistake: they're not just rights. They're duties. If you don't fulfill your duty to express your dissatisfaction about what your corporate-controlled government is doing to you, you're telling all those corporatists that you're OK with what they're doing to you.

"Are you happy with what your corporate overlords are doing to you?"

A general full-throated murmur of "No's" went through the crowd.

"How do you truly feel about your corporate overlords at work in your Legislature and in your Congress?"

"**Fuck O-ver-LORDS**!!" the chant began. And continued. For almost five minutes.

"OK, so we're all in agreement," Franklin said, motioning the crowd to ratchet down the volume. "We don't like being screwed by all the corporatists out there.

"So, let's do this: let's insist – politely but firmly – that our corporatist drone officeholders and the officeholders who are afraid of those corporatist drones all start to take the USA-SBR seriously.

"Let's compel our elected officeholders to **go on the record** either in support of the USA-SBR or in opposition. If they won't go on the record or if they actively oppose the USA-SBR, then let's find USA-SBR supporters to run against those corporate drones in each and every election until voters finally remove them from office.

"That's how we make change happen. It won't be easy. It won't be quick. But here's what we promise you: someday it **WILL** be worth it. Someday your children and grandchildren will thank you with all their hearts for having the courage and commitment to overcome the corporate behemoths which are out to crush the middle class.

"But we have to support each other's efforts first.

"So, enjoy your clean underwear you got here tonight. Enjoy the ramen noodles you got here tonight. But if you want more than one night of enjoyment – if you want more pride than just knowing you're on the right side of history, you have to make an effort.

"We look forward to your commitment in writing to distribute copies of the USA-SBR to your neighbors, your friends, your kids' schoolteachers, your elected officeholders. We look forward to you committing to contact those elected officeholders and reporting back to us what THEY do or do not commit to do themselves.

"If each of us does our part for the USA-SBR, ten years from now, things like "too big to fail" and "too rich to do a perp walk" may simply be embarrassingly awful footnotes for the history books.

"Let's make this happen, Flagstaff. Enjoy the movie!"

And "Capitalism: A Love Story" began to roll, as the crowd responded with a standing ovation. Their responses on the sign-up forms and on the USA-SBR website and Facebook page showed the enthusiasm had been genuine.

∗　∗　∗

El Canon Grande and a Chance Furry-Faced Encounter

The group left by mid-morning the next day, heading west on Interstate 40 for their scheduled stops at UCLA and San Diego State University.

The weather was starting to turn wintry, with high winds and blowing snow as they left Flagstaff city limits and passed to the south of the San Francisco Peaks.

All but Franklin had been leaning against making a side trip to the Grand Canyon, as each of them had already seen it – in fact, Pongo and Harry had hiked to Phantom Ranch via the inner gorge almost 10 years earlier during their college winter break.

But, at Pongo's suggestion, they had discussed whether to go forward with the side trip while Franklin was showering in his Flagstaff hotel room that morning. Everyone agreed that it would be cruel to bypass a chance for Franklin to have his first opportunity to explore Grand Canyon trails on foot.

As they were heading toward Williams, AZ on I-40, they advised Franklin that their schedule had been revised to allow for a full-day visit to the Grand Canyon so Franklin could hike the Kaibab Trail down to the Colorado River and the Bright Angel Trail (the less steep of the two) back up to the South Rim (14-plus miles total). The rest of the group would hike around the top of the South Rim for an hour or so by mid-morning and then kick back in their rooms at the Maswik Lodge until Franklin returned from his solo hiking adventure.

"Kick back" in this situation, though, actually was a euphemism for hours of intimate fluid exchanges between Pongo and Heather in their suite plus Harry and Bianca in their own suite on the next floor up. And, unknown to the rest of the group, Marcia and Idris were exchanging some fluids of their own in a suite at the opposite end of the lodge. It had been many weeks since each of the 'kicking back'-ers had enough free time for hormonal recreation, so there was much energy to be expended. Phil, pathetically, was left to his own DIY gratification and an extended nap.

While mattress springs were being put to the test at 6,800 feet elevation above sea level, Franklin was enjoying the lightness of downhill travel on the trail a few thousand feet below the south rim. At Phil's insistence, he was carrying 1-1/2 gallons of water – even though it was about 39F when he started down from the south rim, Phil knew it would be at least 20 degrees warmer in the inner gorge. And at least ¾ of that H2O supply would be needed on the 10 percent uphill grade coming up Bright Angel Trail on the way back.

Franklin was so thrilled at being in the heart of, arguably, the most scenic place in the world, he didn't even mind having to occasionally dodge piles of mule feces and puddles of mule urine on the trail. He even got used to its pungent aroma. Thousand-foot high red and orange cliffs as far as the eye can see will do that.

Franklin noticed that almost every person heading uphill on the South Kaibab Trail was smiling, despite lots of huffing and puffing. He even saw one young man in his late 20's smiling in spite of having to carry his pretty – but worn out – young bride uphill on his shoulders.

"Why didn't you two take the Bright Angel Trail going uphill? It's about half as steep," Franklin said, sympathetically.

"It's our honeymoon," the young man said. "We just go where our hearts take us. Right now I wish they'd take us to a surprise Beautyrest mattress with crisp clean sheets in a shady spot alongside the trail. You haven't seen something like that have ya'?"

"If I had, I'd be taking a nap there right now! Besides, you two look like beauty sleep would just be redundant. Young love – wish it were as contagious as festering athlete's foot."

"Now, there are two concepts not often in the same sentence," the young shoulder-mounted wife laughed as her devoted husband plodded up the trail.

As the couple was almost out of Franklin's view, he saw a stain the shade of a Red Delicious apple spreading above the heel of each of the young husband's hiking shoes. "*True love that is,*" Franklin thought. "*Would I ever have done something like that for Eleanor? Or Lucy?*" He wasn't sure, but he wanted to think so.

It was another two miles on the trail before Franklin encountered any other hikers – uphill travel on the Kaibab was about as rare as an environmentalist at a Koch Family Thanksgiving gathering. Along the way, Franklin noticed pronghorn antelope, rabbits (both roaming freely and in the jaw of a smiling - ? – coyote), porcupines, javelina, mule deer, two bighorn rams and the occasional rattlesnake.

As Franklin watched the rams prepare to head-butt – no doubt vying for the affections of a lovely ewe spectator somewhere nearby – he neglected to notice a two-inch-high spike-shaped chunk of Coconino sandstone protruding from the trail.

He helplessly tumbled head over foot, forgetting to watch where he was rolling as he tried to keep a grasp of the canteen and jug that had been slung over his shoulder. Had he been less focused on protecting his water supply, he'd have noticed the 350-foot precipice just beyond the outer edge of the trail.

Just as he was about to roll over the side, he felt a pair of thick legs move in between him and gravity's worst punishment.

The thing he saw was a 70-something 6-foot-3 white guy wearing a windbreaker with a "Texas Tea Party Patriots" logo and the name "Pick-Ax Paxton" embroidered below the left shoulder reaching down to help him to his feet. Another four persons, three women and one man, wearing similar windbreakers were just downhill on the trail, jogging to catch up.

"Certainly would appear I owe you one," Franklin/Percy said. "I'm Percy Van Mullder – but some of my friends call me Scruples. I'm from Poughkeepsie, New York."

"Glad to make your acquaintance, young man. I'm Jeff Paxton. This (pointing to a 50-something blond to his left) is my wife Darlene and that's my son Paul, his wife Becky and Becky's best friend Courtney. We're from Anarene, Texas."

"Are you that young fella from New York who's been goin' round the country tryin' to get Congress to take up another Bill of Rights?" Becky, 27, a registered nurse, asked. "Courtney and I were watchin' you and the others on YouTube last week. I thought I recognized you when you said Poughkeepsie."

"I would be he," Franklin/Percy said. "Was wondering when I'd actually get to meet some real-life Tea Partiers in the flesh. Sure am glad your father-in-law here was spry enough to serve as a human guard rail just now."

About that time, Franklin noticed each of the five Texans were sporting varying thicknesses of the tell-tale visible-only-to-Franklin (and some others?) fine sensillum-like fur, the kind which divulged the bearers' predisposition to being self-serving. He'd last seen a smattering of those fur-bearers at the Utah State University rally in Logan and had been grateful not to have noticed any since then. They made him feel like a bighorn sheep lamb surrounded by a pack of wolves.

Then, suddenly, Franklin had a picture in his mind of a boulder cascading down the side of a nearby cliff and landing on his furry rescuers, popping open their brains like so many casaba melons. In his quick vision, he saw himself stumbling toward the cracked craniums and instinctively scooping out the ganglia and other innermost brain tissues, head by head. He could almost taste the mouthwatering savoriness of the spongy tissues. Then, just as quickly, the rational part of Franklin's mind snapped himself back to reality.

"I'm a little surprised to see Tea Party folks enjoying a National Park," Franklin/Percy said, smiling. "You folks do realize this park doesn't generate a profit for anyone, correct?"

"Percy, my friend, seems like everyone is under the impression that all of us Tea Partiers are Ayn Randians who want everything to be corporatized," Jeff said. "Just ain't so. We take pride in our National Parks."

"Seems like most people in your organization don't realize almost all of the organizational strategy and funding for it came from huge corporate interests trying to create an astroturf group," Franklin/Percy said.

"By astroturf group, I take it that you mean a phony grassroots group," Courtney, a 29-year-old auburn-haired accountant, said, grinning.

"That's correct – it's Courtney, right? If you Google Tea Party and Dick Armey – he's a former Texas Republican congressman – you'll see that he funneled lots of corporate cash into the original Tea Party organizing efforts in 2010.

"The corporatists behind that Tea Party financing are **deeply** into privatizing currently not-for-profit government services, whether it's National Parks, Social Security, Medicare or programs for the poor. They're the ones who seem to like government shut-downs as a negotiating tool. The Corporatist-in-Chief in 1982, your Tea Partiers' sainted Reagan the Gipper, didn't have House support to privatize national parks, but he signed into law the largest user-fee increase for the parks in decades after it was passed by the Republican-controlled U.S. Senate.

"Of course, part of what we're trying to do with our USA-SBR rallies is help educate people to realize that the only way corporations can successfully privatize not-for-profit government services is by charging hefty fees against people who use those services. Profits aren't magic – they have to come from **_someplace_**, and those profits for previously non-profit government services would come right out of your pocketbook and mine.

"If there's one thing I hope you can take with you from this little encounter we've had, it's that you'd probably be paying as much as $100 a person just to set foot on this trail if National Parks were privatized. And you're monthly Social Security payments might have been cut by as much as half, Jeff, if "W" Bush had gotten away with privatizing the most successful social program in history.

"And those same privatization-obsessed corporatists wanted numerous mines plus at least two dams to be built in the Grand Canyon, dams which would've flooded vast portions of the inner gorge and done untold damage to this gem of a park. It was environmentalists – not Tea Party corporatists – who stopped those projects."

"Well, what you liberal-types don't seem to get is that Tea Partiers HATE – I mean **_HATE!_** – taxes," Paul Paxton said. "We don't give a piddlin' piss-ant pecker's puddle what the taxes go for. If the guv'mint has to go broke an' stop pavin' streets, some company'll come along an' fill that void. An' if it costs a little more, it's worth it not to have to pay taxes, 'specially if we know that little bit's gonna maybe make more real private business jobs 'stead of jobs for lazy guv'mint slobs."

"For non-Ayn Randians, your son here sure sounds like he and Ayn came out of the same government-hating mold, Jeff," Franklin/Percy said. "Guess he hasn't heard about Tea Party-backed Republican pols like Texan Rick Perry and Indiana Mitch Daniels who privatized highways and sold off 75 to 99 years' worth of rights to set toll road fees to Spanish billionaires. Or other Tea Party-backed Republicans who passed a bill in Congress that allowed mega-banks to manipulate and corner the market on aluminum so every person who buys a can of soda pays an extra nickel or so straight into mega-billionaires' pockets.

"All that hate-the-guv'mint talk almost sounds kind of bigoted, if you asked me – but you didn't. The only career government workers I've known in all my years were dedicated to serving the public – and their supervisors made sure they put in a full day's work for a full day's pay each and every day.

"If they hadn't, the voting public – and the newspapers which held them accountable - would've made sure they lost their jobs. And you should remember: those 'real private business jobs' most of the time are non-union jobs which often don't have any benefits at all, whether that's sick pay, vacation pay or health insurance.

"Want your burgers made by a cook who's had to come to work with a severe respiratory infection because his employer doesn't offer health insurance or have paid sick leave?" Franklin asked Paul.

"I ain't worried none. That cookin's gonna kill all them germs REAL good," Paul said.

"But what about between the cookin' and when the meal is handed to you?" Becky asked her exterminator husband. "I can't help but think Mr. Van Mullder here's makin' some sense."

"Becky, all y'all nurses is just obsessed with all that health-related crud," Darlene said, nose pointing slightly skyward. "If your father-in-law had had all these hoity-toity libtards to deal with when he started his bug-poisoning bidness, you'da had to meet Paul at the local Wal-Mart instead of Texas A & M, 'cuz we wouldn'ta been able to affard to send him even to Archer County Community College."

At that moment, Franklin saw something he'd never seen before – either in his previous life or since Pongo and Harry found him revived in 2010. The sensillum-like fur showing on the necks, faces and ears of Becky and Courtney appeared to be slowly falling out – slightly faster on Becky than on Courtney. The sight of it was a moment of rejuvenated hope for Franklin, a pureness of pleasure in the thought that it was possible even for those exposed to the harshest prejudices and snideness to reverse course, on their own, once exposed to knowledge.

"Mama, I don't know that Becky's all that obsessed," Jeff said. "There's got to be room for people to disagree with respect – to agree to disagree. If there's real science behind what Percy's saying, then we should try to be open to re-thinking some things."

"I think that's true for all of us," Franklin/Percy said. "You wouldn't be here right now if your heart weren't full of love for this beautiful landscape. I can see that you'd never want this precious treasure to be jeopardized for someone's profit. Am I right?"

"You couldn't be more correct if you was sittin' at God's right hand," Jeff said.

"And I don't doubt for a second that, when you stood between me and a life-ending tumble, you knew you might be risking your own safety at least a little bit. Am I right there, too?"

"Well, young man, let's just say that I couldn'ta slept well for the rest of however many nights I've got left if I'd just let ya' do the Wile E. Coyote dive without at least _tryin'_ to keep ya' trail-bound."

"OK, let's say that. Purely sleep-related self-interest on your part," Franklin/Percy laughed. "That's another thing there we've got in common: Looney Tunes. _Alta cultura_, the finest."

"Shit, Dad, we don' know no Al Taculturra. Don't know how these liberal snobs expect us to know all their fancy heroes," Paul muttered under his breath – just loudly enough for Franklin to hear it.

"I think Percy just was saying we both have a genu-iney appreciation for high culture," Jeff said. "Any man who likes the likes of Foghorn Leghorn and Bugs and Daffy and Pepe LePew and Elmer Fudd must have a durn good corry-zone – that's Mexican for heart, son. I'm right pleased we could help keep ya' safe, sir."

"Back at ya', Jeff. You Lone Star friends watch out for that first step off the side the rest of the way up – it's a doozy. Hope we can meet again someday – would love to see you at one of our rallies."

"Don't know that I'd hold my breath on that one," Jeff said, "but if you're ever down Anarene way, we'd love to show you some bona fidey Texas hospitality."

"Mr. Paxton, I promise I'll let you know if I'm ever within 50 miles of your fine community, OK?"

"I'll hold you to that, commpaddree," Jeff said.

As the Texans walked uphill in the opposite direction from Franklin, he saw Becky and Courtney both give him the sign language for 'love you,' which he realized later probably meant "hook-'em horns." Maybe not, though, he thought. Unknown to Franklin, they actually *would* show up later on at one of the USA-SBR rallies, sans Paul.

* * *

The rest of the hike was an exercise in joy for a man whose legs had been fairly useless for more than 30 years. Crossing both of the footbridges across the Colorado River in the Inner Gorge left him at a loss for words. It was one of those days a person wishes could last forever. The sun was blanketing the red, pink and purple canyon walls in a soft, warm golden glow as it set during Franklin's final mile up the Bright Angel Trail to the canyon rim. He'd have arrived 45 minutes earlier had he not taken a detour to Plateau Point from the Indian Garden watering hole on his way out of the canyon. Staring down over the edge of Plateau Point, he had thoughts of admiration for the Native Americans who'd managed to preserve all of the natural beauty of the region for millennia before Europeans "discovered" the Americas.

By the time Franklin reached the south rim, there was just a faint glow of twilight to the west. All he wanted to do was go to his room and have room service bring a couple of grilled cheese sandwiches, thick New England clam chowder and fairy toast, but he'd already agreed to meet the rest of the group for dinner at 6:30 p.m. at the El Tovar Dining Room.

When he got there, he expected to see all of the group rested and refreshed, but every last one of them – although looking vaguely happy - seemed to be worn out, appearing as though they'd just carried their own heavy backpacks up and down the steps of a stadium dozens of times during a fitness workout. "*Must have done some hiking of their own along the rim today while I was gone*," he thought to himself.

Franklin recounted with them an oral catalog of the sights and sounds he'd experienced on the South Kaibab and Bright Angel trails, including his near-fatal stumble on the Kaibab a couple of miles from the canyon bottom.

They all enjoyed his account of the encounter with the Texans, especially his description of the "invisible" sensillum-like fur slowly sloughing off the two younger women as they waved goodbye. Harry was confused about why Texas women would be furry, though.

"I'll explain it to you later, genius," Pongo said.

The Poughkeepsians finished their evening by looking over the edge of the south rim in the starlight and counting the number of pinpoints of light in the canyon from overnight hikers' campfires.

* * *

TRAIL-TIME REPERCUSSIONS, THEN
MOUSE EARS- & BEACH-BOUND

The group got a 7:30 a.m. start for the metropolitan Los Angeles region the following morning, all of them feeling fully refreshed after an exceptional night's sleep.

After stopping for lunch in Barstow, CA at Lola's Restaurant, they arrived two hours early for a 5 p.m. press gathering at the conference room in the Courtyard Century City hotel where they were staying for two nights. Their rally was set for the following day at UCLA's Pauley Pavilion. The group had decided to forego a separate rally at USC simply because the two universities were only 13 miles apart.

Marcia had received advance confirmations that reporters from the Los Angeles Times, the LA Weekly, NPR and each of the local broadcast TV network affiliates would be attending the conference. Almost all of the questions were virtually identical to questions asked in every other community where they'd held a rally. The only new line of questioning came from the local Fox network affiliate's reporter.

"Do you have any comment, Mr. Van Mullder, on the report out of Anarene, Texas that you accused Tea Partiers of wanting to flood the Grand Canyon?" asked Bambi Acquavite, a pert and distractingly buxom bleached blond in her early 30's with a barely noticeable lisp.

"I don't recall saying any such thing," Franklin/Percy said. "I did meet a family from that community while hiking through the canyon just yesterday. I reminded them about something I'd learned during a U.S. History course: that certain corporatists lobbied hard for decades to try to have a couple of dams built in the canyon, but were stopped by environmentally-sympathetic members of Congress.

"If you or anyone else knows of any Tea Party plan to flood the canyon, I hope you'll let the rest of the country know so we can try to stop that. I'm sure if Edward Abbey still were alive, you could get some great quotes from him, Monkey Wrench Gang-style."

There were a few questions about their planned guest speaker, Tom Hayden, former member of the California Legislature for 18 years and one of the Chicago Eight who were tried on charges of inciting riots at the 1968 Democratic National Conviction (his and others' convictions were overturned on appeal). They anticipated Hayden would speak out in support of the USA-SBR's ban on hydraulic fracturing (fracking).

A couple of reporters, including the L.A. Times' columnist Dick Muley, asked if the Poughkeepsians were worried that featuring a guest speaker known for his strident progressive views might energize "wackos" from the opposite end of the political spectrum.

"History has come to vindicate virtually every single stance on the issues taken by Mr. Hayden over the decades," Pongo said. "If we still were in the mid- to late-'60s, it might be newsworthy to take note of people calling Mr. Hayden a radical. Based on the actual events of the past 50 years, we feel he should be considered a moderate voice of reason. Anyone still considering him a radical is simply someone trapped in an anachronistic bubble.

"In fact, if there were any justice in this life, Mr. Hayden and government whistleblowers everywhere would be considered national heroes of the most deserving and lasting patriotic burnishment. Persons who repeatedly dared to speak the truth when the truth was unwelcome by most."

"Well, shit, maybe we ought to make some more room on Mount Rushmore, Mr. Podrowski," Muley grunted.

"We're happy to leave that to the next Gutzon Borglum," Franklin/Percy smiled. "No hurry."

* * *

The rally the next day – for which Marcia had purchased three days of locally-broadcast ads – was set for 7:30 p.m.

The Poughkeepsians decided to take advantage of the good weather for a day trip to Disneyland, mainly because Franklin had never been. In addition, they pointed out to Franklin that the day coincided with his namesake's 21st birthday. "Percy Van Mullder" now could legally imbibe – a fact which left Franklin with decidedly mixed feelings. In his previous life, he'd been known to knock back more than his share of martinis, even fancying himself as something of a mixologist. For the life of him, though, he couldn't remember why he thought all the hangovers were worth it, other than the fact that all his friends did the same thing. *"Just maybe it's appropriate to be at a place where no alcohol is served to the general public on 'Scruples' Van Mullder's 21st birthday,"* he thought to himself. (At Disneyland, alcohol is served only at special private events and at the hyper-exclusive "Club 33," where memberships are sold to the super-wealthy.)

Pongo reminded Franklin that, even though Franklin persuaded Walt Disney to produce some anti-Nazi cartoons during World War II, Disney actually had some serious anti-semitic sympathies and had visited Nazi Germany in 1935.

"Do they refuse to let Jews and pro-Jewish into their amusement parks?" Franklin asked.

"Don't think so," Pongo said.

"Then let's just focus on having a great old time," Franklin said.

Thanks to finagling by Marcia, Franklin and the others were able to take advantage of the Dream Fastpass ticketing feature at the Indiana Jones Adventure, Splash Mountain, Space Mountain, Big Thunder Mountain, Pirates of the Caribbean and Haunted Mansion sites, meaning their in-line wait times were dramatically reduced.

By late afternoon, Franklin was sporting the radar-dish ears of a Mickey Mouse cap. His fingers were blue and sticky from eating cotton candy. Phil, who'd been accompanying Franklin on most of the rides, told Franklin they needed to start heading back to the parking lot. Franklin responded to Phil by compelling him – with all the eloquence of a man who'd kept a nation listening week after week to Presidential fireside broadcasts – to go on "just one more ride, OK? OK? C'mon, Podrowski! Just one more!"

One more turned into three more before Phil realized it. Finally, Phil had to remind Franklin there were as many as 9,000 or 10,000 persons wanting to hear what Franklin and former Sen. Hayden had to say about the USA-SBR. "Which is more important to you, Sir? Riding some rides or preparing for tonight's rally?"

"Let me think..." Franklin snickered.

By 6 p.m., when they needed to leave to make their way to Pauley Pavilion, they all were a little sad at how quickly their day had passed. Franklin, wide-eyed as a pre-teen, said he wanted to return the following day, but Marcia reminded him that they'd planned to visit Newport Beach, Knott's Berry Farm and the LaBrea Tar Pits the next day before their scheduled 5:00 p.m. press conference with San Diego news media.

Attendance at the Pauley Pavilion rally far exceeded their expectations: of the 13,800 seats in the arena, fewer than 10 percent were empty. When Marcia and others tallied the sign-up sheets after the rally, they were surprised to find significant numbers of ralliers had come from as far away as Santa Barbara, Fresno and Merced, not to mention Riverside, San Bernardino and Palm Springs.

Former State Sen. Hayden gave an impassioned speech about the lunacy of poisoning groundwater accumulated over hundreds of millennia simply to produce a few weeks' or months' worth of natural gas. That "W" Bush signed a law exempting frackers not only from complying with the Clean Water and Clean Air acts, but also from even disclosing the chemicals they were injecting into the groundwater, was nothing less than corporatists' collusion to risk poisoning every family which depends on water out of the taps, the safety of which had been promised by governments for more than a century, he said.

Franklin/Percy pointed out later in the rally that the risks to the groundwater promised a huge benefit for one industry above all others: the for-profit water-bottling industry. Now, he said, the average homeowner all over the country risked being in the same position as Navajo Tribe members whose groundwater sources were permanently tainted by corporations which mined uranium for nuclear bomb and reactor fuels decades before. "Many of those tribal members must truck water 50 to 100 miles simply to be able to take a drink of water, much less a shower," he explained, to a chorus of boos.

"How should we thank all those corporate overlords who are convinced our lives are just too darned easy with clean water coming out of our taps at home?" Franklin/Percy asked.

"FUCK O-ver-LORDS!" came the repeated chants in response. For a full five minutes.

The screening of "Capitalism: A Love Story" was a huge hit – it appeared most of the audience hadn't even seen or heard of it before.

At the conclusion of the rally, as was now their practice, they had a full minute of silence for Sally Rose Cummings and her children Royal and Chloe, as a family picture of the three of them illuminated a large TV screen at one end of the pavilion.

There was more activity, both that night and the next day, on the USA-SBR website and Facebook page than Marcia, Harry and Bianca could keep up with.

It boded well. They wouldn't know just how well for another few election cycles, though.

∗ ∗ ∗

They had a blast while visiting Knott's Berry Farm, the LaBrea Tar Pits and the Newport Beach area from mid-morning to late afternoon the next day. By the end of the day, there was only half of one bottle of sunscreen left as they lay warming on one of the few trash-free spots of sandy beachfront.

"You guys keep soaking up all those rays and pretty soon someone's gonna think we've got the same Mama," Idris said.

"Or we're all gonna need melanomas sliced out," Pongo said.

"I just wanna know where the Orange County topless beach is," Harry whispered to Idris, out of earshot for Bianca and Marcia, both of whom were virtually awe-inspiring in their string-y swimwear. "Anyplace with all these bikinis has got to have at least a little stretch of sand for ladies who like their headlamps unobstructed."

"We've got to make that 5 p.m. press conference, ladies and gentlemen," Franklin quasi-shouted out. "When the big hand is on 3 and the little hand is on 4, we've got to pack up and go."

"Yes, Mother," Pongo said as he relaxed with his head on Heather's bare midriff as she lay on her towel on the beach. "Uhhrrkk, crap - I didn't really say that, Sir…it's just the luxuriant comfort of this nice lady-pillow talking."

At which point Heather dumped a nearby child's bucket o' sand on Pongo's face. "Fear itself 'tis nothing compared to a woman's wrath," she laughed.

"I could not agree more," Franklin said, adding, just as Pongo started to ask a question, "- no, please don't ask me to explain why."

"Aw, shucks," Pongo said, with a piss-poor North Carolina affect, snapping his fingers with an exaggerated arm swing. "Ah thawt yew wuz agonna gimme somethin' rat stimmallaytin' to dee-skuss at that thar rally tew-morry nat."

"How's this: I'll give you my Mama's recipe for fruitcake," Franklin said. "That ought to keep them enrapt for, say, a half-hour?"

"Dude, you're one fly oratorical prodigy," Harry said, shielding his eyes from the sun.

"I've been called many things in my public career, but never a fly. Don't they have very, very brief lifespans?"

"It's an adjective the way he used it, Sir," Pongo said. "It means 'awesome' or really cool."

"I thought I was just joking about the fruitcake recipe," Franklin said. "So, you really think I could make some fly-ey fruitcake oratory that would impress the younger crowd?"

"Harry's just yanking your chain, Franklin," Pongo said.

"It sounds like you mean he was kidding me."

"Now you're cookin' with gas, Sir," Harry said.

"OK, now I understand. They used that phrase about the time my final term started."

Eyes were rolling all the way around. Even Phil knew Franklin's vernacular needed a serious overhaul; he made a mental note to have the O'Learys conduct an in-home seminar for Franklin on 21st century idioms and colloquialisms before Franklin's spring break from Dutchess C.C.

* * *

FOURTH ESTATE TANTRUM: TAKING THEIR BALL AND GOING HOME; CORPORATE TANTRUM: THREATENING TO TAKE THEIR BALL AND LEAVE (BUT NOT DOING THAT)

When the Poughkeepsians convened their press gathering at the San Diego Mission Valley Marriott's Board Room, reporters showed up from the San Diego State Daily Aztec, U-T San Diego (a daily formerly known as the Union-Tribune; owned by a wealthy San Diego real estate developer with no prior journalism background, it would go on to be purchased by the Los Angeles Times in June 2015), the San Diego Reader and from each of the local network television affiliates.

The questioning was some of the sharpest yet – which was greatly gratifying to Phil simply because it meant their local TV ads were having an impact.

The U-T's Sally Tealtent, a hyper-conservative columnist and occasional author of union-hating screeds who'd literally made her entire journalistic career out of sucking up to ultra-wealthy Ayn Randians, opened the questioning with all the tact of a turd-dumping T-Rex.

"Just why in the effing hell should my employer give you a single column inch of coverage when one of the major provisions of your USA-SBR is to put a stranglehold on his ability to buy more media outlets?" Tealtent asked. "Do you think we're stupid? Do you think our devoted readers are idiots?"

"Why are you here, then, Ms. Tealtent?" Franklin asked. "Your employer has no ties to journalism whatsoever other than the ability to read and to have been rich enough to buy the Union-Tribune so he could employ people like you.

"He was so insecure about dissent he wouldn't even tolerate a sportswriter who didn't respect his lack of journalistic bona fides. He even hates unions so much, he won't even use the traditional name of the newspaper any longer: 'U-T' instead of _UNION_-Tribune.

"As a mega-millionaire real estate developer, was he just out to get free advertising for himself? Or was he just bored from counting all his cash? Last time I checked, the newspaper business wasn't dying because it had just too darned few jazillionaire owners telling middle class folks how to think.

"So, really, why are you here if our effort is so bogus? Don't you have some working class union folks to go out and vilify because they make just '_too darned much_?'"

"I'm just here to do my job," Tealtent said. "You've just made it clear my publisher's inclination not to give you any coverage is correct."

"So, we can all take it that you and your employer feel strongly that ownership of news media outlets should be in the hands of as few mega-rich folks as possible, is that correct? Your publisher and you both feel that's a healthy direction for democracy?" Phil asked.

"If the founders had intended for this to be a true democracy, we'd all be in the midst of anarchy," Tealtent said. "Everyone would think his own vote was the most important vote of all – no one would respect the opinions of anyone else."

"So, you're saying the founders of our country wanted the wealthiest members of society to perpetually have disproportionate influence and control over the levers of government?" Pongo asked. "You really believe having one person or one corporation own dozens and dozens of media outlets promotes a healthier and more diverse society?"

"Quit putting words in my mouth, you overgrown ankle-biter. Something is really wrong with this country when a person of independent means is automatically seen as greedy and unsympathetic to minorities."

"At least we have **some** common ground – it looks like we agree that greed is something to be avoided," Franklin smiled, gently laughing. "Please let us know if your publisher decides to join the Occupy Wall Street movement, OK?"

Tealtent calmly rose from her chair and waved her hand dismissively as she headed for the rear exit. Just as she was almost all the way out of the room, her forearm lurched back through the doorway to launch a middle finger salute in Franklin's direction. As she pulled it back through the doorway to finish her exit, the heavy solid-framed oak door slammed squarely on that same middle finger. An outbreak of muffled giggles and guffaws erupted around the room as a "Yeeooowch!" echoed in the hallway.

"If there still are any other hardcore political columnists or TV anchors here," Phil said, "to paraphrase Crosby, Stills and Nash, please feel free to let your freak flag fly now so we can get on to more substantive details, OK?"

A hand went up from a 40-something woman near the back of the room.

"We've been reading copies of the 38-page USA-SBR document we were provided. I'm just wondering if any of you are worried that its details are too overwhelming for the average middle-class person to comprehend," said Amelia Maximillian of the San Diego Reader.

"It's all written at about a 9th grade reading level," Phil responded, "except for Latin terms like *de facto*. Did any of you have any problems grasping the gist of any part of it?"

"I don't think so," Amelia said as she looked around at her fellow journalists. "But we're all college graduates."

"Our feeling was, basically, in for a penny, in for a pound," Franklin said. "We intentionally set a high bar for our goals. Women's groups worked hard for a dozen years to gain approval of the Equal Rights Amendment, only to come up short.

"We figure, if our supporters are going to work as hard as ERA supporters did for passage, let's make it count for more than just one major issue.

"There's something for everyone to love in the USA-SBR."

"Others might say there's something for everyone to hate in it," said Dolores Desempares, a reporter for the local CBS affiliate. "What's your strategy for coping with naysayers?"

"Our strategy is to educate everyone we can why the USA-SBR is beneficial to them," Pongo said. "Shills for huge corporate interests will always be trying to twist its contents around to jack up fear. It's in their interests to preserve the current system, the system which is rigged to favor monopolies, hedge funds, offshore foreign bank accounts, tax shelters – legal welfare for the super-rich.

"We're here to put a stop to **that**.

"*Once and for all.*"

"If the super-rich want welfare so badly, what's to keep them from quitting the game and taking their ball home – as in taking all their jobs overseas - if they don't get their way?" asked Jillian Pleonecious of the local Fox TV affiliate.

"Well, they'll surely whine and whimper about an end to welfare for the rich if we're successful," Franklin/Percy said. "But there's one simple truism which will always guarantee they'll never abandon the good ol' U.S.A. – even if they despise the working stiffs whose consumer demand created all their wealth."

"What's that?" Ms. Pleonecious asked.

"Business goes where the money is. The U.S.A. is, if nothing else, a prized marketplace. Even with a dying middle class, we still have one of the most envied customer bases in the world – after Europe, at least."

"But what happens when business interests like the U.S. Chamber of Commerce start airing scary ads on TV about the USA-SBR intimidating so-called job creators into fleeing overseas?" Ms. Maximillian asked. "Especially if they feature some folksy avuncular middle-aged couples in those spots, the way health insurers did when they stopped health care reform in the early '90s?"

"There will always be people who are susceptible to fear-pandering," Franklin/Percy said. "It's human nature to spread rumors about scary things. But it's also human nature to share knowledge, to share hope.

"Which will prevail? It's the job of the news media not simply to spread information, but to filter out unfounded rumors rather than pretend the unfounded rumors simply are part of their effort to pursue 'objectivity' by giving quote-unquote 'all sides' of a story.

"The Salk polio vaccine prevents untold millions of cases of that disease worldwide. Suppose a determined group of hundreds or even thousands of unbalanced people insist that the vaccine will cause mad cow disease. Anyone in this room want to defend the news outlets who would label that kind of unfounded rumor with a headline like, "Allegations against vaccine being investigated"?

"That's how complete lunacy ends up being portrayed as having the same credibility as settled science.

"We have to hope that you members of the Fourth Estate – including your publishers and station owners - will take your jobs seriously enough to make filtering out lunacy a top priority.

"If you're approached by an organized group hell-bent on undermining the USA-SBR, we have to hope you will pass along to the public only their most rational objections. Should they approach you claiming that our requirements for paid leave and a clean environment will put millions of corporations and small businesses out of business, please try asking them to explain why that hasn't happened in Europe or Canada.

"If that kind of organized group tries to claim that stopping at-large elections for city and county boards and commissions will somehow lead to anarchy, ask them why that hasn't happened in Phoenix, Arizona.

"If that kind of organized group tries to claim that banning gerrymandering will somehow lead to radicals running the government, please ask them why that hasn't happened in a host of other countries, like Canada.

"If that kind of organized group tries to claim that publicly-funded elections will mean that local and state governments will end up being run by ignorant and inexperienced amateurs and hoboes, please ask them why that didn't happen in Maine and Arizona.

"If that kind of organized group tries to claim that working to make government more small-d democratic – by proportionally adjusting memberships of institutions as population grows or shrinks, by electing previously appointed key cabinet positions, by electing half of the Supreme Court, by guaranteeing a right to vote at any polling place, by extending election day to a 25-hour period, by creating a national initiative process, by implementing a binding referendum process for wars, by allowing private citizens to present true bills of indictment to grand juries and by requiring broadcasters to solicit support of small investors to be re-licensed – then please ask them what they don't like about small-d democratic government. Please ask them what it is that they prefer about non-democratic government.

"If that kind of organized group tries to claim that replacing all varieties of regressive taxes – the taxes which hurt the middle class and poor the most and leave the super-rich virtually unscathed – (except for 'sin taxes') with a progressive tax on incomes will somehow lead to huge numbers of employers fleeing the country, please ask them why that hasn't happened in countries with more progressive tax rates than ours, like France. And please ask them if they truly, honestly believe those employers really would abandon a thriving consumer-driven market like the one in the good ol' U.S.A.

"If that kind of organized group tries to claim that keeping candidates with known racist sentiments off the ballot will somehow muzzle all dissent in the country and deprive voters of highly qualified lawmakers, please ask them if they've noticed that dissent actually comes from all varieties of officeholders, not just the bigoted ones. And please ask them why persons with racism in their past are more highly qualified than candidates without racist backgrounds.

"If that kind of organized group tries to claim that a uniform Federal system of child support enforcement and parental visitation facilitation will somehow impoverish non-custodial parents and enrich custodial parents, please ask them if they're happy with the _current_ under-funded state-by-state patchwork system with virtually no Federal enforcement once the paying parent crosses state lines. And please ask them to cite specific examples of custodial parents who've become wealthy from child support payments – WITHOUT including the ex-spouses of professional athletes and hedge fund managers. They won't have much of a list – because it exists only in their imaginations.

"So, all we're asking is that you fine folks of the Fourth Estate do your due diligence. Due diligence in the longstanding tradition of the likes of Edward R. Murrow, Ben Bradlee, Matt Taibbi, Bill Moyers, James "Scotty" Reston, Molly Ivins, William Greider, Christopher Hedges and such. Please hold everyone accountable, us included, **but _not JUST_ us.**

"Look, we don't want to leave any of you with the feeling that we actually _want_ to tell you how to do your jobs. Obviously, WE don't know how to do your jobs. You're the news professionals, each of you dedicated to writing that first rough draft of history every day. So, please don't bristle at us when we politely suggest what you might ask those who, out of the most craven motivations, would undermine our sincere, genuinely altruistic efforts. Our suggestions for questions are borne out of the knowledge that sometimes superb reporters simply aren't allowed to **_DO_** their jobs by their publishers and station owners. Especially when it comes to holding the most powerful of the elites accountable.

"We know the natural inclination of any good journalist is to be skeptical. Maybe even a little cynical. We get that. We simply ask that you consider the possibility that we *are* the real deal: people who are tired of being ground down by a system which overwhelmingly favors the elite – people who are tired of being ground down by defeatist cynicism – people who want to be optimistic, realistically optimistic, about what this country can be, based, if nothing else, on this country's proud history of courageous, creative leaders from its distant past.

"If this country has nothing else, it's a history of everyday people finding the fortitude to step up when the chips are down. We're just trying to encourage those hard-working people out there to step up with us.

Sustained applause suddenly spontaneously began from the Poughkeepsians listening to Franklin's words and, surprisingly, from a small group of hotel housekeepers and food service workers who had paused, unnoticed by the reporters in the room, a few minutes earlier in the hallway just outside the meeting room to hear Franklin's strong, articulate delivery of his heartfelt expression. Even a couple of the local television network affiliates' camera operators were applauding – to the visible consternation of at least one of the affiliate reporters. One of the camera operators not working with the ticked-off reporter saw the sneer on her face and started to flip a middle finger up, but drew his fist back at the last second. (His salary with *his* affiliate employer was barely enough to keep his rent and student loan payments up to date, even with his wife's income included from her full-time job as a second grade teacher; the USA-SBR did more than resonate for him – it gave him real hope for his children's future.)

"OK, thanks for that vote of support, especially those of you hard-working folks passing by in the hallway," Phil said. "Let's take a couple more questions and then call it a day so we can prepare for the rally tomorrow, OK?

"Jack Corona, from the local CBS affiliate," a tall Hispanic man halfway back in the room said, hand raised.

"Mr. Van Mullder, I was wondering if your group would consider full passage and ratification of the entire USA-SBR as the only measurement of success for your campaign, or if there's some goal short of full passage which you'd recognize as a barometer of accomplishment."

"I don't know if I speak for the entire group of supporters, but I'm pretty sure our goal always has been for full passage and ratification," Franklin/Percy said. "When you start setting your sights lower, it tends to be a slippery slope. Every single part of the USA-SBR is there for a reason: to make life more secure, enjoyable and predictable for working people.

"Whether full passage and ratification occurs in five years or fifty years, I would consider what we're doing a success if it leads to most people once again believing in *their own power* to make their government work for them, rather than for the very richest, least needy among us, like the Kochs.

"When the Borax Soap and General Electric spokesman who once said 'the most terrifying words are the government is here to help' is finally exposed as the craven corporate shill he truly was, that will be another sign we've succeeded. A truly small-d democratic government is the most powerful tool working people have for keeping corporate greed in check. If we cede that tool to the cynics and the corporate shills who stoke their cynicism, then there truly can be no hope short of a revolution – or a series of national general strikes.

"OK, so your main focus is complete success with some moral victories along the way," Mr. Corona said. "Conversely, is there a low point on the barometer which your organization would recognize as a point of failure, an indicator that it's time to abandon the effort?"

"Once again, I don't know if I would want to speak for our entire group," Franklin/Percy said. "But I would consider our efforts a failure **_ONLY_** if a time comes when a significant portion of working class Americans completely abandons all hope of compelling their elected officeholders to work for them.

"And I wouldn't consider that so much our failure as the failure of an arthritic, metastasized capitalism which consumes the very flesh of the host populace it supposedly was created to sustain."

"How will you know if and when that happens?" Mr. Corona asked.

"I imagine a sign of that might be something like only 40 percent of eligible voters showing up to vote in a Presidential election. Or, perhaps, hordes of non-wealthy people fleeing our borders for countries where they can become sick without going bankrupt and where they can have college educations without being in debt 'til middle age.

"You know – like Canada. I had a nightmare the other night: I dreamt that, instead of fundamentally reforming our corrupt economic system, our corporatist Congress decided to spend many billions of dollars creating a 21 Century version of the Berlin wall. To keep U.S. citizens in our country, instead of keeping immigrants out."

"Last question," Phil said. "Let's let one of our superb women organizers field this one."

"Martha Riddex, local ABC-TV affiliate," an emaciated somewhat hung-over-looking middle-aged bleached-blonde at the back of the room said, pointing her finger in the air.

"What's your strategy for appealing to the so-called 'low-information voter'? You know, like that family on 'Raising Hope'."

Pongo whispered into Franklin's ear about Virginia, Burt, Jimmy, Sabrina, Maw Maw and Hope Chance from the TV series: "They're so dumb-but-sweet, they're always saying malapropisms like 'lost Limberger baby,' 'procrasturbating,' 'hermeditary,' 'philostrophical,' 'vaginacologist,' 'ecclesiastical waistband' and so forth. Better let me take this one, Sir...

"When it comes to the 'Raising Hope-ers' of this world," Pongo said, back at full volume, "we're pretty confident that if we focus our message on the basic reason the USA-SBR is needed, they'll recognize how important their support is. Helping them understand the USA-SBR is the only way to get the government to go to bat for THEM instead of their corporate overlords. We're hoping just the prospect of free college education, free health care and lower pay TV bills from increased competition will alert them to what this could mean."

"Let *me* give this a shot, Pongo," Bianca whispered.

"I'm Dr. Bianca Swanson – I'm in my final year of medical residency. I became involved with the USA-SBR through my friendship with the Podrowskis and Mr. Van Mullder. I'm someone who's repulsed by the idea that a doctor's time is valued at $1,000 an hour while the time of the custodian who sanitizes the doctor's office is valued at one-one-hundredth of that amount. No human being's value should ever be one hundred times another human being's. That kind of disparity is what leads governments to believe souls are disposable, like cannon fodder for the latest in our series of perpetual wars.

"To answer your question about supposedly 'low-information voters': it's our job to pique the interests not just of political junkies and the Occupy Wall Street crowd, but of the people most affected by economic and social injustices. Namely, those people who are laid off by their employers every time a Wall Street bubble bursts. Or laid off every time a supposedly well-regulated corporation sneaks malfeasance by an understaffed regulatory agency. Or laid off every time a huge corporation which contributed massive sums to a presidential candidate massages approval of a merger with a rival so they can lay off thousands of people.

"People like Burt and Virginia on that show, people who clean pools and mow lawns and do housekeeping – when unfettered greed and fraud cause Wall Street bubbles to burst, the clients of the country's Burts and Virginias start doing those jobs themselves, so landscapers' and housekeepers' incomes drop off a cliff.

"It's *our* job to help all those unemployed and under-employed people, all those people lined up outside the Food Stamps offices each morning, to help them to connect the dots – to help them realize the cause of their predicament is not just some 'business as usual' development out of their control, but is, instead, the calculated craven decision by the corporatists who control our government to favor perpetual enrichment of the already rich over working peoples' financial stability.

"And it's our job to make it clear to those same people that there will be fairness in the way parents are required to support their children – that neither men nor women will ever again be allowed to shirk with impunity their financial responsibility for the souls they bring into this world, and that neither men nor women will ever again be allowed to withhold court-approved children's visitation from a fit parent regardless of how much that parent can afford to pay in child support.

"When the word gets out to people at the bottom of the business food chain that the USA-SBR will put a ***FULL AND FINAL STOP*** to corporate mergers designed to increase profits by eliminating competition and laying off vast multitudes of people, they'll sit up and take notice.

"They'll recognize those of us supporting the USA-SBR are the real deal. People motivated to do the greatest good for the greatest number of people. People motivated by altruism rather than what's best for the price of some shares of stock they happen to own.

"Whether that recognition will be enough to motivate ***them*** to put aside their Playstations, their Netflix and their smartphones long enough to actually make a difference – well, we're hoping the remaining clear-thinking journalists out there, like yourselves, will help to remind them that the kind of change we're advocating happens only when there's ***active*** widespread grassroots support all over the country."

"How do you expect us to do that?" Ms. Riddex, smirking, asked.

"One way might be to request – through the Freedom of Information Act, if necessary – that each member of each chamber of Congress and each member of each chamber of each state's Legislature disclose monthly the number of contacts they're received from constituents in support of the USA-SBR," Bianca said.

"Of course, the flaw there is that we'd be relying on officeholders to be honest about the statistics they're providing, realizing that officeholders opposed to the USA-SBR might be tempted to fudge the numbers somewhat. We'd have to hope that even among the officeholders who oppose it, there would be staff members who'd hold their lawmaker-employer accountable to be honest, through leaks to the likes of you folks if need be.

"Another way journalists like yourselves could remind the general public of the value of activism for the USA-SBR would be to cover candidacies of those wanting to replace officeholders who oppose it. Your employers managed to spend lots of time covering Tea Party candidacies in 2010 – surely there'll be time to cover a grassroots movement from the other direction, especially considering that, this time, it won't be an astroturf movement. No corporate slush funds funneled through Dick Armey for ***us***, we're proud to say.

"We don't expect that there will be a single, one-time mass candidacy of pro-USA-SBR supporters around the country, though. We foresee this as a gradual movement, with more and more state legislators and members of Congress sympathetic to this cause gaining traction with voters every two years, especially during Presidential elections."

"So, exactly where does your funding come from?" Ms. Riddex asked.

"We have pre-printed handouts at the back of the room detailing our individual contributions from private donors so far," Phil said. "We've declined to accept donations larger than $200 and have kept a database showing the names of each donor. The information on the handouts also is available on our website. You'll also find information on the seed money for the USA-SBR which comes from my own family. The Podrowskis have decided to devote virtually our entire financial assets to this project, in honor of the man whose legacy inspired us as we grew up in Dutchess County: Franklin Delano Roosevelt."

"So it's a *new* New Deal?" Ms. Maximillian asked, in her mind already thinking of a tag line for the segment her producer would prepare.

"It's the USA-SBR," Idris said, stepping forward. "But the New Deal is the sustenance that's nourishing its roots. If FDR had lived long enough, this is the kind of change we believe he would have achieved."

"Thanks for your participation today – our very best wishes to every member of the Newspaper Guild here today," Phil said. "We will always value your professionalism."

∗   ∗   ∗

Alerting San Diegans to Reality, Then Back to Pueblo Viejo to Fly Home

The Poughkeepsians spent the next morning and part of the afternoon mostly resting – although Franklin, Pongo, Harry and Idris decided to spend a few hours at the San Diego Zoo. Franklin appeared to soak up information at the exhibits about endangered species, population pressures on wildlife and global warming.

By the time they were ready to start the 7:30 p.m. rally, the organizers were fully refreshed and prepared to give a thorough presentation. They welcomed local progressive media celebrity Juan Emilio, who provided liberal perspectives on a network-owned local TV station, as their main master of ceremonies.

Compared to previous rally gatherings, attendance was slightly off. Phil attributed it to the U-T newspaper's coverage blackout, although local television coverage from the previous evening had been fairly positive.

The crowd, however, was as enthusiastic as at any of their previous venues. There was even a locally-organized section of "Drooling Fair and Balanced Cadavers" (as the banner below their seating area declared), all dressed in pants belted halfway up their chests in stained white T-shirts, an homage to the legions of Fox News cultists around the land. Appropriately, they were among the loudest to salute the ramen-slash-clean underwear package-tossers mid-way through the rally.

Franklin/Percy gave a rousing talk on the dangers of over-militarization, one which the other Poughkeepsians worried might go over like a lead balloon in a community with as many Department of the Navy links as San Diego. But Franklin peppered the speech with proud tributes to the service branch of which he'd been assistant secretary almost 100 years earlier. He pointed out that Navy personnel always came to know the locals – "and not just the 'ladies of the night' " (to much laughter) - whenever their ships were in safe harbors around the world. Because of that, he said, they were perhaps the least-prejudiced, slowest to advocate hostilities among the millions of service personnel in the many branches of the armed services.

"As one of my favorite authors once said, travel is fatal to prejudice, bigotry and narrow-mindedness. If only there were more like Samuel Langhorne Clemens today," Franklin/Percy said. (A blow-up of a photo of Mark Twain graced the screen behind him as he spoke.)

"One of the things for which he was proudest to be known was his anti-imperialism. He wrote eloquently about the brutality of the U.S. Army's 1899 invasion and occupation of the Philippines, a purely imperialistic exercise in violent annexation of a foreign land.* We all should recall that President George W. Bush cited that shameful period of our history as our "model" for the Iraqi occupation.

"We all should be afraid of the horrific balance that's accrued onto our karma account over the past century-plus. If we are to get this nation right with history, we have to take with visceral seriousness the future impacts of our decisions about when to use and not to use violence against other nations' peoples. We should always use non-violence as our preferred baseline, as long as there is no existential threat against our own home soil.

"The next time a deceptive Secretary of State says she doesn't want a smoking gun to turn into a mushroom cloud, we should hold her feet to the nuclear fire, figuratively speaking. Those who would use the fear of nuclear war *to send us to war* bear the utmost hyper-penetrating scrutiny there is to be had.

"For that remark alone, a remark which led directly to hundreds of thousands of deaths, a remark she knew to be a manipulative lie, Condoleeza Rice probably deserves a special place in hell, if there is such a destination.

"We absolutely _must_ do our best to demonstrate we're better than that, that we will achieve positive change for the very least among us through persistently peaceful means. Means like what we're all here tonight to champion.

"And, make no mistake, we can't achieve this change without you – and you – and you – and you. (Franklin/Percy pointed to each section of the crowd.) Each and every one of you taking the time to put down your smart phones, to turn off your video games, to switch off your pay TV long enough to write an E-Mail or – even better – a letter to the elected officeholders who are representing you.

"Remember that archaic phrase? 'Representing you'? Always, ALWAYS remember: they work for *each.* *of.* *you.* They are paid *by* you, out of YOUR

---

* "History is a Weapon, Comments on the Moro Massacre," *Voices of a People's History*, Zinn and Arnove

taxes. Sure, they take a lot of money from sleazy corporations. But they still, officially, work for YOU. You have the right to hold them to that concept. And, again, make no mistake: they MUST be held to that concept. Most of them, even many of the better ones, will _not_ do it voluntarily – if for no other reason than the fact that they've got to be constantly on the phone raising money from people with stacks and stacks of lucre to compete with candidates who take unlimited amounts of dirty corporate money.

"But YOU can change that. Your support for the USA-SBR can create a system where all elections are publicly funded, where there are strict limits on donations, where candidates can actually be removed from office for breaking election rules.

"_Without_ your active – emphasis on ACTIVE – your ACTIVE support, though, we're stuck with what we have now. Corporate overlord government.

"Is that what you want?"

Then the chant began.

"Fuck O-Ver-LORDS! Fuck O-Ver-LORDS! Fuck O-Ver-LORDS!"

And it continued for minutes.

"You can do this!" Franklin/Percy said. "On with the show…"

And the rally, like the others, ended with "Capitalism: A Love Story" and the tribute to Sally.

By the end of the night, almost every last USA-SBR packet had been taken and perhaps 95 percent of those in attendance signed pledges promising to pressure their elected officeholders to support the USA-SBR.

* * *

They left at 2 a.m. the next morning for the long drive back to Tucson International Airport to drop off their rental van and catch their marathon flight back to New York via Atlanta. They stopped quickly for breakfast at Carl's Jr. in the former 'fan belt capital of the world,' Gila Bend, AZ. On the way in to the otherwise spotless restaurant, Idris and Harry stomped on a family of two-inch-long cockroaches just outside the sparkling-clean glass door entrance.

"What with global warming, I don't think they've had a frost here since the '70's," Phil said, watching the bug guts squirt out onto the sidewalk with each stomp. "We'll probably be lucky if this doesn't turn into some modern version of that good ol' sci-fi movie, "Them!" You know, the one where the giant desert ants start eating everyone."

"I wouldn't worry," Harry said. "These are just the only Arizona residents now exempt from 'Show me your papers' jackboot ID inspections by Sheriff Joe. And as soon as he can figure out how to force them to verify they're not **Mexican** cockroaches, they won't be around any longer to potentially mutate."

They consumed their surprisingly savory breakfasts in the rental van as they headed east on Interstate 8; roach innards were soon forgotten.

On the flight back from Tucson International, the featured movie was "Tower Heist," a Ben Stiller vehicle which Franklin enjoyed for its accurate depiction of the super-wealthy – even if the ending was less than 'feel-good.' Franklin asked his seat-mate, an elderly Jewish woman from Tallahassee, why it was that more movies couldn't have happy endings. He wasn't prepared for her response.

"Some of those artsy-fartsy Jackass Hollywood dicks seem to think we all need to be reminded what a shitstorm life can turn out to be," she said, gently grasping Franklin's forearm. "Call me a pussyass Nancygirl, but I'll take a sweet-finished flick from that Opie kid any day over most of the pig turds these so-called comedians churn out. Maybe you don't agree – do downer endings make your dick hard?"

"I, uh, er, uh, well, I s'pose I agree with you," Franklin said, blushing.

Which led to two hours of not-so-delicate conversation about her grandchildren's promiscuity, hemorrhoidal inflammations, bunion removal surgery, diverticulitis, goiters, drywall mold, conservative talk radio (blessedly, she disliked it), athlete's foot, body odor among her neighbors at the assisted living facility, driver license re-licensing hurdles for the aged, root canal surgery and removal of abscessed back cysts – among other things. Franklin tried repeatedly to offer her her choice of free hard liquor drinks, a sure-fire anesthetic, but she wouldn't hear of it.

Fortunately for everyone, the otherwise kind-hearted but conversationally diarrhetic grandmother got off the plane in Atlanta. The Poughkeepsians actually got to stay on the same plane for the remaining leg of the trip to New York. Franklin's next seat-mate was a 20-something man who knocked back multiple shots of whisky as soon as he could, admitting his strategy for air travel anxieties was to drink himself into a stupor as promptly as possible. It worked, to the relief of both men.

By the time they got off the New York-to-Poughkeepsie Amtrak train at about 10:20 p.m. that night, they were so grateful to be able to return to their own beds, there were virtually no complaints about jet lag.

*   *   *

LIZ SHINES AGAIN; MR. PLAID PANTS DISCLOSED

Franklin quickly found himself back in his usual college and part-time job routine at Adams Landscaping, with classes starting two days after the group returned. Holly Van Arsdale appeared just as potentially affectionate as ever during the two classes they shared together at Dutchess C.C. – Franklin was always catching her glancing at him, and vice versa. This was growing into something more than a simple nuisance for Franklin. If only he could control the spontaneous erections, he kept thinking to himself – and then he would remember each time just how fortunate he was to be "young enough" again to even have those.

He was grateful to find out from Holly's friend Nancy that Holly now was working at least 20 hours a week north on Albany Post road at the Eveready Diner in Hyde Park. Knowing her time was mostly occupied made the temptation to 'meet cute' with her someplace a little easier to resist.

A week after classes started, he and Pongo took the day off to travel to NYC to see Elizabeth Warren again on the Daily Show. They got two of the last dozen stand-by tickets.

U.S. Senate candidate Warren didn't disappoint: she pointed out to Jon Stewart that 30 of the largest U.S. corporations were currently paying more on lobbyists than they were in Federal income taxes. As a result of dramatically reduced tax revenues, she added, the U.S. is spending barely one-fourth of what China spends on infrastructure maintenance and improvements – and less than half of what European nations spend. Even worse, she said, cuts in tax rates on the wealthiest have translated into dramatically reduced government spending on scientific research and public education programs. Thanks to slashes in tax revenues from wealthy individuals and corporations, according to Ms. Warren, traditional government investment in the middle class has all but evaporated. Her animated, passionate arguments on behalf of working families left both Pongo and Franklin convinced of her genuine devotion to the have-nots of the 21st century.

Once again, as they rode back to Poughkeepsie on Amtrak, Franklin asked the obvious question: when will someone convince her to run for the Presidency?

"All we can do is hope it's as soon as possible, as in 2016," Pongo said. "Looks like President Obama has a strong chance for re-election this year."

"All I can say is, the Democrats and independents both would be fools not to beg her to run the first chance she gets," Franklin said.

"Well, Ms. Hillary Rodham Clinton just might have a little to say about that – when she's not busy sucking up to Wall Street bankers, at least."

"You should know about an encounter I had while we were in Tucson the first time, Pongo," Franklin said.

He went on to explain the details of Mr. Plaid Pants' intimidating conversation that night at the Hampton Inn, about the Wall Street consortium's plans to put Hillary Clinton into the Presidency in the 2016 election – and, most importantly, the not-so-veiled threats against the Poughkeepsians, were they to forge ahead with their USA-SBR rallies.

"No shit!" Pongo said. "Would've been nice to know this a little sooner, Sir. Any reason you waited 'til now to share that?"

"Well, it's not like _you_ have any huge secrets to worry about, Pongo – or do you??"

"Oh, you mean my secret homosexual trysts with the local high school football coach and his pet emu – along with my online gambling addiction?"

"My blessed Jesus!" Franklin said, his face suddenly blanched.

"I'm just screwin' with ya', Sir! Cool your jets, OK?

"But what if the rest of us had some bizarre secrets you didn't know about? You know, like a former President who's come back to life after 67 years? I think we deserved to hear this a little sooner.

"Anyway, what's done is done – we'll pass the word along to the rest of them when we get back to Poughkeepsie, OK? I think everything will be fine, as long as my Dad hasn't turned into some kind of terrorist in the past week."

Phil hadn't. Everything *did* turn out OK...for the time being, at least – but it was still more than four-and-a-half years 'til the election that might put another Clinton back in the White House. A Clinton who would be *even more* corporate-kissy-face than the last Clinton who led the country.

The other Poughkeepsians all looked a little sick to their stomachs when they heard Franklin re-tell his story of the encounter with Mr. Plaid Pants. Heather, like Pongo, selfishly thought first about how deeply she would miss the weekly late night carnal adventure tradition she and Pongo had been sharing for so long in the back seat of his Civic at their "special place" in the Dutchess County backwoods. Franklin could see the wheels turning in all of their heads as he continued to divulge the details of the contentious conversation. One was thinking about how he liked to masturbate under the stars in the forest during warm new moon nights, another was thinking about how she liked to masturbate on her rooftop deck on the same kind of warm nights, a couple were thinking about they enjoyed giving each other hand jobs under a blanket in the back row at the Hyde Park Drive-In Theater on the same kind of warm nights and another person was thinking about how he liked to give his wife orgasms in the back of their minivan while it was parked in their garage. All each of them could think about was someone spying on the most intimate moments of their lives.

"Do you think we should hire someone to make sure whether our homes need to be de-bugged?" Phil asked Pongo and Idris.

"It might be the prudent thing to do, as long as we find someone willing to indemnify himself or herself in a BIG way in the event someone with their firm breaches a confidentiality agreement with us," Idris said.

"Then let's get on that right away," Phil said. Each of the others present (including Bianca, Harry, Grandpa Tom, Orvis, Karin, Annie, Mel and Cherisse) nodded their assent or said things like "Damn right!", "Shit, yes," or "Fuckin' A."

"Does any of us have any surprises we want to share now, before we see some headline about it in the newspaper a year or two or four from now?" Phil asked. "I feel like the guy in the scene from John Carpenter's "*The Thing*" movie – if we **_DO_** have any surprises for each other, I don't know if we're in much of a position to do anything about it at this late date."

Harry raised his hand.

"You don't need to raise your hand, Harry – it's not Mrs. Pruitt's Second Grade room," Pongo said. "What is it?"

"Ten years ago, I got pissed off at Vice Principal Preston 'cause he confiscated my Penthouse magazines, so I took a shit on the hood of his car. I printed out fifty copies of a picture of it and taped 'em on every car in the school staff parking lot with a note on each saying, 'You're next, prick!' On the back, I wrote, "Wanna suck my dong? Call 1-800-Clarence Thomas"

"Cuhh-lassssy, dumbass. Don't think we need to worry about high school pranks."

"Anything else, folks?" Phil asked.

Silence. Phil, Franklin and others were becoming worried. Mr. Plaid Pants appeared to be having his intended effect.

"Let's just agree to recognize that there probably will be an unpleasant surprise or two dug out of the rectums of our collective pasts," Phil said. "Let's just plan now to respond assertively and rapidly when that time comes, OK? We'll plan for either me or Franklin or both of us to respond to national media the same day anything weird comes out in the news, OK?"

Silence again. But this time almost all heads were simply nodding, nervously.

* * *

UNWELCOME PURSUIT BLAZES
TRAIL BACK TO DEVOTION

The spring semester at Dutchess C.C. seemed to Franklin to be plodding along by the end of February. He'd been tempted to ask Holly out on a date, but the repercussions of the exchange of saliva and other bodily fluids kept it easy for him to bite his tongue, so to speak.

He was grateful for the frequently challenging manual labor tasks he was given at Adams Landscaping – when he was moving pallets of mulch or loading stacks of 2"x6" pine boards into customers' trucks or unloading shipments of 8'x8' sheets of oak plywood, he wasn't reflecting on how lonely his private life could be.

Chet Dale became so worried over Franklin's/Percy's lone wolf ways Chet even tried to match Franklin up with his pretty young niece, Janeene White, 20, the youngest daughter of Chet's sister Margaret "Maggie" White. Unknown to Franklin, Chet started having Janeene deliver homemade cookies to Franklin and his co-workers twice every week. At her Uncle's suggestion, Janeene made a special point of lingering in Franklin/Percy's vicinity, always asking him what was happening in his life.

Franklin appreciated the attention and was struck by Janeene's good looks, but he quickly figured out that Janeene simply didn't 'float his boat.' If proper chemistry were a requirement, the product of their attempted combination was far more like gentle fizz than explosive jizz – one of those potential hook-ups that just might work only if both partners were the last of their species on the planet. **_And_** needed body heat to survive.

After nearly a month of cookie deliveries, a progressively more revealing wardrobe each week (Franklin privately joked that she might end up a walking strip of X-Ray film by the end of the year) and almost comically pathetic 'come hither' gazes aimed in Franklin's/Percy's direction during nearly pointless conversations, Janeene's patience expired. It was clear to her she might as well be trying to have a random 'meet-cute' with Justin Timberlake at the Marist College Cannavino Library periodicals archives as expect affections from her Uncle's favorite drudge. She decided her time socializing would be better spent swimming and running at a local gym. (Six years later, she would find herself marrying a local charter school shop teacher she met at the gym; unfortunately, three years after that, her husband would beat her 'til she was nearly blind in one eye for using the wrong kind of dressing on his salad – though the real-but-unstated reason was she didn't give him as much head as he thought he deserved.)

Franklin was relieved to find out Chet was OK with Janeene and Franklin not hitting it off. But Chet told Franklin/Percy more than once he needed to "get out there and let those juices flow once in a while" if he wanted to "keep an even keel."

An avid yachtsman in his earlier life, Franklin knew better than most the value of an even keel. But there were times when his most prized private part lately was feeling like a fin keel he was constantly having to avoid stumbling and fumbling over. Amputation definitely wasn't an option. And DIY self-gratification was getting seriously tedious. But, most of all, the simple lack of opposite-gender companionship – the pleasure of an intelligent woman's stimulating conversation, if nothing else - was weighing like the heaviest anchor on this old salt from Hyde Park.

Franklin's thoughts kept coming back again and again to the lovely Ms. Van Arsdale. There simply must be a way to develop a relationship without risk to her health and safety, he told himself, but he was barely half-convinced.

His internal debate continued off and on 'til the Dutchess Community College spring break. When he wasn't busy using massive exertion as a stand-in for human companionship, he was pestering the O'Learys to watch videos with him. They convinced him to watch "Kick-Ass," even though he was supremely skeptical about its appeal. But he absolutely loved its upbeat ending.

A day later, he remembered Bianca mentioning 1-1/2 years earlier a television show which had intrigued him because it had something to do with bringing deceased people back to life. "Pushing Up Daisies?" he asked himself. "No, 'Pushing Daisies,' that's it...I've got to see that."

And he did.

Binge-watching the series' two seasons of sweetly formulaic episodes with the O'Learys, he had an epiphany about a possible future with Holly. The kind of epiphany that comes not from kissing-through-cellophane strategies, but from accepting the simple validity of 'love finds a way' kinds of truisms.

The following Monday on campus at Dutchess C.C., he made a point of tracking down Holly during lunch at her favorite Atrium Café table in Conklin Hall.

Her latest would-be suitor – Corpsdur Grandspieds, a second-generation Franco-American starting forward on the D.C.C. Falcons' soccer team - was sitting across from her at the time. Seeing Franklin/Percy approaching, she explained to Corpsdur (pronounced "corder") that her friend 'Scruples' was her calculus tutor. She asked him to excuse himself because Scruples needed to provide crucial preparation for a test – a completely imaginary one - scheduled for 4 p.m. that day. Corpsdur saw a vaguely passionate look in Holly's eyes as she looked at 'Scruples' and was immediately skeptical. But, testosterone notwithstanding, he wasn't particularly interested in ferreting out a probable lie by a beautiful young woman who hadn't even agreed yet to a date. He left with all the grace and aplomb which an emotionally bruised star student-athlete could muster.

'Scruples' asked Holly how she felt about him, as compared to Corpsdur.

She told him he already knew.

He did.

She asked him how he felt about her.

He told her she already knew.

She did. Mostly.

"What do you say we re-locate ourselves someplace more private so we can speak more freely with each other?"

She was agreeable. Franklin drove her to a small house owned by a young couple – the Wallaces - who were friends with Holly and had recently gone on a month-long trip to Scandinavia; they'd asked Holly to keep an eye on it and make sure their fish were fed.

"So, it's been a good long while since we had that long talk while we walked," he said, shortly after they sat down on the Wallaces' leather couch a few feet apart from each other. "Do you still feel like pleasing your father and your church are the most important things in your life? That you can only please them the best by being with a sweetheart who is as devoted to your church as he is to you?"

Tears started to slowly trickle down her cheeks. She appeared deep in thought for what seemed like many minutes as she choked back sobs and looked off in the distance first right, then left and then, finally, directly into Franklin's/Scruples' eyes. She fell into his suddenly-open arms.

"Jesus forgive me," she whispered into his right ear, "but my church and my Daddy can go screw themselves if it means I can't be with the man I care the most about. You're all I've been able to think about – at least, when I'm not focused on school – for the last year and a half."

"Me too."

"So what do we do now?"

"That depends, Holly: do you still feel like you have to share every detail of what happens between us with your church leader?"

"No, CHRIST, no! I'm not a teenage girl any longer. I have my own mind. No man in ANY church is entitled to know what I do with my own body, with my own private life. My conscience belongs to me and me alone, not to some group of patriarchs whose primary purpose in life is to make sure women have as many babies, as many new church members, as possible."

"Thank Jesus," Franklin said, a few drops of ocular liquid tricking down his own cheeks. "You can't imagine how much I hoped to hear exactly that from you, Darling."

He kissed her gently on the neck and cheek. When she looked him in the eye again and seemed curious why she wasn't being kissed straight-on, he backed away a little.

"This is where it gets, well, seriously peculiar, my sweet Holly.

"If we're going to make what we have here work, you're entitled to know some things. The most important is that I have what probably would be considered to be a disease. It's not AIDS. It's not even something I 'caught' from someone else through sex or anything like that.

"But it's something that could – well, probably *would* – sort of infect you if I exchange fluids with you or even kiss you. It wouldn't kill you, but it could give you a kind of temporary rabies-type thing every time you were near someone with an open head wound."

"What do you mean by temporary rabies-type thing?"

"Er, uh, um, well, it would make you want to dig out the insides of the person's head and eat it."

"You mean, like in the '*Night of the Living Dead*'?"

"Sort of. I'm not actually sure if it even kicks in fully if the person with the head wound still is alive. But I wouldn't bet my life that it doesn't."

"OK, so it wouldn't kill me <u>and</u> I'd have to avoid people with open head wounds at all costs. What if we decided to have a child together someday?"

"I have no idea. Maybe the child has it too, maybe not. No idea. None at all.

"There's another thing too: I'm not who you think I am. I'm not ready to be more specific than that, because I don't know if you'd believe me."

"Try me, Honey."

"OK: I'm actually a hundred years older than I appear."

"And I'm really a Russian spy who's here to steal boner pill technology for limp-pricked middle-aged ex-commies."

"Honest. I used to be someone fairly important. I was born when the only conveyances were powered by equine energy, except for railroad cars. My initials at birth were F, D and R."

"You're saying you're FRANKLIN DELANO ROOSEVELT? Oh, c'mon, Honey – I've seen what 'one can short of a sixpack' looks like and your cans are all there – er, so to speak. You really don't expect me to swallow that, do you?"

"What you swallow is entirely up to you. But, seriously, does the USA-SBR we've been promoting read like something your average – or even above-average – community college student would compose?"

"Well, Dear, let's agree to this, OK? I'll keep your theory about actually being a very old man to myself if you'll take my word that what you share with me stays with me and if you'll not tell anyone that I'm on the pill to keep you from knocking me up – at least 'til I'm ready for that, if ever."

"It's not a theory, Sweetheart. There are people who were there when I was brought back to life. People who could confirm it for you.

"Make no mistake: you need to understand that none of what I'm sharing with you can be spread beyond the two of us and the core group of USA-SBR organizers from Poughkeepsie. You can't mention any of this to your parents, your bishop – not even Nancy or any other BFF.

"If you were to slip up and spread around these things about me, there are lives which could be at real risk. Like being an involuntary lab rat for the rest of your life risk. I am not – how do they say it now? – shitting you."

"Most people say, 'I shit you not,' " Holly offered.

"Whatever scatological expression works best, as long as you understand me. If you and I start exchanging saliva and other personal fluids, you're going to be almost as much of a scientific oddity to the folks in lab coats as I am. I don't think either of us wants to be hauled off in a windowless government van by some Men In Black to a Black Ops site, right?

"And maybe as important as anything: I have no guarantee that I won't wake up one morning and be fifty years older than I appear to be right now. Something like that happened once and a dear friend of mine had to take some pretty drastic actions to stabilize my appearance."

"What kinds of drastic actions? No one was killed, were they?"

"Just some smart birds."

"Well, I have no guarantee that I won't come down with some awful disease that kills me or deforms me. You know, a lot of women die from breast cancer, from ovarian cancer, from cervical cancer – some as young as their 30's."

"So, you're OK with this, with all these risks? You don't think I'm some kind of bizarre lunatic for claiming to be the revived-slash-rejuvenated corpse of the thirty-second President?"

"Just a compulsively-idealistic guy who's obsessed with making the world a better place. A nut who doesn't realize when someone's been waiting a year and a half for him to kiss her. Waiting very patiently, I should add." She smiled with a coy, yet deeply felt, passionate glance out of the corners of her eyes. A glance which expertly disguised the reality that she was risking the harshest kind of hurt, the most lasting kind of fractured heart, were Franklin to turn away, to reject the emotions she no longer wanted to suppress.

But, at that moment, Franklin needed no further encouragement. He kissed her gently, fully, directly on those wonderful, sensuous lips. Moments later, their tongues penetrated deeply into each other's mouths. That was only the first of many delightfully comforting, yet energetically stimulating medleys of penetrations they would experience that afternoon and evening. Within three minutes, Franklin had unzipped Holly's snug-fitting floral print dress and let it glide smoothly to her feet. Between kisses on her mouth and neck, he marveled at her ever-so-perfectly curved figure. He tried to permanently store in his mind the exquisite sight of the lines of her brassiere and panties against her smooth, blemish-free skin, the outlines of the untanned strips from last summer's string bikini, the Michelangelo-like symmetry of her sweetly cleaved trampoline-taught buttocks begging to be freed from the sheerest of lavender panties - silken bikini briefs tasked with the enviable duty of insulating those delicate cheeks from undesired friction. _Desired_ friction, however, was at the top of the priority list at that moment for both Holly and Franklin.

Twelve and a half hours later, their relationship had been fully consummated - more times than Holly could count, for her part, at least. Their first orgasms occurred almost simultaneously, as Franklin was softly tongue-caressing Holly's erect nipples while providing vigorous manual stimulation below the waist at the same time Holly was finishing rolling a condom (just retrieved from her handbag) onto Franklin, who was rock hard. Fortunately, she had at least a half-dozen more lambskins, all of which would end up being used that night. Franklin couldn't recall a time when he'd been physically intimate with someone who was as consistently aroused as the beautiful Ms. Van Arsdale – and his all-night-long stamina surprised even himself. Quite the passionately unselfish feedback loop they created for themselves, he thought, with no small amount of joy.

Earlier, Franklin was stunned to notice something he had never experienced before – and never would with anyone else other than Holly for the rest of his life – as he was trying to simultaneously use his tongue and the two longest fingers on his right hand to help her come the second time. As he caressed her stiff-nippled right breast with his left hand while both orally and manually stimulating her clitoris and vagina, he felt orgasmic uterine spasms so stunningly strong that they literally began to vibrate his tongue. A millisecond later, Holly let out a succinct orgasmic shout of "Percy," a shout which seemed to be intentionally cut short.

Franklin was so full of joy over the pleasure he'd just been able to give to Holly, shortly after the spasms stopped he raised his head up with an earnest almost ear-to-ear smile. He started, proudly, to ask Holly if she'd really felt as wonderful as she'd sounded, but then he saw what seemed to be a look of restrained embarrassment on her face.

"Did I just do something to make you feel ashamed or guilty or something?" he asked.

"Omigod, _no_, Honey!" she said. "Nothing could be further from the truth."

"Well, I'm glad, Sweetheart. There's nothing that could make me happier than to help you feel that way. I was just confused because the look on your face just then seemed like I had embarrassed you."

"You saw that – I am sooo sorry, Percy. I couldn't help it. It's from something my mother told me."

"I don't know if it's right for me to ask, so tell me if it's not, but what are we talking about?

"Well, when my Mama gave me the birds and bees talk, er, uh – oh, and you should know that my Papa was sitting nearby with us. He wanted to make sure what she told me was in line with our church's teachings. Anyway, she told me that, if I ever had an orgasm, I should make sure I didn't let on to my lover – my dad corrected her to say my 'husband' – anyway, she told me to never, ever let my lover know just how much I enjoyed the orgasm."

"Why would she tell you that? That's just weird."

"She said if my lover realized just how much I enjoyed my orgasm, or realized that I even HAD an orgasm, he'd feel like he had a blank check to just stick his dick into me whenever he felt like it."

"What a sick, sick thing to tell an impressionable young girl. I'm sorry, I don't mean to be bad-mouthing your mother, but there's no excuse for telling your daughter something like that when giving her the 'facts of life' talk."

"Well, the first boy I was with – a full year before I met you – seemed to think that way."

"When you realized that, did you stay with him?"

"No, of course not."

"Almost all sixteen- and seventeen-year-old boys are unmitigated dick-sticking idiots about showing affection. All they think about are their penises and their girlfriends' breasts.

"I imagine most mothers giving the birds and bees talks to their daughters focus more on being careful about really getting to know a young man before letting him make love with you. If you know your lover is a genuinely unselfish person, someone who puts your emotional and sexual needs before his own, you probably never have to worry about him feeling like he has the right to poke you with his johnson whenever his johnson tells him to.

"I'm so sorry you thought you had to suppress your enjoyment that way. I can't believe someone like your mother would distrust men so much as to tell her own daughter something like that. I hope she never had experiences like that. I wonder if she would even share something like that with someone else."

"If she did, it probably would've been with one of our church bishops. But our church bishops – they're all laymen who've never been through any lengthy in-depth seminary training – anyway, they're not known for their pro-feminist sentiments. *Producing children* with sex is just as important as *enjoying* sex in our church teachings."

"I hope you won't think me an apostate of some kind for wanting to focus just on the enjoying part."

"Let me show you just how mistaken you are about that."

Whereupon she mounted Franklin vigorously and lowered her left nipple right into his slightly opened mouth.

The rest of the orgasmic expressions that night were neither pianissimo nor staccato.

Just before they returned to their respective residences an hour or so after Holly's fourteenth (??!) orgasm, he got Holly to agree to call him by his true given name from then on when they were in private or among his closest friends. She was too satiated, too enthralled by Franklin's earnest selflessness as a lover to question that kind of request – but she wondered if she could avoid letting that name slip in front of her roommate and longtime BFF Nancy Perez.

Holly managed to return to her apartment around 1:30 a.m. without waking Nancy. When Holly awoke the next morning, she noticed the horribly-impacted wisdom teeth she'd had surgically removed the previous summer had grown back – but this time, they were straight as an arrow and weren't crowding any of her other teeth. No repeat surgery needed. Which was a good thing, because neither she nor Franklin would've wanted medical journal publicity for such an unheard-of occurrence. She also noticed that the crooked little finger on her left hand – a casualty of a broken bone sustained during a softball game when she was eight years old – was no longer crooked; likewise, the enlarged joint where the break occurred no longer was enlarged. It looked just as it did before that long-ago game on the Violet Avenue Elementary School playground.

Then she discovered something that caused her to feel stupid at having insisted on Franklin wearing so many condoms the night before. She forgot there might be a risk involved from the oral copulation they'd had off and on during the night. Sure enough, she felt between her legs and there it was, the little friend she'd had for most of her first two decades on the planet: her hymen had re-grown itself. This, she thought, just might make lovemaking a little less enticing for both of them. But after being on the receiving end of Franklin's stamina for more than half of a day and experiencing more than a dozen orgasms over the course of one night, she decided she could live with that trade-off – if Franklin could, anyway.

"*So, **this** is what my church bishop warned me would send me straight to hell?*" she thought to herself. "*What an absolute dick.*"

Later in the day, while she was in her Sociology 202 class at Dutchess C.C., she noticed that she didn't need her contact lenses any longer. At her next eye exam, her ophthalmologist, Dr. Pete Peckinpah, told her that her uncorrected vision had gone from 20-80 in both eyes to 20-10. He said he'd never witnessed such a change in a patient who hadn't undergone a Lasik procedure. He asked if he could document her case for an ophthalmology journal. She politely declined, explaining that she attributed it to a new nutritional supplement she'd been taking (wondering all the while if a doctor like Dr. Pete, were he to know the truth, would try to find a way to market Franklin's semen as a vision cure-all; she briefly envisioned little refrigerated jars at pharmacies around the country labeled "Dr. Pete's Two-Nut Extract Vision Correction Cream").

"What did I say to make you choke back all that giggling?" Dr. Pete asked. She hadn't even realized she was smiling at the time. When she heard the word choke, she started laughing out loud.

"N-n-n-n-ooothing," she snorted, laughing still harder. "I don't know why talking about taking a nut extract (*more raucous laughter*) would make me laugh so hard."

He pressed her about what kind of nut extract she'd been using, but her laughter by then had escalated to loud guffaws, so loud he worried his assistant might think something strange was going on. So, he dropped it. But he was more curious than ever. Over the next three months, he started taking every form of nut extract and fresh nuts known to humankind, hoping to experience a similar improvement in his own vision, which was 20-60 when not corrected with eyeglasses.

But the only thing he came away with was more than five extra pounds of cushioning around his waistline.

∗ ∗ ∗

PRECAUTIONS

Franklin, Phil and the others were relieved to find out the following day that the contractor they hired to search for spying devices in each of their homes and vehicles had come up with nothing.

The contractor cautioned them on several fronts, however:

\# First, finding no bugging devices in their homes and vehicles didn't preclude someone from using sound magnification and filtration devices to listen through walls and vehicle doors.

\# Second, National Security Agency operatives – and, presumably, private parties – were rumored to have the capability to listen in on conversations in any room where a landline telephone was located, *even if the phone was hung up*, <u>without</u> needing a physical bugging device attached to the phone.

The best way to avoid that kind of spying, according to the contractor, was to discuss confidential issues only in a basement *without* any exposed above-ground walls and *with* any basement landline phones unplugged from the wall. As the contractor explained those details, Pongo was reminded of a plethora of scenes from submarine warfare movies when, without fail, someone always would accidentally drop a wrench during 'silent running' and cause destroyers overhead to start dropping depth charges. There would be no such ***immediate*** sign – with either literal or figurative explosions – if someone were successfully surveilling them. Not 'til it was too late to do much about it.

The USA-SBR organizers immediately all agreed to conduct all their business and other confidential discussions in the Podrowskis' basement. Whether they could stick to that pledge was another matter. *"Have you **ever** tried __not__ talking about something you **REALLY** wanted to discuss while riding in a car with a good friend, much less a lover?"* Pongo thought to himself, a question which answered itself.

As March rolled around, Franklin asked Holly – who had been hoping to spend her spring break with Franklin between her legs for several days straight, **reeealllly** straight – if she wanted to join the USA-SBR organizers on a tour with rallies at the University of Virginia, West Virginia University, University of North Carolina and North Carolina State University.

Holly had seen almost all of the YouTube videos of their previous tours. She'd been genuinely moved by what she'd seen. But what the Poughkeepsians were doing seemed like work to her. She needed her break for a real break; maintaining her 4.0 average took its toll on her mental stamina. Much as she would've liked to drain Franklin's essential bodily fluids every night during the tour, she decided she'd be more of a distraction than a source of support. So, she lovingly declined Franklin's offer – on the condition that he submit to as many oral orgasms as she could induce during the last couple of hours before the group departed. She did not have to point a gun to Franklin's head to compel his agreement – but just to be sure, she pointed her 34C-caliber bare breasts against his face.

∗ ∗ ∗

GOIN' SOUTH: MORE NATIONAL PARKS

The group left Poughkeepsie for Virginia – with a semi-conscious but goofy-smiling Franklin taking up most of the back seat of the airport shuttle bus – at the crack of dawn on Saturday March 10. Their first rally was set for two days later at the University of Virginia John Paul Jones Arena; they arrived via US Airways at the Albemarle Airport outside Charlottesville, VA.

After checking in at the Hampton Inn and Suites, where they would be holding a press conference late Sunday afternoon, they drove straight to nearby Shenandoah National Park so they could hike to the top of Old Rag Mountain. Franklin simply could not get enough good use out of his rejuvenated legs – the 32nd President looked forward to some serious rock climbing. He was not disappointed.

They summited Old Rag by late afternoon and were treated to a spectacular sunset as they scrambled down the rough metamorphic rock boulders on the way back down the trail. About a mile down the trail from the summit, all of the group had to scramble up mature maple and ash trees to avoid an encounter with a black bear sow and her two cubs which had just emerged from an abbreviated

363

hibernation. The group was well aware just how dangerous a mama bear could be when she was shadowed by new offspring.

After a well-earned night's rest (which was punctuated by a resumption of the less-than-completely secret hotel room dalliances between Idris and Marcia), the group rose early the next morning to return to the park for a hike up North Marshall Mountain, followed by a hike up Stony Man Mountain on their way back to Charlottesville. The bleary-eyed Mr. M'Benga and Ms. Dirkenstack begged off from the day's hiking agenda at the last minute, each suggesting they needed to take the Sunday morning off and then help set up for the 6 p.m. press conference. In fact, however, they both simply wanted to get in a couple of hours of sleep before resuming the process of banging each other's brains out from every geometric angle biologically possible. They planned to stop the bodily fluid transfers before the group got back from the park. They just barely made it, however, due to a spontaneous decision to engage in shower coitus – their genital collisions in the shower stall were so vigorous that a couple of tile squares were cracked; and an elderly couple on the floor below complained to the front desk staff about the noise, mostly out of envy (told the noise sounded like a pair of gorillas wet slapping each other while doing chin ups on a tree branch, the staff – stifling hard laughs between words – gave the old couple a made-up story about a movie director editing a documentary about Appalachian black bear mating habits and asked their indulgence during waking hours). Both Idris and Marcia sported barely-dried-at-all hair when the group met them at the hotel conference room at 6 p.m. – which wasn't all that inappropriate simply because the rest of the group had just showered off all their trail dust from the day.

Idris and Marcia shared laughs with the rest of the group as they recounted the day's events on the hiking trails, which included Franklin accidentally stepping in a heaping, steaming pile of bear scat shortly after they started up the North Marshall trail, as well as their vivid description of Pongo being surprised by an elderly Catholic nun hiker as he was in mid-stream urination half-way up the same trail. "I thought he was about to go all 'Something About Mary' the way he zipped his fly up so fast," Harry said. "I could just see him getting his dick caught up in a bloody zipper mess and having to ask for help from this old lady in her penguin outfit. But all he ended up with was a big ol' stream of hot piss down his pantleg. Don't think he'll be asking Heather to dress up as a novitiate any time soon for one of their backwood trysts."

Phil chuckled as he recounted a separate incident on the Stony Man trail as they ate lunch on the trail. Harry and Bianca had finished their sandwiches quickly and had excused themselves to explore off-trail while the others finished eating; they'd promised to return within 15 to 20 minutes. Phil noticed that, after they walked about ¼-mile through the stand of hardwood trees, they'd just suddenly disappeared behind some bushes.

He convinced Pongo to sneak over to those bushes with him, as quietly as humanly possible. When they got within about 30 yards of the bushes, Phil told Pongo to follow his lead. At that moment, Phil executed an impressive imitation of a cougar's high-volume stay-away-from-my-fresh-meal screech. Pongo promptly joined in, sounding – appropriately – like the hungry offspring of a mama cougar.

Almost immediately, Bianca popped up – sans blouse and bra with her hand still grasping Harry's rapidly shrinking penis – with a piercing scream. She rapidly realized she and her randy lover had been pranked.

"You fuckhead pricks!" she yelled, covering her exquisitely lovely – if slightly asymmetrical – breasts with her free forearm, still not letting go completely of Harry's hairy member. "Your friends are nature pervs, Harry – they seem to get off on cock-blocking you, Sweetie. Not to mention getting a free peep show."

"Hey, we're not the ones breaking Federal laws about indecent exposure in a National Park," Pongo heckled. "Anyway, who'd want to take on the impossible challenge of preventing premature speculation by Harry's Hairy. Yes, I _meant_ 'speculation' 'cuz once his rocket goes off it's pure speculation whether it'll be a week or a month before it'll be Launchpad-ready again."

As Phil was finishing up the description of a beet-red-faced Harry raising his drawers and hiking shorts to full staff, Marcia could only think how grateful she was that she and Idris hadn't done the same sort of thing the previous day. Especially 'cause that's almost exactly what Idris had suggested to her just under his breath as the others had gone around a bend in the trail. Just the idea of it had gotten her significantly auto-lubricated at the time; she hadn't taken him up on it simply because she'd forgotten to put any condoms in her fanny pack, even though she still was on the pill. At almost 44 years old, she wanted no risk what-soever of unplanned maternity – and she didn't want the expense and time off of work required to get an abortion, much less risk having to encounter bizarro religious fanatic abortion haters during a protest outside a clinic.

But everyone else laughed hard at the Phil's good-natured teasing, even Harry. And, especially, Franklin. At that moment, he wished so very much that Holly had wanted to come along on the trip, thinking just how ecstatic he'd be just for the chance to share both emotional and physical intimacy with her in such a beautiful setting as a national park.

∗   ∗   ∗

The first of the local Charlottesville media arrived for the pre-USA-SBR rally news conference just as the Poughkeepsians were finishing up their laugh-fest.

Franklin and Phil introduced themselves and their fellow rally organizers to the representatives from the Charlottesville Daily Progress, the Richmond Times Dispatch, each of the local network broadcast affiliates (including PBS) and the local NPR affiliate.

The questions took on a politely dismissive, if slightly passive-aggressive tone. The general theme seemed to be, basically, "How dare you Noo Yawkuhs have the audacity to come here and try to radicalize our polite and hard-working rabble?"

Franklin explained in detail how each provision of the USA-SBR was designed to return to the middle class and working poor the power which had been seized from them through corporate mergers combined with influence-purchasing power wielded by billionaires (like the Kochs) and mega-millionaires through campaign contributions.

"It is no small thing that, since the Citizens United ruling, the richest 1 percent now have carte blanche to purchase as much political TV advertising as they'd like," Phil chipped in.

"And the concentration of wealth in the media continues to metastasize. For example, two of the top three newspapers in Virginia now are owned by billionaire Warren Buffett's Berkshire Hathaway Inc. conglomerate holding company."

"Yes, that would be your employer," Franklin said, pointing to Daily Progress reporter Pete Preston, "and," he added, pointing to the Times Dispatch's Larry McMuffett, "your employer too.

"Is there anyone here who'd like to defend the concept of more and more billionaires owning more and more newspapers? Anyone who believes it improves news coverage? Anyone who believes it means more of a diversity of viewpoints?

"Anyone who's convinced that the news filtered through a billionaire's ownership means more empathy for those among us who are struggling the most financially?

"Anyone here who's convinced that one corporation – Gray Television – owning three different network affiliate stations in this city alone is a good thing? Is there anyone here who believes that even the local PBS affiliate being owned by an out-of-town corporation (based in Richmond) is a good thing?

"Is there anyone here who understands what the word plutocracy means?"

Crickets, for a half-minute or so.

"So, if I understand you correctly, if ownership isn't local and if ownership of multiple news and entertainment broadcasting sources is concentrated under one corporation's control, that necessarily must be a nasty, repugnant thing," Fox TV affiliate reporter Seamus McFecklesh said, half-sneering.

"I never used the words nasty and repugnant," Franklin said. "What we're saying with the USA-SBR, essentially, is that concentration of ownership of media outlets and other large corporations, as well as concentration of political influence, is destructive to the diversity of expression and to the diversity of representation.

"When we have those kinds of ownership concentrations, we have plutocracy. By commonly-accepted definition, definition going back thousands of years, plutocracy destroys democracy.

"That is not what this nation should be about. We're out to stop that. We're out to help return power to the many millions of hard-working Americans who've been screwed over so long by for-profit mega corporations, they don't even realize how much they're being economically fucked on a daily basis. Please pardon my French."

"But Americans seem to be pleased with what their corporations are providing for them and they seem to believe they're being charged a fair price," said local NBC (i.e., Comcast) affiliate reporter Reptility Poindextrous.

"I don't know what your source is for that – maybe the Koch Industries monthly newsletter? - but if you honestly believe that, I have some wonderful beachfront property in Yuma, Arizona you'd probably love to buy," Harry quipped.

"Perhaps someone among you can help us understand how forcing the government to make sure working class families get a fair shake is a danger to democracy," Franklin said. "It always seems like Chamber of Commerce types are accusing progressive organizations like ours of hating business. I've never seen a regional daily newspaper or local TV station refuse to use a red herring phrase like that.

"What we'd like to know is, when will corporate media start to hold businesses accountable for hating their labor force? When you hear someone like the head of Papa John's Pizza say he hopes the Affordable Care Act will be repealed because being forced to provide health insurance for his employees will lead to pizza prices going up 15 cents each, why don't you hold his feet to the fire? Why is it OK for a business to have such contempt for its own workers, so much contempt that they don't care if their own uninsured employees' medical expenses force them into bankruptcy?

"Is it really that hard to imagine yourselves being in the same position as those employees whose employers don't want to provide health insurance for them?"

"Yes," came a half-whispered smart-assed reply mumbled by an unseen reporter at the back of the room.

"It's nice that you can think these issues are funny," Bianca said, then introducing herself. "Please ask yourself right now, though: what if it were my own 20-something daughter or son whose employer refused to provide health insurance or paid time off for illness?

"Would you want your own child – or anyone else's for that matter – to have to overcome a medical bankruptcy before she turned 25?"

Nearly every reporter in the room was looking down at their shoes, unexpectedly chagrined, envisioning being compelled to provide food and shelter for their college graduate adult children.

"We would simply ask you not to place some sort of simplistic label on the USA-SBR movement," Franklin continued. "It's about economic justice and social justice, but it's a system intended to facilitate lasting change, changes which can make this country a healthier and more prosperous nation for millennia to come, not just from one election to another."

"We understand that you're taking some real heat for your proposal to guarantee only one U.S. Senator from each state, with the second senators from so-called over-represented states being re-distributed based on population," said Lucious MacVenial of the local ABC (Disney) broadcast affiliate. "What do you tell people who are incensed at potentially having to lose a favorite U.S. Senator to another state?"

"I would ask them why they think it's fair for them to be disproportionately represented in Congress," Franklin said. "The original requirement for two U.S. Senators per state was created, in part, as an incentive for sparsely-settled states to have a disproportionately-greater voice in Congress. It was hoped that would help stimulate westward expansion into those sparsely-settled states.

"It's been about 240 years since that experiment began. The time draws nigh for that experiment to end. Those states which still are sparsely settled are not going to see their populations magically mushroom simply because they're disproportionately represented in Congress. If you're from those states – like Wyoming, Alaska, Montana and Hawai'i – and you want to maintain your U.S. Senate representation, you need to come up with compelling reasons to attract more people to move to your states.

"Would someone in this room please help me understand why it's appropriate that the District of Columbia. – which has more residents than Wyoming and Vermont and almost as many as all of Alaska – gets **_ZERO_** voting membership in either chamber of Congress while Wyoming, Vermont and Alaska each have two voting U.S. Senators and one voting U.S. House Representative?

"That goes against the most fundamental of our small-d democratic principles as a nation. It means that hundreds of millions of U.S. citizens – in states like California, New York, Texas, Illinois and Pennsylvania - go under-represented in the U.S. Senate. All for a population re-distribution scheme which should've gone the way of the dinosaurs at least 50 years ago.

"And I'm waiting for someone, anyone – other than massive corporations which find it easier to control a Congressional chamber with fewer members – to explain why being unable to expand membership of each Congressional chamber as the nation's population expands is in line with small-d democratic representation.

"Being unable to adjust the number of seats in each Congressional chamber as the population grows simply makes it more likely that the very richest of the rich will continue to exert their financial muscle to control the rest of us.

"Mr. Orogrande, from the local CBS affiliate, are you aware how much the membership of the U.S. Congress would've needed to expand since women received the vote in 1920 to keep up proportionately with population growth?"

"No idea, sir, but it's not really my job to know that," said Abel Orogrande, a bearded 40-something Hispanic man of wide girth. "I would guess maybe at least double what it is now."

"Try more than triple," Franklin/Percy said.

"So, does anyone here believe a representative with 710,000 constituents can give the same quality representation as one who has 250,000? C'mon, please feel free to raise your hand if you do.

"No takers, eh? Excellent, everyone here understands basic arithmetic. We're confident pretty much everyone else in the country does too. People understand that the power of each working-family voter gets progressively diluted as the population grows – **unless** the seats in Congress are increased to match those changes in population.

"So, your group believes making big government bigger will solve problems for the average voter, is that right?" Orogrande asked.

"Please don't put words in our mouths, OK, Abel? What we're saying is that making the constituencies of each Senator and each Representative *smaller* will enable each voter to hold each member of Congress more accountable."

"So, based on that logic, why not simply make every single voter a member of Congress?" asked Beth Ricosuerte, a local PBS affiliate reporter.

"Because this is a democratic republic, not a pure democracy," Franklin said, "not to mention the obvious fact that 320 million members of Congress could be pretty unwieldy and expensive. Still, in an ideal world, voters would be so motivated to hold their elected officeholders accountable that they'd show up for weekly or even monthly meetings with their members of Congress.

"But this is not an ideal world. Voters have their own lives to live and their own full-time jobs and families to look after. They have to let their elected Representatives and Senators pursue the day-to-day responsibilities of governing.

"Which is not to say that Representatives and Senators couldn't use sophisticated opinion surveys to better represent their constituents' day-to-day inclinations on major issues."

"How about a final question?" Phil asked. "Yes, you sir, in the orange sweater." He pointed to a gaunt 20-something man sitting in front of a tripod-mounted HD video camera with a FoxNews logo above the lens.

"Jeff Carson, local Fox TV affiliate. Just wondering if there's anything to rumors on the web and elsewhere that the Wall Street wing of the Democratic Party – the Clintons, Emanuels, the Gerry Connollys, the Jim Himeses – are working behind the scenes to torpedo what you're trying to accomplish."

"The so-called Wall Street wing of the Democratic Party is nothing more than a subset of closet Republicans who've been taking Wall Street campaign donations and who know they can't get elected as Republicans because their constituents won't vote that way. And they know the base of the Republican Party won't vote in primaries for officeholders whose social views have evolved past the 19th Century," Franklin/Percy said.

"To answer your question directly, no one claiming to be affiliated with any wing of the Democratic Party has approached us so far about threats to undermine our efforts. If that ever happens, you'll hear about it from us first, because we'll want voters to know.

"If officeholders from **_ANY_** party won't formally commit to support the USA-SBR, we will actively seek out candidates to run against them in primaries.

Americans deserve better than corporate oligarchy and plutocracy. It's way past time for the USA-SBR.

"We hope you'll find personal gratification in the USA-SBR's provision to require _**all**_ government proceedings to be open to the public, with no restrictions on pooled news video and radio coverage."

The Poughkeepsians went around and personally thanked each reporter for showing up and urged them to read the 38-page USA-SBR thoroughly before finishing their report from the press conference. They were surprised at the number of times they heard reporters admit that, even though they were charged with being impartial, that – off the record – they found very little in the USA-SBR which didn't seem appealing on multiple levels.

* * *

The Poughkeepsians decided to take a break during the day Monday to recover from their weekend of hiking – except for Idris and Marcia and Harry and Bianca, who, in their respective suites, spent most of the day exchanging bodily fluids.

Phil and Franklin spent the day driving around Charlottesville, stopping at nearby Monticello for a tour, followed by a matinee viewing of the movie "John Carter," which Franklin thoroughly enjoyed, having read and liked one of the John Carter books while he was Assistant Secretary of the Navy. He especially liked that the actress who played the princess character in the movie bore a faint resemblance to his beloved Holly.

That evening's rally featured a guest appearance by a semi-retired Oscar winner who lived nearby – Sassy Spudnut – who'd spent lots of time on line blogging about what an utter embarrassment Sarah Palin was to her gender.

Sassy – who was most enthused about the USA-SBR's provisions for wage equality, free college educations, and elimination of corporate personhood – urged the 10,000 persons in John Paul Jones Arena to use the same kind of strategy that Tea Partiers' behind-the-scenes corporate puppeteers had advocated in 2010.

"When the officeholders and candidates who oppose us hold public events, **show up**. Ask them tough questions. When they try to evade your questions, though, don't act like bullies the way the Tea Partiers did. Just don't back down from your questions – if they don't answer your questions, keep reminding them that it's their duty to respond directly. Not to dissemble. Not to distract. Stay respectful, but be assertive.

"If corporate media don't cover the event, YOU cover it, even if it's just with your phone camera. Post your videos to YouTube. Alert your local TV stations if you get particularly interesting video.

"Remember: you pay elected officeholders' salaries, not the corporations they think are their masters."

Franklin/Percy went on to explain other provisions of the USA-SBR. As always, he ended the presentation by asking how much fealty those in attendance owed to their corporate overlords.

As always, their response was the same: several minutes of "Fuck O-ver-LORDS!" cheers, which went up in volume each time Pongo and Harry tossed out more ramen and clean underwear. And, as always, there were tears after the video memorial to Sally – followed by lots of laughs mixed with anti-corporate boos during the viewing of "*Capitalism: A Love Story.*"

There were just about as many pledges to contact elected officeholders and candidates as at previous rallies. It was clear they would need to increase their spending on USA-SBR copies being picked up by attendees for later distribution: they always seemed to run out or come close to running out. The ongoing conclusion was that their local media advertising the two weekends before the rally continued to be successful.

And, once again, they were surprisingly gratified by the local news coverage the rally received. Even on the local Fox affiliate, the coverage appeared respectful, even if there was a special emphasis on potential sabotage by so-called "Blue Dog" Democrats.

There was, after all, some truth to that. The full extent wouldn't be known for more than a year.

* * *

Their next rally stop was the following day at West Virginia University at Morgantown. The Poughkeepsians had decided in advance to minimize their time in the Mountain State. They were motivated mainly by their impression that, with the state's mining and resource extraction culture so deeply ingrained combined with the tendency by politicians there to suck up to the good ol' boy corporate power structure embodied by Massey Energy's former CEO Don Blankenship (described as "coal country's dark lord" by Rolling Stone), it might be futile to expect deep support for the USA-SBR there. [Massey went on to be indicted 2-1/2 years later for alleged willful conspiracy to violate mine safety standards involving an accident which killed 29 miners in 2010.]

They arrived at the Fairfield Inn and Suites at about 4:30 p.m., about an hour before their scheduled press conference at the Mountaineer Meeting Room there.

The Times West Virginian (a small Fairmont-based daily paper, one of approximately 90 owned by Community Newspaper Holdings Inc., a subsidiary of the State of Alabama Retirement System) and the Dominion Post, Morgantown's only newspaper, each with barely 20,000 paid subscribers, both sent reporters; likewise, management from the nearby CBS, NBC and Fox affiliates also sent reporters. They all looked barely old enough to buy a beer.

The Poughkeepsians were surprised to see a couple of Pittsburgh network affiliates' reporters there 'til Marcia explained that Morgantown was part of the Pittsburgh television market.

Bill Verrue, the reporter from the Dominion Post, whose publisher was a hard-core Republican with multiple failed attempts to win elective office, was the fly in the ointment that particular afternoon.

"Why shouldn't our readers view this USA-SBR thing as just another scheme to help big government take over our lives?" asked Verrue, a 50-something rotund white guy with a stain on his necktie, which was tied with the skinny part sticking out far below the wide part, a la Otis Campbell on the Andy Griffith Show. "Every 15 or 20 years, there's always some poindexter out there who thinks he's got it all figured out: just give the guv'mint enough power and everything'll be real good."

"Actually, Bill, that's a right good question," Phil responded, stepping to the front of the group. "Anyone who hasn't actually read the USA-SBR itself or who hasn't read an in-depth analysis of it by one of those poindexter-eggheads they don't trust just might jump to that kind of conclusion.

"But one of the main reasons we're here today, one of the main reasons we've been running those promo ads on local TV the past two weekends, is to encourage people *NOT* to jump to conclusions.

"Once you and your publisher have had a chance to read all 38 pages of the USA-SBR – really, it'll only take you about 15 or 20 minutes at the most – you'll see that it doesn't actually give the government any more power whatsoever over little people, people like you and me.

"It restores to government the power the people once were grateful for the government to have to protect them from abuses by wealthy corporations and rich individuals – individuals and corporations which have used their massive financial resources to successfully turn the government into their own wholly-owned subsidiary over recent decades.

"Our experience in our travel to rallies all over the country is that people are aching for government to once again be the impartial referee it was always intended to be, the referee who's unafraid to whistle a foul on even the most influential of corporate overlords when an injustice is committed. For at least the past 30 or 40 years, that referee has been bought off. Bought off with direct contributions by big business and by the schemes of lobbyists controlled by corporate manipulators – most of them puppeteered by barons of the energy industry, including the likes of Massey Energy.

"What once was a state full of proud, hard-working members of the United Mine Workers of America now sees those union jobs being slashed as mining corporations pressure local and national elected officeholders to allow more and more moutaintop removal mining. Mining which depends far more on huge machinery than skilled labor.

"There are so damnably many mountaintops being destroyed in this state, the state flag should be changed to show a flattened mountaintop alongside a rock-covered stream full of dead fish as the new state symbol."

"Y'know what, you Noo Yawk prick?" Verrue said. "Y'all don't like it, y'all can just take your spoiled little asses back to the Empire State. Won't bother us one little bit."

"I don't know that Mr. Verrue speaks for all West Virginians, Mr. Podrowski," said Wilbur Wallop, of the Times West Virginian. "But is it really realistic to expect most people to take 15 minutes out of their day to read this USA-SBR tract, assuming they can track it down on line or get an actual hard copy?

"I mean, after all, this isn't the Revolutionary War when Thomas Paine's leaflets were peoples' main source of mental stimulation.

"What's your real hope here about stimulating the public's participation?"

"Maybe it's a pie in the sky kind of hope," Franklin/Percy said. "But we'd love to see every person who gets one of the hard copies of the USA-SBR we've been circulating pass it on to someone else who wants to read it. We'd love to go to every airport and train station in the country and see someone sitting on a bench reading a ragged copy of it that's already been read by 15 other people.

"We hope the enthusiasm for this kind of empowerment for the rights of average working folks spreads so quickly and thoroughly that most people's exposure to it will immunize them against the kind of hard-core cynicism expressed by the likes of Mr. Verrue and his publisher.

"The success of this effort will depend almost entirely on people like those hard-working UMW members calling, writing and visiting their elected officeholders to pressure them to support the USA-SBR. And on them finding someone sympathetic to the USA-SBR to run against the craven corporatist officeholders who refuse to support it.

"There's nothing we'd like better than to see a multiple-decade veteran coal miner take on a corporatist like Evan Jenkins and win a seat in Congress on a platform of support for the USA-SBR."

That exchange between Franklin/Percy and Wallop was followed by several basic information-seeking questions by the local television reporters, questions about the details of the USA-SBR – mainly because the reporters had no idea what was in it, despite Marcia having circulated copies of the USA-SBR to producers and editors at every news outlet within 100 miles of Morgantown.

Pongo and Franklin responded to each question with aplomb and patience; by the time the press conference was over, all of them were confident the local press actually had a thorough understanding of the details of the proposal.

* * *

During the day the next day, the group drove around the area to view the results of mountaintop coal mining. They visited a handful of residents' homes where mining and fracking had virtually destroyed their supply of fresh water. By the time it came for them to prepare for that evening's rally, all were somber, reticent and more or less depressed at the environmental destruction they'd witnessed in West Virginia. More than one of them wished they still were in East Virginia, as Edward Abbey used to jokingly refer to West Virginia's eastern neighbor.

They'd decided to dedicate the rally to Edward Abbey, who was born not far from West Virginia (in Indiana, PA) and who expressed his love for the Appalachian mountain landscapes of Pennsylvania and West Virginia in much of his writing.

Edward Abbey, Franklin intoned for the 5,000-plus at West Virginia University's Coliseum, would've done everything in his power to protest the now-routine practice of mountaintop removal mining.

"To paraphrase Mr. Abbey's writing as a college student of a Louisa May Alcott statement, 'man will never be free until the last conscienceless corporatist – pardon the redundancy there - is strangled with the entrails of the last global warming denier.'

"Please, all you Fox News acolytes out there, *please* take note that we're not speaking literally here, OK? I can almost see already the breaking news bulletins that the USA-SBR organizers are advocating literal evisceration of climate change deniers.

"Hey, if some of them accidentally have botched appendectomies and there's some leftover entrails lying around, I suppose it couldn't hurt to have some of that on hand. You never know, just in case there's a corporatist zombie out there who needs to be put down."

"Anywho, what's say we try to remember, every day, in honor of Mr. Abbey – known to his family as Ned, you know, as in Flanders – what's most important about winning back control of corporations by the government: namely, saving this irreplaceable planet for many, many generations to come.

"If the corporatists win, this planet may become too hot for our grandchildren to survive beyond the end of this century. This is not hyperbole. There are climate scientists, like Prof. James Hansen, who believe the moonscape-style extraction of Canadian tar sands oil may already mean 'game over' for the climate.

"If we, as a species, are to have any chance at all for survival, it's imperative that we all rally behind the USA-SBR, to put an end forever to the concept that profits come before humanity.

"Unless you worry more about the well-being of your favorite corporate overlord 'person.' Do you?"

You know the crowd's response. The chants went on for five full minutes – plus another two minutes after the final tossing of the ramen and clean underwear.

The rally ended with the usual sequence of events. Except for the near news blackout by the Republican-prismatic Dominion Post, the local news coverage once again was remarkably positive.

* * *

They spent the next day traveling from Morgantown to Chapel Hill, NC for their rally the following day at the University of North Carolina's Dean Smith Student Activities Center. They arrived about 4 p.m., two hours before the scheduled press conference at a meeting room at the Aloft Hotel where they were staying. They scheduled just one press conference for both the UNC rally and the rally two days later at North Carolina State University in Raleigh, about 40 miles away.

Present at the press conference were reporters from the Charlotte Observer and the Raleigh News & Observer (both papers owned, along with another 29 daily papers, by The McClatchy Co., of Sacramento, CA), plus reporters from each of the local affiliates for national broadcasting networks, including, as always, PBS and NPR.

After introducing each of the Poughkeepsians, Phil opened the conference with praise for the McClatchy Co., pointing out that theirs was the only major news organization in the country to not consistently parrot pro-war propaganda disseminated during the Iraq and Afghanistan wars of the previous decade.

"As long as truly independent ownership of print media like the Observer and the News & Observer are surviving, ownership which doesn't see bottom line profits as the sole goal for existence, there will be hope for our descendants' future in this country.

"Now that we've buttered you up thoroughly, please feel free to start picking us apart, OK?"

Gil Messier of the Observer obliged.

"Really, what makes you think people out there still have hope? There are a lot of liberals who thought President Obama would be the boldest president yet for progressive causes, only to see him denying a record number of Freedom of Information Act requests, pursuing record numbers of deportations and caving in to Republican threats to cut unemployment and nutrition assistance benefits.

"So, just how do you motivate people to stop playing video games on their phones and computers and start becoming press-the-flesh activists?"

"Honestly, Gil, we actually don't know how much hope people still have," Franklin/Percy said. "Our goal is at least to show them what their potential is for creating real, lasting change. We can only do that if we can try to convey our message to as many folks as possible in as unfiltered a way as possible."

"Thus, the local TV ads over the past two weekends," Messier said.

"That's correct," Franklin/Percy said. "We hope people took notice – I suppose we'll find out tomorrow night and the following evening just how well our message resonates so far."

"Wilton Smithson, News & Observer, Mr. Van Mullder. Is it enough just for large crowds to show up the next two evenings? How long do you hope it'll take before you know if those seeds of activism you're trying to plant actually germinate?"

"Someone recently asked me if I'd ever heard about the cross between an elephant and a rhino. ''Ellifiknow'! (Mild laughter ensued.) It may be six months, it might be six years. Some seeds take longer than others to start growing.

"And some seeds produce fruit trees with nice big juicy fruit, while other seeds just sit there 'til some raccoon with the runs comes along and defecates on them.

"We're hoping our seeds have the good sense to get up and out of the way of sphincter-challenged colons on the loose…Time will tell."

Alice Stuyvesant, a reporter for the Chapel Hill PBS affiliate, asked if all the restrictions on corporations and elections could impact corporate sponsorships of public television programs.

"Only if those corporations expect something in return for their donations to PBS and NPR," Franklin/Percy explained. "If they insist on conditions being attached to their financial underwriting, I believe the USA-SBR would require that to be interpreted as a form of privatization. The USA-SBR is not sanguine about privatization.

"If they want control over creative processes, the corporations can always try to organize their own broadcast for-profit networks as spelled out in the USA-SBR. But they'll have to play by the FCC rules as set forth in the USA-SBR. The airwaves, after all, are owned by all citizens and by law, must be regulated by the government on behalf of all citizens, not corporations.

"We hope that will restore the creativity and editorial freedom which once flourished in public broadcasting, but which had the life sucked out of it when the Congress' reduced funding forced PBS and its affiliates to prostitute themselves to for-profit businesses all around the country.

"Won't you feel like a huge burden has been lifted off of you when you no longer have to worry about whether a report you do might ruffle the feathers of a local tobacco mega-corporation or bank which donates big dollars to your station?"

"I'm just a reporter – I literally have almost no say in the final cut of the reports I do. I suppose you'd have to ask my producer about that," Ms. Stuyvesant explained. "As far as any kind of quid pro quo goes, though, I think there'll always be something like that hanging in the air just because, if they don't like what we do, they can always simply stop contributing."

"We understand that reality," Franklin said. "Our hope is that, once the USA-SBR dramatically reduces the role of corporate money in politics, elected officeholders will feel more responsibility to properly fund public broadcasting. Once again, time will tell."

The group went on to answer somewhat routine rally-related questions for another 45 minutes before wrapping up. They knocked off early that evening because they were looking forward to meeting their featured guest host for the next day's rally, UNC alumnus Lewis "Back in Black" Black the next morning. Marcia had arranged for them to have breakfast with Lewis – flown in the night before at the Poughkeepsians' expense - and spend the morning with him discussing the USA-SBR. They were sure he could mine its details for some comedy gold at the expense of its adversaries.

By the end of the day, he'd put together almost 30 minutes of classic stand-up about:

- what would happen to big dick financial manipulators ("Once the USA-SBR is done with them, their pricks are gonna shrink so small, they'd fit inside a flea's pussy with so much room to spare that Michelle Bachman's husband's gonads would fit right in too");
- what would happen to voter suppression-obsessed racist GOP thugs ("They're each gonna get a jury duty summons for juries with 11 other jurors, all of 'em Mexicans and blacks, for the trials of white guys who went around shooting black kids in hoodies because they read in the KKK Weekly Defecator that dark-skinned kids in hoodies all are queer bank robbers – and they're gonna have to wear T-shirts to deliberations every day saying 'I voted for Klansman David Duke even though he wasn't quite white enough' ");
- what would happen once middle class and working poor people didn't have to pay out of pocket for health care ever again ("They're all gonna be able to afford to get their pooches trained by Cesar Millan so they can teach 'em to piss and shit on command at all of John McCain's and Mitt Romney's luxury estate lawns all over the country – but don't worry, they're only going to evacuate their doggy bowels with the finest digested PetSmart cuisine – stuff people on Food Stamps would kill to eat; they're even gonna train their dogs to use Mitt's car elevator so they can piss all over the tires on his upstairs limousines – striking a decisive blow for all car-top caged canines from sea to shining sea")
- plus what would happen once Wyoming no longer has the same number of U.S. Senators as California ("Free Yellowstone bison burgers for everyone in Oxnard, with a side of fried elk mountain oysters!").

Needless to say, the rally was a stunning success. Most of the time usually devoted to Franklin's detailed explanation of the reasoning behind the provisions of the USA-SBR was taken up with Q & A's for Lewis. By the time he was done, there was almost no one left in the arena who hadn't been doubled over with drippy-tear laughter.

The next evening's rally in Raleigh at PNC Financial Services Arena featured as co-hosts Amy and David Sedaris, siblings who'd grown up in Raleigh. More silliness and lampooning of the rich comedy vein known as ultra-conservative homophobic Republicanism ensued. They shared their memories of growing up in a relatively conservative environment and, like Lewis Black the night before, predicted funny consequences for political Neanderthals when the USA-SBR someday is ratified for passage by the states. And when they were almost done, Lewis Black made a surprise appearance, reprising most of his stand-up from the night before.

As the rally neared its end, Amy, in a break for her comedienne character, took the time to introduce the memorial segment for Sally, with personal comments about her own life which brought the crowd close to tears before the video about Sally even began.

When the two successive days of rallies were done, the Poughkeepsians felt a real sense of accomplishment, feeling like this is more than just a pie in the sky dream, this USA-SBR. It's something which just might happen. That is, if the closet Republicans who label themselves as Democrats – like Hillary Rodham Clinton – don't intervene behind the scenes in such a way as to intimidate true progressives.

A fairly large "if," that was.

∗ ∗ ∗

The next morning the USA-SBR-ers rose early for a half-day drive from their Chapel Hill hotel to the Great Smoky Mountains National Park on the opposite side of the state. Visiting another relatively close by National Park simply was not something Franklin, now a nearly-obsessive hiker, was willing to pass up.

By early afternoon, they reached the Oconaluftee visitors' center to see the well-preserved Mountain Farm Museum and the nearby Mingus Mill. They then drove to the Pigeon Creek trailhead at the Mingo Falls Campground on the Cherokee Reservation just outside the National Park boundary, taking the just under a half-mile (one-way) hike to the spectacular 120-foot high waterfall. They found an amazing variety of multi-colored salamanders in the pool at the base of the waterfall. By the time they returned to the parking area, daylight was waning as was their stamina, so they decided to check in at the Chestnut Tree Inn in nearby Bryson City for an overnight stay.

After the hotel's complimentary breakfast the next morning they headed off on the road to Clingmans Dome. They were fortunate enough to arrive at the road entrance when a Park Ranger was temporarily opening it for travel about 10 days earlier than scheduled, thanks to good road conditions and a promising weather forecast. Led by Franklin, they took the 1-mile round trip hike to the Clingmans Dome summit, which is the highest point in the park, followed by a short hike to Andrews Bald to see if the rhododendrons were in bloom yet. They weren't. But there were black bears grazing on plants at the far edge of the meadow, seemingly oblivious to the New York tourists.

Their park exploration had to end by mid-morning so they could make their way back to Charlottesville for a 6:00 p.m. flight back to New York, which gave them plenty of time to make the 8:55 p.m. Amtrak train back to Poughkeepsie that evening.

By the time they reached Pougkeepsie, they all were ready for a long weekend of R & R. But both Franklin and Pongo had to return to work the next morning, as did Bianca, whose new career as a full-fledged physician was about to begin. She'd taken a full-time job at an urgent care center affiliated with Vassar Brothers Medical Center. To make sure she got a full night's sleep, she was only too happy to "spontaneously" fellate Harry once they returned to her apartment. Which worked just fine for her. 'Til he woke up at 2:30 a.m. in a frisky mood, that is. She thought about kicking him in the nuts, but, hell, she was almost as horny as she was sleepy, so 'what the heck,' she thought. Her flexibility was rewarded barely 10 minutes later with a monumental orgasm. Must've been all that fresh National Park air, she thought. Harry barely thought anything, because, by the time she helped him complete his orgasm just seconds later, he had remained semi-conscious through the entire process. Sometimes Bianca wondered what exactly she saw in her often silly-slash-sometimes unambitious beau – besides a really hard body and an even harder dick, that is.

Pongo and Franklin slogged through their work weekends doing the bare minimum they each could get away with without appearing to be slacking off. Franklin's stamina was sorely tested after a particularly passionate welcome home from Holly after work that Saturday evening. All she'd thought about every evening while the group was on the rally tour was when she'd get to feel Franklin harden up next to her again, when she'd get to feel his delicately adhesive kisses on her nipples again. She was not disappointed. In fact, she was not disappointed at least four times that night. For his part, Franklin was so aroused he didn't even notice the resistance of Holly's re-grown hymen as he plunged into her remarkably wet depths.

When their final semester at Dutchess C.C. resumed the following Monday, they were both full of optimism about the months and years ahead. Franklin had received remarkably good news from Marcia that morning: the USA-SBR website and Facebook pages were on fire with activity. Their rallies, especially in North Carolina, appeared to have struck a real chord with the mostly under-40 crowds which had taken to their presentations like they were minor rock and roll gods.

It appeared they were going to need to hire more staff just to co-ordinate all the on-the-ground grassroots organizers in the various states they'd visited. Marcia recommended they seriously consider opening at least a half-dozen field offices with local managers in key states as soon as they could agree on budgets for each office.

In the back of Franklin's head, though, were the warnings he'd received in Tucson from Mr. Plaid Pants. Something unsettling was in the works. He could feel it.

∗ ∗ ∗

SCRUPLES THE 'TERRORIST'

By the time he'd completed his last Dutchess C.C. final exam about seven weeks later and was sure he'd maintained his 3.9 GPA, Franklin received his letter confirming he'd been admitted to Marist College's Bachelor of Social Work program. He was feeling sanguine about not just his academic prospects but the prospects for progress of the USA-SBR as well.

Which was when he got calls from two of his professors, calls which perhaps shouldn't have shocked him but, nevertheless, made his heart flutter a little.

Each of the two professors had been approached by tall, imposing, football linebacker-sized men in dark suits bearing what appeared to be FBI agent identification. They'd pressed each of the professors for information about Franklin/Percy, claiming to be investigating under the authority of the Patriot Act.

Nothing like implying "this young man could be a terrorist" to make a man in his (sort of) mid-20's feel optimistic about his future. Franklin made it a priority to discuss this latest intimidation strategy with the other USA-SBR organizers, as well as with Holly.

Pongo and Phil reminded him how, in the years right after 9/11, the FBI used paid informants to infiltrate anti-war groups composed of elderly activists, not to mention how the FBI had a long history of looking for communists behind every bush, tree and boulder in the land, imagining massive conspiracies to turn every red-blooded Amurricun into flag-hating comm-symp peacenik fairies.

"Let's not overthink this just yet, OK, Franklin?" Phil recommended. "They may just be trying to shake us up, trying to get us to overreact."

A couple of hours later, over dinner, Holly was somewhat less circumspect with Franklin.

"Those fuckers should be in jail," she said, practically growling. It was the first time Franklin had heard her say the F-word. "I think we should contact Sen. Gillibrand's office and demand an investigation. These asshole bastard salamander dicks need to face consequences for these kinds of dirty tricks. I'd like to personally squeeze each of their nuts into tiny little diamonds."

"Well, thank goodness you're able to have a calm, reasoned perspective on this," Franklin smiled.

"Here's what I think," he said. "If they keep this kind of chicanery up, we should figure out a way to use it to our advantage. Like, say, by leaving around phony evidence for them to find or, say, having people they might contact give them false leads for wild goose chases. Things that, if they ever were dumb enough to use to charge us with some kind of Patriot Act violation, we could use to show them to the world as the McCarthyist hatemongers they are."

"But who in heck do you think put them up to it?"

"I'm thinking just maybe supporters for someone who stands to lose the most if the USA-SBR gains even more traction. Supporters for someone who wouldn't want to look like a stodgy Wall Street establishment-type Presidential candidate in another four years."

"Maybe someone whose initials match the words Hyper-phony Republicanesque Cuntometer?"

"I was thinking more like Huge-butt Repellent Cookiebaker, but yours works too. Who knows?"

"So, we just watch our backs for now?"

"For now, unless they turn up the burner a notch or two."

* * *

NEW EXPEDITION: GETTING THE HANG OF THIS

Cookiebaker/Cuntometer debate notwithstanding, once finals were over for Franklin and Holly, the Poughkeepsians decided to depart for their latest rally tour, visiting Georgetown University, the University of South Carolina and Penn State University.

On this go-round, however, Pongo and Bianca both had to bow out due to employment obligations, what with the FDR facilities in Hyde Park being in their busy season and Bianca still without much earned paid leave time at her new Urgent Care Center job in Poughkeepsie. But, to Franklin's surprise, Holly decided to come along for the tour.

They decided to fly from New York City to Columbia (SC) Metropolitan Airport. From there, they would drive their full-size rental van north to Washington, D.C. and, finally to State College, PA before driving back to Pougkeepsie.

They held their usual routine: press conferences in late afternoon the day before the rally; there were the usual reminders by Franklin and Phil of the dangers of media consolidation.

In Columbia, SC, Phil lamented that the major daily newspaper there, The State, was part of a national chain of newspapers (McClatchy) rather than being locally owned, although he emphasized it appeared to be part of a chain devoted to reasonably good journalism and diversity of opinion.

In D.C., the Poughkeepsians questioned whether the rumored sale of the Washington Post to an internet billionaire was likely to lead to a return of the kind of quality investigative journalism which uncovered the 1972 Watergate plot to subvert a presidential election.

In State College, PA, the group again expressed sadness that the local paper (the *Centre Daily Times*) also was owned by a national chain (McClatchy), but praised the consistent quality of journalism practiced by the chain. For now.

Questions at each of the press conferences covered almost entirely the same ground that had been covered at previous press conference locations. There actually were few surprises, unless the group's consensus that the Southerner reporters were uniformly pleasant and polite could be counted as a surprise. Probably not.

Marcia pulled off a major coup in convincing Stephen Colbert to perform as the emcee for their rally at the Colonial Life Arena in Columbia, SC, where he was raised, on the condition that he perform in-character as though it were a Colbert Nation crowd, which, actually, it was. From start to finish (sitting behind a replica of his iconic Comedy Central desk), Colbert painted a "nightmarishly dark picture" of what could happen if the USA-SBR were someday ratified and made part of the U.S. Constitution. However, the nightmarishly dark picture was only nightmarishly dark in the way that the Newt Gingrich-themed parody sketch on Saturday Night Live of "It's A Wonderful Life" was nightmarishly dark. Which is to say, brilliantly optimistic (to anyone other than a corporate bean counter). The crowd was ecstatic.

Marcia took a different strategy for the Georgetown University rally at the Verizon Center arena: she managed to convince Joan Claybrook, formerly of Ralph Nader's Public Citizen organization, to be the guest speaker. She was more than up to the task: she led off by joking that the group had tried to get fellow Georgetown alumnus Jack Abramoff, but he was too nostalgic for his post-bribery-conviction pizza job he left two years earlier to consider the gig. Then she segued into how the USA-SBR potentially could forever eliminate incentives for lobbyists to manipulate politicians with money and fancy favors. The crowd tried to bribe her with ramen and clean underwear to do an encore. She obliged, but declined the bribes.

The rally at Penn State University in State College, PA posed a different challenge. Marcia finally decided to convince Rob Boston, an author on church-state separation issues who grew up in nearby Altoona, PA, to act as emcee for the gathering at the Bryce Jordan Center arena. She urged Boston, Communications Director for Americans United for Separation of Church and State, to try to broaden his presentation beyond church-state separation issues. He didn't disappoint.

Boston led off with praise for local State College, PA author James Morrow, whose humanistic-themed anti-war, pro-feminist fiction writing often probed inconsistencies in traditional religious philosophical underpinnings about the workings of the universe. There was a smattering of earnest applause; but, clearly, most in attendance weren't literature critics.

Boston then went on to focus on the threats which surely would be posed against passage and ratification of the USA-SBR by radical right-wing religious fundamentalist groups like the Family Research Council. He cautioned not to underestimate their organizational skills and reach. Specifically, he explained, they likely would go ballistic over provisions in the USA-SBR against blending of church and state, against limiting the civil rights of minorities, against prohibiting adults on record expressing bigotry from holding public office and against preventing same-gender couples from marrying.

As they listened to Boston's presentation, the Poughkeepsians couldn't help but feel a little disheartened. There had been the occasional organized protest against their efforts – such as in Utah and Idaho – but those protests had been relatively small and toothless. The picture painted by Boston now was one comparable to protests routinely held outside abortion clinics. Hyper-religious partisans are among the most radicalized persons within the human species, he said.

"*Oh, shit,*" Phil thought to himself. "*We should've prepared for this long ago.*" He envisioned significant expenses for a security staff presence at all of their upcoming rallies.

But, on the positive side, Franklin announced near the end of their rally that evening that a baker's dozen regional USA-SBR organizational offices would be opening in September around the country at leased brick-and-mortar locations in Washington, D.C., Atlanta, Los Angeles, San Francisco, Seattle, Chicago, Phoenix, Las Vegas, Richmond, Madison, Rapid City, Portland and Philadelphia. Marcia was spending perhaps 60 hours a week co-ordinating the hiring of office managers for each of the regional offices. Their primary goal would be to make educational appearances at high schools, universities, local government meetings, civic groups and local rallies, he said. (Privately, he worried how well those offices would be received in communities with large military bases; the USA-SBR was not military-industrial complex-friendly. Just conscience-exercise friendly.)

Their overnight stays and dining experiences during the road trip back from Columbia, SC to Poughkeepsie merged into a kind of blur, especially for those who were travelling with their significant others (like Franklin and Holly and Idris and Marcia). The compressed driving schedule usually meant everyone was too worn out at the end of the day for much in the way of recreation or physical intimacy. Which wasn't that bad: there weren't any National Parks along the way that they either hadn't already visited or thought were worth seeing, at least in the late spring.

The return home to Poughkeepsie on the Friday afternoon before Memorial Day was a huge relief even though, once again, Franklin was expected back at work at the following morning at Adams Landscaping.

∗   ∗   ∗

Meeting the 'Kenyan'-der in Chief; Romney's Bizarro Anti-Reality

T he month of June was unremarkable for the group: mostly mundane business-related preparations for the field office openings, the occasional drive to New York for media interviews and the weekly (at least) dates with their lovers, all juggled with full-time day job schedules.

Phil and Franklin decided on July 4 to hop in the car the following morning to drive to Pittsburgh so they could attend an Obama campaign rally on July 6. They managed to get spots in the crowd relatively close to the President – Franklin even had the privilege of briefly shaking the President's hand! The President briefly seemed to recognize Franklin and quickly said, as he walked away, "YouTube guy!" with a thumbs-up gesture. Franklin noticed none of the tell-tale fine sensillum-like fur on Obama, except a light coating on his ears – but Franklin suspected that was some natural middle-aged male random growth.

Franklin was pleased, if not viscerally gratified, with Obama's references during the speech to the good that government did for his grandparents and others – how he decided to be involved in government to give back some of what government had given him and his family. It was such a refreshing, non-cynical contrast to the classic Reagan remarks about government, brimming with contempt.

On the drive back to Poughkeepsie that evening, Franklin expressed his high hopes that a second term for Obama wouldn't feature the continued compulsive obstructionism from Republicans which was the dominant feature of Obama's first term.

"Wouldn't hold my breath on that, Sir," Phil said, grimly.

Eleven days later, on another whim, the two men decided at the last minute to drive to Irwin, PA to see Mitt Romney up close. Once again, Franklin – who went unrecognized, except for a brief high-five and fist bump from a couple of maintenance staff workers – was fortunate enough to be close enough to Romney to shake his hand. This time, however, Franklin was struck by the fairly dense growths of fine sensillum-like fur which protruded from Romney's collar, shirt-sleeves, pant legs, ears, nose, and even his palms. This, Franklin thought to himself, is one supremely financially self-focused human being. Then, while Romney gave his speech, as soon as Franklin started hearing Romney claim President Obama wanted to "punish success," Franklin tapped Phil on the shoulder.

"Let's shake the dust of this place off of our backs and get the hell out of here. These people reside in a different reality from everyone else."

As they were leaving, Franklin thought to himself that he wished there were snow on the ground, "so I could write 'ROMNEY=TAX-DODGING DICK' in big bold yellow letters." Alas, not much snow in Pennsylvania in July.

Their trip back to Poughkeepsie was long and boring, except for almost hitting an elk in western New York.

Four days later, however, as Franklin prepared to leave for work, he wished he could have some boring days back as he heard on the morning news radio report that a lunatic had shot 12 persons dead and wounded another 70 at an Aurora, CO movie theater the night before.

No motive. No reason. No logic. A lunatic with access to weapons. Nothing more. Nothing less.

Franklin went to work, depressed, but re-assured by the knowledge that Americans come together to do the right thing, to make sure no one like that shooter ever gains access to deadly firearms ever again. Never.

Pongo asked him later that day, after Franklin expressed the same sentiment to him, "Man, you been asleep the last 50 years or so? How could you think that?"

"Not asleep, just deceased."

Sure enough, in the days, weeks and months following the Aurora shooting, not only was nothing done to limit access to deadly firearms, but firearms sales nationally spiked. "Can't beat the lunatics? Hey, just join 'em!" Phil later opined.

As Franklin soon would learn, the National Rifle Association controlled so much campaign cash from its membership fees that elected officeholders of all political stripes – conservative, liberal, Tea Party, Independents, you name it – virtually every last one of them in Congress was in terror of voting in favor of restrictions on firearms access. Even for the mentally ill. In the end, no new law was passed.

Which was only appropriate, because passing such a new law might've cramped gun manufacturers' style so much that a certain little incident which occurred during Franklin's Marist College finals week the following December just might not have occurred.

But we'll get to that later.

After a crushingly hot, humid summer of work at Adams Landscaping, Franklin's enrollment at Marist College for the fall for his double major in Social Work and pre-med/pre-health went smoothly. He had no illusions about being able to coast through the science classes: it would take lots of hard work and late nights, as science was not his forte, except for the science of botany, especially involving trees. But he was determined to eventually have the option of becoming a physical therapist. He felt strongly about giving back to others the kind of support he received from *his* physical therapists 80 to 90 years earlier.

His Marist professors for Poly Sci and Social Work courses - who were well aware of his USA-SBR activities from YouTube videos, the USA-SBR website and the USA-SBR Facebook page – each recognized the importance of what Franklin/Percy and his associates were trying to accomplish. They didn't all agree with every detail of the USA-SBR, but, to a person, each of them wanted the Poughkeepsians to succeed.

In fact, each of them got together, separately, with Franklin and agreed to base 50 percent of his grade on his USA-SBR activities, while allowing Franklin to effectively choose his own curriculum for each class.

Franklin, however, demurred. He insisted that he be expected to fulfill the same coursework requirements that every other student in each class was expected to complete. Once again, though, to a person, each professor insisted that they were going to give Franklin/Percy extra credit for his USA-SBR work. Whether he liked it or not.

In fact, when he went to pay for his class fees, he discovered that one of those professors – aware that Franklin/Percy had been paying his own way through college to that point – had successfully applied on Franklin's behalf for a merit-based scholarship to cover all tuition and fees for the remaining two years of his undergraduate classwork.

As someone who'd never needed financial assistance in his previous iteration of life, Franklin was touched and humbled to the core by that level of caring. He vowed to himself to pay back every penny of the tuition and fees to Marist – anonymously if need be - once it was clear that the USA-SBR project no longer needed his support to thrive.

He continued to work 20 hours a week at Adams Landscaping through the fall semester while once again juggling time for his studies and weekly dates with Holly (which usually lasted from 8 p.m. Saturdays 'til just past noon on Sundays). As time passed he became more and more grateful for his basement apartment at the Podrowskis', not to mention their unexcelled ability to be discreet about his relationship. Although Pongo *did* keep asking Franklin how it was that Holly went from looking like a 23-year-old to resembling a molten-hot 16-year-old since their relationship had grown intimate. Not that there was anything whatsoever wrong with that, Pongo added, *emphatically*, under his breath.

"Y'see, Franklin, Sir, it's just that every time I see her around the house with you, I have to start thinking about wrinkly, saggy 95-year-old great-grandmothers to keep from having to sit down with my legs crossed. Whatever you two have been doing with each other, it's certainly given her a special, uh, er, uh, *ambiance*."

"Well, friend, I'm going to take that as the sincerest kind of compliment. Just please – again, *pleeeeze* – try to keep any thoughts you have about her to yourself, OK? I promise I'll do the same about Heather."

"It's a deal," Pongo said, relieved that Heather hadn't heard this particular conversation.

✳ ✳ ✳

KOCH-FREE DAILY SHOW: "THEY DON'T WATCH, THEY WON'T COME"

When October 2012 rolled around, Franklin took Pongo up on an offer to go and see the Daily Show again on Tuesday, Oct. 9, the day after Columbus

Day. As before, they lucked out and got two of the last six stand-by tickets for admission. The featured guest on the show was Ben Affleck, who directed the new hit movie, "Argo," about the rescue of six U.S. Embassy personnel from Iran in 1979 after they escaped capture by the Iranian Revolutionary Guard and were hidden by Canadians; the Iranians kept another 52 Americans hostage for 444 days.

During the pre-taping question-and-answer session between Jon Stewart and the studio audience, Franklin and Pongo noticed that an audience member suggested to Mr. Stewart that he might consider starting a nightly gimmick to try and shame the Koch brothers into appearing on his show. The same way David Letterman tongue-in-cheek shamed Oprah Winfrey nightly until she finally appeared on his show. The audience member said he was frustrated by the way the Koch family kept funding and influencing content on things like the PBS Nova program without ever having to be held accountable.

Stewart responded that he didn't think the Kochs ever bothered to watch his show and that, even if they did, he didn't think they'd be susceptible to that kind of gimmick. They simply wouldn't care what he or his viewers think about them, he said. It was up to people like his viewers, those in his audience, to try and hold the Kochs accountable.

But just after that, another audience member asked Stewart how he could just give up on the idea of trying to get the Kochs on his show, of trying to show them for what they truly are. If someone as influential as Stewart, the modern generation's Walter Cronkite, is so quick to give up on holding the Kochs' feet to the fire, then how can Stewart expect simple average folks like his audience members to make any headway? she asked.

Stewart said she might have a point, but insisted there was little he could do.

During the episode itself, Franklin enjoyed a brief pre-recorded piece by Jessica Williams reporting from Utah. The piece was about "mythical creatures, the unicorns of politics," black Mormons. During the piece, African-American Mormons argued with each other about whether to support President Obama; Jessica tried to get the interviewees to finish the "roof is on fire" hip-hop lyrics to determine whether they were more black or more Mormon. One female interviewee did finish, but without including the lyric "motherfucka." Jessica put her down in the "more Mormon" category. He could almost envision the fine sensillum-like fur on the African-American Mormon wearing a white shirt in the back row who kept carping about Obama adding to the national debt.

"Guess the poor guy just forgot about the trillion or two 'W' Bush added to the debt in the past decade for the Iraq war and rich peoples' tax cuts," Pongo whispered, laughing.

During the commercial break, they were treated to a brief off-camera in-person visit by Ms. Williams, who received a standing ovation.

"If I were an old-timey Mormon, I'd try to get her for my No. 2 girlfriend-slash-wife," Pongo said, clearly smitten. "Think Heather would mind?"

"You don't want to go there, partner," Franklin said.

On the way back to Poughkeepsie, the thing about the Kochs kept coming back to Franklin.

"I guess I don't get it. Jon Stewart is, arguably, the most influential person in the news business today. Even if what he does is called 'fake news,' it's more real than anything else on live television that I've seen.

"Why would he be backing down from that kind of challenge? Isn't taking on the super-rich who manipulate government what the founders **intended** for the press to do?"

"EllifIknow," Pongo said. "The Kochs do produce a lot of consumer goods, which means lots of potential TV ads. Maybe he just doesn't want to alienate a major source of income for his employer. For all we know, it might be in his contract."

"You don't really believe that, do you?"

"*SHIT*, no. But I couldn't think of anything else to say. I can't accept that my idol Jon is flawed in any way. I just won't." Pongo moved his fists up and down like a faux 2-year-old in tantrum mode as he said the words.

"OK, OK, I'll let it go," Franklin said. "Maybe the USA-SBR can do what even the cream of the television journalists can't."

"I fucking hope so, pardon my French, Sir."

✳ ✳ ✳

Hurricane Blows in Obama Victory, New Jersey Destruction & Another Blow to Global Warming Corporate Shill Deniers

Back at the ranch, so to speak, Franklin plowed ahead with his classes, with his work and with Holly; he always put his favorite plowing last, though – delayed gratification, as it's said, is a reliable habit of the most successful people.

Only 20 days after their visit to the Daily Show, though, the entire New York/ New Jersey area was inundated by Hurricane Sandy. Suddenly, the Republican global warming-denial election strategy didn't seem quite so brilliant. Especially when master corporatist New Jersey Republican Gov. Chris Christie appeared arm-in-arm with President Obama to thank him for FEMA crisis funding.

Within another few days, it appeared the President had a near lock on re-election. On election day, that lock was welded shut. Forever.

Pongo, Phil, Franklin and the rest of the USA-SBR crew, including Phil's parents, all watched the returns late into the night. But what they enjoyed most was watching the Daily Show the next day as Jon Stewart re-played FoxNews non-fact belchers repeatedly insisting that exit polls predicting Obama winning the State of Ohio were wrong, wrong, wrong.

Ooops on them.

Still, when the dust settled, the Poughkeepsians – and every other progressive-slash-liberal in the country remembered, somberly, that the U.S. House – thanks to grotesque gerrymandering in 2011 – remained in Republican control, despite more people nationwide voting Democratic in U.S. House races than Republican.

"At least that's another selling point for the USA-SBR and its anti-gerrymandering requirements," Tom Podrowski, smiling optimistically, told Pongo's Grandma Annie.

"You honestly believe people will remember that gerrymandering kept the U.S. House in the hands of the lunatic party?" Annie asked.

"It's up to our son and his friends to keep reminding them," he said, voice raised and aimed in Phil's direction on the other side of the TV room.

"She's got a point there, ladies and gentlemen," Franklin said.

And, over the following four years, they did their best to remind anyone who would listen. Which, sometimes, wasn't very many anyones.

∗　∗　∗

The Shots Heard Round the World: Jesus' Birthday Marred by Dead Innocents; Jesus: "Dad Let Me Down"

Franklin and Holly were just starting up their week of final exams at Marist when the next shocking, sobering national calamity occurred. It was Dec. 14, 2012. A day almost as shocking as that other infamous December day Franklin would always remember.

Franklin was on his way to meet Holly for a mid-morning soda between classes at about 10:45 a.m. at the Library Coffee Bar when they saw on a television screen a breaking news bulletin about an elementary school shooting about 60 miles east-southeast of Poughkeepsie at Newtown, Connecticut. The school name was Sandy Hook.

As they watched the story unfold, both Franklin and Holly – and just about everyone else at the coffee bar – started crying spontaneously. There were 26 victims at the school (not counting the shooter and the shooter's mother, killed by the 20-year-old shooter at their home perhaps a half-hour or so before the other murders). The victims included 20 children, ages 6 and 7 (12 girls and eight boys), along with six adults, including the school principal plus a behavioral therapist hired just a week earlier, all women. The shooter shot his way into the school past locked doors, using weapons that belonged to his murdered mother, who kept at least 10 firearms in her home and had trained the shooter how to use guns at a local firing range.

It later was reported by a former teacher of the shooter that he had an obsession with writing about battles, destruction and war. Investigators later discovered the shooter suffered from severe obsessive compulsive disorder, anorexia and Asperger's Syndrome. Published photos of the shooter showed an eerie resemblance between the shooter and the late anorexic singer Karen Carpenter. They also found that the shooter had written a Word document about the supposed inherent selfishness of women, according to Wikipedia.

"Surely, this time," Franklin told Holly, tears streaming down her face, "**surely** elected officeholders will stand up to the NRA lobby and put some kind of firewall between gun sellers and the mentally ill. SURELY, right?"

Not so much.

Shortly after the shooting, polling showed 92 percent of Americans favored new Federal laws requiring background checks of all gun buyers. But 92 percent simply wasn't enough for lawmakers, because 100 percent of NRA lobbyists opposed laws requiring background checks.

The weeks and months passed and Federal lawmakers failed to pass a single bill creating new barriers for purchases by potentially mentally ill gun buyers.

Christmas 2012 was the most somber holiday Franklin had experienced since Christmas 1941. Something about toddlers being murdered and servicemen being massacred in a sneak attack that just puts a damper on all the joy. His prayer just before the Podrowskis' Christmas turkey dinner was just what the doctor ordered. It was among his most tersely eloquent compositions.

"Dear Father in Heaven," he began, "help us not to abandon our faith in the justice and compassion promised through your love. Help the loved ones of those who recently lost their lives find some sense of meaning from those senseless acts. Something besides, 'it's a mystery we mere mortals can't grasp,' if you please? Please soften the hearts of the grieving and provide the comfort they need in a form they can understand. And please help us find a way to end mental illness in in the minds of the tortured souls you've allowed to come into this life."

* * *

Lone Star, Okie, Wassamatta State & 'Husker Travels: More National Parks

By the time New Year's Day 2013 was over, Franklin and the others simply wanted to get out of town and expend some of the energy from their pent-up frustrations by convincing people of the need for the USA-SBR. Privately, Phil worried that the group might just be too damned pissed off to be very effective with reasoned persuasion.

But they were heading to Texas: where reasoned persuasion sometimes goes to die – execution-style - and gut emotions often rule the day.

The day after New Year's Day the group boarded a Southwest Air Lines flight from New York to Austin, TX, where their rally tour would take them to the University of Texas-Austin, Texas A & M, University of Texas-El Paso (UTEP), Texas Tech University, the University of Oklahoma, Oklahoma State University, Wichita State University, Topeka, KS and the University of Nebraska-Lincoln.

They'd already had Marcia arrange not just for all their routine lodging, but also for a two-night stay near Big Bend National Park plus a two-night stay near Guadalupe Mountains National Park and Carlsbad Caverns National Park on their way to El Paso from College Station, TX. It appeared to be another exhausting couple of weeks on the way for the Poughkeepsians.

It was.

Their news conference in Austin featured reporters from the local American-Statesman, the city's daily paper; the Texas Observer, the regional monthly newspaper perhaps best known for its late columnist Molly Ivins and each of the city's local network broadcast affiliates, including PBS and NPR. Franklin and Phil once again thanked the local reporters for all their hard work, but lamented that the city's newspaper of record was yet another owned by an out-of-state chain (Cox Media Group).

"We just think it's pretty obvious that a local owner and publisher has the best grasp of the old pitchforks and torches concept," Franklin said. "That local owner is probably just a tad less likely to support something – like massive numbers of explosive oil train cars coming through the city or, say, a nuclear waste dump – which locals ferociously oppose.

"That said, though, it would appear at first glance that Cox has done a passable job keeping subscribers satisfied. Still waiting for that first Pulitzer, though, right?"

(Scattered laughs briefly ensued.)

"Well, at least they don't own both the paper and a couple of TV stations."

The USA-SBR questions were fairly predictable and the Poughkeepsians provided answers which appeared to address the reporters' curiosity head-on.

But then...

"Were you aware that a group of unidentified so-called consumer activists has decided to go negative on your efforts with local TV buys this past week?" asked Rip Majorca of the local PBS affiliate.

"No," Idris answered, stepping up.

"How does that affect your organizational strategy?" Majorca asked.

"That all depends on what the ads say. We hope our own ads these past two weeks have stated our case effectively," Phil said. "What do they say?"

391

"Their theme is that corporations and their stockholders are going to be hard-pressed not to raise consumer prices once higher taxes on corporations and the wealthy required by the USA-SBR take effect," Majorca said.

"Just a red herring," Phil said. "If you look back at the history of proposals to make the tax system more progressive, as in fairer to the non-wealthy, every single time the ultra-conservatives sound the knee-jerk alarm that prices will go up. Then when something else – like a spike in oil prices – causes inflation, they can falsely claim they were right.

"If they can't win on reality-based facts, they always resort to unfounded fears. The facts are that, once the wealthy are made to pay their progressive share of taxes, the government not only can stabilize the tax burden on the middle class, but it can better fund safety net programs for folks who've been laid off, not to mention public works programs – like highways, bridges and schools – which put people to work at living wage jobs.

"And those living wage jobs put lots of money right back into those business-es' pockets when people have enough *dinero* to buy their products and services.

"So, to answer your question, our strategy to cope with false, half-true and misleading negative ads by corporatists will be to quickly come to you members of the Fourth Estate to ask you to set the record straight.

"*And – just as importantly* – to ask you to ferret out whose money is really be-hind those phony ads. I suspect it might be money from someone whose surname rhymes with 'joke' and 'smoke,' as in the blowing kind.

"Once people know it's money from the same kinds of fat cats we've designed the USA-SBR to protect us from, we believe they'll see through the craven selfish-ness of the faceless billionaires who bought the ads."

The Texas Observer's reporter, Micah Tarantino, asked if a USA-SBR field of-fice might soon be opened in Austin or somewhere else in Texas.

"I can assure you the next field office we open will be in Texas," Franklin said. "We promise. It should be no later than the end of the year. I'm pulling for Austin."

The remaining questions covered no new ground, except to allude to the USA-SBR's intended effects of rolling back Texas Republicans' efforts to suppress votes of the poor and minorities while removing from office dozens of Texas lawmakers with past records of racist comments. But Franklin and the others pretended that they'd never heard the questions before and responded with en-thusiasm to each and every one.

The appearance the next evening by acclaimed movie director and Texas fa-vorite son Richard Linklater as the emcee of sorts was well-received by the crowd, to put it mildly. He received a five-minute standing ovation before he could even get a word out.

Linklater praised the portions of the USA-SBR which would make it easier financially for families to stay together and would reward their frugality. He also said he was proud of the way the USA-SBR would make it more likely people could avoid unjust consequences from breaking the law, especially the death penalty. He had unkind things to say about former Gov. Rick Perry's enthusiastic authorization of the 2004 execution of Cameron Todd Willingham, pointing out that investigations by both Rolling Stone and PBS' Frontline ("Death by Fire," 2010, followed by a 2014 update) appeared to show the evidence leading to Willingham's conviction was thoroughly bogus.

Linklater expressed hope that the USA-SBR's provisions would help protect working families from the soul-crushing avarice of soul*less* corporate behemoths, especially the behemoths which think nothing of laying off thousands of hardworking folks during mergers just to increase their stock price a few pennies or a few dollars per share.

"The good of the public at large, not just the good of a company's stock price, must be considered when the government decides whether to approve corporate mergers," he said.

The nearly-overflow crowd at the UT-Austin Frank Erwin Center rewarded Linklater's thoughtful remarks with yet another standing ovation. Franklin encouraged the crowd to remember to check out "this cinema rock star's new creations each time a new one appears, especially his latest, now on video, '*Bernie*,' with Jack Black – great non-fiction story, pure Texas gold." Hundreds lined up to intercept the 'rock star' on his way out of the center for his autograph when the rally was over. Linklater was gracious almost to a fault with his fans.

* * *

Reporters from the Bryan-College Station Eagle and the local television network affiliates out of nearby Bryan, TX appeared at the next day's news conference in College Station.

Once again, Franklin and Phil thanked the reporters for coming but expressed sympathy to the Eagle's reporter - who, bless his heart, definitely looked like he'd bought his work clothes at a Wal-Mart clearance sale - for having to be employed by an out-of-state billionaire's mega-corporation (Warren Buffett's Berkshire-Hathaway). The reporter was gracious, however, and re-assured them that none of the Berkshire paychecks had bounced – yet. And the reporter assured them that he'd seen no direct evidence of routine interference with news coverage from the parent company – at least as long as they continued to generate an advertising profit.

The main focus of the reporters' questions revolved around the USA-SBR's provisions to ban hydraulic fracturing – or fracking – for natural gas and oil extraction.

"Is there anyone here who believes it should be controversial to protect a clean supply of groundwater?" Franklin asked. "C'mon, let's see a show of hands.

"Alright, no hands? Then I'd say that seals it for today, at least: banning fracking is indisputably a good thing. We all need pure water to drink to survive – last time I Googled the words 'science + hydration for survival,' at least.

"Anyone here with any breaking news on how to survive without water? No? Alright, let's move on.

"No, wait, I forgot: without fracking, we'll have to get used to ground that just sits there and does nothing all over again. Yes, I know some of you will be missing the little bouncy-wouncy that fracking gives you in the middle of the night. Kinda makes the bedrock deep beneath your house come alive, doesn't it? Well, sorry, but we've got to satisfy these folks who are obsessive-compulsive about not having water that catches on fire."

The remaining questions, once again, had been heard by the Poughkeepsians multiple times on previous tours, but they'd gotten pretty darned good at pretending it was the very first time each one had been asked.

The next day's rally at Texas A & M's Reed Arena featured none other than the great Bill Moyers, PBS' most respected commentator of all time, nee press secretary to the late President Lyndon B. Johnson of Texas. A Baptist seminary graduate, Mr. Moyers could've kept the crowd enrapt for hours just by recounting the most interesting interviews he'd had on *Now with Bill Moyers*, *Moyers & Company* and on *Bill Moyers' Journal*.

Much to the crowd's delight, he did just that.

Most of the crowd got goosebumps as they listened to Moyers' inspirational discussion of FDR's advocacy for the Four Freedoms, freedoms upon which the USA-SBR was attempting a long-overdue expansion.

Perhaps the best received among the vignettes he shared were his recounting of how former Republican stalwarts – such as Kevin Phillips – had come on his programs to lambaste the latest obstructionist obsessions of the modern-day Republican Party and its members of Congress.

Many of the subjects Moyers recalled could've been lifted right out of the USA-SBR. Franklin was thinking that he just might have inadvertently transplanted Moyers' own words onto the USA-SBR after watching some of Moyers' PBS videos with the O'Learys a year or two earlier.

Moyers appeared so invigorated by the College Station crowd that, after his presentation was done, he spontaneously started helping Idris, Heather, Holly and Harry throw ramen noodles and clean underwear into the mostly 20- and 30-something crowd. They all noticed, though, that there were a significant number of people in their 50s, 60s and 70s who'd come to see the lion of PBS elder statesmen broadcasters – perhaps the only public affairs broadcaster more respected than the genius of so-called fake news, Jon Stewart.

The crowd was even more moved than usual by touching introductory remarks Moyers gave before the video memorial tribute to Sally. Moyers had always had a special place in his heart for victims of domestic violence, as he explained while recalling a 2009 interview he'd had with the president of a San Antonio domestic abuse shelter.

* * *

After Moyers finished shaking hands with his fans and well-wishers once the rally was over for the evening, he approached Franklin/Percy, apparently with some trepidation.

"So, I understand some of these folks call you Scruples," Moyers said.

"Yes," Franklin laughed, flashing a broad smile which now featured virtually perfect braces-free teeth, since he'd had them removed the week after Christmas. "I put up with it – I know they mean well."

"Well, I know what I'd call you, but you might not like it," Moyers said.

"What's that, a gasbag?"

"I'm pretty sure it'd be Franklin. Or, Mr. President."

Blushing a fairly bright pink, Franklin said, "No, my given name is Percy. Don't know if you've noticed, but I'm only in my mid-20s."

"No, I don't think you are. But I know I can't prove it, not right away, anyway. And I don't think I want to. I don't think I want to do anything that could imperil you or what you're trying to do with this.

"Maybe, someday, if I'm still on this side of the ground by that time, you'll feel safe enough to share with me what's happened to you, how you made your way back to us.

"No matter what happens to me, I hope you stay with us for a long, long time, Mr. President," he said, just above a whisper.

Franklin gave him a strong, silent embrace. The kind you give to a long-lost friend you know you might not ever see again. He didn't even notice when a tear of his fell off his cheek and onto Moyers' forehead, cascading down into Moyers' own eye, as their embrace ended.

"Preaching's loss has been the rest of the world's gain," Franklin said, pointing at Moyers' heart.

(Days later, Moyers woke up and saw a different face in his mirror, a face which was about 40 years younger, although his hair still was white. He remembered feeling that moisture from Franklin get into his eye. He was starting to put two and two together...)

* * *

The next day, they all rose early, early enough to be there when the very first of the continental breakfast set-ups was being done adjacent to the lobby of their hotel. They were on the highway barely an hour later, heading for Big Bend

National Park six-plus hours away, to spend that afternoon, all of the next day and all of the following morning taking scenic drives and hikes.

By the time the sun had set that day, they'd just about exhausted the batteries on their digital cameras and camera phones taking a combined total of perhaps 1,500 photos of sights along the Ross Maxwell Scenic Drive, including views from the Burro Mesa Cliffs Trail, the Mule Ears Viewpoint (where they hiked two miles to a verdant spring), Tuff Canyon (featuring steep but crumbly volcanic tuff formations) and the stark, sheer cliffs of Santa Elena Canyon, through which the Rio Grande flows smoothly. The group hiked a couple of miles up Santa Elena Canyon with inflatable rafts and then floated their way back. The water was too cold for comfort, but the scenery made up for it.

That night, they stayed at the Chisos Mountains Lodge near the Chisos Basin Visitors' Center so they'd be close to their starting point for the next morning's all-day hike. When they left the lodge at 8 a.m. the next day, they headed up the Chisos Basin Trailhead to the Pinnacle Trail and then on to the Emory Peak Trail (10.5 miles of rugged hiking round trip) to reach the peak's summit (7,832 feet above sea level), the highest point in the park. They were lucky: the weather was unseasonably warm, clear and dry – but seasonally windy, as in 60 mph windy. Harry lost his favorite Yankees cap as he was scrambling up the last bit of the trail to the summit. He blurted out an unusual wind-morphed version of the F-word expletive, but immediately said the view was worth it.

On their way back down the trail the middle of the afternoon, they saw several black bears about a hundred yards downhill, two whitetail deer, a mule deer buck, a coyote, two javelinas, dozens of jackrabbits, cougar tracks and what might've been fox tracks.

They also came across a young couple from El Paso heading toward the summit who were wearing Sierra Club sweatshirts and carrying backpacks with the same logo. One of them, the wife, said she recognized Franklin and Pongo from YouTube videos of one of their Montana rallies she'd seen. They both gave the group big thumbs up and encouraged them to "keep up the good fight." They also warned the Poughkeepsians about a cougar they'd seen following them as they came up the trail about a mile further back.

"Don't want you to become some mountain lion's Meow Mix," the husband said.

That night, back at the lodge, each of the Poughkeepsians was almost too tired to lift a finger, much less think about any amorous intentions. They each slept deeply and peacefully - even Franklin, whose dreams that night were about traipsing with Holly through flower-adorned meadows and free-flowing knee-deep streams.

Remembering that Big Bend was considered "a geologists paradise," the next morning, before making their way out of the park, they drove north from the Rio Grande Village Visitors' Center on the Old Ore Road to the trailhead leading to the Ernst Tinaja (tinaja means "large jar for liquid" in Spanish), a natural funnel-shaped 13-foot rock formation where water pools. The rockhounds in the group insisted on seeing it, mainly because it was the only formation of its type anywhere in the region. It did not disappoint – although they wanted really, really badly to jump into it. But that was *verboten* by the NPS (mainly because, when the water in it is low, it's almost impossible for a person to climb out of it).

Once they got their fill of the tinaja, they headed north to the Guadalupe Mountains National Park.

After staying overnight at the Whites City, NM (the word "city" is used very loosely here) Rodeway Inn, they headed out early the next morning from the park's Pine Springs Visitors' Center to the Guadalupe Peak Trailhead near the Pine Springs Campground.

Along the first mile of the trail, in the early morning hours, they saw another javelina, more deer and a raccoon rummaging around in the shade. They spent the next three-and-a-half hours hiking to the summit of the peak (the highest point in Texas, 8,749 feet above sea level), where, once again, despite otherwise near-perfect weather, there were near hurricane-force winds. After resting their calloused feet and taking scads of digital photos, including one of the entire group (except for the photographer, Phil) next to the summit monument, they headed back down the trail. About a mile or so from the original trailhead, they veered off to the north for the 2 mile hike to Devil's Hall. On the way there, they encountered the same El Paso couple they'd met the previous day.

"They just don't make these parks big enough, I guess," the husband laughed. "Glad to see the cougar didn't get to munch on any of you!"

When they arrived at Devil's Hall, once again, they were not disappointed: imposing rock walls, caves, natural rock stepping stones. They all wished the day could've been longer so they could've seen more. But, it was January. Daylight waned.

The next morning, they checked out of the Rodeway Inn and headed to the visitors' center at Carlsbad Caverns National Park's cave entrance. They opted to go on the King's Palace and Left Hand Tunnel guided tours. Pongo and Harry wanted to go on the guided Spider Cave tour, where significant crawling was required, but it wasn't scheduled for that day.

By the time they left the caverns about four hours later, all Franklin and the others could think about was when they might get to come back. As they strode through each tour, they were virtually dumbstruck at the majesty of the huge calcified limestone formations extending from the cave ceilings (stalactites) and growing up, drip by drip, over hundreds of centuries, from the cave floors (stalagmites). The expanse of time involved in the creation of such overwhelming mineral beauty was almost mind-numbing, something which made their silly little human lifespans seem as puny as a housefly's. But it was also something so viscerally compelling, like being able to grasp a century between your fingertips.

They drove on that afternoon to El Paso, TX for their 5 p.m. press conference at their hotel in advance of the next day's USA-SBR rally at the Don Haskins Center.

There were reporters present – all very young, but very bilingual – from the El Paso Times (owned by Digital First Media of Denver, CO) and each of the local network television affiliates – all but two of which (the ABC and PBS affiliates) were owned by out-of-town or out-of state corporations.

Franklin gave his standard gracious praise for the reporters' participation combined with his commiserations for the reporters having to answer to non-local ownership. Virtually all of their questions were repeats of questions from previous rallies. However, there appeared to be great anticipation for the guest speaker who had been recruited by Marcia for the El Paso rally: George Takei, best known as Mr. Sulu from the original Star Trek television series. She'd convinced Takei that appearing in El Paso for the USA-SBR cause would be an excellent way to honor the memory of Star Trek creator Gene Roddenberry, who was originally from El Paso.

Heather explained that backdrop to reporters, while adding that Takei probably intended to praise provisions in the USA-SBR which would make it impossible that there would ever again be anything like the internment camps where Japanese-American citizens like Takei and his parents were imprisoned during World War II. She added that he might have been mildly influenced by Marcia pointing out that two of the principal organizers behind the USA-SBR – including herself and Idris – had Japanese-American grandparents who were subjected to that same injustice.

It was clear, briefly, that at least a couple of the young television reporters present might have nodded off during their U.S. History classes when the subject of World War II internment camps came up. Franklin and the others could see them frantically doing internet searches on their smart phones as soon as the phrase internment camps was uttered.

* * *

The rally the evening of the following day brought out, for the first time, literally an overflow crowd. Perhaps a third of those attending were wearing Star Trek regalia, including lots of pointy Spock ears.

Mr. Takei, while proud to see that kind of fan respect and graciously grateful to all who took the time to attend, was quick to point out the serious goals which led to the rally even happening.

He reminded the attendees that, without the USA-SBR in place, it was, as of that very day, legal for businesses in some states to refuse to provide services to customers if they believed those customers' so-called lifestyles – as in homosexual gender orientation – contradicted the owners' personal religious beliefs. Just as egregious, he said, those same business owners might be allowed by the U.S. Supreme Court to refuse to provide contraception coverage to employees through their employer-provided health insurance – even if the coverage had $0 additional cost to the employer…something about preventing pregnancies that made some employers' pricks go limp for religious reasons. A case on exactly that issue was about to head to a Federal Court of Appeals, he explained, and probably would be fast-tracked to the U.S. Supreme Court.

The USA-SBR would, once and for all, stop all that idiocy, he said. At long last, public discrimination – against women, the elderly, homosexuals, transgendered persons, intelligence-challenged persons and everyone else it previously was OK to treat like shit – would go the way of the hulking, sluggardly, tail-dragging, tree-chomping dinosaurs. Of course, those 21st century dino-farters still could verbally bash anyone they wanted in the privacy of their own homes. Alone. Over a cold TV dinner. Watching Gilligan's Island re-runs.

The audience consumed Mr. Takei's presentation. With relish.

After the rally ended that evening, Franklin made a point of approaching Takei. Away from everyone else's earshot, he asked him what he remembered the clearest about his time in the internment camps. He asked him what happened to his parents. He asked if Takei and his family had ever been able to forgive President Roosevelt.

He whispered something to Franklin/Percy. Then Franklin whispered something back to him. Then the two men embraced. As they parted ways, Pongo could see a few tears rolling down Franklin's cheek. Pongo decided their conversation probably should remain private. He didn't ask Franklin about it. Franklin didn't spontaneously bring it up.

* * *

The next morning the group drove back up U.S. Route 62 to Lubbock, where they had a press conference scheduled at 5 p.m. in advance of the following day's rally at Texas Tech's United Supermarkets Arena. Franklin and Phil had wanted to take a side trip to see the still-radioactive Trinity Test Site where the first atomic bomb was exploded on July 16, 1945 on what's now the White Sands Missile Range, but Marcia nixed it: turned out the site is only open to tourists on the first Saturday of every April. (Can't have people traipsing around all that plutonium dust and getting themselves all glow-in-the-darky whenever they feel like it, Marcia explained…pesky ol' cancer, y'know.)

Reporters from the Lubbock Avalanche-Journal (one of 11 daily newspapers owned by Morris Communications of Augusta, GA) and each of the local network broadcast affiliates showed up at the Poughkeepsians' hotel meeting facility.

After the usual welcoming and sympathies for having to answer to out-of-state employers, the questioning began. Many of the questions revolved around the group's decision to convince Natalie Maines, nee of the Dixie Chicks, to be the featured speaker the following evening. Idris explained that she was a natural choice, as someone born and raised in Lubbock who graduated from high school there. Franklin remarked that they'd hoped there might be some focus on the recent Sandy Hook Elementary School massacre and what could be done to prevent a recurrence.

Once again, almost all of the reporters' questions had been fielded at previous press conferences, so the Poughkeepsians worked hard to appear candid and unrehearsed. The press session went smoothly and was over within 45 minutes.

The appearance by Ms. Maines the next evening was greeted with unmitigated wild enthusiasm by her hometown fans. She even surprised them by singing "Without You," "Not Ready to Make Nice" and "Taking the Long Way" to a karaoke accompaniment. But before she started, she dedicated her appearance to the children and teachers of Sandy Hook Elementary School and asked that everyone observe a moment of silence for the victims and their families.

When the standing ovation for her vocalizations subsided, she spoke about the importance of doing what's right, even when you're not sure everyone agrees with you.

"That's what these good folks from New York and their supporters all over this country are all about with the USA-SBR. It may not sound patriotic to admit that our country needs to be 'un-screwed.' But, if it's the truth, it's unpatriotic *NOT* to admit it.

"More important than that, it's undeniably crucial that we all try to get over this idea that we all need to out-patriotic each other. People who are all wrapped up in might supposedly always making right have re-defined patriotism in a sick way.

"It used to be that being patriotic simply meant showing courage on your country's behalf by doing what you know in your heart to be righteous. In the past 50 years, being patriotic's been re-defined to mean doing what warmongers want you to do, without questioning whether it's the right thing to do.

"If we can try to get back to that older meaning, maybe we can get ourselves right with the rest of the world. Maybe we can get to the point where most of the rest of the world doesn't hate us.

(Rousing applause ensued for more than a minute.)

"The USA-SBR is the kind of foundation upon which we can build that kind of courage. By keeping bigots out of government, by severely limiting how much money rich warmongers can contribute to campaigns, by making sure every single person 18 and older can vote, no matter how poor they are and no matter how brown or black they are, no matter whether they slept the night before on silky satin sheets or on wood chips in a railroad yard – the USA-SBR is an equalizer. It's the potion that gives the weakest kid in the schoolyard the strength to stand up to the bulkiest bully.

"It's the medicine we need to cure a critically ill system. Please have the courage and the energy to tell EVERY. SINGLE. ONE of your elected officeholders they need to actively support the USA-SBR if they want *YOUR* continued support at the polls.

"It's worth every ounce of effort you have. For the sake of your children and grandchildren if not your own."

(Another standing ovation began, lasting almost two minutes.)

Finally, motioning the crowd to calm down, she introduced Franklin, who went through each of the USA-SBR's provisions. When he was done, Natalie introduced the video memorial to Sally, encouraging all of the victims of domestic abuse in the audience to begin charting a different course for their lives starting the next day.

When the rally ended and all of Natalie's fans were done shaking her hand and getting her autographs, each of the Poughkeepsians gave her a huge hug and thanked her profusely. They made her promise to drive up from her New York City home to Poughkeepsie the next chance she had for an extended visit, including a tour of FDR's Springwood home.

* * *

The next morning they loaded themselves into the van for the five-hour drive to Norman, OK for their 5 p.m. press conference at that day's hotel meeting facility, in advance of the next day's evening rally at Lloyd Noble Center.

They arrived three hours early, giving each of them plenty of time for a two-hour siesta. Some of them used the siesta time to exchange bodily fluids, particularly Marcia and Idris – which led to a moderately embarrassing moment when one of Marcia's adult children showed up unexpectedly at her hotel room door 90 minutes later. ("Just thought I'd come and see in person what all this YouTube excitement is about, Mom! Hey, that some Victoria's Secret special there? Uh, who's that squirming around under the sheets??") Some pleasant surprises are less pleasant than others, Marcia thought. But most everyone else just snoozed away on the pleasant January day in central Okie-land.

Reporters at the press conference included Dusty Magnitudinale of the Oklahoman (a daily paper owned by Denver, CO billionaire Philip Anschutz) plus an assortment of 20- and 30-something reporters from each local television network affiliate, plus a local NPR affiliate reporter.

Same routine: introductions, bienvenidos to everyone and sympathies for having to work for rich out-of-state people. This time, in addition to all of the usual questions – including the now, sadly, routine questions about negative TV ads funded by unknown Koch-like anti-reform groups – a main focus was on the guest speaker Marcia had recruited a month earlier: Brad Pitt, a native of Shawnee, OK who, like fellow Oklahoma native Bill Moyers, was raised a Southern Baptist, and was a former journalism student.

What would Brad be telling the legions of his fans at the Lloyd Noble Center the next day? they asked.

"EllifIknow," Franklin said, smiling. "Whatever he wants, I guess."

(The journalists all laughed.)

"Actually, we're hoping he feels like focusing on the USA-SBR's provisions to ban discrimination, to make health care more affordable and to compel wealthy individuals and corporations to finally pay their fair share of taxes so our country can afford to do good in the world once again – like for overseas disease epidemics – instead of constantly waging war."

Brad did just that the next evening. And he even brought along his lovely wife and beautiful children, who listened enrapt to their beloved daddy address the adoring mass of humanity. Although the mass of humanity had a couple of spontaneous giggling outbreaks as they noticed Pitt's 4-year-old twin son and daughter alternatively doing some deep nose-mining and tickling each other.

"Geez, if I ever go into stand-up, I need to bring them along for the jokes that go splat."

Brad went on to emphasize just how much good the U.S.A. could do for the world when the USA-SBR's provisions to get money out of elections lead to military-industrial complex whores getting voted out of Congress. "We spend as much on our military now as do the next ten largest countries combined. We spend *five times as much* on our military as China does on its – even though China has more than **FOUR TIMES** as many people as the U.S.A.

"And we do all that spending on the tools of death with the wealthiest individuals as well as the corporate overlords in our country paying a nearly record-low proportion of overall tax collections.

"What's wrong with this picture?"

The crowd started the "Fuck O-ver-LORDS!" chant, but Brad quickly motioned them to be quiet, pointing at his little ones nearby.

"Sorry, folks, let's keep this one PG-rated tonight, OK? For the munchkins' sake, not for your friendly neighborhood corporatists."

The crowd, embarrassed, happily complied, quickly switching to: "Screw O-ver-LORDS!" "Screw O-ver-LORDS!"

"Way better, y'all!" Brad yelled, gratefully, over the shouts.

As was normal, Franklin went on to highlight the USA-SBR details, occasionally exhibiting his penchant for passionate rhetoric. When he finished, Brad gave the introduction for the video memorial for Sally. His voice cracked as he spoke of an unidentified actress friend of his who also had been a victim of domestic violence.

Once again, the evening ended on a successful note: a happy crowd, many with autographs in hands which wouldn't be washed for a day or two (to preserve that Hollywood hunk's touch, of course); massive stacks of USA-SBR copies distributed and thousands of signed pledges to contact elected officeholders to compel their support for the USA-SBR.

These Poughkeepsians – they were getting pretty good at this.

* * *

The next day, they all got to sleep late, as they only had a comparatively short drive to Stillwater, OK for that afternoon's press conference in advance of the next day's rally at Oklahoma State University's Gallagher-Iba Arena.

Reporters showing up for the press gathering included Peaches McTavish of the Stillwater NewsPress (a daily paper owned by Community Newspaper Holdings of Montgomery, AL), plus a handful of television reporters from network affiliates operating out of Tulsa. (Phil was tempted to ask if they all were 'living on Tulsa time,' but thought better of it. *"Guess it wouldn't be the first time they heard that one, you numbnut,"* he thought to himself.)

Yet again, there were all the same questions usually asked at their press conferences. The local reporters actually appeared offended at the vitriol in the negative ads being run against the USA-SBR. One of the reporters asked if the organizers wanted to go on record with an admonishment for Chesapeake Energy's Chairman of the Board Aubrey McClendon, the self-proclaimed "World's Biggest Fracker," whom local media speculated might be behind the ads because of the USA-SBR's ban on fracking. (Narrative intermission: four months later, the Chesapeake Energy Board of Directors booted McClendon from his post after revelations of an unauthorized $1 billion "loan" he approved for himself from company funds.)

"That would be shamefully premature," Franklin said. "There are so many possible suspects who could be behind the blatantly false and malicious TV and radio ads, there's no way we could consider any particular individual as a likely culprit at this stage. After all, this negative advertising has been going on for a while now in several states, not just states where Chesapeake does business. OK, well, **mostly** in states where they do business, but that doesn't mean anything.

"So let's just let this one die a natural death for now, OK? Our business manager Marcia has distributed to you a press release which categorically debunks every single detail of these phony negative media ads. If there are any of the points we've addressed in the handouts which are unclear, please feel free to ask us about them now, OK?"

They didn't; the reporters considered the ads debunked and their coverage over the next two days spelled out the debunked falsehoods.

The remaining few questions were about why they'd chosen two guest speakers – Wes Studi and Kristin Chenoweth - for the next day's rally instead of the usual one.

Phil explained that both Studi and Chenoweth were native Oklahomans who grew up and graduated from public schools in the state and had Native American backgrounds (Chenoweth is one-quarter Native American). Both have a keen appreciation for the effects of discrimination, whether it's for racial slights they've known personally or same-sex preference discrimination victims who were close to them. Likewise, he said, both had witnessed firsthand the effects of poverty during their formative years. They both understand the true meaning of the Golden Rule, he added, and believe in the positive things government can accomplish when those in charge don't conspire for it to fail.

Franklin encouraged all of the reporters to attend the rally and meet the speakers in person.

*　*　*

The gathering the next evening at Gallagher-Iba wasn't overflowing the way the attendees were for Brad Pitt and Natalie Maines, but there were significant numbers of Native Americans who'd apparently driven long distances to see, primarily, Mr. Studi, who had received praise for his performances in multiple movies (including *Dances With Wolves, Mystery Men,* etc.) and television roles (playing Lt. Joe Leaphorn in the PBS films *Skinwalkers* and *A Thief of Time*). And it appeared a large contingent from Ms. Chenoweth's hometown, Broken Arrow, had driven the 85 miles to see her in Stillwater.

The pair took turns praising their favorite parts of the USA-SBR. Mr. Studi recalled his first-hand experience of harsh discrimination at Wounded Knee, SD from late February through May of 1973. Had there not been hard-core bigots controlling the levers of government from the earliest days of the country through that time, he said, it would've been far more likely that the U.S. would've fulfilled its treaty obligations to Native Americans whose lands and buffalo had been stolen under the color of law. The USA-SBR's ban from holding public office on persons with records of bigotry during adulthood is long, long overdue, he said.

Chenoweth echoed those sentiments, recalling how several of her friends who were gay had repeatedly suffered malicious attacks on their character throughout their lives.

"This is 2013, not 1813," she said. "We should be way past the point where there's any excuse whatsoever for giving someone who's gay anything less than full respect or anything less than the widest opportunities to fulfill their chosen goals and their chosen relationships.

"Telling someone they can't marry the gay love of their life is like telling someone they can't have two legs because their skin is brown. It's just stupid mean for no reason other than to be mean.

"The USA-SBR would compel people to treat each other like real grown-ups. Or face consequences."

Then she did something that surprised not just the audience, but the Poughkeepsians too. She broke into a song she composed herself during the previous week as a tribute to the USA-SBR; unknown to the organizers, she'd arranged with the audio-visual director at the arena to play pre-recorded music for the song on her cue. She tore away the quick-release outfit she was wearing to reveal a Yankee Doodle-style outfit with a red, white and blue twirlable cane. As she sang, she danced her own self-choreography to the song, which took advantage of her amazing four-octave vocal range.

Not only did Harry manage to get the performance on digital video, but hundreds of supporters in the audience did likewise on their phones.

When she finished her performance, the entire arena erupted into cheers with a standing ovation. Within 30 minutes, the performance was on YouTube, the USA-SBR website and 5,000 Facebook pages. Within a day, it had gone viral with 100,000 hits. With Chenoweth-Cute (and talent) on your side, you just can't go wrong, Phil said that night, the obvious understatement of the year.

After the rousing response to her performance, Mr. Studi introduced Franklin for the specifics of the USA-SBR. "How in the Wide, Wide World of Sports do you follow that, Percy?" he asked.

"Not sure if I have any choice," Franklin/Percy laughed.

When Franklin finished, Mr. Studi returned to the podium and gave the introduction for the video memorial to Sally. He reminded the many Tribal members present at length that their isolation on reservations was no excuse for not dealing with domestic violence.

The rally concluded with another crush of autograph-seeking, handshake-seeking fans. Some of whom even wanted autographs from Pongo, Franklin/Percy and the others they'd seen over the past year-plus on YouTube. There was an abundance of adulation and commiseration over the negative ads by the phantom opposition bankroller(s).

Needless to say, the Poughkeepsians all slept the sleep of deserved accomplishment that night.

∗ ∗ ∗

The following morning they made their way up Interstate 35 north to Wichita in advance of the next day's rally at Wichita State University. The rally promised potentially to be in the most contentious setting yet for them for at least three reasons:

- First, there had been advance negative press – mostly among local network television affiliates – in which local media flacks for area aviation companies had painted a doomsday scenario for their industry if the USA-SBR were to be ratified. Seemed they were assuming the requirement for non-fossil biomass renewable fuels for aircraft engines meant it would be impossible to create such engines, even with a significant lead time for conversions.

- Second, the rally for the proposal which would ban fracking was to take place in the national hotbed of fracking activity – at an arena named for Charles Koch, no less.

- Third, Marcia had arranged for the featured speaker to be one of the national celebrities arguably most associated with opposition to fracking,

Matt Damon, whose anti-fracking movie, *"Promised Land"* had just been released a couple of weeks earlier.

So, when the reporters from the Wichita Eagle (a daily owned by McClatchy Co. of Sacramento, CA) and each of the local network television affiliates (all - except the PBS affiliate - from stations operated by out-of-state conglomerates) showed up for their 5 p.m. press conference at one of the Wyndham Garden Hotel's meeting rooms, the tension in the room wasn't just palpable, it was electric.

Phil gingerly introduced the Pougkeepsian USA-SBR organizers and extended compliments to the Eagle's reporter, Kelsey Ryan, for her paper's relatively even-handed coverage of fracking issues.

Then the questions started flying, hot and heavy.

The repeated theme, especially from the 20-something local television reporters, was that thousands of Wichitans would end up being laid off if the USA-SBR someday were to be ratified, victims of the inability of the industry to meet requirements for engines propelled by renewable biomass fuels.

Franklin jumped right in: "Not only would there not likely be layoffs, there probably would be an employment boom. There would be an urgent demand for new aircraft and new aircraft engines to meet the USA-SBR requirements."

But it's not clear the technology for those engines even is possible, the reporter said.

"Au contraire, mon ami," Franklin smiled. "Check it out: major state universities, like Washington State University in Pullman, already are working on technology to allow jet engines to burn biomass fuels from logging and sawmill waste products and other similar source materials.

"This not only is going to happen it NEEDS to happen. Don't know if any of you have noticed lately, but the world is becoming a warmer and warmer place. More than 97 percent of climate scientists keep warning us that the CO_2 from burning fossil fuels is a recipe for climate disaster. Virtually all of the remaining 3 percent or so of climate scientists have ties to the fossil fuels industry.

"And as global warming progresses, droughts in Kansas and throughout the Midwest will become longer and more severe, putting the water that's accrued over thousands of centuries in your aquifer under more and more stress.

"Which brings us to fracking: if you like clean water which doesn't catch fire, you really want to avoid fracking. Check out the documentary movie, *"Gasland."* It may be nice to have a big check from leasing out the ground under your home for fracking, but it's getting harder and harder to drink natural gas. Tried a glass of methane the other day – just didn't go down smoothly...maybe it was the vintage.

(Handful of camera operators and two reporters laughed loudly at that one – then saw the frowns on their colleagues' faces. Back to crickets.)

"And another little problem with fracking – besides all the carcinogenic chemical crap they pump into the ground from their wastewater – turns out it causes earthquakes. Everywhere they do it."

Why should Kansans in the aviation industry whose jobs could be on the line believe a small group of mostly 20-something folks from Poughkeepsie? a reporter asked.

"Because our veracity has nothing to do with where we're from," Pongo chimed in. "This isn't a theme we've drummed up just for Wichita. Check us out. We've been driving home the truths behind the USA-SBR everywhere we've been. And millions of hard-working folks all over the country have come to realize that it's corporatists and their greed-based fear-mongering which are endangering the very future of human habitation on this planet.

"I mean, what difference will it mean to have a job building an old-technology fossil-fuel burning jet engine if the only water left to drink is heavily contaminated with fracking carcinogens *and* recycled from urine?

"And what difference will it mean to have that job if the outside temperature is 130 degrees Fahrenheit and your employer can't afford to cool your workspace below 95 degrees because energy needed for that cooling comes from sources which ratchet up CO_2 and make the climate-warming feedback loop even worse?

"So, these corporatist employers are pretty good at spreading fear about losing paychecks, but the fear they really SHOULD be stoking is over what happens if they do nothing to moderate their carbon footprint on the planet."

"That's right," Franklin said. "Those protesters planning to brandish scary signs tomorrow about losing paychecks – if all I'd heard from my employer was that these 'out-of-state commie agitators' want you to lose your jobs, well, Christ help me, I'd be doing the same thing.

"On the contrary, we're using the USA-SBR to sound the alarm to _prevent_ hard-working folks from losing their livelihoods over corporatists' intransigence.

"For this civilization – not just in our beloved America, but *all over the planet* – for this civilization to be saved from the planet's surface becoming a scalding, unlivable Venus, we have to depend on the news media and enlightened social media to inform the public of the reality of what's ahead if corporatists aren't motivated to change.

"If they knew what we know, your children and grandchildren would demand nothing less."

The reporters appeared a little less hostile than when the conference began.

The Poughkeepsians answered their questions about why they'd offered the guest speaker spot to Matt Damon, explained why it was important to severely restrict the financial influence of billionaires like the Kochs on elections and then urged the local press to see the next day's rally in person.

Almost all of them did. Although there was at least a half-minute of the next day's coverage on each broadcast news station devoted to images of Tea

Party-style middle-aged couples protesting "Comie soshalist ley-off agitaters" outside the arena carrying signs with multiple misspellings of words more than four letters long.

The arena crowd was among the smallest the Poughkeepsians had seen on their latest rally tours: perhaps 5,500 persons, about 100 of whom were noisy, heckling protestors. Late-arrivers – mostly under-50 women who hoped for an up-close handshake with the featured speaker – eventually swelled the crowd to about 7,500.

Mr. Damon delivered his presentation with class. He encouraged everyone present to see the fracking-related movie "*Promised Land,*" if only to gain a greater appreciation for its classic theme dating back to Biblical times: that short-term large financial gain often is at the expense of long-term negative consequences.

As a surprise to everyone, he announced that, out of his own pocket, he'd purchased 5,000 copies of "*Gasland,*" which would be distributed free to everyone, first-come/first-served, as they left the arena later that evening. He pleaded with everyone to share their free copy with a friend, neighbor or extended family member once they watched it themselves.

Later on, most of them did just that.

He pointed out during his presentation that the USA-SBR's goals appeared to be very much the same as the foundation ONExONE, which is devoted to improving lives of at-risk children in the U.S.A., Canada and elsewhere, as well as other causes he's supported including Water.org and Feeding America.

He predicted that, if the USA-SBR someday were to be ratified, income inequities, taxation inequities, education inequities and health care inequities throughout the nation likely would be minimized if not altogether eliminated.

He urged the attendees to learn to recognize the true existential threats ahead from climate change and dwindling worldwide food and fresh water supplies, while at the same time learning which fears trumped up by corporatists and their FoxNews shills deserved to be ignored.

Except for the 100 or so hecklers scattered around the crowd, Damon's earnestness was recognized and appreciated by every soul in attendance.

After Franklin's detailed step by step analysis of the USA-SBR, Damon was gracious enough to give a heartfelt introduction to the video memorial to Sally, followed by an introduction to "*Capitalism: A Love Story.*"

Everyone, except for about half of the hecklers, stayed to the very end.

As the movie ended, Damon stepped up to the microphone and yelled out, "Warren for President, 2016!!" (But most of the Kansans in attendance didn't know much about Sen. Elizabeth Warren at that point.)

* * *

CLOSE ENCOUNTERS OF THE VICIOUS KIND

P rotestors notwithstanding, the Poughkeepsians were prepared to count their Wichita visit as another success. Until they were exiting the arena, that is. As Marcia, Heather and Franklin passed a small group of protestors in their late teens or early 20's while they were walking down steps leading to the parking lot, one of the protestors – wearing an "Obama=Chimpanzee/Nugent=Chief Squaw Fucker" T-shirt – lunged first at Marcia and then at Franklin, slashing a deep cut across the top of Marcia's left forearm and then stabbing deep into Franklin's side just above his left waist. Heather got a good camera phone photo of the assailant and of the getaway truck before he dashed away and jumped into the back of a beat-up mid-'70s Ford F150 pick-up.

Franklin was bleeding profusely, but within a minute the deep puncture wound stopped bleeding and tissue promptly grew back over the wound, just leaving a wide scar. Meanwhile, Marcia's bleeding stabilized as Heather put pressure on the cut. Pongo, who was just running down the steps to Heather as the attacker was being driven away, called 9-1-1 on his cell phone and gave the 9-1-1 operator the getaway truck's license plate number.

A Wichita Police cruiser arrived within five minutes; an ambulance arrived two minutes later and rushed Marcia to Via Christi Hospital, where she was treated and released, with a dozen stitches on her arm. The group decided not to disclose Franklin's wound to police investigators or medical staff – simply because it would be impossible to explain how a life-threatening injury healed itself in less than five minutes.

Within about 45 minutes, police had found both the getaway truck, the driver and the other two passengers, including the stabber, who would be charged with first degree assault with a deadly weapon for the attack on Marcia. The attacker, "Gootchie" Gunderson, a 22-year-old white high school graduate who'd been a "solid-C" student, would later plead guilty to second degree assault with a deadly weapon and receive a five-year prison sentence. Turned out he was a machinist with two years of experience at a private non-union aviation plant named Winger's Waddlers (some kind of take-off on Howard Hughes' Spruce Goose multi-engine airplane) and his boss had been spewing verbal excrement around their workplace about the Poughkeepsians for a week before the rally organizers arrived in Wichita.

After agreeing to his plea bargain, the attacker told police he used a knife because existing criminal law could've given him a dramatically increased prison sentence if he'd used a gun.

During extended questioning, though, Gootchie was constantly worried police would ask him about the odd middle-aged man in plaid pants who'd approached him 10 days earlier with $5,000 cash in exchange for a "disfiguring attack" on one or more of the Poughkeepsians. Gootchie had found a manila envelope with the cash taped to the steering wheel of his pick-up the day before the rally; he'd promptly buried the cash in a coffee can next to the crumbling masonry barbecue grill in his back yard. He knew that, even if he were arrested, the cash probably would still be there once he was released.

But he need not have worried: every single investigator simply assumed Gootchie was acting out of loyalty to his employer. Gootchie was only too happy to nurture that assumption. It was the only kind of nurturing he understood, unless you count an obsession with self-stimulation while playing every iteration of Grand Theft Auto.

What Gootchie didn't know was that, once he'd been in prison for a week, Mr. Plaid Pants would arrange through his Department of Corrections contacts for Gootchie to be alone with Buford Opelousas, a middle-aged lifer convicted for road rage murders of two teenage high school seniors, in a remote corner of the prison library late one Saturday afternoon. Buford thought anyone with a goofy nickname was a queer who might feel free to engage in some backdoor anal lock-picking whenever Buford dropped his shower soap. DOC staff knew this from previous beatings by Buford. This time, they made sure Buford found a premium Buck knife on a chair across from where Gootchie was reading a magazine article about cures for genital warts. When Buford saw the magazine article title over Gootchie's shoulder, he knew his plan to make Gootchie extinct – originally by strangulation – was a vision from God. Before Gootchie could look back to see what this heavy-breathing 6-foot-3, 280-pound homophobe was doing, the 8-inch blade of the knife was plunged into Gootchie's back all the way to the hilt, severing his inferior vena cava. Slightly more than two minutes later, Gootchie's potential ability to bear witness against Mr. Plaid Pants was somewhat impaired. Mainly because he would never breathe again.

The DOC's investigation into how Buford came up with the knife fell apart when the knife went permanently missing the day after the attack. Custodial staff were blamed for "accidentally" leaving the evidence room unlocked overnight.

The assault on Marcia was just a small sidebar next to the Wichita Eagle's main coverage of the rally the morning after the attack. But local network TV affiliates led their late news broadcasts with the stabbing, making it sound like some re-telling of "In Cold Blood."

It bled. It led. What else is new?

Before long, though, the Wichitans had mostly forgotten the minor stabbing and water cooler talk at area aviation companies was about the possibility of increased hiring and long-term career security from business demand for new distilled biomass deriviatives-fueled jet engines, rather than about fears of layoffs.

✳ ✳ ✳

The next morning they embarked on the next-to-last drive of the tour, to Topeka, KS for the rally scheduled the next day at Landon Arena there. They'd invited news media from Topeka, Manhattan and Lawrence to attend that afternoon's press conference at their hotel's meeting facility.

They didn't really expect the reporters from the Lawrence Journal World or the Manhattan (almost daily) Mercury to show but, sure enough, they both did, along with a reporter from the Topeka Capital-Journal. Both the Journal World and the Mercury were locally owned (the Capital-Journal was owned by Morris Communications of Augusta, GA), so Franklin elected to skip the spiel about how sorry he was they had to answer to out-of-state owners, even though all of the area television network affiliates were owned by out-of-state interests. Instead, he took the opportunity to praise the owners of the Journal World and the Mercury for their devotion to their local communities and their determination to stick with a profession which didn't always lead to affluence.

"And, no, ladies and gentlemen, this is not some craven strategy to suck up to those two newspapers," he said. "We really mean it. And, if there's anyone from Gannett here in the room, we just hope your corporate overlords will be nice to us."

(Lots of genuine laughs broke out briefly.)

The Poughkeepsians answered the usual assortment of questions about their 38-page proposed Constitutional Amendment. When one of the reporters asked if the Poughkeepsians agreed with the treatise in Thomas Frank's "*What's the Matter with Kansas?*," Harry quipped, "I always thought there was nothing the matter with Kansas that a nice ocean beach, a Disney amusement park and an alpine ski resort wouldn't fix."

(Lots of genuine laughter, but a little briefer...like they'd all heard that one sometime in their past.)

"Seriously, though," Franklin said, winking at Harry, "one of the main points of Mr. Frank's book was that life in Kansas for the middle class and the working poor is tough. He said it's tough partly because well-paying union jobs are almost extinct and because the Republican Party power structure has been so successful here in slashing tax collections, which has forced the social services safety net to be shredded.

"One of the goals of the USA-SBR is to compel Federal, state and local governments to return to the tried and true best method of funding government and stimulating the economy: the progressive income tax, which takes a disproportionately larger amount from the rich simply because the wealthy have many, many times the amount they need to live a comfortable life.

"They can afford it.

"The middle class and working poor cannot afford to be nickeled and dimed to death by higher and higher sales taxes, user fees, gas taxes, property taxes and so forth.

"The USA-SBR would change all of that. It would make taxes, once and for all, a matter of fairness. The revenues the government had in the 1950's and early 60's which were used to build interstate highways and bridges would come back. And, you know what? Rich people would stay rich – because that's what they do."

The final question was about the next day's featured speaker: Marcia had convinced environmental law activist Erin Brockovich – played in the movie of the same name by Julia Roberts – to appear.

"Why her, you ask?" Phil said. "Because she's demonstrated over more than a decade that she appreciates how people without a voice can be abused by huge corporations, how a massive, heartless corporation can simply render hundreds of families' homes virtually worthless. Just to make a corporate buck.

"She knows what fracking is doing to family farms and homesteads in this state. She knows we're trying to change that.

"Plus, she was born in Lawrence and she went to college down the road in Manhattan. She's a born and bred Kansan."

That last part satisfied the local journalists.

✳ ✳ ✳

The evening of the next day, Ms. Brockovich arrived just a few minutes before the rally was set to begin. She explained that she'd been interviewing a family in a neighboring county who suspected that a nearby fracking well had ruined their groundwater. They'd contacted her on her website after hearing she'd be in Kansas that day.

"No rest for the wicked," she laughed.

Her presentation, which recounted her efforts to hold chemical and energy companies accountable for the pollution they inflicted on average folks in several states, was well received. The Poughkeepsians could tell that the audience genuinely appreciated Ms. Brockovich's shared Midwestern roots. They seemed convinced she wouldn't mislead them.

Which was even more gratifying to the organizers as they heard her give kudos to them for the provisions of the USA-SBR which would make the EPA and U.S. Justice Department more accountable to aggrieved individuals.

"When the USA-SBR is ratified someday, you will be able to go on line on your computer and get instructions on how to submit a true bill of indictment to a sitting Grand Jury. And the Prosecutor will have to respect the Grand Jury's wishes about whether to investigate your true bill and whether to go forward with an indictment.

"And, if a Prosecutor fails to do her or his duty, her or his due diligence, that Prosecutor would be subject to criminal charges under Federal law.

"How's them apples for ya'? Sorry, didn't mean to sound like Sarah Palin, there. 'Course, y'know I'm not her. She'd be trying to find a definition for the word indictment right about now."

("*Go, Erin!*" several different 20- and 30-something men cheered from the crowd.)

"What gives me the greatest hope about the USA-SBR is the prospect for holding big corporations accountable," she continued. "Once this is ratified (holding up a copy of the USA-SBR), corporations once again **won't** be the same as flesh and blood human beings. Normal people – the ones like us who don't sit on the Supreme Court – we always *knew* corporations weren't real flesh and blood. Makes you wonder if at least some of those Supremes are some kind of artificial intelligence robotty Terminator type lawyers.

"What we need is an anti-corporatist Terminator Ahhnuld to come back and take out some of those creeps!"

("*Erin rules! Erin rules!*" echoed again from the young men in the crowd.)

By the time she was done, the Poughkeepsians thought she'd stirred up enough anti-corporatist testosterone to fuel the USA-SBR for at least another year or two.

They just might've been right.

By the time they returned to their hotel rooms that night, the Poughkeepsians found at least three different offers from Kansans to operate and staff a USA-SBR field office in Wichita or Topeka for the foreseeable future. (Of course, there were also a couple of complaints on the website about the "real" Erin Brockovich not being at the rally – from people who thought Julia Roberts actually was going to be the speaker.)

* * *

The final leg of this rally tour started the next morning, when they gassed up the rental van they now had and headed north to Lincoln, Nebraska in advance of the next day's rally at Pinnacle Bank Arena on the University of Nebraska campus.

Their press conference in their hotel's meeting facility was set for the usual 5 p.m. start time. Which was good, because it gave them time to get the flat they had 50 miles south of Omaha fixed.

When they arrived at the meeting facility an hour early, the reporter from the Lincoln Journal Star (a daily paper owned by Lee Enterprises of Davenport, IA) already was there working on something on his laptop. Franklin went ahead and handed him a copy of the USA-SBR, which he accepted, although he said he'd already read it – he said he wanted a copy just for his managing editor's kid who was a high school senior. Reporters for the locally-owned ABC network affiliate and PBS affiliate showed up next, followed by reporters from the other network affiliates operating out of Lincoln and Omaha.

Questions progressed, pro forma, with expertly-feigned 'heard that for the first time' expressions from the Poughkeepsians. There literally was nothing new for them to answer, but they bent over backwards to make sure the reporters were satisfied with the details they were providing.

The reporter from the Journal Star, smiling broadly as he laughed under his breath, asked, "How come the other rallies you guys did had speakers like Bill Moyers, Brad Pitt, Natalie Maines and Erin Brockovich and we get a Cornhusker poly sci prof?"

"Honestly? Well, we tried to find a marquee name as the guest speaker, but, for all of the stability and perceptiveness you Nebraskans routinely exhibit, the folks from this region seem to be fairly white bready. No celebrities with close Nebraska ties who aren't billionaires. Our goals, for the most part, don't synch up well for most billionaires.

"But don't get us wrong: we believe that the long term effects of the USA-SBR will mean billionaires don't just stay billionaires. As the USA-SBR re-grows the economy from the ground up, not just workers on the lower strata will prosper, but billionaires will too.

"Anyway, we think Professor Arty McComen will spell out quite nicely why middle class and working poor Nebraskans would be smart to put the USA-SBR in their backpacks and run with it. All the way to the bank."

The journalists didn't seem impressed.

But they should've been.

∗   ∗   ∗

To the extent that it's possible for a political science professor to dazzle a crowd, Professor McComen did just that.

He brought his own Powerpoint presentation with funny, genuinely funny, animated characters interspersed with the Powerpoint slides. There were illustrated, detailed slides for each section of the 38-page USA-SBR, including what appeared to be humorous editorial cartoons directly related to each part of the USA-SBR.

"Christ," Pongo whispered to Franklin, "it looks like he's been working on this thing constantly for almost a month."

McComen clearly had a gift for comedy; in fact, after the chorus of loud laughter he received repeatedly during his presentation that evening, he decided in the following months to start a part-time stand-up comedy avocation. By a year later, a Comedy Central executive visiting a relative in Wichita caught McComen's act and, three months later, McComen had a half-hour special on the network.

But, back to our story: once the Professor's presentation was completed, it was clear that the crowd had absolutely loved his skewering of bigots, the obsessively greedy in the financial world, the obsessively greedy in the health care profession, the obsessively greedy among the military-industrial complex, the obsessively greedy among traditional automaker corporations, the obsessively greedy among the energy industry, the FoxNews alternative reality crowd and the obsessively hypocritical whistleblower-punishing-obsessed members of the Executive Branch and of the Republican Party.

None of which prepared the Poughkeepsians for what came next.

Before anyone knew what was happening, McComen yelled out in Looney Tunes Cecil Turtle voice (the one Jon Stewart imitates oh-so-well), "Uh-yeah, uh-bite uh-this, Turtleman Muh-McConnell!" and dropped trou, mooning the audience.

Another YouTube hit. Perhaps, though, not necessarily for the best reasons. But, when you need publicity for your campaign, you take what you can get.

Fortunately for McComen, he had tenure and there was nothing in his contract which specifically said he couldn't moon a group of consenting adults. And, as far as anyone knew, no one could confirm there were any minors in that audience and none of the adults who were there filed any complaints with authorities about indecent exposure.

Bottom line: the rally was another success, possible morals charge notwithstanding. All was good.

* * *

They flew back to New York from Omaha on United at mid-day the next day. Fortunately for Franklin, he was going to have the following two days off from work, to give him some time to unwind with Holly before getting back to the university-work-study-sleep-reset grind.

A day later it occurred to Franklin he'd never realized how winded a person could get from unwinding – after they spent their entire overnight unwinding together. At one point during the night, Holly asked him how he could keep himself up, so to speak, so continuously without pharmaceutical assistance from those little blue pills.

"Just looking at my beautiful Holly makes me as hard as one of those stalagmites in the caverns, Darling," he said, with a sly smile at the end.

"And as wet too, Honey," she added. "That's important. A scratchy ol' dry rock would not make this young woman pleased."

"Of course, it helps too to be back in one's early 20s. You might not be so thrilled by an old man stalagmite."

"You might be surprised," she said as she moved her head down below Franklin's waist.

"The blessings of having functional legs," Franklin thought to himself. *"Thank God for Dr. Salk!"*

At the same moment, Holly was thinking to herself, *"Thank God for blessed testosterone – may it flow forever!"*

* * *

415

Resuming the Grind; Celebrity Jeopardy?!

It would be the last extended time Holly and Franklin would share together for months. On Jan. 14, full-time class schedules began for both of them. At 4 p.m. the same day, Franklin returned to work for Chet Dale at Adams Landscaping. Chet was pumped to have Franklin/Percy back for his four-hour shifts.

"Good to have my own YouTube celebrity back pilotin' his own special forklift. Less work for me, Scruples!" Chet smiled.

But Chet noticed that, at least once a week, regional and national news media reporters were stopping by to talk to Franklin/Percy – sometimes on camera or audiotape, sometimes not – to get up to speed on the latest USA-SBR developments. After every visit, co-workers would razz Franklin/Percy trying to get his goat with remarks like, "When's your next U.N. appearance going to be, Scruples?" or "Trebek gonna have you on Celebrity Jeopardy yet?" or "Been screwin' any Senators' wives lately?" or "Brad Pitt let you feel up his wife a little when you met 'im?" You know, classy stuff.

Chet mentioned to Franklin/Percy that, if those visits became more frequent, they'd need to be scheduled after work hours or re-routed to Phil. Franklin told him he was OK with that. But the frequency didn't change much right away.

* * *

More Midwestern Thrills

Once spring break rolled around, Franklin, Phil, Holly, Harry, Marcia, Idris and Heather departed on March 9 for a three-stop rally tour at the University of Wisconsin-Madison, the University of Iowa and Iowa State University.

They arrived early that afternoon in Madison, Wisconsin for their 5 p.m. press conference in advance of that Sunday evening's rally at the university's Kohl Center arena.

They were pleased to see reporters arrive from both the Wisconsin State Journal (a Madison daily paper owned by Lee Enterprises of Davenport, IA) and the Milwaukee Journal Sentinel (a locally-owned daily out of Milwaukee which would be purchased in July 2014 by the E.W. Scripps Co. of Cincinnati, OH). In addition, reporters from each regional television network affiliate (all but PBS owned by out-of-state corporations) showed up, once again almost all of whom appeared to be under 30.

Their questions mostly covered the same ground as previous press conferences, but there was a special emphasis on Workers' Compensation, manufacturing of machinery and motorcycles and the strengthening of the food safety system through the Secretary of Health and Human Services' mandate for stricter food safety inspections. Marcia had told them in advance, fortunately, that Madison and Milwaukee were known for a concentration of insurance businesses, Harley-Davidson Inc.'s headquarters and their meatpacking industries.

Asked about the potential loss of jobs resulting from Workers' Compensation insurance being nationalized, Franklin was quick to point out purchases of supplemental Workers' Compensation coverage through private insurers still would be allowed; only certain persons in the new Workers' Compensation agency, members of Congress and their staffs, lobbyists and extended family members of those persons would be prohibited from purchasing such supplemental coverage.

Asked whether the proposed ban on fossil fuel-using internal combustion engines could kill the domestic motorcycle industry, Phil said he, a Harley-Davidson owner himself, had no such worries. All motorcycle manufacturers, not just American ones, would be required to make the switch for units sold in the U.S.A. He was confident there would be minimal reduction of demand for motorcycles using biomass-fueled engines and electric engines. In fact, he said, there likely would be an increase in manufacturing jobs stemming from the need to convert gasoline-powered motorcycle engines into engines using alternative fuels.

Asked whether the area meatpacking industry could see layoffs resulting from dramatic increases in surprise safety and health inspections, Idris explained that meatpacking companies likely would need to hire more staff in order to pass the increased scrutiny by those inspectors. The resulting increases in food safety and quality likely would increase demand for those meatpackers' products, he predicted.

Asked why the group had invited actor Mark Ruffalo to be their guest speaker, Heather explained Ruffalo had spent almost all of his childhood growing up in Wisconsin and that he was selected for his outspoken advocacy for bans on hydraulic fracturing, or fracking.

"Being a handsome hunk of a man who's a phenomenal twice-Oscar-nominated actor had *absolutely nothing whatsoever* to do with it," she added, to a chorus of laughter from the journalists.

The reporters, without exception, showed professionalism and respect for the Poughkeepsians. Franklin decided it would be unwise to engage in a debate with the Journal Sentinel's reporter – someone who had no control over editorial decisions - about the paper's use of far-right-wing hyper-conservative columnist Jonah Goldberg. *"You know enough to pick your battles,"* he thought to himself.

∗ ∗ ∗

The next day's rally gathering was a nice rebound from attendance at the Wichita rally. It was a near-overflow crowd, with a more-than –usual number of under-50 women, many of whom were carrying autograph books and glossy photos of featured speaker Mr. Ruffalo, hoping for his signature.

Mr. Ruffalo didn't disappoint, either about autograph signings or his presentation.

He started off with some touching anecdotal memories of his childhood in the Kenosha area. Then he went on to offer praise for the USA-SBR's ban on fracking, mentioning how his anti-fracking advocacy had landed him on a *terror watch list* (something which the Homeland Security Department had denied, but Ruffalo pointed out, "What would you expect them to say?").

Like Matt Damon in Wichita, Ruffalo had purchased 5,000 copies of Josh Fox's "*Gasland*" documentary video with money out of his own pocket to be distributed free to attendees at the very end of the rally, first come, first serve. Also like Damon, he said, in accepting those free copies, he considered each attendee to be promising to share them with at least one other friend, co-worker or extended family member.

"It's all about preserving those most precious of things we humans require to stay alive: clean water and clean air," he said. "The USA-SBR would revive and restore the Clean Air Act by banning fracking and preventing corporations from poisoning our soil, water and air with those horrifically toxic secret fracking chemicals.

"We've GOT to do this thing. You've GOT to put your elected officeholders' feet to the fire on this. If they won't stop shilling for fossil fuels corporatists, then you've GOT to run against 'em. It's that simple."

Ruffalo then lauded other provisions of the USA-SBR designed to limit the influence of money in politics and preserve the environment.

He listed the advantages of each part of the USA-SBR and compared them to what's currently allowed under the law and under the Supreme Court's interpretations of the law. He praised the USA-SBR's expansion of representation in Congress and on the Supreme Court. He predicted that USA-SBR opponents would accuse the proposal's backers of wanting to politicize the court.

"Anyone bother to read the Gore v. Bush decision that invalidated Florida voters' votes in 2000? Anyone bother to read the Citizens' United ruling? Anyone bother to read the Supreme's ruling eviscerating the 1965 Voting Rights Act? Anyone actually want to contend with a straight face that the court isn't ***ALREADY*** politicized?"

(A standing ovation occurred lasting a full minute.)

By the time he was done, he'd gone through the entire USA-SBR, saving Franklin from that job. He went on to an earnest, emotional introduction for the video memorial for Sally. He said he wished he'd had the privilege of getting to know her the way the Poughkeepsians got to.

Once the rally was done, the Poughkeepsians took Ruffalo out for an enjoyable vegetarian meal. When they saw him off at Dane County Regional Airport for his flight back to New York City the next morning, they were genuinely sad to see him go. But he promised to visit them in Poughkeepsie the next chance he got.

"You probably say that to everyone," Franklin joked.

"But this time I mean it," Mark smiled.

* * *

They went in their rental van from the airport southwest on U.S. Route 151 for the three-hour ride to Iowa City, where they had a 5 p.m. press conference scheduled in advance of the next day's rally at the University of Iowa's Carver-Hawkeye Arena.

After stopping for lunch at Short's Burger & Shine – where Franklin simply couldn't resist getting a shoeshine, something he hadn't had since 1945 – they checked into their hotel and got much-needed naps (they hadn't finished their dinner and dessert with Mark the night before until about 1 a.m.). As he was nodding off, Franklin remembered how 'shoeshine boys' from his time were virtually all African-American men, despite the 'boys' moniker. Because employers wouldn't hire them for most other things.

Some kinds of nostalgia were much more bitter than sweet.

Reporters from the Iowa City Press-Citizen (owned by Gannett Corp.), the Cedar Rapids Gazette (a locally-owned daily) and the Des Moines Register (also owned by Gannett) were present for the press conference, along with very young reporters from the local television network affiliates.

Besides the usual torrent of questions about the USA-SBR, the reporters appeared to be concerned with how effective the USA-SBR's proposals to rein in global warming would be. Marcia had emphasized before the press conference that the main engine of the economy in the area was agricultural.

The Des Moines Register's Jason Noble asked if it was already too late to offset the worst impacts of global warming – he wondered if the 'tipping point' had already been reached.

Franklin/Percy stepped up to the plate: he emphasized that USA-SBR requirements to wean consumers from the use of fossil fuels and to embrace the expansion of solar energy generation would produce real results in slowing global warming's effects. That slowing would, in turn, reduce the need for agricultural insecticides as well as forestall cyclical droughts. He explained that, due to the physics of increased CO_2 emissions during previous decades of fossil fuel consumption, there would be a lag time before there could be any actual reduction in global warming. However, that only underscores the absolute urgency for every consumer in the U.S.A. to support the fossil fuels restrictions required by the USA-SBR, he said.

Unless the USA-SBR's provisions to stem the effects of global warming are adopted, Franklin said, Iowans could expect extreme weather events like extended droughts, massive flooding, tornadoes and severe hurricane-strength windstorms not just in the near future, but for at least the next couple of centuries.

There could even be huge firestorms during the warmest parts of summer which could wipe out thousands of acres of crops in just a few hours, he warned.

There didn't seem to be a single global warming denier among the reporters. "*That's a refreshing surprise*," Phil thought to himself. "*But that doesn't mean one or more of them won't reach out to a denier for so-called journalistic balance. What horseshit. How can scientific fact be balanced??*"

As if weirdly on-cue to Phil's thoughts, Franklin then held forth in his most serious the-Japanese-just-attacked voice (which raised a few eyebrows among the oldest reporters, who wondered if it was Franklin/Percy 'Rich Little-ing" FDR, in marginally bad taste).

"I implore you not to look to the deniers of the facts of global warming when you are reporting on this issue. It is not only impossible to 'balance out' a scientific fact, it is a betrayal of your own subscribers and viewers to suggest that there is an alternative kind of lens of reality through which the threat of global warming can be viewed.

"Don't. Do. It."

At least four of the reporters present took Franklin's urging seriously, successfully convincing their editors and producers not to include remarks by global warming contrarians in their reports. But did they hear about it later. From every "angry uncle" Fox News viewer nut job between Coon Rapids and Sac City.

* * *

The next evening's rally featured guest speaker James Hansen, a University of Iowa alumnus and NASA climatologist who had announced his upcoming retirement from NASA a month later so he could accept a professorial position at Columbia University which would allow him to speak out with more candor on the threat of global warming.

Prof. Hansen prefaced his remarks by emphasizing his opposition to the USA-SBR's anti-nuclear energy provisions. He was convinced that the only way to save civilization from the effects of global warming was to use **ALL** strategies to reduce CO2 emissions, including expanding nuclear energy as a resource, simply because there are no CO2 emissions with nuclear reactors. And because CO2 emissions are what are destroying the climate.

However, he acknowledged the hyper-toxicity of conventional nuclear wastes and stressed that nuclear energy should be generated through new-generation "fast reactors," which consume nuclear waste, and thorium reactors which produce waste that's toxic "only" for a couple of centuries instead of the 200,000 years-plus of deadly toxicity for conventional nuclear wastes. Likewise, the thorium wastes, unlike conventional nuclear wastes, aren't usable for generation of nuclear weapons materials. (Unfortunately, virtually none of the existing nuclear power generating stations use 'fast reaction' or thorium technology.)

Those objections notwithstanding, he said, the USA-SBR's provisions to reduce greenhouse gas emissions make passage and ratification of the USA-SBR essential.

Without reduction of those gases – and a halt to the moonscape strip mining of Canadian tar sands oil deposits – it is, without a doubt, "game over for the planet's climate," he said.

"It's not like we have anywhere else to go, you know. This planet is *it*, for the foreseeable future."

He also slammed mountaintop removal mining, as well as the idea that there is any such thing as "clean coal." He defended his protests against mountaintop removal mining, which resulted in him being arrested twice, once in West Virginia in 2009 and once at the White House in 2011.

He reiterated his call for the elimination of coal-fired energy generation by 2030. However, he didn't repeat his description of trains hauling coal as "death trains," as he had described them when he appeared before the Iowa Utilities Board in 2007, a characterization which drew flak from a utilities organization for its unintended comparison to Holocaust victims, an unintended comparison for which Hansen subsequently apologized.

He repeated his urgent recommendation (originally mentioned in 2008) that fossil fuel company executives should be tried for "high crimes against humanity and nature" due to their intentional spreading of doubt and disinformation about global warming, disinformation which threatens the continued existence of human civilization as it's now known.

In addition, he had more than a few unkind things to say about the enormous volume of methane gases released into the atmosphere through hydraulic fracturing, or fracking. Methane gas, he explained, is 20 times more potent as a greenhouse gas compared to carbon dioxide.

When the rally was completed that evening, virtually all of the attendees felt invigorated about fighting against global warming. If there had been an XL Pipeline flack or a Massey Energy shill standing outside the arena as they exited, it probably would not have been a pretty sight.

Hansen's conditional support for nuclear energy notwithstanding, the Poughkeepsians counted the evening's rally as a qualified success.

* * *

The next morning, the Poughkeepsians drove Prof. Hansen to the East Iowa Airport at Des Moines and dropped him off for his United Airlines flight to New York City. Then they headed north to Ames, IA for the 5 p.m. press conference they'd scheduled there in advance of their rally the following day at Iowa State University's Hilton Coliseum.

After driving around from mid-morning to noon to see the Ames sights, they were a little underwhelmed, though they did enjoy their stop at Reiman Gardens. Phil convinced them to see a matinee of the recently released hunger-related documentary, "A Place at the Table." They all gave it a big thumbs-up. But Franklin was sad to see, even after LBJ's War on Poverty in the mid-'60's and enactment of the Food Stamps Program nationwide effective July 1974 (after pilot programs under the Food Stamp Act approved by LBJ in 1964), that hunger still was an issue for many of the nation's poor.

They got out of the theater more than an hour before their press conference at the Hampton Inn meeting room. They were somewhat disheartened when the only media person to show up for the press conference was Julie Ferrell, a 20-something woman from the Ames Daily (almost) Tribune (owned by GateHouse Media of Pittsford, NY). They concluded there were no television media present simply because they'd all already attended the press conference they'd had two days earlier in Iowa City.

But Julie's questions showed she'd prepared thoroughly for the press conference and apparently had read the entire text of the USA-SBR.

When they were done, they told her they hoped all the other young reporters across the country were at least as dedicated to their craft as she was.

That evening the group decided to see another movie, "*Emperor*," about Gen. Douglas MacArthur's dealings with the Japanese Emperor in the months following the end of World War II. Franklin liked it, mainly because it shed some light on the months after his previous life ended – but the others got the impression he might've enjoyed an old Marx Brothers movie a little more.

∗ ∗ ∗

The rally the following evening at the Hilton Coliseum had an underflow crowd, the smallest yet for any of their latest tours, perhaps 4,500. The consensus was the crowd was so small simply because they didn't have a 'marquee name'-type person as their guest speaker.

Their featured speaker that evening was Riceville, Iowa native Jane Elliott, a graduate of the University of Northern Iowa. She was best known for her experiment (shortly after Martin Luther King Jr.'s assassination) in *temporarily* convincing her mostly 8-year-old white 3rd graders that blue-eyed children were "better" than brown-eyed children (and vice-versa) so those white children would better understand the kind of discrimination experienced by African-Americans.

Her experiment was filmed in 1970. The film, titled "Eye of the Storm," was viewed by millions nationwide and she subsequently appeared on "The Tonight Show with Johnny Carson" and many other television programs, including being featured on a PBS Frontline episode and five appearances on Oprah Winfrey's show. She became recognized as a pioneer in the field of diversity education training.

Ms. Elliott gave an inspiring talk for the crowd on both progress and barriers to progress in the fight against racism, discussing at length the Trayvon Martin shooting from a year earlier, as well as other instances of people being arrested or shot for the crime of "walking while black" or "breathing while black."

She expressed regret that so many persons once misinterpreted what she was trying to do, and expressed great gratitude at the appreciative contacts she's received over the years from the African-American community for her efforts to help people understand the real effects of racism.

She shared supportive sentiments for the USA-SBR's ban from holding public office on persons who were on record as adults with racist remarks. But she was just as concerned that such persons receive help to escape the culture of ignorance and bias which clearly had swallowed them up at an early age.

Likewise, she had nothing but praise for the USA-SBR's guarantee of equal rights and opportunities to all persons regardless of race, gender, same-sex orientation, transgender orientation, etc.

As the evening progressed, it became clear to the Poughkeepsians that Ms. Elliott had, arguably, the biggest heart of any of the persons they'd invited to be guest speakers. The attendees appeared to feel the same way. Perhaps a thousand of them lined up to thank her for her dedication to bringing the races together. She was gracious to every one of them, almost to a fault.

Another successful rally, *sin dudo*, Phil said as they left the arena that night.

$$* \quad * \quad *$$

BEANTOWN COMFORTS

Their trip back the next day from East Iowa Airport to New York City's JFK International Airport was once again on Delta ("Jesus, Delta AGAIN?" Phil had said when Marcia gave them their itinerary), but the flights were uneventful, although they barely made the connecting flight in Detroit, thanks to the gate for the connecting flight being almost a full mile away from where they disembarked. They encountered only one surly flight attendant, a young apparently gay man who appeared to have had his customer service training from the late Benito Mussolini. "*Well, anyone can have a bad day*," Phil thought to himself, "*so need to give him the benefit of the doubt.*"

Fortunately for Franklin and Holly, they didn't each have to be back to work or school until the following Monday. So they decided to kick back for a day (including some intimate overnight friction) before taking a scenic drive northeast to Boston for the weekend. It was just the tonic they needed to come down from the stress of the latest rally tour. When not enjoying each other's company in the cozy confines of a downtown Boston hotel, they explored the red-striped Freedom Trail and, after inspecting Old Ironsides, ventured onto the USS Cassin

Young, a World War II-Korean War era destroyer moored in dry dock near the end of the trail.

Franklin couldn't recall if he'd ever set foot on this particular vessel – probably not, he thought. Listening to him reminisce about his travels about Navy vessels, though, Holly began (finally!) to step into his reality. Franklin could see the change in her eyes as it happened and did his best to comfort her, to promise he'd never just up and disappear from her life...although, after looking into the mirror lately and thinking he looked maybe eight or ten years older than he had the month before, he wondered if he could really keep that promise.

But maybe, just maybe, it was only his insecurities twisting his imagination...

* * *

Booming Beantown; Dungeons
for the Messengers

B arely a month later, as Franklin's 3 p.m. Anatomy 102 class was about to start at Marist on April 15, everyone in the back row of the classroom suddenly urged everyone else to turn on their smart phones and catch the latest news report on the internet.

Within seconds, everyone was looking at the terrifying images of the Boston Marathon pressure cooker bombings. Having gone through two entire World Wars without a single terror bombing on U.S. soil, this was an experience Franklin simply couldn't wrap his head around. *"How could someone have that much hatred build up in his system? How could someone want to kill unarmed people they'd never even met? Not just unarmed people, but **peaceful** people trying to expend energy constructively?"*

When he met Holly shortly after the class finished, just before he was to leave for his evening job, Franklin mentioned his inability to understand the violence behind the bombings. Holly reminded him of the violence inflicted on Palestinians by Israel (and vice versa) and how Arab nations sympathetic to Palestinians despised the U.S.A. for its unquestioning, unconditional ongoing financial and military support of Israel. In addition, she reminded Franklin of the unpopularity of the U.S.A.'s pre-emptive war against Iraq, as well as the ongoing war in Afghanistan, wars which regularly featured mass deaths of innocents killed by remotely-piloted U.S. drone attacks, often at weddings and family gatherings.

"I know we used to think of ourselves as the 'good guys' in these kinds of conflicts, but it's just not so simple any more," Holly said. "The Taliban and Al Qaeda are pretty horrific in many ways, but I don't really know how much better we are. We seem to have quite a bit of blood on our hands.

"When you get a chance, you should check out the embarrassing stuff about the U.S. military shared with the press by Julian Assange and Wikileaks, not to mention what's happened to Corporal Chelsea Manning – formerly Bradley Manning – since she decided to be a whistleblower about what most people would consider to be war crimes committed by our armed forces in Iraq and Afghanistan.

"What our government did to her makes me kind of ashamed to be an American. Same for Julian Assange. They should've been seen as the most courageous kinds of patriots. But two months ago, Manning got a 35-year prison sentence and they want to do the same kind of thing to Assange. Shameful beyond words.

"Anyway, hatred for horrible things our country has done still isn't an excuse for trying to kill innocent people. I don't understand that logic – never will."

"Maybe once they find and arrest the bombers and put them on trial, maybe their blood atonement will quench the thirst for revenge so many Americans seem to be thriving on these days," Franklin speculated.

"I thought Americans were itching for war after December 7 – this kind of lust for vengeance goes way beyond what I remember from back then."

"Maybe it's because the victims – both on 9/11 and today in Boston – the victims all were civilians, innocents," Holly said.

"I suppose that could be it. I hope there's some forgiveable excuse besides simple blood lust."

"I dunno – I doubt anyone ever lost money betting on Americans' ability to hate people back who hate us. Just doesn't seem to be a grasp for the concept of an eye for an eye making the whole world blind."

"That sounds familiar. Who said that?"

"I think it was Mohandas Ghandi's biographer."

"Ghandi...I should know that name."

"You and I can watch an excellent movie about him and how he got the British to grant India independence in '47 without a shot being fired."

And they did, late that night. The Mahatma's end (by assassination) brought back stark memories for Franklin of the time he lost a close friend – Chicago Mayor Anton Cermak - to an assassin who wanted Franklin dead as well, less than three weeks before Franklin's first inauguration.

"*Gunman Giuseppe Zangara: yessirree, could've been a modern-day poster boy for the NRA's Second Amendment rights crusade,*" Franklin thought to himself, in no small way pissed off.

* * *

HEADING WEST, AGAIN, FOR A GOOD CAUSE

Less than a month later, Franklin's and Holly's finals at Marist were done and they both were a semester closer to their Bachelor's degrees. Their plan was to take about two weeks off to resume their USA-SBR rally schedule, this time at the University of Nevada-Reno, the University of Colorado, Colorado State University, the University of New Mexico and New Mexico State University.

Unfortunately, Pongo and Harry wouldn't be able to join them due to their day job requirements. But Phil, Marcia, Heather, Holly, Idris and the O'Learys were going to be joining Franklin this time.

Franklin convinced them to make the first stop at the University of Nevada-Reno – mainly because he wanted them to explore Great Basin National Park on their drive from Reno all the way over to the next rally stop at Boulder, CO. As an avid arborist, he really, REALLY wanted to see the super-old bristlecone pines growing at the park's highest elevations.

They arrived at Reno-Tahoe International Airport, via American Airlines, at mid-afternoon on a Saturday. Other than three different screaming 2-year-olds on each leg of their flight, the trip was uneventful; by this time they'd all learned to bring along noise-cancelling headphones. Most welcome was that every last flight attendant was gracious, patient and kind – a true rarity for 21st century travel.

They went straight from the airport to their hotel's meeting facility for the usual 5 p.m. press conference in advance of the next day's evening rally at the University of Nevada-Reno's Lawlor Events Center.

A reporter from the Reno Gazette-Journal (a Gannett Corp. daily) showed up, along with a reporter from the university newspaper, plus reporters from each local network television affiliate. With the exception of the Gannett reporter (who, understandably, looked like he'd prefer having a fishing line hanging off a long boat in the middle of Lake Tahoe), they all looked like they'd never, ever be able to buy an alcoholic beverage without photo identification. The NBC affiliate reporter looked so young that she might even be forced to use a fake ID. It was widely known that the youngest staff get assigned the weekend shifts. Barring something like a major volcanic eruption, at least.

Questions weren't exactly fast and furious, but it was, gratefully, apparent that most of the reporters once again had at least read the full text of the USA-SBR.

The most critical questioning came from Gannett's Gazette-Journal reporter, who asked Franklin/Percy how the group expected to garner support from the mining industry when the USA-SBR provision to scuttle the 1872 General Mining Act appeared to be designed to gut mining companies' profits.

"Honestly, we don't expect to have the support of the mining industry," Franklin said. "If we did, that would tell us we haven't done our jobs.

"The 1872 law is a dinosaur in the Federal code. It's pure corporate welfare in its worst form. The law was passed to help encourage development of what then was the sparsely-settled western half of the country. Guess what? It's not sparsely-settled any longer and mining companies know how to rake in profits without having the government hold their hands.

"The only reason the law hasn't been repealed already? Three words: Big. Money. Lobbyists.

"As for gutting the industry, try asking miners who know they're risking their lives every day for employers who cut safety corners whenever they can get away with it:

- "Do you want to keep working for a company which considers high risks to your life just another cost of doing business?
- "Or do you want to work at a government-operated site where cutting safety corners will mean the boss gets fired? A government-operated site where you have guaranteed retirement, production bonuses plus union representation? Where there's no motivation to cut safety corners or environmental corners because there's no shareholder value to be augmented?

"I know which option I would choose if I were a mineworker. Plus, knowing that mining profits would help pay down the national debt, well, what's more patriotic than that?

"If mining companies want to whine about losing the 1872 law and having to pay real market value-based royalties, they're more than welcome to take their ball home and look for a pick-up game in a different country – you know, maybe a banana republic where corruption is endemic and they have to pay weekly bribes to keep their sites open...or, maybe, a middle eastern country where their workers might be beheaded for getting paid in dollars."

A few of the reporters' questions suggested that there was genuine appreciation for the USA-SBR provisions to establish and protect National Parks and National Monuments. Franklin proudly referred to those as the "Edward Abbey Provisions."

Which, unfortunately, led to the reporters asking if the Poughkeepsians were closet EarthFirst!-ers or Earth Liberation Front-ers, groups associated with sometimes popular, sometimes radical environmental actions.

"We consider ourselves more aligned with Greenpeace's goals," Phil asserted. Which was true.

"But there have been times when we've felt sympathy for the goals of the more 'out-there' environmentalists. It's important to try to remember that there is an overwhelming body of scientific work out there which appears to show that our planet just might be impossible to live on in another century or so – the more radical groups have taken the urgency of that threat to heart.

"The main difference between them and us, though, is that we would never, _ever_, **_EVER_** advocate destruction of private property as part of a pro-environment strategy. That philosophy simply doesn't comport with the Golden Rule we've always tried to live by."

"Amen, brother," Franklin seconded.

The remaining questions covered old ground for the Poughkeepsians, but they did a remarkable job once again of feigning surprise at each individual inquiry.

*   *   *

That evening, the group decided to go their separate ways to explore the Reno-Lake Tahoe area, an area of remarkable alpine scenic beauty.

Phil, Heather and the O'Learys elected to go on a drive through some of the more beautiful lakeside neighborhoods. Phil tried to keep the 'When are you and Pongo going to tie the knot' conversations with Heather to a minimum, although even the minimum seemed several hours too long for Heather. Fortunately, sitting in the very back of the rental van by herself, her eye-rolling was fairly difficult for anyone else to see.

Marcia and Idris elected to drive to the southern end of the lake, where they found a remote area to park and test their rental car's rear end suspension system with some extraordinary back-seat rollicking. Idris had high praise for Marcia's own rear-end suspension system. "Shockingly good your rear shocks are," he said in his finest faux Yoda voice shortly after her third orgasm. Which harvested hearty laughs from her and a quick resumption of deep osculation and further suspension testing.

Franklin and Holly chose to go on a long, long walk along the lakeshore beach as the sun set and the twilight gave way to a clear glimpse of the Milky Way galaxy arcing from north to south overhead. There were many embraces and moist kisses. Finally, in a more secluded area of beach, at Holly's suggestion they decided to disrobe and swim au naturel. It would be the first, though not the last, time they would share physical intimacy in the water. Fortunately, the water was just barely warm enough to be tolerable, thanks to a near-record high that day at almost 90F. They ended up making love among the trout fingerlings for more than four hours, starting at twilight about two hours before the tiny sliver of moon was to set and finishing up around midnight, alternating between standing in water neck deep and lying in water together less than a foot deep.

There was great relief when they returned to the beach edge nearest the trees and found their clothing still there, undisturbed – but then they saw a note left in the pocket of the beige guayabera shirt Holly had gotten Franklin a week earlier. Using his keychain LED light, they saw that it read:

"My wife of 57 years and I were walking by this evening and saw the two of you in the waning light 100 feet out from shore, so overcome with your love for one another, so unselfishly focused on pleasing each other. Just wanted you to know *that you two brought back irreplaceable memories to us. You made us grateful once again for the passions we were able to share in our youth, for those bonds that last a lifetime. And please know, all we could see was from your shoulders up. Thanks again for helping the 80-year-old blood in our hearts feel 60 years younger,*

Bob and Melody J."

As they read it together, Holly's face blushed with color in the LED light-illuminated darkness. "What a touching note," she said. "I'm so glad we didn't notice them – how kind and sweet of them to be so discreet.

"Do you think we'll be able to reminisce the way they were someday?"

"I think we should come back here in 60 years to give it a try," Franklin said, punctuating his suggestion with a gentle, lasting kiss.

∗　∗　∗

The next evening's rally's featured guest speaker was the co-founder of the non-partisan Progressive Leadership Alliance of Nevada (PLAN), Bob Fulkerson.

His presentation began with a detailed Powerpoint display of a plethora of PLAN's progressive goals, including a continued fight against the Yucca Mountain nuclear waste repository, preservation of water quality, thorough restrictions on mining development and preservation of pristine forests, wetlands and deserts, with a particular emphasis on protecting Nevada from future environmental scarring from things similar to its embarrassing history of nuclear weapons testing.

"Nevada deserves to be known for more than being the setting of the Kevin Bacon movie '*Tremors,*'" he said, to much laughter. "OK, it was pretty entertaining, I grant you."

Fulkerson then went down a slide presentation showing just how each of the USA-SBR provisions would help PLAN achieve their economic justice, pollution control, climate healing and social justice goals for Nevada, not to mention the rest of the nation.

When he was done, he asked the crowd, "So, would you be better off with the USA-SBR or the continued plutocratic corporatocracy we have now from our corporate overlords? You tell me, OK?"

To which the crowd responded with the time-honored YouTube-inspired chant:

"Fuck O-ver-LORDS!" "Fuck O-ver-LORDS!"...for at least two minutes.

"Well, let's hope it actually doesn't come down to that **literally**," Fulkerson laughed once the chanting died down, gently covering his crotch with both palms downward-turned and a faux grimace on his face. "It would be just too darned much work!"

(More laughs ensued...)

The rest of the rally presentation went pro forma and was enthusiastically received, especially the ritual tossing of the free ramen and clean underwear. In shamelessly continuing to copy Michael Moore's strategy of fake-bribing young people, the Poughkeepsians hoped they were starting a lasting tradition for all college rallies. Maybe someday the tradition would graduate from ramen to mac & cheese boxes, though, Phil thought to himself. More calcium, better nutrition.

* * *

O'LEARY LEMONADE AND OTHER PARK FEATURES

Their travel the next morning took them east to Great Basin National Park, at which there was the lowest-latitude year-round ice field in North America on Wheeler Peak.

The Poughkeepsians decided to start with the Lehman Caves tour, mostly to get out of the heat.

Discovered by rancher Absalom Lehman circa 1885, the huge cavern rooms immediately impressed the New Yorkers, with an abundance of flowstone, helactites, cave popcorn growths, massive stalagmites and stalactites. They soon noticed, though, that there'd been significant damage done to many of the stalactites. The tour guide explained that most of the damage was done by visitors who knew no better before the park was created in 1986.

The Poughkeepsians once again virtually exhausted their digital camera batteries taking hundreds of photos of the cave and each other, including some silly shots of Franklin with Holly on his shoulders trying to look like some kind of cavern monster. They'd been especially amused over the fact that a large room in the cave known as the "Dance Hall" was used as a speakeasy during Prohibition, as well as a set for a low budget science fiction B-movie.

Other parts of the cavern looked disturbingly similar to the interior anatomy of the female body, which Franklin later realized was more than appropriate, considering they were inside Mother Earth, after all.

They were kind of sad when the tour came to its end – Franklin told the ranger tour guide that it sure seemed like there were lots more areas to explore than what they'd seen. The guide explained that, yes, there were, but that several large rooms had been closed off for safety reasons. There were dozens of other caves in the park which might be enjoyable for professional cavers, he said, but only one of them was officially approved for permit-only caving by experienced spelunkers. In addition, he explained, there were mountain ranges in the area around Ely, Nevada which also contained significant numbers of caverns.

With only an hour or two of daylight left when they emerged from the cave, the group decided simply to check into their rooms at Hidden Canyon

Ranch Bed & Breakfast at nearby Baker, Nevada, so they could get a good night's rest for the following day. They were planning to complete the Wheeler Peak Summit Trail (8.6 miles from the parking area round trip) as well as the Bristlecone/Glacier Trail (4.6 miles) the following day, so they would need early wake-up calls.

They got 'em. But the pancake breakfast was worth the bleary-eyed semi-consciousness that went along with getting out of bed at 5:30 a.m.

They were at the Summit Trail parking area (more than 10,000 feet above sea level elevation) by about 9:00 a.m. Phil made sure everyone had at least a gallon of water to carry along. They ended up needing it in the warm air as they trudged up another 2,900 feet in elevation to the Wheeler Peak Summit. All but Idris got to take many dozens of digital shots of the phenomenal view – Idris forgot to re-charge his camera battery, so his photography ended after about a dozen pics. A tourist from Salt Lake City who summited about the same time as the Poughkeepsians mentioned that the famous (infamous?) Area 51 "secret" military installation was faintly visible to the north of the peak.

Phil had to explain to Franklin what Area 51 supposedly was. "When you get a chance, watch the sci-fi movie, '*Independence Day.*' Or, heck, if we stay here past dark we might just get to see one of the Area 51 experimental flying saucers. Y'never know!"

Franklin gave an utterly perplexed look in Holly's direction, along with a shoulder shrug. "I'll explain later, Darling," she said.

The hike over to the glacier was – well, let's just say it: it was sad. It was the most pathetic looking glacier anyone in the group had ever seen.

"Shit, I think I've got more ice in our basement freezer back home than is in that thing," Phil said.

"It's probably a miracle there's even enough ice there for a Big Gulp soda," Heather said, "what with global warming and all."

"Christ, I've taken in so much water on this. damned. trail," Orvis O'Leary said, out of breath, "I may just exercise my biological imperative and turn that itty bitty patch of ice into some O'Leary ammonia-flavored yellow lemonade."

Karin O'Leary slapped Orvis hard on the hand just as he was reaching to pull down his fly. "Not on my watch, Mister," she said. "If you've gotta go that badly, there were some noxious hoary cress weeds along the side of the trail about 100 yards back. So, if you can't wait, go back there, unzip and knock your little self out. And tell your *little self* I said, 'Hi!,' Sweetie."

A few minutes of weed-killing later, the trail-weary Poughkeepsians headed back downhill in the direction of their rental van.

There was nothing but restful unconsciousness for the exhausted New York tourists once they returned from their trip up Wheeler Peak and finished their dinner at the lodge. Franklin was pretty near ecstatic over the workout he was giving his legs, over the sights those legs were allowing him to experience. Things he never would've dreamed he could experience 68 years earlier.

It was back on the road the next morning and back to the challenge of getting people with little or no interest in civic issues to believe they could effect change in their daily lives by trying to tackle government issues on a macro scale.

Leaving at 6 a.m., they headed east via U.S. Route 6, Interstate 15, Interstate 70 and U.S. Route 93 for the 10-hour drive to Boulder, Colorado, where they had a 5 p.m. press conference set for their hotel meeting facility in advance of the following day's evening rally at the Coors Event Center.

Reporters from the Boulder Daily Camera (a daily owned by Digital First Media of Denver) and the Denver Post (same ownership) were already waiting for them when they strode into the meeting room at about two minutes 'til 5 p.m. (Marcia carped at Phil and Franklin for the last two hours of their drive, complaining that they had no business making such a tight schedule for their long drive and press conference. "What if we have a flat tire? What if we get a speeding ticket?" she kept asking. Phil finally had to ask her – as politely as possible – to 'stow it.' But he told himself that would be the last time the group tried to fit too much into one day.)

The convoy of local network television affiliates showed up about 5 minutes later, once again all appearing to have just stepped out of an ad for a low-budget Abercrombie & Fitch knockoff store. Soooo young, Franklin thought to himself.

The main focus of their questions revolved around damage to water quality from fracking and fracking wastes as well as dwindling potable water supplies as mountain snowpacks seemed to be shrinking almost every year and melting more quickly every year.

Franklin stepped right in to list the provisions of the USA-SBR which would ban fracking and which were designed to combat the effects of global warming.

The reporters appeared enthused about the guest speaker scheduled for the rally: highly respected University of Colorado physics Professor Emeritus Albert Allen "Al" Bartlett, whose specialty was the mathematics of overpopulation.

Phil explained that they hoped the professor would be able to keep his promise to appear, but that he was reported in frail and failing health from his recently diagnosed lymphoma. (They would read on-line less than four months later that he had succumbed to his ailment.) If he was unable to appear, Phil explained, Franklin would fill in – and they might even be able to fly in someone else (he was thinking, maybe, Michael Moore) at the last minute.

The reporters' other questions were asked and answered in fairly quick succession, allowing the exhausted rally organizers to retreat to their rooms for some much-deserved rest – including sleeping 'til almost noon the next day.

By rally time the next evening, none of them had heard from Prof. Bartlett; they'd hoped to get a confirmation call during the day. But they finally were able to breathe that clichéd-but-welcome collective sigh of relief together when the good Professor showed up about one minute before the rally was to begin.

To say he did not look well would've been like saying Chris Christie appeared ready for an obstetrician. Painfully obvious, but not necessarily the complete story. Despite looking every single day of his 90 years and two months of age, as soon as Phil and Franklin felt the Professor's handshake and saw his more or less ear-to-ear smile, they knew he probably could make it through his presentation without faltering. It was a good thing, though, Franklin thought at first sight, that the Prof wasn't there to lecture the crowd about the best ways to maintain a youthful appearance. But then he thought to himself, "*You jackass, this man is* **90 YEARS OLD***! What a great thing it is that he's even here!!*")

Professor Bartlett gave a phenomenal presentation of his 1-hour "Arithmetic, Population and Energy: Sustainability 101" lecture which he'd given in person approximately 1,750 times over his life. It would turn out to be the final time he gave the lecture, which has been viewed literally 5.2 million times on YouTube. The basic message: the arithmetic behind exponential population growth is simple. And it is unsustainable, in terms of energy and resources: no way to keep up with the demands for fresh water, healthy food, housing and other basic consumer goods.

Essentially: population growth, at its current rate worldwide, will literally starve civilization in the foreseeable future.

Prof. Bartlett praised the USA-SBR for its provision to reform tax codes throughout the U.S.A. to disincentivize families from conceiving unlimited numbers of children. Likewise, he emphasized that such disincentives would result in smaller carbon footprints by humanity, prolonging the sustainability of human civilization.

The Professor also praised the USA-SBR's provisions for weaning consumers from fossil fuels and encouraging the use of alternative renewables like wind energy and non-food biomass waste fuels.

By the time he was done, there were chants of "Pro-fes-sor AL!" "Pro-fes-sor AL!" "Pro-fes-sor AL!" throughout the center which continued for minutes.

His talk seemed to fly by, as did the subsequent discussion of additional USA-SBR specifics by Franklin. When the O'Learys, Heather, Holly and Idris began tossing the free ramen and clean underwear packets out to the crowd just before they were to show "Capitalism: A Love Story," Professor Al surprisingly shuffled up to the microphone.

"Let me ask one more thing of you," he said. "I know what they're doing here with the ramen packets and the underwear packages is in good fun, I know it's kind of a joke about the so-called slacker generation.

"But let's remember this: there are real, genuinely hungry people out there, not just in Denver, not just in Los Angeles, not just in New York, but right here in Boulder too. People to whom a small packet of ramen means another day of survival. People to whom a clean set of underwear maybe just might mean staving off infections from parasites or dysentery.

"Instead of just grabbing these items up and taking them home, or even putting them in a scrapbook or some such thing, why not deposit them in a barrel or box or something on your way out tonight, so the rally organizers here can distribute them to the Salvation Army or Goodwill Industries or a local homeless shelter?

"Please consider that, that's all I ask."

The crowd immediately responded with a standing ovation and more shouts of "Pro-fes-sor AL!" "Pro-fes-sor AL!"

And when all was said and done, the exact same number of ramen packets and clean underwear packages which were tossed into the crowd were found in a large box next to the exits by the Poughkeepsians as they exited the center that night. Franklin promised to deliver them to a local homeless shelter the next morning before they left for Fort Collins. He did exactly that, telling the shelter director the donations were from Professor Al Bartlett.

* * *

Their trip to Fort Collins the next day for their 5 p.m. press conference there in advance of the following day's rally at Colorado State University's Moby Arena was blessedly short compared to the previous leg of their tour drive: just slightly over an hour. Once again, except for Franklin (because of his shelter visit), they were able to sleep in 'til 11 a.m. before departing.

They decided to stop for a leisurely lunch at the Silver Grill Café. After consuming a thick hot turkey sandwich, Franklin decided to try one of their city-block size cinnamon rolls and was instantly hooked. "Just might have to start adding up the frequent-flier miles to come back here again and again," he said. His Homer Simpson-style 'aggghhhhhh' and slight drooling at the corner of the mouth induced the other New Yorkers to give the rolls a try. They were *all* hooked.

"Christ, did they put opium in these things?" Orvis said, only half-joking. (For the record, they did not.)

A pair of pert young college-age women, one a bleached blonde and the other a natural blonde, ambled over as Franklin was finishing his roll. They were both wearing shorts which just *barely* covered what the law required to be concealed. They both said they recognized Franklin from his YouTube video appearances. They both asked Franklin if he felt like taking a stroll back to their apartment for "some fun."

Holly, who'd been sitting about 10 feet away with Pongo, belatedly noticed what was happening, seeing each of the coeds place the palms of their hands on each of Franklin's upper legs, and ventured into the middle of the conversation, just as Franklin was about to politely decline their offer – though his private area already was involuntarily stirring to life. Visibly.

"I hope you'll understand if he remains here with me, ladies," she said. "We're actually something of 'an item,' y'see."

The coeds, red-faced with embarrassment, each patted Franklin on the leg and exited discreetly, giggling at each other.

It was Franklin's first encounter with groupies. Holly figured it wouldn't be his last.

The L-tryptophan kicked in quite nicely after their lunch, so they all splurged on themselves with a nice, lengthy siesta. So lengthy this time, in fact, that they almost overslept past the start time for the press conference. From that point forward, whenever they discussed whether to nap during a travel day, they always cautioned each other against '*cinnamon roll naps.*'

The reporters attending the news conference included a representative from the Fort Collins Coloradoan (another in the vast number of Gannett empire dailies) along with the usual local television network affiliates' barely middle-school-age-looking journalists.

The journalists questioned whether the provision in the USA-SBR allowing individual citizens to submit true bills for indictment to grand juries was intended as a method for holding law enforcement officials accountable for abusive actions by police officers and sheriff's deputies. They pointed out that Fort Collins police had 2-1/2 years earlier fatally shot a low-income man wanted on warrants for non-violent felonies simply because the man pointed a flashlight at them from his front porch. The officers were exonerated by the Larimer County District Attorney without charges being filed.

They also explained that local authorities were in the process of establishing what appeared to be a potentially unconstitutional ordinance making it illegal for poor people to solicit financial help from strangers.

"Sounds like your law enforcement folks don't have much patience for those at the low end of the socio-economic spectrum," Idris said.

"The USA-SBR, including the provision you've asked about, is intended to bridge the gap between the haves and the have-nots. Our observations in our travels appear to be that major institutions, institutions controlled by elected officials put into office through large donations from lots of 'haves,' those major institutions seem to be accountable first and foremost to the haves, not the have-nots.

"We want to change that. When a homeless man or woman is approached by a law enforcement officer, we want the homeless man or woman to know and to have every right to expect that they will be treated with the same respect that officer would give to a member of the City Council who called to complain about a theft.

"And if that homeless man or woman receives anything less than that level of respect, we want there to be a system in place – call it an ombudsman, call it an independent prosecutor if you want – a system in place through which that victim of disrespect can be made whole."

"Every soul on this planet, every person who is physically and mentally able to express themselves coherently and thoughtfully should be seen as a potential asset to their community," Franklin asserted.

"When we stop seeing people as having value simply because there is no value in their pockets, or in their wallets, we have truly lost our way. This community and every community like it across this wonderful land need to appreciate the undervalued individuals who struggle and strive each and every day simply to avoid being overcome by the elements.

"If we don't even attempt to appreciate the potential those individuals have to make our communities a better place, we've abandoned our claim to what it means to be better than feral. As so many have recognized over time, there but for the grace of God go we."

When Franklin and Idris finished, the journalists looked like they were ready to reach for their wallets when the collection plate was coming down their row. The Poughkeepsians had made an impression.

They were confident, Franklin said, that their featured speaker the next evening, Sister Mary Alice Murphy, founder of the Sister Mary Alice Murphy Center for Hope, would finish the impression, with an exclamation point, so to speak.

She did.

Sister Murphy praised the intent of compassion which was evident throughout the USA-SBR, whether it was from the provision dedicated to Robert Kearns – an inventor who was the victim of legal intimidation by major automakers, so much intimidation that it caused his marriage to fail and placed him under psychiatric care for a time – or the provision requiring that government benefits for the poor be indexed annually to inflation, preserving their purchasing power, or the provision guaranteeing decent homes for all families and guaranteeing gainful full-time employment, or the provision requiring an increase in the nationwide minimum wage, with annual indexing for inflation.

She also had praise with provisions which would make it far easier for the poor and homeless to vote, to have a real say in who represents them as elected officeholders.

She truly hopes, she said, that the USA-SBR can eventually put her namesake Center for Hope out of the homeless shelter business and into a different kind of dispensary for hope, perhaps exclusively as a training or adult education center.

Sister Murphy's emotionally thoughtful introduction to the memorial video for Sally brought every last one of the rally organizers to tears just when they thought their repeated viewings of the video had permanently fortified them against the pain of Sally's loss.

The Poughkeepsians could compare Sister Murphy's unmitigated goodness of heart only to that of their earlier featured speaker Jane Elliott. They seemed like two seeds from the same pod.

So it was with genuine sadness that they had to shake hands and give their farewells to Sister Murphy at the end of the evening. Each one of the rally organizers – even including the normally hard-shelled Orvis – pleaded red-eyed with her to someday visit them in their humble upstate New York community.

It was one of those rallies they all wished they could re-play whenever they felt low or cynical about the prospects for the future of humanity.

* * *

After a hearty continental breakfast the following morning, the Poughkeepsians packed up the rental van for the long drive to Albuquerque for that afternoon's 5 p.m. press conference in advance of the next day's rally at the University of New Mexico's Pit arena.

They thought the previous night about detouring to the Four Corners Monument, but Marcia emphatically warned that they didn't have time, reminding them about the last time they squeezed too much travel into one day.

"Jeez, all it is, is a concrete square on the ground with a cross in the middle to show you how to be in four states all at once. Yawn. Big. Time. Yawn," she snickered.

"OK, straight through it is, with just some fast food on the way," Phil said. "As long as you agree to the route through the Arapaho, San Isabel and Carson National Forests. It's only an extra 45 minutes and I'm tired of driving on Interstate freeways."

Then Franklin made his pitch for a detour near Colorado Springs to see the Garden of the Gods Park. He'd seen photos of it on the internet and showed them to his travel mates. The others agreed, but that meant leaving a full 90 minutes earlier and a slightly different route using I-25 to Colorado Springs and then U.S. Route 24 west.

"Works for me," Marcia said. "As long as lunch is quick."

The detour to the Garden of the Gods Park was nothing less than spectacular. Many, many digital photos were taken and posted to the USA-SBR website and Facebook page.

Their lunch a few hours later was just as Marcia had asked: quick and with real ice cream milkshakes to boot. They stopped at arguably one of the finest dining establishments in Monte Vista, Colorado: the Dairy Queen Grill & Chill restaurant.

Town wasn't much to look at, but it was a fine lunch nonetheless, Franklin thought. Berkshire Hathaway billionaire mogul Warren Buffett would've been proud of that little microbe-size bit of his business.

As the Poughkeepsians were being served their meals and ice cream, Franklin noticed a young mother, maybe 23 years old, approaching to order her food with two small children, a son maybe three and a daughter about two, trailing behind their momma single-file like little ducklings.

The young mom was dressed in ragged thrift store jeans and a dingy white top which looked like it could stand a couple dozen bleachings to get the body oil discoloration out of it. She was wearing old canvas deck shoes which were thoroughly perforated from lots of wear and tear, with soles which were almost completely worn through in spots. The children's clothing was only marginally better. Each of the children looked like it had been at least a couple of days since they'd had a bath.

Franklin watched as the mom pulled out a small tattered coin purse and began counting out how much she had for their meals. She first pulled out three one-dollar bills and then proceeded to count out what looked like about $1.50 in change.

At that point, Franklin had had all he could take. He walked over to the DQ front counter order-taker and handed him $100 in cash. He whispered to the young man to give the woman and children *whatever they wanted* and to let him know if he needed more money for it. He told the young man to make sure the mom got back every penny of whatever change there might be. And he told the young man simply to tell the young mother that the meals were courtesy of someone who'd come in earlier in the day and left cash to buy meals for whomever appeared the hungriest. All Franklin could think about was that, but for a quirk of fate, *his own grandchildren* might have ended up with the kind of lives those two little ones had ahead of them. Lives often spent wondering where the next full meal would be coming from.

While he and the other Pougkeepsians were eating their lunch, he looked over at the young mother and children having what he was fairly sure was their first filling meal in days. He noticed that, right after the mother handed napkins and drinking straws to her children, she started gathering packets of condiments, salt and pepper and discreetly stowing them in the canvas bag she was carrying. "*I hope to God that's not their dinner,*" Franklin thought to himself. As the Poughkeepsians were on their way out a few minutes later, he noticed the young mother wiping moisture out of her eyes as she lovingly caressed each of the small children.

It was almost more than Franklin could take.

As they walked back to their rental van, Pongo sidled up to Franklin.

"I think the rest of them are embarrassed to say anything to you because it's obvious you didn't want anyone to see, but I'm not: that was one of the kindest gestures I've seen in a long time. I have a feeling that, if we weren't here, you'd probably try and take that woman and her kids home and adopt them like an abandoned puppy."

"You're probably not too off the mark there, son."

$$* \quad * \quad *$$

Endangered Species Welcomed; Belated Murder News

They arrived at their Albuquerque hotel with 30 minutes to spare before their press conference was to start in the hotel meeting facility.

Phil and Franklin were, literally, thrilled when a reporter, Nicole Perez, from one of the last independently owned and operated daily newspapers, The Albuquerque Journal, showed up. They treated the strikingly beautiful young woman virtually as though she were royalty, or among the last of an endangered species. They heaped praise upon her employer and wished her well personally. Franklin said they hoped her publisher would find a way to continue to operate the paper independently for at least another 200 to 300 years.

"And, honest, we keep having to say this, but we're not kissing up here. We're just so grateful that we're not dealing with someone else from Gannett, you know, the Dark Side," Phil said. "JUST KIDDING, all you Gannett-ers swarming all over the surface of the planet!"

(Not really.)

Ms. Perez smiled graciously, expressing her gratitude for the kudos. "Just doing my job, that's all," she chuckled.

The remaining reporters arrived from each of the local network television affiliates and questions began, as with their previous press conference, focusing on potential abuses by law enforcement officers.

Phil and Frank gave, essentially, the same responses they'd given in Fort Collins, expressing hope that the USA-SBR provisions for holding prosecutors accountable would help stem the tide of questionable arrests and police shootings.

They had no idea at the time that the Albuquerque Police Department had already been embroiled in excessive use of force controversies for more than three years and would be the subject of a national scandal over excessive use of force within six months, what would be perceived as part of an epidemic of law enforcement abuses all over the country, often aimed at persons of color and/or the poor.

Ms. Perez and her fellow reporters and editors already had come to realize that enactment of the USA-SBR, if it ever happened, would occur far too late to help with their community's law enforcement problems.

Ms. Perez mentioned that it appeared that anti-abortion extremists had recently moved into the Albuquerque area. She asked if the provision in the USA-SBR about all persons being protected from interference involving medical procedures by persons or groups acting out of religious concerns was intended to be an absolute protection for abortion rights.

"Yes," Heather said.

"Did you want to add anything else, Mr. Van Mullder?" Ms. Perez asked.

"Heather said all that needs to be said."

A reporter from the local PBS affiliate, a Native American man in his late 30's, asked if the provision in the USA-SBR to make it easier for a President to create National Monuments and National Parks was intended to help protect areas threatened by development such as the Petroglyph National Monument.

"Absolutely," Idris said. "Under the USA-SBR proposal, if the President declared such an area a National Park and the Congress didn't override that declaration by a ¾-majority vote within 90 days after the declaration, the area would be permanently protected."

"You guys seem to have thought out just about everything here," the reporter said.

"I doubt we've thought out every little thing, but we've tried to cover what's important," Franklin said.

As the reporters finished with their final questions, Marcia handed out copies of the USA-SBR for them to share with their editors and producers. A couple of the TV reporters asked about the long scar on her left forearm. "Just a minor combat injury sustained on the front lines in Wichita," she said.

"Did you hear that the man who slashed your arm was stabbed to death about a month ago?" Ms. Perez asked.

"No, uh, er, uh, that's remarkable," Marcia said. "I never thought the young man meant any deadly harm, to me at least. Did they get the perpetrator and figure out a motive?"

"They got the stabber, but I don't think they ever really figured out a motive, other than the stabber thought your attacker was gay."

"Wish I could say I'm relieved by that, but it doesn't sound quite right on the face of it to me. There are lots of gay and gay-looking people in prison, but not very many of them are stabbed to death."

"Maybe the guy's parents will wring some answers out of someone," Ms. Perez said. Realizing Marcia was shaken by the news, she gently patted her on the back of her shoulder. "It'll all come out OK, don't you think? It's not like the killer lives in Poughkeepsie, right?"

Marcia – and the rest of the USA-SBR organizers – didn't know **where** the killer lived, except that he was in prison for now.

Marcia shared her misgivings about the prison murder with Phil and Franklin and asked what they thought.

"Ellifino," Phil said.

"Whatever happened, we need to find out more," Franklin said. "Marcia, tomorrow, let's find out if there's a victim's advocate in Kansas who can help you figure out more about this. I'd be interested to know if they discovered how the murderer got his weapon."

"I'll follow up in the morning," Marcia said. "I just think this is too much of a coincidence. Something's not right."

＊　＊　＊

Information Marcia received the following morning over the phone from Kansas wasn't even slightly re-assuring. Hearing that the murder weapon apparently was stolen from a supposedly-secure evidence room, her urethral sphincter let loose just a little.

"Was anyone disciplined or even fired over that?" she asked the victim's advocate 600 miles away.

"Not so far," the advocate said.

"Is there an actual investigation?"

"Looks like it wrapped up a week ago. Probably no charges, except the murder charge against the inmate, unless something else shakes loose."

*   *   *

That evening's featured speaker was ProgressNow NM's Executive Director Patrick Davis.

Mr. Davis' greatest praise for the USA-SBR involved the provisions for expanded immigration rights, as well as for protections from discrimination based on gender orientation, including the right of same-sex persons to marry.

He described the USA-SBR as a progressive's dream come true, a once-and-for-all levelling of the playing field to allow "the little guys" to go head-to-head against the huge corporatist plutocrats without having to back down.

The Pougkeepsians deserved singular praise for trying to build a consensus among progressives all over the country, especially the younger under-30 crowd who find it hard to fathom why their elders seem so reluctant to hold the feet of corporatists of both political parties to the proverbial fire.

As a former police officer, Davis was especially enthused about provisions of the USA-SBR which would enable average citizens abused by "bad cops" to submit true bills of indictment to grand juries when prosecutors refused to pursue charges against officers accused of wrongful actions.

"Anything which compels the justice system to be accountable to those in the community who lack financial power to retain their own representation, that's a positive thing. Something which is many, many decades overdue.

"One can only wonder, if those USA-SBR provisions had been in place five years ago, would our Albuquerque Police Department be in the horrible mess it's in now?"

Davis highlighted each provision of the USA-SBR which he and his fellow ProgressNow NM associates felt particularly strong about. He urged each of the attendees to turn off those video games and to take a break from mindless texting to actually try to compel their elected officeholders to take a stand on the USA-SBR.

"If they're against it or if they decline to take an official position on it, tell 'em either you're going to run against them or you're going to find someone else who will. Make it crystal clear that you're not joking."

The crowd, which filled about two-thirds of The Pit arena, seemed to take this ex-cop seriously. There also seemed to be far fewer clouds of acrid smoke in this arena – only one which Idris had noticed - than previous ones. Which Idris thought was kind of funny. *"Did they think this one strong, handsome dude was going to swoop down from the podium and personally collar two or three hundred dope smokers?"* he thought to himself, chuckling.

They thanked Davis profusely when the rally was concluded, asking him if he had any ideas about how to better move their efforts forward.

"Was thinking you might just want to schedule a national convention once you've finished all your rally tours...Y'know, something where you could have 100,000 or 200,000 people show up, say, at the National Mall the way Jon Stewart did a few years ago. Something that might put that metaphorical image of pitchforks and torches firmly in the minds of all the mouth-breathing knuckle-draggers in Congress like Mr. Gohmert from our lovely neighboring state."

"Not bad, Mr. D, sir, not bad at all," Phil said.

"You're welcome, don't mention it."

"No problem, we'll just make sure the person who thought it up is the principal organizer as well," Franklin smiled slyly.

"As Keith Jackson might say, wuuhooaa, Nellie!" Davis laughed. "Let's pull that one back a bit..."

They all shook hands and went their separate ways, knowing it wouldn't be the last time they saw each other.

* * *

The next morning, like *"Groundhog Day,"* they hit the snooze buttons on their alarm clocks, got up again around 11 a.m., re-loaded the rental van and headed south on Interstate 25 to Las Cruces, where their next 5 p.m. news conference was scheduled in advance of the next day's evening rally at New Mexico State University's Pan American Center.

The Las Cruces Sun-News (yet another daily owned by Digital First Media of Denver) sent its reporter, as did one (the ABC/Disney television affiliate) of the four area network affiliates, all based in El Paso. But, having already covered the Poughkeepsians when they previously were in El Paso, it was clear from the outset that the lone 'local' TV reporter was there just to go through the motions. She told the Poughkeepsians later just before she left that, if she'd known none of the other competing El Paso stations would be coming, she wouldn't have either.

So, the news conference was relatively brief, but not for lack of interest from the Sun-News' man (who Phil thought looked remarkably like Jason Jones, a 'fake news' correspondent on The Daily Show). Ironically, the reporter's name was Jones Jasonne.

Jasonne asked if the USA-SBR's union representation provisions would forever eliminate so-called "right to work" laws or, as described by union advocates, "right to work for less" laws – laws which allow employees of a business with an NLRB-certified union to opt out of paying union dues.

"Yes, those laws would be eliminated nationwide," Franklin said proudly. "Unions able to convince half plus one of any employer's work force to support union representation would be entitled to collect dues from all employees of that business. It's only fair that unions have funds so they can function as workers' representatives.

"And, more importantly, those employers would be **required to negotiate in good faith** with those unions for improved pay, benefits and working conditions. In addition, those employers would be barred, under threat of Federal prosecution, from trying to intimidate or otherwise threaten employees to convince them not to sign a union representation card.

"The middle class would, finally, be back on its way up out of the hole that corporatist plutocrats have dug them into over the past 45 years or so."

Jasonne also asked if the USA-SBR organizers were concerned about the prospect of reduced revenues for law enforcement organizations if and when the USA-SBR proposal severely restricting asset forfeiture statutes were to take effect.

"Let me answer that, Phil," Franklin said. "No."

"Why not?" the lone TV reporter asked.

"Simple. Because due process rights should never be trumped by a law enforcement agency's need to augment its budget.

"If those laws were allowed to stand, before long some brilliant legislators in Podunk, North Dakota would convince their governor to sign a law allowing for vehicles to be seized every time a meter maid issues a ticket for an expired meter.

"It's a slippery slope. It's one thing for the government to seize huge stacks of cash from the back of a drug cartel kingpin's truck. It's a whole other thing to allow the government to seize a farm that's been in a grandfather's family for 100 years because they found a tiny marijuana patch cultivated by his grandson in one remote corner of the property.

"It's happened. We want that idiocy to stop."

By the time the press conference was done, the reporters felt like they'd gotten story angles no one had ever gotten before. They were more or less correct.

∗ ∗ ∗

The featured speaker for the next evening's rally, the final rally of their latest tour, was Dan E. Arvizu, a NMSU alumnus and director of the National Renewable Energy Laboratory in Golden, CO.

Arvizu, a handsome middle-aged nattily dressed gentleman sporting a thick shock of snow-white hair, said he was surprised to be invited by the Poughkeepsians.

"After all, I was appointed to my current job by George W. Bush, who also appointed me to the National Science Board, which I've chaired since last year.

That was after President Obama re-appointed me to that board in 2011. We oversee the National Science Foundation.

"I'm someone who's probably never going to sign on to the provisions in your USA-SBR which would try to ban privatization – I cut my teeth in my profession working for some outstanding private corporations. Companies like CH2M Hill which were pioneers in cleaning up contaminated nuclear weapons production sites like Hanford in the State of Washington – a company which has had to cope with sometimes unfair allegations of fraud, kickbacks, violations and cover-ups, not to mention some mass layoffs despite taking $2 billion in stimulus funds.

"My career roots also include a company – Sandia National Laboratories, an organization which tests certain components of nuclear weapons – a company which is a wholly owned subsidiary of Lockheed Martin, which the USA-SBR organizers have described as an ex-corporate felon. And which was a pioneer in something not so popular right here in Las Cruces and elsewhere in the country: red light cameras.

(Mild choruses of 'boos' from the crowd briefly ensued.)

"And you likely won't see me signing on to the USA-SBR provisions which tend to make it hard for the government to keep secrets. One of my jobs at NREL is to keep our operations out of the public eye. If you try to walk into my workplace, you'll be escorted away by a security guard.

(More smatterings of boos ensued...)

"Not to mention that a lot of people with this organization may frown on the fact that, as a government employee, I'm paid a seven-figure salary, more than double what we pay the President of these United States. I'm part of those 1-percenters out there that folks like you are always railing about. But I live my life *every single day* determined to **earn** every dollar of that salary.

"So, you're probably not going to hear my sing the praises of the *entire* USA-SBR from the rooftops.

"But you **will** hear liberal praise from me for the provisions of the USA-SBR which are intended to wean this fossil fuels-addicted country from oil and natural gas and switch over to solar and wind energy. And you'll hear me passing along lots of kudos for the provisions which make it easier for people to live in the countries they choose with full citizenship privileges.

"When I was a kid, having immigrated from Mexico to Texas with my parents, I was around kids who could rarely afford things like superhero comic books. But kids always seemed to find a way to enjoy them. As soon as the kids I knew could read, they all looked forward to seeing what the Flash, Green Lantern and Superman were doing to keep the bad guys in check.

"With all those superpowers those guys had, I don't ever once remember reading about one of 'em who did something as amazing as turn simple rays of light from the sun into enough power to run entire cities.

"Do you folks get it? What our scientists at NREL and other labs around the country are doing is creating superpowers, the kind Jerry Siegel and Joe Shuster never dreamed of.

"Superpowers which could save the planet from the kind of destruction that only a Lex Luthor could've conceived, you know: global flooding, massive power blackouts, anarchy in the streets.

"Think about it:

"Solar panels on a chunk of the Sahara Desert the size of the State of West Virginia would be enough acreage to power the entire planet.

"**REALLY**, stop and think about that. And that's just with *current* technology. We may reach the point someday where our solar panels are so efficient we can cut that acreage down to size. I'm not saying we'll power the planet with panels set up in the back yard of that neighbor with B.O. who sits on his patio in his underwear scratching his nether regions all day long. But we might be able to shrink that acreage down to the size of a smaller state. One that doesn't quasi-nuke mountaintops just to get at nasty, dirty, glacier evaporating coal."

(Massive, enthusiastic applause...)

Concluding his presentation, he thanked the rally organizers profusely for giving him the opportunity to speak at his alma mater before such a significant crowd (approximately 7,500 persons) on such important topics.

After the tribute to Sally and the showing of the "Capitalism: A Love Story" movie, as the center was emptying out, each of the Poughkeepsians took turns shaking Dan's hand and congratulating him on his life achievements.

"Y'know, we're not writing you off on convincing you about trying to stop privatization," Franklin/Percy said. "Really, we hope you'll make the time sometime to speak with people on the lower rungs of those corporations you used to work for, especially any that were forced to take early retirement or laid off, to get their take on what it's like not to have guaranteed retirement benefits."

"And we're not going to give up on you when it comes to working to make government more transparent, more thoroughly open," Phil added.

"Hey, friends, I didn't say I was opposed to government openness – don't get me wrong. It's just that, when it comes to major developments in renewable energy, there are lots of entrepreneurs out there who'd give their eye teeth to snatch up the secret details on our projects so they could race out there and get 'em patented. You know what I'm talkin' about."

"We get it, Dan – we're just not sure why it wouldn't work to keep the details open to *everyone, everywhere,* so *everyone* had the same chance to benefit from the advances coming out of our taxpayer dollars, that's all...," Idris explained.

"I hear you," Dan said. "I really, truly wish you all well. Godspeed, brothers and sisters."

(When Dan announced his retirement from NREL two years later, the Poughkeepsians arranged for the local Baskin Robbins in his community to deliver a huge ice cream cake to his home, with the words "Enjoy your old age out in the sunshine!" printed on it, surrounded by sugar-decorated images of solar panels.)

* * *

Their flight back to New York's JFK International Airport from El Paso International Airport on American Airlines was the most pleasant yet, even with having to change planes at the Dallas/Fort Worth airport. Every single flight attendant appeared to be mature, respectful and patient. The only time a small child started squealing halfway back in the cabin between Dallas and NYC, an attendant moved quickly to the parents' seats and did something, something the Poughkeepsians couldn't see, which seemed to magically calm the child within a couple of minutes.

Once they arrived back on the late Amtrak train from Penn Station, they all spent a half-hour or so perusing the USA-SBR website and Facebook page for the latest data with Marcia at their business office. It all looked promising.

Then they all headed to their respective homes for sack time. For Franklin and Holly, it was back to their full-time summer work schedules the following day. Franklin knew Chet was itching for him to get back from "all those damn tour appearances to get your mug on YouTube again and again and again."

* * *

GOVERNMENT VS. WHISTLEBLOWERS: PICK A SIDE

It was about a week later when Franklin picked up the newspaper in the Podrowskis' driveway just before he was to leave for work when he saw a large headline about major leaks of secret government information. The leaks had been orchestrated, it said, by an obscure government contractor's employee named Edward Snowden. The leaks painted a chilling picture of probably-unconstitutional widespread government wiretaps not just of virtually every citizen's phone calls and E-Mails, but even of high-ranking elected government officials among the closest of U.S. allies.

All in the name, supposedly, of fighting global terrorism.

(Less than three weeks later, the U.S. Supreme Court went on to strike down the Defense of Marriage Act, enabling individual states to decide on their own whether to allow same-sex marriages. Because the USA-SBR's provisions were stronger than the court's action, the Poughkeepsians, while happy about the development, otherwise paid little attention – they were much more focused on the Snowden revelations.)

446

"Just how is having access to the E-Mails and phone calls, or even just phone records, of an elderly grandmother in Indiana helpful in fighting terrorists?" Franklin thought to himself.

The proverbial fecal matter had just hit the proverbial electric air circulation device for the corporatist plutocrat permanent war culture assholes in the government.

Which was phenomenal news for the Poughkeepsians. By the end of the day, the USA-SBR website and Facebook pages had almost a million new contacts; the most popular YouTube videos from their rally tours had almost as many new hits, especially the videos of Matt Damon and Mark Ruffalo.

"People finally are realizing they need to pick a side, either the USA-SBR or apathy and more of the same," Franklin thought to himself.

Their initial enthusiasm, however, was tempered somewhat when Marcia told them the demographics behind the new contacts: 85 percent of the new contacts were by people under 30. Older voters still appeared to need more convincing.

Still, Phil said, the spike in interest could only be a good thing.

And it was. Donations from average, concerned citizens to the USA-SBR spiked as well. It looked like their nest egg for upcoming TV ads could continue to be preserved.

As the weeks and months passed, Franklin and the others followed developments on the Snowden case.

Both President Obama and Hillary Clinton joined conservatives in claiming that the revelations by Edward Snowden about the National Security Agency's illegal surveillance "helped our terrorist enemies." Obama implied that Snowden *exhibited infidelity* about protecting classified information. Obama, Hillary Clinton and Secretary of State John Kerry all implied, directly or indirectly, that Snowden *was a **pussy** for not returning home to try and vindicate himself before a court of law.* Hillary even said Snowden had exhibited "outrageous behavior" with his disclosures – even though Snowden had first tried to resolve his concerns through contacts with National Security Agency staff attorneys.[*]

Of course, **none of them** explained that Snowden literally would have no defense to make in court simply because the broadly written, draconian 1917 Espionage Act makes no distinction between being "a spy" and being a whistleblower for government contractor employees like Snowden. (The Whistleblower Protection Act only applies to actual government employees, not persons working for government contractors.)

Hillary Clinton even claimed – falsely - that Snowden was _voluntarily_ "seeking refuge" in Russia when, **in fact**, the U.S. government cravenly revoked Snowden's passport while he was travelling through Russia with the goal of him being trapped there, to make it appear (falsely) that he was some sort of Putin-sympathizing quasi-Communist.

---

[*] Jan. 2014 Politico; July 2014 Guardian

Hillary, who'd just stepped down as Secretary of State the previous Feb. 1, even accused Snowden of making information available to foreign governments and potential U.S. enemies when, **in fact**, all he did was disclose what *should've been* public information to an intentionally-limited number of news media professionals under carefully controlled circumstances.

Every time Franklin would read some new remarks by Hillary Clinton and other corporatist Democrats about the Snowden issue his blood would boil.

"That young man put his entire career, his entire life on the line because he felt so strongly that his country had lost its way, had gone against everything the Constitution is supposed to stand for when it comes to protecting individual rights. And the very people who should be defending him and praising the courage he's shown are then ones implying that he's a traitor," Franklin complained to Phil and Pongo one afternoon in the late fall of 2013.

"Surely this couldn't all be because Snowden contributed a couple hundred dollars to the Presidential campaign of that wacky Ron Paul anti-government guy in 2012. Could it?"

"Doubt it, Sir," Phil said. "Ron Paul never had a chance. He was the darling of the Libertarian fringe – the people who are just a couple hairs shy of wanting complete anarchy. Doesn't believe in government having a role in much of anything at all. A true corporatist's corporatist. A real Ayn Randian – even named his son after Ayn Rand. His son's a U.S. Senator from that hotbed of advanced academia and progressive knowledge otherwise known as Kentucky."

(Many laughs ensued over that description of the Bluegrass State, a state known primarily for its sod, its carcinogenic burley tobacco crops, its turtle-resembling U.S. senator and an annual **_two-minute_** horse race where women show up wearing exotic hats.)

"I don't know how to explain this, but I've got a truly compelling feeling in my gut that I need to see Ms. Clinton in person, to observe how she functions," Franklin said. "I feel like, if I can just see her in real time, I can get a better feeling for just how genuine – or how phony – she really is."

"You know what I think?" Pongo asked, not waiting for a response. "I think you just want to see if she's got that fine sensillum hairlike fur stuff that only a tiny number of people like you can see. The people with that stuff are the ones who give you those weird brain food cravings, aren't they?"

"Since you asked, I *have* actually noticed a correlation between those weird, almost uncontrollable cravings and being in proximity to people who have that fine hairy fur growing where there should just be bare skin.

"*So far*, though, I've been able to keep those cravings under control, at least when the people are alive and well.

"But to answer your question, I want to see her because – well, OK, I want to see her because **what** I see – or *don't* see - will give me insights into just how truthful a person she is."

He didn't share with the Podrowskis the massive anxieties he'd been having lately about his aging process accelerating and how he suspected it might take more human amygdala-type tissue to stabilize his condition. Every gaze into a mirror gave Franklin a little esophageal reflux.

The Podrowskis, for their part, had noticed no significant change in Franklin's appearance. Nor had Holly. But, then, they weren't really looking for any.

The fall 2013 semester at Marist progressed uneventfully, although there was great distress nationwide over the Republican-induced Federal government shutdown in October. News video images of a shutdown-supporting Republican Congressman using caustic verbiage to intimidate a female National Park Service Ranger at a Washington, D.C. park when the Ranger declined to admit visitors due to the shutdown (she was simply doing her job) went viral for a time. The Poughkeepsians decided not to spend any time on a rally tour that fall out of concern for what might happen with air travel and other issues indirectly related to the shutdown. Plus, both Franklin and Holly wanted to make sure their GPA's stayed at or near 4.0 – graduate programs tend to like those stellar grades when reviewing applicants for admission.

Turned out they probably needn't have worried: they both went into each of their final exams only needing B- grades to end up with an overall 4.0, but they both aced all of their finals. None of their professors was even remotely surprised.

* * *

MIDWEST TOUR REDUX: COLBERT NATION; PLUS, YOU ARE SOMEBODY!

Immediately after the Christmas and New Year's holidays, with the shutdown a distant memory – and *completely erased* from the memories of *most* Americans, sadly – the Poughkeepsians decided to embark on a rally tour with visits to the University of Illinois, Northwestern University, Indiana University, the University of Minnesota, the University of Michigan and Michigan State University. Since their last tour, they'd added an additional video memorial dedicated to Prof. Al Bartlett, their guest speaker at their rally at the University of Colorado, who had died Sept. 7, 2013 from lymphoma at the age of 90.

Their first stop was Chicago's O'Hare Airport via American Airlines on Jan. 2, 2014 for a 5 p.m. hotel meeting facility press conference in advance of the next day's rally at Northwestern University's Welsh-Ryan Arena.

The group was pleased to see reporters from both the Chicago Sun-Times and the Chicago Tribune (both locally owned as well) in attendance, as well as one from the locally-owned Champaign-Urbana News-Gazette who was there in advance of their rally two days later at the University of Illinois. The Poughkeepsians had considered in advance whether to hand out "officially-sanctioned" USA-SBR Freedom of Press Awards to each of the reporters on behalf of their newspapers for having the highest concentration of locally-owned newspapers found during their rally travels. However, Pongo pointed out that the Tribune's ownership also controls dozens of television stations all over the country. And the leadership of Wrapports Inc., which controls the Sun-Times Media Group, looks like a Who's Who of Chicago-area 1 percenters, he added. So, they decided to forego that kind of journalistic brown-nosing, unintended snub to the News-Gazette's reporter notwithstanding.

Questions from the newspaper journalists and area network television affiliate reporters tended to focus on issues related to privatization, what with Chicago-area politicians – including Clinton family crony Rahm Emanuel (former Clinton White House Senior Advisor), Chicago Mayor since 2011 – famous for setting up outsourcing contracts for their favorite campaign contributors.

Franklin/Percy was quick to list all the benefits – including corruption prevention benefits – flowing from the USA-SBR's provisions to discourage or ban privatization and outsourcing.

"Once the average person can understand that privatization usually is nothing more than a way to cheat taxpayers and Federal employees so private business people can get richer, they'll embrace that part of the USA-SBR like a long-lost rich uncle," he said.

"What makes you think a government-employed supervisor will be more honest than a corporate owner?" Tribune reporter Pete Pewsillanime asked.

"Transparency," Franklin said. "Openness would be required for all government employees. Private businesses, not so much. It would be a lot easier for someone wanting to keep folks honest to look over a government manager's shoulder than a corporate CEO locked away in a downtown penthouse office.

"Plus, government employees are far more likely to pursue their careers out of a genuine dedication to serving the public rather than being in it for the money. As in, 'WHAT money?' civil servants would be asking right now. Private sector workers, not so much – they tend to be more compensation-motivated."

Sun-Times reporter Melvin Masterber asked what kind of reaction the USA-SBR organizers anticipated from their proposal to tighten gun ownership rights. (There had been a record number of firearm-related deaths in northern Illinois during the previous 12 months.)

"We expect a full-court press from firearms manufacturers and the NRA when they come around to recognizing that the prospects for the USA-SBR are fairly positive," Idris said.

"So, what's your strategy?" the reporter followed up.

"Our strategy is not to give them any ammunition – and to let the course of current events speak for itself," Bianca said. "For every NRA lobbyist or firearms industry lobbyist – pardon the redundancy – we've got a thousand emergency room health care professionals who can attest first-hand to what loose controls over firearms sales cause. There are weekend evenings in Chicago – as you already know – when E.R.'s look like combat MASH units.

"When the NRA decides to confront us head-on, we'll look them right back in the eye. We can afford some pretty hard-hitting paid advertising of our own, you know."

"So, is your USA-SBR anti-hunter?" a reporter from the local Fox affiliate asked.

"Could. Not. Be. Further. From. The truth," Franklin said. "Hunters – except for a certain former Vice President and, no, it's not Mr. Gore – are typically the most cautious people when it comes to handling guns, especially those who've been through NRA-endorsed hunter safety courses.

"And the truly dedicated hunter who takes real pride in her, or his, craft would no sooner feel a need for a 50-round magazine or a rapid-fire weapon than a surgeon would feel a need for a chain saw.

"Folks who value hunting for the true sport that it is will recognize that the USA-SBR is no threat to their pastime."

Before taking final questions from the reporters, Phil and Franklin took special pains to give kudos to two Chicago Tribune reporters, Patricia Callahan and Sam Roe. Their investigative reporting in May 2012 exposed lies by *supposed* expert witnesses (funded by the tobacco industry) to various state legislative committees in support of requiring that carcinogenic flame retardants be added to furniture (instead of requiring cigarette manufacturers to design cigarettes to extinguish themselves when not being smoked). Confronted by Callahan and Roe, one of the expert witnesses acknowledged his testimony before various committees wasn't truthful, but excused it, in part, by pointing out that he "wasn't under oath."

(Callahan and Roe went on to be featured in a September 2014 documentary, "*Merchants of Doubt*," exposing in detail how fossil fuels, tobacco and other industries switched from **denying** responsibility for their products' adverse effects to a strategy of asserting _doubt_ about responsibility, usually through secretly **_industry-subsidized_** phony 'experts.' The Poughkeepsians would view that documentary during a rally visit to Columbia, Missouri in March 2015.)

The reporters wrapped up their questions with few surprises for the Pougheepsians. Franklin, Phil and the rest had high hopes for that evening's coverage. They weren't disappointed. Whether it was the concern for continued firearms violence in northern Illinois or weariness over the state's century-long tradition of political corruption, the local broadcast media's coverage of the press conference was nothing short of gratifying.

Print media coverage of the Poughkeepsians, however, with reporters seeking out 'balancing' reactions from their NRA and hard-core conservative contacts, was about what was expected: Page A-14 in the Tribune and page B-22 in the Sun-Times, with a small photo in the Tribune and no photo in the Sun-Times.

* * *

Marcia once again used her gift for persuasion to convince Northwestern University alumnus Stephen Colbert to be the featured speaker at Welsh-Ryan Arena the following day.

Appearing in his "Colbert Report" character, Colbert was satirically relentless with his faux condemnation of the USA-SBR organizers for having "the audacity to empower the little people, those embarrassingly financially puny hourly wage slav – I mean, workers. You know, the silly working class drones with the delusion that they deserve luxuries like health care, consistent nutrition, PERManent shelter…Ramshackle shacks were good enough for the Bonus Marchers in '32, but, NOOOO, not for these $7.25 an hour welfare queen snobs." (Looking off stage, under his breath, "Bonus Marchers were beaten and burned out by the Army? Meh, had it coming – bad hygiene.")

"These punks from Poughkeepsie don't seem to understand – when they're not picking their feet there, that is – that the concept of American Exceptionalism means little people are **required** to be silent, humble and grateful to be in a country as generous and powerful as this. They know they can always get free food and shelter just by enlisting in the military, don't they?" (Looking offstage, and under his breath, "No, they don't need to be told about this Permanent War culture thing – it's just their little sales tax for expecting the privilege of being part of exceptionalism.")

The overflow crowd of "Colbert Nation" fans consumed his hour-long presentation like caramel kettle corn. They just couldn't get enough. The audience was so laugh-silly-teary-eyed, the Poughkeepsians probably could've foregone the ritual tossing of the free ramen and clean underwear without anyone noticing, but they went ahead with it – didn't want the Evanstoners thinking they weren't exceptional.

They all were stunned when, just before the end of Colbert's performance, he stepped out of character and encouraged the crowd to take up the USA-SBR's cause even if – like himself – they didn't necessarily agree with every last detail of it. Sounding very much like the Sunday School teacher he was, he told them it was part of their duty to leave this world a better place than they found it.

Following the rally, the Poughkeepsians insisted on treating Colbert to dinner at the place of his choosing. As long as they serve uncontaminated shrimp and/or hominy, he said, it didn't matter.

They went on to have the most memorable dinner they would have on any of their rally stops, at Pete Miller's Seafood & Prime Steaks – despite lots of autograph requests from restaurant staff for Stephen. All of which he graciously accepted.

In fact, Colbert was graciousness personified, from the moment they met him at the arena until they dropped him off at O'Hare Airport the next morning on their way south to Champaign.

* * *

The next evening's rally at the University of Illinois' State Farm Center arena ("*Don't you just love all those corporate sponsorships at taxpayer-funded institutions?*" Franklin sarcastically thought to himself, pissed) featured long-time Chicago-area icon Jesse Jackson as the guest speaker.

Thanks to the Rev. Jackson's cachet, the arena crowd was near-capacity – and with a significantly greater than average proportion of folks with 'snow on the roof,' so to speak – but plenty of fire in the hearth, as the good Reverend often said. Marcia's scheduling of Tavis Smiley as Rev. Jackson's introductory speaker certainly didn't hurt attendance either.

Smiley spoke eloquently of how he was influenced not just by Rev. Jackson's activism, but also by the former mentor from his young adulthood, Maya Angelou. Exceptional role models for youth of all ethnic and economic backgrounds are easy to find, he exhorted the audience.

Jackson took to his task as featured speaker as though he'd personally authored the entire USA-SBR and had been giving a sermon on it every Sunday for 10 years.

He said, though, that he was tempted to view the reparations payments provision as "too little, too late," but thought better of that.

"Justice delayed may be justice denied, but even delayed justice is a blessed thing," he said. "Just ask any one of our brothers who's been released from prison after twenty years when a DNA test showed his conviction was completely wrong.

"When the USA-SBR becomes law, we should file our reparations claims and make the wisest possible use of the damages payments we receive. I urge each of you to set aside most of those funds for your children's college living expenses.

"No student, not at ANY age, should have to juggle a full-time job and full-time school enrollment. But those who do, God bless them."

At the end of his presentation, when he was done pumping up the crowd ("You **ARE** some_BODY_!") to contact their elected officeholders, their families and their neighbors to urge support for the USA-SBR, the audience was so worked up that Franklin was afraid they were going to start knocking on neighborhood doors as soon as they left the arena late that evening.

They were worked up, all right, but not quite *that* worked up. The organizers found out later, though, that many members of the audience went around their neighborhoods the following morning before church and later that afternoon, after church. Distributing copies of the USA-SBR, no less. (Not so much in upscale neighborhoods, though.)

Every last one of the Poughkeepsians felt honored to have Mr. Jackson in their midst, flaws and all, and they went out of their way to make sure he knew how they felt. When they dropped him off at the Willard Airport, they presented to him a poster-sized collage photo, created by Marcia during the week before the rally, showing a historical progression of his activism, from standing side-by-side with Martin Luther King Jr. in Selma, Alabama to his many appearances on behalf of the Rainbow Coalition to his presentation in front of the crowd of about 18,000 at the State Farm Center the night before. On the back of the poster were individual, personal notes of gratitude from every one of the Poughkeepsians. After he read each of the notes, he shared close embraces with each of the New Yorkers. As he headed to the check-in counter, there were heartfelt tears of gratitude leaking out of the corners of his eyes.

* * *

The Poughkeepsians went in their rental van directly from the airport to I-74, State Route 63 and I-70, via Terre Haute, to Bloomington, Indiana for that evening's 5 p.m. press conference in advance of the next day's evening rally at Assembly Hall on the Indiana University campus.

They welcomed reporters from the Bloomington Herald-Times (a daily owned by Shurz Communications of Mishawaka, Indiana) and the Indianapolis Star (owned by the Gannett empire, but previously owned by former Vice President Dan Quayle's grandfather and step-grandmother). Ever-so-young reporters from each of the local network television affiliates later showed up in succession for the conference.

Most of the questions centered on the proposal in the USA-SBR to eliminate privatization of government services and, specifically, to ban Charter Schools, citing them as a drain on funding for conventional public schools and unfairly cherry-picking students who would otherwise be attending conventional public schools.

One of the local television reporters knew his aunt had invested in an area charter school, so he asked emphatically why the USA-SBR organizers were targeting "an honest effort" to improve education.

"If it were all that honest an effort, management of all Charter Schools would either decline taxpayer funding or agree to accept any and all students for enrollment with no tuition or fee costs, regardless of the students' testing scores and financial backgrounds," Phil said. "If it were all that honest, they would agree to fully fund employee benefit and retirement programs matching the programs offered in regular public schools and allow full union representation for all their employees.

"But they won't. Because they know that would impact their bottom line. That's what Charter Schools really are about. The bottom line. And, in a lot of instances, being able to teach certain dogma which regular public schools – *and the courts* – don't recognize as reality, like so-called intelligent design theory."

There were other questions about the legislature being in the process of legalizing possession of firearms stored in car trunks on public school campuses, as well as about major tax cuts on wealthy businesses resulting in dramatic revenue shortfalls combined with increased state income and property taxation on non-wealthy individuals.

"You know, there's some truth to the notion that state and local governments are remarkable laboratories in the science of democracy," Franklin/Percy began. "But then there are things like making it legal to take high-powered, high-capacity magazine firearms in car trunks to public school grounds.

"That would seem to suggest that some democracy laboratories maybe need to be inspected for some sort of communicable brain-wasting disease.

"And don't get us started on cutting taxes on the rich businesses so the non-wealthy can make up the difference. That trickle-down crap should be injected into an old fracking well and **permanently** abandoned – except that it might permanently taint everything in the ground with toxic stupidity.

"If I live to be 200, I hope the time comes that people stop unquestioningly soaking up that business propaganda bullshit – pardon my French, I usually don't engage in that practice – that bullshit that wealthy corporations are job creators.

"For the ten-thousandth time, they only create jobs if there is a consumer demand for what they create or for the service they provide. Got it? Hope so."

Whether they got it right, at least they quoted him right. Even if it was on page B-5 of the Star the next day. The Herald-Times actually put the rally organizers on their front page. First time that had happened. The Poughkeepsians were not displeased.

* * *

As Good as They Could Get

The featured speaker arranged by Marcia for the following evening was Indiana native Greg Kinnear. His presentation was a tribute to Robert Kearns, whom Kinnear portrayed in the 2008 movie, "*Flash of Genius.*"

Kinnear pointed out that the Ford Motor Co. actually had a car plant in Indiana – a full 75 years earlier (there were a number of component manufacturers in the state since then, but no car plants). The automaker, like most other major automakers, had since outsourced manufacturing plants all over the globe, mainly in Third World countries. Their goal, he said: finding places where they could pay their workers the least money.

What happened to Robert Kearns, he said, was just a symptom of that corporate bottom-line mentality, albeit a cruel and stark example.

Kearns had the audacity and courage – after winning a struggle with severe depression stemming from efforts by Ford and other auto manufacturers to cheat Kearns out of his rightful compensation for his home basement-laboratory invention of the intermittent windshield wiper – to take up his own cause in court when he was denied representation by private attorneys.

Although his inexperience with the legal system literally cost him judgments against other auto companies, he was successful in winning a $10.1 million jury verdict against Ford and later received another $18.7 million from Chrysler Corporation.

Kearns clearly was the exception to the rule, though, Kinnear emphasized. For every individual like Robert, he said, there surely must be dozens or hundreds of others who were steamrolled by law firms of corporate bullies.

Going all the way back, for example, to Beaver, Utah native Philo T. Farnsworth, a lifelong Mormon. Farnsworth battled the RCA Corporation over his invention of cathode ray tube television in 1927 after originally imagining broadcast television signal waves at age 14 in 1921 as he looked down at row lines while he plowed a field on a Rigby, Idaho farm. His legal battles with RCA and the ensuing financial strain on his family – combined with the death of his 13-month-old son Kenny - led to severe depression and, at the end of his life, serious alcohol abuse, which contributed to his death from pneumonia at 64.

What the USA-SBR would do, Kinnear emphasized, is make predatory corporatists think twice before figuratively defecating all over one of the "little people" who have the kind of genius to actually come up with the ideas those large businesses **need** to make beaucoup bucks.

The crowd liked that. A lot.

The USA-SBR has all the potential to make domination by corporate overlords a matter of distant history – someday, he said.

And the chant from the crowd began: "FUCK O-ver-LORDS!" "FUCK O-ver-LORDS!"

Franklin went on to highlight the other specifics of the USA-SBR and the rally concluded without incident.

That is, until four 30-something men in camouflage fatigues (with "T-Par-T Militia" emblazoned on their backs) tried to rough up Kinnear and the Poughkeepsians as they were leaving the facility.

Idris, Phil and Franklin gave as good as they got, though. And Kinnear managed to unstraighten the nose of one of the assailants. By the time the fisticuffs were done, the bold T-Par-T militiamen were scampering off – considerably worse for wear - to an idling Ford Bronco with no license plates almost 100 yards away being driven by a 60-ish man in dark sunglasses. Franklin wondered if it was Mr. Plaid Pants or one of his surrogates, but it was too dark to get a good look. The Bronco sped away at about the same time that Heather was getting through to a 9-1-1 operator. They were never seen again, but the abandoned Bronco (stolen a day earlier) was found three miles away that night in front of a Chick-Fil-A restaurant. Police were later told that the security video system at the restaurant was malfunctioning that evening.

The Poughkeepsians apologized profusely for the dustup to Kinnear, who was exceedingly gracious.

"Occupational hazard," he said, laughing. "Just might decide to participate via Skype next time, though."

He politely declined the Poughkeepsians' offer of transportation to the airport the next morning, saying he already had it covered.

"If I get beat up by some elderly Skycap, though, I might start to have second thoughts about visiting my native state again. I could be crazy, but I've been getting some weird vibe from people – like they think I'm gay because I played that gay guy opposite Jack Nicholson."

"Forget about it, Jake – I mean, Greg," Pongo said, channeling the ending of 'Chinatown.' "It's Bloomington."

"Good one," Greg said, laughing hard. "Gotta start using that next time I visit someplace intimidating, like Leisure World!"

∗ ∗ ∗

Their next morning's itinerary took them on a full day's travel to Minneapolis for a 6 p.m. press conference at their hotel in advance of a rally at the University of Minnesota's Williams Arena the following day.

Reporters attending included Ron Vortisees of the Minneapolis Star Tribune (a locally-owned daily) and Lacey Vivace of the St. Paul Pioneer Press (a daily owned by Digital First Media of Denver), plus a reporter and camera crew from each local network television affiliate's news department.

The major local issues addressed in reporters' questions involved area conservatives' opposition to anti-bullying legislation affecting public schools and risks of sulfide mining.

"Conservatives are stridently opposed to anti-bullying legislation?" Franklin/Percy asked. "Why am I not shocked?

"Nevertheless, you've got to admit they've got – what is it? Cajones? I mean, to risk – very **reasonably** risk, I might add – being seen as pro-bully: that's as brazen as you can get. What will they be doing next, those Tea Partiers? Maybe fighting to outlaw lactation because it might mean babies of poor people receive as high quality nutrition as babies of rich people?

"These 'R's' – they should pass a special income tax on stand-up comics, 'cause their careers would be nowhere as lucrative without the material the 'R's' give 'em."

Bianca answered the questions about sulfide mining.

"Things like sulfide mining and its consequences are why the long, LONG-overdue replacement of the 1872 General Mining Act is a key feature of the USA-SBR," she said, burnishing her physician's credentials again.

"No longer will there be deference to those who would permanently scar the environment – either physically or chemically – to worship at the altar of unlimited profit.

"Mining organizations will face serious consequences for damage they cause to the environment. Serious prison time. If their organization causes a death, they could potentially face life in prison.

"The mining industry, whether it's miners using sulfides in Minnesota or copper miners in Arizona or coal miners in West Virginia, will be forced to put the health and safety of both their own workers and the general public at the top of their priority list."

"Do you think we can expect the mining industry to be fleeing out of the country once your USA-SBR becomes the law of the land?" asked Mr. Vortisees, echoing a repeated corporatist-inspired theme.

"If they choose to do that, we can't stop them," Phil said. "But we can't imagine that they'd give up the rich resources available in the U.S.A., not to mention the stability of local schools, infrastructure and governments, in exchange for the unpredictability of some regime controlled by drug cartels – or even 'those darn way-too-polite Canucks.' Their only predictability is how dang nice they can be."

(Plenty o' laughter ensued.)

* * *

I'm Good Enough. I'm Smart Enough. and, Doggone It, People Like Me

The next day's rally featured guest speaker and former Air America talk radio host U.S. Sen. Al Franken, D-MN, nee Saturday Night Live's Stuart Smalley.

Introduced by Pongo to overwhelming applause from a packed-to-the-rafters Williams Arena crowd, Sen. Franken looked back at the Poughkeepsians and spoke to them first, paraphrasing his most popular Stuart Smalley line, in character.

"You're good enough. You're smart enough. And, doggone it, people should like you!"

(The crowd erupted in laughs, as well as a brief standing ovation.)

"Seriously, what you've done here – even if it's not absolutely perfect for everyone, including me – it's a huge step toward making our system of government fair to the have-nots.

"You know, that "forty-seven percent" of have-nots who were perceptive enough not to put this country in a cage on top of Mitt Romney's station wagon for four years."

Franken went on to heap praise on the USA-SBR's provision opening up foreign trade as a huge boon to Minnesota's agricultural community, although he predicted that at least one major market – Cuba – would be opened up to U.S. farmers by President Obama by, perhaps, the fall of 2015.

"For gosh sakes, it's not like those wily Cubans are planning to invade us or welcome in evil space aliens or even crazed San Diego Comic Con costumed superhero wanna-bes."

He had strong support for USA-SBR provisions to ban voter suppression, calling that one less tool in the Republican's election trickery utility belt. "If we can just keep removing those utility belt tools, pretty soon they won't be able to keep their pants up. UUUggghh, on second thought after that mental picture, we'll have to make sure we replace the utility belts with some other kind. To hear them talk, they'd probably be OK with the chastity variety."

Many, many laughs later, Franklin/Percy went through the remaining details of the USA-SBR and the remainder of their usual presentation, including the video memorials to Sally and Prof. Bartlett.

The line to shake hands with and get autographs from Sen. Franken must've had 2,000 persons. At 11 p.m., citing a need for "all the beauty sleep I can get," the Senator asked them to excuse him and apologized for any autograph-seekers who were disappointed by his exit. "I promise, you'll get lots of chances to meet me in person during the next election season. Honest. Just think (holding imaginary banner in his hands): COMING SOON to a city bandstand near you, handsome comedian seeking your support. Plus, guest appearance by Al Franken."

(More laughs from exiting fans.)

The Poughkeepsians fawned over the good Senator so much, Holly thought he might joke about getting a restraining order.

But he did not.

After they delivered Sen. Franken back to his lovely wife Frannie, who was waiting patiently in the parking lot to drive him home, Phil said quietly to Marcia-the-expert-booking-agent, "Young lady, you deserve a raise."

"I'll be sure to remind you of that after I get my next paycheck or after I pay for my daughter's next set of college textbooks, whichever comes first," she said.

"I said 'deserve,' _not_ 'you're going to get,' " Phil smiled.

[Little did they know, barely a year-and-a-half later, Sen. Franken would go all Wall Street on them and announce his endorsement of Hillary Clinton for the Democratic Presidential nomination. Franklin and all his Poughkeepsie friends – not to mention millions of Sen. Franken's fans - were **stunned** by the news. There were rumors – but only rumors – that Ms. Clinton was seen on security video entering the hotel where the Senator was staying the night before his announcement – she was said to be carrying a large plastic bag which appeared to contain a pod-shaped item. (See back cover.)]

* * *

Suing Rape Victims; Right to Work for Less; Moore Is Better; Ayers on Perpetual War Culture

Like two days earlier, their next day started at the crack of dawn because they had an all-day eastward drive to get to Ann Arbor, MI for their 5 p.m. press conference in advance of the following day's rally at the University of Michigan's Crisler Center. Thankfully, the roads were mostly snow and ice-free, although there was a huge snow and ice storm forecast for later in the day behind them.

Both the Detroit Free Press (a Gannett-owned daily) and the Detroit News (a daily owned by Digital First Media of New York City) sent reporters, as did the Ann Arbor News (a bi-weekly owned by Booth Newspapers of Grand Rapids, MI) and the Ann Arbor Independent (a local weekly). Local television network affiliates also sent their usual contingents.

Most of the questions revolved around Michigan's two-year-old – as Franklin put it – Right To Work For Less law which was designed to suppress union membership.

"It's just plain wrong," Franklin/Percy said. "It's designed to prevent employers from having to engage in good faith negotiations with their employees. It's designed to make sure employees have as little power as possible and as low a wage as possible.

"The USA-SBR would fix that, once and for all, with card check and with a ban on union members being allowed to consider their dues payments optional. How many of you would pay your taxes and mortgages and utility bills if they were simply optional? That's the logic of the anti-union Tea Partiers and Republicans. Let's see a show of hands."

None was raised.

"OK, argument settled."

Most of the remaining questions involved the so-called Right to Life movement's increased activity in Michigan.

Asked by Laura Calcitrant of the Free Press whether the USA-SBR provision preventing interference with medical procedures would alienate so-called Pro-Lifers, Bianca was quick to respond.

"You mean the ones who want women to always carry their babies to full term even if they have severe birth defects or are the result of rape? The ones who don't give a shit whether the mother can afford to raise the child they demand she carry to term? They **want** to be alienated. They don't believe in a woman's right to control what happens to her body.

"This is one of thirty-one – I repeat once again, THIRTY-ONE states which allow a rapist to sue his victim for custody or visitation with the child who's a product of his rape. It's also a state which forces a waiting period for abortion even upon rape victims.

"That is an unforgivable travesty. It speaks to the truth that women are bereft of power in state and federal governments throughout the nation.

"It is something which should make you ashamed to admit that you are from this state. But, at least, you won't be alone. Remember: THIRTY-ONE states.

"We intend to fix that, **_FOREVER_**."

"Geez, are you guys just itching to be called baby-killers by those Kansan wack-os, or what?" Clive Messyawnack of the Independent, half-joked.

"You mean those knuckle-dragging Westboro Baptist Church _homo_-sapiens wanna-bes?" Harry asked. "Off the record – everyone agree? (all nodded) – I say fuck 'em."

(Considerable laughter ensued.)

"OK, Harry, enough of that," Phil said, but he noticed Bianca nodding vigor-ously in support of her beau's candor.

"We believe strongly in the right of every person – regardless of race, gender, religion, culture, sexual preference or state of health – to control whatever hap-pens to their own bodies. As she said, the USA-SBR will guarantee that, once and for all."

"So," Becky Peligrosita of the News asked, "that includes the right to die?"

"You bet it does," Pongo said. "My maternal great-grandmother was forced to die a slow, agonizing death from lung cancer 15 years ago simply because there was no doctor within thousands of miles who would risk losing his license to prac-tice by prescribing a lethal dosage of drugs for her.

"Do I blame right-to-life nutjobs for her agony? Damn straight.

"What they don't seem to understand is: it's all about treating people the way you'd want to be treated – even when they sometimes don't treat _you_ that way. The Golden Rule. As a dear friend likes to say, it's not rocket surgery."

* * *

Featured speakers at the next day's rally were Michael Moore – whom Phil praised for graciously waiving any screening fees he might otherwise be due for their showings of "Capitalism: A Love Story"- and University of Illinois-Chicago Prof. Bill Ayers. Ayers was a University of Michigan graduate and Chicago area liberal activist whom the far-right despises with relish for simply being barely ac-quainted with then-legislature candidate Barack Obama in the mid-'90s (they were in the same rooms together a handful of times at different organizations' gatherings). Conservatives viscerally loathed Ayers mainly because in the '60s and '70s he was a proud member of the anti-war Weather Underground and ad-vocated limited violence toward war-related properties (but not people), as well as then being an unabashed believer in communism.

"Whether the USA-SBR becomes a reality of the legal system, whether the have-nots and other human corporate drones and wage slaves – like yourselves - who are invisible to the one-percenters out there ever gain real power in this life…that's entirely up to each of you," Moore said, pointing at different parts of the audience.

"YOU have to act. YOU have to take responsibility for your civic duty, as corny as that sounds. YOU have to hold elected officeholders accountable for what they do AND what they don't do.

"NO. ONE. ELSE. WILL. DO. IT. FOR. **YOU**!!!"

"Please get that through your heads, OK?

"Now, before the free ramen and clean underwear – trademark Michael Moore Enterprises, just kidding! – Mr. Ayers would like to speak. Or, as I like to call him, the only American human hated more than me. Again, just kidding! Clearly, I'm most hated of all!!"

Prof. Ayers went through the USA-SBR and pointed out all the ways, if it had been part of the Constitution as early as the '60s and '70s, it might have prevented major instances of _social injustice_, including:

- The Dominican Republic War
- The Vietnam War
- The Lebanese "peacekeeping" war
- The Grenada War
- The Panama War
- The Nicaraguan Contras' proxy war
- The Somalian War
- The Haiti War
- The first Persian Gulf War over the invasion of Kuwait by Iraq (the first blood-for-oil war)
- The Bosnian War
- The Kosovo War
- The war in Afghanistan
- The Iraq War (second Gulf War)
- Race riots in each decade from the '60s forward (because civil rights for all would've been enshrined and on-the-record bigots would've been banned from holding public office)
- Environmental disasters in each decade from the '60s forward (Love Canal, Alaskan Exxon Valdiz oil spill, other oil spills, fracking and associated ruined groundwater and earthquakes, Gulf of Mexico oil spill disaster, ongoing PCB contamination etc., etc., etc.)
- Cancer epidemics (from exposure to environmental disasters and Monsanto products, among others) and health problems from pharmaceuticals approved by the FDA at the behest of Big Pharma lobbyists
- Worst effects from global warming (with solar energy enshrined rather than removed from the White House roof, as done by Pres. Reagan in 1981).

- Shortened lifespans when compared to all other industrialized countries (due to not having the USA-SBR's right to health care without out-of-pocket expense).
- Unstable employment from frequent economic 'bubbles' bursting (due to not having the USA-SBR's limitations on manipulation of the national economy by huge so-called too-big-to-fail banking interests and corporate lobbyists)
- Executions of wrongly-convicted prisoners (such as Cameron Todd Willingham, due to not having the USA-SBR's severe limits on capital punishment and disincentives for criminal justice system participants to authorize an execution when there could be even the slightest doubt about guilt)
- Massive government deficits (due to *not having* the USA-SBR's requirement for progressive taxes, elimination of tax loopholes for the wealthy individuals and corporations plus elimination of tax cuts for wealthy individuals and corporations whenever the government has a deficit balance)

About the only thing not in the USA-SBR that he'd like to see, he said, would be the due process permanent deportation or imprisonment of the billionaire Koch brothers. "Just kidding," he said. "Hmmm, on second thought, well, let me think about that."

The Crisler Center crowd appeared to soak up the presentations with gusto. By the end of the rally, there were perhaps 500 persons lined up for Mr. Moore's autograph and, once again, many thousands of new signers of pledges to contact elected officeholders to compel them to take a stand on the USA-SBR.

And, thankfully, this time no parking lot assailants. "Maybe they were just afraid I'd stumble on top of them and turn 'em into road kill," the still-rotund Moore said, chuckling.

* * *

FUCK 'EM! AND GIVE 'EM HARTMANN, WHILE YOU'RE AT IT

The following morning, they made the comparatively short drive to East Lansing for a mid-day news conference in advance of their rally the next day at Michigan State University's Breslin Student Events Center.

The only print newspaper participant at the news conference was a reporter, Billy Joe "Limpy" Brennan from the Lansing State Journal (a daily owned by the

Gannett empire). But reporters from each local television network affiliate eventually showed.

Limpy Brennan asked the group about Michigan lawmakers' fixation on reducing pay and benefits, including pensions, for workers paid out of state revenues.

"The USA-SBR's provision for a minimum wage based on at least $15 an hour annually adjusted based on 2012 dollars would mean a significant pay increase for many, many low-wage workers," Heather said.

"Plus, its provisions requiring that retirement plans be in the form of defined benefit plans – rather than the far less lucrative 401K accounts – **and** prohibiting the benefits in those plans from being reduced, except during times of deflation – those provisions should prevent state legislatures from creating a bleak old age for their retirees."

"Sure sounds like that means more taxes on the wealthy," said Lucille Cupiditous, of the local Disney (ABC) television affiliate.

"Considering that taxes on the wealthy - with the exception of the Clinton years - have been *systematically slashed* since 1980, that would appear to be something long overdue. For the economic health of the middle class and the rest of the nation," Franklin/Percy said.

"And please take note: we take the provisions of the USA-SBR about businesses being labeled 'economic traitors' very seriously. Wealthy lawmakers around the country – mostly Republicans – never hesitate to play to the prejudices of their base by putting silly restrictions on how people can use their welfare benefits. Some states keep them from using welfare benefits for their kids to use city swimming pools. As though they honestly think poor people believe they can use welfare benefits to get rich. Yeah, right.

"It's far past-time for turnabout being fair play with those businesses which would actively seek to avoid paying their fair share of taxes. As well as those who would outsource their labor forces to foreign countries to save a few bucks on products they bring back here for their ex-employees to buy."

"You know what I say?" Harry asked the reporters. "And this is off the record, right? (All reporters nodded.) I say FUCK 'EM!"

"Jesus, not again, Harry," Phil said. "We apologize for that (once again, he noticed Bianca mouth the words, '*Fuckin' A!*' as he was apologizing).

"What Harry meant to say is, middle class and working poor families have had the deck stacked against them all over the country by the wealthy and super-wealthy. Provisions requiring that certain businesses be labeled "Economic Traitors" are simply one way to achieve some social justice and encourage those businesses not to abandon the country which created their ability to prosper, their ability to exist as the artificial limited liability-protected entity known as a corporation."

"Oh, yeah, sure," several of the television reporters said, almost in unison, each privately admiring Harry's signature candor.

* * *

The following day's evening rally had as its guest speaker former Air America talk show host Thom Hartmann, a Lansing Community College and Michigan State alumnus and author of multiple books (including "*SCREWED: The Undeclared War Against the Middle Class*," 2006) who had once been a country music disk jockey in Lansing.

Hartmann was in excellent form that evening. As his format, he welcomed members of the audience to come on-stage and each engage in a question and answer session about the USA-SBR.

The first person to come up from the crowd, a Charlie Bingham from Corpse Pond, MI, took a microphone at stage right after shaking Thom's hand and then said, "Here's what I think of our Corporate Overlords!"

With his right hand, he then took the microphone, jammed it into his rear exhaust area and expelled the loudest, juiciest and longest-lasting flatulence ever heard by most of the audience.

As First Amendment free speech expressions go, it was 'eeenuque,' as Slim Pickens would've said.

Hartmann graciously thanked the young man and quietly asked Marcia to cleanse the mic with a handi-wipe. Marcia inadvertently cleaned it with a rapid up and down gripping motion, which caused the crowd, in unison, to let out orgasmic gasps followed by more laughs. She shook her finger at the audience in that stern schoolmarm fashion.

Hartmann also took telephone calls from those who heard the rally broadcast over WDTW-AM radio. It seemed like another Air America broadcast.

The calls from "angry uncle" Fox Newsy-types were the most entertaining, not because Hartmann belittled or insulted the callers (he didn't), but because of his skill at getting the callers to acknowledge their own prejudices and ignorance.

By the time Hartmann's presentation was over, the crowd felt both entertained and considerably more knowledgeable about what the USA-SBR was **NOT**. As in:

- *not* a communist takeover;
- *not* a fascist plot to seize weapons,
- *not* a secret strategy to raise *everyone's* taxes (just the wealthies'),
- *not* a plan to disarm the military,
- *not* a way to put everyone on welfare,
- *not* a communist plot for the government to take over everyone's businesses (just the ones who engage in massive fraud and those who would suck at the privatized government teat at the expense of their employees' wages and benefits)
- *and* <u>*not*</u> a concept for the inmates to run the asylum, as Fox News was wont to claim.

When all was said and done, when the memorial videos were played, when the "Capitalism: A Love Story" was run, everyone at the rally had had a ton of fun.

* * *

The next morning, Franklin asked if it was possible for them to visit the Isle Royale National Park off of Michigan's Upper Peninsula before they flew back to New York.

"It's a no-go," Marcia said, after checking the National Park Service website. "They're snowed in up there 'til April or May. We could go to the Sleeping Bear Dunes National Lakeshore, but I expect you'd just be looking at a lot of frozen lake."

"Oh, well – didn't hurt to ask, right?" he said.

"If you'd have been out of bounds, I'd've given you a nun-slap on the hand, Sir," she joked.

So, by mid-day, they were on a non-stop flight out of Detroit to NYC. They'd thought about flying on Spirit Airlines, but Marcia ("She's so damned smart!" Phil kept saying, usually immediately followed by Idris saying, "Of course, that's why she's shtupping yours truly!") quickly pointed out that Spirit charges a fee for everything but inhaling and exhaling – and a charge for those might be on the way. So United it was (which was OK with Orvis O'Leary because he liked their "*Rhapsody in Blue*"-themed commercials; "Hope Georgie Gershwin's getting some hefty royalties for that in heaven," he'd say to Karin every time it was on TV).

By the time they all were back in Poughkeepsie late that evening, they were thrilled to be back in their own homes, headed for their own beds and able to return to their various routines.

"How long do you think we're going to be able to keep up the energy and passion for these rallies?" a weary Phil asked Franklin.

"Hell, if a 132-year-old guy can keep going, I think you've still got some juice left in your batteries, Phil."

"No, really, what do you think?"

"Let's say, for now at least, we just try to make it through at least part of the 2016 election season, OK? Assuming Mr. and Mrs. John Q. Public don't decide we're no longer the flavor of the month before then."

"I can live with that – I hope."

He did.

* * *

Seeing the Fur Fly; No, Not
a New Insect Species!

Mid-January 2014

Franklin returned to his school/work/study/sleep daily grind fairly seamlessly. His and Holly's classes at Marist were challenging, but not overwhelming.

Seven weeks later, he decided to take a day off from classes to fly roundtrip to Los Angeles to see Hillary Clinton speak in person at UCLA, a speech for which she demanded (and got) a $300,000 fee, all of which was paid to the Clinton Foundation.

During the speech, she called Russian President Vladimir Putin a 'tough guy with thin skin' for his reactions to criticism of Russia's partial invasion of Ukraine's eastern periphery. She contended Putin was trying to "re-Sovietize" Russia's edges with such incursions. She compared Putin's excuse for invading (to protect ethnic Russians in Ukraine) to Hitler's excuses for invading Germany's neighbors in the run-up to World War II.

As interesting as her belligerent critique was, though, Franklin was just as interested in one other thing: her appearance. He made sure he got a seat near the front of Royce Hall.

Would he see that fine sensillum hairlike fur - fur visible only to Franklin and others with that special gift of vision - bristling and shimmering on Hillary's skin? Would it be thick and lush as it was on the nitwits who dug him up and on the husband and wife he met on the Grand Canyon Kaibab Trail?

He did. And it was.

The fur on the former Ms. Rodham was so thick and lush - even on her squirrel-like cheeks, forehead and the tops of her hands – Franklin felt a little dizzy just looking at it. Much of the time, as he listened to her speech with the occasional faux Arkansas inflection, he kept thinking to himself, "*Please don't crack your head open. PLEASE don't crack your head open. **PLEASE** do **not** crack your head open!!!*" Because he knew what might happen. Her lustrous sensillum-like fur was the thickest, healthiest looking coat he'd ever seen in all his years – and he'd seen hundreds, perhaps even thousands. A hard crack of her cranium and his self-control just might evaporate into those unseasonably warm Santa Ana winds whirling outside Royce Hall. He did **NOT** want that to happen.

And, of course, it **would** not happen. Ms. Clinton was not about to crack her head open. And without any uncontrollable urges for cranial nutrition by Franklin, he could've done just about anything in that dimly-lit audience – nose-mining, toenail trimming, Three Stooges-style eye-gouging/head hammering/

nose-slapping antics, teeth-flossing, crotch-scratching, you name it – and he might as well have been a cockroach crawling under a sink on Uranus for all she knew. She was as safe as a newborn baby in a neonatal nursery. And Franklin was relieved about that.

So, no more mystery about Hillary's core beliefs. It wasn't just all those belligerent, pusillanimous, Wall Street-friendly cravenly bottom-line-ing politically-calculated *remarks.* It was her very nature.

When he awoke the next morning in his hotel room to prepare for his return flight to NYC and saw the first few white hairs in his eyebrows – not exactly what you'd expect to see on a 22-year-old-seeming body, more like a mid-30s thing – he wondered if he might be compelled someday to take advantage of Hillary's specially-infused mind. He doubted it.

Well, he doubted it conditionally. *As long as* her specially-crafted mind didn't bode poorly for the middle class and working poor who might someday **depend** for survival on her core corporatist-amicable personality traits shifting 180 degrees, he was fairly sure he could keep himself from literally violating that mind.

In other words, he hoped and prayed she'd never come close to getting the nomination of her party to be their presidential candidate. *"Maybe she'll hold off on running 'til someone decides to form the party that most closely aligns with her political philosophy,"* he thought to himself, *"as in the* 'Closet-Republican Democratic Party.' "

"Yeah, sure," he thought. *"About the same chance of that as of Dick Cheney joining a Greenpeace expedition to save the whales – unless it were to save them for his daughter Liz's target practice."*

But he refused to give up hope. There was always that chance Sen. Warren might run.

Yeah. Sure.

✳ ✳ ✳

Northwest Passages

About 10 days later, spring break 2014 arrived and the group – this time minus Bianca, Idris and Heather, but with Tom and Annie Podrowski and Harry's parents Dr. Cherisse and Mel Peterson (as well as their son) for the first time - headed west again for USA-SBR rallies, this time to Gonzaga University in Spokane, Washington; Washington State University in Pullman, WA, the University of Idaho in Moscow, Idaho and the University of Washington in Seattle.

Their first stop was at Spokane International Airport (airport code GEG, standing for "Geiger Field"), located on the western edge of Spokane near Fairchild Air Force Base and the City of Airway Heights.

As Franklin was waiting at the gate for the rest of the Poughkeepsians to exit the US Airways flight, he overheard an interesting conversation. A middle-aged man was standing across the cell-phone/laptop re-charging station from a 30-ish mother and her 8- or 10-year-old son as the child was sipping from a Coke in a plastic bottle.

"Y'know, you can thank our wonderful American predatory capitalism for getting to choose from just one brand of soft drink here in the entire airport," the man said, smiling and half-laughing, to the child and his mother.

The mother, visibly surprised that a friendly stranger would have the audacity to voice criticism of capitalism in one of its primary arteries for commerce, gently turned her son's face in her direction before speaking a response directly to her son, not to the friendly stranger.

"You need to know," she told her son, looking him right in the eye, "that capitalism is what _gives_ _us_ _food_."

"Sonofagun," the stranger said, chuckling. "And, all along, I thought it was hard-working farm families who were trying to avoid selling their farms to massive agribusiness corporations. Last time I checked, capitalism was what gives us food thoroughly infused with preservatives from thousands of miles away."

The young mother and son, as well as the friendly middle-aged man, moved a few feet further apart from each other at that moment.

Another nearby middle-aged man then asked the man who'd been conversing with the young mother and child, "Is that really true, what you said there about why there's only one brand of soft drink in the entire airport?"

"You bet. The Airport Board's contract for the food service provider is written in such a way that the provider is allowed to work out a sweetheart deal with suppliers that's to the financial advantage of both the country's largest soft-drink business, Coke, and the food service provider. It has **absolutely nothing** to do with the Airport's customers' preferences and **everything** to do with people making additional profits behind the scenes.

"You can only speculate why the Airport Board would write up contract language allowing their food service provider to limit product availability that way. It leaves you to wonder if someone on the Airport Board could have some financial gain coming either from the Coca-Cola Corporation or from their contracted food service provider.

"I doubt the Board would jump at the chance to disclose how they try to prevent that kind of behind-the-scenes manipulation. Maybe even because it _is_ happening. Who knows? No way for us to know, not easily, anyway.

"For that matter, it could just be incompetence on the part of the person who wrote the contract. But I kind of doubt that, simply from the level of detail which is included in those kinds of contracts. Allowing the food service provider to limit major-brand availability had to be an intended feature of the contract. Lots of other airports don't appear to allow their food service contractors to limit product availability that way.

"This guy I know says he actually asked the airport manager about it and the manager refused to discuss it. Said he only answers to the State Auditor."

"Forget about it, guy - it's Airport Town," chuckled another middle-aged man (in a faux-dramatic tone of voice) who'd overheard the two men talking. Seemed to be a lot of "*Chinatown*" closing-line references in Franklin's orbit lately.

By that time, the last of the Poughkeepsians (Orvis and Karin O'Leary) had exited the enclosed ramp from the plane. Franklin shared the conversation he'd overheard while he was waiting for them.

"Incredible," Phil said. "Capitalism is to greed like blood is to a vampire. Greed's like a cancer. It pops up everywhere there's a weakness, everywhere a small part of the system is allowed to be weak, to be vulnerable to profit predators."

"Must work for **somebody**, if they're willing to say, essentially, '*go fuck yourselves*' to everyone who doesn't like Coke products," Harry said. "Or maybe they're just hoping people who hate Coke products will drink themselves under the table with their expensive booze."

* * *

MR. PCB THE FLY-FISHING CARCINOGEN MAN

Their press conference at the Red Lion Hotel's meeting facility was set for 5 p.m. that afternoon in advance of the following day's evening rally at Gonzaga's McCarthey Athletic Center. Attending from the Spokesman-Review [a daily locally owned by Republican-friendly siblings W. Stacey Cowles and Elizabeth Cowles' Cowles Publishing, which also owns numerous Eastern Washington and Montana television stations, including the NBC (Comcast) local affiliate in Spokane] was political reporter Jack Rutgers. Also there was Robin Harbinger, political columnist for the Pacific Northwest Inlander (a locally-owned Spokane free weekly), Rollie Wiggum, reporter for the Coeur d'Alene Press (a Coeur d'Alene, Idaho daily, one of multiple small Idaho newspapers and upscale hotels owned by the Hagadone Corp.) and Gerry Masticateur of the Moscow-Pullman Daily News (owned by TPC Holdings Inc. of Lewiston, ID, which owns multiple small newspapers). Reporters for local network television affiliates, all appearing to be in their mid-20s, also showed up, at least one carrying his own camera.

The crux of the questioning revolved around environmental, mining and privatization issues.

The Inlander's Mr. Harbinger appeared most sanguine about the USA-SBR's provision to replace the 1872 General Mining Act and to once again hold polluters responsible for cleaning up massively-polluted Superfund sites.

"Considering that the entire bottom of North Idaho's tourist centerpiece, Lake Coeur d'Alene, is infused with toxic hard rock mining wastes generated for more than the past 125 years, how do you anticipate the USA-SBR will resolve that problem?" Harbinger asked.

"We would want to leave that to the professionals at the EPA," Phil said.

"Could it mean draining the lake completely and dredging out millions of tons of contaminated sediments? That could take more than a decade," Harbinger said.

"Once again, you'd need to ask the professionals at the EPA. As I understand it, so far that hasn't been an option. But, if you recall, one of the USA-SBR's provisions is to make leadership of the EPA elected, so as to make the agency more accountable to voters. With a new agency director being directly accountability to voters, just about anything is possible.

"You'll want to keep in mind: the mandate of the EPA is the public's health and safety.

"One could imagine that concerns about people downstream continuing to be exposed to lead, arsenic and a whole witch's brew of toxic crap from people who mined for a quick buck and then abandoned their claims – you can conceive that those concerns *just might* be placed ahead of the impact of that pretty lake going missing for several years could have on the tourist economy.

"And as I understand it, Mr. Rutgers, your employer owns the Inland Empire Paper Company, which is a major emitter of carcinogenic PCB's into the Spokane River. I believe the PCB's have been found to come from the paper company's recycled newspapers. Seems like they discharge lots of phosphorous into the river too – you know, the stuff that sucks the oxygen out of the water and makes fish sick.

"Any idea if the Cowles are going to finally stop weaseling around the fact that their discharges screw up the river, Mr. Rutgers? They keep implying that what they're doing is peachy-keen because they have a permit from the State Department of Ecology to do it."

"I can't speak for my employer," Mr. Rutgers said.

"That's not a problem, we understand.

"Guess the city leaders won't be promoting to sportsmen tourists any time soon the recreational possibilities for fishing the Spokane River. Since the EPA recommends not eating the fish caught there."

"I wouldn't know," Mr. Rutgers said. "Haven't heard any plans by the city to do that, though."

"Just think of the possibilities," Phil said. "You could have a little mascot, like the Mr. Butts cigarette pack character in Doonesbury. Maybe Mr. PCB, like a lump of black crap with a tumor-spotted head on top and tumor-pocked legs and arms. He could be outfitted with a fly rod and a fisherman's cap. Great way to pack in the tourists!"

Franklin addressed questions relating to the USA-SBR's provisions to undo and prevent privatization.

"It's a mission of education," he explained. "Educating people that, when it comes to social services, there's no room to allow private companies to take over government services for profit. Simply because it's a scam: the only way private businesses can make a profit providing social services is to cut corners on those mandated services – essentially, to violate the law and hope no one holds them accountable. That, and cutting pay and benefits for the employees providing those services, which virtually guarantees that the professionals currently providing those services will go elsewhere – and be replaced by not-so-professional folks.

"Privatization of government services is like trickle-down theory: it sounds great, but in reality, it's a clusterfuck of a massive failure designed to enrich corporatists who already are rich at the expense of the middle class and working poor.

"We've got more than 45 years of proof that trickle-down is a myth. If you look hard enough over the past 15 years or so, you'll find plenty of proof that the theory of prosperity through privatization too is pure myth. Unless you **only** look at the CEO's of Maximus and other privatization-specialized crony capitalist businesses.

"It's been like finding the Lost Dutchman Mine for those guys."

Rutgers and Wiggum both had tough questions about how the Poughkeepsians were funding their drive for passage and ratification of the USA-SBR.

"We've addressed that before: our funding comes from the personal assets of the Podrowski family and from lawful donations by supporters all over the country," Mel Peterson explained. "The data on those donations is updated regularly on our website and on our Facebook page.

"Considering that it was family wealth which enabled the creation of each of the enterprises for which the two of you work, I hope you'll cut us a little slack there."

They didn't – well, not much, anyway.

Rutgers saved his most potent salvo for his final question:

"Are you guys absolutely out of your minds – as in living on another planet - when it comes to this reparations thing? You're talking about something that'll cost the taxpayers as much as the Afghanistan and Iraq wars combined. And you seem to think Wall Street's going to take that transaction tax in quiet repose."

"You tell us, Mr. Rutgers:" Franklin responded. "Which do you think is better, the non-existent economic stimulus we got from throwing a trillion dollars down a combat rathole in the Middle East or the solid, lasting economic stimulus we would have from using a trillion dollars – paid for, mind you – a trillion dollars to commit the longest-overdue acts of social justice in the history of humankind?"

"That's not up to me to decide," Rutgers said.

"That's right. That's why we're here. To try and make sure Americans of all stripes and all walks of life have a chance to decide for themselves whether the USA-SBR is worthy of their support.

"All we ask you to do is make sure they have a chance to understand what it's all about – without any phony fear-mongering by people who have axes to grind.

"We're confident you and your colleagues here today are more than professional enough to achieve that level of communication with your subscribers and viewers."

"Methinks you may be giving us a little too much credit," Rutgers chuckled.

* * *

Double Dose of that "Smoke Signals" Guy

Their featured speaker at the following day's rally was Sherman Alexie, a best-selling author specializing in Native American issues and an alumnus of both Gonzaga and Washington State University.

Mr. Alexie praised the USA-SBR for its provisions to try and give power to the powerless. He praised the USA-SBR's provision for reparations payments, but cautioned against viewing it as a cure-all for centuries of oppression and existential pain inflicted by the U.S. government.

He described in detail what it was like to grow up among one of the most powerless groups on the planet, Native Americans – a people violently colonized against their will on their own lands.

Alexie went on to praise the USA-SBR's provisions to heal the Earth, to help it overcome the centuries of abuse by those who were determined to exploit its resources, no matter the cost to those who depended on those resources for their day-to-day needs.

He recounted the history of the tribes who depended on subsistence fishing along the Columbia and Spokane rivers for thousands of years, regularly netting massive salmon as they stood on rocks above the torrents. He lamented that virtually none of the tribes' most sacred places – like the Spokane Falls - ended up in the reservations on which they were forced at gunpoint to settle. The tribes' history of sustainable resource management simply ground to a halt once the rivers most important and most sacred to them were dammed.

Alexie said he wasn't surprised that the government trod all over the tribes' rights by damming those rivers, nor was he surprised that the government cheated the tribes out of proper compensation – USA-SBR notwithstanding - for the damage those dams did. Damage that destroyed a way of life.

And he shared his humorous perspectives on how Native Americans see themselves, playing a clip on-screen behind him from his 1998 movie "Smoke Signals" about how some Native Americans believe they have to "look mean" to be respected, like they just returned from killing a buffalo.

"Thomas" character in movie: "But our tribe never hunted buffalo, we were fishermen."

"Victor" character: "What? You want to look like you just came back from catching a fish? This ain't 'Dances with Salmon,' you know."

Maybe the tribes needed their own 'Monkey Wrench Gang,' he joked, with apologies to Edward Abbey.

Alexie touched on both the "sins of capitalism and the sins of socialism," but cited simple "human cruelty" as leaving the most lasting scars.

His vignettes alternatively left the audience laughing, sad and angry at the injustices he and his ancestors had lived through and learned about. When he was done, there was not a soul in the overflow McCarthey Center crowd who was unmoved by Alexie's presentation.

* * *

Their following evening's presentation was set for Beasley Coliseum on the Washington State University campus in Pullman. The Poughkeepsians enjoyed Mr. Alexie's presentation so much, they asked him to reprise it. He graciously agreed – he said it gave him an excellent excuse to visit some dear friends in Pullman and Moscow.

The presentation at WSU was dedicated to the late CBS Television newsman Edward R. Murrow, a WSU alumnus.

Though his talk at Beasley was somewhat different from the previous evening – he spent considerable time lamenting that there were so few, if any, journalists of Mr. Murrow's caliber still in existence, journalists with the courage to speak truth to power and advocate against systematic abuses of poor - the result was the same.

He heaped adulation on Bill Moyers as one of the last few Murrow-like journalists in existence. He recalled how proud he was to have been asked by Moyers to appear on Moyers' most recent PBS program.

He spoke at length of Native Americans' challenges overcoming the prejudices of whites and of living down the stereotypes of Native Americans as portrayed in popular culture. The stereotype of Native American alcoholism actually isn't a stereotype, he said, but a "damp, damp reality," a raging deadly epidemic resulting from the use of alcohol to kill the pain of the soul instead of the use of more traditional ways of coping, like singing chants of lamentations.

But the misguided choices also are deeply affected by the generational poverty most Native Americans had come to accept as part of their reservation culture, an artificial culture that replaced the balanced, spiritually healthy culture destroyed by the reservation system. He went on to speak of Native Americans who had succeeded in breaking out of that generational cycle, persons like himself who'd found ways to successfully live between cultures. It's a "magical thing," he said, to find acceptance in both white and Indian cultures and move back and forth between them at will, something even "liberal whites, the ones who adore us the most" can't seem to do.

"I guarantee you I know far more about living like a white person than any of you non-Indians out there know about living like an Indian," he laughed.

He said he hoped the removal of Native Americans' financial pressures through the proposed reparations payments would help motivate Indians to find the inner peace which could come with a return to more traditionally spiritual Indian practices.

"But we'll probably never be able to get back to the fulfillment of netting huge salmon from outcroppings over the Spokane Falls," he lamented. "The EPA says they're so contaminated with PCB's it probably wouldn't be a good idea anyway – especially since the dams keep them from returning there anyway."

He cautioned that the large reparations payments to younger (18- to 25-year-old) Native Americans might result in unintended consequences, what with many young people of *all* cultural backgrounds not necessarily having the best financial acumen.

The audience, about 13,000 strong including perhaps 8,000 members of various regional tribes, was moved in myriad heartfelt ways – as well as earnestly motivated to pursue support for the USA-SBR from their elected officeholders.

* * *

DEEP THROAT'S DEEPER COURAGE

James Blakely, the Sierra Club's Idaho Chapter Conservation Program Coordinator and University of Idaho alumnus, was the featured speaker for the following evening's presentation at the University of Idaho's Kibbie Dome arena.

Blakely started his talk by pointing out that, his graduation notwithstanding, the University of Idaho was famous for graduating large numbers of far right-wing politicians – like Sarah Palin – and successful business persons who likely wouldn't want anything to do with the USA-SBR. Simply because their "constituencies" were of the scorched-earth philosophy: extract profit at all costs and leave the mess for others to deal with.

However, he reminded them, there was at least one graduate who, despite his well-burnished conservative bona fides, found the courage to stand up for what mattered at a time when it could've cost him his career and, just maybe, even his life.

"Deep Throat sound familiar to you?" he asked the crowd. The majority of the crowd was under 35, so they had puzzled looks on their faces, conjuring up images of fellatio.

"Perhaps the least-famous alumnus of this institution, when compared to the impact he had on our society, is the late Mr. Mark Felt. With the help of some dedicated young journalists – Mr. Bob Woodward and Mr. Carl Bernstein of the Washington Post – he was their secret source, 'Deep Throat,' who guided them to evidence which led to Dick 'I Am Not A Crook' Nixon having to resign the Presidency."

He was no liberal, Blakely said: Felt actually was convicted of a felony in 1980 for violating the civil rights of persons he suspected of being involved with the radical group the Weather Underground. His identity as Deep Throat was revealed shortly after his death in December 2008. President Reagan pardoned him in March 1981 for the felony.

But, when it mattered most, Felt risked everything important to him to do his civic duty and protect the country from abuses by a criminally misguided, mentally unstable President, Blakely recalled.

"That's the kind of courage you fellow Idahoans now need to summon to take time from your mundane day-to-day fixations to help propel the USA-SBR toward reality," he said.

Blakely praised the USA-SBR's provisions to wean the country from the atmospheric death brew created by the combustion of coal and by the proliferation of oil extracted by the most destructive of mining techniques. Namely, the tar sands oils with which fossil fuels mega corporations, like Koch Industries, were determined to impregnate the world, like it or not. "Boreal forest rape followed by atmospheric rape," as he described it.

"These fine people from Poughkeepsie are going up against the most daunting obstacle you can find in a mega-capitalist nation: massive corporate money.

"The only way they will overcome that obstacle is with the human footpower each of you kind souls possesses. If you can wear through several pairs of shoe leather, and several layers of fingertip flesh from phone calling and E-Mailing, you can make this happen.

"If you can't, it won't. But you know you can. It's _**THAT**_ important.

"If I can give up a day or two of hiking every week to work on this, you guys can give up some video game time and smart phone time every week for it. If I can do this, YOU. CAN. TOO."

The crowd appeared to be in agreement. Perhaps only a hundred out of the entire audience did **not** sign up to contact their elected officeholders about a commitment to support the USA-SBR.

* * *

The Poughkeepsians spent almost all of the next day traveling to Seattle for their 5 p.m. press conference in advance of the following day's evening rally at the University of Washington's Alaska Airlines Arena. They left extra-early so they could take in the sights at Palouse Falls State Park on the way. Before they started on the latest tour, Pongo showed them a YouTube video of a kayaker going over the falls: they were hooked. Once again, they were, to a person, awe-struck at the grandeur of the falls. They spent about two hours having a picnic lunch, hiking on precipice trails and taking photographs.

As the others were finishing their picnic sandwiches, Pongo noticed Franklin had wandered off on one of the trails and appeared to be crouching down, talking to something. Curious, Pongo quietly wandered over with Phil at his side. Moments later they saw what it was: smiling ear to ear, Franklin was feeding, by hand, a friendly, chirpy, sort-of-smiling little furry marmot and talking to it as though it were his favorite puppy.

"Should we tell him it's probably not allowed to feed the marmots?" Pongo asked his Dad.

"Let's let this one go, son – whaddya think?" Phil asked.

"I'm with you, Pop."

* * *

They arrived in Seattle just a half-hour in advance of their press conference. Reporters from the on-line Seattle Post-Intelligencer, the Seattle Times, the Stranger and the Seattle Weekly showed up, along with on-air talent from each of the local network television affiliates.

The reporters' questions involved the USA-SBR's provisions for a higher national minimum wage, a ban on gender discrimination, the right to housing and eventual elimination of fossil fuels.

As they were all questions the Poughkeepsians previously had addressed – many times – at previous press conferences, there was plenty of smooth sailing for this one. Until, that is, a reporter for the local Disney (ABC) affiliate asked what would happen to television affiliates which didn't have their FCC broadcasting licenses renewed under the drastically different licensing provisions in the USA-SBR.

Phil's response, essentially, was, 'tough luck.'

"Your station owners have, basically, had government-endorsed monopolies to make profits off of publicly-owned airwaves for a good, long time," he said. "This change is long overdue. If your ownership is smart, it will figure out a way, as required under the USA-SBR, to attract massive numbers of small investors.

"If they can't figure out how to do that, then I would recommend they start looking for the very best auctioneering firm to help with the sale of all their hardware and so forth, because the nearly-free ride on their gravy train will be ending.

"It may seem like harsh medicine but, remember, those airwaves your owners have been renting out for a pittance over the decades literally belong to every last citizen of these United States.

"As for individual employees of any station owners whose licenses aren't renewed, I think we can confidently predict that those employees will have the inside track for positions under the owners of the newly-licensed stations."

If the quickly-reddening faces of the television reporters there weren't already a clue, the next two days of local television coverage of the USA-SBR organizers' efforts turned out, not so shockingly, to be just a micro-millimeter shy of outright hostile. Franklin said later he was surprised one the petite bleach-bottle blond television reporters – whose face had turned nearly tomato red and was giving him a sneering stink eye to boot – didn't pull a shiv on him as he was returning to his hotel room.

"Don't think I'll be inviting her to my next birthday party," he said. "Unless she wants to pop out of my cake."

That last remark drew a whole other kind of stink eye from Holly, Karin and Cherisse.

"We need to have another talk about women's perspectives, Franklin, Sir," Phil said.

"I was just joking, ladies," he said.

"That's what they all say," Cherisse fired back, briefly forgetting whom she was addressing. She decided then and there that she had a date with her hotel mini-bar. She kept it – before Mel could break it, anyway.

* * *

Re-Animating Dead Ideas

Most of the following morning was spent by the Poughkeepsians on a self-guided tour of the Pike Place Market and the surrounding waterfront attractions. The group then went in a rental van on a ferry across Puget Sound for a drive to Olympic National Park via Port Angeles and Forks. They were gone for a good six hours. The scenery was stunning, except for large swaths of private property and reservation land where massive fir tree stumps stood, a somber testament to the craven greed motivating the clear cutting of huge swaths of old-growth forest.

On their way back through Port Angeles, Franklin asked the group to promise to take him on the ferry to Vancouver Island, British Columbia, if they ever returned to the Olympic Peninsula. Promise they did.

The guest speaker for that evening's rally couldn't have been better recruited by Marcia, considering the buzz saw they'd run into the previous day over media ownership.

Prof. Robert Waterman McChesney, a University of Washington alumnus and University of Illinois Department of Communications Gutgsell Endowment faculty member, was co-author of *"Dollarocracy: How the Money and Media Election Complex Is Destroying America."* Phil once again spoke of Marcia's need for a raise for convincing Prof. McChesney to fly across the country for their rally (at the Poughkeepsians' expense, naturally).

After hearing Prof. McChesney's presentation, it was clear to the organizers that the good Professor probably would've traveled there on the back of a mule if that had been required. He was **_that_** devoted to the cause of getting the influence of big money out of broadcast media.

McChesney began his presentation with a big-screen re-play of a Nov. 8, 2013 segment of PBS' '*Moyers & Company*' featuring him and the Nation magazine's John Nichols, who co-authored the 'Dollarocracy' book with him.

When the re-play was finished, McChesney said his favorite line from that broadcast was when Nichols explained how the big money from the super-rich who've created 'Dollarocracy' "***can re-animate dead ideas***," like cutting Social Security and Medicare benefits. Even though those cuts, favored by Mitt Romney and his running mate, were soundly defeated in the 2012 election, less than a year later a Washington, D.C. panel of so-called experts was proposing the exact same thing.

McChesney, labeled one of the 50 most influential visionairies changing the world by the *Utne Reader*, explained in detail how 'Dollarocracy' means "one dollar=one vote" instead of Democracy's "one person=one vote" system. He lamented that at the same time a record amount - $10 billion – was spent on media in the 2012 election season to manipulate voters, the jobs of as many as 10,000 "in the trenches" news reporters around the country were eliminated. "Those were reporters who could've helped filter out the B.S. spread around by all those paid ads," he said.

The result, he added, is a grim reality where the most dollars for media buys mean the most wins at the ballot box – and it happens, at times, on both ends of the political spectrum. Just as bleak, he said, was that 85 to 90 percent of political advertising in 2012 was negative, designed entirely to alienate the viewer from the target of the ad with minimal focus on the qualities of the candidate for whom the ad was purchased – leading to de facto voter suppression by turning politics into drudgery for most prospective voters.

McChesney explained that journalism – once considered the antidote (as Moyers put it) to political propaganda ads – has taken a huge hit in the past decades due to massive staff layoffs as print advertising revenues shrank and advertising spending shifted to the internet.

Internet advertising tends to shift internet users away from journalism rather than toward it, he said, and on-line content providers have recognized that. In fact, after AOL bought the Huffington Post, the AOL chairman directed that all new Huffington Post stories would have to pass a "profitability considerations" test before getting into print. Time magazine has a similar set-up, he added.

In short: if it doesn't potentially contribute to profits, it doesn't get printed. Meaning stories about the problems of the working poor and minorities living in ghettos likely will no longer see the light of day.

McChesney reprised his final remarks from the Moyers program:

"The system is collapsing. We're living through the pain now of a corrupt system that isn't delivering the goods. It's not addressing the great crises of our times and that great despair that that brings.

"And then ultimately what every individual has to do is very simple: you've got to look in the mirror and understand, if you **act** like change for the better is impossible, you **guarantee** it will be impossible. That's the one decision each individual faces."

McChesney then made it even simpler:

"You can step away from that crushing hopelessness corporate media wants you to see when you look in that mirror. You can make this USA-SBR happen, with hard, persistent work. Just don't expect big corporate media, you know, like Kabletown on Tina Fey's '*30 Rock*' – which actually was a poke in the eye at NBC/Comcast – don't expect them to cover the progress you make.

"If you expect pats on the back for doing the right thing from a system which *does **NOT** want* you to do the right thing, you're guaranteeing disappointment for yourself. The ultimate reward will come when you see that final state legislature ratify the USA-SBR, not when Brian Williams finally decides it deserves to be covered.

"As Gil Scott-Heron wrote, 'the revolution will not be televised.' And make no mistake: the Koch brothers of this world see the lawful Constitutional Amendment you support as a revolution.

"Surprise them: go make it happen!"

What followed was a prolonged standing ovation with the traditional "FUCK O-ver-LORDS!" chants interspersed.

After the rally's end, as the Poughkeepsians were congratulating and hugging McChesney, most of them thought – some for the first time – that this thing *ACTUALLY COULD* happen. Franklin was thinking the same thing, but with a significant modifier: "*But probably not with a closet Republican corporatist like Hillary Rodham Clinton in charge.*" He'd learned long ago of the wisdom in thinking years ahead of others.

* * *

Their flight back the next day from Sea-Tac Airport to NYC on United Airlines was delightful, except for the usual lack of legroom in coach. Franklin had originally found the cramped seats assigned to air travel's hoi polloi hard to accept, but every time he'd feel a negative thought about that forming, he'd remind himself of one simple fact: he could walk again. Cramped quarters were:

No. Big. Deal.

Once again, blessedly, no bizarre elderly woman was sitting next to him for the five-and-two-thirds hour flight. And, amazingly, no screaming babies or toddlers for the entire ride.

The next day, it was, yet again, back to the good ol' school/work/study/sleep/re-set routine for Franklin and Holly. Enough to do to keep their minds off the gremlins and hobgoblins which might be lurking out in the void somewhere to obstruct their plans for a happy, if not joy-filled, future together. By now, Holly had noticed the re-growth of her hymen after each intimate encounter with Franklin became thinner and thinner, so as to be almost non-existent. She rarely thought of him any longer as this person who literally had been resurrected by some bizarre force of nature. He was just Franklin-slash-Percy. Someone who had finally come to understand – with lots of help from Phil and Pongo – what it meant to be a supportive, easy-going partner and lover with a 21st-century woman. A woman who would never, ever make conceiving a child her *primary* focus in a relationship. But she occasionally wondered to herself as she lay in bed late at night waiting for sleep to roll over her mind whether never, ever having a child would be a deal-breaker in this relationship. Especially considering the culture in which she was raised.

But, then, each time, she'd remind herself, "*That's crazy talk. You're in your early twenties, pinhead! LOTS of time to worry about that.*"

And that would be when she'd slip into the dream.

∗ ∗ ∗

SOMNOLENT VISIONS, PART IV

*S*he suddenly saw herself in the delivery room. The obstetrician was heaping encouragement on her. "Just another push or two and you'll be done, Holly. You've got this.

"All the vital signs are good. Wait, it's feet first – that's OK, feet first is the way I like it. A change-up is always good. No evidence that the cord's around the neck. Still good vitals.

"Skin tone's good. There it is: now you know, like it or not. It's a boy. It's a strong, ten-toed full-blooded male of the Van Mullder-Van Arsdale species. This little man is going to ge..."

"Going to get what, doctor?"

"Hold on, we've got a little anomaly here. Nothing we can't fix."

At that moment, she looked down and saw that her top of the now-emerged head of her newborn son had not fully knitted itself shut during fetal development.

As she recognized the textures of the boy's visible brain matter, something came over her like the jolt a do-it-yourself handyman feels when he inadvertently touches an unshielded live wire in a light fixture box.

It was then that the delivery room suddenly seemed to pull back 30 feet from her eyes. She seemed to be watching everything unfold from a distance. She watched as her instantly-strong arms shoved both the obstetrician and each of the delivery room nurses against the walls so hard that their heads broke the ceramic tiles on the walls.

She watched as matter from each of their brains stuck to the tiles as their limp bodies slid to the floor, one at a time. She knew they would be next.

Then she watched as her hands started scooping out her newborn son's brain matter and cramming it into her grotesquely salivating mouth. Just as she was about to feel the first particles of infant amygdala touch her taste buds, she woke up, drenched in sweat and overcome by horror.

Fortunately for her roommate Nancy down the hall, Holly's nightmares never were accompanied by screams, just frantic gasps for air.

And those dreams would persist. Sometimes a day or a week after sexual congress with Franklin. Sometimes a month later. But, always, they followed.

"*Helluva price to pay for the most fulfilling and joy-filled pleasuring I might ever experience in my life,*" she thought to herself.

"*Was Daddy right?*" she wondered.

*   *   *

NON-VIRGINAL SUMMITTING

May 2014

The finals for the spring semester at Marist arrived at breakneck speed. Once again, no one was surprised when both Holly and Franklin maintained their 4.0 averages. Well, Franklin was a little surprised. There were times when he still thought of himself as the 'C' student he'd been, for the most part, during his previous college iteration.

Their next rally tour was set to start the day after they received their grade reports. They discussed their routes two weeks before departing and agreed they would visit the University of Oregon, Oregon State University, Stanford University, the University of California-Berkeley, San Jose State University, Sacramento's Sleep Train Arena (where the NBA Kings play) and Fresno State University during a 17-day period; they planned for a combined press conference for the Bay Area and other northern California schools, except for Fresno State, which would get its own. The 'down time' they had scheduled during the tour were side trips to Timberline Lodge (a WPA-built facility) at Mount Hood, Oregon, Crater Lake National Park, Lassen Volcanic National Park, Redwood National Park and Mount Shasta National Natural Landmark. Pongo wouldn't be going due to his own National Park job duties.

"Sure seems like a lot of volcanoes on this intinerary," Franklin said. "Hope we're not planning to sacrifice any virgins on some Mount Hood fumarole."

"We need one more talk," Phil said, noticing the wincing expressions from the women in the room.

"I was only *JOKING,*" Franklin said.

"Let's cut him some slack this time," Harry said. "I was actually about to say the same thing – only I was going to offer to provide a life-saving cure for any virginal rectitude we encounter."

"Don't think we should be looking to HP here as a sterling example of feminist forward thinking," Bianca said, with a joking smirk on her face. "But I think we should let that one go too. I thought it was funny. Besides, I don't think there are any virgins anywhere near this group."

At which point, Karin said in a faux Georgia accent, "Y'all should speak for y'all's seff, chald. Frankly, my de-ah, you embarrass me no end. Please excuse me, should I be blushin' in this moment of indeescreshin, you young hahlut, you!"

A good laugh was had by all, including Franklin, who would always look forward to visiting mountains with holes in the middle – which he coined as 'non-virginal summits' - from that point forward.

∗ ∗ ∗

After arriving at Portland International Airport early in the afternoon, their latest tour began with a stop at Corvallis, Oregon for a 5 p.m. press conference in advance of the next day's rally at Oregon State University's Gill Coliseum.

Reporters attending included journalists from the Corvallis Gazette-Times (a daily owned by Lee Enterprises of Davenport, IA) and the Portland Oregonian (a daily owned by Advance Publications of Staten Island, NY), as well as the usual throng of barely-old-enough-to-imbibe reporters from each of the local network television affiliates.

The usual USA-SBR-related questions started the press conference. About mid-way through it, the 20-something reporter from the Oregonian, Larry Fromager, asked why the USA-SBR didn't address what the government should do if there's an invasion by outer space aliens.

"Yes, OK, I get it," Franklin said. "You're using the classic tried-and-true class clown strategy to try to imply that our provisions cover too many issues. I don't see you complaining about the provision to ensure the continued existence of quality investigative journalism, a provision which Scandinavian countries adopted years ago.

"How's this for a more substantial question you just maybe *could* have asked, although it's not of the space alien variety:

"'Will the USA-SBR's provisions to end the U.S.A.'s culture of permanent war and to prevent unnecessary wars result in there being more money available in the budget for genuine emergencies?'

"The answer there is an unambiguous **yes**. For example, the U.S. government currently doesn't have in place a plan for responding to potential global extinction level events like a major meteor impact or a massive eruption of a huge volcano, such as the Yellowstone caldera.

"If we can prevent trillion dollar sums from being spent in the future on military-industrial complex-friendly fiascos like the Iraq War, we'll have the resources to plan for _those_ kinds of **genuine** existential threats which we know are likely to occur, but which we can't forecast with adequate accuracy."

Mr. Fromager had nothing further to ask or say.

Other reporters' questions involved ground already covered in previous press conferences; those interactions with the Poughkeepsians went smoothly.

* * *

INTO THE NOT-SO-WILD CONSTITUTION

The following evening's rally at Gill Coliseum featured Corvallis High School graduate and best-selling author and mountaineer Jon Krakauer, author of "*Into the Wild*," "*Into Thin Air*," "*Where Men Win Glory: The Odyssey of Pat Tillman*" and "*Under the Banner of Heaven*."

As someone who in his many mountain-climbing treks witnessed first-hand the effects of global warming, including vast swaths of pine bark beetle-infested dying pines, Krakauer poured out his heart in support of the USA-SBR's provisions to protect the environment and combat global warming.

Likewise, he praised its provisions for establishing a right not to be unwillingly proselytized by emissaries from various religious faiths, citing his first-hand research for "*Under the Banner of Heaven*" documenting how church leadership can be prone to re-writing sanitized versions of history and excommunicating members who try to hold them to account.

"There is a mountain of social justice to be achieved in this life," he said. "You can summit the goals set forth by this document (holding up the USA-SBR), but only if you start climbing now and only if you don't stop 'til you can see from the top.

"There will be lots of super-wealthy people ahead of you at the summit sending rockfall your way, so stay vigilant on your way up.

"You. Can. Do. This."

Many, many books were autographed before the evening was done.

* * *

A WPA GEM

The Poughkeepsians left early the next morning for Timberline Lodge, the beautiful Mount Hood gem which wouldn't have been built but for Franklin's inspired creation of the Works Progress Administration (WPA).

It was an emotional nostalgia-filled visit for Franklin, who had dedicated it in person as it neared completion in September 1937.

This time, unlike his previous visit, he was able to bound up the front steps of the lodge with Holly, climb part-way up the side of Mount Hood and enjoy a ski lift ride up its slopes to take in the spectacular view to the south, where he and his sweetheart could see the slopes of the Three Sisters volcanic peaks near Bend, Oregon in the distance. Watching the smiling faces of the nearby snowboarders doing their 360's and 720's, he was tempted to grab a board and join in. But, thinking about the remote – but real – possibility of a broken back, he demurred. He knew all too well that the ability to walk and run was not something to be unnecessarily risked…not for him, anyway. But Holly leapt at the chance. Turned out she was a natural at snowboarding – at least when it was 65F outdoors.

Franklin took special enjoyment in going up and down the wooden staircases inside the lodge and, later in the afternoon, swimming with Holly in the pool at its west edge. As he tossed beach balls back and forth with kindergarten and 3rd-grade-age children there with their Bozeman, Montana family, he briefly thought about many laughter-filled memories from his visits with families of other polio victims in the pools at Warm Springs.

When Holly wasn't wondering what the faraway looks on Franklin's face meant, she thought a lot about how fit Franklin looked in his swimming trunks. All of that heavy lifting at Adams Landscaping had sculpted some serious biceps, triceps and abdominals.

While Holly's mind was pondering an extended intimate visit with Franklin in their bedroom at the lodge, Franklin's still was on both Warm Springs *and* what the WPA had accomplished.

"And to think: this lodge functions as a not-for-profit U.S. Forest Service facility for tourists, not for a mega-corporation's shareholders – with no exclusive members-only fees required or systematic price gouging designed to appeal primarily to that 1 percent at the top of the income ladder."

If he'd dropped dead at that moment, he'd have been satisfied to the core, comforted by the feeling that his return to this life had truly counted for something. But, as things turned out, he still had many more meaningful contributions to make.

Not the least of which was a contribution to the mutual satisfaction of his and Holly's steaming libidos about 15 minutes later, a contribution which not only lasted the next three hours, but kept on giving. And giving. And giving. Every night for the rest of this latest tour.

The other Poughkeepsians spent the day exploring Mount Hood, climbing up its side to view the gas-venting fumaroles, snowboarding, riding the ski lift up and down several times and goofing around with chipmunks and marmots. As at Palouse Falls, a certain one of the New Yorkers (with the middle name Delano) didn't notice a sign asking that the critters not be fed. As a result, one of those *naturally*-furry friends slept that night with a tummy chock full o' Cheeto's – as well as a handful stored away for the coming winter. Not exactly naturally-occuring nutrients found in the wild. Unless you're a naturalist in New York's Central Park.

Idris and Marcia decided to explore the forests below the lodge, venturing into a particularly dense thicket, where they elected to emulate the copulating squirrels they'd witnessed several times exchanging fluids – with the males finishing in under a minute each time - in vertical alignments clinging to tree bark.

"If you don't take more time with me than those boy squirrels did with their sweeties, I may just decide to remove your stored nuts for the winter, young man," Marcia said.

"Yeeooowwch," Idris said, under his breath. "Can't have that!"

They were there more than two hours: nuts remained in place.

In fact, they were there so long that they even saw Harry and Bianca passing by looking for their own secluded spot for intimate probing. Fortunately for both couples, Mr. Peterson and Ms. Swanson kept going, finding a deeply-shaded spot padded with soft grasses among a dense stand of trees about a quarter-mile to the south.

By the following morning when it was time to return to the rally schedule, every last Poughkeepsian hoped for a chance to return to Mount Hood sometime before they got old and crotchety.

∗   ∗   ∗

They arrived at Eugene, Oregon around lunchtime, giving them a considerable cushion to prepare for their 5 p.m. press conference in advance of the next day's rally at the University of Oregon's Matthew Knight Arena.

Reporters were there from the Eugene, Oregon Register-Guard (a locally-owned daily) and the Eugene Weekly (also locally owned). A reporter from the local National Public Radio network affiliate also showed up, but there were no local television reporters there simply because they'd all attended the press conference in Corvallis.

Register-Guard reporter Soccoro Plantureuxeuse wanted to know how the government would meet the USA-SBR's requirement for everyone to have a decent home during economic slumps.

"Honestly, Soccoro, we're confident that the Congress will feel compelled to comply with what would then be its Constitutional imperative," Franklin/Percy said. "We're pretty sure members of both chambers would want the issue kept in their own hands rather than have one or more constituents obtain a court order which would tie their hands and severely limit their options.

"But the Congress does have the occasional habit of not doing the smart thing. (Howls of laughter.) We're fairly confident that, once the USA-SBR removes the influence of corporatists' massive donations from the election system, the collective Congressional I.Q. will rise sharply.

"The Louie Gohmerts of the world, we hope, will soon be sent packing back to their home states to harangue the locals about 'terror babies,' who gays should be forced to have as sex partners, forcing women to carry unwanted or deformed fetuses to full term and encouraging oil pipeline construction supposedly as a way to improve caribou sex."

✳ ✳ ✳

D'OH BOY

The next evening's rally at Matthew Knight Arena (named for the late adult son of Nike Inc. Co-founder/Chairman Phil Knight, foreign outsourcer *extraordinaire*) featured Portland, Oregon native Matt Groening, creator of *The Simpsons*, who brought along Harry Shearer, voice of "Springfield" nuclear power plant owner and all-around craven greedhead C. Montgomery Burns.

Marcia got Shearer to agree to introduce Groening in Shearer's C. Montgomery Burns character voice. It *killed*.

Groening thanked the Poughkeepsians for inviting him back to his native state, praising its residents for consistently being ahead of the curve.

He spent most of his comparatively brief talk praising the provisions in the USA-SBR focused on achieving social justice and preserving the environment.

"My silly little efforts at animation just make people *laugh* about injustices and prejudices. You guys actually can make some real, lasting **change** happen there," he said, looking at Phil and Franklin/Percy.

"We joke about the three-eyed fish swimming near the Springfield nuclear plant, but things like virtually eternally-toxic nuclear wastes and so-called 'clean coal's' filthy CO_2 defecation into our atmosphere are real existential threats to your families and my family.

"Y'know, when we depict the Republican Party leadership as a bunch of craven, out-of-touch greedheads and crotchety near-zombies sitting around a huge table inside a castle on top of a stormy hill, it's not just for comedy. Someone said that in every example of great comedy there are at least a few kernels of truth. Man, their kernels would fill a trainload full of tar sands oil barrels.

"If you know what's good for you, you'll get out there and kick some far-righties' butts and make this thing happen."

Shearer stepped up to the mic with the perfect C. Montgomery Burns-voiced coda: "Exxxxxcellent!"

Franklin went on, as usual, to explain the remaining provisions of the USA-SBR in detail. He saved some remarks for Phil Knight 'til the end of his presentation.

"Mr. Knight, if you're out there in the audience somewhere, please know that the USA-SBR provision requiring products distributed in the U.S.A. by companies obsessed with foreign outsourcing to be labeled "Made By Economically Traitorous Company" was not a provision _directly_ inspired by your command of Nike.

"Nevertheless, please **also** know once the USA-SBR is the law of the land that – unless you change your outsourcing practices in Asia, where you pay your impoverished employees a teensy-tiny fraction of the hourly pay they could earn here – we _will_ have a raffle.

"The proceeds from that raffle, donated to charity, will determine who gets to be the first person to imprint that 'traitor' stamp (with the co-operation of the Secretary of Commerce) on a pair of shoes made at one of your greedy-ass Asian textile plants.

"I intend to be the first person to buy one of those raffle tickets. Who else here will join me in sending a message to this particular corporate overlord?"

Then, once again, the chant:

"FUCK O-ver-LORDS!" "FUCK O-ver-LORDS!" "FUCK O-ver-LORDS!"

It was a raucously enjoyable rally. Home Jay Simpson woulda loved it (maybe with some bleeping out of the F-words).

Actually, his creator sorta DID.

＊ ＊ ＊

Hasta Be Shasta; No Lessening of Lassen; All Redwoody

The next morning, before heading southward to the Bay Area for their next press conference three days later, they detoured to Crater Lake National Park, driving all the way around the rim road and spending time at the visitor center.

Franklin was impressed, especially at what he couldn't see: the complete depth of the lake, almost 1,950 feet, the deepest lake in the U.S.A. But he would've preferred an area with more hiking trails, especially those that were more challenging. They did not linger there.

The next leg of their touristy side trip took them two hours down U.S. Route 97 to the City of Mount Shasta in Northern California. They stopped to feed the trout fingerlings at the fish hatchery next to the Sisson Museum. Holly, Heather, Marcia, Karin and Cherisse stood around and giggled like pre-school kids at the frenzied way the fish attacked the feed pellets every time they threw a handful into the crystal clear water. The men enjoyed watching the women laugh as much as anything else they'd seen on the tour to that point. Once both the women and the fish got their fill of each other, the group then took in the historical exhibits inside the museum before driving to the end of the highway going up the mountainside. One of the museum exhibits mentioned people in the early 1900's seeing glowing red-hot luminescent boulders tumbling down from the top of one of Mount Shasta's four volcanic cones.

The Poughkeepsians were awed at the sheer mass of the mountain. Like so many other mountains in the West, it dwarfed anything they'd experienced in New York and New England.

They went on to spend the night at the Oxford Suites in Redding, each of them hitting the sack relatively early to be ready for a long day of National Parks exploration the next day.

The next featured site on their itinerary was about 45 minutes away at Lassen Volcanic National Park in Northern California. They took the park highway through the center of the park – stopping numerous times for scenic photography – and then backtracked to loop around its southern border to the Warner Valley Campground road.

They hiked from the Boiling Springs Lake Trailhead near the Warner Valley Campground on to Boiling Springs Lake.

Franklin's favorite part of the day was the stop at Boiling Springs Lake – he wanted to test the 125F waters there, simply because he'd always enjoyed the therapeutic benefits of hot springs baths in his previous iteration of existence. Enjoy he did, although he came away fairly well-caked in mud.

"Good for your skin," Holly said, standing in the water next to Franklin, as she smeared some of the mud on her own alabaster curves. After the others headed back onto the trail to Terminal Geyser, the two of them stayed behind to thoroughly and sensuously remove the mud from each other in a clear-water part of the lake. Coital friction ensued as soon as the others were out of sight.

After Franklin and Holly caught up with the rest of the Poughkeepsians at Terminal Geyser (which isn't actually a geyser – it's "just" a fumarole) along the Pacific Crest Trail, they headed back up the park trail to Devil's Kitchen, where there were lots of steam vents, fumaroles and mud pots to marvel at.

By the time they were done hiking and picture-taking, daylight was starting to wane, so they headed back to Redding.

The next morning, they all rose relatively early again, this time for a drive to Redwood National Park via State Route 299 and U.S. Route 101. At the park, they stopped at the Kuchel Visitor Center, watched videos, reviewed exhibits and mapped out the itinerary for their drive through the park, which included a drive to the Klamath River Overlook, where they saw several gray whales breaching. Then they went up Coastal Drive to Crescent Beach Overlook followed by a 1-mile hike to Enderts Beach. After that, they took the Drury Scenic Parkway south to Davidson Road and watched Roosevelt elk grazing at Elk Meadow.

"Those were named after my favorite uncle-by-marriage," Franklin proudly reminded the Poughkeepsians, "after he approved the creation of Olympic National Park. I just thought you might be interested."

A couple of them were. The rest already assumed as much. *"You really don't need to try to impress us,"* Phil thought to himself, and then remembered just how much Franklin admired cousin Theodore.

From Elk Meadow, they went on to take a 2-1/2 mile hike on Trillium Falls Trail to see one of the few perennial waterfalls in the park.

There were minor skirmishes each time they returned to their rental van over who got to re-charge their digital cameras. Harry kept fixating on trying to find where scenes from *"Star Wars Return of the Jedi"* were filmed. He finally gave up when he realized that, after a while, massive stands of redwoods all start to look pretty much alike. At least when compared to the scenes from the movie he kept playing on his smart phone – when he could get a signal, that is.

* * *

SIX FLAGGIN' IT: THE EXOTIC ANIMALS DILEMMA

By late afternoon, they all were ready to head for their hotel at the Marriott Courtyard in Vallejo, where their press conference was set for 5 p.m. the next day for all of the rallies they'd scheduled in the days ahead at Sacramento State University, Stanford University, the University of California-Berkeley and San Jose State University.

What Marcia hadn't realized when she'd booked the hotel, however, was that, while first-rate in every way, it was located close to the Six Flags Discovery Kingdom theme park, which featured lots of exotic zoo, avian and marine animal exhibits. So, they had to get used to tourists' small children, pre-teens and teens running up and down the halls until about 10 p.m. Marcia decided to make lemonade out of the lemon they'd gotten, though: she bought day passes for the theme park for the Poughkeepsians.

So, the entire group got to spend about eight hours the next day meeting exotic animals up close and going on various and sundry carnival and thrill rides. The weather even managed to co-operate. It was another chance for Franklin to step out from the memories of his heavily-shielded childhood experienced courtesy of his often hyper-protective mother and the private tutors he'd grown up with. He relished the opportunity, especially with Holly along to help him feel like less of a dork.

Which he inadvertently and repeatedly resembled. His relatively brief earlier visits 2-1/2 years earlier at Disneyland and Knott's Berry Farm seemed like a decade ago. He appeared clumsy trying to get on rides which 4-year-old children slithered onto smoothly; he appeared to have no idea what to expect from modern upside-down-rolling roller coasters (he hadn't gone on any in Southern

California), he kept welcoming people to cut in line ahead of him and he even tried to tip a ride operator with Roosevelt dimes, thinking dimes still were something big spenders handed out (something he'd meant to do at Disneyland and Knott's, but he'd always been without any 'coppers,' as he liked to call change, while he was there) – the awkwardness list went on and on.

But Holly, realizing her lover's unique background, literally held his hand throughout the entire day, 'til it was time to leave for the press conference. By the end of that day, if Franklin hadn't already been passionately in love with her, he'd have been as smitten with her patience and devotion as a person of the heterosexual male orientation could possibly be.

* * *

Holly asked Franklin as they were about to leave the theme park if he had any misgivings about the wild animals there – especially the high-functioning ones like dolphins - being held in captivity, unable to roam freely through an expansive habitat like the one they – or their ancestors – had originally considered their home. Held captive simply so tourists could gawk at them.

It did bother Franklin.

So, Holly asked, should there have been a provision in the USA-SBR banning zoos and parks from artificially confining wild animals unless injuries or habituation to humans would prevent them from surviving in the wild?

"Zoologists – except perhaps for a few of the ones employed by for-profit amusement parks like Sea World – they're already fairly vigilant about making sure animals who can survive in the wild are returned to the wild," Franklin said.

"Once people become more educated about how detrimental most zoos and animal theme parks are to the long-term health of wild animals, I feel fairly confident most people won't want to pay to see them living in what amount to abusive habitats. It may take time, but I'm pretty sure that will be a natural consequence of the provisions in the USA-SBR for improved public education.

"Besides, we've got to convince voting humans to support the USA-SBR. Until all those critters compel Congress to give them the right to vote, we need to keep our focus on persuading residents who walk upright."

"Including the knuckle dragging ones in the Tea Party?" she asked.

"Including knuckle draggers of all persuasions: we don't discriminate."

* * *

FUNKY FRACKERS INC.

Reporters attending their press conference that afternoon represented the San Francisco Chronicle (a daily owned by one of the first huge media

491

conglomerates, the Hearst Corporation, originally of San Francisco), the San Francisco Examiner (previously a Hearst paper but now an independently locally owned free daily), the San Francisco Weekly (with the same ownership as the Examiner), the Oakland Tribune (a daily owned by Digital First Media of New York City), the Vallejo Times Herald (also owned by Digital First Media), the locally-owned Palo Alto (almost) Daily Post, the locally-owned Palo Alto Weekly, The Sacramento Bee (a daily owned by McClatchy Co., based in Sacramento) and the San Jose Mercury News (a daily owned by Digital First Media of New York City). Reporters from local affiliates of television networks also attended, as well as Jerry Whiterock, a CBS News correspondent based out of San Francisco.

It was the first time that many members of the 'fourth estate' had attended one of the Poughkeepsians' press conferences. To say tension was heightened among the New Yorkers would've been like saying it was difficult for someone wheelchair-bound to break out of the not-so-distant Alcatraz.

The bulk of the questioning involved the environment, with multiple reporters pointing out the epidemic of destructive wildfires in and around heavily populated California cities and suburbs, as well as an ongoing drought throughout the state.

Franklin/Percy listed – as he had so many times before at press gatherings – all of the reasons why the anti-global warming provisions in the USA-SBR would help heal the planet's climate.

Carl "Lucky" Lache, who covered environmental issues for the Sacramento Bee, asked why the USA-SBR was so fixated on stopping fracking when it was clear the expansion of that technology has driven down energy costs significantly, especially considering the industry's claims that the science shows "less than significant" impacts on groundwater and seismic incidents.

"Mr. Lache, if some executive from the California Independent Petroleum Association told you that you should sign a contract allowing Funky Frackers Inc. to drill a well in your back yard in exchange for a one-time $100,000 payment because they were '*pretty sure*' the effects on your drinking water supply would be 'less than significant,' would you sign?"

"Well, that'd be up to my wife. She's the family accountant."

(Lots of muffled laughter from the other journalists.)

"Levity aside, if you're willing to trust the fox to guard your groundwater henhouse – pardon the mixed metaphor, please – then you're nowhere near as bright as you seem to be.

"There are thousands of examples all across this country of groundwater supplies being destroyed for millennia because of fracking. Hundreds of examples of repeated incidents of earthquakes in areas of fracking where earthquakes previously were an extreme rarity.

"If you, as someone who covers the environment, are unwilling to apply more scrutiny to the fracking industry's claims, it certainly doesn't bode well for your subscribers who enjoy pure unadulterated H2O coming out of their taps. Unless they routinely need to light a blowtorch in their sinks."

"So, Scruples – if that _really_ _is_ your nickname – what do you feel is the most important thing we in mass media can do to help people understand issues involving fracking?" Lache asked.

"Simple: stop publishing and repeating verbatim claims from industry representatives – whether it's in your news coverage or your opinion pages – that fracking poses minimal or no threats to the environment. Those. Are. Lies.

"When you print that kind of B.S. what you're doing is along the same lines as giving coverage to people who claim the Nazi Holocaust never occurred in World War II. Only, in some ways, it's worse: the Holocaust deniers are motivated by hate – their shitty hate probably can't give you cancer. The fracking industry is motivated by craven greed – and the shit **they** stuff down their wells _can, in fact,_ give cancer to you and me and everyone else. Through the water we drink, no less.

"Ever try putting cigarette-style cancer warning labels on water coming out of the tap? Let us know if you solve that one, OK?"

What had been a shit-eating grin on Lache's face had now transformed into either red-faced embarrassment or anger. Unclear which. Franklin himself was blushing considerably – he was embarrassed at the ease with which profanity had started spontaneously coming out of his mouth in recent months. "_Suppose I can blame that on my exposure to all these 21st century young folks,_" he thought to himself.

(For what it's worth, eight-and-a-half months later the Bee ran a lengthy op-ed piece from a spokesman for the California Independent Petroleum Association claiming that the 'latest science' showed fracking wasn't a significant risk to groundwater, surface water and seismic activity. When Franklin later read that, he thought to himself, "_McClatchy, you know you can do better. Who got to your editorial board?_")

The remainder of the press conference focused on social justice and immigration issues, for the most part.

Judging from the remarks of the journalists to each other as they left the hotel meeting facility, the rally organizers acquitted themselves well. On all counts.

The coverage the next day – both locally and even on the CBS Evening News – appeared to bear that out. Even Mr. Lache's piece in the Sacramento Bee was nothing less than an accurate depiction of the press conference. Upon reading it, Franklin immediately felt guilty for having addressed the reporter somewhat harshly. He consoled himself with the fact that pretty much all reporters – from the beginning of time forward – develop a fairly thick skin pretty quickly. If they're any good, anyway. He hoped Lache hadn't taken what he'd said personally. In fact, he hadn't, at least not once the conference was over.

✳ ✳ ✳

Speak, Forrest, Speak!

Marcia all but guaranteed herself a raise with the featured speaker she'd corralled for the next day's rally at Sacramento's Sleep Train Arena: none other than multiple-Academy Award winner Tom Hanks, who'd attended Sacramento State University and had lived with his family in Sacramento for an extended period long before moving to Los Angeles.

Hanks right away made his affinity clear for the environmental and gender orientation rights protection provisions of the USA-SBR.

"The USA-SBR can help us to make the use of fossil fuels as extinct as the dinosaurs they come from," he said.

"If we want to keep our planet from turning into a furnace, to keep the entire surface of this Earth from becoming one big Death Valley, each and every one of you needs to get to work, tomorrow, putting your elected officeholders' feet to the fire on this.

"Unless, that is, each of you plans on magically turning yourselves into the Human Torch from the Fantastic Four. Seems like your monthly deodorant budget would be the size of General Motors', though."

He also expressed his hopes that the USA-SBR's provisions to discourage wars, especially Iraq-style so-called 'pre-emptive conflicts,' would lead to more government money being available for space exploration and research for disease prevention.

"Those real-life heroes depicted in "*Band of Brothers*," they didn't give their lives and lose their limbs just so the military-industrial complex could take us down a cultural path of permanent war, just so massive corporations could enrich their management and shareholders at the cost of the blood of our youth."

He added praise for USA-SBR provisions to ensure openness in government and to minimize the influence of corporatists' money and lobbyists at all levels of government.

"Keep the faith, and keep buying electric cars and hybrids. We can do this."

* * *

Double Standard Justice

The following day's rally at the University of California-Berkeley's Haas Arena featured Berkeley native and Academy Award winner Ben Affleck.

Affleck, a longtime fan of the late Howard Zinn and Zinn's "*A People's History of the United States*," provided his almost unqualified endorsement for almost every provision of the USA-SBR, with a few minor exceptions.

He was especially hopeful that its provisions to incorporate annual minimum wage increases (including a large one-time minimum wage increase at the outset or ratification) and to promote union organization would lead to a dramatic reduction in income inequality.

Perhaps among the more hopeful provisions, he said, was the one which would create access for regular citizens to grand juries when they felt that their local prosecutors were trying to protect members of the elite political establishment from being held accountable for corruption or other crimes.

"The justice system we have now – where there is one standard for those who have plenty of money and a completely different standard for everyone else – it simply cannot continue to stand. It has become virtually as un-American as Jim Crow. And it continues to disproportionately imprison people of color, especially African-American men.

"The existence of a law enforcement system in which an African-American male of almost any age can be shot and killed with impunity by a police officer for the offense of breathing while black – that system must end. With all deliberate speed."

(Massive applause.)

Needless to say, the lines for handshakes and autographs after the rally concluded were Afflleck-buddy Matt Damon-long, or longer. Affleck stayed as long as he could, but left after an hour, explaining that he needed to catch a flight south to return to his family in Pacific Palisades.

$$* \quad * \quad *$$

Joan's Amazing Grace

The next day's rally at Stanford University's Maples Pavilion in Palo Alto had Joan Baez as the guest speaker. Baez participated in her first act of civil disobedience as a Palo Alto High School student in 1958 when she declined to participate in an air raid drill (designed to give students the impression they could survive a Cold War-era nuclear bombing).

Baez' virtual mission in life was to educate the public about the senselessness of war and the myopic greed, manipulation and fear which propel nations into war.

For that reason, she was only too happy to applaud the USA-SBR's provisions to discourage and prevent armed conflicts.

She shared harsh criticism of Stanford University for its ties to those she considered warmongers, such as Edward "Dr. Strangelove" Teller and "W" Bush's "(Iraqi) smoking gun to be a mushroom cloud" former Secretary of State Condoleezza Rice.

Baez heaped praise upon the provisions for immigration relaxation in the USA-SBR.

"It's the first time human beings would be treated with more respect when crossing borders than truckloads of the farm produce they've picked," she said, laconically.

(Massive cheers and a standing ovation followed.)

Once the rally was done, Baez's line of hand-shakers and autograph seekers wasn't Matt Damon-long, but she stayed 'til every last person had a chance to shake her hand or give her a hug.

She told some of them that they could do far, far worse than to emulate the political philosophy of the man who was President the first four years of her life, Franklin Delano Roosevelt; she said she could vaguely recall the grief of her family members upon FDR's death. She told one autograph-seeker that her paternal grandfather, the Rev. Alberto Baez, once even wrote a letter to FDR in 1935, a letter which remains in the New Deal Network archives, offering to help the President with any initiatives to assist Spanish-speaking Puerto Rican American citizens in Brooklyn to find jobs.

Overhearing that, Franklin – not one to have ocular leakage in public – teared up a bit. He made sure he got his turn at a hug when the rally attendees were done getting theirs.

After dropping off Ms. Baez at San Francisco International Airport late that evening, each of the Poughkeepsians agreed among themselves that she probably was the most spiritually balanced of all the guest speakers they'd been fortunate enough to welcome into their midst. A non-violent soul through and through, to her very core.

$$* \quad * \quad *$$

POUGHKEEPSIANS ALWAYS LIKED HIM BEST

The Poughkeepsians welcomed to their rally the following day at San Jose State University's Event Center Arena comedian Tom Smothers, a long-time activist on behalf of anti-war and civil liberties issues, as well as a former San Jose State University track and field athlete, as their guest speaker.

Smothers' '*Smothers Brothers Comedy Hour*' variety show with his younger brother Dick was cancelled by the CBS Television Network in April 1969 despite years of stellar ratings after the network's entertainment division became uncomfortable with outspoken opposition to the Vietnam War by several of the show's guests.

Ever since, Tom – whose own father died as a World War II prisoner of war on a Japanese ship - has been a steadfast opponent of armed conflicts and outspoken advocate for civil rights.

Tom had nothing but praise for the USA-SBR sections involving the erection of barriers to unnecessary wars. What a different world it would be today, he said, if there never had been a Vietnam War, not to mention all the other wars since then.

Likewise, he threw his full support behind provisions of the USA-SBR which mandate openness in government, remove big corporate money from government, ban suppression of voting rights and change Federal Communications Commission broadcasting licensing requirements to make broadcasters reach out to lots of small investors.

"Where were you guys fifty years ago, anyway?" he asked, looking at the Poughkeepsians, briefly in his old 'goofy-Tom' character. "Oh, uh, right, little eggies inside your 10-year-old Mamas. Sorry 'bout that. Would've been nice, though, to see CBS have to suck up to lots of average folks to keep their broadcasting licenses."

Tom went on to play his guitar and sing a couple of funny songs he'd written the previous week in tribute to the USA-SBR. The performance was an instant hit on YouTube among Baby Boomers; it got 100,000 hits within a week after the San Jose Mercury News ran a brief piece on it.

To further exemplify his humility, Tom shared the spotlight before he wrapped up, providing a brief but heartfelt and eloquent tribute to the late Gary Webb, the San Jose Mercury News reporter who exposed a Reagan-era conspiracy between the CIA and drug smugglers but was reviled by traditional corporate media, mainly for working at a comparatively small newspaper. He urged everyone to go out and see the movie about Webb ("*Kill the Messenger*") when it came out six months later.

[Unfortunately, only a few remembered to.]

By the time the rally was done, those who weren't already fans of this Smothers Brother had fallen in love with him.

Before he returned to his Kentwood, CA area vineyards two hours north of SJSU the next day, the group insisted on treating Tom to a nice sit-down lunch. He graciously accepted. It was another one of those many moments shared in their organizing tours which they would remember the rest of their lives. It was easy to see why this particular man – whose mother didn't "like him best" – was an icon of entertainment history.

* * *

The group left shortly after their lunch with Tom Smothers to get to their 5 p.m. press conference in Fresno in advance of the following day's rally at Fresno State University's Save Mart Center arena.

The only newspaper reporter present was Josh Silliphant of the Fresno Bee (another daily owned by the McClatchy Co. of Sacramento), but reporters from each of the local network television affiliates also showed up. A few of them looked too young to drive.

One of the main issues of concern for the local reporters was hydraulic fracturing. Turned out that local fracking allegedly had killed all the trees in a cherry orchard two years earlier (due to fracking chemicals causing saline contamination in groundwater) and was threatening to kill off almond orchards in the area.

"Wish I could say we're surprised at that," Orvis said. "If the USA-SBR is ratified, fracking will become as extinct as the do-do bird."

"But what will happen to all the orchards and farms that get destroyed in the meantime?" Silliphant asked.

"'Til the USA-SBR is the law of the land," Orvis said, "the farmers' only recourse will be the courts. And everyone knows how expensive and drawn out that process is. Just check with Erin Brockovich or the folks in Hinkley 3-1/2 hours to the south."

Another huge issue was the increasing number of potable water wells of private residents drying up as an extended drought began to emerge in the region and as population in the area continued to grow.

"What will people in this part of California do if their taps literally start running dry, their water wells spitting out sand?" Silliphant asked.

"It's difficult for anyone, including scientists, to manufacture water out of thin air," Phil said.

"The best we can do is try to approach global warming head-on. Our USA-SBR does that with its provisions to end our country's addiction to fossil fuels. It won't happen overnight, but, make no mistake: when the USA-SBR becomes the law of the land, it _will_ happen."

"The other major issue behind that," Franklin/Percy said, "is the increase in demand for potable water by growing populations and by the agricultural industries growing to match the demand from those growing populations.

"The USA-SBR's provisions to discourage large families – specifically by ending the tax code rewards for having larger families – will _begin_ to change the way people think about large families.

"Our goal is to make reproductive fecundity such a socially embarrassing fact of life that the only people who would want to watch television programs like the ones about the Duggar and Bates families will be mentally defective individuals. People who aren't exactly the sort of folks advertisers are interested in spending their dollars on.

"Once both news and social media have exposed the connection between large families and depletion of worldwide resources, that should give everyone a sobering wake-up call about how they need to plan their families. **For their own self-interest**, not to mention the interests of the planet itself.

"Those in your profession, Mr. Silliphant, could do far worse than to read '*Countdown*,' by Alan Weisman – and encourage your readers and viewers to do the same. It's a compelling and hopeful examination of the achievements and possibilities of family planning worldwide.

"If we could afford it, we'd include a copy of '*Countdown*' with every copy of the USA-SBR we distribute."

The other primary issue for the local reporters was immigration reform.

Franklin's detailed explanation of the USA-SBR provisions to open up borders in both directions all around the world – for persons without violence-related criminal convictions – kept them rapt with attention.

As he spoke, Franklin thought he could almost see the wheels turning in the minds of a couple of reporters, reporters who appeared to have wistful visions of living in exotic places along the lines of New Zealand, Bali, Australia and Thailand.

"But, uh, er, sir, aren't a lots of folks gonna see just lettin' peoples live wherever'n they please as to be un-American?" asked Wilton Abeille-Bourdon, a mid-20-ish reporter for the local Disney (ABC) television affiliate.

"We would hope most folks would see allowing people to live wherever they want, without threat of persecution, to be perhaps the most humane and decent way to live," Franklin said.

"If you fell madly in love tomorrow with a beautiful woman living in Uzbekistan and she couldn't leave her job to come here, wouldn't you at least want to have the *choice* of going there to live?"

"My waff and two little-un boys prob'ly wouldn't take too kindly to that," Abeille-Bourdon said.

"Sorry – didn't picture you as someone with multiple children at your age… Anyway, if your son were grown up and that happened to him, wouldn't you at least want him to have the choice about which country he could live in?"

"Ah s'pose so, since you asked."

"Hooray for one less thing to be called un-American," Franklin said, raising his hands in triumph.

* * *

Pioneer of Protest

The Save Mart Arena rally at Fresno State University the following evening featured a rare appearance by author David Harris as the group's guest speaker. Harris, ex-husband of Joan Baez, was a Fresno native and Fresno High School graduate who went on to notoriety during the Vietnam War for organizing "The Resistance," a movement encouraging young men to refuse to cooperate with the Selective Service System. (The Selective Service System was the government mechanism which drafted young men for induction into the U.S. Army.)

As the result of his activism, Federal prosecutors decided to make an example of Harris, arresting the former Stanford Student Body President in July 1969 and convicting him of draft evasion. He served 15 months in various Federal prisons. Ironically, while he was at Stanford University, Harris was the dormitory resident advisor for one year for future Presidential candidate Mitt Romney.

Phil's introduction of Harris to the crowd urged their respect for the unjust persecution successfully imposed on him by Federal prosecutors.

"Think about this, good people of Fresno: on August 11, 1967, the all-time champion of unfettered predatory capitalism – Ayn Rand – went on the The Tonight Show with Johnny Carson and told a national audience that no government and no group of men had the moral right to force a man to submit to conscription.

"She said young men should resist the draft to keep from serving in Vietnam.

"She did virtually the same thing David here was arrested for less than two years later. Do you know how many days, much less months, she spent in prison for urging men to resist conscription?

"If you guessed ZERO, you win a gold star and a pat on the back.

"So, exactly how was it that David was imprisoned for 15 months while the author Ms. Rand, darling of the far-right wing, wasn't even charged with a crime?

"Well, I suppose it could've had something to do with David's hard work registering minorities to vote during the summer of 1966 in Mississippi. Mr. Hoover at the FBI was none too fond of that kind of activism. He thought most civil rights activists like David were Communists.

"But I suspect it had a lot more to do with Ms. Rand's unflagging activity as an unapologetic proselytizer for unfettered predatory capitalism. She called the selfishness behind unregulated capitalism the main reason for the survival of modern civilization – in the same breath that she **admitted** altruism – self-sacrifice for the good of the community – is *incompatible with capitalism.* Throw in a grain of truth there with all those compulsive lies and you're bound to convince someone you sound good.

"Never mind that her so-called rational self-interest – otherwise known as 'I've got mine, who cares if you get yours' – is the philosophy of predatory animals. Not human communities.

"And – get *this* – she claimed there is no relationship between capitalism and our country's penchant for going to war. She said that with a straight face, even though she certainly realized that perpetual war – as lubrication for the profit-intensive military-industrial complex – is the natural and inevitable outgrowth of unfettered predatory capitalism.

"So that woman, a woman whose mean-spirited sociopathic philosophy to this day drives a huge majority of the Republican Party, was able to flitter around the country with impunity urging young men to break the law. She even alleged that the movie "*It's a Wonderful Life*" was anti-capitalist pro-socialist communist propaganda.[*]

"So, David, in case military conscription ever makes a comeback just remember this simple strategy to keep yourself out of prison: go around the country and call out as a communist everyone who shows a shred of human decency.

"'Cause everyone knows, to keep our modern civilization healthy, we've gotta keep on throwing everyone who's even temporarily on the skids – their children included – *into the woodchipper.*

---

[*] Josh Jones, Open Culture, 12/25/14

"If they don't make each of us personally richer, what good are they, right? Anyone besides me getting a little fascist vibe off of that Rand chic?

"Anyway, we should all hold David here in as high a regard as there can be. Someone who was unjustly persecuted and imprisoned for simply trying to walk the walk and talk the talk of social justice could easily have been excused for giving up and dropping out of this bizarre contradictory stew known as American culture.

"David did not. David picked himself up and became a respected journalist and author. He remains an icon from a period of our time when whatever social justice took place was mostly a cosmic accident, like a gold nugget sneaking through a tiny opening in a sieve and returning back to the stream from which it was unwillingly wrested.

"He deserves our heartfelt thanks for living a life of courage and principle."

(A standing ovation lasting a full minute ensued.)

Harris promptly showered flattery on the Poughkeepsians for their idealism expressed in the provisions of the USA-SBR. He said he was surprised that, with the potency of those provisions to achieve social justice, the New Yorkers hadn't been targeted for sham prosecutions and constant undercover surveillance. As soon as he said that, the Poughkeepsians thought of Mr. Plaid Pants, as well as the two assaults on them at previous rally sites.

"I hope you continue to be successful in avoiding persecution by the military-industrial complex," he said, glancing at the Poughkeepsians. "Their mission is simple: keep government under the control of oligarchs and corporatists – people whose sole focus is on profits at the expense of lots of human cannon fodder – and everything else they want will fall into place.

Looking into the crowd, he added, "These mostly very young people care a great deal about the thousands of you out there – not to mention your families back home.

"It's time now for you to do them a solid. Because the only way they're going to stay protected from trumped up charges and phony prosecutions orchestrated by corporate shills in government is if each of you takes responsibility for your own part of getting this (holding up the USA-SBR pamphlet) done.

"It's not a mystery how you make this happen: you put peoples' feet to the fire. And if they say they like getting their feet singed, then you go out and run for office against every single person who wraps corporate currency around their singed toes.

"As Jean-Luc Picard would say on '*Star Trek: The Next Generation*,' Make. It. So.

"NOW.

"Don't let another soul go to jail or die in the name of Wall Street profit for the One Percent.

"It's in your power to do this."

When the rally was done, with all the usual memorial videos and "Capitalism: A Love Story" done playing, the Poughkeepsians made it a point to thank Harris one at a time on stage and shake his hand in front of the crowd.

"This is a MAN," Franklin said, "a man who was willing to go to prison for the modern equivalent of stealing a loaf of bread, only this loaf was to sustain the courage of his brothers targeted for wartime combat in a war contrived for one purpose only:

"To send a political message to non-capitalists. Fifty-eight-thousand-one-hundred-fifty-one U.S. soldiers dead to send a political message. Fifty-eight-thousand-one-hundred-fifty-one soldiers dead fighting against a country which never had the slightest, most remote intention of attacking or invading our shores.

"This is a MAN, a man who, like every other Vietnam War draftee, deserves reparations from his government for it trying to send him to war under false pretenses.

"Until we get this USA-SBR passed and ratified, it should never surprise us again when the corporatists who control our government conspire to gin up another phony list of reasons for going to war – whether it's about Iraq again or Iran or anywhere else on the planet.

"This man – and all other men and women like him, young and old – deserve your honest efforts to make this (holding up USA-SBR) happen.

"Don't let any of this slip out of your mind between now and when you wake up tomorrow morning, we implore you."

(Lots of thoughtful applause, quite a few shouts of "Hero Harris!" and just a smattering of "FUCK O-ver-LORDS!" chants.)

There were a few tears of appreciation slipping down Harris' cheeks as the Poughkeepsians walked with him out of the facility and escorted him to his car. They made sure he knew he'd made a difference in their lives.

* * *

The Poughkeepsians took a one-stop early morning flight back to New York City from Fresno Yosemite International Airport the following day via American Airlines and U.S. Airways. Gratefully, their travel was uneventful, except for someone on the leg of the flight between Dallas-Fort Worth and LaGuardia whose bathroom emissions somewhere over Tennessee suggested a massive intake of vintage Mexican food.

Their return to their usual warm weather routines was a comforting change, not to mention being back in their own beds again for the first time in almost two weeks.

The statistics on the USA-SBR web and Facebook pages suggested steady organizational progress. They were starting to receive about six contacts a day – both electronically and via the U.S.P.S. – from elected office holders who either wanted to go on record in support of the USA-SBR or who had well-thought-out questions about it which implied potential support.

All seemed well.

* * *

HRC on NPR

Franklin and Pongo were driving around Poughkeepsie running errands on the afternoon of June 12, 2014 when they happened to catch a Hillary Clinton interview on National Public Radio's '*Fresh Air*' program. She told NPR's Terry Gross that nothing positive came from Edward Snowden's disclosures and she continued to mislead the public about Snowden's options for working within the system, falsely faulting him for not resolving through 'proper channels' his objections to widespread illegal surveillance and systematic deceit by the U.S. government.

Channeling her inner Joe McCarthy, she directly implied that Snowden intentionally ended up in Russia because he knew the Russians could use their technology to uncover the information he had. Ms. Gross didn't bother to point out what Ms. Clinton surely already knew: that Snowden had, in fact, tried to get his superiors to disclose wrongful surveillance and, more importantly, that he had no choice but to remain in Russia because the U.S. government revoked his passport while he was there on his way (probably) to Venezuela. [Ms. Gross appeared much more interested in trying – unsuccessfully - to get Ms. Clinton to admit that she'd supported same-sex marriage for a much longer time than when she officially announced her support for it in March 2013 - and that the delay in that announcement was influenced by political strategy. Ms. Clinton sternly denied that, essentially saying she grew into her support for same-sex marriage along with the rest of the country over the past 25 years.]

She went on at great length with her takes on how she and others in the Obama Administration had restored the role of pre-eminent world leadership to the U.S.A. since the fiasco (not *her* word) of the George W. Bush Presidency.

"I wish I could understand why all these closet-Republican Democrats like her have such a hard-on to throw Edward Snowden in a dungeon and toss away the key," Pongo said. "Maybe they're afraid their stock in corporations manufacturing drones and spy gear will tank."

"Can't fault her for her testiness, I suppose," Franklin said. "I wouldn't turn my back to her when she's fighting off those same-sex marriage questions like she was in that interview. She sounded like she was in a contract negotiation."

"Did you notice how she had *absolutely nothing to say* about the Firedoglake report the other day that the Director of National Intelligence (James R. Clapper Jr.) had pursued NSA employees for alleged Espionage Act violations over leaks to news media **despite the fact** that government employees are _exempt_ from that law when they're acting as whistleblowers?"

"Well, it would've helped if Ms. Gross had asked her about that. But I liked that Ms. Gross got her to go on record as being OK with same-sex marriage being decided state-by-state and in the courts instead of through a Federal civil rights-type law. Goes to show her states' rights-ey closet Republicanism."

"If we were to catalog all of the important issues she's had little or nothing to say about – _other_ _than_ **non-specific platitudes** or things most people already have come around to support, like gay marriage and equal pay for women – we probably would end up with about a thousand pages of great ideas needing to be embraced by a great leader," Pongo said.

"Has she come out in support of sunshine, lollipops and rainbows yet?" Franklin asked.

"I think she's waiting to hear back from her platform consultants and private pollsters – probably wants to see how many 1963 Lesley Gore records were sold last year. But word in the 'beltway' is that she's *leaning against* **sunshine** – has just *too darned much* of a transparency cachet to it…"

✳ ✳ ✳

DEAR LADIES: KEEP THOSE LEGS CROSSED – WITH LOVE, YOUR SUPREME COURT

Another 18 days passed and it became painfully obvious that U.S. Supreme Court jurists weren't influenced in the slightest by the growing grass roots support for the USA-SBR evident from activity on the Poughkeepsians' blog and other social media sites.

On that day, June 30, just four weeks after returning from their latest rally tour, the Poughkeepsians were infuriated to read about the latest landmark decision from the Supremes.

Known as Hobby Lobby.

"What. The. FUCK!" Harry said, as he walked briskly into Pongo's living room with that morning's newspaper in his hands.

"These Republican-appointed ass-wipes are saying that a for-profit corporation employer can use its supposed religious beliefs as a valid excuse for not complying with a law that contradicts those religious beliefs, specifically a law that requires them to cover women's birth control through the company health plan.

"First, has anyone besides this non-mental giant (pointing to himself) noticed any corporations sitting in church pews on Sunday?"

"Like you'd be in a church pew," Pongo deadpanned.

"No, seriously, I mean, what would a corporation look like in church? Would it be some Terminator-type robot wearing a dress shirt that said 'Praise the Lord' on the front and 'Fuck the Poor and Unions' on the back?

"Those Supremes, shit, they need to smoke some better dope. If they can imagine some corporate avatar shitting – oops, I meant sitting – in a church pew, surely they can imagine it, like, dispensing free birth control pills out its ass or free automated nut nips for guys in some little room attached to its back.

"What's happened to all those old codgers' imaginations, anyway?"

"Beats the shit out of me," Pongo said. "Thank God Heather doesn't work for those Hobby Lobby fuckheads. Last thing we need is a rugrat crawling around pumpin' poop into a diaper.

"What say we go to the nearest Hobby Lobby and tape a few free Planned Parenthood condoms to the shelves next to their romantic candles section?"

"Fuck. 'n. A.!"

And they did just that. They made sure to include Franklin once he got off work from Adams Landscaping.

"Are you kidding me?" Franklin asked. "How in Jesus' name can a business have a religion? And, even if it did, how could it legally force its beliefs on its own employees?? How could that possibly be American? That's hardly different from the *government* forcing a specific religion on its people."

"Well, yes, Sir," Pongo said, "but the Supremes say all the person has to do to exercise her own freedom of religion if they're offended by that is **to quit**."

"Oh, hell, no. They expect a person to, basically, risk destitution and homelessness to get out from under their own corporate employer's so-called religious strictures?

"What the fuck is this, a fucking Middle Eastern theocracy?" (Harry's jaw dropped open at this new penchant of the former President for using the F-bomb.)

"You mean, like Idaho and Utah?" Pongo asked. "You remember Utah County, where you could get evicted for putting Sports Illustrated swimsuit model pictures on your apartment wall."

"Point taken."

* * *

They'd thought the idiotic Hobby Lobby decision – which was just a logical extension of the idiotic Citizens United decision – might cause interest to skyrocket on the USA-SBR's internet links.

But it didn't. Activities on those links remained steady.

They theorized that it probably prompted just as many people to give up altogether on hope for social justice as it prompted to get pissed off enough to act. They probably were right.

* * *

Hillary & Jon – Sittin' in a Studio; Softballs Were Tossed

Fifteen days later, Franklin convinced Pongo to go back to New York City with him to see Jon Stewart interview Hillary Clinton. She was appearing to hype her new book, "*Hard Choices.*" After reading a few reviews of the book - which uniformly trashed it as little more than a high school-y exercise in name dropping about everyone she'd met as Secretary of State - Franklin and the Podrowskis decided it was **NOT** a hard choice to forego reading it.

Franklin wanted to see if Stewart shot any hardball questions at her or if they would mostly be little slow-pitch pre-school-style softballs.

Unfortunately, it was mostly the latter.

But, as Franklin fought against being distracted by her shimmering thick sensillum-like fur – which only he could see – protruding around her hilariously round cheeks, neck and forearms, he heard the former U.S. Senator say something which made the entire trip worthwhile, if only to confirm his fears about her.

She actually said much of what's wrong about America's image problems with other countries, countries which have been starting to despise the U.S. government in recent decades, *could be solved simply by starting up a new system of pro-U.S.A. radio and television broadcasts into those countries, a la the old Cold War era Radio Free Europe stations.*

"So, a healthy dose of Cold War-style pro-U.S.A. propaganda is all we need to make it all right," Franklin whispered to Pongo, both of them shaking their heads, both disgusted and embarrassed for their own country. "She actually thinks **that's** all it takes to distract people from our drones murdering innocents gathered at family weddings and such.

"Just. Incredible."

Stewart did not verbally pounce on her for that assertion, sadly, although Pongo could tell he was truly tempted to.

After her interview was done, she'd made it clear her intention – were she to someday be elected to a certain higher office – was to be a "morning in America again" Reagan-y kind of President.

"God help us all," Franklin said. By this time he considered himself a virtual scholar of all things Reagan-fucked-up-ity.

* * *

Mmmm...Throaty Goodness!

About three weeks later Ms. Clinton appeared on Comedy Central's The Colbert Report. What took place on that night's show should've been an embarrassment to both Clinton and Colbert.

They went through what clearly was a pre-rehearsed back and forth comedy skit which was so un-funny – except to Hillary fanatics in the audience – that it was nearly painful to watch. And listening to Hillary's throaty laugh was like putting a frosted turd topping on a curdled milkshake.

"Just how in the FUCK could any political party think it might be smart to put that corporatist-shill Wall Street crony phony on their Presidential ticket?" Pongo asked as he, Phil, Heather, Holly and Franklin watched the show.

"She certainly doesn't appeal to me," Heather said. "But what do I know? I'm just some libtard who works for the government helping disadvantaged folks.

"Maybe she can get me some Wall Street-y privatized version of my job for lower pay and no benefits!! It would be sooo good for my soul to know that my hard work was helping make rich stockholders get richer."

"Hey, I hear, Colbert's about to retire," Phil said. "You should apply for his job, Heather!"

"Fuck you," she said, joking, with a smile.

* * *

Furry Faced Former First Female Back at It

The next-to-last undergraduate semester for Franklin and Holly at Marist began just four weeks later. They both were relieved to get all the classes they needed – otherwise, they might've been stuck with a summer session in 2015.

Things progressed as expected during the fall semester; part-time jobs sandwiched between class time, studying and sleep.

On Oct. 14, Franklin, Pongo and the others took note of a speech made by Hillary Clinton at the luxury Bellagio Resort Hotel in Las Vegas on behalf of the University of Nevada-Las Vegas Foundation,

The speech aroused controversy because Clinton insisted that a $225,000 honorarium be paid to the Clinton Foundation in exchange for her appearance, while she used part of her speech to call for more affordable tuition for college students. The event was organized to honor two major UNLV donors, including a contributor of massive donations to Republican candidates, Sheldon Adelson.

What sparked Franklin's attention was not so much the possible hypocrisy of taking a huge honorarium to appear at a university function where she lamented high costs of tuition (the honorarium came from funds specifically donated for the event) or the potential hypocrisy of honoring a billionaire favorite of Republicans (after all, most progressive Democrats consider Hillary a closet Republican).

What sparked his attention was the fact that, during her speech she said **_not word one_** about:

- Abuses of high-tuition **for-profit** universities, colleges and trade schools causing students to rack up monumentally huge student loan debt, often with minimal prospects for living wage careers. (This was a frequent bone of contention for U.S. Sen. Elizabeth Warren; Hillary Clinton, not so much.)
- The role which government could play by levying sufficient taxes on wealthy individuals and corporations to enable the government to offer free undergraduate tuition to *every single student* at **all** state-operated post-secondary education facilities.
- The roll which government could play by **forgiving all student loan** debt for deeply-indebted students, students with loan balances continuing to exist once they reach middle age.
- Massive inflation in costs of mandatory college textbooks.

Her primary focus was calling for businesses to collaborate with universities to make college more affordable. College shouldn't be affordable only for students from wealthy families, she said. Oh. Yeah. Simple. Platitudes: *that's* the ticket!

Once Franklin shared the reverberations from this latest Hillary Clinton performance with his fellow Poughkeepsians, the response was fairly uniform, following a continuing pattern:

Why in the fuck would a progressive-slash-liberal political party consider her a great prospect for the presidency?

Simple answer, Pongo said: "She's still married to her cheating, slimy, slick-but-way-popular oratorically-gifted husband. And she's as politically clever as they come. People **don't watch** where her money comes from or the Wall Street billionaires she schmoozes with.

"They **do watch** her on the Daily Show. They **do watch** her on the Colbert Report. They **do watch** her on lots of corporate news media. The watch her pretty much only when she's at her best. And when people are tough with her, what they _see_ is, 'Oh, that poor cheated-upon wife, mother and grandmother. She's had to put up with *SOOO* much and now the mean ol' reporters are being nasty to her.'

"*That's* why."

So, so far, she'd received $300,000 for a speech at UCLA which Franklin viewed the previous March, as well as a significant fee the previous February "from a Republican donor" for a speech at the University of Miami, according to her husband's ex-Health and Human Services Secretary.[*] All that after telling the media she and her husband were "dead broke" once his Presidency ended. While her husband had earned $104.9 million in speaking fees since leaving the White House, according to the Wall Street Journal as of June 2014.

Huge mystery (being facetious here), Franklin said: who can afford to pay $104.9 million to Bill Clinton in speaking fees? Answer: corporatists who see those fees as a good investment, considering his wife's a solid prospect for a future Presidency.

Small (very small) joke, Franklin added: What's a worse laundry problem for the Clintons than blue dress stains?

Answer: Pocket stains from all that dirty quasi-quid pro quo money.

Keeping everything in perspective, though, Franklin had to wonder to himself: *"If Bill and Hillary had come from 'old' money like I did, would they perhaps have schmoozed around with a better class of people? Would they just maybe not have sucked up to Wall Street crony capitalists the way they have so consistently?"*

It took only a moment for Franklin, recalling all the latter-20th century history discussions he'd had with the O'Learys, to answer his own questions.

"No. Fawning over the super-rich is just as much in their genes as is rubbing elbows on camera with low-income African-Americans and Hollywood celebrities. They have hyper-phoniness reduced down to a science."

∗ ∗ ∗

ROCKIN' THE (SUPPRESSED) VOTE; 'R's SOCK IT TO 'D's

The next event of note in the Poughkeepsians' fall was the 2014 general election. With President Obama's popularity on the skids as Republicans found him not sufficiently bloodthirsty-slash-warmongering and progressive Democrats were exasperated over his verbal abuse of anti-secret surveillance/government openness heroes Edward Snowden and WikiLeaker Julian Assange, no one should've been surprised that national voter turnout (36.4 percent) was the lowest since 1942. Of course, as Phil pointed out to Franklin, **part** of that was the result of Republican efforts to suppress voting rights with voter ID laws aimed directly at Democrats' core constituencies (minorities and low-income voters).

And, of course, when voter turnout tanks, Democrats take it in the shorts. They lost control of the U.S. Senate and lost additional seats in the already Republican-controlled U.S. House.

---

[*] 6/27/14 ABC World News

Notably silent on major campaign issues throughout the campaign season: none other than Hillary Clinton. Though she did stay busy gathering speaking fees.

In fact, Franklin noticed, Hillary spoke out pretty much only when it appeared to serve her own interests. Or, when she was forced to, as when Republican members of Congress, obsessed with Hillary hatred, subpoenaed her to speak before them on the Benghazi terror attacks, the Republicans latest flog-the-dead-imaginary-horse issue.

She appeared to be of the Ayn Rand school of political advocacy: so-called rational self-interest (i.e., selfishness up to the point of breaking the law or ruining your reputation) trumps idealistic altruism, every. single. time. As Ms. Rand said so many times, altruism and capitalism can't co-exist. It seemed clear to Franklin that, for Ms. Clinton, broad-scoped altruistic progressive political advocacy and personal political capital can't seem to co-exist (except for her *lip service* to women's issues plus a *few* other priorities among liberals like same-sex marriage and simplified voter registration).

"Maybe when she's actually running for something, she'll have more courage to speak out on a wider range of issues," Phil suggested.

"I'm sure she'll speak out on a wider range of issues," Franklin said. "Just don't hold your breath for her to have the courage to challenge her Wall Street cronies.

"Remember, even a street wise urban community organizer like President Obama was in his youth pretty much swooned like a starstruck schoolgirl when he came face to face with Wall Street.

"And Hillary was no urban community organizer. She was an attorney for Wal-Mart, remember?"

"So just what do we do when 2016 rolls around if Sen. Warren isn't a candidate?" Pongo asked.

"As they used to joke about pre-flight airline emergency instructions, '*fasten your seat belt, put your head between your legs and **kiss your ass goodbye**,*' politically speaking, anyway," Phil said.

* * *

EYELASH JAVELINS WITH AMAZING AERODYNAMICS

Little more than a week after that election, the European Space Agency landed a space probe on the surface of a comet for the first time in human history. Fifteen million miles away.

It was a feat akin to tossing a javelin the size of a human eyelash across 100 miles of end-to-end football fields at a target the size of a flea's mandible.

And it got the attention of pretty much every one of the Poughkeepsians.

"You'll notice it was the European Space Agency that did this, not NASA," Phil said, as they were reading in their morning *Poughkeepsie Journal* (the local tentacle of the Gannett Company) and on their smart phones about the Rosetta spacecraft's Philae lander's successful touchdown on Comet 67P.

"Hey, whaddaya expect from the good ol' U.S.A.?" Pongo said. "We're too busy **_not_** budgeting for the latest chapter in our Permanent War reality to find any bucks for all that silly space exploration stuff most people **_absolutely fucking love_**."

"Please don't drop those F-bombs in our home, OK, son?" Phil asked.

"Well, shit, after all, it's just research into what might someday be an existential threat to the entire planet, you know, just some dumbass comet wiping out every living being larger than a mouse," Pongo said.

"Hey, it's not like it's ever happened before, right? Oh, yeah, that's right, now I remember: there's that little comet-y collision on the Yucatan Peninsula that wiped out the dinosaurs a while back."

A long-time admirer of his uncle-by-marriage's exploratory expeditions, Franklin decided to chime in.

"It docs kind of make me want to get out there and – what's that saying you folks have now? – you know, line up every last person in Congress and 'bitch slap them silly' 'til they admit we should've put scientists on the surface of Mars at least 10 years ago instead of fixating on new and more efficient ways to kill people with brown skin."

"A. Men. Brother," Pongo said.

∗ ∗ ∗

Hunting the Fabled Kin Species in Its Own Habitat

Once final exams were done, Franklin asked Pongo if he'd consider accompanying Franklin to look up at least some of his grandchildren during the week between Christmas and New Year's Day.

Pongo was incredulous.

"After all this time, why are you suddenly wanting to see the grandchildren now? Is there something I'm missing here? I thought you didn't want to impose yourself on their reality – I thought seeing them would simply remind you of the loss of all your children. What's changed about this since we found you there at Hyde Park that night 4-1/2 years ago?"

"I got to thinking that it would feel good just to see them, not to actually try to insert myself into their lives in some weird fashion. I have come to accept that my children are gone and that my grief over losing them won't change that reality. And, most of all, I've been worrying lately that, if I wait much longer, the choice of whether to see them will be taken away from me. You know, Pongo, by something like the failure of their health. I remember, every day, that I never got to say goodbye to _any_ of them."

"Alright, I get that," Pongo said.

"But, what the heck? Why aren't you asking Holly to go with you? If anyone could provide moral support on a trip like that, it's a lot more likely she could give you what you need than I could. I don't get it."

"Holly means the world to me. It's taken her a long time to get used to the idea that I'm not really someone from her generation. And, yet, she still loves me with all her heart. There's no accounting for taste, I suppose.

"At any rate, it seems to me that probably the least smart thing I could do would be to give her lasting visual reminders of the fact that I'm about a hundred years older that she is. The first time she'd see an elderly person I pointed out as my grandchild, I'm pretty sure that would be a sobering memory Holly just might never be able to shake.

"I've already told her that you and I are simply traveling downstate for some boring consultations with a law firm about the best way to organize donations on our web links."

"Well, Sir, if that's what you prefer, who am I to second-guess how you manage your most important personal relationship? Count me in."

"Thank you, Pongo – this really means a great deal to me.

"Please let me re-iterate: I don't want to meet up with any of the grandchildren in person – that would be just too strange. Most of the ones I knew were in their mid-teens or pre-teens when I passed away. There were several who were only infants.

"I just don't feel right not to at least _see_ them, even if it's from a distance."

Pongo and Franklin decided to more or less stake out the homes of the grandchildren who were healthy enough to be out and about. Their first visit was to the home of his oldest grandchild, Anna Eleanor Roosevelt Seagraves (nee Dall), 88, a retired teacher and librarian living in Washington, D.C., who still was active in Democratic politics. She was about 18 when Franklin died.

They waited outside her home in Pongo's Honda on the opposite side of the street a half-block away for almost an entire day before giving up. Franklin was disappointed to the core. Pongo was **bored** to the core, but didn't complain, not once.

Franklin had next wanted to see his daughter Anna's child Curtis, who'd taken Roosevelt as his surname. But a search of the web and the FDR Presidential Library archives before they left on their trip had disclosed that Curtis had moved to Spain. No time for that trip.

They then went to the home of granddaughter Sara Wilford, 82, an award-winning Sarah Lawrence College faculty member specializing in childhood psychology in the Yonkers, New York area.

After a few hours parked almost a block away, they saw her emerge, but this no longer was the girl Franklin had last seen when she was 13. Tall and lithe, bundled in a dapper shin-length black wool overcoat, she had her grandfather's winning smile and a smooth, barely-wrinkled skin tone suggesting someone **at least** 10 years younger than her birth certificate would state. While Franklin lay at rest for so long, she'd become a mature, elegant, confident-looking, stately woman - but a woman whom Franklin wouldn't have recognized if he'd met her on the street, even though she did bear a bit of a resemblance to him even beyond that smile. He wondered if Sara ever heard from her younger sister Kate.

Then they saw a slightly younger woman emerge from Sara's home and follow her out to the frozen street.

For a moment, it appeared that they were walking directly over to Pongo's Honda parked parallel to the curb. As they stepped gingerly through a half-foot of snow, each of them slipping and almost falling onto the icy pavement, they veered away from Pongo's Civic just as they were about 25 feet away– and got into a full-sized sedan parked two cars behind the Poughkeepsians. A moment later, Sara was driving away, headed with her friend to her favorite grocery store.

"You really don't want to let an opportunity like this pass you by," Pongo said as he started his Civic and began following Sara's car, careful to stay about a block behind.

"What in the heck are you doing, young man?!" Franklin asked, taken aback. "This isn't what I wanted. I **told you** that."

"I think it _is_. You're the same man who looked that mass killer Joseph "Uncle Joe" Stalin in the eye and didn't blink, the same man who jousted verbally with Winston Churchill over whether to invade France in 1942 or 1944, a man who was never once intimidated when it came to speaking truth to power. A man who had the righteous confidence to send thousands of young men to risk death for the defeat of the worst kind of fascism.

"And you want me to believe you're not strong enough to come face to face with a granddaughter you've missed for a long, long time?"

"There are different kinds of courage," Franklin said. "I'm afraid I may be fairly overdrawn on this particular variety."

"_I_ don't believe you are, Sir. I have every faith that you can get through this with the same kind of aplomb which got you through your years with Eleanor. And you know what? Every time you mention the phrase 'I'm afraid,' I wanna pinch your ear and drag you to see the YouTube video of your first inauguration speech. I'm not sure you **_GET_** to be afraid. Not when it's not exactly a state secret that you understand the dangers of irrational fears."

"I am just a human being. I am entitled to be afraid of whatever scares me. Just because I wasn't afraid of a lot of pain and hard work after I got sick doesn't mean I'm impervious to all things frightful."

"Oh, piss-in-a-teacup! This person is not Hitler. She's not a serial killer. She's not a blood-sucking vampire. She's your *granddaughter*, for chrissake. She's a scholar. She's widely respected. She's not exactly known for confronting people in public and going into rants.

"So, to paraphrase Archie Bunker, please stifle yourself and listen up, __now__: here's what we're going to do…"

* * *

When Sara and her friend (a fellow college faculty member she'd known for 20 years) arrived at the Morley's Food Store on Yonkers Avenue, Pongo and Franklin watched them get out of the car and go into the store.

Once they were through the store's front door, Pongo and Franklin got out of Pongo's car and made their way quickly into the store. It would be Pongo's job to casually monitor Sara and her friend while Franklin picked out some random items to buy.

Pongo was to watch Sara and friend 'til they began moving in the direction of a check-out line. Then he was to wave – as inconspicuously as possible – to Franklin, who would be faux-browsing shelves near the opposite end of the check-out lanes. At that point whichever of the two Poughkeepsians was closest to the check-out line Sara selected was to get in line right behind Sara while the other quickly joined the first in line. Then it would be the responsibility of the Poughkeepsian closest to Sara in line to start up a casual conversation.

It all went according to plan. Up to a point.

Defying his own expectations by, say, a mere light year or so, Franklin merged into the check-out line right behind Sarah and, clumsily at first, began to engage her in conversation. He didn't realize the items he'd absent-mindedly tossed into his hand-carried shopping basket included several packs of condoms, tubes of both anti-fungal cream and Preparation H, wart remover and bottles of fortified wine.

"Hi, there, er, Mis-, wha-, uh, Ma'am, uh – are you Ms. Wilford, the famous psychology professor, the one with the well-known grandfather?" he asked.

"Why, look at you!" she said. "You're that young man in the YouTube videos – and you too," she said, reaching out to shake first Franklin's and then Pongo's hands. "You're the one who kind of looks a little like my late grandfather – and you sound a little like him too. Must be something in that Dutchess County water, I guess. Looks like you've got quite the weekend planned there (pointing to his basket)."

"*Dear God*," Franklin thought to himself in a semi-panicked frame of mind. "*Does she recognize me for who I really am?*!!" He thought he could feel his urethral sphincter starting to loosen. "*Christ, not a plumbing failure, not right now!!?*"

"Whu-, ye-, erg-, yes, my name is, well, they call me Scruples, Scruples Van Mullder, or Percy. Always wondered if it was just the under-30 crowd who watches those YouTube-y things."

"Great to meet you, Scruples. Yes, I'm Sara Wilford and this is my friend Professor Douglas. How did you know who I am?"

There were a few seconds of awkward silence as Franklin did a bang-up impression, unintentionally, of a tongue-tied fan meeting a matinee idol.

"We both have psych minors," Pongo jumped in, "from Marist – we read about some of your work with children when we were doing some research and, to put it mildly, we were favorably impressed. I'm Pongo Podrowski."

"Very nice to meet you, young man," Sara said. "What brings the two of you down this way?"

"We, eh, were, um, well, we had to drop off one of our staff members after a meeting we had downstate with some strategists about our rally tours," Franklin said.

"This meeting you here is such sweet serendipity," Sara said. "I was planning to log onto your website this weekend to sign a pledge to contact my elected officeholders from Westchester County to convince them to support your USA-SBR. Love that title you gave it – Un-Screwing of America. Couldn't be more apt.

"If my Granddad were alive, I'll bet he'd be volunteering to go around the country with you for this cause.

"Professor Douglas and I wish you nothing but the very best on this."

"Well, if you ever want to be a guest speaker at one of our rallies, all you have to do is call," Franklin/Scruples said.

"At my age, I imagine the best thing I could do at one of your rallies is not block the aisles when people are showing up and leaving. No, I'll be happy to support your cause any way I can – except for that."

"You can't imagine how much that means to us," Pongo said. "Please come and visit us if you're ever in our neck of the woods, OK?"

"Just might do that, Pongo. I've been known to visit there from time to time. Thanks for boosting an old lady's ego, you two!"

And, as clunkily as their encounter had begun, it concluded with heartfelt handshakes and encouraging pats to the shoulder for each of them from Sara. To say Franklin was relieved was like saying Ronald Reagan despised people who received welfare. The understatement of the year.

As Pongo drove Franklin out of Yonkers, Pongo saw that the earlier uncharacteristic look of vulnerability on Franklin's face had been replaced with a kind of puppy-dog look of humility.

"I think what you made me do here – I think they call it 'manning up' now, right? – what you did was the kind of candor a person can only **hope** they'll be lucky enough to earn from their very best friend. I hope I can return the favor for you someday."

"Everyone needs a figurative swift kick in the butt from time to time, Sir. Today was your time. I'm sure my handsome butt will be a deserving target sometime down the road."

It was, in fact, a lasting comfort to Franklin to see that Sara hadn't become a frail, homebound friendless shut-in. But it was hard to see little Sara all grown up and be unable to say once again those things a grandfather says to a favored granddaughter. He no longer thought what they were doing was a bad idea, but he still wasn't completely sold on the notion that it would help his heart to heal over the decades of separation from his family.

He and Pongo then tried to find the home of Kate Roosevelt Whitney, 78, sister to Sara and daughter of his son James, who dropped out of her life long, long before he passed away. Kate had married Democratic campaign consultant William Frederick Haddad.

They couldn't even find anything at all about her: not a current or former employer, not a residential address, not a public library account.

Franklin felt horribly depressed over being unable to find Kate, although he was relieved to know that his oldest grandchildren, at least, had ended up neither destitute nor, apparently, alone and friendless.

Grandson Elliot "Tony" Roosevelt Jr., 78, it turned out, apparently was working in the oil business in central Texas. He seemed to be doing well, according to an almost two-year-old Bloomberg News article.

Elliot Sr.'s daughter Ruth Chandler Roosevelt, 80, who went by Chandler Roosevelt Lindsley during her 55-year marriage, was a Dallas, TX widow since the death of her husband Henry Lindsley III, 82, a prominent businessman, of natural causes at their home in April 2011.

Sadly, though, Texas was too far for Franklin and Pongo to travel on this Christmas break, even with a chance to see two adult grandchildren.

There were no other grandchildren who'd been old enough for Franklin to really get to know before he died, so he decided he should be grateful for at least getting to see and even speak with one of them. But *all of those decades* lost to the ages – it seemed to him that he was a real grandfather for such a tiny fragment of time in the great scheme of things.

Anyway, nothing ventured, nothing gained, he told himself. Maybe he'd try again to find some of them – maybe take that trip to Texas. "*My grandson a Texas oil man? Suppose he wouldn't be crazy about what we're doing. Still, would be nice to see Tony and Chandler. Maybe in another year or so.*"

✳ ✳ ✳

BUCKEYE STATE ADVENTURE

Three days after Pongo and Franklin returned to Poughkeepsie, it was time for the group to head off again for another USA-SBR rally tour. This time they'd be going to Kent State University, the University of Toledo and Ohio State University. In that swing state that usually decides the Presidency.

The group, which this time included pretty much everyone among the Poughkeepsians' inner circle (Phil, Pongo, Franklin, Tom, Annie, Orvis, Karin, Heather, Harry, Bianca, Idris, Marcia, Mel and Cherisse) flew into Cleveland early in the afternoon of Jan. 2, 2015. They drove their 15-passenger rental van south to Kent State University for their 5 p.m. press conference in advance of the following day's rally at the Memorial Athletic and Convocation Center.

There were reporters at the press conference from the Kent Record-Courier (a daily owned by Dix Communications, a media conglomerate out of Wooster, OH) and the Cleveland Plain Dealer (a daily owned by Advance Publications, formerly Newhouse, of Staten Island, NY), as well as from each of the area's local television network affiliates.

The cluster-fucked economy was the main focus of the journalists' questions.

Franklin spent more than a half-hour listing the myriad ways the USA-SBR would stimulate the economy and help balance governments' budgets by strengthening the progressive income tax system throughout the country, discouraging businesses from outsourcing and elevating incomes of working poor and middle class families.

"When the USA-SBR is passed and ratified, we'll finally be able to take the middle class off the endangered species list," Franklin said, only half-joking.

"The one thing which contributed more than anything else to our last enduring period of prosperity from 1993 to 2000 was the increase in Federal taxes on wealthier Americans signed into law by President Clinton in 1993. Yes, Republicans demagogued the issue to death and re-took the House the following year, but the results of that increase in tax revenues couldn't be disputed: high employment, stable government revenues, a vigorous stock market and a healthy annual government surplus by the time Clinton left office.

"And, of course, the fact that our country wasn't involved in any major armed conflict during that period – unless you count the Somalia skirmishes plus airstrikes in Bosnia and Yugoslavia – well, that absence of expensive boots on the ground combat probably had a little to do with that prosperity too.

"If you hadn't also noticed, the USA-SBR will make it harder for politicians and shills for the military-industrial complex to goad us into wars and other armed conflicts."

He explained the specifics.

Another series of questions involved actions by far-right hyper-conservatives in several Ohio school districts trying – and, so far, failing – to implement teacher censorship requirements through so-called "controversial issues policies." The requirements would restrict what historical facts teachers could discuss and would require teachers to include 'creationism' discussions in their curricula, as well as discussions about the United Nations' "Agenda 21."

Ultra-hyper-conservative reactionary extremists around the country were contending that "Agenda 21" was a conspiracy to undermine traditional U.S. freedoms when, in fact, it was a program designed to encourage sustainable – rather than haphazard - development and to prevent environmental damage associated with population growth.

Under the reactionaries' proposals, every discussion of accepted scientific theories, such as evolution, would have to be balanced out by alternative, **non-scientific** speculation based on teachings by mental midgets like Glenn Beck, with a heavy emphasis on *supposed* conspiracies by environmental extremists. (A few months later, a small group of like-minded far-right legislators across the country in Idaho would actually jeopardize $16 million annual Federal child support enforcement funding in their state – 70 percent of their total support enforcement budget - because they were afraid a law requiring Idaho, like **all** states, to conform to new Federal regulations was a conspiracy to give Muslim countries' courts authority to impose Sharia law over Idahoan single parents.)

Phil explained that the USA-SBR provisions requiring that all education be *based on empirical reality* should protect students all over the country from efforts by "fringe lunatics" to eviscerate core curricula. Schools operated by religious institutions would continue to be free to discuss ideas about imagined supreme beings, he emphasized.

"Jesus, Vishnu, the Great Spirit Cucumber, whatever religious figure a church-owned school wants to highlight in its lessons for the day - that still will be their right.

"If students are going to be able to rely on consistently thorough elementary and secondary school education around the country – education which will prevent them from being at a disadvantage when competing for college scholarships – that provision of the USA-SBR is crucial.

"Which is not to say that there won't be disputes settled by the courts over what constitutes empirical reality. We're reasonably confident that the courts will continue to find as the Federal District Court in Harrisburg, Pennsylvania did 10 years ago: that the teaching of non-scientific theories such as so-called Intelligent Design is *nothing more than a **pretext** for the teaching of religion in public schools.*"

(The Poughkeepsians in the room erupted in immediate applause, as did a couple of the local television network affiliates' camera operators.)

* * *

LITTLE BIG MAN

Their guest speaker the following evening was no less than an Ohio icon: former Cleveland Mayor, former member of the U.S. House of Representatives and former Presidential candidate Dennis Kucinich.

Kucinich stressed the senselessness of war and bigotry. He insisted that the courage of the 13 unarmed student protestors who were shot by National Guardsmen at Kent State during Vietnam War protests in May 1970, including four who were murdered and one permanently paralyzed, matched the courage of any soldier sent to war.

While Kent State always will be remembered by many for that atrocity, he said, the more lasting effect for the university will be the degree to which the students who graduate leave with broadened understandings of the diversities of existence.

"For every student who comes to understand that the hopes and wishes of a struggling poor peasant farmer in Afghanistan are not unlike those of a patio enclosure factory worker in Parma, for every student who begins to realize that the goals and dreams of a low-paid textile worker in Iran are little different from those of a meat processing line laborer in Waynesville, for every student who leaves here able to accept that people in Tehran, Iran really are profoundly similar to people in Cleveland, Ohio –

"This university has made the world a better place."

Kucinich dedicated his presentation to the memory of Kent native John Brown.

"When Mr. Brown concluded that the moral stain of slavery could not and would not be removed from this country without each person taking a principled stand, a stand of willingness to sacrifice his own life for lasting social justice, he leapt into the fray more than a year before the Civil War began.

"He recognized that, sometimes, for a democratic republic to face up to its own hypocrisies, it takes the actions of a brave person to slap it into full sentience. Even if it meant the loss of his own life.

"This country once again needs principled people, like Mr. Brown, like each of you in this audience, like those brave people from Poughkeepsie who started this thing, who are willing to 'put themselves out there' to risk their reputations, their personal finances and even their own health in the cause of making this (holding up the USA-SBR) into the law of the land.

"Before you leave this beautiful building this evening, become the integral part of this effort to make history which we all need for you to be. Make that simple pledge to contact your elected officeholders to compel them to display whether they have the same kind of courage you do.

"Hold. Them. To. Account."

Kucinich and his beautiful wife, the former Elizabeth Harper, herself an England native and food safety activist, embraced as the crowd rewarded his presentation with a long standing ovation. After the rally ended, the Kuciniches welcomed the attendees to the front for book signings, handshakes and such.

Quite a few of the audience members hugged Dennis and thanked him tearfully for standing up to the Cleveland banking interests and refusing in the late '70s to sell the city-owned Muni Light electric utility, saving residential customers perhaps thousands of dollars a year each over the decades.

"You're our Anti-Privatization Jedi Knight," a middle-aged woman told him, smiling. "We're sure there are bankers out there who still are seething over the fact that the mafia didn't succeed with their contract hit they put out on you."

Yes, there really was such a thing. The mafia hitman didn't succeed because a hospitalized Kucinich missed the event where the shooting was to happen.

Franklin/Percy told Kucinich he was in the same company as two polar opposites: FDR and Reagan, who both survived assassinations plots, though neither plot was the product of hyper-capitalists.

"I'm proud to be in the company of the former, ashamed to be in the company of the latter," Kucinich said. "Mr. Reagan would've sold Muni Light to a crony capitalist buddy so fast it'd have made every light bulb in the city spin right out of its socket."

* * *

The next morning, the Poughkeepsians took their rental van to Toledo for a 5 p.m. press conference later that day, in advance of their rally the following day at the University of Toledo's John F. Savage Arena.

Those attending the press conference included reporters from the Toledo Blade (a locally-owned daily operated by the same company which owns the Pittsburgh Post-Gazette), the Toledo Free Press (a locally-owned Sunday-only rival paper) and each of the area's local television network affiliates. The television reporters at each press conference seemed to be doing the Benjamin Button thing – they simply appeared to be uncontrollably regressing in age (*"They should try eating lots of hot dogs,"* Franklin thought to himself). One of them at the current press conference – who clearly wasn't planning to actually be on camera for her report – a pretty, gum-chewing blond who had to be at least 15 (OK, 21), was wearing the uniform from what must have been the moonlighting job she'd just come from: it was an Arby's shift manager outfit.

The press gathering was most notable for its politeness. Franklin and the others were deeply disappointed: it seemed like forever since they'd had a reporter or columnist storm out of a room flipping them off.

Most of their concerns were directed at the effects of the gradual elimination of fossil fuels required by the USA-SBR on the thousands of automotive-related jobs with Toledo businesses operated by General Motors, Chrysler and Dana Holding Corp.

The group decided to let Mel, the Dutchess County Roads Department supervisor, tackle those questions. As the group previously had explained at previous press conferences, Mel detailed the many opportunities for GM, Chrysler and Dana Corp. to plan ahead for re-tooling machinery and filling lots of new jobs which would be created with the increased demand for new non-internal-combustion technology.

"If they don't anticipate that demand soon enough, companies like First Solar will fill that void. The new jobs are right there, just over the horizon. Ask Elon

Musk with Tesla – a little bird told me they're planning to pay a _minimum_ of about $23 an hour at their huge new battery manufacturing plant near Reno, Nevada.

"That, my friends of the Fourth Estate, is what's known as a living wage."

* * *

FEMINISM'S STILL KICKING BUTT

The following evening's rally at Savage Arena was another feather in Marcia's cap: she'd convinced Toledo native Gloria Steinem to travel from her New York City home to be their guest speaker, despite some health challenges for the 80-year-old women's rights icon.

No one in the crowd was thinking about her age as they listened to her presentation. It was filled with her trademark zingers aimed at the misogynistic corporatist far-right wing bloviation culture best exemplified by Fox News and Rush Limbaugh.

She recalled her early advocacy, going back to a 1970 Time magazine article, for LGBT rights and social acceptance, including same-sex marriage. She was glad Ms. Clinton finally "came out" in support of those rights in March 2013, but wished she'd found her way sooner.

Steinem went on to praise advances in equal rights for married women, explaining why she no longer considered marriage a destroyer of relationships.

There was a cornucopia of kudos from her for the pro-women provisions of the USA-SBR. She urged women everywhere, including Ms. Clinton, to emulate elected officeholders like Sen. Warren by advocating for specific changes in laws which would benefit single parents of both genders and non-wealthy couples of all stripes.

"It's not enough to say you want to see tuition become more affordable. It's not enough to say that you want to see pay rates increased for the middle class. It's not enough to say it will be nice when same-sex marriage is legal everywhere.

"If you're an elected officeholder or you **want to be one**, you have to articulate clearly how you want that to happen. That's the only way we worker drones can hold you accountable."

She saved her most poignant remarks for her introduction to the memorial videos for Sally Rose Cummings and Prof. Bartlett. Referring mainly to Sally, she urged women everywhere to be prepared to defend themselves against violence and to welcome into their lives a 'little village of like-minded assertive friends' as a support system barrier against unforeseen threats.

"My heart goes out to Sally's family. No one can know how much their loss hurts. Make no mistake, their loss will never stop hurting altogether. They will feel that loss every day for the rest of their lives. How do you replace your beloved daughter and grandchildren?"

One of the next social justice movements across the country, she said, needs to be mass reviews for pardons of women who are imprisoned for killing or seriously injuring their abusers. "Let's hope, as more women are elected or appointed as prosecutors around the country, imprisonment of abuse victims by our criminal justice system will go the way of the do-do bird."

(There was long, sustained applause.)

Upon completion of the rally, Ms. Steinem was gracious enough to pose for many, many photos, including more than a few with the Poughkeepsians. She promised to visit them sometime between rally tours. She said she loved traveling through Dutchess County and the rest of the Hudson River Valley.

That night they made sure there was an armed pair of security guards to escort Ms. Steinem from the arena to her parked car. Just wouldn't due to have a stabbing or beating on this particular occasion.

There was none.

✳ ✳ ✳

The following morning, the group bundled up against the cold and loaded themselves into the rental van for the drive south to Columbus for their 5 p.m. press conference in advance of the following day's rally at Ohio State University's Value City Arena.

A gaggle of reporters arrived early for the conference, including one each from the Columbus Dispatch (a daily locally owned by the Wolfe family), the Columbus Weekly (a local paper devoted to African-American issues), the Dayton Daily News (part of the Cox Enterprises empire based in Atlanta, Georgia) and each of the local television network affiliates. Yet again, the local television reporters seemed barely out of teenhood: one of them had a tube of Clearasil sticking out of his coat pocket; a glance at him from less than 10 feet away proved one thing. He needed it.

Besides the usual press conference questioning, there was a focus from the press in this university town on legalization of marijuana. A Dispatch reporter, Sid Marsalado, a hulking football offensive lineman-shaped guy with what looked like pizza and Doritos stains on his dress shirt, asked if the Poughkeepsians anticipated much blowback over the USA-SBR's provisions allowing individuals to grow their own marijuana and other natural substances approved for medicinal use.

"We've received virtually nothing but positive responses to that provision," Franklin/Percy responded. "We understand that, the closer we come to approval and ratification, the higher the value of the common stock for PepsiCo, the parent company for Doritos – as well as common stocks for Yum! Brands, parent company of Pizza Hut plus all the other pizza chains and General Mills, parent company of Totinos pizza and Betty Crocker-brand brownies."

"Right on," Marsalado said, fist-bumping a cameraman standing next to him. "Too bad the USA-SBR's got that provision against big corporate donations – you guys probably could clean up with dough from those companies."

The remainder of the press conference questioning covered a lot of what was, to the Poughkeepsians, old ground. But they'd become pros at reacting with surprise and/or wide-eyed enthusiasm to each question. Once the USA-SBR becomes the law of the land, Phil thought more than once, they all probably could get jobs as corporate press flacks. That is, if they hated themselves.

$$* \quad * \quad *$$

Second Chances for Better Choices

Their guest speaker the following night was legendary former President of the Planned Parenthood Federation of America (from 1978-1992), Faye Wattleton, an Ohio State University nursing alumnus. She was only the second woman to lead Planned Parenthood and the first African-American woman to do so. She was currently the managing director of a consulting firm specializing in business turnarounds.

Wattleton's primary focus, understandably, was on the USA-SBR's provisions for protecting and expanding the rights of women and have-nots all over the country, as well as ensuring access to health care with no out-of-pocket costs.

She was especially thorough in her kudos for the USA-SBR's provisions to guarantee the right of persons to have a second chance at life.

"So many persons," she said, recalling her early Planned Parenthood work, "are forced into decisions at a young age when they simply don't have the maturity or life experience to make the right choices.

"Being pro-choice isn't just about having the right to make a choice on your own, it's also about helping people achieve the kind of personal growth in a way that makes it more likely they'll make choices that lead to lasting happiness. Whether it's about choosing their life partner or their career or even the best way to commute.

"Most people aren't born into wisdom. Most people need the patience and understanding of caring teachers, professors, mentors – the list goes on.

"I'm hopeful that the economic and social justice that comes out of the USA-SBR will lead once and for all to there being plenty of government funding for post-secondary education and mentoring programs.

"If the kind of prosperity promised by the USA-SBR actually comes to fruition, I can imagine a future where far fewer people will need those second chances in life. But, if they do, the USA-SBR should help ensure that those barriers to second shots at opportunity are easily hurdled.

"But the obstacles to this (holding up USA-SBR) becoming the law of the land can be overcome only through active participation by each of you.

"Calling each of your elected office holders, talking to your friends, even going door-to-door – all of those things won't *by themselves* cause you to become infused with great insight and wisdom leading to lasting personal success. But they will give you a keen perspective on the kind of persistent efforts which are a key component of success and those unselfish actions will cause you to feel a deep sense of satisfaction, of accomplishment when the time comes that the final state legislature ratifies this monumental document.

"We **all** have a dream. We **all** can make this happen.

"Keep the hope of this alive every single day in your heart and every single day *on your feet* as you spread the word of this inspired work of conscience."

Once the memorial videos and "*Capitalism: A Love Story*" were over and the rally was adjourned, so to speak, by the Poughkeepsians, Ms. Wattleton remained behind, offering to meet with a group of a few dozen young women seeking general career advice. When it came to walking the walk of her credo, this particular mentor meant every bit of the talk she talked.

Serendipitously, Ms. Wattleton ended up on the same flight back to New York the next day as the Poughkeepsians, so they got to save her shuttle fare to the airport when they dropped off their rental van.

And Franklin got to sit next to her on the plane. He was rewarded for his seat selection with Ms. Wattleton's shared stories of her youth growing up with her construction worker father and minister mother in Missouri. The memories of her mother's Church of God sermons kept Franklin's attention all the way back to LaGuardia. Her stories were so compelling, he barely noticed the fit-pitching 2-year-old three rows behind them. (The fits stopped about 20 minutes after the child's mother gave him a full dose of Nyquil.)

* * *

Improved Womanhood via 'Manning Up'

About a month after he got back into the school/work/study/sleep grind, Franklin (along with Pongo and Phil) read on-line in a *Guardian* article about Hillary Clinton telling a Silicon Valley audience of technology moguls in California that a key to being a successful female executive "is developing a thick skin" and preparing lots of clever comebacks for inevitable sexist remarks by men.

In other words, becoming more like men.

In the same presentation, she applauded efforts to fight discrimination against women in Silicon Valley and elsewhere.

"As though anyone *other than* a sliver of far-right Republicans and religious extremists would **_support_** gender discrimination," Franklin told Phil and Pongo. "This is like observing that kid running for grade school class president who opposes crappy cafeteria food. Like there's someone who *favors* crappy cafeteria food?

"She's a master at the straw man argument. Gotta grant her that."

"Hey, aren't **ALL** Republicans – *and* closet-Republicans?" Phil asked.

"So it would seem," Franklin said.

*   *   *

GOIN' SOUTH PART 2

Their next series of rallies was set for Spring Break. They were scheduled to leave the morning of March 14, 2015 for their tour of sites at the University of Arkansas, the University of Mississippi, Mississippi State University, Louisiana State University, Memphis State University, the University of Tennessee and the University of Missouri.

Their first press conference was scheduled in Fayetteville, Arkansas at 5 p.m. that afternoon in advance of their rally at Bud Walton Arena the following day.

There were reporters at the conference from the Arkansas Democrat-Gazette (a daily owned by WEHCO Media Inc., a Little Rock media conglomerate owning 10 newspapers in three states plus cable television outlets), the Arkansas Times (an independent weekly locally owned out of Little Rock), the Northwest Arkansas Times (another tentacle of WEHCO) and from each of the local television network affiliates. This time, the local television reporters looked so young, they could've been mistaken for a group of early-teen door-to-door Girl Scout Cookie salespersons. Except for the pimply-faced young man wearing weirdly out-of-date glasses who was sporting a Wal-Mart hoodie (with a Boyz II Men logo on the back) over his dress shirt and doing a little surreptitious nose-mining when he thought the others weren't looking. For a moment, Franklin would've sworn he saw a merit patch-adorned Girl Scout sash sticking out of the jacket pocket of one of the young women.

Turned out that the USA-SBR folks had just stepped into a hotbed of controversy: the Arkansas Legislature appeared to be on the verge of sending to the Governor a bill which would allow private businesses to decline to serve LGBT persons on the basis of the religious beliefs of the business owners. A similar bill appeared to be on the verge of passage in Indiana.

"Do you believe local support for those bills will damage the prospects of the USA-SBR in Arkansas and Indiana?" asked the Democrat-Gazette's Wallace Filtrevisage, a thin, gray-skinned man who appeared to have streaks of cigarette ashes on the front of his Wal-Mart-sold blazer.

"My name's Scruples Van Mullder," Franklin said. "I'll take this one."

"No, on the contrary, we think any legislature which is so tone-deaf as to pass a law like this is going to find out it's just stepped into a pile of dog feces so massive and fresh that they'll need a snorkel to breathe out of the top of it and hydraulic jaws of life from the local Fire Department to be extracted from it.

"And they'll find out at about the same time that businesses and non-profit organizations all over the country can find lots of alternative states in which to conduct their commerce.

"In other words, we suspect those kinds of anachronistic laws – Jim Crow-ey turds rightfully belonging in the 1950s – will drive people _toward_ the USA-SBR. Like the sea of humanity that was the '49-ers rushing to the California gold fields.

"Those mean-spirited bigoted hate-inspired laws probably are the weirdest-but-biggest blessing in surprise we ever could've hoped for.

"Does that answer your question?"

"Uh-, well, yes, sir. How do you spell anakkratistic?"

(*"With a dictionary"* was what Franklin/Scruples was tempted to say, but he thought better of it: *"This guy's probably a product of the South's public education systems which traditionally have been the worst in the nation – it's not his fault he's only semi-literate."*)

"Marcia, would you please help that gentleman and conscientious speller with that word? Thank you so much, Dear." (Marcia hopped off the stage, stood next to Mr. Filtrevisage and wrote the word for him on his Reporter's Notebook.)

Another reporter, Delta Connard of the Northwest Arkansas Times, asked if the USA-SBR's ban on holding public office for persons who'd gone on record as adults as having bigoted viewpoints would blunt chances for its passage in the South.

Orvis O'Leary, cheered on by his wife Karin, leapt into action.

"Are you saying that the South is full of bigots? If you are, we certainly don't believe that – otherwise, we wouldn't be here. We believe just the opposite: that the South is full of genuinely polite, hospitality-driven kind souls. Kind souls who, incredibly, for reasons difficult to understand, considering the War Between the States ended 150 years ago, have a habit of electing racist ex-Klan sympathizers to public office.

"We simply want, so to speak, to fumigate their ballots so that their choices for public officeholders aren't limited to those kinds of nitwits.

"Y'know, sometimes if you have an infestation in your home, after a while, if you just keep the pests out of your food, you begin not to notice that they're still just about everywhere else.

"We're convinced it's way past time to get those bigots not just removed as a source of mental malnourishment, but out of public life altogether.

"Take our word for it: it'll be good for your families' mental health. We guarantee it."

* * *

ROCK STARS IN FAYETTEVILLE

The headliner for the University of Arkansas' Bud Walton Arena rally the next day was Bob Estes, Board Chairman for the Arkansas Coalition for Peace and Justice (ACPJ).

Estes spoke eloquently in opposition to the Arkansas Legislature's efforts to legitimize discrimination and passive aggressive hatred against the LGBT community under the pretext of religious freedom.

"To use religious freedom as an excuse to discriminate debases the character of the First Amendment," he said. "It's an abomination of the Constitution. Just like the Citizens United decision."

He went on to praise provisions in the USA-SBR which encourage non-violent resolutions of disputes involving both local and national issues.

The ban against holding public office on persons who, as adults, expressed racist views "will be nothing short of transformative," he said.

Likewise, the USA-SBR's provisions encouraging fresh starts and early releases from prison for non-violent substance abusers would free up money otherwise wasted on expensive prison cells.

"With some luck," he said, "the USA-SBR just might put the private for-profit prison industry out of business! No more corporate overlords controlling not just us, but our prisoners too. No more sending prisoners convicted of marijuana possession in Batesville to a more profitable prison 2,000 miles away in Idaho, for Christ's sake!"

To which the crowd responded with a standing ovation.

This being a crowd of polite Southerners, there was only the tiniest smattering of "FUCK O-ver-LORDS!!" chants. You really had to listen *closely* to pick them up.

After the "*Capitalism*" movie was done, Estes approached the Poughkeepsians one at a time, shaking their hands and, basically, treating them like rock stars.

"What you guys are doing – that's our future," he said. "If we can achieve that kind of change, there's nothing we can't accomplish. If we *can't*, though, it's just maybe game over in a generation or two."

"We get it," Franklin/Percy said. "We intend to succeed. As long as there are no mafia or CIA hits out on us, at least. If they couldn't get Dennis Kucinich, I don't think they can get all of us."

"Well, he had to be kind of a quick, small target – you know, hard to hit," Harry joked.

"I'll have to try and stay low, drag my knuckles like some of those Tea Partiers," Franklin/Percy, with just the very mildest laughter, told Estes. It was a chore to laugh for a joke about someone being shot when you were the target once. Even if it was 82 years earlier.

* * *

NOT IN KANSAS ANYMORE – OR MAYBE THEY ARE

They left early the next morning out of Fayetteville for their six-hour drive to Oxford, Mississippi for their 5 p.m. press conference that afternoon in advance of the rally the next day at the University of Mississippi's Tad Smith Coliseum.

Those attending the press conference included a semi-conscious reporter from the Oxford Eagle (a Monday-Friday local paper), plus others more sentient from the Oxford Citizen (a local weekly), the Jackson Clarion-Ledger (a daily Gannett Co. tentacle) and the Jackson Advocate (a weekly focused on the African-American community) as well as journalists from each of the area television network affiliates. As the 'go-young' trend among local broadcast media appeared to be continuing across the country (Phil called it 'go cheap'), the local TV reporters in Mississippi were so puerile a couple of them appeared to be wearing Pull-Up underpants, plus little ID tags like some parents pin to their children so strangers can help them find their way home if they get lost. We shit you not. (Well, maybe a little.)

The first question of the day had to do with privatization. The Poughkeepsians were about to find out they weren't in Kansas anymore. So to speak.

"Do y'all think there's even a single living breathin' pawLITtikul soul within the confines of ah state's borders who'd be a-willin' to go on rekkurd supportin' takin' jobs outta the private sektur and puttin' 'em inna the guv'mint?" asked one of the pre-teen looking TV reporters.

"I'm Scruples Van Mullder – I can answer that.

"We're confident that Mississippians can do basic arithmetic just as well as anyone else in the country (*but Franklin/Scruples knew test scores showed the opposite was true*).

"When Mississippians become aware that virtually all of the so-called savings that come from paying less for privatized government services actually goes to private companies' *out-of-state stockholders at the expense of crappy service to their clientele* while those companies' in-state employees use up more welfare and Medicaid benefits than their government employee counterparts, we think they'll grasp what a bad deal that is.

"It's sooo simple: owners of businesses providing privatized government services **have to find profit someplace** where the non-privatized government agency **could not.**

"They do that

- "by cutting corners on services doing things like ignoring Federal requirements for productivity and deadlines;
- "by cutting their employees' pay and benefits (which often sends them directly to the Food Stamps and Medicaid office);
- "by laying off more experienced, more efficient older workers to hire replacements who are inexperienced and cheaper and
- "by hiring staff who are outright unqualified for job openings so they can pay them less.

"In other words, they cheat the system to make a profit."

"So y'all are sayin' that Yancey Thigpen's newspapuh ovah they-uh in Bumpass Corners that does them out-sauced printin' jobs fo' the guv'mint is a-gonna lose all them jobs, be that raht?"

"That's probably correct. What's going on there is Yancey's papuh – I mean paper – is able to make a profit because they're paying marginally qualified printing staff a non-living wage with **few or no benefits**. That makes his employees a financial burden to the state when they apply for Food Stamps, Medicaid and maybe even welfare payments.

"Do you think that's fair to taxpayers that Yancey should get to profit off of the taxpayers' subsidizing his employees' basic needs? And it's not just Yancey who profits from that – a huge percentage of people who work at Wal-Mart around the country are receiving Food Stamps benefits.

"Look. It. Up."

Much of the remainder of the press conference revolved around the Poughkeepsians defending the USA-SBR's provisions guaranteeing nationwide same-sex marriage rights and the nationwide right for adults at least 21 years old to grow at home natural substances (such as marijuana) which the FDA hasn't declared to be toxic or carcinogenic.

"Just imagine how much taxpayers will save when all those people in jail or prison only for recreational marijuana convictions are released back into the community," Franklin said. "Just imagine the kinds of good that could be done with those funds: new parks, deteriorating bridges replaced, more research into cures for disease – you name it!"

The Poughkeepsians closed the news conference by heaping kudos on the citizens of Mississippi for implementing tough requirements for childhood immunizations.

"You faced down the goofy vaccine conspiracy theorists and, in doing so, you guaranteed that the health of everyone in this lovely state will be improved for the long term. We applaud each and every Mississippian for having the courage to compel your residents to do the right thing," Karin O'Leary said, leading the

12 Poughkeepsians (Bianca and Pongo stayed home for this tour) in a standing ovation for those at the conference.

* * *

Norman Rockwell's Bravest Model

The guest speaker at the following evening's rally at Tad Smith Coliseum was Mississippi native Ruby Bridges Hall. Ms. Bridges Hall in 1960 was the first African-American child to attend an all-white elementary school in the South under Federal court de-segregation orders. Her walk to school that first day of classes was depicted in an iconic Norman Rockwell painting showing her in a spotless white dress carrying a book while surrounded by tall, business suit-attired Federal marshals shown just from the shoulders down.

Ms. Bridges Hall spoke eloquently and at great length about the sanctity of the provisions in the USA-SBR to cleanse the collective souls of the nation of the infection of racism and bigotry.

As a child who had to face the consequences of overt racism every day she went to school, she recalled, she never would've dreamed of a day when the law might simply ban from holding public office any and every person who'd ever expressed a racially bigoted belief during their adult years.

"Of course, the first repercussion of that provision of the USA-SBR may be that racists' families train their children to never utter bigoted remarks in public, while they continue to think and believe those hateful ideas. But if public expressions of that hatred can be stemmed, then it will be like keeping a poisonous plant in constant shade. Eventually, it will wither, waste away and die, turning into nothing but a bitter bit of dusty ephemera.

"The remaining hatred-consumed souls who continue to exercise their right to spew that meanness in the light of day – well, you know what they say about sunlight being the best disinfectant. That section of sunlight in the USA-SBR will disintegrate those public expressions of oral fecality, over time. I know that in my heart."

Ms. Bridges Hall shared many of the anecdotal memories contained in her 1999 book, "*Through My Eyes.*" By the time she was done, she'd won over every last soul in the crowd.

She urged her listeners to do everything in their power to make sure the USA-SBR becomes the law of the land so African-Americans and their Native American brothers and sisters could finally receive some measure of delayed justice through the provision for reparations payments.

"It would be nothing less than a down payment on a permanent place in the middle class, a financial shield against the vagaries of the lives of financial struggles so many of us have led from time to time," she said.

"Let no one – whether they're white, black, green or purple – try to tell you that reparations are undeserved. We all know better. If nothing else, we've earned the reparations by enduring decade after decade of irrational hatred.

"If we still are stopped for the dastardly crimes of breathing while black or driving while black, at least we won't have to worry about being unable to pay the fine – before we have it **overruled** by a judge, that is."

She introduced the memorial videos on Sally and Prof. Bartlett with heartfelt empathy and laughed along with the crowd throughout the "Capitalism: A Love Story" showing.

By evening's end, the Poughkeepsians once again expressed individually to their guest their honor at her choosing to share a tiny bit of her life with them. And they once again gave Marcia lots of hugs for her skills at booking such great featured speakers.

∗ ∗ ∗

The next morning, on a surprisingly brisk late winter day, they headed in their rental van to Starkville, Mississippi for their 5 p.m. press conference there in advance of the following day's rally at Humphrey Coliseum on the Mississippi State University campus.

They were somewhat disappointed when the only reporters showing up were a 25-ish newsman from the tiny Starkville Daily News and from the local major network television affiliates. There wasn't even a PBS or NPR affiliate reporter present. And the television reporters who did show up – well, let's just say the scene reminded the Poughkeepsians of an orthodontist's waiting room full of pre-teens with lots of metal in their mouths. The only thing missing was the Mommies and Daddies sitting next to each of the reporters waiting to pay their next installment for their teeth-straightening services. At least there was no annoying smacking from gum-chewers.

There literally were no new questions that the Poughkeepsians hadn't heard before.

So, after the standard questions were asked, Heather took the lead: she told the reporters that residents in their state could expect improvements in child support enforcement efficiency through new, quicker administratively-established support orders (in addition to routine court-ordered child support) and streamlined uniform Federal Civil Contempt proceedings for chronically non-paying parents. In addition, she emphasized that the new Federalized Support Enforcement Officers would receive higher pay than the state-paid positions they were replacing and would have more incentives to remain in their positions, improving experience and efficiency among enforcement staff.

"How many of you here are single custodial parents?" she asked. Three persons, two women and one man, raised their hands.

"I guarantee you, you will like what the USA-SBR has in store to motivate your children's other parent to keep paying consistently. Besides that parent's own motivation to be a good Mom or Dad, obviously."

"There are states which currently don't have provisions under their laws to charge a non-custodial parent with Civil Contempt for non-payment, like Montana. There are other states that have such provisions in state law, like Hawaii, which *rarely* pursue contempt simply because they feel like it's too costly for their budget. When the USA-SBR becomes the law of the land, every single county in every single state will be subject to Civil Contempt referrals through the new Federalized support enforcement system.

"Once and for all, there will be 'nowhere to run to baby, no place to hide,' to paraphrase *Martha and the Vandellas*. Especially considering that their passports already would be invalidated for non-payment.

"So, to all the corporatist, pro-privatization, knuckle-dragging naysayers out there, if you don't like the improvements that go along with the USA-SBR, better start working on that time machine to take you back to the '50s. 'Cause this sweet ride's going to the future."

And, with that, the press conference was done.

∗ ∗ ∗

The Jean ValJean-ing of America

The Humphrey Coliseum was nearly full for the next evening's rally, which featured Gulfport native Tavis Smiley, one of only a few guests who would be making a second appearance at their rallies (after giving an introduction speech for the Rev. Jesse Jackson during their Champaign, Illinois rally).

Smiley's presentation focused on the social injustices visited upon the Scott Sisters. The sisters, Jamie and Gladys, both African-Americans, were convicted of orchestrating a 1993 armed robbery in Forest, Mississippi which netted them a grand total of $11.00. That's 1,100 cents, not dollars.

For their dastardly crime, which was the first offense for both of them and which involved no physical harm to anyone, _each_ _sister_ was given **double life-in-prison** sentences.

Despite staunch advocacy on their behalf which led to a review of their convictions by the U.S. Supreme Court, both of their convictions and their sentences were upheld. Mississippi Gov. Haley Barbour, a Republican (of course), denied their petition for clemency in 2006. However, he agreed on Dec. 29, 2010 to release them on the condition that Gladys donate a kidney to Jamie, who was suffering from end-stage renal failure – **AND** on the condition that they each pay $52 per month to the State of Florida, their new state of residence (where their mother lived), for costs of administering their parole *for the rest of their lives.* They were released Jan. 7, 2011 after 17 years in prison for their $11 robbery.[*]

It probably should be pointed out, Smiley said, that Mississippi is among those states with the largest number of correctional facilities which have been privatized, with five prisons operated by for-profit corporations there, including scandal-ridden Corrections Corporation of America (based in Nashville, Tennessee) and Management & Training Corp., a Centerville, Utah-based company.

A May 30, 2013 *Reuters* article spelled out just how bad it got at one Mississippi privatized facility. Smiley read from it:

> *"A Mississippi prison for severely mentally ill inmates is infested with rats that prisoners sell to one another as pets, two civil liberties groups claimed in a federal lawsuit filed on Thursday.*
>
> *Inmates at the East Mississippi Correctional Facility near Meridian live under "barbaric" conditions, in filthy quarters without working lights or toilets, forcing them to defecate on Styrofoam trays or into trash bags, the American Civil Liberties Union and the Southern Poverty Law Center claimed in the lawsuit.*
>
> *Beatings, rape, robbery and riots are commonplace, and inmates are denied access to medication and psychiatric care, the 83-page complaint stated.*
>
> *The privately run prison "is an extremely dangerous facility operating in a perpetual state of crisis" and inmates' human rights are violated daily, according to the groups. Some prisoners set fires in a desperate attempt to get medical attention in emergencies, the lawsuit said.*
>
> *"I've been in prisons all around the country, and this is the worst I've ever seen," said Gabriel B. Eber, staff counsel for the ACLU's National Prison Project.*
>
> *The class action lawsuit says state prison officials have been aware of the conditions at the facility for years but have not remedied the problems.*
>
> *In one instance, according to the lawsuit, an otherwise healthy inmate had to have a testicle removed after prison officials repeatedly denied his request for medical help when it swelled to the size of a softball from cancer.*

---

[*] San Francisco Bay View, 1/10/11

The abundance of rats has resulted in some prisoners using them as currency, trading the captured animals for cigarettes or selling them as pets with makeshift leashes, the lawsuit said."

"I suppose the Scott sisters could take some comfort from the fact that they weren't in one of those five Mississippi privatized for-profit prisons," Smiley said.

"But it's got to make a person wonder if it's more important to Mississippi's Republican governor to keep those privatized prison beds full than it is to mete out actual social justice.

"Come ON, brothers and sisters: **SEVENTEEN YEARS FOR ELEVEN DOLLARS – ON A <u>FIRST-TIME</u> OFFENSE**??!!"

"And Gov. Barbour kept them in prison more than *<u>TWO YEARS</u>* after the Wall Street financial melt-down? I guess he knew he didn't need them out to make room for J. P. Morgan Chase Bank's CEO, right?

"Let's count up how many Wall Street CEO's were thrown in prison for ripping, literally, **BILLIONS** off of Mom's and Pop's all over the country, even *all over the WORLD.* Bear with me while I use my calculator here – wait, just a second (feverishly punching buttons on his pocket calculator); OK, just figured it out!

"Here it is (holding the calculator out for the crowd to see): Z. E. R. O.

"So, here's the tally: 17 years for African-American sisters on their first offense during which no one was harmed. Zero years, zero months and ZERO DAYS for Wall Street CEO's who intentionally destroyed millions of homeowners' lives, leading to countless layoffs, suicides and divorces. Plus – *get this* – **those same CEO's ended up getting taxpayer-funded bonuses**.

"And guess who voted for the bailout? Seventy-five out of the ninety-nine senators who voted, ***<u>including</u>*** then-Senator Obama and then-Senator Hillary Clinton. *Only **nine** of the twenty-four Senate nays were Democrats.* Shameful.

"So, if you ask me whether I support the USA-SBR's provision requiring that first-time offenders who haven't physically hurt anyone be diverted away from prison sentences, I have one response: **damn *<u>right</u>* I do**. And *YOU HAD BETTER TOO*, unless you like being overwhelmed by all that social justice floating around out there, especially for us folks of color."

There was a new chant: "U-S-A...S-B-R!!" "U-S-A...S-B-R!!" "U-S-A...S-B-R!!"

The Poughkeepsians got goosebumps, as did just about everyone else. There was enough electricity in that audience to keep Starkville's lights on for the rest of the week.

Smiley finished his talk by urging his African-American brothers and sisters to support the USA-SBR provision for reparations payments. But, like Jesse Jackson, he pleaded with them to remain circumspect about how to use not just those potential funds, but *<u>any</u>* financial windfalls they have in life.

"The three most important factors in a sound, grounded future: education, education and education. If this becomes law you will be tempted to go forth and brighten your garages and homes with lots of shiny bling.

"Do. Not. Do. That.

"Prove to everyone else that the human race is at least as smart as a squirrel: put away as much of that money as you can, not just for a rainy day, not just for a cold winter, but for a college career, for a home down payment, for your future children's unforeseen emergencies."

The ralliers appeared to listen attentively. Smiley was confident his message was taken to heart.

From that evening on, in the Poughkeepsians' eyes at least, Tavis Smiley was a rock star.

They made sure he understood that before they bade him farewell.

He said the feeling was mutual.

$$* \quad * \quad *$$

JINDAL'S SPECIAL REALITY

The next morning it was a Van Arsdale van driver ("Say that fast five times in a row," Franklin joked with Holly) all the way to Baton Rouge for their 5 p.m. press gathering in advance of the following day's rally at Louisiana State University's Pete Maravich Assembly Center.

Those attending the press conference included reporters from the New Orleans Times-Picayune (a daily owned by the Advance Publications empire out of Staten Island, NY), the Baton Rouge Advocate (a daily locally owned by John Georges) and each of the local television network affiliates.

Their focal point was on the environmental provisions of the USA-SBR.

Harry Peterson and his dad Mel volunteered to tag-team the specific ways each USA-SBR provision would help forestall or prevent another Hurricane Katrina.

The reporters' environment-related questions were resolved in less than a half-hour.

At that point, Heather Griffin took it upon herself to point out the myriad ways the USA-SBR would neuter Louisiana Gov. Bobby Jindal's positions which she characterized as:

- *Starkly* anti-women's rights (for his opposition to pro-choice rights)
- *Starkly* anti-environment (for continuing to support government subsidies for Gulf of Mexico drilling even after the British Petroleum oil spill disaster of April 2010)

- *Starkly* anti-health (for opposing almost all provisions of the Affordable Care Act and voting to deny care to Medicare patients who can't afford co-pays)
- *Starkly* anti-middle class (for voting to make it harder for unions to organize to negotiate living wage jobs with employers and for not supporting the latest calls for minimum wage increases)
- *Starkly* anti-minority and anti-low-income voters (for voting to require all voters, including minorities and the poor, to produce photo ID's at their voting precincts during elections).
- *Starkly* anti-immigration (for supporting barriers to immigration and expensive security fencing along the U.S.-Mexican border).
- *Starkly* anti-economic justice (by supporting continued tax cuts for the wealthy and elimination of the progressive income tax, which requires that the wealthy pay a greater share of their income than the middle class and working poor do).
- *Starkly* opposed to church and state separation (for supporting tax dollars going to faith-based charter schools and for his unwillingness to offend fundamentalists by embracing evolutionary biology theory despite having an honors degree in biology from Brown University).

The list goes on and on and on, Heather said. "Empirically-based reality and Bobby Jindal's version of reality each reside in parallel universes.

"Thankfully, the USA-SBR resides in our universe, in our reality."

$$* \quad * \quad *$$

LONG-LASTING PALAST-ING

Their guest speaker the following evening at the Pete Maravich Assembly Center was investigative reporter, author and documentary filmmaker Greg Palast, whose documentary, "*Big Easy to Big Empty: The Untold Story of the Drowning of New Orleans*" was made to commemorate the one-year anniversary of Hurricane Katrina. It was released in 2007, two years after the storm.

Palast kept the crowd on the edge of their seats with almost two hours' worth of anecdotal stories from his years of investigative reporting.

His main focus was on crony capitalism, from the "W" Bush Administration awarding a major post-Katrina contract to a company whose primary qualification was large donations to Republicans on to multiple 'red' states' use of electronic vote tally-processing companies (like Diebold) whose main qualifications for such sensitive contracts were close ties to Republican movers and shakers.

He made a convincing argument that "W" Bush's 2004 re-election was stolen from John Kerry, based on an analysis of a disproportionately large number of ballots cast by likely Democratic voters being declared 'spoiled' by Republican-affiliated county officials around the country, *especially in Ohio.*

With the Poughkeepsians' permission, Palast screened the 30-minute "Big Easy to Big Empty" documentary for the audience. Afterward, he offered to take questions from the crowd. That led to another hour's worth of entertaining exchanges between Palast and attendees as Marcia, Holly, Heather, Karin, Orvis, Mel and Cherisse passed microphones around in the crowd.

Franklin had seen the occasional *"Tonight Show"* episode during which Jay Leno did his *'Jaywalking'* routine featuring hilariously stupid Los Angeles-area people displaying their nearly complete ignorance of current events. So, he was pleasantly surprised at the consistently well-articulated understanding of the political system by the audience members in Baton Rouge as they questioned Palast.

By the end of the evening, Franklin/Percy told Palast he wished he could spend a few days with him picking his brain. (*"Heard that as soon as I said it –* probably *wasn't the best metaphor for* **me** *to use,"* he immediately thought to himself.)

As it turned out during the following week, the Baton Rouge stop was beneficial for both the Poughkeepsians – who noticed an even larger-than-normal spike of activity on their website and Facebook page – and for Palast: more than 2,500 copies of his "Big Easy to Big Empty" documentary were sold on-line by just five days later.

* * *

Their next day's travel took them to Memphis, Tennessee for a 5 p.m. press conference in advance of the following day's rally at Memphis State University's FedEx Forum arena.

The travel was starting to wear on the Poughkeepsians, so they agreed to switch off driving duties every 90 minutes or so. It seemed to work better, unlike two days earlier when Holly had to fight off sleep a couple of times on the way to Baton Rouge.

"Don't wanna have an accident on the interstate and end up with our brains smeared all over the pavement," Phil said.

"OK, I heard it as soon as I said it," he said apologetically to Franklin.

"There's a lot of that going around. No need to apologize – it's not the sound of words that affects me, just the fragrance of open head wounds. C'mon, you know that."

* * *

There were reporters at the press conference from the Memphis Commercial Appeal (a daily owned by Journal Media Group of Milwaukee, WI), the Memphis (almost) Daily News (published Mondays through Fridays and apparently locally owned) and from each of the area local television network affiliates.

The local TV reporters – like everywhere else – had taken the Benjamin Button thing to yet another level: a couple of the reporters were wearing Oshkosh B'Gosh overalls and had small dentist office-sized lollipops sticking out of the front bib pockets – and even the ones in normal clothing appeared to be not just nose-mining occasionally, but crotch- and butt-mining as well.

Franklin made a mental note to make sure to watch at least a couple of local newscasts late that evening to see how the reporters' producers managed to get them camera-ready.

"You can't photo-shop live action broadcast television in real time, can you, Harry?" Franklin asked, under his breath.

"If you can, I'd sure like to know how to do that. You just gave me some cool ideas I'd like to try the next time I record Bianca and me together."

"We're bordering on too much information there, friend."

* * *

Stepping Back in Time – Wait, No, It's Just Tennessee

The reporters' questions involved the latest actions considered by Tennessee's hyper-Republican, hyper-Tea Party Legislature, which included:

- Making it harder for women to exercise their pro-choice rights.
- Cutting taxes on the wealthy.
- Allowing people to take guns to local parks and even to work in the trunks of their cars, employers' policies notwithstanding.
- Blocking the Federally-funded expansion of Medicaid, despite the benefits to the middle class and working poor.
- And making it harder for women to choose what happens to their bodies. Already mentioned that? That's OK, they're really, _really_ into that – after all, barely 17 percent of the Tennessee legislators are women. (Which isn't even close to the state with the fewest women lawmakers, Louisiana, at 11.8 percent.)

"Well, it certainly sounds like we might be wasting our time in Tennessee, since every single one of those Republican goals will be thwarted by the USA-SBR," Phil said.

"Except for one thing:

"We hope to convince grassroots Tennesseans to replace **each and every one** of those corporatist, Astroturf-phony conservative populists with bona fide, genuine anti-corporatist, anti-plutocrat, anti-Wall Street pro-middle class real-to-the-bone populists who will speak truth to power as long as they're able to breathe.

"That is why we're here.

"We won't give up on Tennesseans unless they give up on us.

"And we have no reason to expect that they will, as long as you dedicated members of the Fourth Estate do your jobs fairly and remain grounded in **fact**, as opposed to negative speculation and fear *induced by those who stand to gain most* from that negative speculation and fear."

* * *

High Voltage from Hightower

Their featured speaker the following evening was none other than populist extraordinaire and author Jim Hightower. Although the Poughkeepsians weren't aware of Hightower having any direct ties to Tennessee, he was only too happy to weigh in on a pending piece of legislation in the Tennessee Legislature.

The bill was being pushed by the Association for Responsible Alternatives to Workers' Compensation (ARAWC), an industry-sponsored group trying to undercut businesses' liability for on-the-job injuries and deaths suffered by their employees.

As he had recently reported in his monthly newsletter, he explained to the crowd that ARAWC's lobbyists were putting heat on lawmakers to allow large employers to **opt out** of state benefit plans so the employers could substitute their own, cheaper highly-restricted benefit plans.

In his home state of Texas, he said, once the ARAWC-sponsored plan there took effect, more than half of the new corporate Workers' Comp plans stopped paying anything whatsoever to families of workers killed as the result of accidents on the job. The Tennessee version **wouldn't even cover funeral expenses, artificial limbs or in-home care**.

The companies' total liability would be limited to three years or $300,000, whichever was less. He pointed out that the CEO mastermind behind those ARAWC-sponsored bills was none other than the head of risk management for – *wait for it* – Wal-Mart.

Hightower kept the audience spellbound for more than an hour with his many and varied tales of corporate soul-crushing of the middle class and working poor.

He pledged to contact every single elected officeholder in his home county, as well as his U.S. House Representative and his two U.S. Senators to get them to go on record for or against the USA-SBR.

"As those two great guys on that "*Rock the Park*" TV show like to say, 'If I can do this, you can too.' So, what the heck, make it happen! You know you don't have anything existentially better to do, right?"

And he *was* right.

Once again, Marcia had hit another home run by booking Hightower, who'd been a frequent guest on Bill Moyers' PBS programs. The Poughkeepsians asked him if he'd hop on their van for a repeat appearance at the University of Tennessee's Thompson-Boling Arena two evenings later.

"What the heck, my schedule's clear for the next week or so," he said. "Let's do it. Let's go after those corporate flimflammers 'til they say uncle."

He even agreed to participate in their usual 5 p.m. press conference the following afternoon in Nashville.

And he did. He killed.

✳ ✳ ✳

Hightower's performance at the University of Tennessee's Thompson-Boling Arena the next evening was every bit as witty and wisecracking as it was two evenings earlier. He went into the ARAWC controversy again, as eloquently as ever.

And then he surprised the Poughkeepsians by going through a whole new litany of Wall Street-shaming, not once repeating any of the issues he'd brought up in Memphis – but still managing to connect every single bone of contention he had with a provision in the USA-SBR which would remedy it.

As Hightower spoke, Franklin whispered to Phil, "Think we could get this guy on retainer? He is one clever man. Why isn't he on PBS or his own talk radio show?"

"You already know, Franklin," Phil whispered back. "You remember why we have that provision in the USA-SBR to break up the broadcast media virtual monopolies. I **know** you do."

"Oh, right – they're not about to allow an anti-corporatist on the air, **especially an entertaining one** like Jim - no way, no how, not from what the O'Learys showed me. Moyers was the only one who could finagle that – and that probably was due to the latitude he got for having on his show some endangered species-*conservatives* who openly resent Tea Partiers' ignorance."

After the rally was over, Franklin actually asked Hightower if there was any way they could make it worth his while to become an integral part of their little group.

His reply: "You get enough people elected to Congress who are willing to get this passed and then we'll talk, OK?

"In the meantime, I'm still waitin' t'see if that Hillary character even mentions you guys once. Except for supporting *state-by-state* approval of same-sex marriage – which is way weaker than what your USA-SBR would do – she hasn't even supported **a single part** of your project, not specifically.

"I don't know if it's just me, but I sure enough do wonder if her progressivism might be the mile-wide quarter-inch-deep variety. It's hard not to forget how she once was beatin' those pesky drums for war against **I-*ran*.**

"I recommend, as long as you keep getting lotsa folks to support what y'all are doin' that you remember to do *one basic thing* about Ms. Rodham Clinton and her ilk."

"What's that, Kemosabe?" Franklin/Percy asked.

"Watch thy backside."

* * *

ARCHETYPICAL ARCH-Y FUN

The next morning the Poughkeepsians headed off for the final leg of their current tour: the University of Missouri in Columbia. They left plenty early that day for the 6-1/4 hour drive so they'd have time to stop for lunch in Saint Louis and ascend through the 630-foot Gateway Arch over the west bank of the Mississippi River.

After they had a fast-food meal at a KFC franchise, they made their way over to the Arch. Like an excited pre-teen kid, Franklin had scarfed down his chicken tenders and biscuit as fast as his esophagus would allow so he could make his break for the tallest arch in the world. Franklin's enthusiasm reminded Harry of actor Jim Parsons' Sheldon Cooper character's frenetic behavior on '*The Big Bang Theory*' every time something related to Star Trek came up. Come to think of it, Harry thought, that arch resembles the Star Trek Federation logo. Just a wee little co-inky-dink, he mused.

Franklin scrambled through the visitor center and on to the end of the line for the tram to the top of the arch like a kid afraid he was going to miss the neighborhood ice cream truck. He was half-wishing that the trams and elevators would go out of service so he could test his leg strength going up the equivalent of 63 flights of stairs. But he was bright enough not to mention that to Holly, who was perfectly happy, thank you, to take advantage of the trams.

Holly practically had to offer to fellate Franklin in the Visitor Center restroom to get him to come down from the viewing area at the apex of the arch. In the end, she kept it to a whispered informal implication. Once he was back down, he thanked her for prodding him to get back on schedule – and said he wouldn't hold her to what she'd implied 630 feet higher up. That evening, it turned out he didn't have to, as it were. *She* did all the holding.

* * *

ENCOURAGING GOOD JOURNALISM WHERE ITS BEST STUDENTS ARE NURTURED

They made it to Columbia with a good 15 minutes to spare before the 5 p.m. press conference at their hotel meeting facility. There were reporters there from the Columbia Daily Tribune (a locally-owned daily), the Columbia Missourian (the University of Missouri paper staffed by journalism students); the Saint Louis Post Dispatch (a daily owned by Lee Enterprises of Davenport, Iowa) and from each of the local television network affiliates the usual blemish-faced romper room graduates trying their hardest to pass as journalists. At least one of them appeared to have arrived on a recumbent bicycle with training wheels. It might've been the one wearing dainty little pink mittens, but Harry wouldn't swear to it.

Most of the questions gravitated to three issues:

- High rates of violent crime, usually involving firearms, in urban parts of the state such as Saint Louis.
- Freewheeling gun laws.
- Religious "freedom to discriminate" laws popping up around the country.

Phil told his parents, Tom and Annie Podrowski, to jump right in.

They did.

They took turns pointing out step-by-step how each relevant portion of the USA-SBR would address and solve each of those problems.

"Of course, you have to remember: just outlawing sales of firearms to certain at-risk buyers is only a start," Annie said. "There still will be a staggering number of handguns circulating – legally or otherwise – out there for a long time to come, considering that during the Obama Presidency, gun sales skyrocketed.

"Some bells are hard to un-ring. But solving a problem – whether it's large as in huge numbers of injuries from firearms, or diminutive, as in keeping smaller children from bringing toy guns to school in their backpacks – either way, a solution always begins with small, persistent one-at-a-time steps."

Franklin/Percy finished off the responses to questions by fielding one involving voter suppression efforts by Republicans who were – incredibly – continuing to boast about how their clever actions would keep African-Americans from going to the polls in large numbers. It was almost like they already knew the 'fix' was in at the Supreme Court.

Which, of course, it had been when the Supremes gutted a huge portion of the 1965 Voting Rights Act in their June 2013 landmark decision.

With no small amount of pride, Mr. "Van Mullder" pointed out precisely how the USA-SBR would restore those eviscerated portions of the Voting Rights Act.

"If only there were real justice in this life: all of the Antonin Scalia's of the world would be required to show certified copies of their birth certificates at the polls every two years and the rest of us would simply be trusted not to commit any voter fraud felonies.

"Now there's a radical idea: giving people the benefit of the doubt."

Franklin also aimed praise at the University of Missouri's long tradition of producing quality journalists. He encouraged current journalism students to emulate the likes of Chicago Tribune reporters Patricia Callahan and Sam Roe. Callahan and Roe were featured in the documentary "*Merchants of Doubt*" (based on the 2010 book by Naomi Oreskes and Erik M. Conway) for their work exposing the carcinogenic fire retardant chemical industry's use of deceptive lobbyists at various state legislatures to keep bans on those chemicals from becoming law. *Despite support for those bans from firefighters' unions, children's advocates, health insurers, etc., etc.*

He pointed out that the carcinogenic chemicals industry was, *at that very moment*, in the process of successfully blocking approval of such a ban in the State of Washington Legislature's Republican-controlled Senate despite the same ban being approved in the state's Democratically-controlled House on votes of 95-3 and 92-3.[*] All of that despite the documentarians showing how the **cigarette industry** was behind the original subversive push for carcinogenic flame retardant chemicals as a way of blaming supposedly 'highly flammable' consumer products for cigarettes smoldering for hours after being partially smoked – instead of going to the expense of simply designing a cigarette which would extinguish itself soon after being removed from the smoker's mouth.

And the topper, Franklin said: the carcinogenic flame retardant chemicals in children's clothing, furniture, mattresses and bedding *don't even work – they have virtually no effect in slowing the growth of a fire in a home.*[**] He encouraged the Columbia journalists to hold their legislators accountable if there was no such ban in Missouri.

And, finally, he extolled the USA-SBR's provision which would outright ban exposures of the public to carcinogens in air, food, water, clothing, furniture, building materials and other products.

Most importantly, he said, the ban has real teeth: Class B Federal felony charges for individuals and businesses who defy the ban.

* * *

'MR. GRANT' GOES LONG AND SCORES BIG

The featured speaker at the Mizzou Arena the evening of the following day was none other than Lou Grant himself: Missouri native Ed Asner.

Mr. Asner had huge volumes of praise for the USA-SBR's provisions to ensure single-payer Medicare for All health care coverage with no out-of-pocket payments for anyone.

---

[*] 5/2/15 Spokesman-Review
[**] "Merchants of Doubt," 2014 Sony Pictures Classic

"Maybe someday someone can help me understand why Ms. Clinton of the Clinton Dynasty is so dogged about opposing single-payer health care. What is it about her and all the other closet-Republican faux Democrats getting in bed with all these billionaires at the drop of a hat?"

Mr. Asner was red-hot effusive with kudos for the USA-SBR provisions which would encourage more effective union organization, as well as a significantly increased minimum wage.

He called the provisions making it harder for Congress to start unnecessary wars "a turning point for civilization" and a "long-overdue dose of saltpeter" for the greed-obsessed military-industrial complex and its hordes of highly-paid huckster lobbyists.

In addition, he heaped accolades on the Poughkeepsians for including severe restrictions on the use of the death penalty.

"Those restrictions should, if I'm reading them correctly (adjusting his reading glasses to his squinty eyes), effectively **abolish** its practice except for the very, very worst of serial killers and mass murderers. And, even then, the Prosecutors and jurors are required to bet their own lives on no one having stacked the deck against the alleged perpetrator."

Mr. Asner's saved his strongest praise 'til last: namely, his admiration for the courage of the Poughkeepsians for including a provision enabling average citizens to submit a true bill of indictment against a sitting elected official – including even the President – for committing felony or other criminal infractions, including felonies involving illegal surveillance of private citizens.

"What this USA-SBR does is, figuratively speaking, give average working people the legal cajones to hold the powerful accountable.

"If the rest of us can just have their back, you know – make sure these pithy protectors of the peace from Poughkeepsie don't get pulverized by pervasive palavering pusillanimous pit bulls and pinschers, then this thing has a chance.

"But it's up to each of us to re-direct our energies at each and every office holder who won't commit to supporting this.

"As Lou Grant might say, get your ass in gear and get to work on this!"

(Lots of sustained applause.)

As Mr. Asner was wrapping up his presentation, the Poughkeepsians once again each hugged Marcia for having the skill and good sense to convince 'Lou Grant' to participate. "Someday you're gonna get that raise," Phil joked.

Mel and Tom mainly wanted to know from Mr. Asner what Alex Trebek was like when Asner was on Celebrity Jeopardy. "These lips will never tell," Asner laughed, with that expression of pouty faux embarrassment shown by someone whose secret lover has just been discovered.

* * *

Mirror, Mirror on the Wall

Marcia had booked them on a non-stop flight from Saint Louis to La Guardia the next day leaving shortly after lunch. Their 90-minute drive from Columbia to Saint Louis seemed more like 30 minutes, as they were fortunate enough to have Mr. Asner along for the ride – although he snored in the back seat for most of it. His flight was in the opposite direction: back to his Santa Monica, California home via Los Angeles.

Once again, the Poughkeepsians were thoroughly relieved to step off the Amtrak train onto Poughkeepsie soil again that evening. There was no time for Franklin and Holly to relax, though: their first day of classes for the final half of the spring semester started early the next morning.

But when Franklin awoke and looked in the mirror the next morning there was more than just the weariness of a stressful rally tour on his face.

It was happening once again: he definitely was getting older. His appearance now was that of someone in his early to mid-40's.

* * *

He quickly shared his discovery with Phil and Pongo. The consensus was that he needed to let Bianca cull more crows so he could have another birdbrain-infused fruit smoothie. But, as hopeful as he wanted to be, it occurred to Franklin that, if that were a 'cure,' so to speak, for stabilizing his aging, he wouldn't have to be going through this again.

Still, it was worth another try, even if the effect was only temporary, he thought to himself. After all, life itself is only temporary – a blink of an eye in geological terms, right?

* * *

Duck Turd of the Free World

By the following weekend, Bianca and Heather had had enough time to cull crows from the cropland and fruit groves of the same farmers Bianca had approached earlier. Around breakfast time that Saturday morning, Bianca delivered a birdbrain-infused blueberry and huckleberry smoothie with a special spicy taste – she called it a '*Caw-cophany*' flavor shake – directly into Franklin's slightly unsteady hands. She noticed – but said nothing about – the new white streaks in Franklin's moustache.

He choked it down and the wait began.

As the days progressed, he found himself checking the mirror every time he went to take a leak at Adams Landscaping and during his lunch break at Marist.

By the third day, he could tell a difference. The crow's feet (yes, the irony was not unnoticed by him) at the outer corners of his eyes had faded almost completely away. But the whiteness in his eyebrows and moustache had only changed a little. He'd gone from, say, a mid-40s appearance to mid-30s. He was fairly confident no one at school and, especially, at the rallies would notice this supposedly mid-20s virile guy was aging rapidly all of a sudden.

It was clear Chet had noticed, though. Chet kept telling him not to stay late on his shifts at Adams and to make sure he got to bed at a reasonable hour.

"You look like a walking, talking duck turd – compared to a year ago, anyway," Chet had said a few days earlier.

Not something anyone likes to hear – especially a former Leader of the Free World.

* * *

Freedom to Discriminate: Find Another Store, Same-Sex-ers!

As March 2015 drew to a close, there were lots of reverberations in the news media and cyberspace about the legislative fiascos in Indiana, Arkansas and elsewhere over attempts to codify individual states' rights (there's that wonderful Confederacy avatar again: States' Rights) to allow their residents with businesses to inflict their religious beliefs (i.e., prejudices) upon their customers. By refusing to serve them if the customers were gay, pursuing same-sex marriage, etc.

Apparently influenced by the State of Washington's successful lawsuit against a small-town florist who refused to cater a same-sex wedding (she claimed it violated her Southern Baptist beliefs; never mind that lots of other Southern Baptists, like Bill Moyers, disagree), the Republican-controlled Indiana Legislature and their Republican Governor actually passed a bill to protect business owners like that florist.

Which led to a complete meltdown: a national 'Boycott Indiana' movement quickly spread, a prairie-fire-in-a-drought-style conflagration. Within weeks, a new bill invalidating the previous bill's offensive language was signed into law. The Indiana Republicans looked, for all the nation to see, like the very worst kind of cravenly bigoted assholes who still would jump at the chance to cave on their so-called 'principled stand' if it meant preserving business profits.

Never fear, some of them said, they'd be back next year to try again at protecting the right to be a bigoted asshole.

* * *

HYPOCRISY – AND YOUR TAX DOLLARS –
AT WORK, HILLARY-STYLE

It was around that same time that prospective Presidential candidate Hillary Rodham Clinton was forced to admit that she had intentionally wiped clean her personal E-Mail records, some of which involved information being sought under subpoena by a Congressional committee on the imaginary dead horse-flogging 2-1/2-year-old Benghazi attack issue. Turned out she'd used her personal E-Mail account(s) for government business while she was Secretary of State. She claimed she just didn't know any better.

The former Secretary of State who'd repeatedly verbally blasted Edward Snowden for disclosing unlawful National Security Agency monitoring of hundreds of millions of private citizens' E-Mails and phone calls now had decided that, not only did her E-Mails deserve to remain secret, but that the scope of government surveillance of citizens *just might* be too broad - though she'd reserve final judgment on the 'too broad' part for later.

With not even a microscopically-sized scintilla of a hint of irony displayed.

Nor – none too shockingly – anything even remotely resembling an apology to Mr. Snowden.

"Cuh-lassy," Franklin thought to himself.

* * *

AND IT BEGINS

A week or so later, on April 12, 2015 while Franklin was on his lunch break at Adams Landscaping, he saw on his smart phone the video circulated by Ms. Clinton announcing – prepare to be shocked! – that she was running for President. The slick ad worked hard to imply that she wanted to be president for just your average run-of-the-mill folks whose lives revolved around taking out the garbage without their dog eating it, going on walks with their same-sex partners, starting small businesses, anticipating childbirth, planting a garden and so forth. She wants to be "a champion" for those everyday folks, she said.

"If," Franklin thought to himself, *"and **only if**, she can find time for all that championing when she's not schmoozing with her Wall Street 'Best Friends Forever' buddies."*

* * *

"Hey, Mr. President, Sir," Pongo said when Franklin arrived home from work that evening, "did you catch Hillary's announcement video today?"

"I did."

"Did you notice her new campaign logo?"

"Yes, now that you mention it."

"Did you catch the not-so-subtle symbolization there?"

"You mean with the big red arrow?"

"Not just the arrow itself. Look at it again."

"Jesus, you're right. It's pointing hard right, in a big, unmistakable way. Not up, not down, not left, but as right as right can get."

"Sure looks like she wants people to think of her as heading way off to the right. Just so it'll be clear she's not like that so-called Obama radical, y'think?"

"I'm thinking there should be a little icon of a cliff-face drawn in just to the right of the bottom of that arrow," Franklin said. "Truthfulness in advertising, y'know, that sort of thing."

*　*　*

PAYING FOR KIND THOUGHTS, THAT'S ALL – YEAH, THAT'S THE TICKET!

In anticipation of her announcement, allegations emerged four days earlier of apparent unseemly big-money influence on Ms. Clinton during her tenure as Secretary of State.[*]

It all began while she was a U.S. Senator in 2005.

The Clinton Foundation had entered into an agreement with Vancouver, Canada billionaire mining and oil exploration financier Frank Giustra. Giustra pledged in 2007 to donate $100 million plus half of all his future earnings toward a Latin American 'sustainable growth initiative' partnership with the Clinton Foundation.[**]

It turned out that Giustra had good reason to be grateful to the Clintons.

Bill Clinton had first met Giustra during a 2005 charity tsunami victims' fundraiser at Giustra's Vancouver, British Columbia home in Canada. As Clinton's friendship with Giustra developed, Clinton introduced Giustra to then-Colombian President Alvaro Uribe, who was wanting to privatize his country's state-owned oil company, Ecopetrol. Clinton helped smooth the way for a partnership deal between Uribe and Pacific Rubiales, an oil company co-founded by Giustra.

The main controversy?

Despite Hillary Clinton (and, similarly, Barack Obama) pledging during the 2008 Presidential campaign to "do everything (she could) to urge the Congress

---

[*] 4/8/15 International Business Times

[**] 6/21/07 Toronto Globe and Mail

to reject the Colombia Free Trade Agreement" both she and President Obama reversed course and supported it by 2010.

However, there were allegations in 2011 that the Colombian military had rounded up at gunpoint Colombian oil workers who were striking against Giustra's company and threatened violence against them if they didn't disband, **all in violation** of the Colombia Free Trade pact negotiated by Hillary Clinton and President Obama.

Human rights groups and union leaders urged Secretary Clinton to pressure the Colombian government to protect the union organizers, using her leverage to potentially shut off hundreds of millions of dollars in U.S. aid to the Colombian military if the Colombian government didn't comply.

But, *guess what*! Clinton eventually responded by authorizing a formal State Department announcement *publicly praising Colombia's progress on human rights*. Result: all those millions of dollars in U.S. aid ended up with the same military goons who'd been intimidating the union organizers.

A giant middle finger in the direction of struggling Colombian oil workers. Can't risk rubbing one of their most powerful donors the wrong way. A donor, who by the way, now sits on the Clinton Foundation Board of Directors.

"*Hope she's not holding her breath waiting for lots of donations from rank and file union workers in the U.S.A.*," Franklin thought to himself.

(According to the International Business Times, neither the Clinton Foundation nor the State Department responded to a request for comments on their story; Pacific Rubiales denied to the Times that it was involved in government military violence against its striking oil workers.)

At around the same time Bill Clinton was becoming close to Giustra, Giustra also was starting up a uranium mining firm, UrAsia, which would – with Bill Clinton's assistance – win a deal with Kazakhstan's state-owned mining company and go on to merge with South African company Uranium One.

Uranium One would later become majority-owned by Russian firm Rosatom, upon approval by members of the Committee on Foreign Investment, including then-Secretary of State Hillary Clinton, allowing Russians to have legal control over extensive uranium mining rights in the U.S.A. (such as in Wyoming) through Uranium One's leases.

During that extended process, donations to the Clinton Foundation included $31.3 million from Giustra, $2.35 million from Uranium One Chairman Ian Telfer, plus millions more from others peripherally involved – not counting a $500,000 speaking fee paid to Bill Clinton for a speech in Moscow in June 2010 by a Kremlin-related Russian investment bank promoting Uranium One stock purchases.[*]

More revelations followed during the weeks following Hillary's announcement of her candidacy: turned out that the Clinton Foundation had promised in writing as a condition of Hillary's appointment to become Secretary of State

---

[*] New York Times, 4/23/15

to disclose **_ALL_** of its foreign donors annually, **including** those donating to the foundation's Canadian affiliate.

Small problem: more than 1,100 of those foreign donors *were **NOT*** reported, prompting the foundation to announce it would have to file multiple amended tax returns.[*]

And every time Hillary was *specifically asked* at the time of those new disclosures whether there were any actions she took as Secretary of State *on behalf of donors to the foundation*, she simply blew off the questioners, rather than just saying 'no.'[**] Instead, she claimed that the suspicions of corruption circling around previously undisclosed foreign donations were simply the result of the political "silly season" blooming due to her newly-announced candidacy.

The Clintons' penchant for friendships with Hollywood movers and shakers like the billionaire Giustra produced some unusual coincidences.

Giustra was founder and Chairman of the Board of LionsGate Entertainment (a Vancouver, B.C. firm with headquarters in Santa Monica, California) around the time Michael Moore's "Fahrenheit 9/11" was greenlighted. LionsGate ended up distributing the film after Disney/Miramax dropped out of a distribution agreement on orders from then-Disney CEO Michael Eisner. Though Giustra had left LionsGate by the time it was released, it went on to become LionsGate's highest-grossing film, winning the Palm d'Or at Cannes. Giustra returned to the Lions Gate Board of Directors in 2010.[***]

The director of LionsGate's highest-grossing film, Mr. Moore, has consistently criticized Hillary Clinton for her willingness to accept massive campaign donations from for-profit health care corporations. During her tenure in the U.S. Senate, health care industry donations to her were exceeded only by those made to Republican Rick Santorum, according to Moore.

Seems like a fairly clear bottom line here, Franklin thought to himself:

- If you're a billionaire, expect Hillary and Bill Clinton to put their reputations on the line for you. *Even when the hypocrisy of it is **glaringly** embarrassing.*
- If you're an 'everyday person' appearing in her campaign video, just make sure you're paid up front. And don't get your hopes up over finding a well-paying union job if she's elected.

Working at Hillary's former law client-slash-low-wage employer Wal-Mart, though – well, that's another matter altogether: hiring is constant.

✳ ✳ ✳

---

[*] National Public Radio, 5/2/15
[**] *The Daily Show,* 4/30/15
[***] Wikipedia, 5/2/15

Three days after Hillary's announcement, there was an unexpected news item out of Washington, D.C. which should've portended poorly for Wall Street-embracing candidates like Ms. Clinton.

On his day off, U.S.P.S. letter carrier and Navy veteran Doug Hughes – after telling authorities of his plans in advance – successfully flew his small, low-priced gyrocopter at low altitude over Washington, D.C. and landed safely on the lawn of the U.S. Capitol.

His primary goal, he stated both before and after his flight, was to make a delivery of his own personal mail. Turned out he was carrying 535 letters – one for each member of Congress – letters which featured an eloquently-worded plea (including even a quote from then-U.S. Sen. John Kerry) to remove the influence of corporate money from Congress.

Of course, corporate media being what it is, the main focus of news coverage was not about Hughes' eloquent plea. Rather, it was about the fact that he was able to fly undetected by Homeland Security onto Capitol grounds.

Seeing evildoers everywhere, 'inside the beltway' commentators threw up their hands – figuratively and literally – pointing out that 'he could'a had a bomb!'

Message sent, but not received. (At least the *Daily Show* was able, sort of, to point out the misplaced priorities of the beltway pundits, considering that Hughes discussed his planned "Freedom Flight" with the Tampa Times *the previous year* and obviously had no malicious intent.)

$$* \quad * \quad *$$

The Faux Populist Peeks
Out from the Cracks

On April 21, 2015, the *New York Times* reported that Ms. Clinton, *trying* to appeal to supporters of Sen. Elizabeth Warren, had **privately** called for a "toppling" of wealthiest 1 percent. Despite the fact that her campaign **was being bankrolled by that very same 1 percent.** Her top campaign donors throughout her political career look like a list of the Who's Who among the financial institutions of the 1 percent (Citigroup, Goldman Sachs, JP Morgan Chase Bank, Lehman Brothers, TimeWarner, Cablevision, Merrill Lynch, Credit Suisse, etc.).* The *Times* also reported that she spoke *in generalities* (of course) about wanting to reduce corporate welfare, raise the minimum wage, guarantee sick leave for low-wage workers and close tax loopholes.

---

* Anti-Media, 4/21/15

All of that, however, occurred barely a month after she announced that Iowan Jerry Crawford, a *long-time Monsanto Corp. lobbyist and attorney* who'd known Hillary from her previous Presidential campaign, would serve as adviser for her Ready for Hillary Super PAC. Since her last Presidential candidacy, Crawford had successfully backed a Monsanto-endorsed <u>Republican</u> running for State of Iowa Agriculture Secretary. He'd also represented Altria, parent company of tobacco mega-corporation Phillip Morris USA. Monsanto is vilified among many farmers and progressives for its heavy-handed pursuit of monopolies on seeds, often **suing** farmers for using seeds from a current crop grown from Monsanto products to plant their following year's crop – a farming practice going back, literally, millennia.[*]

Hillary also was well-known for pressuring foreign governments to purchase Monsanto products while she served as Secretary of State.[**] Her ties to Monsanto go all the way back to her employment at the Rose Law Firm. The Rose Law firm represented Monsanto, which during Bill Clinton's administration obtained FDA approval for the notorious bovine growth hormone used on dairy cows, for many years.

Franklin shared those just-discovered news items with Phil when he got home from work that late April day in 2015.

"No doubt," Franklin said to Phil, tongue firmly in cheek, "all those 1 percenters out there are simply shaking in their boots and loosening their sphincters over the prospect of such an arch nemesis as Hillary becoming President."

"I foresee *Depends* sales soon peaking," Phil said, voice dripping in sarcasm. "Good to know Hillary has the middle class' back."

To punctuate the continued sarcasm, Phil cut loose a particularly loud fart.

∗ ∗ ∗

A SHAMEFUL TREND EMERGES INTO BROAD DAYLIGHT – FINALLY!

On April 12, 2015, Freddie Gray, a 25-year-old African-American man, was forcibly arrested by Baltimore, Maryland police for alleged switchblade possession and dragged into a waiting jail transport van. During the trip to the jail, with police officers inside the van accompanying Gray, Gray went into a coma and was taken to a trauma center where he died a week later. Turned out his spine had been severed and he'd suffered a serious head injury while in the police van; the head injury matched the shape of a bolt sticking out of the interior of the transport van.

---

[*] AlterNet, 3/9/15, culled from NYT, Washington Post, etc.

[**] Max Ocean, *Common Dreams*, 7/3/14; Tom Philpott, *Mother Jones*, 5/18/13

His death prompted a series of peaceful street protests on April 25, 2015 which eventually turned into violent riots after his burial two days later. The violent riots subsided after a few days and turned into victory celebrations when the State's Attorney announced on May 1, 2015 that six police officers (three white, three African-American) would face felony charges, including a 2nd degree murder charge against the van driver.

It was at least the *fifth* time in the previous nine months that **unarmed** African American men died during interactions with police or while in police custody.

Those victims included:

Eric Garner, 43, who died July 17, 2014 as the result of a police chokehold ("I can't breathe") as a group of officers forcibly arrested him for selling untaxed cigarettes; a Staten Island, NY, grand jury on Dec. 3, 2014 declined to indict the officer who applied the chokehold, despite the medical examiner's ruling that the death was a homicide. Widespread protests followed in the U.S. and even in London, England. But no officer was charged or disciplined for Garner's death.

Michael Brown, 18, in Ferguson, Missouri. After he was stopped by an officer on Aug. 9, 2014 for walking in a residential street, Brown (who had no criminal record) was shot six times, including twice in the head despite witnesses saying Brown had his hands up above his head; he was suspected of shoplifting a $5 pack of Swisher Sweets cigars after a convenience store customer called police when she saw Brown shove a male store clerk and glare at the clerk after the clerk put his hands on Brown as Brown tried to leave; video later showed Brown appeared to try to buy the cigars, but apparently didn't have enough money for the purchase. Peaceful protests followed, but law enforcement responded by allowing a police canine to urinate on a makeshift memorial to Brown and by bringing in a day later 150 officers decked out in riot gear and accompanied by military-style assault vehicles, shooting tear gas cannisters and rubber bullets into crowds and at reporters. Officers were seen forcibly dismantling journalists' television camera equipment and assaulting reporters. Burning and looting ensued. Protests continued through much of October and resumed after a grand jury on Nov. 24, 2014 declined to indict the officer who shot Brown. The protests flared again when the Ferguson Police Chief resigned on March 11, 2015 and it was announced he had a golden parachute ($96,000 severance pay plus a year of health benefits). A Federal review later determined the officer who shot Brown hadn't violated Brown's civil rights based on the officer's unconfirmed claim that Brown tried to assault the officer as the officer sat in his patrol car.

Eric C. Harris, 44, who was accidentally shot April 2, 2015 by a 73-year-old Tulsa County reserve sheriff's deputy as a group of deputies pinned him to the ground (he'd fled on foot from arrest for the alleged illegal sale of a firearm in a sting set-up; the deputy was charged with manslaughter; as Harris was pinned on the ground dying, he complained of "losing my breath," to which another deputy said, "Fuck your breath").

Walter Scott, 50, who on April 4, 2015 ran from a police officer after he was stopped for a broken brake light – the officer shot at him eight times, hitting him five times, after a taser hit failed to incapacitate Scott (the officer was charged with first degree murder only after a private citizen's video of the shooting came to light).

Based on the April 2013 study, "Operation Ghetto Storm," showing an African-American was killed by law enforcement, private security or self-appointed vigilantes every 28 hours in 2012, those deaths perhaps shouldn't have been shocking. But the video and eyewitness evidence accompanying the killings seemed to paint a fairly clear picture that African-American men's lives – including the lives of men with no prior criminal records like Michael Brown – mattered far less to authorities than uncharged white-collar felons still allowed to roam free on Wall Street.

In other words, if you're an African-American male, you can be *de facto* <u>executed</u> over stealing $5 worth of stuff; if you're a white Wall Street mortgage instruments manipulator involved in billions of dollars of fraud, you get a **huge raise at taxpayers' expense**.

This did not sit well with Franklin and the other Poughkeepsians.

To put it mildly.

Phil wondered if it was what modern-day mental health experts would call transference: racists in law enforcement at the street level so inconsolably incensed over having an African-American President, a President relentlessly vilified daily on an entire news network (Rupert Murdoch's Fox News), that they looked for chances to manhandle, abuse and even kill African-American suspects whenever the opportunity presented itself.

Franklin disagreed: "It's nothing more than gutter-level racial hatred. It wouldn't matter whether the President were black, polka-dotted or as white as that Johnny Winter musician on those old albums of yours, Phil. A bunch of rapscallions who will take their viciousness to their graves."

"There's one of those words again, Mr. President," Pongo said.

"Oh, yes, 'rapscallions.' OK, I'm trying to do better – I am, aren't I, Pongo?"

"Yessir, you are. Just a reminder."

* * *

FROM PRESIDENT EMERITUS TO PHYSICAL THERAPIST

The home stretch at Marist for Franklin and Holly before their anticipated May 22, 2015 graduation was hectic, as it was for most fourth-year students. Franklin/Percy cut back his work schedule at Adams Landscaping by four hours a week, but Chet was OK with that – as long as Franklin would promise to stick with Adams 'til his final career plans were firmly in place.

Franklin already had been admitted two months earlier to the fall 2015 Doctor of Physical Therapy program at the State University of New York-Albany. He promised Chet he'd continue to work every weekend at Adams for as long as he could, making the 1-1/4- hour commute back to Poughkeepsie every Friday as soon as his last class was over.

But he wondered how long he could keep up that commitment, not to mention his continued promise to participate in the USA-SBR organizational efforts: after all, it was a *doctoral* program, not an on-line class to become a Notary Public.

$$* \quad * \quad *$$

OVER THE CLIFF?

On May 7, 2015, as the bleary-eyed Franklin and Pongo sat down in the early A.M. at their breakfast table to munch on muffins and omelets, they were confronted by a headline in the *New York Times*' science section: "Amount of Carbon Dioxide in Air Keeps Rising, Hits Milestone."

It was a relatively brief Associated Press story (based on a story the previous day in *The Guardian*) with no local sidebars added by the *Times*, but it packed a wallop: the global-wide measurement for Carbon Dioxide had hit 400.83 parts per million (ppm) for the first time in recorded history.

The new National Oceanic and Atmospheric Administration (NOAA) study on which the story was based stated that the new worldwide measurement was the highest **in two million years**. Worse, it stated the rate of increase now is 100 times faster than any previously-recorded (pre-industrial) natural rate of CO2 increase. It occurred almost 30 years after the level considered safe by climate scientists – 350 ppm was eclipsed for the first time worldwide. Sadly, that announcement essentially made the 350.org campaign (to reverse the huge human exacerbation of global warming) virtually hopeless, though its mission would continue.

"We have to have hope for humanity's ability to head off the climatic train wreck our species has our planet steaming into, Pongo," Franklin said.

"We have to keep reminding our ralliers of their individual responsibility to minimize their carbon footprints, every chance they get. Unless they're OK with the surface of this planet hitting a couple hundred degrees Fahrenheit in a couple of centuries."

"Maybe we should start handing out oven mitts at the rallies instead of clean underwear," Pongo said.

"Let's do both, OK?" Franklin suggested.

"Mitts? Sure," Phil said, overhearing. "We'll introduce 'em by clarifying that the mitts aren't for holding any hot balls while donning clean skivvies – rather, they're for keeping their hands from looking like KFC Original Recipe chicken wings by the time they walk from their commuter trains to work.

"But they'd work just fine on balls too…"

"Nice and subtle," Franklin said.

"I've got a knack," Phil proudly smiled.

* * *

Part Three

COLLEGE GRADUATION AND FINAL
RALLIES... ATTACKS AND UNCONTROLLED
AGING SPUR PLAN... UNWELCOME
AND WELCOME CONSEQUENCES

Graduation Consummation

The Marist graduation 15 days later came off without a hitch. Holly's parents showed up, beaming – but Franklin/Percy thought he detected a mixture of both stink-eye and worry aimed his way.

He was pretty sure it had something to do with the prematurely gray streaks in his hair and moustache. He told himself not to take it personally: after all, he was the one who was sleeping with their unmarried daughter.

He and Holly decided to celebrate their college graduation by taking a long weekend trip to Bar Harbor, Maine. It was spectacular, if crowded, on the Bar Harbor sidewalks and oceanfront. But they only ventured out for a few hours on Saturday afternoon. They chose to spend the remainder of their time re-acquainting themselves with their favorite parts of each other's epidermis inside their hotel room overlooking the Gulf of Maine.

It. Was. Perfect.

But it was way too short.

They had to return the following Monday for their latest USA-SBR rally tour, this time to the University of Alabama, the University of Florida, Florida State University and the University of Georgia. It was to be the first of their final three tours before the 2016 general election.

They still didn't know what to make of their success in ramping up support from genuine grassroots "everyday people" like the ones in Hillary Clinton's weird video. Likewise, they didn't know what to make of Hillary's continued complete silence on each of the specific provisions of the USA-SBR.

Other than the most logical inference: a persistent snub usually means you can go fuck yourself.

* * *

They broke down and agreed with Marcia to take the only non-stop from LaGuardia to Birmingham, Alabama for their visit to the University of Alabama in Tuscaloosa. Even though it was on Delta. With two additional Poughkeepsians attending this tour – Penny and Mitch Duarte (Heather's Mom and Step-Dad) – they wanted as few complications as possible, including minimal connecting flights.

(Delta's latest public relations turd dump involved their demand that musician passengers with cellos buy an extra seat for their instruments **while refusing** to grant those passengers frequent flier miles for the cost of that extra seat. Delta didn't just refuse to grant miles for the required extra seat for one passenger, renowned cellist Lynn Harrell. When Delta discovered he'd been granted miles for his extra seat purchases, they not only disallowed those miles, they *revoked Harrell's <u>entire</u> SkyMiles membership*, wiping out *a half-million miles* he'd earned just for himself - and they even banned him from the program. "*Absolute, unequivocal dickheads, those Delta management folks,*" Franklin thought to himself.)[*]

Except for one uber-Nazi-style flight attendant who didn't like a passenger's attitude when she told the passenger he'd have to wait to go to the bathroom 'til they were done serving drinks in First Class, the flight went well. (Both of the rear bathrooms were occupied. Unfortunately, the passenger, a terminal cancer ostomy patient, couldn't wait that long. The flight attendant succinctly asked the passenger to please 'suck it up' for another 15 minutes. Harsh words were exchanged. The flight attendant grumpily relented at the last moment, just as an Air Marshal was about to intervene. All in all, one of the more pleasant Delta travel experiences.)

*   *   *

Their one-hour drive west to Tuscaloosa was mercifully uneventful. They arrived for the 5 p.m. press conference at their hotel meeting facility about an hour in advance.

Reporters were present at the conference from the Tuscaloosa News (a daily owned by GateHouse Media of Perinton, NY), the Montgomery Advertiser (a daily tentacle of the Gannett empire), the Birmingham News (a three-day-a-week paper owned by Advance Publications) and from each of the regional television network affiliates which, like virtually all other local TV affiliates around the country, appeared to have a rule against on-camera talent looking more than 21 years old. One of the local TV reporters had a skateboard sticking out of her backpack.

As predicted by Marcia on their way to the hotel, the first and foremost concern of the reporters was how the USA-SBR would affect the latest same-sex marriage controversy in Alabama.

---

[*] Wall Street Journal, 3/13/13

Turned out that, three months earlier, their State Supreme Court Chief Justice Roy S. Moore had ordered Alabama probate judges to refuse to issue marriage licenses to gay couples, despite the fact that a Federal District Court judge appointed by President George W. Bush had ordered Alabama courts to honor such requests. The Federal judge had explicitly ruled that Alabama's ban on same-sex marriage was unconstitutional.

Moore had previously been ousted from his position on the Alabama Supreme Court more than 10 years earlier for judicial misconduct as the result of refusing to honor a Federal judge's order to remove a monument to the Ten Commandments from a government building in Montgomery. However, he'd run again for election to the post and won.

Unlike most high school civics students, Justice Moore apparently was sick or asleep on the day it was explained that states' courts are bound under the U.S. Constitution to follow the orders of Federal courts.

In any event, this was low-hanging fruit for the Poughkeepsians.

"The USA-SBR resolves this issue once and for all," Penny Mitsuhama Duarte explained.

"There should never, ever again be some kind of weird, balkanized patchwork of laws around the country stating one kind of marriage is OK in one state and isn't OK in another.

"Human beings have the right to be treated the same way in each and every state. This is not the DIS-United States of America – it is the _U_-nited States of America. No matter what a person's perspective is on the old issue of State's Rights – an issue that began with slavery and continues to dog folks in states where slavery once was legal – *NO STATE ANYWHERE* has the right to treat one person differently from another.

"Every last person has the right to equal treatment under the law regardless of whether they're white, black, brown, beige, Simpsons-Yellow, purple, Boehner-Orange, polka-dotted or primer-tone same-sex.

"If anyone – including a judge or Supreme Court justice – can't grasp that, they simply do not deserve to hold office.

"And, by the way, we have another provision in the USA-SBR about that. It's the Roy S. Moore Provision."

Franklin and Penny's husband Mitch went on to answer the reporter's remaining questions, which all had been answered in earlier press conferences. But Franklin mostly deferred to Mitch, as this was all relatively new to him (though he'd watched lots of YouTube videos of the rallies) and he needed some experience jawing with news folks.

As Mitch interacted with the reporters, Franklin noticed they seemed to hang on his every word – and they seemed afraid to ask something which might be cause to take offense. Franklin was thinking it just might have something to do with what an imposing hulk of a man the part-time Homeland Security Air

Marshal was. *"Probably should've brought him along sooner,"* Franklin thought to himself, *"like before the rallies where we had the stabbings and fights."*

Mitch was only thinking about what milquetoasts the reporters seemed to be. He wished they'd brought some of the 'big guns' from Fox News. *"Woulda ate 'em for breakfast,"* he thought.

*   *   *

Slaying Organized Hatred

The crowd at the next evening's rally at Coleman Coliseum seemed strangely calm. Which seemed appropriate, considering the guest speaker for the evening was a man of quiet, reserved eloquence: Morris S. Dees Jr., Southern Poverty Law Center co-founder.

Mr. Dees applauded the USA-SBR's provisions for keeping known bigots and, by extension, any member of known hate groups out of public office.

However, he urged those in the audience to always hold out hope for young persons raised in an atmosphere of racism and bigotry. He told of his own background, having been raised on a cotton farm in the South during the Great Depression, in an era when everyone, including himself, thought racial segregation was normal and worthy of preservation.

He explained how his transformation occurred during his college years, how the sheer violence of racism shocked his conscience into embracing a different reality, the genuine reality of the potential worth of **every** member of humanity, regardless of race or religion.

One of the elements of the USA-SBR most worthy of everyone's support, he said, is the provision to ensure every person's access to four years of tuition-free and fee-free post-secondary education.

The ability to move beyond the orbit of a person's own parents and extended family and into the realm of a diverse set of peers at the college level is that special ingredient needed as a catalyst for every individual to reach her or his full potential for personal growth, he said.

If all persons who were intelligent enough to pass college entrance exams and qualify for admission actually were able to enroll and progress through their studies without having to stress out about the cost of enrollment, the world would be a far better, far less hateful place, he added.

Dees was among the most articulate and insightful of all the guest speakers featured at the rallies. But he was not one to vilify the roles corporatists and plutocrats like the Koch brothers have played in contributing to economic and social injustice. His focus was almost entirely on groups and individuals who have preyed on minorities.

Nevertheless, the Poughkeepsians were grateful for his encouragement about the USA-SBR provisions designed to level the economic playing field for both minorities and the poor of all ethnicities. He was especially complimentary about its provisions to prevent voter suppression.

Perhaps most of all, by the time the rally was finished, the Poughkeepsians were relieved that none of the hate groups targeted by the Southern Poverty Law Center had chosen that evening as a chance to get even somehow – through the use, say, of something like explosive devices.

The only time during the presentation that they were worried was near the beginning of Dees' talk, when approximately 25 young men sitting together in the upper level of the arena simultaneously pulled their pants down, pointed their bare buttocks toward the dais and lit their farts. The sheer number of anal releases at the same time amplified the sound enough that the audience 50 feet away could hear them – but the stage was a good 100 feet away.

All Dees could see in the darkness of the arena seating was the brief illumination from the orchestrated flipping of the butane lighters (only a couple of the flatulators' farts actually ignited). At the time, he thought it was some sort of concert-like tribute to him. Little did he know it was just – literally – redneck assholes in action.

Despite the skinhead-ish Alabamans' efforts to undercut Dees' message, the rally nevertheless resulted in several thousand more attendees signing pledges to put their elected officeholders' feet to the fire about the USA-SBR.

$$* \quad * \quad *$$

GAGGING THE HOI POLLOI – AND NOT FOR FUN, EITHER

The next morning, the Poughkeepsians rolled down the road in the direction of Tallahassee for a 5 p.m. press conference in advance of the following day's rally at Florida State University's Donald L. Tucker Civic Center.

There were reporters at the conference in the Poughkeepsians' hotel meeting facility from the Tallahassee Democrat (another daily tentacle of Gannett Co.) and each of the local television network affiliates. The local TV reporters were so young, each time a woman nursing a baby walked by the door leading into the meeting room, they began salivating and getting fussy. Franklin could've sworn he saw a couple of them slap their own hands as they started to put their thumbs into their mouths.

The hot topic of the day was the ongoing reverberation from Republican (of course!) Florida Gov. Rick Scott's order to state employees several months earlier that they were not to utter the phrases "climate change" or "global warming" while on duty.

In early March 2015 it was confirmed that one state Department of Environmental Protection employee was ordered to take two days of personal leave and obtain a mental health evaluation before being allowed to return to work. All as the result of using the phrase "climate change" while at a Florida Coastal Managers symposium on environmental issues.

The state employees' union director said, "If anyone needs mental health screening it is Governor Rick Scott and other officials telling state workers to pretend that climate change and sea-level rise do not exist." [*]

"Gag orders? Is this the old Soviet Union? Isn't that what a totalitarian state does?" an incredulous Franklin/Percy said in response to the Tallahassee Democrat's reporter.

"Is this state still part of the U.S.A.?

"Please tell us Clarence Darrow or some other great litigator from the past has come back to life to represent that employee and kick some Rick Scott ass.

"I know Scott just started a new term in January, but surely there's got to be some way to remove him from office. He only won by a one percent plurality, right?

"In any event, the USA-SBR confronts the reality of global warming. It requires specific actions. It will have no truck with the totalitarian bullshit that's been spewed by Gov. Scott's administration.

"Enough said. Gov. Nero can go back to fiddling."

And, with that, the reporters went on to other more mundane questions about the USA-SBR. Franklin – still red-faced with anger at Gov. Scott - handed the questions off to Orvis, Karin, Tom, Annie, Mitch and Penny.

* * *

GRAYSON REDUX

The next evening's rally featured a return appearance of a previous guest speaker, U.S. Rep. Alan Grayson, D-FL.

Grayson's presentation was fairly similar to his talk at the Boise rally, but without the references to problems in Idaho. He did add some acerbic remarks about Florida Gov. Scott's Stalin-esque language pogrom against the words global warming and climate change and against the state employees who continued to use those banned words.

"If we are to judge people's virtuousness based on the enemies they have, then those poor state employees who continue to choose to express observations of

---

[*] 3/18/15, SaintPetersBlog

reality – i.e., global warming, despite risking being 'Ricked' (that's my newly-coined term for wrongful termination) – they are the most virtuous persons in the state.

"They deserve to be at the top of the political food chain, not Gov. Scott. Let's all work hard on the USA-SBR to make sure that every last person who's been 'Ricked' can have that chance to prosper again someday."

"We cannot rest until we remove ALL the Koch brothers' shills and other corporate overlords' shills, like Gov. Scott, from public office.

"Please make this fine document (holding up the USA-SBR) one of your missions in life to bring to fruition. No matter how long it takes."

For the first time in a while, the "FUCK O-ver-LORDS!" chant resonated loudly in the arena for the Poughkeepsians.

If the crowd had other more important missions in life to accomplish, they weren't evident that night.

* * *

The Poughkeepsians convinced Rep. Grayson to hop on their bandwagon – literally – for the next two rallies in Florida, including the one two days later at the University of Florida's O'Connell Center in Gainesville and the one two days after that at the University of Miami's BankUnited Center.

He even agreed to participate in what turned out to be some very spirited press conference questioning with the Poughkeepsians in Gainesville and in Miami. During the Miami press gathering, he said he'd risk his political reputation on the righteousness of the USA-SBR's provisions to reduce the influence of money on politics, especially its influence on the passage of the "economically rancid" Trans Pacific Partnership.

By the time the next two rallies were over, the Poughkeepsians – not to mention Florida's political beat reporters – were wondering if Grayson just might be tempted to run to replace the head - as in the "Ricker" - of the Russian – oops, they meant Florida – Supreme Soviet, i.e. state government.

Out of respect for Rep. Grayson, the Poughkeepsians kept their speculation to themselves.

* * *

MITCH STEPS UP TO THE PLATE: GRAND SLAM

Marcia booked a flight for the Poughkeepsians from Miami to Atlanta for the morning after the Miami rally so they could make their 5 p.m. press conference in Athens, Georgia near the University of Georgia. To a person, they were all grateful they could avoid the nine-hour drive between the two cities. Even if it might mean again flying on – *ugh* – Delta.

During the blessedly brief flight, Franklin told Phil it seemed unlikely that the Cox Media Group's ownership of seven daily newspapers, including Atlanta's Journal-Constitution, plus dozens of television and radio stations (including Atlanta's ABC-TV network affiliate) could contribute greatly to the diversity of opinions and coverage needed for a healthy democracy. (Franklin didn't realize 'til later that the Cox Media Group was directly connected to Ohio Gov. James M. Cox, the 1920 Democratic candidate for President who chose Franklin as his running mate.)

"That FCC re-licensing provision you included in the USA-SBR should eventually take care of that," Phil responded. "'Til then, though, we have to work the best we can with what we've got: a mostly homogenized corporate press with tons of young reporters worried more about their job security than about conveying unpleasant facts."

There were reporters at the press conference from the Journal-Constitution, the Athens Banner-Herald (a daily owned by Morris Communications of Augusta, Georgia) and from each of the area's local television network affiliates. The local TV reporters this time around were so young and baby-faced, Phil suspected they all used Johnson's 'no more tears' baby shampoo. Except they all were paid so little, it was much more likely they bought the generic brand. You know, the kind made in Outer Mongolia with a label saying "*No Tearz Morely.*"

The main substantive issue on the reporters' minds was the recent failed effort – supported by Southern Baptist lobbyists – in the Georgia Legislature to pass an 'OK to use religion as an excuse to discriminate' law which seemed to be targeted at the LGBT community.

"Just what is this obsession with putting LGBT persons at the back of the bus?" asked Franklin/Percy in response to a question from Journal-Constitution reporter Gregoire Frankencyan.

"Just how does allowing religious extremists to refuse to provide services to people on the basis of their genetic sexual orientation make the world a better place? Does Georgia want to go through the whole lunch counter sit-in thing all over again?

"The USA-SBR fixes all this idiocy once and for all. Enough said."

Another reporter, Hallie Humperdinck, of the Banner-Herald, asked what the Poughkeepsians thought of the University of Georgia trying to potentially expel a student who was arrested while engaging in a non-violent "Moral Monday" protest on State Capitol steps March 2. Accused of a university "Code of Conduct" violation, the student, along with 11 other arrested activists from the group Athens for Everyone, protested the State Legislature's refusal to pass the Federally-funded expansion of Medicaid in Georgia under the Affordable Care Act.

The student, Adam Veale, 20, insisted that his protest was a legitimate expression of non-violent free speech protected by the First Amendment and that the charge of blocking the south steps of the rotunda was simply a pretext for violating protestors' free speech rights. (The protestors were jailed overnight in Atlanta.)

Veale declined to accept a 'plea bargain' of sorts which would've included 16 hours of community service and lunches with faculty members. He told the Journal-Constitution the protestors refused "to stand idly by" while the Governor and Legislature declined to act on expanding Medicaid at virtually no cost to the state – apparently out of contempt for President Obama.

Fortunately, on April 24, 2015, Veale was, in effect, acquitted of the alleged Code of Conduct violation at a university Student Judiciary Committee hearing. Score: First Amendment Social Justice 1, Asshole Georgia Truth to Power Suppressors 0.*

"That Georgia voters would put in power politicians whose hatred of the President would keep them from putting in place a virtually cost-free program which could alleviate pain and suffering and financial heartbreak for their most vulnerable residents – what can we say?" Franklin/Percy said, throwing his hands up in the air.

"Georgians have to figure out for themselves the lunacy at work there. And it literally is the job of each of you journalists here today to help them to understand that it is just that: lunacy. There's no better way than to describe that level of hatred. Whether it's hatred of the President, hatred of the poor or both.

"Passage and ratification of the USA-SBR would've made all of this controversy moot. It puts into place, essentially, Medicare for All with no out-of-pocket costs for _**anyone**_.

"It would finally make our country as civilized and humane as the rest of the developed world.

"By the way, guess who one of our guest speakers is at our rally tomorrow evening! You got it, Adam Veale. You go, Adam!"

Sissy Guilleret, a reporter for the local PBS affiliate, asked the Poughkeepsians for reaction to the resignation six weeks earlier of the Georgia State Elections Director due to an illegal purge of voters before their 2014 statewide primary elections.

(Secretary of State Brian Kemp pressured Linda Ford, his long-time friend whom he selected as Elections Director, to resign after an audit disclosed a mistaken purge of 8,000 voters less than 90 days before the May 2014 election, a violation of the National Voter Registration Act. The local NAACP president said Kemp should've accepted responsibility for the mistake instead of offering Ford as a "sacrificial lamb." The purge kept at least one person from voting in

---

* 4/17/15 Journal-Constitution; 4/17/15 Red & Black, independent University of Georgia student newspaper; 4/25/15 Online Athens Banner-Herald.

the primary. It followed a lawsuit about a controversy over an unrelated alleged purge of more than 40,000 voters.)*

Mitch Duarte volunteered to take on that question; he'd been doing some studying on that issue.

"Kind of puts the U.S. Supreme Court's June 2013 landmark decision on the 1965 Voting Rights Act into even better perspective for being the utterly unambiguous clusterfuck fiasco that it was, doesn't it?

"The court declared that, because the database on voter registration discrimination from sixteen states used to craft the Act was 40 years old, then the presumption must be that, without new data, the discrimination must no longer exist. Before the government can resume enforcement of voting rights under the act, the court said, Congress must pass a **new** authorization based on **new** data.

"Those sixteen states included Alabama, Alaska, Arizona, Georgia – **yes, GEORGIA** - Louisiana, Mississippi, South Carolina, Texas, most of Virginia, four counties in California, five counties in Florida, two townships in Michigan, 10 towns in New Hampshire, three counties in New York, 40 counties in North Carolina and two counties in South Dakota.**

"Now, I don't know about you, but if I visually observe someone systematically allowing their pet to defecate all over my front yard, I don't need to do a statistical study to know that lots of dogshit is piling up.

"Guess what! Lots of voter discrimination dogshit is piling up again in a lot of those states – including mostly Old South former slavery states like Georgia. And guess what else! It's not even on the radar for the current Republican-controlled Congress to pass a new authorization bill based on new data.

"Anyone here want to venture a guess why? Wouldn't have anything to do with all the Republican efforts to stamp out non-existent voter fraud by requiring photo ID's, would it? You know, those photo ID laws that Republicans get caught about on video every once in a while bragging up how well they'll keep minorities and the poor away from the polls?

"It's this simple: the USA-SBR will do away with all of that bullshit. Once and for all. Everyone will automatically have the right to vote at age 18. No ID required, simply because voter fraud is virtually non-existent. Anyone who wants an excellent portrayal of how silly the idea is of a person trying to influence the outcome of an election needs to watch the episode of "Family Guy" where Stewie tries to fly all over the country to cast ballot after ballot after ballot on election day.

"And guess what else! Anyone who gets caught trying to vote twice *already* – as in *right now!* - *gets to go to prison*. Who would want to risk that over voting one or two extra times? And how could anyone keep secret a conspiracy among the huge number of people needed to do that to actually affect the outcome of an election?

---

* 4/3/15, Journal-Constitution
** Leadership Conference on Civil and Human Rights website, viewed 4/20/15

"If there's a _real_ risk of true voter fraud, it's with the Republican-connected companies hired to process electronic ballot counts, like **Diebold** in Ohio in 2004. You remember, the state just barely won by Bush in 2004 that gave him the Electoral College re-election victory?

"You don't see Republicans rushing out to demand photo ID's _for Diebold executives_, do you? Just wondering...

"In any event, the USA-SBR is the answer to all of this – and a lot more."

∗ ∗ ∗

A Brave Young Soul Plus a Top-Notch Comic

The youthful Mr. Veale, speaking for the first time in front of a packed venue at the University of Georgia Stegeman Coliseum the next evening, showed the poise of someone twice his age. He later would attribute that to a combination of his experience dealing with customers at the Ben & Jerry's where he worked plus the fact that the bright lights facing the stage made it impossible to see just about anyone except the people sitting on either side of him.

His eloquence on the subject of the economic and social justice aspects of Medicaid expansion appeared to come naturally – which shouldn't have been surprising, as he'd spent considerable time researching the subject as a political science major.

He asked the crowd to imagine what it would've been like if each state, one at a time, tried to refuse assistance through the Federally-funded Food Stamps program.

"Impossible to imagine that, right?" he asked. "Just think of the visuals: starving men, women and children lined up on courthouse steps with signs asking, 'Why do you let us go hungry? It costs you nothing to take the Federal money!'

"In my mind, I can imagine a President sending National Guard troops in to distribute the Food Stamps, with the President shaming the governor of each state refusing the assistance on national TV every night, until the radical conservatives relented.

"In these modern times, though, when a group of extremists like the Tea Party paint almost every action by the Federal government as evil and/or some sort of communistic 'taking' from the well-off, we almost take it for granted that conservatives will put the needs of the few ahead of the needs of the many.

"Largely gone is the recognition that the Progressive Income Tax - the fairest tax in the land, the tax that takes the most from those whom it affects the least – is the tax which has **made this country great** and which has given the middle class the modern infrastructure and services which make our lives safe, simpler and more comfortable.

"Because these radicals, these Tea Party Republicans, are afraid expanding Medicaid – literally improving the health of their most unfortunate constituents – might lead quote-unquote '*someday*' to tax increases for their wealthy patrons, they would sooner have their most unfortunate constituents – literally – suffer.

"What they fail to understand – or intentionally refuse to admit – is that at-risk health of the unfortunate among us literally means at-risk health for **all** of us. Microbes and viruses affecting poor schoolchildren can't be trained not to travel from a poor child's hand to a rich child's hand.

"Of course, though, that might explain why the far-right is so fixated on creating government subsidies for private schools and charter schools which can cherry pick which children they choose to admit for enrollment.

"In any event, the passage and ratification of this document (holding up the USA-SBR) would almost overnight achieve more social justice and economic justice than this country has experienced over the past two centuries combined.

"To think just of the possibilities for ending our culture of Permanent War – that alone is worth getting this thing done.

"Let's each and every person here not leave Stegeman tonight without pledging to contact each of our elected officeholders, one at a time, to compel them to commit to whether they support or oppose this.

"If they oppose this, you know what to do. To paraphrase Jenny in one of my favorites, '*Forrest Gump*,' "Run, people, run!!"

Veale later introduced "*Capitalism: A Love Story*" with an enthusiastic flourish. Turned out he's a Michael Moore fan. The Poughkeepsians thought Mr. Moore would be proud to know that.

Marcia also had convinced comedian David Cross to appear in honor of his nearby Atlanta birthplace. He killed with some stand-up mocking southerners' apparent preference for being depicted by certain comedians and popular actors as ignorant, know-nothing hicks. The crowd ate 'er up. That morphed into some funny speculation about why "The Walking Dead" producers selected Atlanta as the setting for the series about hungry, hungry zombies.

Recalling his experience doing voiceovers for the Alvin and the Chipmunks movies, he mused about what it would be like to have a zombie Alvin and the Chipmunks series of movie sequels. He went on to speculate that, if the corporatists running the government continued to expand their influence unchecked by things like the USA-SBR, it might not be too long before Food Stamps recipients might have to take up zombie cuisine habits or maybe some new GMO-ed breakfast foods like Soylent Green Wheaties. The crowd found that pretty savory too.

When the rally was done for the night, it turned out to be the highest percentage so far of attendees who signed pledges to contact their officeholders. Mr. Veale and Mr. Cross were godsends. The Poughkeepsians each wished Mr. Veale a long, bright future of continued 'truth to power' courage. When it came to Mr. Cross, though, they mainly nagged him to keep up with more episodes of "*Arrested Development*" on Netflix. Huge fans, they were.

* * *

Idyllic Summer Fun – Oh, and Work Too

Their trip back to LaGuardia Airport the next day via, once again, Delta ("Oh, <u>shit</u>," Phil said as soon as Marcia handed him his boarding pass) turned out to be not so bad. No quasi-Nazi flight attendants this time and there seemed to be plenty of access to bathrooms. Franklin did read, however, in an old Journal-Constitution copy he found in the waiting area that airlines were planning to cram an additional 15 to 20 seats on each of the newly-manufactured 737's being built by Boeing.

"*That's so special,*" he thought to himself. "*They must **really** be trying to bring back train travel.*"

It was back to the usual full time work grind at Adams for Franklin the following day. Holly would be returning to her usual full-time summer job as a waitress at the Eveready Diner in Hyde Park until her graduate classes for her pharmacy doctoral program at Albany College of Pharmacy and Health Sciences started on Aug. 31, 2015, the same day Franklin's classes were scheduled to begin at Sage Colleges in Troy.

* * *

Invoking FDR to Re-Start a Faltering Campaign

June 14, 2015

Franklin noticed while reading the Sunday *New York Times* over the Podrowskis' breakfast table that Hillary Clinton had chosen to make her campaign 're-start' speech the previous day at the Four Freedoms Park on New York's Roosevelt Island to a non-overflow crowd of 5,500 hard-core pre-invited supporters. The park was named for Franklin's Jan. 6, 1941 speech, which laid out his rationale for the idea that there should be a worldwide right to freedom of speech, freedom of worship, freedom from want and freedom from fear.

In her speech (a video of which showed her reading haltingly in a stilted, uninspiring voice, speaking as though she were reading the speech for the first time), Hillary claimed to be on the side of the middle class – despite declining *within the previous 24 hours* to specifically support the push for a national $15 per hour minimum wage.

She said she supports the push for paid family leave, but, unlike Sen. Bernie Sanders, specifically did NOT claim support for paid vacation time for every worker.

She also claimed to be on the side of reducing income inequality – despite her long history of cronyism with Wall Street insiders and billionaires.

In addition, she didn't *specify* how she – a politician who, along with her husband, had become dependent on massive speaking fees from billionaires - would narrow the gap between the top 1 percent and everyone else.

She said she would re-write the tax code to remove favoritism for the ultra-rich, but she neglected to say how she would do that with a Congress controlled by the ultra-rich.

She claimed to be supportive of quality pre-school education and child care services for all children, but didn't explain how she would achieve that with a Republican-controlled Congress.

She spoke of relieving the burden of college students "drowning" in debt but did **not** endorse Sen. Sanders' push for free college for everyone pursuing a bachelor's degree.

"*Is she thinking of giving students discount cards for the local A & P?*" Franklin thought to himself.

Most gratingly to Franklin, this billionaire-schmoozing former attorney for Wal-Mart's Board of Directors' mega-billionaires had cited in the speech her respect for Franklin's own "enduring vision" for the country and belief in the importance of economic opportunity and jobs for everyone wanting one and ending "special privileges" for the very few.

"*If she has all that much respect for my enduring vision,*" he thought to himself, "*why has she kept brown-nosing the billionaires and hedge-fund managers and Wall Streeters and trickle-downers and multi-national corporations she was disparaging in her speech? Do people really take what she says at face value?*"

Pongo walked into the kitchen and saw Franklin's now reddish-hued face.

"Reading about Hillary's speech yesterday?" Pongo asked.

"How could you tell?"

"You looked a little less than pleased."

"How would you feel if an ex-Republican buddy to billionaires was invoking your 'enduring vision' when you knew it was purely for phony political posturing?"

"I guess my face would be a little red too."

"She did say some great things about advocating for women and children, equal pay, paid family leave, making quality pre-school or day care 'available' and such. She just didn't seem very convincing to me – and probably not to anyone else who knows her history of rubbing elbows with Wall Street cronies."

"I heard," Pongo said, "not to put too fine a point on it, that she gave new meaning to the word awkward with her reference to the Beatles song 'Yesterday' when she was trying to put in a dig at the Republicans. Heather said she was reading the lyrics to their song sort of the way a first grader would read from a Jack and Jill book."

(The following Tuesday, even Hillary's friend Jon Stewart would publicly and punnily admonish her on his show to "let it be" with using the Beatles' lyrics for political put-downs.)

"I vaguely remember listening to some of the Beatles' songs on one of our road trips – Pongo, I'll take your word for it that Ms. Clinton lacks the *je ne sais quoi* of a rock and roll star.

"It would have been nice to see her devote some of her speechwriters' creativity to come even close to vilifying the billionaire class for its compulsive greed the way Sen. Sanders has. She said nothing about the union-killing parts of the Trans Pacific Partnership, the Keystone XL pipeline's contributions to global warming,* how the renewal of the Patriot Act would neuter many civil rights or her vote to go forward with the Iraq War.

"She did say she would do '*whatever it takes*' to keep America safe. I'm wondering if that means she's still ready to go to war against Iran."

"God help us. No word about whether she would support a new Bill of Rights?"

"She said that '*if necessary*' she would support a constitutional amendment to overturn Citizens United, but nothing else. I suppose it's fair to infer she's confident our ever-so-functional Congress can fix everything else piecemeal."

"*Dee-lightful*, as your favorite uncle-by-marriage would say."

$$* \quad * \quad *$$

So What If TPP Causes Economy to Hemorrhage Jobs to Southeast Asia? Slick Willie Says Just Get Your ISP to Boost Your MBPS!

J ust three days later, the guest on "*The Daily Show*" was none other than Hillary's husband Bill. Bill spent much of his time defending the union-killer otherwise known as the Trans Pacific Partnership, arguing earnestly that it should be fast-tracked through Congress, its secret provisions notwithstanding.

---

* On Sept. 22, 2015, Hillary Clinton announced her opposition to the Keystone XL Pipeline, *specifically NOT* because of its greenhouse gas-related existential threat to the continuation of most mammalian life on the planet, but, rather, because it had "become a distraction" for her campaign (what with Sen. Bernie Sanders gaining widespread support among progressives for his long-standing opposition to the pipeline and the moonscaped strip mining of Canadian boreal forests it would further facilitate). Likewise, sensing desperation among corporate donors in the wake of a mass murder at an Oregon community college, her campaign advisers convinced her on Oct. 5, 2015 to end her near-silence on gun violence and promote several new gun control proposals rivalling those of Sen. Sanders. In addition, on Oct. 7, 2015, with Sen. Sanders' support in polls yet to crest, the former legal counsel for Wal-Mart and other bastions of American anti-union Wall Street corporatocracy suddenly flip-flopped her history of corporatist support for the Trans-Pacific Partnership (TPP) over the previous five years, apparently vying for a spot in the "*National Pretending to Be Something You're Not Hall of Fame*" alongside charter inductee ex-Sen. Larry E. "Wide Stance" Craig, R-Idaho. Her husband Bill apparently wasn't aware of her TPP misgivings during his June 17, 2015 appearance on The Daily Show – perhaps because those misgivings *have never actually existed.*

The ex-President and arch-corporatist Democrat *actually said* that Americans could overcome the worst effects of the TPP, which *actually has* provisions for retraining of the **millions of persons in the U.S.A. whose jobs it would cause to disappear**, with one simple fix:

Increasing everyone's high-speed broadband internet access.

And he said it with a straight face.

* * *

Terrorist Massacre of Christ's Lambs: Time to Furl that Flag

Because it's just not America any more if there's not a slaughter every few weeks, there was a certain sense of numbness when Franklin and the other Poughkeepsians woke up four days later to see plastered all over television and newspapers the news of a terrorist killing near the birthplace of the old Confederacy.

Turned out a 21-year-old Confederate flag-waving white supremacist had decided he needed to do his part to initiate a war between the races by executing nine peaceful African-American worshippers the previous evening at Emanuel African Methodist Episcopal (A.M.E.) Church in downtown Charleston, SC. The victims actually had welcomed the shooter into their bible study meeting an hour before the shooting. Among the nine dead was the church's senior pastor, State Sen. Clementa C. Pinckney. A tenth person who was shot survived.

In the wake of the shooting, the usual far-right-wing zealots refused to characterize the shooting as a homegrown terrorist act, refused to lay blame for easy availability of semi-automatic weaponry, refused to join a growing movement to stop the sales and government/commercial displays of Confederate flags and refused to label the shooting as purely racist, claiming it was primarily part of an ongoing attack on Christian worshippers.

Franklin said if he'd still been in office, he'd have signed an executive order immediately banning the sale of all semi-automatic weaponry "as an urgent matter or public health and safety, and let the lawyers wrestle over the fallout. Enough is enough."

Unfortunately, he was no longer in office. The NRA (decidedly *not* FDR's National Recovery Administration), apparently, <u>was</u>.

* * *

Sum-, Sum-, Sum-, Sum-, Sum-, Sum-, Summertime: Sunny Prospects...

The summer which began a four days later was as special a summer as any two young college graduate lovers like Franklin and Holly could hope to have. Thoughts of past conflicts, of weird intimidating characters like Mr. Plaid Pants, of hatred-obsessed right-wing extremist cranks – all those thoughts hibernated far in the back of the Poughkeepsians' minds, especially after the U.S. Supreme Court delivered surprise rulings on June 25 supporting the Affordable Care Act and on June 26 supporting the right of persons with same-sex preference to marry each other. ("Where are the Republicans going to direct all their hatred now that those two issues are off the table?" Phil had asked Franklin over breakfast on June 27. "What new issue are they going to dream up to convince middle class and working poor folks to vote against their own best economic interests?" That same day former Arkansas Gov. Mike Huckabee gave a clue: "MLK-style" civil disobedience against gay marriage rights. Old hatreds die hard.)

∗ ∗ ∗

The corporate money-inundated Democratic Presidential front-runner, Ms. Clinton, on July 13, 2015 made a "major presentation" of her "bold economic vision" at "The New School," a private university in lower-Manhattan's Greenwich Village.

As "major presentations" go, it was among the better cures for insomnia: although she gave standard (if 30 years too late) critiques of the ludicrous silliness of trickle-down Reaganomics and emphasized the importance of the middle class deserving a raise, she didn't bother to give many specifics, other than promising to go after employers who mis-characterize employees as contractors to cheat their workers out of benefits and overtime pay.

She said she would support a minimum wage raise, but didn't specify by how much...maybe 5 cents an hour, who knows? She didn't even mention social justice activists' efforts to raise it to $15 per hour.

Rah.

Oh, yeah – rah.

∗ ∗ ∗

As Ms. Clinton continued to remain silent about the specific provisions of their USA-SBR, the Poughkeepsians got into what felt like a safe routine: following up on requests for individual appearances by grassroots organizers in the area, keeping tabs electronically with USA-SBR activists around the country and holding press events whenever it seemed appropriate – usually to react to some shockingly bizarre remark by Louie Gohmert, Slash Lugbuch, Rick Scott, Rush Limbaugh or some other semi-sentient conservative bomb-thrower.

Franklin took advantage of the pleasant weather to make trips every other weekend with Holly to Bar Harbor to hike the trails, watch for whales and make each other wail indoors (and occasionally outdoors too) with the joys that young lovers experience as no one else does.

Mental pictures of hiking the Beehive Trail, the Bubble Rocks Trail and the Cadillac Mountain Trail in Acadia National Park were etched into memories that would stay with them as long as they kept breathing. There were a couple of especially lovely secluded spots on the Schoodic Head Trail that were especially memorable after that summer. Every year after that, whenever they'd tell each other it was time for some Schoodic Head, they'd both blush with anticipation and know exactly what – and who – was coming.

* * *

By the time the end of August rolled around they decided to take that next step: finding an apartment to share on the outskirts of Albany. It seemed like a big deal to both of them – even though, as it turned out, Holly would usually spend at least part of every other weekend back in Poughkeepsie at her friend Nancy's apartment and Franklin would spend almost every weekend at the Podrowskis' because of his job at Adams. Holly managed to juggle her job at Eveready with her classes fairly well – for a while.

After a couple of months, both of them decided the weekend commutes – 80 miles each way – were squeezing their schedules too tight, not to mention leaving a fairly significant carbon footprint. They both gave their two weeks' advance notice, Franklin to Chet at Adams and Holly to Terry Bloomquist at Eveready – but only after each of them got jobs with similar employers in Albany.

Chet was visibly moved by the prospect of no longer having around the clock-work-reliable hard-working witty young laborer he'd come to know so well over the previous five years.

Turning his back to dab at his eyes, he told Franklin/Percy, "Scruples, if I'm ever so crazy in the future as to hire some spunky pup like yourself who gets me so used to his wisecracks that I let him have six weeks off every year to run around all over the country, I'm gonna call you so you can tell me what an idiot sucker dumbdick I am."

"Happy to do it, Dumbdick," Franklin/Percy said, serious and straight-faced – for about three seconds, that is, 'til he laughed and reached out to hug Chet.

"You prick," Chet said. "If you're not back here to pester me at least once a month, I'm gonna drive up to Albany and pummel your arse 'til YOU need a physical therapist."

"It's a deal, Chet."

* * *

Mid-November 2015: Looking Ahead

The last six weeks of the fall semester flowed by as swiftly and smoothly as the nearby Hudson. Both Holly and Franklin looked forward to spending the holidays with their respective families. Franklin finally was starting to feel accepted as a quasi-member of the Van Arsdales. He thought, privately, that the time was approaching when he would feel compelled to 'make an honest woman' of Holly. Maybe after the 2016 general election lunacy was over and done with. The Poughkeepsians already had agreed that that would be a good time to take at least a three-month holiday from the USA-SBR. This would be the first general election, though, when they had a slate of candidates all over the country running to knock off USA-SBR opponents and running on a USA-SBR platform to win both open seats and incumbents' seats in the Congress and in state legislatures.

By the morning of – or maybe even afternoon of – the following November 9th, they would have a fair idea if their grassroots organizing was ready to bear fruit…or if their grassroots needed more aeration and fertilization.

* * *

Their first Christmas together in their own apartment made memories they would cherish for many years. After an intimate Christmas Eve spent alone together, they had Pongo, Phil, Heather, Bud and Ellie Van Arsdale and Nancy Perez over the next day for a complete Christmas dinner. Both Franklin and Holly worked hard on the cuisine. The chestnut dressing Holly concocted was perfect.

Thankfully, there was not a single instance of stink eye detected from Holly's parents.

And everyone was delighted with Franklin's traditional reading of "A Christmas Carol." It was like sitting across the table from old man Scrooge himself.

* * *

Re-Assuring Insurers & Ensuring Prosperity

Their next to last rally tour was set to begin on Jan. 4, 2016 in New Haven, Connecticut at Yale University, followed by stops at the University of

Connecticut in Mansfield, Connecticut; at the University of New Hampshire hockey Monarch's Verizon Arena in Manchester, New Hampshire, and at the University of Maine in Orono, Maine.

They made clear to the area news media in advance that their Jan. 4 press conference was intended to cover both the rally at Yale and the rally at UConn. The 5 p.m. press gathering at their New Haven hotel meeting facility was attended by reporters from the New Haven Register (a daily owned by the Digital First Media empire of New York City), CTNow (a free weekly based in Hartford, Connecticut), the Hartford Courant (a daily owned by the Tribune Publishing empire of Chicago), the Connecticut Post (a Bridgeport, Connecticut daily owned by the Hearst Corp. of New York City), the Stamford Advocate (another daily tentacle of the Hearst Corp.) and from each local television network affiliate. Yet again, the local TV reporters were soo damned young – Phil made a mental note to point out to the other Poughkeepsians that none of the reporters, including both men and women, was wearing footwear with shoelaces.

As Connecticut is a state in which many, many insurance businesses are headquartered, many of the reporters' questions were aimed at what would become of their state's primary industry were the USA-SBR to become the law of the land.

Bianca volunteered to take a stab at this knuckleball.

"The most profitable part of Connecticut's insurance industry – the life insurance industry – would be completely untouched. At the outset at least," she said.

"I say 'at the outset' simply because what almost surely will happen down the road to your insurance industry eventually will be – wait.   for.   it. – that your profits will start to skyrocket.

"How can that be? you ask. Well, for those of you with insurance risk analysts in the family, I suspect you already know the answer.

"As the USA-SBR's requirement for full health insurance coverage for _**every-one**_ kicks in – including medical, dental and optical without any out-of-pocket costs – you'll see virtually everyone's health improve. It's like a feedback loop, but instead of the feedback being negative from people spreading disease, the feedback will be positive from the health care system containing *and preventing* disease. Lifespans across the board gradually will creep higher and higher.

"Of course, what does that mean for all those fine Connecticut actuarial folks selling life insurance? You got it! Lots more green stuff to pocket.

"And lots more profit greenery for your insurance folks to harvest means lots more of that greenery circulating and recirculating in the economy – meaning more to spend, more consumer demand and more jobs to meet all that consumer demand.

"Which also means more tax revenues going into the government for things like infrastructure and funding of essential government services, like Medicare.

"It's as win-winny as it gets."

* * *

VOICES OF REASON – FOR LAUGHTER

The Poughkeepsians' featured guest speaker the evening of the follow-ing day at Yale's Payne Whitney Gymnasium was "*Family Guy*" creator and Connecticut native Seth McFarland.

McFarland entertained the crowd for more than an hour with his takes on how each of the most important provisions of the USA-SBR would be received by Peter Griffin, Glen Quagmire, Stewie Griffin, Tom Tucker, Carter Pewterschmidt and Griffin family doctor Dr. Hartman, using each character's voice.

In Peter's voice, he praised the USA-SBR for "helpin' me keep those damn GMO-ey things out of my gut because I got stuff plugged in there *already* I been tryin' to get out for the past 20 years. That GMO shit – it'll make ya' start growin' little mini-me's on your neck – like I had in Episode 2 of Season 12."

In Glen's voice, he aimed kudos at the Poughkeepsians for making the Consumer Product Safety Commission more accountable. "If you've ever had your, eh-, uh-, hot glue gun malfunction while it was, er-, uh-, plugged into an overcharged re-, uh-, re-ceptacle, well you know just how dangerous that static electro-friction can be if your *device* is defective. The flight attendants deserve for my er-, um-, *product* to function properly. Thank you, commissioners, for allowing my *product* to be consumed safely."

In Stewie's voice, he thanked the Poughkeepsians' USA-SBR "for helping en-sure that Peter's wife Lois has a no-cost dependable supply of contraceptive pills and devices. I mean, can you imagine what it would be like if the next one that popped out of her finally looked like her husband? Dear sweet Jesus. I'd have to work twice as hard to keep from getting lost and forgotten in those fat folds."

In Tom Tucker's voice, he panned the USA-SBR: "So you Poughkeepsie Poindexters want to create an investigative journalism fund??!!! Do you not un-derstand the sweet gig I've got? You're gonna make me stop reading from the teleprompter and get out there and meet Congressional perverts trying to hook up on line with 12-year-old girls?...

"Uh-hmmm – well, let me give this a little more thought. Maybe investigative journalism can be back in vogue again. I'll get back to you after we go to to Ollie Williams for the Blaccuweather Forecast."

In Carter Pewterschmidt's voice, he lambasted the USA-SBR for "trying to take a couple of the hundred billion dollars in my bowling shoes account just so you can help some brown-skinned children buy second-hand shoes. Soak the rich, soak the rich, that's all you socialist Jeopardy-watchers do in your spare time. Isn't that right, Ollie? Ollie's my personal bidet operator when he's not doing the Blaccuweather forecast. Grab your Playtex gloves, Ollie, it's time for another cleansing treatment. Chop-chop!"

In Dr. Hartman's voice, he minced no words about the USA-SBR: "When I think of all the mansions I could've had, all the Aston Martins I could've kept, all the Mitt Romney garage elevators I could've owned – but, NO, pansy working families make my reimbursements 10 percent smaller because they *just **HAVE*** to *have* their doctor bills covered. Don't they know?!! Medical bankruptcies just make you **stronger** – er, uh, if they don't kill you, that is.

"Socialist futhher muckers! By the way, that'll be $190 for that tissue of Kleenex, Mr. MacFarlane! And if it's not paid within 30 days, I'll be by to screw your wife. Twice daily – takin' with food."

And, in his own voice, he was effusive with earnest praise for the provisions in the USA-SBR which would permanently ensure everyone would be able to marry – and divorce – the person of their choice, "no matter what standard equipment they came with off the showroom floor."

It was another one of those evenings when pretty much every one of the Poughkeepsians made it a point to tell Marcia to hold out for her raise.

"How did you book this guy?" Phil asked.

"I told him we'd let him sing and dance if he spoke for an hour."

She was just kidding, but at the end of his presentation, MacFarlane did exactly that, performing a song he wrote just for the rally, singing along with music he had recorded for it earlier in the week in California. It was a YouTube sensation the next day. Near-record number of hits.

He topped off his song and dance by joining Pongo, Heather, Holly, Harry, Idris, Franklin, Marcia, Tom, Annie, Phil, Cherisse, Mel, Penny and Mitch in the ritual tossin' of the ramen and underwear. Unable to restrain his gusto (shocked, right?), Seth showed a real flair for different kinds of pitches: screwball, knuckleball, fastball, curveball, slider – you name it. Although there was one tighty-whitie fastball he'd have liked to have back that almost took the glasses clean off a 52-year-old lady librarian from a Wallingford junior high school.

* * *

MacFarlane enjoyed the rally so much, he volunteered to do repeat his performance the next evening at the University of Connecticut Harry A. Gampel Pavilion in Mansfield.

Once again, he killed. If it was possible, his second night's performance was even better than the first. Perhaps one-fourth of the attendees were dressed as "*Family Guy*" characters. And it was standing room only.

"We shoulda found this guy a couple of years ago, Marcia," Phil said. "You really fell down on the job, there, y'know – bein' dilatory 'n all. No raise for you!"

They both laughed at each other. A lot.

With no small amont of sadness, they parted ways with Seth that night after considerable jocularity and imbibing. The wish to reunite in the future was reciprocal. Seth said he just might even try to include the Poughkeepsians in a future "Family Guy" episode. Jaws dropped in all directions. "And I might not even try to embarrass you – not **too** much, anyway."

* * *

POWER TO THE PEOPLE – ROCKIN'
THE UNDERGROUND, BABY!

They arrived the next afternoon right on time for their standard 5 p.m. press conference in Manchester, New Hampshire.

Those attending included reporters from the Manchester Union Leader and Sunday News (a daily owned by the local ultra-conservative McQuaid family), the Concord Monitor (a daily locally owned by the Newspapers of New England chain), Foster's Daily Democrat (a daily owned by Local Media Group out of Middletown, NY), the Portsmouth Herald (another Local Media Group daily) and from each of the area television network affiliates.

Without fail, each of the local TV reporters once again appeared so incredibly young – so much so as to seem to have just graduated from junior high school. At least one of the female reporters appeared to be wearing her parochial school plaid-skirted uniform. Pongo noticed a wide-eyed expression, probably involuntary (like a gag reflex) on Harry's face as he saw the skirt.

"Rein in those horses down there, podnuh," Pongo said, hoping to snap his BFF out of that glazed-over look – and to arrest any involuntary below-the-belt construction in its tracks.

It worked. Barely.

The first questions addressed the USA-SBR's ban on utilities' above-ground power transmission lines.

"You realize, don't you, that every last utility in North America is going to throw every lobbying dollar they can scrounge up to keep the USA-SBR from becoming law, don't you?" asked Brad Morve of the Union Leader.

"From what I read in the media around here, the Northern Pass proposal for massive power lines from Canada down through New Hampshire's pristine forests won't exactly be helpful for the lobbyists' efforts," Franklin/Percy said. "I would think that, if the utilities truly wanted people to accept their monstrous power lines, the *very LEAST* they could do would be agree to bury them underground.

"And, like the USA-SBR says, if they don't like it, they can be nationalized. And if they don't like getting rid of fossil fuels once and for all, they can be nationalized too. Taking the profit out of utility services *always* results in lower bills for customers. Every. Single. Time.

"And I gair – ron – teee you, the administrator of a nationalized electric utility isn't going to be paid the jazillion dollars a privatized utility CEO is paid every year. Let's just see those lobbyists keep trying to put lipstick on **that** CEO pay pig of an issue.

"Our goal, regardless, is not just to make corporatist lobbyists an endangered species, it's to make them as extinct as the fabled so-called moderate Republican."

(Much laughter, especially from the camera operators, union members all.)

* * *

Abby Lays It All Out, with No Ab(by)Stractions

With the assistance of New Hampshire Peace Action, the Poughkeepsians were able to get journalist Abby Martin, host of the cable news show *"Breaking the Set,"* as their guest speaker.

Ms. Martin favored the crowd at Verizon Arena with an impressive array of documented campaign donations and speech honorariums paid to Presidential candidate Hillary Rodham Clinton during and after her time as a U.S. Senator and Secretary of State.

The list showed *multiple* contributions of many hundreds of thousands of dollars funneled to her and to the Clinton Foundation by military-industrial complex corporations and foreign government interests.

She documented numerous private meetings between Hillary Clinton and Wall Street corporate interests, including the Carlisle Group. She documented how Hillary's peers always found her to be supporting the most belligerent, most hawkish options she was offered by the President when she was Secretary of State. She even recalled an occasion when Hillary visited Russia primarily to solicit a contract from the Russians for aircraft to be built by defense contractor Boeing. And not to forget: Hillary's frequent shilling for Monsanto's GMO products when she was Secretary of State – as in, 'buy their frankenfoods seeds and their cancer-causing weed killers if you know what's good for you.'

The most telling thing about Hillary, Ms. Martin said (besides the gizzard-choking mountains of moolah taken from all the billionaire predatory crony capitalists), is *her complete and utter silence* about any of the specifics in the USA-SBR. She'll dance around the edges of a tiny number of certain little passages of it, but actually commit to something concrete? Don't bet the farm on it.

The closest Ms. Clinton came to supporting a specific provision of the USA-SBR, Ms. Martin said, was eight months earlier when she promised that opposition to the Citizens United decision would be a litmus test for anyone she might nominate to the Supreme Court.

"Surely she must realize that at least **one** – if not **_both_** – of the next President's first two possible nominations to the Supreme Court would be to replace justices *who voted with the minority* on the Citizens United decision. Their replacements literally **could have no effect** on overturning Citizens United.

"Justice Ginsburg, who voted with the minority, is the oldest justice on the court at 82 – and she's fought off cancer, so _far_. Justice Breyer, the other oldest justice who voted with the minority on that case, is 77.

"Sure, two of the justices who voted with the majority on Citizens United – Kennedy and Scalia – they're both 79. But, for all we know, they might stay on the court 'til they're 95.

"The big question is: why hasn't Hillary come out in formal support of a Constitutional Amendment, like the USA-SBR, which would effectively *once and for all* ban the legal fiction of 'corporate personhood' as well as ban the idiotic legal concept that money equals free speech?

"Could it be that she's not quite as uncomfortable with Citizens United as she claims? Let's hope not."

Ms. Martin's message: if you want Hillary in office, expect to get more permanent war culture. Don't expect corporate control of both chambers of Congress to abate anytime soon. And expect the government to give more preferential treatment to major defense contractors like ex-felons Boeing and Lockheed Martin, as well as other deep-pocketed corporate interests.

And expect her to continue to schmooze with her many, many longtime billionaire buddies all over the world. Shamelessly.

But don't fret, she said: Hillary will still continue to schedule the occasional meetings with pre-screened acolytes, to 'make clear' the **appearance** that she '*listens to the little people.*'

* * *

A MAINE-LY NATIONAL EMBARRASSMENT OF A GUV, LUV

The next afternoon the group rolled in to Bangor, Maine for their usual 5 p.m. press conference, this time in advance of the following day's rally at the 8,000-seat Cross Insurance Arena, the occasional venue for the basketball program at the University of Maine in Orono 10 miles away.

Journalists attending the press conference included a reporter from the Bangor Daily News (a locally-owned daily), the Ellsworth American (a locally-owned weekly based in Ellsworth near Bar Harbor), the Portland Press Herald (a locally-owned Portland daily), the Boothbay Register (a locally-owned weekly based in Boothbay) and from each of the area local television network affiliates. The TV affiliate reporters all seemed to be just old enough to drive.

Pongo half-expected to see that one or more of them had made their way to the press conference on mini-scooters. When he looked out into the hotel parking parking lot, sure enough, there were two of them, one with a Comcast Cable logo (NBC) on the side of the seat and the other with a Disney (ABC) logo on the side of the toenail-size gas tank. He looked to see if there were any reporters resembling one or more of Disney's Seven Dwarfs (he was really hoping to see a live version of Bashful), but the closest he could find were a couple of pizza-faced young guys who looked like they'd been hunched over with their elbows between their knees for a couple of hours.

Most of the reporters' questions involved USA-SBR details already discussed many times by the Poughkeepsians at previous press conferences and rallies.

However, there were several questions regarding Maine's wacko, Limbaugh-on-steroids governor, Republican Paul LePage. LePage won re-election the previous November with 48.2 percent plurality of the vote in a three-way race.

That victory came despite LePage:

- Vetoing a bill which would've prevented the financial industry from using fraudulent or inaccurate documents to foreclose on homeowners.
- Praising global warming for opening up the Northwest Passage through the Arctic Ocean despite global warming decimating the Maine shrimp industry and threatening other Maine coastal shellfish by stimulating populations of invasive green crabs, as well as endangering Maine coastal communities through rising sea levels.
- Falsely claiming that illegal immigrants were threatening Maine by bringing tuberculosis, HIV and Hepatitis-C into the state, despite no scientific evidence to support his fearmongering.
- Setting aside special time to meet with an extremist group affiliated with the "Sovereign Citizens" movement which: (1) advocated arresting Democratic leaders of the Maine Legislature and hanging them for supposed treason; (2) claimed the government was conspiring against Christians by planning to seize their weapons; (3) alleged the government was performing 'mind control' activities and (4) encouraged citizens to refuse to pay taxes.
- Supporting removal of child labor restrictions so that businesses could employ 12-year-old children as part-time laborers (though he personally felt businesses should be allowed to hire 11-year-olds as well).
- Bullying Maine Department of Labor employees to skew disputed Unemployment Compensation claims in favor of businesses rather than laid-off employees. Department of Labor employees told the *Maine Sun Journal* they felt "abused, harassed and bullied" by the contacts from LePage and believed their own jobs were being threatened if they didn't yield to the Governor's pressure.
- Proposing to raise state workers' minimum retirement age and cap retirees' cost of living adjustments. *Because pressuring 90-year-olds to be in the labor force is just as work ethic-ey as pressuring 12-year-olds into it.*
- Forcing state employees to remove a mural honoring the history of laborers in Maine (including scenes from a 1986 strike) from the ***Department of Labor*** which had been on display for five years, claiming it supposedly

was biased against employers; he called those who wanted to protest the mural's removal "idiots." He also ordered the re-naming of rooms in a Department of Labor building which previously had been named in honor of various historical labor leaders.

- Claiming, in 2013, that his "greatest fear in the State of Maine (is) newspapers." He told a group of 8th grade schoolchildren that reading newspapers "is like paying somebody to tell you lies," according to the *Central Maine Morning Sentinel.*[*]

"This is a man who clearly is determined to represent only the monied interests in the state," Franklin/Percy said. "His philosophy for governing appears to have been traced directly from that of Benito Mussolini: whatever corporations want is what's best for everyone.

"Literally trying to erase history from the walls of a state agency. That Maine voters could be persuaded to extend his employment is a profound statement on the corrupting influence of money in the elections process. Gov. LePage chose not to use his state's public financing process in his campaign. He calls the Maine Clean Elections Act 'welfare for politicians' – instead of what it is: medicine for a democracy infected with dirty money.

"The USA-SBR is exactly what Maine and the rest of the U.S.A. need to disinfect the entire political system of craven crony corporatist hyper-capitalists. With it, there is the promise of cleansing sunshine and openness. The promise of public participation without threat of oppressive surveillance and even arrest – like the arrest of filmmaker Josh Fox in February 2012 simply for trying to film a supposedly open-to-the-public Congressional committee hearing.

"To be opposed to something like the Maine Clean Elections Act is like being opposed to motherhood and apple pie. Since the Citizens United Supreme Court decision, the world appears to be turned upside down, whether it's in the Maine Governor's office or the board rooms of Halliburton Corporation or the halls of the Department of Justice where men like Edward Snowden and Julian Assange are seen as existential threats to the military-industrial complex instead of the heroic men of principle they are.

"Don't let someone like Governor LePage succeed in brainwashing schoolchildren – and their parents, for that matter – into thinking that the Constitutional bulwark against the corruption of business and government – the nation's newspapers – are anything other than guardians against half-truths, outright lies and subtle manipulation by those who bask in the comfort of their massive accumulations of wealth.

"And don't be too ashamed or embarrassed – all of you - to admit that you, the news media, have consistently failed to perform your duty over the past half-century to shed sufficient disinfecting light on the craven corporatist shills and

---

[*] All collected from Huffington Post web entries on 4/24/15

manipulators who've gone on to take control of government at virtually all levels nationwide.

"That would be a fine first step toward resuming the role the Founders intended for you to play.

"The alternative role would simply be more of the same.

"You make the choice."

∗　∗　∗

BRINGING DEAD BRAINS BACK TO LIFE AS ONLY THE KING CAN

Their guest speaker at the next day's rally was none other than Maine favorite son Stephen King, who's sold more horror and fantasy fiction books that just about everyone with a pulse combined.

King lamented the five-year tenure of Gov. LePage, whom he previously called one of the Three Stooges (along with fellow hyper-anti-labor and global warming-contrarian Republican governors Rick Scott of Florida and Scott Walker of Wisconsin).

He derided the unspoken presumption among all Republicans and Wall Street Democrats that a culture of Permanent War is what the U.S.A. is stuck with, thanks to the influence of the military-industrial complex.

King heaped praise upon USA-SBR supporters for their provision to make it harder for Congress to enter into war or hostile overseas actions by requiring a three-fourths majority vote from both chambers of Congress.

In addition, he threw his support behind the USA-SBR's provision for a Federally-funded gun buy-back program aimed at getting semi-automatic weaponry off the streets. If semi-automatic weaponry no longer were easily available to the general public, he said, lunatic mass murderers probably would have a harder time splattering peoples' brains all over the sidewalk.

"Do all those manly men out there who have a heartfelt love of hunting really, _truly_ believe they'll be outgunned by Bambi and Thumper and Yogi and Boo-Boo if they can't have their AK-47's with 50-round drum magazines?

"It's amazing to me that the National Rifle Association has somehow managed to launder the minds of gun-owners everywhere to believe they're some sort of pink-panties-wearing effeminate Nancy-girls – my apologies to all Nancy's everywhere – if they're not carrying around enough firepower to wipe out a platoon of invading Russians.

"Last time I checked, we had a pretty darned reliable Army of our own we could count on for that sort of problem – which would be a potential problem **only** if our nation were situated about 5,000 miles to the east."

King went on to detail each of the specifics in the USA-SBR which he said promised to make life in the U.S.A. far better and far less stressful for the middle class and working poor.

"Y'know, FDR proposed his own Second Bill of Rights a year or so before he died – I just wish **he** could be here to make the case for the USA-SBR. I'm sure he could do a far better job at this than I am. I can certainly appreciate his strength of character – my own fight to recover from being mowed down from behind by a minivan was nothing compared to his struggle just to be vertical again. Polio, that monster you can't see coming, is a much more fearsome foe than a shitty old van.

"I've brought so many characters back from the dead in my books – maybe I can figure out a way to do that for him. A version of 'Pet Sematary' for dead Presidents, maybe? And while I'm at it, maybe I can figure out a way to bring Gov. LePage's dead brain back to life."

For the Poughkeepsians, Mr. King was a rock star – and not just because he played in his own cover band, the *Rock Bottom Remainders*. He wanted to breathe life into the very man who was largely responsible for him appearing at the Cross Insurance Arena that evening, the Poughkeepsians' favorite Dutchess County historical figure.

Right idea, but Mother Nature already beat him to it.

After the rally was done, the Poughkeepsie organizers treated King to a fish dinner followed by his favorite cheesecake. During dessert, Pongo overheard Franklin/Percy negotiating with King about co-writing a book with him about trees coming to life and eating alive the humans who'd been cutting them down with abandon, with the trees then producing seeds which germinated human-tree hybrids. Franklin still was proud of his partiality for arboreal life.

It wasn't the first time a fan had suggested co-writing a book with Stephen. However, for reasons he couldn't quite comprehend, FDR fan King actually felt *weirdly drawn* – and that's the *best kind of drawn* for him - to those ideas being described by that Scruples dude. It just might've been the beginning of a beautiful friendship, as Mr. Bogart once told Mr. Rains.

$$* \quad * \quad *$$

A HUFF-LESS HUFFY

The Poughkeepsians headed back south the next morning along Interstate 95 toward Albany and Poughkeepsie. It was back to work and doctoral classwork the following Monday for both Franklin and Holly – once again, they looked forward to returning to their usual routines for a few months before their last rally tour in advance of the 2016 general election.

It was just as they opened the door to their Albany apartment in the early evening when Franklin and Holly saw the dog. Holly's immediate reaction was a muffled scream abbreviated by a retching reflex in her esophagus.

The lifeless shape of the poodle-chihuahua mix Franklin recognized as Huffy, one of the dogs he, Pongo and Harry used to walk, was nailed by the ears to the door of the coat closet just inside their apartment's front door. Huffy had been slowly eviscerated and then strangled with the strap of a bag bearing a USA-SBR logo. A small computer-printed note in Century Gothic font was taped to the bloated tongue hanging out of Huffy's mouth.

"*Want more of same? Do nothing differently. Want less? Do Nothing*"

"Dear Jesus," Franklin said. "Huffy's owners must be beside themselves."

Both Franklin and Holly knew Huffy's family: Tim and Sherry Geist, both 42, and their 6-year-old son Tim Jr. Huffy was their only pet.

"We've got to call them," Holly said, sobbing.

"Are you sure?" Franklin asked, his eyes watering. "This, this ki-, kind of thing could set back what we're trying to do a long ways."

"I'm sure that's what the man who did this wants. But if we cover this thing up, we could just be playing into his hands."

"And if we just call the police right now, every bit of this is in the newspapers, on TV, on the internet within hours. Let's take enough time to know what we want to say to the outside world, OK?"

"If Huffy were *your* dog, would **you** want to know right away that this had happened to her?"

"I'm not sure I would. If it were a choice between *wondering* if someone found her and gave her a good home and **knowing** she'd been brutally killed by some perverted sadist or sociopath…well, I might just prefer the anguished hope of the unknown over the certainty of knowledge."

"Let's call Phil and Pongo and the others, right away. I just don't feel comfortable right now trying to keep this thing just to ourselves."

"I'm with you on this. Let's call. Right now."

* * *

They first discussed over the phone whether it was wise to even have the conversation over the phone, what with the chance of surveillance by persons in the NSA or other Federal agencies who might be taking it upon themselves to find juicy tidbits of personal information which could be used to discredit the Poughkeepsians.

Phil first suggested an immediate meeting at the Eveready Diner.

"I am not setting foot outside of this apartment with that poor little soul still nailed to that closet door," Holly said, serious as the proverbial heart attack. "And law enforcement won't want us touching it until they've had a chance to examine the scene."

"Do you want to stay there while we talk about it?" Phil asked.

"You can't be serious," Holly said.

"I'd stay," Franklin said.

"Are you OK with that?" Phil asked Holly.

"I suppose. It sounds like the best way for us to talk about this with the lowest risk."

"OK, Holly, the rest of us will meet you at Eveready as soon as you can drive down here. Franklin, you call us pronto if anything happens between now and when we all get to Albany," Phil said.

Within two minutes, Holly was out the door and driving away from the apartments' parking lot.

About five minutes after that, there was a knock at Franklin's door.

"Don't tell me you forgot your key, Honey," he said as he opened the door.

But it wasn't Holly.

✳ ✳ ✳

To Report or Not to Report, That Is the Question

Every one of the rally tour organizers was at Eveready Diner waiting for Holly when she pulled up 45 minutes later. It was a minor miracle she wasn't pulled over for speeding.

Seeing her tear-reddened eyes as she walked in, her Eveready co-worker Melissa Pudnoquer asked if something was wrong – Holly convinced her it was simply a reaction to being exposed to mold in the air at her new apartment.

Sitting around a large table at the back of the restaurant, the group got right down to business.

"There's no time to spare on this," Pongo said. "As someone who's been trained in law enforcement, I can tell you it doesn't reflect well on a complainant if it comes out that the person voluntarily delayed reporting an incident."

"So, are we all agreed that we must report this thing and report it right away?" Phil asked.

Lots of nodding around the table. Except for Tom.

"Geez, it's sad and all, but it's just a little dog. The boy who owned it probably will just assume it ran away and either got hit by a Wal-Mart big rig or got stolen.

"It's not going to turn that kid into a serial killer if that little dog ends up in a garbage bag in the Albany landfill."

"So, what if the killer is watching while one of us disposes of that dog and then calls in an anonymous tip to police?" Mitch asked. "Anyone have anything to tell the police when they ask us about that?"

"You're right," Mel said. "There's no way around it. This thing's got to be reported. Without any delays."

"So, assuming we simply tell the police the truth about how Franklin and I found little Huffy, what do we tell all of our supporters about this?"

"Let's have a press conference tomorrow and condemn this thing for what it obviously is: an attempt to intimidate us into backing off of our organizing," Idris said. "An attempt to make us look like we think the lives of people's pets are way less important than us trying to promote the USA-SBR."

"Well, the animals' lives **are** less important, aren't they?" Cherisse asked.

"The general public will figure that out without us taking an official stand on that," Orvis said.

"Yup, officially stating we feel pets' lives are secondary to our cause, that's all we need," Karin said. "I can see the headlines now: 'FIDO'S PROSPECTS PER USA-SBR-ers: CANINES' RISK WORTH ORGANIZERS' REWARD'"

"Let's get ahead of this thing, Marcia," Phil said. "Please schedule a press conference for 8 a.m. tomorrow, OK? But wait to schedule it for an hour or so, so Franklin and Holly have a chance to get this reported once she gets back to Albany."

"Consider it done," Marcia said.

* * *

As the hulking figure shoved his way in through Franklin's apartment door, all Franklin noticed was the black (or was it dark blue?) duster coat the man was wearing. No plaid pants on this one, just dark slacks. He was wearing slick black leather gloves and a dark wool cap covering his face.

"I'm just here to retrieve the evidence, now that you've seen it," a mechanical-sounding voice coming from the man's chest said. "We know you haven't called the police yet. This friendly little animal who gave up his life for a Milk Bone treat – he's got a happy resting place waiting for him in the incinerator where my benefactor works.

"Here's the deal: you fucking pinheads stop annoying my boss and his friends in high places and your pals stop losing their beloved pets. You stop this USA-SBR shit or dial it back to next to nothing and everyone – carpet butt-rubbers included – gets to die a natural death at a ripe old age, or not.

[At that moment, Franklin noticed the "H-arrow" symbol on business cards in the hulking man's shirt pocket, as well as a "Beretta" insignia pinned to the inside of the man's coat lining. (Unknown to Franklin, the H-arrow cards had been placed in the man's pocket as a diversion.) It appeared to Franklin that the man had forgotten the insignia and cards were there. Franklin would find out later that Beretta – ironically, an Italian company – was the sole manufacturer of sidearms for the entire U.S. Department of Defense. Franklin had no idea if the insignia meant an affiliation with the manufacturer or if the dog-murderer received it as a souvenir the last time he attended a convention for sociopaths. SocioCon '16?]

"And what happens if we try to have you tracked down and prosecuted?" Franklin said, wide-eyed at the sheer volume of sensillum-like fur all over the hit man's face, what appeared to be new growth, growth so thick it almost seemed to be crawling with life as it protruded through seams in the mask.

"Good luck with that, Dickhead."

At that moment, as if to 'reward' Franklin for his potential defiance, the Black Duster Man slung a Ziploc bag full of dog guts into Franklin's face. Duster Man pulled Franklin's cell phone from his pants pocket and destroyed it as Franklin was choking on bits of doggie digestive tract. The canine hit man then rummaged through the apartment looking for other phones, but found none. He sat Franklin down in a desk chair, tied him tightly to it, then tied the chair tightly to the steam heat radiator next to the outside wall of the apartment. Franklin was too stunned to react much.

$$* \quad * \quad *$$

MR. PEABODY'S FRACTURED TAIL; WHACK A MOLE, ANYONE?

Phil first noticed something wasn't right as he and Pongo pulled into their driveway 20 minutes or so after leaving the diner.

Their garage door was up. Neither of them ever left the door up. And their Uruguayan immigrant housekeeper never left it up.

As they got out of Pongo's Civic, they both noticed the lock on the door from the garage into the house had been jimmied, apparently with a crowbar.

Stepping into the hallway leading to the TV room past the laundry room, what *had been* spunky little Mr. Peabody stared back at them through dilated, lifeless brown eyes. As with Huffy, Mr. Peabody had been nailed up by his little ears, this time to the plastered drywall above the Podrowski's old Janssen piano.

It appeared, though, that little Mr. Peabody has expended no small effort in fighting off his attacker: there were shreds of human flesh in his little mouth, along with what seemed to be a human fingernail pulled right out of a middle finger. Unknown to everyone at the time, most domesticated canines, including Mr. Peabody, had the same ability to see the fine sensillum furry coats – visible among humans *only* to those with Franklin's gift of sight – of select members of homo sapiens who were moderately to severely conscience-challenged. That ability had allowed Mr. Peabody at least a fighting chance – but, at 22 pounds versus 252 pounds, it had been a fairly brief fight. If Mr. Peabody hadn't had the savvy to 'play faux friendly' when his attacker first showed himself, it would've been no fight at all.

But Mr. Peabody had not died quickly. The consummate asshole pet destroyer had broken each of Mr. Peabody's legs – his rear legs twice each – and pulled out three or four of his rear teeth before making a harikiri slice through his abdomen.

"Fucking evil bassa, b-b-b-bastard," Pongo said, weeping uncontrollably. He had had Mr. Peabody since he was 12 years old. Mr. Peabody was only the second dog he'd ever had. As it turned out, Mr. Peabody would be the last dog he would have. Some losses are never overcome.

As with Huffy, there was an unsigned note in Century Gothic font; this time it was attached to Mr. Peabody's shriveled penis, which seemed to have been slit open several times before he died:

"Couldn't keep him from spilling his guts to me. Want to keep _yours_ all to yourself? Back the fuck off, Commies!"

No visible prints. No apparent DNA or fibers from the hit man. No nothing.

The Podrowski men immediately went into their backyard to look for any additional evidence – and to see if the killer had broken into, or out of, their home through a rear window. They were in the back yard for about two minutes before they satisfied themselves that the killer must've gotten both in and out through the garage.

When they stepped back inside, Mr. Peabody's carcass was gone.

Vanished.

The note was still there, now on the floor beneath where Mr. Peabody had been affixed to the wall. But that was all.

No bloody footprints, no handprints on the garage egress. Nothing.

"Christ, we've got to get through to Holly," Phil said, stifling sobs.

They did – she finally picked up their call just in time for her to find Franklin tied up in their apartment. She hadn't called the police yet. She told them what had happened to Franklin.

"Dear God," she said, "what are we dealing with here?"

"It would seem that we've managed inadvertently to antagonize some folks who are only too willing to use whatever tools are at their disposal to intimidate us," Phil said. They're not going to let us succeed without inflicting all of the pain they're able to. At the same time, they don't want to leave us enough evidence to be able to track them down.

"Needless to say, without either Huffy's or Mr. Peabody's little bodies as evidence, we might just look like fools if we report these killings to the police."

"You didn't take any photos?" she asked.

"No – and even if we had, who's to say what was shown in the photos wasn't a stuffed animal?" Pongo said, still choking back sobs.

"What I don't understand is, how in the hell did he know exactly when Pongo and I would be gone from the house here just now? How did he time this thing so perfectly – even to be inside the house just as we arrived, ready to leave without us finding him?

"Is there any chance we've got a mole in our group?"

"Christ, Phil," Holly said. "Exactly what would a mole's motive be? Isn't what you're asking exactly what these perverse bastards would want us to be doing – suspecting each other?"

"All I know is, we need to make sure – before we make any strategic decisions of any kind, we need to make sure we're not giving an opponent ammunition to use against us," Phil said.

"I agree with my Dad," Pongo said. "And if there *IS* a mole, someone who had a hand in this thing happening to Mr. Peabody, I'd like to personally be the one who gives that ass-wipe a plunger-handle enema."

They then promptly had Marcia pull back the plans for the next morning's press conference.

* * *

MORE AGING, MORE CULLING

The next morning, Franklin awoke to find his hair had turned about 50 percent white, somehow dissolving the coating of his most recent regular two-week self-applied black dye job. Same with his moustache and eyebrows. Overnight, he suddenly had the appearance of a man in his early to mid-50's instead of his mid-20's.

Bianca and Heather quickly got on the job of culling crows again.

"This has got to be the last time," Bianca told Phil before heading out that morning. "I don't think I can get the farmers' co-operation more than this one additional time. Not without raising lots of suspicion."

But she succeeded; by late evening, Franklin had another fruit flavored bird-brain shake.

By morning, he did look younger again. But this time he appeared to be in his early 40's. The birdbrains appeared to be losing their effect.

The next time he jumped ahead in age, for all anyone knew, it might be to age 90.

* * *

THE FINAL 2016 TOUR; TO MR. MURDOCH'S MINION: TAIL'S WAGGING THE DOG

With relatively few acquaintances at Sage Schools near Albany, Franklin's latest aging episode was barely noticed.

Rolf Reticulando, Franklin/Percy's supervisor with his new part-time employer, Pearl Landscaping & Patio Co., remarked briefly that it seemed like Franklin/Percy had been "burning the candle at both ends a little too much," but otherwise didn't seemed alarmed at Franklin's appearance.

By the time spring break rolled around, Franklin and Holly decided circumstances had stabilized enough for them to go forward with their final rally tour before the general election. However, with all the stress from the dog murders, Annie, Karin and Cherisse decided to sit this tour out and remain in Poughkeepsie.

Since the killings of Huffy and Mr. Peabody, they'd continued to do occasional speaking appearances at public schools and civic groups, as well as promote their website and Facebook pages, without any apparent additional threats.

So, off it was to New York City's Madison Square Garden, the TD Garden in Boston and Marist College's James J. McCann Center arena at Poughkeepsie for their latest rallies. Their plan was to drive to the rally in New York City, after which they would fly to Boston's Logan International Airport; they were saving the Marist rally for last simply because it was in their own back yard.

Their press conference on a Saturday afternoon at a Four Seasons meeting room in New York City was attended by reporters from the New York Times (locally owned by Arthur Ochs Sulzberger Jr.), the Village Voice (a locally owned weekly), the New York Daily News (locally owned by billionaire Mort Zuckerman), the New York Post (a daily owned, along with Fox News, by Rupert Murdoch's News Corp.), Newsday (a Long Island daily owned by Cablevision of Bethpage, NY), the Wall Street Journal (a daily owned by Rupert Murdoch's News Corp.), the New Yorker (an almost-weekly magazine owned by Advance Publications of Staten Island, NY) and from each local network TV news affiliate. The Poughkeepsians were shocked to see that a couple of the local TV news reporters actually appeared to be over 40. "Must've been a World War Z thing strike down all the other reporters in the last day or two," Pongo speculated.

The first question was from a Rupert Murdoch drone, Milt Chiffre, who writes for the Wall Street Journal.

"What have you dudes been smoking to think that K Street and Wall Street lobbyists aren't going to do everything short of setting off a nuclear weapon to keep you from getting a transactions tax for reparations passed into law?" he asked.

"Actually," Franklin/Percy said, "we're all non-smokers. Well, I should say non-TOBACCO smokers, right Idris? (Mild laughter from the dais.)

"The last time we checked, though, decisions about what does or doesn't become law rest with the Congress and state legislatures, not the lobbyists who constantly try to schmooze them into ignoring their constituents' priorities.

"Does the Wall Street Journal believe reparations payments are undeserved by Native Americans and African-Americans?"

"I don't represent the editorial board," Chiffre said.

"We understand that. But do you know what their position is?"

"Yes, they oppose reparations payments funded by a transactions tax, even a temporary tax."

"Does it not make sense to you to have the institutions which have built their wealth over the centuries off of land and resources taken by force from Native Americans bear some responsibility for undoing some of that harm? Does it not make sense to you that institutions which built their foundations off of the blood, sweat and tears of brutalized slaves should in some small part be responsible for correcting some of that injustice?"

"Wasn't that what the forty acres and mules were supposed to do for the slaves?" Chiffre asked.

"You've got to be kidding," Phil said.

"OK, then, why should an 18-year-old half-blooded Cherokee in Oklahoma and all of his over-18 siblings each become a millionaire overnight?" Chiffre asked.

"Because it took hundreds of years of highly-orchestrated brutal government oppression to inflict systemic poverty and pain-killing addictions to alcohol and other substances onto previously self-reliant, ecological and spiritual indigenous cultures here," Phil said. "Their most sacred lands were turned into shopping malls, oil wells, superhighways, airports and landfills, not to mention heavily polluted waterways.

"When it comes to the scales of social and economic justice, a million here and a million there will barely start to tip them back into balance."

Many of the reporters' other questions were about police brutality against minorities, especially African-Americans.

Phil explained the USA-SBR's requirements for head-mounted cameras, as well as the provision allowing private citizens to submit true bills of indictment to grand juries.

And, not surprisingly, another of Murdoch's reporters, this one from the New York Post, had lots of questions about how the USA-SBR supposedly would drive all right-thinking capitalist businesspersons overseas.

Pongo explained, as in previous press conferences, that if businesspersons were foolish enough to abandon the markets in the most stable democratic republic on the planet, there would be more than enough entrepreneurs who would step in to replace them.

"There would be a bumpy transitional period," he explained, "but things would return to comparative normality quicker than you might think."

Wall Street Journal reporter Max Gierkopf asked if the Poughkeepsians really were delusional enough to believe major media corporations were going to allow to become law the provision of the USA-SBR giving preference to licensees with the most investors regardless of dollar amounts invested.

"You just don't get it yet, do you?" Franklin asked. "Corporations are the tail trying to wag the dog in a democracy. Voters always have had more power than Wall Street – they've just not realized YET how it would benefit them to fire Wall Street's shill cronies who sit in Congress.

"Once our provisions to remove the influence of big money in Congress take effect, the corporatist cronies will need to put on their water wings, because there'll be a tidal wave coming with their names on it.

"And they probably shouldn't be holding their breath for lifelines from their middle class victims when that time comes. The average time card-puncher will be about as sympathetic to those bankster cronies as working folks were to those corporatists' ancestors at the start of the Great Depression.

"Those Wall Street apologists sometimes like to say that, with great wealth comes great responsibility. Well, the time is rapidly approaching when they'll have the responsibility to eat crow and beg for mercy. And, knowing the generosity and the amazingly short memories of the American public, they'll probably find forgiveness – eventually.

"My personal hope, though, is that once the sea change in Congress has come and all the craven corporate toadies are tossed aside, a new law will be passed requiring that the CEO's of the Fortune 500 will always be the first 500 infantry soldiers sent to fight overseas wars.

"It will be a glorious day when the era of businesses' privatized profits dependent upon socialized risks is forever at an end, along with every other form of profit-padding corporate welfare."

Rupert Murdoch's paid propagandists could only shake their heads side to side. Pongo joked that they probably could get jobs as catchers for the Mets with that waving-off-the-pitch motion pretty much perfected – and because they were so good at digging their bosses' garbage pitches out of the dirt.

$$* \quad * \quad *$$

Huffpost Toastin' & Roastin'

The Poughkeepsians' featured speaker for the next day's rally in Madison Square Garden was New York resident Arianna Huffington.

She spent much of her presentation imagining what various Republican superstars' reactions would be if they woke up and suddenly found that the USA-SBR were the law of the land.

"Turtle Man (Mitch McConnell) has been getting 84 percent of his campaign donations from large donors (57 percent), PACs (21 percent) and himself (6 percent). So, he's probably going to wake up in a trembling sweat from a nightmare about having to go door-to-door with a rotating cast of grandchildren in his arms – and people asking if he can match Jon Stewart's imitation of him. Under the USA-SBR, he 'don't need no steenkin' big donors,' 'cause they no be legal, senor.

"Orange Man (House Speaker John Boehner) has been getting a big chunk of his campaign contributions from the fossil fuels extraction and production industry. So, he's probably going to wake up screaming with sweat-soaked sheets after a nightmare about having to buy solar panels for his roof from a Home Depot clerk who looks just like his quote-unquote 'Kenyan' president, only to go home and find both his chauffeur and his butler both also look exactly like his quote-unquote 'Marxist' President.

"Marco Rubio probably will wake up terrified from a nightmare in which he dreamt that the only way he could finish reading a speech without needing to glug down a quart of water was to read from a teleprompter which forced him to say every 30 seconds, 'this teleprompter is being operated by union professionals who earn living wages with guaranteed retirement benefits.' Followed by him being chased out of the TV studio by pitchfork and torch-wielding Tea Partiers carrying signs with his name misspelled.

"Rand Paul probably would wake up screaming like a little girl because his nightmare featured toddlers brandishing immunization hypodermic needles chasing him into an alley with junk diploma auditors at the other end all the while he's trying to find someone who isn't an internet-certified surgeon to remove his appendix at the old skid row Travelodge Motel turned into a privatized county hospital.

"Ted Cruz probably would be waking up with his head spinning like Linda Blair's in *The Exorcist* and screaming incoherently about his nightmare that there were *too many* people with USA-SBR-created health insurance who were *too healthy* and had too much money left in their pockets, enabling them to go out and buy Progress Texas literature about him."

She continued in the same vein for almost an hour, skewering the likes of Jeb Bush, Mike Huckabee, Carly Fiorina, Chris Christie, Lindsay Graham and Rick Perry.

It was like a gold mine that just kept pumping out nuggets. She even saved some keen observations just for Louie Gohmert, the dumbest member of Congress – ever ("We know Al Qaeda has camps on the Mexican border... people...trained to act Hispanic...""")

It was one entertaining evening. And productive too: a record number of USA-SBR pledge signers for one appearance.

Franklin, Holly, Phil and Pongo weren't as thrilled by the positive developments as they thought they'd be, though – their minds were still on the fates of those sweet little canines whose lives were ended by someone or some group which hated every last word of the USA-SBR.

* * *

---

* Rolling Stone, 12/4/13

TRAINED MONKEY PRIESTS

The next morning they took their flight to Boston's Logan International. Their afternoon press conference included reporters from the Boston Globe (a locally-owned daily), Boston Herald (a locally-owned daily), the East Boston Times Free Press (a free weekly) and from each of the local network TV affiliates. For the second press conference in a row, there actually were two reporters present who appeared to be out of their 30s. "Everyone who's under 40 in the entire city is probably at the gym getting in shape to try out for the Patriots," Harry said.

He might not've been far off.

Melinda Crispe of the Globe asked the Poughkeepsians if the USA-SBR's provisions for equality between the sexes would mean the Catholic Church would be forced to ordain women as priests.

"Even though most of us believe that is long overdue, the fact of the matter is, all religions still would be able to follow their own articles of faith, as long as their faith doesn't involve taking away someone else's rights," Franklin/Percy said.

"So, in response to your question, no, the Catholic Church leaders could ordain trained monkeys as priests if they wanted, as long as it doesn't allow them to roam around the city defecating on park benches, MBTA subway seats, movie theater seats and so forth.

"Well, I suppose they could let them roam around the city if they followed along completely prepared with sanitary hygienic procedures to disinfect their hairy priests' blessedly feculent uh-, er- uh- leavings.

"Now monkey priest flatulence – that's another repugnance altogether. We're thinking some sort of custom-fitted cork would be the only way the monkey priest could assume his time-honored social roles."

The remaining questions were mostly non-simian-related. All asked and answered before at other venues – but the Poughkeepsians pretended otherwise.

* * *

CARL SAGAN'S PROTÉGÉ: USE $$ FROM USA-SBR TO GO TO THE STARS

The guest speaker at the next day's rally in TD Garden was Neil deGrasse Tyson, Hayden Planetarium director and long-time Nova ScienceNow host, not to mention frequent guest on Jon Stewart's Daily Show. (He occasionally pointed out to Stewart that the rotating earth globe for his show always was rotating backwards. Jon never fixed it, though.)

✳ ✳ ✳

Tyson, who's long advocated for continued exploration of space, said the prospect of wealthy individuals and corporations finally paying more of their share of taxes under the USA-SBR might mean there finally would be enough NASA funding to expand human space travel.

In the past, he reminded the audience, great leaps in manned space travel occurred only as part of the Cold War space race when American prestige was on the line: our space scientists versus their space scientists.

Once the Cold War ended, so did the race into space, he said.

Corner-cutting by a for-profit contractor, PerkinElmer Inc., to meet budget limitations and deadlines led to the Hubble Space Telescope nearly being a complete failure,[*] he reminded listeners. Only through the creative thought processes of a group of brilliant NASA scientists was a lasting fix for the Hubble's defectively-ground mirror able to be implemented.

More of that kind of creative thought enabled NASA to squeeze enough productivity out of a still-shrunken budget to succeed with multiple unmanned rover missions to Mars, missions which still produce significant scientific discoveries every day, he said.

The possibility that there would be sufficient government revenue not only to fund ongoing social and health issues, but also to support renewed space exploration efforts should be something that makes every Star Trek and Star Wars lover a little giddy.

But making the USA-SBR happen would take more than giddy feelings, he quickly added.

He urged everyone in the audience to set aside their recreational web surfing and game-playing for a handful of minutes every day instead to devote their efforts to trying to compel elected officeholders to commit to support the USA-SBR.

Those who won't commit to supporting it can be replaced, he said. "It's the American way. Vote out the ones who won't listen to reason and vote in the ones who will.

"With enough funding and the will and vision to go forward – based on pressure from the American public – there's no reason why a *government-funded* mission to Mars can't succeed within, say, ten years. As I've said before, if the Chinese government announced a goal of building a military base up there, it probably would happen even sooner than that.

"But foreign governments' plans aside, it should be our pride as a nation for our history of exploration and scientific curiosity – not to mention the potential

---

[*] Wikipedia as of 4/26/15; Los Angeles Times, 10/5/93

long-term economic benefits – which causes us to insist to our lawmakers that they fully fund that ambitious mission.

"And they probably could do it for an additional half-cent per dollar of tax revenues.

"I'm willing to pay that. Are all of you?"

Lots of cheers.

"So, please get off your duffs and honor Carl Sagan's memory in the best possible way: demand that your lawmakers support the USA-SBR and that they use the revenues it will produce to explore Mars and the stars.

"Don't let our local star up there set another day without taking some action on this (holding up USA-SBR)!"

Chants of "USA-SBR!" "USA-SBR!" continued for a few minutes.

As the crowd chanted for deGrasse Tyson, the Poughkeepsians once again cheered on Marcia for her amazing guest speaker booking skills.

After the rally was done, the group hung out with deGrasse Tyson 'til the wee hours closing time at his favorite Boston bistro. If it had stayed open longer, they could've listened 'til dawn just to hear him talk about his long-time mentor, Mr. Sagan.

✳ ✳ ✳

Driving While Black? Police Headcams Will Protect You

Their drive the next morning southwest toward Poughkeepsie for their local press conference in advance of the following day's rally at Marist College's McCann Center included a beautiful ride along the Taconic State Parkway, the same route Phil had explored with Franklin more than five years earlier. Surprisingly, a few of the Poughkeepsians had never taken that drive before.

Those attending the press conference that afternoon in one of the Poughkeepsie Grand Hotel's meeting rooms included reporters from the Poughkeepsie Journal (another daily tentacle of the Gannett empire), the Hyde Park Townsman (a weekly originally part of Dutchess Suburban Newspaper Group), the Albany Times Union (a daily tentacle of the Hearst Corp.), the Kingston Daily Freeman (a branch of Digital First Media of New York City) and from each of the local ABC and Fox network TV affiliates out of Albany, along with the Real News Network local radio network affiliate out of Kingston. The local Albany TV reporters, yet again, appeared to be barely old enough to imbibe. "Is there some kind of virus that just causes them to drop dead once they hit age 25?" Phil whispered to Franklin, only half-joking.

Most of the reporters' questions had been asked and answered dozens of times at the USA-SBR press conferences over the years.

However, there was some focus on the contention by a Vassar professor a little more than a year earlier that the Poughkeepsie area was unfriendly to non-whites. The professor, an African-American, partly based his assertion on being stopped by local law enforcement for, essentially, driving while black – he said the officer asked him if the truck he was driving was stolen,[*] something the officer could've found out with an electronic check of vehicle registration records without even having to stop the driver.

"That's why the USA-SBR requires constantly functioning head-mounted cameras to be worn by law enforcement officers at all levels nationwide," Phil said. "Audio and video recordings don't lie – and it would be a felony to tamper with the recordings.

"That's also why we have the provision banning on-the-record bigots from holding any kind of public office. It's just something that's long, long overdue.

"By now, hopefully, everyone realizes that bigotry isn't confined to a specific region of the country, like the South. There are bigots and racists pretty much everywhere, in all walks of life.

"If the USA-SBR works as intended, those bigots – at worst - will be forced to keep their twisted views to themselves. Making it lots less likely they'll pass along their hatred to their children.

"That's a big deal."

The reporters didn't question that.

* * *

Nucky Gets Plucky, Keeps It from Getting Sucky

The next day's rally featured Hudson Valley resident and Golden Globe Award winning actor Steve Buscemi as the Poughkeepsians' guest speaker. All of the Poughkeepsians except Cherisse, Annie, Karin and Penny were present for the rally; Phil had called Franklin and Holly to make sure they knew a handful of the regulars wouldn't be showing up, so they'd have some additional duties. They were still fairly shaken up by the dog killings and felt they should be home to 'hold the fort,' so to speak, Phil explained.

Buscemi, who served four years as a New York City firefighter as a young man and worked several 12-hour shifts as a firefighter-volunteer immediately after the 9/11 attacks, wore his support for the blue collar families and union members on his sleeve.

The USA-SBR, he said, with its provisions making it easier for trade unions to organize at private businesses, would restore a balance that's been missing ever

---

[*] 12/8/14 Poughkeepsie Journal

since the dawn of the Reagan years, he said. Finally, at long last, there would be real, concrete consequences for those who would punish workers simply for trying to have a respected voice of representation on day-to-day issues about fair treatment and fair pay.

Buscemi, himself arrested in New York City in May 2003 during protests over then-Mayor Bloomberg's closure of numerous firehouses as a budget-cutting measure, urged the attendees to have "the guts to walk the walk and talk the talk" of support for the USA-SBR.

"If you want to stop having billionaires control who represents you in the Congress, to stop their corporations from manipulating the FDA over what goes into your food and medicine, to stop their paid lobbyist minions from perpetuating our Permanent War culture...

"There's no better way to do that than telling your elected officeholders you expect them to go on record as supporting the USA-SBR.

"If they don't, then I'd wager there are dozens of people sitting right here in this arena who could un-seat any of those assholes.

"If you have the guts. I don't think you'd be here today if you didn't already know you **DO** have the guts to do that.

"Make. This. Happen. (Holding up USA-SBR)

"Unless you like your corporate overlords, that is."

Then the chants, for the next three minutes:

"FUCK O-ver-LORDS!" "FUCK O-ver-LORDS!" "FUCK O-ver-LORDS!!"

Buscemi, who wore one of his *Boardwalk Empire* fedoras during the speech, tipped it to the crowd, and gave a thumbs-up gesture as he returned to his seat on the dais.

The Poughkeepsians and the crowd gave him a two-minute standing ovation.

Franklin/Percy then was stuck with the denouement duties, introducing the memorial videos for Sally and Prof. Bartlett, followed by "*Capitalism: A Love Story.*"

Buscemi was gracious enough to let the Poughkeepsians treat him to an old-fashioned cheeseburger and onion rings dinner, followed by a blueberry milkshake, at the Eveready Diner up the road after the crowd dispersed.

He volunteered to do a television P.S.A. for the group "if you don't think my goofy mug will turn people off."

Quite the contrary, assured Phil, Franklin, Pongo and the others.

* * *

THE ASSAULT THAT WENT OVER THE LINE

It was shortly after 11:30 p.m. – about 45 minutes after they dispersed from the diner – that Phil and Pongo got a frantic call from Grandpa Tom.

"Christ almighty, Phil," Tom said. "They violated your mother. You've got to come now."

"Is she alright? – I mean, is she alive and conscious?"

"Don't want to talk now, just come – and don't wreck on the way."

Phil and Pongo dashed out of the house. Phil asked Pongo to drive – as they pulled away, Phil called Franklin and Holly, who'd just arrived at their Albany apartment.

"Please get your butt down to my Mom and Dad's as fast as your little car will carry you, OK?" Phil asked.

He briefly repeated what Tom had told him.

When Franklin and Holly arrived at the elder Podrowskis' home near Fishkill, they found Phil and Pongo sitting across from Tom and Annie in the living room. Tom was sitting upright, cradling Annie's head as she lay supine on the couch.

"Does she feel like talking about it?" Franklin asked Phil in a low voice.

"I don't mind," Annie said. "It's not like it's my fault or anything, right?"

"Of course not, Grandma," Pongo said.

"It happened so fast, he was on me before I realized what was going on.

"I heard the doorbell ring maybe 15 minutes after Tom left to go to the rally. I went to look through the peephole and – I swear to Jesus – I saw *your face*, Franklin, looking back at me through the little hole.

"I opened up the door to ask if Tom needed something from the house and – before I could get more than two words out – the man forced his way in and tore off some sort of fancy rubber mask. What was beneath the mask was just a black nylon stocking-type mask – it completely hid his face.

"As he was taking the rubber mask off with one hand, he was throwing me in one sweeping motion across the room and onto our couch, where Tom and I are right now.

"I asked him why he was here and – this was what terrified me the most – he had one of those electronic voice distortion amplifiers. He sounded like a cross between Darth Vader and that IBM computer that beat those Jeopardy champions. I thought I was going to evacuate my bowels right here on the couch, I was so scared.

She started to cry between her sentences at that point.

"He said in that weird, mechanical-sounding voice that this was happening because we wouldn't abandon the USA-SBR, because there were people whose financial interests couldn't be put at risk because of our audacity to presume what working people want.

"He said the next step in our education after this wouldn't be nearly as pleasant as what he was about to do.

"It was then that I noticed he had black latex surgical gloves on both hands. I kept waiting for him to pull out a knife or a scalpel, but he didn't.

"He just pulled my pants and underpants down. So hard that they both tore at the seams a little.

"And then he raped me with his fingers. Dear God, he made it hurt so badly. And when his arm seemed to tire a little bit, he pulled out what looked like a sawed-off plunger handle and he rammed it into my bottom several times, until he could see blood starting to coat the wood.

"He took that handle with him when he ran out.

"The last thing he said was something like, 'Your friends aren't going to keep her from winning. We have too much invested.' But it was pretty garbled from the distortion. He might've said 'running' instead of 'winning' and it might've been 'the mulch' instead of 'too much.'

"All I know is, he was careful not to leave anything at all that would be a clue to who he was."

"Have you already called the police?" Holly asked.

"No, we thought we'd wait to hear what you have to day," Tom said.

"I've heard enough," Franklin said. "We should've called the police after the dogs were killed. They have to be brought in on this. The people behind this are daring us to have law enforcement involved. When evil is given free rein, it will go as far as it's allowed to.

"It's time."

"I agree," Phil said.

* * *

GUT FEELINGS AND STRATEGY

The City of Poughkeepsie Police Department detectives who interviewed Annie and Tom were professional and thorough. However, they predicted that, besides publicity of the attack, little was likely to come from their investigation. There were no other witnesses, no physical evidence, no fingerprints, no DNA, no facial recognition, no voice recognition, no license plate information, no vehicle information, no forced entry, no video, no audio.   Not even an indication of race or ethnicity. Just an approximation of the perpetrator's height and weight.

And motive? Well, there's that: apparent intimidation, aimed more at the victim's family and friends than the victim herself.

Asked by the detectives who she thought the attacker meant when he said Annie's friends wouldn't "keep her" from running or winning, Annie said she imagined the "her" must be Hillary Clinton – if for no other reason than the fact that there had been considerable criticism of Hillary at several of the USA-SBR rallies.

The detectives declined to speculate about whether they might have a basis to question Ms. Clinton.

After the detectives left, Franklin was particularly agitated. He motioned to Phil, Pongo, Tom and Holly to join him in Tom's and Annie's front parlor so Annie wouldn't have to listen in.

"Listen, all of you, please don't think I'm crazed and revenge-driven here, but I have a real gut feeling who's responsible for these attacks," Franklin said.

"We're listening," Phil said. "You already know we don't think you're crazy."

"What it is, is this: I can never prove it, and I don't know if I am sure beyond all reasonable doubt, but I simply know in my heart that Ms. Clinton understands what's been happening here, at least after the fact.

"Make no mistake: I am **not** saying – not even remotely – that she's responsible for ordering some hitman-type person to do what's happened to us, with the dog killings and now Annie.

"But I think she had reason to believe these things were going to happen. And I think, whether she realizes it or not, she probably knows on a first-name basis the person who *did* order these attacks.

"Let's look at the complete perspective here: she's not once endorsed any of the specifics of our USA-SBR project – unless you count supporting police officers wearing cameras, *without* mentioning specific consequences for tampering or turning them off.

"She did make some classic Hillary-esque non-specific remarks recently about "*considering*" whether to ask for elimination of "*some*" tax loopholes for financial institutions and wealthy individuals.

"Whatever the hell **_that_** means. Maybe a non-binding petition to beg Jamie Dimon at JP Morgan Chase and Lloyd Blankfein at Goldman Sachs to stop being assholes?[*] No, wait, their employers are her major benefactors – couldn't be that."

"If there ever were any doubt whatsoever that we have **two systems of justice** –one for the *super-hyper-rich* and one for everyone else – what those dicks did leading up to the 2008 meltdown left no question," Pongo said. "It's like that Taibbi dude wrote in Rolling Stone: can anyone imagine someone arrested for pot possession on the street being able to call the local prosecutor's **_BOSS_** and **insisting** on being able to pay a few months' of his income from selling grass in exchange for *no charges being filed at all*? If that Dimon prick can just order up a crony deal like that from Mr. Holder, then **everyone** should have that privilege.

"Of course, that would require equal treatment under the law – a real deal-killer."

---

[*] *Dimon got a 74 percent raise – while 7,500 low-level staff were laid off - once he manipulated a slap on the wrist record civil fine deal with Attorney General Eric Holder with a tacit agreement for no criminal prosecution for JP Morgan Chase's role in misleading marketing of toxic financial instruments leading to the 2008 meltdown; Matt Taibbi, 11/6/14 Rolling Stone...Blankfein of Goldman Sachs is among the heads of unprosecutable organized crime syndicates who make their profits off of mass fraud; Blankfein ordered his minions to unload toxic sub-prime mortgage-backed instruments on Morgan Stanley luring Morgan by saying Goldman owned $6 million of the instruments when, in fact, Goldman had a $2 billion bet on the instruments tanking – leading to $960 million in taxpayer funds bailing out Morgan; Matt Taibbi, 9/30/13 Rolling Stone.*

"The recipient of their corporate largesse, Ms. Rodham Clinton, has been grabbing all the headlines she can as this 'my man done me wrong' supposedly arch-feminist when, in fact, she hasn't supported any specific measure which actually would help American women," Franklin said. "Like restoring Food Stamps to their pre-November 2013 Republican-imposed cuts. Or increasing funding for work-related day care assistance. Or supporting a law to forgive student loan debt, a major financial burden on lots of single moms.

"She's said some wonderful things about helping women in extreme poverty in Africa and elsewhere. Her specific concrete proposals to help *American* women, though: _mostly_ the sound of crickets.

"She's never discussed how it came out in 1997 that Breast Cancer Awareness Month was conceived and launched 12 years earlier by Imperial Chemical Industries, a British organochlorines conglomerate raking in $14 billion a year off of compounds known to be carcinogenic. Around that same time it was reported 70 percent of breast cancers might stem from environmental exposures to chemicals.[*] Not to mention that the widely varying nature of cancers means that there likely will never, ever be a single 'cure' for all cancers, or even all breast cancers.

"Has anyone heard any cancer researchers suggest there's likely to be a cure for all breast cancers in the next five, ten or even twenty years, the way researchers sometimes talk about cures for diabetes?

"As First Lady in the late '90s – and since then, for that matter – Hillary could've done women everywhere – how do they say it now? – a **_solid_** by calling out the organizations that keep promising women there's a magic cure out there somewhere. **And** by calling out corporations that profit off organochlorines in our plastics, pesticides, paper, foods, prescription drugs and even our water supplies – at the very least to give potential breast cancer victims the chance to avoid putting that crap in their bodies.

"She said *nothing* about those issues."

"Well, of course not – and hardly anyone else did either," Phil said. "A significant chunk of Wall Street profits is dependent on chemical industries which produce organochlorines and organophosphates. Besides, you can't expect her to get all feisty about capitalism's shortcomings – it'd harsh her upbeat Reagan-ey 'morning in America II' theme."

"Let me finish, OK, Phil? (Franklin had been on a roll.)

"When the *Rolling Stone* college rape story fiasco came to a head a year ago, she had an opportunity to stand up for rape victims everywhere by reminding the public that one botched story didn't mean there wasn't a rape crisis on campuses around the country.

"She said nothing.

---

[*] *"There's Nothing in the Middle of the Road but Yellow Stripes and Dead Armadillos,"* Jim Hightower, 1998

"When Jon Krakauer's book about rape scandals in one of the college towns we visited - Missoula, Montana - came out a year ago, Hillary had an opportunity again to weigh in on the problems young women have getting through all the sexual abuse minefields in life.

"She said nothing.

"She and candor, especially about the specifics of policy, are allergic to each other. She simply does NOT spontaneously offer any substantive insights or bold leadership positions on issues the public is more or less evenly divided about.

"*Every single thing* she says, everything she *does*, every *pre-selected group* she allows to interact with her – it's all part of a pre-calculated strategy to *guarantee* she's seen in the least objectionable light, the most artificial lighting this side of a 10-watt fluorescent tube. It's an orchestrated portrayal where she can give off the calculated *appearance* of someone who wants to know what people think without actually having *to prove* she cares. Like a slick TV ad for a mediocre dent and ding appliance store promoting pricey but more or less worthless warranties.

"I'm going to make a prediction here: I predict that, once this story about Annie being assaulted breaks in the national media in the next day or two, Hillary will say *nothing*. Unless a reporter asks her *specifically* about Annie's incident.

"And if that does happen, I am certain I will be able to tell from the level of sincerity she displays with her response whether she knows which of her support-ers was *most likely* behind these attacks.

"Outside of playing cards, I am not a betting man. But I will make this bet right here and now: I wager $5 that she will say nothing about Annie's attack un-less she's asked about it. And I wager another $5 that any remark she *does* make will have all the empathy of her talks in 2008 implying then-Sen. Obama would have a higher risk of assassination than she would.

"Anyone want to take that bet?"

No takers.

* * *

Three days passed after the story of about a USA-SBR organizer's family mem-ber being sexually assaulted in her home was picked up by the major televi-sion network news divisions, the Associated Press and Reuters.

No remarks from Ms. Clinton. Utter silence.

Then, that evening, during a meet-and-greet near a campaign fund-raising event in a Seattle suburb, a young (yes, that's redundant) local network affiliate TV news reporter assertively asked Hillary how she felt about the USA-SBR orga-nizer's family member being sexually attacked in a Poughkeepsie residence.

As she was signing books for two different fans, she said, simply, "Just tragic. Awful thing." She diverted her eyes from her fans and their autograph books for about $1/10^{th}$ of a second between signatures. No offer of moral support.

No insights which might help the victim find meaning or aid in recovery. No suggestions about ways to prevent rapists' home invasions. No expression of sympathy.

It was all Franklin needed to see.

But when he woke up the next morning he saw **more** than he *wanted* to see.

* * *

Botox Won't Fix This

The hyper-aging process had come back, with a vengeance. What Franklin saw in the mirror wasn't the 90-year-old face he'd feared might show up unannounced – but it looked to be at least 75.

This was not something that a fruit-flavored birdbrain shake was going to remedy. Not even close. He needed something which would be lasting. He had some vague ideas about what it might be, but nothing concrete.

After sitting down at the Podrowskis' breakfast table to shocked expressions from Phil and Pongo, the three of them decided to convene an emergency gathering of everyone who knew Franklin's true identity. They needed some brainstorming from everyone in the group with a medical background (Bianca Swanson and her father Sam, Annie and Cherisse Peterson). And fast.

* * *

Cherisse Gets an Idea

The group arrived for the meeting in Phil's basement around 11 a.m. Besides Phil, Pongo and Franklin, it included Heather, Holly, Harry, Orvis and Karin O'Leary, Tom and Annie Podrowski, Penny and Mitch Duarte (Heather's parents), Mel and Cherisse Peterson (Harry's folks), Bianca Swanson and her father Sam, Idris M'Benga and Marcia Dirkenstack.

As their staggered arrivals commenced, each of them immediately saw Franklin's newly aged face. They each took turns embracing him and asking him how he felt. He said he felt OK, just old and achy.

Phil prepared them for what was about to come.

"Franklin woke up to see in his mirror this morning what you're seeing right now. He'd been planning to call all of us together to discuss Ms. Clinton and what he feels are fairly clear indicators that she may, maybe without even realizing it, know the person or organization which was behind the attacks against Annie and those two dogs.

"In fact, he's fairly sure that she's at least in *some* small way <u>pleased</u> those attacks took place. I don't know that I disagree with him. He makes a fairly persuasive circumstantial case. Especially considering what the attacker told Annie and what was written on the notes with the dogs.

"But the main reason we're here now is visible on Franklin's face.

"If the medical professionals among us can't come up with a viable idea for an antidote to Franklin's rapid and unpredictable aging, we're not going to have the privilege of his company a lot longer."

"Who wants to take a stab at this?"

After about 10 seconds of silence, Cherisse, who had been on the proverbial wagon for almost two years by then and appeared exceptionally bright-eyed, raised her hand assertively as though a light bulb had just gone off in her mind.

"Please hear me out on this. If any of you feels that it's too over-the-top or mean-spirited, please don't be afraid to say so. If you feel strongly that it's a non-starter and everyone else disagrees with you, no one will think less of you if you want to drop out of this group.

"This goes back to the way Franklin described Hillary. You'll all recall it, I'm sure. That thick sensillum-like fur that's invisible to everyone here except Franklin. He said it was grotesquely thick for Hillary. Which Franklin says usually is a sign of someone with a profoundly challenged conscience.

"Well, here's what I'm suggesting – and I guarantee no one will be permanently harmed by any of this..."

* * *

Almost 30 minutes later, when she was done explaining her proposal, there were a number of stunned-to-silence faces sitting around the long table in the basement. To her and the Podrowskis' great relief, however, no one had gotten up and left. Cherisse had been especially worried about Penny and Mitch, because Penny was absolutely crucial to her plan.

Phil told them the group would be re-convened once a long list of logistics was worked out. He and Franklin already had concluded that would mean some long discussions with Penny, as well as with Annie, Cherisse, Bianca and Sam.

Phil had one more immediate concern which he needed to discuss as discreetly as possible with Pongo, Harry, Idris, Bianca, Annie, Tom, Penny and Mitch – without Franklin being aware.

Phil was fairly sure – by process of elimination – he knew who the mole in the group was.

* * *

Rooting Out the Mole

T hat afternoon, again in Phil's basement, he met with Pongo, Harry, Idris, Bianca, Annie, Tom, Penny and Mitch.

"Where's Franklin?" Penny asked. "Why are we here without him?"

"I intentionally left him out of this meeting," Phil explained. "I've been fairly sure for a while now that there must be some kind of contact between someone in our group and the person or organization responsible for these attacks and I'd prefer Franklin not be aware of what I'm proposing here."

"Shit, you think Franklin's part of that?" Mitch said. "I'm sorry, I don't buy that. Not for a second."

"No, no, **no**. Hear me out. I'm _not_ saying Franklin's the conduit. But, by process of elimination, I'm pretty darned sure it's that goo-goo eyed sweetheart of his. There's no one else among us who could conceivably have a motive for sabotaging the USA-SBR."

"So what's HER motive, then?" Annie asked.

"That's the thing – I have no idea. Franklin and Pongo have mentioned in the past that she comes from a fairly ultra-conservative anti-feminist kind of family background. I haven't ever heard her share anything remotely resembling those kinds of sentiments, but who can say?

"In any event, here's what I'm proposing: we're going to tell Franklin and Holly that we need them to join me, Pongo, Harry, Idris, Tom and Penny for a trip to Penny's office in New York City to discuss our plans for Franklin's long-term aging therapy there.

"We're going to make it clear that we're leaving Annie behind in Poughkeepsie alone at my house, instead of hers, to divert any possible attack while we're gone. They'll both probably object to that, but Annie, you and the rest of us will point out that it's pretty unlikely the attacker would know Annie would be at my house by herself.

"We'll convince them it'll be OK. If I'm right, though, it _won't_ be OK – the attacker will find out through Holly exactly **what** we've planned and **when** we've planned to be gone and for how long.

"The linchpins to this thing will be us taking two cars into New York City the night before the meeting, so once the car with Franklin and Holly is out of sight, they won't even be aware that I never even came out to get into the second car – that, plus sneaking Mitch into my house at least a day earlier to hide in the basement. We'll set it up so that the people riding in each car are staying in separate hotels, so Franklin and Holly won't even know I haven't come along 'til the next morning at Penny's office.

"That will leave the trap set with Annie as the bait and Mitch and me as the ones who'll stop the attacker. If Holly's the mole, we'll probably have the attacker trying to get into the house within an hour after the others leave."

"So what are you and I going to do if and when this Lurch-ey asshole actually makes his way in here? You have some Bruce Lee-type skills we're not aware of?

"And what if this bastard in black has an actual firearm?"

"This guy is a pro. Even if his intent is actual murder, he's not going to be carrying a gun. A gun produces evidence. Please excuse the picture I'm painting here, Annie, but if, God forbid, he actually wanted to exterminate you as his next step in the process of intimidating us out of business, he's far more likely to employ strangulation, either manually or with a garotte.

"But Mitch and I are going to be armed with tasers, baseball bats, steel-toed boots and injectable anesthesia – unless you've perfected the Vulcan neck pinch, Mitch."

"Nope, not yet."

"In addition, we'll have the element of surprise. This bastard isn't going to know what hit him."

"Sure sounds like you've thought this out fairly well for the most part," Penny said. "Just one thing: what if he doesn't come alone this time?"

"Er-, uh, well, OK, point taken. We'll make it so that Harry and Idris stay here with me instead of getting into that second car with Tom and Penny. Either way, four on one or four on two, our odds of nailing this bastard should be more or less overwhelming."

"Whaddya mean four on one? I'll be here too! I count, don't I?!" Annie asked.

"I just meant, we won't be expecting you to help, Annie. You're just the bait."

"Damn sweet bait at that," Tom said. "She's kept me bitin' for a heap o' decades."

"Oh, kiss my ass, you old lecher," Annie said.

"I'm ready when you are, Dear."

✳ ✳ ✳

SPRINGING THE TRAP – AND MORE SURPRISES

Their plan was set to be put in motion two days later, just after sundown on the Thursday before the Maryland and Wisconsin Presidential primaries.

It came off like clockwork: the car with Franklin, Holly and Penny left first as planned, followed by the car with Pongo, Bianca and empty seats where Franklin and Holly thought Phil, Harry and Idris were supposed to be.

Then the waiting.

As Annie lay on Phil's family room couch, she watched the "Big Bang Theory," followed by a PBS Nova program – which she turned off as soon as she saw that it was funded by David H. Koch. She then put in a DVD of a PBS program about so-called "Intelligent Design" advocates being defeated in U.S. District Court over a fight to have their pretext for religious instruction made part of a Pennsylvania school's curriculum.

Two full hours passed as Phil and Mitch crouched behind the anteroom closet door next to the front door of the house, while Idris and Harry sat behind a sheet wrapped around the legs of a pocket billiards table in the basement. Mitch held a walkie-talkie in his right hand, as did Idris. As soon as an attacker came through the door, Mitch was to click on the 'talk' button twice – Idris was to do the same if the attacker came through a basement window. The two in hiding who heard the signal were to rush to where the other two were, weapons at the ready.

Phil started playing Angry Birds Star Wars II on his smart phone to stay awake. Harry started playing Plants vs. Zombies to fight off sleep.

It was a good thing they did.

Four and a half hours after the two cars left, Annie heard a light knock at the front door. She checked out the peephole and saw Pongo's face. Barely semi-conscious at that later hour, she almost swung the door wide open before she realized it had to be another rubber mask.

As loud as she could whisper without being heard outside the door, she said just one word in the direction of the closet.

"Showtime!"

Two faint clicks could be heard from behind the closet door, followed by faint, stealthy steps coming up the basement staircase.

She slowly opened the door and stepped back as quickly as she could without making it clear she already was on to the attacker's modus operandi.

As the hulking 6-foot-4-inch man covered in black wearing a black duster coat stepped forcefully through the open door, he ripped off the rubber Pongo mask, showing the same black nylon stocking mask as before.

He took a few steps forward as Annie took a few steps backward. It almost looked like some sort of Brazilian dance step.

Then he held out his black surgical glove-covered right hand and curled his index finger in a backward motion a couple of times at Annie. This evening he wasn't particularly conversational.

Annie shook her head right to left a few times.

He took a few more steps toward her – by then, she'd backed all the way up against the far wall.

As he was starting to pull a two-foot-long garotte from right coat pocket, his whole body suddenly felt like when his dentist started his root canal drilling before the anesthetic kicked in. His hands involuntarily spasmed into fist grips so tight that his own fingernails drew blood from his palms.

By the time he realized he'd been tasered, it was too late. He saw four men standing over him with baseball bats. Idris yanked the black stocking mask off of the man's face. None of them recognized the man behind the mask: he was a 30-something round-faced white man with a long-ago broken nose and what looked like scars from multiple beatings. He had three tattoos on his neck: one of a JP Morgan Chase Bank logo, one of the Goldman Sachs logo and another of a beret-wearing Ayn Rand. (The Poughkeepsians couldn't have known at the time that those tattoos were intended to throw them off a trail.)

"What you did to my mother," Phil started, "I ought to pummel the living fuck out of you. But you're lucky she's here right now. I wouldn't want her to see that. Plus, you're not worth what it would cost to clean your putrid guts out of my carpet."

"OK, Son, dial it back," Annie said. "Let's get the police over here **right now**."

When the detectives showed up 25 minutes later, sirens blaring, they could find no identification on the attacker. They started to take a photo of his dental work, with one detective forcibly opening the attacker's mouth while the other was poised to snap the shutter release on a digital camera – but the junior detective dropped the camera when they saw that the man's tongue *had been removed*.

The junior detective regained his composure and snapped the shutter release a couple of times.

Handed a notebook, the man refused to identify himself. He wouldn't respond to the detectives' questions about whether he was affiliated with any kind of campaign, Presidential or otherwise. Asked if he was affiliated with JP Morgan Chase Bank or Goldman Sachs, he wrote nothing.

"We're not going to get anything out of him here," the lead detective, Sgt. Russ Odieux, told his partner. "Let's get him back to interrogation. Maybe a little time out will loosen his tongue – well, *so to speak*, I mean."

"I think this guy's trumpet-playing days are more or less over, Sarge," said the junior detective, Nate Schwachkopf.

"C'mon – outta here, now."

As the detectives walked out the front door and walked toward their police cruiser, the unmasked attacker between them, Pongo thought he saw two sudden small white flashes a few feet apart on a hillside a quarter-mile to the south-south-east. Then the detectives heard what sounded like a super-speed hummingbird followed instantly by a 'sklurrt' sound. The attacker stiffened and then went limp. The detectives looked at his face and saw a bloody red hole an inch above the space between the attacker's eyebrows as well as a red oozing hole where his left eye had been – then they saw a patch of blood and brains flowing from the top of his neck down his back. Just as the attacker's body started to slump to the walkway, there was a second set of hummingbird zip-sounds and the dead attacker's mouth suddenly was a full of shattered teeth – likewise, now his right eye was just another oozing red hole.

At that moment, they heard a final supersonic hummingbird instantly followed by the sound of shattering plastic and glass. The digital camera Detective Schwachkopf had been holding by its carrier strap suddenly disintegrated into shards of plastic, glass and metal. The memory card inside it was instantly va-porized by a hollow-point bullet. There was a hairstrand-thin line of red at the edge of Schwachkopf's palm where a piece of camera shrapnel had grazed his hand.

Then, as quickly as it had started, the sniper attack was over. As was life of the Randian attacker. It was clear that the rifle shots were intended exclusively for Mr. Black Duster, not the police detectives.

"*At least*," Phil thought to himself, "*there's no longer a need for me to beat that bastard prick into worm food.*"

✳ ✳ ✳

It turned out that the attacker's 'voice' Annie heard during the previous assault appeared to have been broadcast through a distortion microphone by a third party some distance away. The attacker had a tiny implanted high-tech receiver device, discovered by the coroner during the autopsy. The attacker's fingerprints had been burned off with acid a couple of weeks earlier – with the attacker's eyes and teeth virtually disintegrated, there was no immediate way to determine an identity.

Detectives Odieux and Schwachkopf scoured the area where the shots ap-peared to have originated, but could find almost nothing, except a few tracks from slick-surfaced bicycle tires. No brass shell casings. No footprints. No spots where they'd taken a leak or pinched a loaf.

Odieux and Schwachkopf took the assassins' arrogance and hubris to target a prisoner standing between two badge-wearing police detectives as a personal affront to their competence. A "we dare you to find us, dumbasses" challenge of major proportions.

They started with Mr. Black Duster's corpse. Surely his DNA would have a match. Somewhere.

Not so much, according to the FBI Crime Lab in Quantico, Virginia.

Surely their facial recognition database would come up with something.

Perhaps in a parallel universe. Not in this one, though, the FBI said.

If Mr. Black Duster was a fiend of diabolical proportions, something would surely turn up. If they just stuck to it.

✳ ✳ ✳

Fast Forward, Temporarily, to 2023

And something did turn up. Seven years later, just a month before Odieux was to retire.

It happened after a 45-year-old Dusseldorf, Germany tavern manager, Beckstead Suffkopf, was arrested and booked for being slightly over the blood alcohol content limit while driving his business van home at 2:30 a.m. on a normally deserted backwoods road.

The police officer made sure Suffkopf submitted to a routine DNA test. He had to make sure Suffkopf wasn't wanted for some heinous deed elsewhere on the globe, as in, say, breathing while black. Oh, yeah, he wasn't black. Well, you get the picture.

Turned out Suffkopf wasn't a modern-day Jack the Ripper. But his DNA showed an identical match to Mr. Black Duster. Mr. Suffkopf was Mr. Black Duster's identical twin.

As soon as they got word of the match, Odieux and Schwachkopf jetted off to Dusseldorf. They met Suffkopf at his tavern.

Suffkopf told how, 7 ½ years earlier, his brother's wife, Christl, had murdered her 3-year-old son Detlef and killed herself a few weeks after Suffkopf's brother Dieter suddenly abandoned them. She'd left a handwritten suicide note. The deaths had stunned Beckstead – he'd always thought his sister-in-law was as resilient a woman as the world had ever seen. She'd had a thriving practice as an orthodontist. In the wake of those deaths, it appeared that Dieter had fallen off the face of the Earth.

It would be another six months before Odieux and Schwachkopf determined what really happened. They deduced that multiple armed men – visiting Christl's and Dieter's home under the guise of package delivery service employees – had forced their way into the house. They used the threat of violence against Christl and Detlef to compel Dieter to travel to Dutchess County first to kill the dogs and then to repeatedly assault Annie. They made Dieter wear a two-way radio with voice distortion on Dieter's end. They told Dieter that toddler Detlef would be tortured and killed if Dieter communicated a single word during the assaults.

By the time they made those threats to Dieter, though, Christl and Detlef already had been dead for days. Unaware, Dieter, a marginally-successful self-employed foreign currency trader, remained compliant throughout. The phony passport they'd had Dieter use had caused his trail to go – and stay – cold.

'Til his brother's arrest.

The Poughkeepsie detectives felt like they'd stepped in a giant 10-foot-wide 5-mile-deep riper-than-ripe column of compressed-but-juicy dog turds. Only a soul-sucking organization like the CIA or some Wall Street lucre-addicted carcinogens-peddling methane-farting cadre of board chairmen sociopaths would have the balls and the wampum to go thousands of miles to make sure they had a reliable-yet-untraceable chump to do their dirty work.

All the Dutchess dicks wanted was: To. Get. Out.

For their own families' safety. Fools they were not.

* * *

WHOLLY MOLE SHE ISN'T – BUT
WHOLLY MOLE *SHE* IS

Two days after the thwarted kidnapping-slash-murder attempt, Phil asked a shocked Franklin and Holly to meet with the rest of the group. It was time for Holly to come to Jesus, so to speak.

Only Holly, who was convinced she and Jesus already were well-acquainted, wanted to know why there had been apparent deception about the meeting with Penny in New York.

Phil laid it all out. In each instance of an attack, there appeared to be no likely way for the attacker to know where to be at the proper time unless either Franklin or Holly passed that information along somehow. And every last person in the group would bet their lives that it wasn't Franklin.

Franklin was stunned that the group didn't feel they could share their suspicions with him.

"Surely you didn't believe I would betray you somehow," he said, shaking his head. "What were you thinking?"

"We were thinking you wouldn't enjoy being a part of a plan to expose your sweetheart as a liar or a spy," Mitch said.

"Did all of you know about this?" he asked, his face flushed.

"Just about," Idris said.

"Did it ever occur to you to just ask her?" Franklin asked Phil.

"People who betray don't usually want to own up to it."

"I'd have been able to tell if she were holding something back. You should understand that about me by now. Besides, she's not one of the hairy-furry ones."

"People don't always betray out of greed or some other form of selfishness," Bianca said.

"Holly, we want to hear what you have to say, what you believe caused you to be involved this way," Phil said.

"About *time*. You've made up your minds without even giving me a chance," Holly said, near tears. "Why would I do anything to endanger the people closest to the man I love with all my heart?

"What's my motive? Do you think so little of me that you believe I could justify betraying all of you, not to mention Franklin, simply out of my own self-interest somehow?"

"OK, then," Pongo said. "Give us another explanation."

"What are you expecting me to say?"

"Just your own account of what actually happened, Dear," Franklin said. "Please know that I'm giving you the benefit of the doubt at this very moment, OK? I want to believe whatever you have to say."

"We all want to believe you, Holly," Phil said. "It's just that, right now, the wanting is outweighed by the evidence."

"Alright, this is what I can tell you: there was only one person I spoke with about where I was going and what our group was doing before each of those attacks happened – besides Franklin, that is.

"You're trying to tell me that my best friend since first grade would betray all of us. I can't accept that. If she did something horrible, there must have been some reason, some justification."

"You mean Nancy, Nancy Perez?!!" Franklin asked.

"I only have one best friend since first grade – you know, the one who encouraged me to reach out to you when I first got to know you."

"Holly, you need to get Nancy over here – as in _**now**_," Phil said.

* * *

Forty-five minutes later, Holly and Franklin returned from a drive to Nancy's apartment with her BFF, arm in arm as they walked into Phil's basement.

"You'll want to hear what Nancy has to say," Holly said. "This thing wasn't her idea. Go on, Nancy."

Nancy was both bleary-eyed from lack of sleep and red-eyed from more than a day of crying. She'd been inconsolable since the latest attack, but she'd kept it to herself - 'til now.

"I got a call out of the blue from a man who said he was with the FBI. It was about three months ago. He knew that my mother's half-brother from Honduras had sneaked into the country and was living with her.

"He demanded that I meet with him at a restaurant in New York City the next day. I did. He was some white guy, older, in these ugly plaid pants.

Eyebrows went up around the room.

"He said if I didn't co-operate with him, if I didn't get all the information I could about your group's day-to-day travel plans, he would make sure my uncle was deported within 72 hours. And he said he'd personally make sure my mother went to prison under the Patriot Act for harboring my uncle.

"He said if I warned you about what I was being forced to do, that they'd make sure both my brother and I would go to prison too – for obstructing justice.

"He told me if I co-operated, they'd give me $1,000 a week and pay off all of my mother's medical debt from her back and foot surgeries last year – but he said the money would be delivered by hand in cash.

"He promised the deliveries would be on my front doorstep by the time I left for work every Monday morning. They were.

"He promised no one would be hurt. When a month passed and no one had been hurt by then, I believed him. After Annie was attacked that first time, he told me it was a rogue operative who'd screwed up – he said the person responsible would be punished. I know now that he was lying.

"Can any of you say for sure you wouldn't have done the same thing I did under the same circumstances?

"Please don't judge me if you haven't been threatened the way I was."

"So," Holly said to the group, "things aren't always so black and white, are they?"

"We're so sorry, Holly," Phil said. "And, Percy, please accept our apology too, but please understand we didn't want you to be in the middle of this mess.

"The real villains here are the people 'behind the curtain' pulling the strings. People whose primary purpose is to stop what we're trying to do. People trying to preserve the artificial power of corporations at everyone else's expense."

"Can you forgive us, dear?" Annie asked Holly.

"If you can forgive Nancy, then I can forgive you."

"I don't think that will be a problem, Holly," Tom said. "What happens from this point forward is what matters most."

"Nancy, what you need to understand now," Franklin/Percy said, "is this Mr. Plaid Pants man probably isn't going to be having anyone deported or jailed. He was using information his people gathered on their own.

"Now that his people have been implicated in a murder – and not just a murder, but a conspiracy to murder to keep their operative from connecting himself to them – he's radioactive to any old friends he may have in Homeland Security.

"In other words – you, your mother, your brother and your uncle all probably are safe."

"Are you sure **you** are safe??" Nancy asked. "You look like death warmed over!"

"You don't need to worry about me," Franklin/Percy said. "I'll be fine soon."

"We have to know, though, Nancy," Pongo interjected, "I mean **HAVE TO KNOW** that if someone else tries to threaten you again, you'll come to us first. Can we rely on you for that?"

"I'd sooner go to prison than do anything again that could threaten what you're doing," Nancy said.

"I think this young lady has been through enough for one week," Phil said. "Holly, would you please take Nancy home and make sure she's comfortable for the evening?"

"Absolutely. I'll be back in an hour or so."

* * *

AND THE PROJECT BEGINS

Once she returned, the planning for the project to stabilize Franklin's age and health began in earnest.

The first step was picking a date: they wanted a date which both would be hard for Hillary's campaign to decline and would be a fit for Penny's boss, megabillionaire H. Fenster Rupphauser, Whittmyer Industries chairman and C.E.O., who kept a fairly full calendar out of his New York City headquarters.

As it turned out, April 25, about four weeks away, would work beautifully: it was the day before four northeastern Presidential primaries, including in nearby

Pennsylvania. And it had been on Fenster's (Fennie, as Penny called him) short list of dates for one-on-one interviews of candidates seeking the blessings of his endorsements to augment both their publicity machines and their financial juggernauts.

Fennie, like his counterpart in the opposite corner of the country in Nevada, Sheldon Adelson (whose personal net worth was $30 billion), reveled in the adulation the politicians showered on him, each hoping to be the most-favored political star in Fennie's personal constellation. His popularity among major Republican candidates was so legendary, they had all secretly agreed amongst themselves never to make mention of Fennie's notoriously bad breath – one described it as "not unlike two-day-old summertime Maine Turnpike roadkill, which probably is an inexcusable insult to turnpike roadkill."

During the previous Presidential election cycle, he'd been visited by every single Presidential candidate except President Obama and Herman Cain (it turned out later that Cain missed his appointment with Rupphauser because he'd given his taxi driver an address on Long Island instead of in Manhattan). Fennie having made his billions through his inherited family company selling ammunition and components for large-caliber machine guns to the Pentagon and Pentagon-equivalents around the world, President Obama felt sucking up to him for money slightly tainted by blood would be unseemly.

Fennie was particularly excited about this go-round simply because he anticipated – and properly so – that everyone from Hillary to Jeb Bush (that *other* dynasty's golden child) would be at his feet to pucker up for a chance to slobber on his backside. The best puckerer probably would get the best check with the most zeroes.

(*Bizarre Fennie Fact #19: his personal checks were printed on 'My Little Pony' paper stock. Penny figured it was because of the birthday checks he sent to his granddaughters; it actually was because Fennie was a latent transsexual who secretly despised how he'd earned his billions. He just didn't despise machine guns **enough** to actually stop helping the grim reaper as long as the financial sustenance for those weapons also fed his lavish lifestyle. Not a big believer in karma, he was.*)

So, Penny had little trouble getting Fennie to sign off on the schedule for April 25: he'd begin seeing the GOP's great white hopes[*] for two-hour sessions at 8 a.m. He scheduled Hillary's two hours for 7 p.m., followed by at least an hour for debriefing.

U.S. Sen. Bernie Sanders, would appear at 9 p.m. and the final invitee, ex-Gov. Martin O'Malley (D-MD) would appear at 11 p.m. And, of course, just to give themselves breathing room, Penny would make it clear to everyone that the "one-on-one" sessions (which actually featured both Fennie and Penny with each

---

[*] It was assumed Bobby Jindal would be forced to drop out long before April 25 simply due to his numbskulledness – he was determined to make opposition to gay marriage the cornerstone of his campaign even if he was the last person outside of Russia to accept that it could be the law of the land anywhere. Likewise, Rick Perry and Scott Walker both were **in**cluded, despite both of them dropping out in September 2015, simply because of their Palinesque Vice Presidential prospects.

candidate) and debriefings both could run long, as in waaaay long. They also emphasized in advance that not all Republican candidates would be invited – just those whom Fennie felt were the least nuts. Likewise, they ruled out inviting ex-Republican-turned-Democrat Lincoln Chafee, former Rhode Island governor, mainly because he was so dumb as to make converting to the metric system a major plank of his campaign platform. And they ruled out former U.S. Sen. Jim Webb simply because they were tired of having to deal with ex-Republicans-turned-Democrats, especially those with no chance in hell of winning. It turned out to be moot anyway, because both decided to drop out of the race and neither had any Vice Presidential prospects.

One of the more worrisome requirements Penny and Fennie laid down for the candidates – at Penny's insistence – was that they submit to transportation **to and from** Whittmyer Industries' headquarters in Whittmyer Industries-provided limousines. Penny explained to the candidates' campaign managers that there was no room for negotiations on that issue because they viewed it as a security matter. In fact, however, it was a crucial requirement to pulling off Cherisse's plan. Much to Penny's relief, every single invited candidate's campaign manager agreed to that requirement, although a couple of them groused about there being no guarantee when the candidates would be returned to their respective hotels.

Penny told each of the campaign managers to plan for the worst: that they might all be returned late in the day.

Penny was fairly sure she could convince Fennie to take a principled uncompromising stand about keeping Secret Service agents out of his one-on-one sessions *as well as* the "debriefing" sessions with the other Poughkeepsians (which actually would be recovery periods). Likewise, she was confident she could convince Fennie to stand up to the Secret Service on the issue of magnetometers.

To require the Park Avenue patrons of the five-star restaurant on the top floor of his corporate headquarters-slash-hotel building (not to mention the candidates' hangers-on) to go through a magnetometer would simply be too gauche for words. Or so Penny thought she could convince Fennie to insist. And she was correct. After all, you couldn't have a meet-the-emperor gathering without also filling the bellies of the supplicants' media entourages full of the finest cuisine while their candidates-slash-meal tickets were subjected by Fennie to a sort of mental colonoscopy.

She'd read enough about the Secret Service to know that they would agree to pat-downs of suspicious characters in place of magnetometers screenings for all attendees - *if* she and Fennie were sufficiently adamant.

Once again, she was correct.

Then came the logistics of preparing the facilities which would be needed by Cherisse, Annie, Bianca and Sam to make the entire plan succeed. It was time to convene all 18 of the Poughkeepsians so their four medical professionals could once again brainstorm their way through those preparations.

* * *

Resolving Logistics

On April 2, 2016, the group settled in for what they figured would be a day-long planning session in Phil's basement.

Maybe the most problematic detail was figuring out how to have the necessary portable neuro ventriculogram equipment on-hand without it being seized and removed in advance by the Secret Service. It was common knowledge that the Secret Service usually does a top-to-bottom inspection of the building where an event is being held on the day before the event and/or the day of the event before it starts, including screenings of all facility employees and dishes being served to protectees.

The problem: how to keep agents from going bat-shit crazy if – more like *when* – they saw the portable radiological equipment, cranial drills and stereotactic cranial frames required for biopsy procedures.

"Would it be smart to try and hide the equipment?" Cherisse asked.

"I doubt it," Sam said. "They have all kinds of detectors, so I think it's likely they'd find the radiological equipment no matter how well it was hidden."

"What if we hide it in plain sight?" Bianca asked.

"Huh?" Annie said. "I don't follow."

"Every large facility has first aid kits, usually lots of them scattered around throughout a building," Bianca said. "Why couldn't we just leave all this equipment out in the open in a large cabinet labeled '*First Aid*' and give them some bullshit explanation that it's something Fennie wanted to have available just in case one of his billionaire-buddy guests had an aneurysm or something? And we could have all the local anesthetic drugs and radiological contrast dyes in there, too, as well as a nitrous oxide dispenser to keep the drillee as unpanicked as possible.

"I know the laughing gas isn't really necessary for the biopsies, what with no nerve endings being in brain tissue, but I thought it could help distract the 'patients' enough to keep them from completely realizing exactly what it is we're doing."

"This pretty young thing brought her thinking cap today," Cherisse said. "I doubt if any of those Secret Service horndogs has much of a medical background. That sounds like a plan, Bianca.

"Anyway, it's not like we've got a lot of options here. If we can't do a ventriculogram, we can't be sure where we're mining for that lost ark of amygdala and basal ganglia gold. It would be just hit and miss.

"I'm determined to keep that promise of no permanent harm. Unless you count a one-centimeter shaved circle on the crown of the head with a micro drill

621

bit opening for the micro needle biopsy. Just for your information, Franklin, neurosurgeons don't."

"What about if one of the candidates has an allergic reaction to the contrast dye infusion?" Sam asked. "Do we really want to risk one or more of them going into severe anaphylactic shock and asphyxiation?"

"That's why God gave us scalpels to incise the windpipe," Cherisse said sarcastically. "Anyway, we're going to use the least-risky contrast dye possible. Besides, as you already know, not all anaphylaxis becomes critical. I'm convinced it's a reasonable risk.

"Besides, we'll have Epi-Pens on hand for each candidate just in case. A little epinephrine would be just what the doctor ordered if their faces start to look like one of those rubber stress squeeze toys – you know, the ones with the cheeks and eyes that bulge out when you squeeze."

"Well, that's nice to know, since I intend to be in there assisting," Franklin said. "Many hands, light work, y'know."

"That's not going to happen, Sir," Phil said. "As I recall, there are issues for you when someone's cranial matter is open to the air."

"We don't know that for sure," Franklin said. "Things may have changed since our visit to Idaho. I think it would be an excellent opportunity for this wrinkly old reprobate you see before you to prove his self-restraint."

"It sounds to me like your taste buds might be doing your thinking for you," Phil speculated. "I know this much: we're going to be under a passel of pressures that day. We want to minimize risks, not tempt fate. I think I probably speak for everyone here when I say we need to try to keep you and the candidates' biopsy procedures as insulated from each other as Hillary and her husband's latest hottie bimbo."

He did, in fact, speak for everyone else – about that, at least.

"Well, if that's the case, then I'm sure no one will be offended if I don't volunteer as a skull for Cherisse and the rest of you to practice on," Franklin joked. "I've already had enough people want to pick _my_ brain in two lifetimes."

"No need to worry about that," Cherisse chuckled. "I must've done a baker's dozen of those cranial biopsy procedures when I went through my neurosurgery rotation."

"How long ago was that, Cherisse?" Sam asked.

"Uh, eh, er, uh – twenty-two years ago."

"Here's the deal, Cherisse – and you two too, Annie and Bianca – I'm going to pull some strings at my old alma mater's teaching hospital and arrange for all of us to have some alone time with a handful of their cadavers this weekend. I know a guy who owes me one big time. We need to have some practice time so we're all confident with what we're doing.

"We can't have any self-inflicted fuck-ups here. There's already plenty of risks for unforeseen shit, so, as Phil was saying, we need to minimize what risks we **can** control."

"So, exactly **_how_** are we going to get each of the candidates to get through this process without kicking and screaming?" Franklin asked.

"Here's what I've got planned," Penny started. "I'm going to convince Fennie the C.I.A. recently discovered that mainland Chinese Communists have surreptitiously planted tracking and listening devices into the brains of every Presidential and Vice Presidential candidate.

"That part will be easy – Fennie's watched "The Manchurian Candidate" so many times, he practically knows the dialog by heart. He's the commie-hater's commie-hater.

"I'll rehearse with him exactly how to present it to each candidate. He'll simply tell them there's a new Homeland Security-endorsed procedure that involves a special cranial exam to ensure no candidate he invests in has a terminal brain illness or is about to have an aneurysm or stroke.

"He'll explain calmly that the total procedure, once his 'one-on-one' session is done, takes about three hours, maybe four, including recovery time and involves no general anesthesia, just laughing gas and a localized painkiller. We're confident that, when each candidate realizes how much campaign cash is at stake, they'll be itching to take the nitrous oxide. Fennie can even offer soft-core porn for the guys to watch while they're undergoing the neuro ventriculogram."

"But what if Hillary balks?"

"We have a Plan B, but we don't want to use it and I don't even want to talk about it," Cherisse said. "Please just accept my assurance that Ms. Rodham Clinton won't be leaving without us getting a look under that fully-cheeked hood. And, if we find any good fishing worms in there, Pongo, we'll save 'em for you for your next trip to the lake.

"Really, don't worry, Franklin – if Hillary's half as furry-conscience-challenged as you described, she'll be seeing dollar signs from the time she sits down in front of Fennie 'til our limo driver Mr. Perspicace spirits her away."

"What if the Secret Service dudes find out what we're doing before we finish with Hillary?" Pongo asked.

"We'll be requiring each person participating to memorize a primary and secondary escape route out of the Whittmyer Building to make it to Penn Station for an Amtrak train to Poughkeepsie," Sam explained. "We'll have a pre-arranged coded emergency signal for everyone to bail and book it double-time out of town – everyone will be carrying a walkie-talkie with a five-mile range tuned to the same channel. We can assume the agents will be monitoring all civilian band channels, so we'll **only** communicate in code."

"And how will we be able to evade identification when they screen the backgrounds of every employee and every invited participant during the 48 hours before the event?" Franklin asked.

"I've got that taken care of," Penny said. "Every one of you will have employee identification cards showing names, titles and hire dates of our restaurant employees whom we're giving the day off that day. The cards will have your pictures on them. I've already pre-screened each of those employees to make sure none of them has any arrests for violent crimes in the past. We wouldn't want the Homeland Security agents to be sending you home in a cab that day."

"But all of our faces have been plastered all over You Tube from all of the different rallies we've held," Phil said. "Exactly how do you keep the Secret Service agents – not to mention their facial recognition technology – from realizing we're not actually Whittmyer Industries employees?? I know it's probably not a problem for Franklin with him looking about 75 now, but what about the rest of us?"

"Great point," Cherisse said. "You won't believe this: there's a big advantage to Penny having access to the resources of a massive corporation. Turns out Fennie's enterprise actually has a staff make-up artist-slash-costume designer. Her name's Shyla Coiffeur. She occasionally moonlights as a make-up specialist on Martin Scorsese movies. She's on-call 365 days a year to help prep Fennie to look younger than his 77 years and to get him ready for appearances on TV and at costume parties and various and sundry galas.

"She's already lined up to apply lots of spirit gum and rubber facial augmentation for each of you early in the morning on April 25th. Right, Penny?"

"You got it – you'll each be expected at Shyla's private uptown Manhattan office by 5 a.m. on the 25th. She'll be there with three of her assistants. They should be done with all of you by 7 a.m., 7:15 a.m. at the latest, depending on how long it takes for your employee photo ID's to be generated there. We've told Shyla all of you are part of a surprise party for Fennie and his grandkids later in the day. Penny will have a technician with an ID card camera and card printer at Shyla's office – you'll each get your cards before you leave for the Whittmyer Building.

"If you have preferences about how you want to be disguised, you need to E-Mail me by tomorrow. I'll cut and paste all of your preferences onto a generic Microsoft Word document, using your ersatz Whittmyer Industries employee names, and have it hand-delivered to Shyla on the 23rd. Obviously, it'll be important for you to remember your names at all times while you're with the make-up staff _and_ while you're at Whittmyer headquarters. You can pick up the info on your employee identities from me before you leave today."

"So, let's say everything comes off without a hitch and we've got all these amygdala and basal ganglia biopsy tissues from each of the candidates," Orvis O'Leary said. "What do we do with them? Does Franklin just gulp them all down at once, or does he take some each day? What happens when we run out of the stuff?"

"We'll keep each tissue sample from each 'contributor' separate and labelled showing whom each one came from," Cherisse explained. "There will be at least two samples from each candidate. Franklin will be consuming one sample at a time daily over the following week. We'll be monitoring to see how each one affects him to see if there are any differences between the individual contributors' tissues.

"While we're monitoring that on an ongoing basis to see what the best level of consumption is to stabilize Franklin's age at, say, no more than 35 years old, we'll be mixing embryonic stem cells with each of the other samples to try to grow full-size amygdalae and basal ganglia which we can preserve and use, potentially perpetually, to maintain Franklin's health and normal aging process."

"Jesus, though, Cherisse," Harry said. "What about all the Whittmyer security cameras? The Secret Service will be hooking into those and monitoring everything you guys do. Do you REALLY think they're going to let you get away with sucking brain matter – even tiny amounts – out of a bunch of candidates' heads while they watch you on closed circuit TV?"

"I'm glad you brought that up, Harry," she said. "Because *YOU* are the one we're going to rely on to cover us on that.

"Ever see Oceans Eleven? The Clooney version, not the Sinatra one."

"Um, yeah – it came out when I was, like, 14, I think."

"Do you remember how they dealt with video monitoring issues?"

"Shit, all I remember about being 14 was getting a hard-on every time my English teacher with the big boobs put her hand on my shoulder."

"I remember that movie," Bianca said.

"Well, of course you do – you didn't have an erection problem," Harry said.

"Yeah, uh, anyway, they wired a parallel closed circuit system and set it up to kick in with a continuous loop of a room which looked identical to the one they were breaking into," Bianca continued.

"Exactly," Cherisse said. "But, instead of us having to build an elaborate duplicate of a huge sub-basement vault the way the heisters did in the movie, all we have to do is go into the empty small banquet room where the biopsy procedures will be done and record video of it empty anytime between now and April 25th. Penny will make sure we have access when the time comes."

"So, you expect me to sneak through air conditioning ducts and shit and hook up a parallel video circuit that'll overcome the Secret Service's system without them noticing," Harry said, his brow slightly damp.

"We expect it only because we know your level of expertise," Pongo said. "You got straight A's in that stuff in college. You *know* your shit, so don't give us this '*I've got performance anxiety*' shtick, OK?"

"OK. I just didn't want to sound cocky. I can do this.

"B'sides, what's the worst that can happen? Twenty years in Federal Prison? I hear they have pretty good cable TV and that soap on a rope stuff that's harder to drop in the shower."

"Shit, you won't have to drop your soap to get corn-holed," Pongo joked. "You're so pretty you'll be a magnet for every guy with a foot-long pussy plunger – they'll be able to rock your world from the opposite side of the shower room."

"Ha.   Ha.   Ha.

"But seeeriously, folks, what about _**Penny**_? Once we get this thing finished, even if my video loop works, every Federale under every rock is going to realize the 'medical services' technicians she supposedly hired to perform Fennie's candidate brain exams were bogus.

"Out of everyone involved here, _**SHE**_ is the only one who's almost guaranteed to end up in Federal prison. Maybe you too, Mitch, since they'll find it tough to believe her husband didn't know what was happening.

"Are we all really willing for her to be thrown under the bus?"

"Not to worry, Harry," Penny said. "You're going to cover us there too. You're going to do a phone system hack on Mr. Rupphauser's phones in this building, specifically the lines into his executive offices, including my office.

"You'll do the hack in such a way that it's traceable only back to some pay phone booth someplace. If you have to actually do the hack from a booth, you'll want to make sure it's not viewable from any nearby security cameras – or you'll need to wear a disguise. I can have Shyla help you with that if need be.

"Your hack will set up our phone system so that any one calling out on our lines here to the real phone number for Manhattan Diagnostic Radiology (MDR) actually ends up connecting with a bogus phone line. You can just make the bogus phone line a number for some enterprise that's recently gone out of business and had its phone service disconnected.

"That way, when I tell the Secret Service later that I was sure the staff conducting the brain exams – and, supposedly unknown to me, the biopsies – were from MDR, I can say that believably and credibly.

"I should come out of this smelling like a rose. And Fennie will go ballistic if they try to accuse me of anything. He's always liked me – a **lot**."

"You're pretty wily, Penny," Phil said. "Have you always known this about her, Mitch?"

"Why do you think I carry a gun most of the time?"

✻ ✻ ✻

How to Get to Whittmyer?
Practice, Practice, Practice

The following weekend's practice cranial biopsy procedures in the Columbia University cadaver lab were not particularly encouraging – at least in the beginning.

The portable neuro ventriculogram device Sam purchased from a medical supplies distributor worked fairly well (it had been designed for use at combat field hospitals), except for one thing: the cadavers didn't have any blood pressure, of course, so there was no way for the contrast dye to circulate through the brain. The Poughkeepsians simply had to make educated guesses as to where to aim the biopsy micro needle. At first, they only hit paydirt one in every five tries. By the end of the evening, though, they were hitting the amygdala and/or basal ganglia on at least every other try.

"When we do this for real," Cherisse said, "it pretty much needs to be a couple of shots and done. Three tries at the very most. The last thing we need is for one or more of our Presidential candidates to come in articulate and leave sounding like a drunk Gomer Pyle.

"I mean, it'd be different if we were preparing them for the Monty Python '*Upper Class Twit of the Year*' sketch where mental defectives have to make their way through an obstacle course."

"Now that you mention that, there *are* worse things that could happen than a little candidate brain damage," Sam said. "I think it'd be great to watch Twit Hillary versus Twit Cruz at the two-inch 'high' hurdle.

"In case you couldn't tell, I am *just **kidding***, Annie and Bianca – you don't need to call the AMA – not yet, anyway."

* * *

SELECTING THE LUCKY DISTINGUISHED GUESTS

As the final 10 days before the April 25th meet-the-Fenster parade of would-be Presidents approached, the Poughkeepsians met at Phil's to decide which of the five Republican hopefuls to invite.

Even though his chances for the Republican nomination (early poll surges notwithstanding) were realistically somewhere between those of Pee Wee Herman and of the turd your neighbor's dog occasionally dumps in your front yard, all the Poughkeepsians voted in favor of Penny and Fennie inviting Donald Trump.

If ever there were a more conscience-challenged hyper capitalist who compulsively wanted to win _only_ the Presidency, they had no idea who that could be. They all imagined that, in Franklin's eyes, Trumpy would have the most wookie-furry face, neck and body of any human on the planet.

When it came to the remaining four they were fairly evenly divided over the top two: former Gov. Rick Perry (R-TX) and former Gov. Jeb Bush (R-FL). So Texas' mental midget executioner and George Herbert Walker Bush's Dynasty Boy #2 were locks.

The final two had to be chosen in a multi-step process because none of the possibilities got more than two votes from the Poughkeepsians.

Ex-Arkansas Gov. Huckabee was weeded out first because, many years earlier, he actually made a populist remark against corporations (he made a few income inequality references in his announcement speech almost a year earlier which were quickly offset by his fixation on preventing gay marriages).

Sen. Graham, Gov. Kasich and ex-Gov. Pataki were weeded out next on the grounds that their charisma already appeared to have been surgically removed.

Carly Fiorina was eliminated next, reluctantly. Even though her corporate leadership was abysmally craven and embarrassing (as droves of folks who purchased an HP computer during her tenure plus the 30,000 people she laid off after driving the company into the ground could attest) - which was a *positive* for the Poughkeepsians' selection criteria – she had past health issues which caused them to worry about the physical quality of her noodle. Since this was mainly about preserving Franklin's life, sub-par reptilian brain parts would be as useless as a dictionary on Dan Quayle's desk.

Ben Carson was the final Fennie Fan to be cut. On the grounds that his hyper-Randian mind was just too darned bizarre, culturally schizoid (somewhat sympathetic to African-Americans' struggles, though despising the progressive income taxes which fund safety net programs benefitting lower-income taxpayers – and completely dismissive toward gays, claiming they "choose" to be homosexual), somewhat simplistic (advocating success through television avoidance and scholastic performance) and frequently self-contradicting.

Franklin said Carson's vindictiveness toward homosexuals reminded him of the contempt shown by William C. Bullitt, Jr., his Ambassador to France, and Cordell Hull, his Secretary of State, toward Hull's Undersecretary Sumner Welles once they found out about an attempted homosexual liaison by Welles in 1940. Franklin said he long suspected Bullitt bribed railroad porters into entrapping Welles, a married man, into suggesting a tryst. Bullitt and Hull gossiped about Welles to newspaper columnists so much that the stress led to Welles having a heart attack, forcing Franklin to reluctantly accept Welles' resignation in September 1943.*

Franklin said he no longer wished Bullitt would "burn in hell" for all eternity: "Probably a week or two would do."

That left noted homophobe former U.S. Sen. Rick "Keep the Moms at Home & Take Away Their Contraception" Santorum and Gov. Scott "I Despise Organized Labor & the Middle Class" Walker.

Phil kept saying, *repeatedly*, that he wanted to vote a half-dozen times for Herman Cain. The others finally had to ask him politely to shut up, reminding him that the competition was only open to greed-consumed Republicans who actually expressed an interested in running during the current cycle.

Appropriately chastened, Phil stopped his own personal Cain mutiny long enough to announce that Sen. Sanders, not so shockingly, had declined Fennie's invitation, as had ex-Gov. O'Malley. As though the only progressives in the race

---

* *"Traitor to His Class – The Privileged Life and Radical Presidency of Franklin Delano Roosevelt,"* H. W. Brands, 2008, Doubleday

(well, maybe it's a stretch to include O'Malley as a true progressive, what with his penchant for accepting campaign donations from wealthy developers) would want to be associated with munitions-tainted money.

* * *

DRESS REHEARSAL

On April 23, 2016, the Saturday before the big day in New York City, the Poughkeepsians met at Phil's home for their final checklist run-through and rehearsal.

Penny had limousine drivers confirmed for each candidate's pick-up time and hotel location on the coming Monday. The drivers each were made aware that the candidate they were picking up probably would be ready to be returned no sooner than three hours after being dropped off at Whittmyer Industries and possibly as late as seven or eight hours later. They were expected to be ready to pick up their candidate at a moment's notice, so there would be no driving assignments for other clients during that entire day.

Penny made sure the driver for Hillary – Willem Perspicace, 28 - was a hard-core Elizabeth Warren supporter. She encouraged him to pester Hillary to formally support a hydraulic fracturing ban and prosecutions of Wall Street executives implicated in the 2008 meltdown. And to try to shame her over the huge sums contributed to the Clinton Foundation by foreign interests while she was Secretary of State, not to mention her acceptance of huge corporate speaking fees she kept for the family foundation. Penny promised Willem there would be no adverse employment consequences as long as he didn't use profane or demeaning language.

She also made sure Willem's limo would be equipped with an audio-video camera aimed at the occupant of the rear bench seat.

In addition, she'd generated an E-Mail to Whittmyer headquarters staff to alert them to all the protocols for the candidates' visits the coming Monday. She explained in the E-Mail that the HQ staff might see some unusual faces around the building who appeared to be new staff. She assured them that it would be nothing out of the ordinary for such a visit and encouraged staff to assume such new faces simply were undercover Homeland Security agents.

She complimented the group's choices on disguises, mainly the selection of wigs, alternative hair coloring and fake facial hair.

"Can't wait to see you in a white Afro wig, Franklin," she said. "You may want to give that a try on an ongoing basis if you like what it does for you."

"Pongo was watching some old ESPN archival footage the other night and I saw some footage of Julius Erving," Franklin said. "Thought I'd give it a try - for a day, at least."

Penny had even found a large Korean War-era wheeled metal cabinet at a military surplus store with a pre-painted Red Cross logo on the front doors which fit their needs for the neuro ventriculogram equipment perfectly. It even had a port with AC electrical outlets with a 50-foot spool of 8-gauge shielded copper electrical extension cord attached to the back of its rear panel. She arranged for Sam to buy it incognito.

Sam found three hospital-quality examination chairs on sale at a medical supplies chain outlet store, a different store from the one he used to buy the radiological equipment. They looked similar to dentists' examination chairs, except they had attachments which allowed the patient to be restrained so as to avoid movement during a surgical procedure. The group would be rotating the chairs in and out of the otherwise-empty banquet room where Cherisse and Sam would be performing the actual biopsy procedures. There would always be one chair inside the room where the 'one-on-one' sessions between the candidate, Fennie and Penny would be taking place.

If the Secret Service accidentally saw any of the chairs, Penny had instructed staff to explain that they were needed for Fennie's back relief in case he had back spasms during the day. The restraints were necessary, they would explain, to eliminate the possibility that Fennie would accidentally fall off the chair while having a spasm. A complete fabrication, but it seemed plausible, which was all that mattered.

The Poughkeepsians all appeared to have their two emergency escape routes memorized. Penny already had reserved seats for all of them on the 10:45 p.m. Penn Station Amtrak train to Poughkeepsie.

The assignments for the 25th included the four medical professionals – Cherisse, Sam, Annie and Bianca – on the biopsy procedures, with Holly, Pongo and Phil as their assistants; Penny would be supervising Fennie's questioning of each candidate; the O'Learys would be escorting the candidates from the lobby and ante-room into the one-on-one meeting area. Tom would be Fennie's 'official' designated representative in charge of finessing the Secret Service, as needed. Harry would be monitoring the security camera video feeds, making sure the loop feed of the empty banquet room was linked to the Secret Service monitors just before the first candidate was taken into that room for the first biopsy procedure. Mitch and Idris would be responsible for making sure each candidate was escorted and placed with the correct limo driver when it was time for each candidate's ride back to her or his hotel. Marcia would be in charge of making sure no unauthorized persons – especially Homeland Security types – entered the small banquet room where the biopsies were being performed.

But Franklin: what to do with him? What would give him significant responsibilities without risking him being too close to open-to-the-air brain matter?

Of course, Cherisse thought: diversion. The man who signed off on Patton's 'ghost army' prior to the World War II D-Day invasion would be perfect to try and divert the Homeland Security staff, especially Secret Service agents, away from the parts of the Whittmyer Building where the 'one-on-one' sessions and biopsy procedures were being done.

And no one would expect an avuncular 80-ish man of anything other than sincere wishes to do his patriotic duty.

If anything went wrong, Penny and Marcia would be responsible to join Tom's efforts in finessing the lead Secret Service and Homeland Security agents. Penny would have the authority at any time to issue the radio command to abandon ship, so to speak.

Barring an Amtrak derailment or a candidate having a heart attack during her or his biopsy procedure, it appeared the Poughkeepsians had minimized all of the foreseeable risks.

Foreseeable was the key word.

Everyone at the run-through session appeared to be upbeat, including – not unexpectedly - Franklin, even though he now appeared to be *at least* 80 years old. He could feel near misses from the Grim Reaper's scythe swinging at his backside.

"*You just have to make it through the **next two days**,*" he kept reminding himself.

✳ ✳ ✳

Caper's Eve Relaxation

On Sunday April 24th, the day before the Big Day, Holly decided to spend the day with Franklin in their Albany apartment. That morning, when she saw his face – now looking, say, 83 years old – she couldn't hide her near-terror.

"What happens to us if this thing tomorrow doesn't work?" she asked, her eyes moist. "Do I have to wonder every time I come to see you if you'll be some kind of mummified corpse when I open your door?"

"You might.

"I can't control how this thing, whatever it is, how it progresses with me. For all I know, I could go to sleep tonight and never wake up again, or I might have some kind of remission and wake up tomorrow appearing 9 years old.

"If that's more than you can cope with, I'll understand if you just want to move on and leave me behind. You deserve some stability and predictability in your young life, Darling, not some knave who lives to pleasure you only to dry up and blow away in the wind like an old maple leaf with the color sucked out of it."

"I didn't come this far with you just to leave you behind, Honey. We're going to get through this thing and it's going to work. I just **know** it.

"And, who knows, it might even be what it takes for the USA-SBR to be successful. Maybe this will be the first step toward you becoming that man who saves this effed-up country again from the chaos of that arthritic 'invisible hand.' It could happen."

"My dearest Holly, do you think we could forego talk of saving the country today? There's nothing I'd like more on this beautiful Sunday than to spend the entire day walking, talking and making love with my beautiful sweetheart. To the degree that an old man can."

"I think we can work that out," she said, slowly unzipping Franklin's denim shorts and reaching inside.

She found her one-eyed target, who was thrilled, nay, even standing at attention to greet her. No chronic dry eye there.

* * *

On Goes the Show

4/25/16: B-Day (as in "B" is for biopsies)

The entire group met at Phil's house at 3 a.m. the next morning for a caravan drive into Manhattan to Ms. Coiffeur's office for the make-up and disguise work. (There was no Amtrak train leaving that early from Poughkeepsie.) Fortunately, there was a large parking garage next door to Shyla's office. They planned to retrieve the cars two to three days later – they'd already concluded the safest, least risky way to get out of Manhattan and back to Poughkeepsie late that evening would be the last Amtrak train of the night out of Penn Station.

Their drive was fairly routine – not counting Phil almost welcoming a full grown doe onto his windshield near Fishkill and everyone in Pongo's car having to dig change out of their pockets and purses at the last moment approaching the Triborough Bridge on their way into Manhattan.

They found Shyla and her staff to be skilled, patient and saucy. Thanks to Penny's E-Mail with the Poughkeepsians' disguise preferences – including photo attachments showing the face of each group member with a foot-long ruler held alongside for perspective – their pre-shaped full and partial latex masks were ready for fitting and fine-tuning as soon as they arrived.

By the time they were ready to leave, their new looks included:

- Phil and Pongo Podrowski: vague resemblances to Albert Einstein and Nikola Tesla.
- Orvis and Karin O'Leary: looking sort of like an aged Walter White and his not-so-aged wife Skyler. Karin simply rocked her new long blond locks.
- Tom and Annie Podrowski: spitting image of an advanced-age Brad Pitt and Angelina Jolie. The Angelina look was a real stretch for Annie, though. She just didn't have the smackers for it.
- Idris M'Benga: his choice of an African-American version of the Pee Wee Herman look was inspired, especially with the tight gray suit and red bow

tie he brought along. ("You have to promise **not** to go around all day saying, '*I know you are, but what am I?*' to people," Pongo insisted to Idris' shit-eating grin.)

- Harry Peterson: a *Simpsons* fan he, his choice was compulsive inventor Professor Frink. As with Idris, Pongo reminded Harry they wouldn't tolerate him repeatedly saying the phrase, "*For crying out glaving*" over and over in a Hank Azaria-Jerry Lewis "*Nutty Professor*" voice.

- Mel and Cherisse Peterson: they chose to be one-percenter Pat "Global Warming Alarmists=Unpatriotic Racists" Sajak and Vanna White doppelgangers – although Cherisse opted for a white lab coat instead of the *de rigueur* floor length evening gown usually sported by Vanna.

- Holly Van Arsdale and Percy "Scruples" Van Mullder aka Our 32nd President: Holly elected to go with the Barbara Streisand resemblance – although she said it was difficult to inhale through her prosthetic schnoz. She also complained that the sheer weight of it was giving her a sinus headache – but a couple of good ol' fashioned generic aspirin helped with that. Franklin had already decided on going as an aged white version of a bell-bottomed Julius Erving. The white Afro wig was over the top, but it didn't look bad as long as you focused on the entire man and not just from the head up.

- Heather Griffin and stepdad Mitch Duarte: she chose a resemblance to suffragette and reproductive rights pioneer Margaret Sanger; Mitch decided to go with an Edward James Olmos look. It was a natural for his chiseled good looks.

- Bianca and father Sam Swanson: Bianca was a huge fan of Reba McEntire's survivalist look in "*Tremors*," so she went with that, sans the handheld artillery; Sam went for the Dr. McDreamy appearance – a nice fit for him.

- Marcia Dirkenstack: she decided to emulate the Lynda Carter look from Carter's Wonder Woman years. Idris would spend much of that day trying to imagine her in the Wonder Woman costume and involuntarily giving himself repeated crotch turgidity. Not a plan for comfort when sporting a tight Pee Wee Herman suit.

The first arriving candidate, the Walking Comb-over otherwise known as Donnie Trump, entered Fennie's inner sanctum with an air of – don't be shocked – haughtiness and self-congratulation, having just deftly dodged a cadre of Mexican-American protestors still outraged over Trump characterizing Mexican immigrants as rapists. Trump – known by 'birth name' Fuckface von Clownstick to Jon Stewart fans – repeated three times to Fennie that he had more money than Fennie's entire family and that he didn't need Fennie's money. He was only there to win Fennie's undying devotion and admiration as a fellow capitalist, he said.

Fennie slathered on the Rupphauser charm. By the time Fuckface and Fennie were done, an obstetrician would've been hard-pressed not to find a new tiny heartbeat in Trump's uterus – or, lacking a uterus, perhaps somewhere in the sheltered smooth-plain ecosystem atop his noggin.

As they shook hands, Fennie motioned Fuckface over to Marcia, who was standing at the entrance to the small banquet room where *los neurologos y medicos Poughkeepsios* were waiting to look into his mind.

As the prospect of dollar signs wafted through his huge head, Fuckface allowed himself to be strapped into the examination chair and submitted to the infusion of contrast dye agent by Bianca. No sign of problems so far.

Cherisse sprayed some sort of antiseptic solution up Fuckface's schnoz. ("*Never saw that as part of this procedure,*" Sam thought to himself.) But Cherisse knew what she was doing.

Once a few minutes passed, they placed Fuckface's head into the stereotactic frame, gave him plenty of nitrous oxide to breathe and started up the neuro ventriculogram device.

Within 15 minutes, they had an image showing fairly precisely where Fuckface's amygdala and basal ganglia were located.

"Fire up that grill, er- I mean *drill,* Baby!" Sam said to Cherisse.

At the same time, Annie injected a healthy dose of local anesthetic into the top of Fuckface's skull. Sam brushed aside the mop head of well-dyed hair to reveal the shiny bare scalp which had Trump **literally** written all over it (the word 'Trump' had been repeatedly tattooed in his own special logo; in much smaller print below each 'Trump' were the tattooed words "fucks long and hard"; apparently, they was intended as a mantra for whomever he designated as privileged enough to scroll back his protective hut cover). First Sam sterilized the small target area. Then with his scalpel he slit an opening less than an inch long and clamped off the bleeding tissue, leaving the area completely prepped for Cherisse.

Cherisse then looked up to see all eyes in the room on Holly. She'd all but forgotten there were fears among some that Holly being exposed to the faint scents of brain matter from the cranial drilling could cause her – not to put too fine a point on it – to go rogue zombie, what with her frequently exchanging bodily fluids with the ex-dead President. As a neurologist, Cherisse – like the other physicians present - wasn't quite as worried about that; she understood how the blood-brain barrier worked and was fairly confident Holly's risk of spontaneous, uncontrolled neuro-chomping was minimal.

So she let the others do the staring and worrying.

* * *

*A*nd then, eyes a-blinking, Trump heard on his skulltip a tinkling and crinkling of each little drill bit.

As he drew in breath frail and got so confounded, down his brain trail needles delicately bounded.

Doc spoke not a word, but went straight to her work, filling tissue cassettes, snips straight from this jerk.

And laying her finger aside of his nose, she squeezed out a booger - up his head it then rose.

She flipped it so high, her group let out a whistle, and down it then flew, just like a green missile.

On the incision it landed, sewn up out of sight, where like Bactine enchanted, the germs it would fight.

Happy brain-suck to all and to all take swift flight!*

(Well, later that night, anyway.)

* * *

FREE ENTERPRISE AT ITS FINEST

The group was starting with Fuckface's noodle mapping when Franklin's plan for diversion began in earnest. Strolling around the Whittmyer Building, he started recruiting boys in their early teens who appeared to be middle school truants. He had about 1,500 fliers to be distributed.

The *sequentially-numbered* fliers read:

---

* With apologies to Clement Clarke Moore

Free $$ in Exchange for Your Urine Samples

No Tricks – No Catches

You Can Help the Advancement of Science
Just by Draining Your Dragon

Simply bring your full bladder to the front of **Whittmyer Industries Building** in Downtown Manhattan and whiz into the plastic cups left in dispensers next to the concrete planters.

No need to be bashful while you're voiding: <u>urination must be in public</u> for study results to be valid. When done, present the number on the bottom of this flier to the same young man who gave the flier to you. He'll be watching to make sure your cup is full before approaching you.

The young man then will obtain a *$10 payment* from the study sponsor in the Whittmyer and bring the payment to you where you filled your cup.

It's that simple.

Sponsored by Akrasia Industries of Sphincterville, Indiana, A Koch Brothers Concern.

Our motto: "More Potent Fracking Chemicals for Tastier Groundwater Because Merely <u>Slightly</u> Flammable <u>Just</u> <u>Won't</u> <u>Do</u>!"

There were more than enough slacker 12- to 14-year-old boys milling around the building to distribute the fliers – he figured each boy could hand out at least a hundred. Franklin explained to the boys that they'd receive $2 for each of the torn-off sequential flier numbers they returned to him along with the payments for the urine donors. The flier numbers would need to be signed by each donor and have one corner dipped in each donor's filled cup for Franklin to release the money. He emphasized that he would be watching the transactions between the pee donors and the flier distributors from inside the hotel, so it would be fruitless to try and scam the Koch Brothers' (phony) Akrasia Industries.

"Just let the Koch Brothers find out about one of you whippersnapper ruffians trying to pull the wool over my eyes," he warned each flier distributor. "They'll pursue each scoundrel to the ends of the earth over each stolen dollar, just because they **CAN**. It's the principle of the thing to them. They need *every last dollar they can get* to make sure Alberta, Canada ends up looking like a moonscape. Who needs all those damn oxygen-producing forests anyway?"

Whether it was the huge, imposing white Afro wig or Franklin's new facial wrinkle fissures – a couple looked deep enough to reach into *his* basal ganglia – or the charismatic 'we'll tackle this together' tone in his voice, he wasn't sure, *but every last one* of the truants bought into his scheme without skepticism.

He urged them to go to the seedier parts of Manhattan or even Brooklyn or the Bronx, where dive bars could be found, to hand out the fliers. In addition, he explained that there might be efforts by certain law enforcers to apprehend some of the urine donors.

"If **that** happens, don't worry too much about it," he said. "If an officer has a donor in handcuffs, when the police aren't looking just cram the $10 bill into the donor's palms or into his pants pocket – but _carefully_. You never know what's been inside those pockets."

The all-too-willing participants in Franklin's scheme began trickling, not streaming, in around 9:30 a.m. and kept trickling in to do their streaming throughout the day. One of the flier-distributing truants asked Franklin what was to be done with the cups of urine.

"Well, you can leave them be. If you have athlete's foot, you can douse your toes with the contents. Or, if you're worried someone might pick one up and try to drink it by mistake, you can pour each one out into the planter or the sewer drain.

"But my recommendation would be to **leave the pee cups undisturbed** so our Koch Brothers urine sample collection trucks – they're disguised as Blue Bell ice cream trucks – can pick them up overnight. Remember: for the study results to be valid, these samples need to spend much of their young lives in the open air."

They all did as Franklin recommended.

As the trickle of streamers grew into a stream of streamers around mid- to late-morning, to speed up the process Franklin simply gave the flier distributors stacks of $10 bills to hand out to the donors *as discreetly as possible* and as quickly as possible once their cups were full, so law enforcers wouldn't notice. He told them to bring back all their signed sequential flier numbers at once so there would be less observable back and forth activity. It ended up producing a steady, natural flow of transactions.

That was when he made sure the Homeland Security and Secret Service agents were aware of the first annual Peeing Man gathering outside the hotel. Up until then, the guardians of candidate safety has been blissfully oblivious to the rash of public urination occurring on their watch.

They began rounding up the donors, one at a time, as the flier distributors did their best to keep up with the Alexander Hamilton handouts. They were able to keep up with the demand for payments until around 8:30 p.m., when police started rounding up the urinators in large groups.

Then the urinators slowly began to get more and more belligerent as a few here and a few there were forced into paddy wagons before the boys could get their $10 bills to them. The police, Homeland Security and Secret Service had gotten more on their hands (no pee pun intended here) than they could cope with. It had kept them well-diverted from the medical procedures inside the Whittmyer Industries Building all day long. But pretty soon, they were on the verge of a urination riot – and not just over inadvertent downtown Manhattan stream-crossings. Although those were fairly disgusting in and of themselves.

The arresting agents and officers tried to point out to the pissed pissers that the fliers they'd received surely had to be bogus. But they were flummoxed by the fact that most of the arrestees were carrying crisp new sawbucks – the same amount promised on the handouts.

* * *

BACK TO 10 A.M., APRIL 25, 2016

As the group was mid-way through Fuckface's biopsies, the encounter between ex-Gov. Perry and Fennie turned out to be a little more interesting.

Ex-Gov. Perry made it clear to Fennie that he would cut down on Federal prison costs and clear out all the prison trash by expediting Federal executions. There were only three Federal executions since 1963, he pointed out angrily, and none since 2003.

"Goddam lily-livered pansies," he said. "All them niggerhead libtards care about is whether we accidentally bump off some innocent little crybaby (he motioned like he had a limp-wrist as he said that) who's already in jail for something else. Goddam slacker loser fags, every fuckin' last one of 'em. 'Specially that goddam Cameron Willingham.

"We ain't bein' recorded or nothin', right?"

"Of course not," Fennie said. (Of course, they _were_; Fennie took promises made to him – both in writing and orally - very, very seriously.)

By the time they were done, ex-Gov. Perry – in addition to promising **not** to execute Fennie, for _any_ reason – had promised:

- To put Fennie on the first flight to Mars.
- To let Fennie tour Area 51 with the hot 18-year-old of his choice, without any escorts.
- To let Fennie fly Air Force One to any location on the globe.
- To guarantee Fennie no IRS audits for the remainder of his natural life plus 50 years (for Whittmyer Industries).
- To guarantee a new overseas armed conflict requiring use of lots of machine gun ammunition every year for the next eight years.
- To share with Fennie at no cost a lifetime supply of the newest boner drugs with the least side effects. He promised Fennie he'd never have to worry about growing a new eye and nose on his back "like that poor dumbass in Oklahoma."
- To nominate Fennie's Kansas cousin Thumper, a personal liability lawyer specializing in incest-related physical deformity claims, to the U.S. Supreme Court (on the condition that Thumper give up his basement meth lab and come out against abortion – including abortions for 'supposedly' raped women - **and** against same-sex marriage, while publicly supporting cousins marrying).

Fennie said the conditions on Thumper's nomination were a non-starter, but he welcomed Perry's other promises.

"It sounds like a good start to me," Fennie told the Rickster, who'd been reading the promises – awkwardly and with lots of mispronunciations – from a list his personal secretary gave him.

"It seems like there were another couple of things I was going to tell you, but – oops! – can't misremember 'em," Texas' second-worst ex-governor said.

"No problem, Rick. Now, Penny will take you over there where that nice lady will let you into the adjoining room for your medical review procedure and debriefing.

"Are they ready for him, Penny?"

She checked with Marcia. At first, Marcia shook her head side-to-side. Then she looked into the small banquet room a second time and motioned for ex-Gov. Perry to amble over.

Amble he did, with that goofy smile on his face. Like an empty headed bovine waddling up to the brain smashers at a slaughterhouse.

As he was being strapped into the examination chair, he noticed Fuckface von Clownstick lying, relaxed, half-asleep on a recovery table at the far end of the room. Bianca was standing over him, examining different pulse points on his body and checking his small incision.

"Now that's what I call getting de-briefed!" he said, leering at the lovely Bianca and mentally undressing her.

"*C'mon, Cherisse,*" Annie whispered, "*from this one **surely** we can take more than simple biopsies! He's really, <u>truly</u> **not using much of anything that's in there** – and probably never will, if he ever did. I bet you a hundred shares of Tesla no one ever would notice.*"

"*Remember our oath, good friend:*" Cherisse whispered back, "*first do no harm. And we're probably fudging that one, seeing as we're doing these procedures without any direct medical benefit to the 'patients' – unless we accidentally discover some sort of nasties going on inside there.*"

"*But, I must admit, I'd love to take your bet if I could! Maybe I'll change my mind by the end of the day.*"

And on went James Rick Perry's neuro ventriculogram and biopsy. No fuss, no muss. As Ricky sat in the examination chair silent and motionless throughout the procedure, Sam marveled at what a childlike mind the Rickermator seemed to have. At least in that moment.

Next up with Fennie (while the Poughkeepsians were mid-way through ex-Gov. Rick's procedure), was ex-Gov. John Ellis "Jeb" Bush.

The most articulate of Barbara Bush's sons (admittedly, a low, low bar), Jebulon was only too quick to please with Daddy Warbucks Rupphauser.

This latest Bush predicted the Republican-controlled Congress would quickly find an excuse to attack Iran once the Jebster took his long-deserved throne in la Casa Blanca on Pennsylvania Avenida. Trying to impress Fennie with his bilingualism, Jebby switched back and forth from English to Spanish and vice versa.

Only problem: Fennie understood Spanish about as well as he understood hieroglyphics. Nonetheless, Fennie nodded along, pretending to comprehend Jebber's gibberish. Midway through nodding, he thought to himself, "*That'd make a great cover band name, Jebber's Gibberish! Mental note to self: trademark that name!*"

Fennie asked Jebmeister how he'd deal with people offended by the notion of political dynasties in a country founded upon resentment for European royal families.

"They'll love me so much that, when they see my face, they'll just see my smile, not my genetic heritage," he said.

"I'm willing to give you a sizeable chunk of change if you'll promise me one thing," Fennie said.

"What's that?" the porta-Jebbie asked.

"That you'll do everything in your power – including signing off on a CIA hitman – to keep another Bush descendant with the "W" mental defect gene from getting into politics."

"But, uh, sir - "

"I am as serious as a heart attack about that."

"Okie-dokie. Done and done." (Jebba the Hutt made a document-signing motion using an invisible pen with his empty hands.)

And that was that. By the time Jibby-Jabby was done sucking up to Fennie, Rickie P. was almost out of recovery and into debriefing.

So, off Jobby-Lobby went for a little shedding of light (or X-rays) and mind-opening. Cherisse was impressed by his politeness and glibness. Less impressed she was by his unambiguous support of big oil, perpetual war and his opposition to tax credits for wind energy.

"A Bushie who supports big oil and fossil fuels!!??!!!" Sam exclaimed, all Scarlett O'Hara faux light-headed-like, with the back of his hand to his forehead. "Why mah dahlin', I do believe I have the vapuhs, Ah am so busaad myseff withun' thuh shawk."

As Jibabba's brain bits extractions were completed and he was heading to the recovery gurney, Fennie and Penny were listening to Rick "Please Don't Google My Surname" Santorum unload his personal views on government in a frothy brown stream of consciousness-raising.

Fennie did his best imitation of the late Edward R. Murrow for a little while.

"Exactly why would JFK's speech about the importance of the separation of church and state make you want to throw up?" Fennie asked.

Lots of stuttering and stupidity and backtracking spewed forth out of ex-Sen. Santorum. None of it worth printing here.

"Umm. OK. Why would you say that people who encourage young folks to go to college are snobs?"

Lots more stuttering and stupidity and backtracking spewed forth from the opening in the middle of that Santorum face. As the blah, blah, blah continued, Fennie marveled at how perfect this other Ricky's teeth appeared to be.

"Ever think that maybe people besides rich folks should be able to get orthodontia if they need it?" Fennie asked, surprising himself so much at that brief foray into populism that he had a brief sort-of seizure-type jerking movement in his back and head.

"That's a trick question, right?" Rick II asked. "It's like a control question in a study just to make sure I have no unconscious socialist tendencies, right?"

"Ummm. OK. Sure.

"Y'know what, Santy? I kind of like you, all that homo-hating notwithstanding. You seem like a stand-up guy who calls 'em as he sees 'em even if it's going to make you look like an absolute dumbass.

"I can't help liking that. I think you'd make a wunnaful, wunnaful (*Fennie liked to throw in the occasional Lawrence Welk-ism*) Vice President. For that reason alone, I'm going to support you in a big way.

"Provided, of course, that you go forward here with your medical examination by our expert neurologists and the debriefing afterward."

(He didn't explain that the debriefing mostly would consist of a discussion with the limo driver on the way back to his hotel.)

It was almost like in the comic books when dollar signs suddenly appear where a person's corneas are supposed to be.

Rickster the Second couldn't get into the adjoining banquet room fast enough. Fortunately, Jebola was already on the recovery gurney and doing quite nicely.

As the Poughkeepsie noggin miners were starting to pipe the laughing gas into Santorum's northern hemisphere blow hole (the opening at the comparatively sweet end of his 33-foot alimentary canal - a gondola-free zone, by the way), the final GOP interviewee was heading into the Rupphauser sacrarium.

Gov. Scott Walker (R-WI) started off by defending his remarks comparing collective bargaining ban opposition from 100,000 union protestors to terrorist plots by ISIS.

"Fighting off union activists really isn't that different from fighting off masked ISIS terrorists overseas. They both could chop off your head if they really were determined to do that. They both could take over your oil refineries if they really wanted to do that. Everyone knows union members would rather strike and shut down plants than actually work and draw a hard-earned paycheck, right?"

"Uhh, er, OK, sure."

"And these welfare mamas. They sit around toking on $50 mary-jane-wanna cigarettes and buying $20 fresh lobsters with their Food Stamps. They'd lots rather have a cushy life off someone else's money than earn it themselves. Everyone knows how much they enjoy going to the welfare office, don't they, eh?"

"Err, whu, jeep-, uh, OK, sure."

"Besides, what's going to happen to our population if we can't stop them promiscuous women from using abortion for birth control – not to mention stopping those perverse lesbian women from marrying each other instead of marrying normal men with normal libidos.

"We can't have our population start to shrink. It might mean employers would have to compete harder for workers, pay them more. It would mean there would be fewer people to buy stuff. Society as we know it would collapse."

"Or, the air might get cleaner and there might be fewer wars over resources like oil, just maybe?" Fennie responded, once again surprising himself so much he almost coughed up a lung. "*I must be listening to Penny's goofy ideas about social justice-y things too much,*" he thought to himself.

"And just maybe any possible reduction in population might have something to do with the fact that male sperm counts have dropped by half since World War II," Fennie went on. "And just maybe that might be the result of some of the 5,000-plus chemicals added to our food, fertilizers and industrial cleaners since then.

"Those chemicals have a way of sneaking into our bodies. And they have similarities to estrogen, the female sex hormone – except they overstay their welcome lots longer and at up to a thousand times normal environmental levels.

"I've read that researchers suspect those chemicals might have adverse effects on parts of our bodies sensitive to estrogen, like the reproductive system, breasts, uteruses, fetuses and such. They think exposures to those chemicals cause infertility, cancers, miscarriages, birth defects and so on.[*]

"So, how do you feel about that?"

---

[*] The Telegraph, 3/17/14

"It's a trick question, right? You're just trying to find out if I'm some kind of subversive liberal plant posing as a Reagan conservative, right? You already knew I'm not, right? You know I wouldn't sign off on anything new that would restrict **how** a business can **do** business, right?"

"Umm, er, yeah, OK. Sure, that's right."

More verbal exchanges like that continued. It took more than an hour for Gov. Walker to explain all the myriad ways he would undo environmental protections, wipe out the last vestiges of organized labor, repeal all minimum wage laws, preserve 'too big to fail' on Wall Street, remove all restrictions on international trade and find new ways to perpetuate the "Permanent War" culture of the U.S.A. throughout the globe.

He even said he hoped to revive the space exploration program with the goal of opening up worm hole travel to reach other far-flung civilizations billions of light years away which might have resources amenable to military conquest.

"Your company could be the first one to produce brass shell casings on planet Altair Four on the other side of the galaxy. Just think about it. It's a mindblower."

"Yup, it's something, alright."

And, with that, Fennie thanked Gov. Walker profusely for his time and promised him a sizeable contribution as a reward for his visionary thinking. But, in Fennie's mind, the donation *actually* was about protecting Whittmyer Industries' backside just in case this lunatic ended up duping a majority of the Teletubbies generation and a majority of the boomers fast approaching senility to vote for his stupid, cravenly myopic ass.

Walker marched on to his neuro ventriculogram examination and skull-plucking. During the procedure, he tried to convince Cherisse, Sam, Annie and Bianca just how wealthy they would become if they supported him and his plans to convert the progressive income tax into a flat tax.

"It'd shift 90 percent of the current tax burden **off** of you well-off hard-working folks and **onto** that lazy 47 percent who think all they need are government benefits and Social Security to keep them happy.

"We'll show those cocksuckers," he said, the laughing gas apparently lifting his speech inhibitions.

"You just try that, Governor," Cherisse said, thinking maybe she could fill a third biopsy cassette from this particular dickwad.

And. She. Did.

Which led to the appearance of their marquee end-of-the-day guest star.

* * *

The Lady of the Hour Enters

Ms. Rodham Clinton arrived in her Fennie-provided limo (with her entourage following close behind) "only" about a half-hour late. The

Poughkeepsians all were relieved that her 'better half' was off somewhere else – either visiting their grandbaby or visiting his latest stacked hottie babe-y. That would've been all they needed, him trying to barge in on Hillary while she was getting something off of her mind. Literally. Better he should be having a head sucking something out of his little Mr. Bill-head someplace else than seeing something sucked out of his bride's head.

She was resplendent in a full length shimmering royal blue Oscar de la Renta gown, dressed as though she were meeting regals – which, in the world of former Arkansans, is pretty much what she was doing. She'd grown tired of having to suck up to Sam Walton's Wal-Mart heirs in Bill's home state. Mr. Rupphauser, whose corporate empire was known mostly for paying living wages to its serfs, was a few steps up the ladder of respectability compared to the Wal-Mart's "$10 per hour minimum pay in 2016 is a living wage" philosophy for its almost completely part-time work force.

Mr. Rupphauser had saved his best impression of Edward R. Murrow for Hillary.

"So, you're a big supporter of Big Pharma, Ms. Clinton," Fennie said. As I understand it, you take more campaign dollars from them than from just about any other source, except maybe Wall Street banks.

"Were you aware that Big Pharma has cut way, way back on research for cures of things like antibiotic-resistant superbugs and diabetes?

"Well, I read the papers just like any-"

"And you certainly must realize that their motivation is all about profit: leaving patients dependent on monthly maintenance drugs guarantees them lots more dollars than providing a one-time cure.

"Except, of course, for companies like Gilead which figure out they can charge $84,000 for a 12-week cure for Hep C. Like just any ol' middle class family can reach into the cookie jar for $84 grand.

"So what would you do about families which can't afford $84 grand and state Medicaid programs which can't afford to pay $84 grand per patient to cure Hep C? Would you do what that USA-SBR proposes?"

"Well, I think companies should be allowed to charge based on market demand for their product because - "

"Because you're one of these closet Randians who's convinced our capitalist system can't survive without giving the robber barons their outsized piece of the pie. At the expense of everyone else."

"Now, sir, please stop putting words into my mouth."

"I've been waiting for many months to hear something definitive about the issues that matter to my children and grandchildren. They want nothing to do with my munitions company, you know. They're hard-working middle class wage slaves just like most everyone else.

"What will you do for them?"

"Umm, eh, well, uh, I will keep food prices stable by encouraging the use of pest-resistant and blight-resistant GMO crops, crops which may need fewer pesticide applications."

"Emphasis on MAY need fewer. All the studies so far show no significant difference in those areas. The main reason you seem to support those Monsanto GMO products is that it puts huge shitloads of dollars into Monsanto because they sue almost every farmer who doesn't buy new seed supplies from them every year. If they can prove the farmer used seeds from his previous year's crop, the farmer is screwed.

"Never mind that using seeds left over each year from the previous year's crop is a practice going back many millennia. A practice which helped our species evolve into more intelligent, more prosperous beings.

"You've fought the single-payer health coverage my grandchildren need. You've fought legalization of marijuana which my niece with cancer in Kansas needs to stimulate her appetite. You've supported the embargo on trade with Cuba which keeps demand for my nephew's potato crop in Montana artificially suppressed. You haven't come out against the fracking being done by Koch Brothers affiliates which has poisoned the groundwater on my sister's ranch in Colorado.

"You've threatened to use nuclear weapons against Iran if they attack Israel, maybe setting off a Third World War. You've supported international trade treaties which would make it impossible for me to continue to have decent profits from the livable wage-paying plants I operate in the U.S. You've consistently supported the Patriot Act despite its privacy-killing elements and you've bad-mouthed Edward Snowden repeatedly for exposing the unconstitutional practices under that law.

"You've kept supporting the cap on Social Security payroll taxes which is welfare for rich people like me even though it threatens to undermine benefits for people like my children and grandchildren. You've not supported – *so far*, at least – _completely_ tuition-free and fee-free college for undergraduates in bachelor's degree programs, something my estranged grandchildren could use.

"You've supported severe limits on the rights of victims of medical malpractice to sue the doctors who harmed them. That's something that would've directly affected my brother's young son, who was permanently injured because of a botched kidney procedure by an incompetent specialist.

"You've not pledged to limit or stop accepting campaign donations from Political Action Committees (PACs) and large corporations like my own. Not to mention big banks. You even voted for a bankruptcy bill – backed by huge credit card companies – a bill which was way more punitive to people like my favorite cousin in Nevada, who had to file a Chapter 7 because of massive medical debt.

"Exactly why should my extended family want you to win the Presidency?"

"Because I support causes which make the lives of women in the very poorest countries better. Because I want to see single parents in this country no longer have to struggle just to pay their rent and feed their families."

"Then why haven't you called for a restoration of the funds cut from the Food Stamps program by the Republicans more than two years ago?"

"I have no authority to make that happen. I am just a private citizen."

"That's absolute bullshit. You have a bully pulpit. Women, especially more mature women, **women all over the country** listen to and read about almost everything you say and do.

"You have influence. You saying you're 'just a private citizen' is one of the larger lies that's been uttered in this room today."

"If you say I have influence, I'll choose to take that as a compliment."

"It's just a fact."

"So, what do you want me to say?"

"I'd like for you to say you'll try to start going on the record more, on the record about *specifics* instead of simple platitudes. I'd like for you to respect the intelligence of most voters out there. And I'd like for you to be honest about your Wall Street sympathies.

"And, yes, I'd like for you to accept a significant contribution from my company. For three simple reasons: you just might win this race. And you just might find your conscience on social issues between now and the time you might take office.

"And I would like to feel welcomed by you if I ever need to speak with you over the phone or visit with you about something that's crucial to me keeping jobs in the country I love most. And no, that's not Indonesia with all its Nike sweatshops."

"I would be proud to accept your donation. However, I'm troubled by your skepticism about my motives."

"Lady, I'm not skeptical. I'm downright disgusted by your motives. You took more than a thousand foreign donations for the Clinton Foundation while you were Secretary of State. You pronounced Colombia as worthy of the best trading status after your husband's Canadian buddy with an oil business there gave your foundation some huge bucks, despite the Colombian government being complicit in intimidation of union organizers at that same oil company.

"But, sadly, your motives seem to be ever-so-slightly less slimy than most, if not all, of the Republicans I've met. And your foundation has done some good work, even if the donations to it were made out of the most craven motives.

"But you and I both know that the good works your foundation does with the dirty money donations you get would be dwarfed by the good works the U.S. government could do if your mega-billionaire donors were required to pay their true, fair, progressive share of the tax burden. Dwarfed like, say, an amoeba compared to an aircraft carrier.

"So, it's simple: you might end up being the best of what's left for all those voting amoebae out there. Unless Mr. Sanders figures out how to be telegenic.

"And best of what's left or not, I truly **do** hope that you'll find your way to more candor and more circumspection about the people who would be most affected by your out-of-the-public-eye companionships with Wall Street."

"Who can possibly know what the future holds?"

"Well, I know a pain-free neurological examination in the small banquet room over there is the closest thing in your future. I hope you find it as comfortable and re-assuring as possible."

And, just like that, escorted by Penny, off Hillary went to have her head examined.

* * *

Unintended Consequences

A half-hour-plus later, as Cherisse and Sam were going over Hillary's neuro ventriculogram, the ripples of Franklin's diversionary scheme at street level were slowly turning into tidal waves.

Franklin had hoped the sight of a few handfuls of self-exposing public urinators would keep Homeland Security and Secret Service staff occupied just enough to ensure there would be no interruptions of Fennie's candidate screenings and the Poughkeepsie medicos' brain tidbit extractions. He figured only maybe one in a hundred of the fliers distributed by the middle school truants would actually produce a urine donor. After all, really, how many people actually would risk arrest and a public exposure (sex offender even?) conviction just for the chance to get a $10 payment? (Franklin had checked with Estelle Suzuki M'Benga, Idris' mother, who had started her career as an attorney in criminal law, before putting his promotion together, though: Estelle said the most serious charge an 'offender' could face would be for public urination, a low-level misdemeanor, and that the arrestee "almost _certainly_" could get the charge dropped if he or she claimed to have been duped. Estelle asked Franklin/Percy why someone would want to dupe someone else into urinating in public and possibly being arrested or cited. "College prank," Franklin explained. Well, he _was_ a college student, after all. And it _was_ a prank, right? Anyway, why would anyone wanna make a Federal case over a simple pranking of the Secret Service? Oh, yeah, that.)

Unintended consequences are a bitch, though.

Franklin was about to get a street-level education in just how abysmal the economy had become for the working poor and the unemployed since "W" Bush got done driving it into the ground almost eight years earlier – heroic, Great Depression II-preventing Obama economic stimulus efforts notwithstanding.

As it turned out, not one in 10, but nine out of 10 of the fliers produced urine donors. Moreover, many of those nine out of the 10 fliers were passed around, shared and photocopied by the area's barflies and homeless men. Not 150 willing men showed up, but _**1,900**_.

Franklin had purchased 1,500 plastic cups just in case he'd been wrong about his participation estimate. When those cups (set up in dispensers looking like free newspaper distribution boxes) ran out, the donors starting finding their own cups and even plastic bags.

Pretty soon the odor of spilled homeless man urine was wafting its way into the Whittmyer Industries Building. The fragrance was, first, whelming and, later, overwhelming.

The _**horror**_...

When the arrests started outpacing the truants' payments, word got around that the 'study' organizers appeared to be welshing on their promise of compensation.

Pretty soon the piss-smelling hordes of pissed-off donors wanting their piss payments surged through the building entrance, almost crushing the Homeland Security and Secret Service agents. Some of whom actually pissed their own pants at the sight of the sea of homeless men (and even a few women). As Franklin watched the drama unfold from the mezzanine above the lobby, he was reminded of a scene from the movie "_World War Z._"

"_This cannot be end well,_" he thought to himself.

By this time, the Federales had caught a couple of the middle school truants pointed out by some of the liquid gold donors – two truants who were so obese they couldn't outrun the agents – and grilled them about who had given them the fliers. Franklin saw one of the truants in the midst of the throngs pouring into the lobby pointing upward at Franklin as an agent stood next to the kid with his hand around the scruff of the kid's neck.

"_Flugnuts,_" Franklin thought, "_the jig's up._"

Franklin quickly summoned the O'Learys and Tom so they all could rush upstairs to warn the others. The O'Learys barely avoided the crush of humanity that was rapidly filling the lobby as their elevator door closed just in time before the crowd could spill in. Franklin and Tom rushed into their elevator as it stopped on the mezzanine level. There was a Secret Service agent in the elevator with them who looked every bit as scared as they were. Tom thanked the agent for his service as he stood behind the agent in the elevator – and then he stabbed the agent in the neck with an Epi-Pen-sized injector of sleep anesthetic. As the 6'2" 260-pound agent slumped to the floor in an opioid haze, a slight smile crept across his previously-stressed face.

Franklin glanced at his watch and saw that it was around 9:45 p.m. It was about the time when Cherisse would be making the first of two or three insertions of biopsy removal micro needles. He actually was off by about five minutes, though.

Because, at that moment, as their elevator rose to the fifth floor, Sam, Cherisse, Annie and Bianca were examining and re-examining the neuro ventriculogram which appeared to show an odd cluster-mass of possibly pre-aneurytic blood vessels in one corner of Hillary's temporal lobe. It didn't create any extra risk for their biopsy procedure, but they quickly debated what to do.

"It's simple," Bianca said. "We leave the ventriculogram inside her clothing, say, inside her bra so she can't miss it, along with a note urging her to visit her neurologist A-SAP.

"Just make sure you don't get any fingerprints on the damn thing."

They all agreed.

The first micro needle extraction was just wrapping up when Franklin, the O'Learys, Tom, Penny and Marcia rushed into the small banquet room.

While Tom was explaining what had happened – without really pinning the blame on Franklin (he was embarrassed enough already; that could wait) – Bianca noticed Franklin now appeared to be about 90 years old.

As the others were fretting over what to do next, she handed Franklin the long micro needle which had just emerged from Hillary's head. (Meanwhile, the nitrous oxide had Hillary in a state of semi-conscious bliss.)

"It's time for you to slurp this up – pretend it's a blueberry milkshake and use your very best suction, Sir. It's good for what ails you, I promise."

So, Franklin did just that. In fact, he didn't just slurp, he licked the micro needle assembly clean from top to bottom. He quickly handed the assembly back to Bianca who sat it down next to Cherisse on the instruments tray.

Nothing much happened to Franklin at first. But then he started shaking uncontrollably, as though he were having a massive gran mal seizure, but with his eyes wide open.

"Oh, shit, you guys," Annie said. "We forgot, her head's still open. Fuck. A. Duck."

It took four of the men in the room to restrain Franklin, despite it being clear he was terrified of what his body was trying to do. As his shaking subsided, the men could feel his magnified strength trying to pull up his forearms to reach at Hillary's skull.

At the same time, Annie and Cherisse noticed Holly, who was approaching Franklin with a panicked expression on her own face.

"You _can_ control this Franklin!" Holly half-shouted as Pongo, Orvis, Tom and Mitch held Franklin back. "You've got to, if not now, sometime soon. What if we hadn't been here?!"

Franklin nodded authoritatively, but his arms still pulled, as though involuntarily, toward Hillary in the examination chair. In Franklin's mind he could imagine his hands ripping the stereotactic frame off of her head and using the pointy parts of it to crack open her skull so he could feast on the innermost parts of her gray matter.

But, all of a sudden, Franklin's arms relaxed. The four men holding him back were able to relax, cautiously. Then they looked at his face. It was an amazing sight, hearkening back to that night more than 5-1/2 years earlier outside the Hyde Park FDR Visitor's Center when the sidewalks were still damp from the huge storm that had brought Franklin back to life.

They watched, transfixed, as the ravines of wrinkles on what then appeared to be a 105-year-old face sort of inflated and disappeared, one by one. His gums, which had looked receded and on the verge of bleeding moments earlier, now looked as healthy as a young man's. Instead of 105 years old, he suddenly looked no more than 35, maybe even 30.

The Rodham Clinton cerebrum slurpee provided by Bianca had worked. Just in time.

Amazingly, while all of that drama was playing out, 10 feet away Cherisse had resumed the biopsy extractions from Hillary's noggin, pulling out two more samples to be placed into a tissue collection cassette.

"OK, you bunch of pinheads," Cherisse said. It sounds like there's a lot of noise on the floor below. I'm thinking we need to rush Hillary here through recovery and get her out the door. I would guess we've got no more than fifteen minutes. Lots less if one of those Secret Service Baby Huey-sized agents bursts in here with his bowels all in an uproar. Hillary's all closed up, so we don't need to worry about Franklin having another involuntary meltdown. I hope. So, get your little Dutchess County asses in gear."

"Agreed," Phil said. "We need to haul ass."

"Christ, I need a drink," Cherisse said, looking skyward.

"Bianca," Phil said, eyes darting from her to Fennie's door and back, "you, Heather and Pongo please get Hillary on the recovery gurney and get that laughing gas turned off.

"And make sure that ventriculogram showing the tangled mass is tucked inside her underwear somehow. That's crucial."

Mitch alerted the limo driver (Willem Perspicace) to be ready for Hillary. Phil, Pongo and Harry, who'd just rushed in from his security video monitoring station, packed away the medical equipment back into the Red Cross-logo-ed metal cabinet. They decided on the move to simply leave it there; Sam had paid for it with cash and was certain there was no video security system at the military surplus store where he'd purchased it. Same for the imaging equipment and other medical items he'd purchased, including the examination chair: cash only, no video security. He'd been careful about all of that.

About then, one of those Baby Huey-sized agents did, in fact, break down the door between them and Fennie's room. They could hear Fennie absolutely furious in the background. "You huckfeds had better have a check in my hands for that damage within seventy-two hours. Or I'll have my buddy Mitch McConnell's turtle beak so far up your ass he'll be able to chew your gucking fum." (Sometimes, when Fennie was stressed he'd get a little orally dyslexic.)

Fortunately, Marcia was standing next to the door with an Epi-Pen-sized anesthetic injector as Baby Huey broke through. When she jabbed the agent in the neck from behind (he was focused on the group standing around Hillary at the far end of the room), it worked as smoothly as a Vulcan neck pinch.

Now, though, it was time to use their pre-planned escape routes. Just to make it official, Penny went ahead and signaled all of them on her walkie-talkie. Mitch and Idris carted the semi-conscious Hillary off in the cargo elevator down to the waiting limo. She was waking a little more quickly than expected and she looked kind of pissed. But she could've just been hacked off over the disgusting aroma of stinky man-piss that had wafted all the way around to the back of the building by then.

Anyway, she was on her way before they knew it. Let her God-forsaken campaign manager deal with that look on her face, Mitch and Idris both thought at the same time.

Sam made sure all of the biopsy tissue cassettes were safely stored in a six-pack cooler with frozen blue ice already inside. He and Bianca headed off on their own escape route, a la "*The Great Escape,*" and wished everyone else luck.

Harry and Mel headed out next – only Penny knew where each pair's escape route went.

Pongo told Phil to go ahead without him because he and Penny wanted to make sure Fennie was OK. Pongo and the others had been able to hear Fennie and Penny through the wall all day and they'd all kind of come to like the guy, dirty billions or not.

While they checked on Fennie, the rest of the Poughkeepsians, including Phil and Franklin, headed off to their escape routes.

"Ten-forty-five Penn Station Amtrak, right Pongo?" Franklin said.

"You got it, Sir," he replied.

Fennie was still white-hot over the ruined solid-core 150-year-old mahogany door the agent now in dreamland had managed to break through.

"That fucking dildo brain must have the strength of a Clydesdale," Fennie said. He sounded like he could spit red-hot nails.

"Will you be alright, sir?" Pongo asked. "I don't want to leave if there's anything I can do. It sounded like you and the agent actually came to blows briefly. You look like you're going to get a black eye."

"Nothing a little raw meat and aspirin won't resolve.

"You need to be on your way, there, lad. I don't want those secret boys thinking you slugged me and knocked out that huge hulk of a man over there."

"What about you, Penny? Should you go too?"

"I'll be fine right here, sir. You and I will set these special agents straight. They're probably just pissed off about all those street people getting out of hand. I'm sure they know we had nothing to do with that."

She and Pongo both knew the ruse about her phone system being hacked probably would keep her in the clear.

Right then, a Secret Service agent started running up the hallway toward the entrance into Fennie's inner sanctum. Knowing that, by then, someone must've gotten word to the agents about the weird brain procedures that had been going on in Fennie's building, Pongo instinctively ran as swiftly as he knew how. He felt like a Big Carl's burger about to be grabbed by Chris Christie.

He didn't leave a second too soon. The chase was on. Pongo's only advantage was he knew where he was going and the agent – or agents – on his tail didn't.

$$* \quad * \quad *$$

Pongo's Getaway, Part II

The shedding of the disguise behind him, the encounters with the uninvited toilet stall would-be visitors completed without incident and the contagious "Africanized-MS" scam on the train now successful, Pongo wondered with knots in his stomach if there would be that phalanx of Federales waiting for him when he emerged from the subway a block from Penn Station.

It was less than 500 feet from the Penn Station stop now and he needed a strategy.

Number 1 on that strategy plan was not getting turned into a lumpy pile of bloody perforated brain goo by a hail of automatic weapons fire from Homeland Security.

Number 2 was making sure the man most responsible for the decisions that defeated Germany in WW II, the former leader of the free world, also didn't turn into bloody perforated brain goo – or perforated _anything_ goo. He knew Franklin was a much taller, much easier target to see than he was.

Number 3 was finding his Pop – who had proven himself over the years to be fairly savvy at self-preservation. Pongo wasn't deathly worried about his Papa – but he knew the reverse would _not_ be true. Phil probably was on the verge of stroking out over Pongo's whereabouts – if Phil wasn't already sitting in a jail cell somewhere.

At the other end of the Pongo chase, the Federal agents who saw Pongo's backside at a distance as he fled Fennie's small banquet room at Warp Factor 8 had encountered an unusual, freakish problem with the subway system. Or with one of its union-member staff, to be more precise.

$$* \quad * \quad *$$

Sticking Up for Your Rights: A Novel Idea

When the Federal agents approached the New York City regional MTA supervisor on duty at MTA headquarters (about four minutes after Pongo scurried out of that small banquet room) to demand that all subway trains be stopped in their tracks immediately, they found that the supervisor knew a lil' sumthin'-sumthin' about civil rights and due process.

"Where's your emergency court order or your court order of enjoinder?" asked Supervisor Barry Menetto.

"Who says we need one? We're Homeland Security."

"The Constitution says you need one. Unless there's someone out there about to detonate a bomb or something that could kill one or more of our fare-payers.

"Is there?"

"No, but th-"

"No 'no buts' allowed on this matter, I'm afraid, sir. If it's not literally a life and death issue, then you need to trot your tight little Federal agent asses down to a FISA Court or some other such court and kiss some judge ass to get that god-dam order.

"I've got maybe half a million people on this system right now expecting to get where those tracks are s'pposed to take 'em. If I stop this entire system right now just so you can check each separate car for your latest boogie monster bad guy, I'm gonna have half a million super-pissed folks calling their aldermen and demanding that my ass gets served up on a platter – and not even some nice silvery thing, probably some cheap Wal-Mart melamac platter just brimmin' with all those nard-killing buto-bite-o feenill-y shitticals.

"So all you big sluggo-luggos there, you head off and do your court-y thing and then feel free to prance right back here, phallic-substitute sidearms drawn if need be, with your order. Then – and only then – will you see me pull the plug on MTA's fucking fantastic transit system.

"And if you bastards try and go all Jack Bauer-y on me, y'know, even torture me or kill me - I swear to Jesus Saves at Costco, I will come back as some shit-stained fuckin' sheet-ghost demon and fuck your bully asses one-by-one with a broom handle in your fuckin' beauty sleep if that's what it takes to get you fuckin' shitheads to follow the fuckin' rules.

"Hey, by the way, a nice early Mother's Day wish for you and yours: go fuck yourselves silly, you dickstained pussy-pissing jackboot fascist thuggies. Hey, do you thuggies wear huggies?? And while you're on your way out, make sure to schedule a little business with those curbside cocksucking prostitutes, OK? I hear you guys like that kind of thing when you're off duty. Just make sure you pay 'em what you promise for a change. Word has it that those hookers in Colombia still are waiting for their tips from you's guys. Hey, I heard some of you's guys told 'em you're only allowed to pay 'em Federal minimum wage. How'd all that go over with the Missus?

"Hey, don't be strangers, sweethahts!"

As the agents left red-faced with rage, their tails figuratively between their legs, Menetto's transit center buddy, Willis "Bugeyes" Washington, whispered to him, "What the fuck was that? Why'd you go off on them like that? Do you want your taxes audited for, like, the rest of infinity?"

"I have some general principles when it comes to law enforcement pricks try-ing to do stuff they aren't actually entitled to do. My great-grandpa was jailed and then hung in a public square by Benito Mussolini for not letting one of Benito's cronies commandeer his truck – his only truck, crucial to his farm – for a ride to a picnic two-hundred miles away.

"Guess you could say I'm not real fascist-y friendly."

"Shit, glad you told me that. I was gonna ask to borrow your Ridgeline this weekend. Whew…"

$$* \quad * \quad *$$

All of the MTA drama was unknown to Pongo. If the MTA supervisor **had** shut down the system, the agents would've reached Pongo long before he was to arrive at Penn Station. Both Pongo and the USA-SBR would've been as impotent as an IUD prescription at Hobby Lobby.

$$* \quad * \quad *$$

BLABBERMOUTH VON CLOWNSTICK AT IT AGAIN

The Poughkeepsians found out later that it was Fuckface von Clownstick (Trumpy) who had contacted the Secret Service late in the day to report something odd had happened to him while he was at the Whittmyer Building. It had taken them an hour or so to interview him in person and another couple of hours to get a neurologist to visit Trump in person to confirm what appeared to have happened.

The neurologist explained that it appeared to be a micro needle exploration of his brain matter, probably for a diagnostic biopsy. There likely was zero perma-nent harm done to von Clownstick, the doctor emphasized.

Fuckface quickly figured out – as all of the other biopsied candidates would as well - that one's political and business prospects wouldn't be helped by the public finding out one had lost a little bit of one's mind.

In no uncertain terms, he demanded that the Federal agents back off, drop their investigation and consider him a hostile witness. As hostile as they come.

Nevertheless, they had to do their due diligence because the other can-didates might not feel the same way. So, back to the Whittmyer Building they went, only to see the sea of urinators swarming the entrance. The rest became history.

$$* \quad * \quad *$$

MEETING AN ADMIRER

Pongo watched the passing brick walls of the subway tunnel outside the windows of his passenger car gradually slow as they approached the Penn Station stop. It seemed like it took an hour to decelerate from full speed to a full stop over the last 500 feet to the platform.

The sweat was pouring down his zitty forehead as the disembodied artificial voice on the subway intercom warned passengers to stay back from the door until it was completely opened. As though people actually paid attention to that.

Pongo thought this was one time it would be prudent not to be the first person out of the passenger car. It was 10:36 p.m. – he still had just enough time to make the 10:45 p.m. train to Poughkeepsie with the others. Provided he wasn't in handcuffs and shackles two minutes from then.

The mother who'd been nursing her baby a few rows away exited first, looking back at him with a stink-eye expression. "*Africanized M.S.*! What an **asshole**," she said as she and her swaddled infant headed to the stairs leading up from the platform.

The others in his passenger car exited from the door at the other end.

It was time to make a decision: get out or abandon the plan to catch the Poughkeepsie train with the others.

Decision made.

He got out. Slowly. Looking both ways for anyone who resembled a hulking, sidearm-brandishing Secret Service agent.

Pongo stepped forward tentatively on the platform. He was sweating so much, he was ripe enough to be whiffed all the way up the top of the stairs leading to the Penn Station main concourse entrance a block away on 7th Avenue.

Where he stood on the platform was almost exactly halfway between the two stairways to ground level. The doors to the passenger cars were just starting to close behind him after the last of the passengers who'd been waiting on the platform got on.

At that hour, there were only a small handful of passengers who were arriving to wait for the next train as the one still there was starting to leave. As Pongo took a step to the right he noticed the shapes of two persons emerging from the shadows at opposite ends of the platform.

He thought he might know who the one on the right was: he was wearing plaid pants and had what appeared to be a 9 mm Glock pistol in his left hand at his side. The man coming out of the shadows on the left was about the same size and shape as Mr. Plaid Pants and was carrying a similar gun in his right hand at his side. There were no MTA security officers in sight – the Poughkeepsians would find out the next day that either Mr. Plaid Pants or his associate had strangled an armed MTA officer to death in the shadows, using a garotte, shortly after the previous train had left.

"Mr. Podrowski, it's time for you to come with us," Mr. Plaid Pants said in as low a voice as possible. "We apologize for not arriving sooner so we could greet your fellow conspirators. We only heard from one of our Secret Service contacts less than an hour ago that some sort of weird thing was going on with those candidates that might have a connection to you. We heard the name Rupphauser and then we thought of your friend Ms. Mitsuhama Duarte.

"She must keep her buddy Fennie well-serviced for him to tolerate her involvement with your pathetic group."

"You are so full of shit."

"That may be – you get to be my age and your insides slow down quite a bit.

"Now, just step this way and we'll get out of here and go find the rest of your commie socialist asswipes and save the Secret Service a shitload of investigation and court work. To be able to find you all, essentially, in one place in a town where people meet their great reward or disappear all the time without much notice – well, it's better than anything we could've hoped."

"Y'know, there are witnesses here and there are security camer-"

"We took care of the cameras. Oh, that's right, the witnesses."

Then Mr. Plaid Pants and his friend calmly started shooting each of the waiting witnesses in the head.

"Now, just come with us. Before we dispatch you, we're going to figure out how to access the money you've been using to finance all your socialist propaganda."

Mr. Plaid Pants' friend at the opposite end of the platform was at that moment re-loading. As he finished re-loading and started to raise his gun, a newly-arrived MTA customer carrying a gallon jug of water leapt over the bodies of the dying passengers and, at full speed, delivered a full-body shove against the gunman. Unprepared for that kind of heroism, the gunman, soaked when the gallon jug burst open, flew all the way to the opposite side of the subway rails. First, when he hit the electrified rail, he was instantly electrocuted. Next, he was sliced and diced as a train coming from the opposite direction ran directly over him just as he was exhaling his last breath.

Pongo used the confusion to sprint past the hero customer and up the stairs to street level. Mr. Plaid Pants ran after him, shooting the hero MTA customer in the temple on the way.

As Pongo sprinted toward the Penn Station concourse entrance, he tried to flag down MTA security officers. After running about 50 yards, he was able to get the attention of two of them.

"MAN WITH A GUN!!" he shouted, pointing behind him. "HE'S WEARING PLAID PANTS. HE'S JUST AROUND THE CORNER BEHIND ME!!"

Unfortunately, Mr. Plaid Pants heard Pongo's shout as well. He retreated in the opposite direction. A block away, he casually hopped into the getaway car he and his associate had parked 20 minutes or so earlier and slowly drove toward the George Washington Bridge and points south.

By the time they turned the corner, the MTA security officers were unable to see Mr. Plaid Pants or anyone resembling him. Moments later there were multiple 9-1-1 calls to the NYPD about dead bodies at the MTA subway platform nearby.

Fortunately for Pongo, the MTA security officers didn't get a very good look at him in the dark. He was able to find the train platform for the 10:45 Amtrak to Poughkeepsie within a couple of minutes. Much to his relief, the train was running about 10 minutes late. Much MORE to his relief, every single one of the Poughkeepsians were there waiting for him. Phil gave him a massive hug.

At that moment, though, he sensed a large figure approaching from behind him. He was about to turn around when he felt a firm, super-strong hand grip his right shoulder. He thought he was about to be handcuffed and hauled off to some European dungeon for waterboarding and eventual death. He bent to the strength of the hand's grip and turned around to see the large – as in massive - man he recognized as the Homeland Security agent who'd slashed the zip line he'd used to get out of the Whittmyer Building just as he flopped through the window of the next building over. Only now he was wearing a fedora which obscured his face somewhat.

"Hi, there Perry," the man said in an almost scary-deep voice.

"Uh, um, actually, I go by Pongo, sir."

"Whatever, I'm Agent Coraje ("korr-AH-hay"). I'm not here to arrest you. I'm just here to make sure you and the others make it onto that last train to Poughkeepsie. Your friends and I have been waiting here for you for a little while."

"Huh?"

"The others will explain in more detail later. FYI, Mitch and I have been good friends for more than thirty years. When things started to fall apart for you earlier this evening, Mitch knew I was stationed nearby and I was able to get to the Whittmyer in less than five minutes.

"He hasn't told me any of the details about what was going on. I just know it was something designed **_not_** to specifically benefit Ms. Clinton. One of my best friends in the agency told me if he had the prospect of being on her protection detail for four years or, God forbid, eight years, he was going to take his own life. I believed him. He'd been on her family's protection detail at their Chappaqua home for most of the last eight years and, during that time, he'd lost his wife and both of his children to cancers. He simply couldn't deal with the prospect of having to be around her corrosive personality again.

"I literally owe my life to Mitch, many times over. And I trust Mitch with my life. And he promises me the rest of you are just as trustworthy as he. That's good enough for me.

"But, just the same, just so you understand, if anyone ever asks any of us, we've never, ever met. And, except for Mitch, we never will meet again. Capiche?"

Every single one of the Poughkeepsians nodded as Coraje looked around at the group.

"You have nothing but my very best wishes," he said with a thumb-up fist as he turned and left. "Stickin' to the union!"[*]

* * *

REPERCUSSIONS AND REGRETS

Pongo shared his brush with extermination by Mr. Plaid Pants with Heather and the others as they waited to board the Amtrak train going north. As he described watching the two men shoot the waiting three or four subway passengers in the head, Bianca and Annie both had to turn and vomit. There was a weird mixture of tearful sadness and relief circulating through the group.

Franklin, not one to be easily saddened, appeared to be on the verge of a complete emotional breakdown.

"This thing was done to help me and people have died," he said, his voice shaking and tears running down the sides of his face.

"No one died at the Whittmyer," Phil said forcefully. "Nothing whatsoever we did there caused anyone any permanent harm.

"Those sociopaths, Mr. Plaid Pants and his associate, they were going to do what they planned to do regardless of what happened at the Whittmyer. They were simply hoping to catch us all in one place, like a subway or train platform, where they might be able to extinguish us all in one fell swoop.

"We can never, ever all be exposed together at once, never again. Especially Franklin."

They all agreed.

"But, we can't let the – what's it called again? – the banality of evil intimidate us into giving up or compromising our principles," Holly said. "Can we?"

"It's not giving in to evil to be prudent about protecting the ones you love," Sam said.

"*Prudence*, that's a good word," Franklin said.

"Let's just let this day settle and get behind us," Cherisse said. "Let's get home and get back to our lives. Let's get back on track and figure out how to make the Second Bill of Rights a reality, no matter whether one of us or all of us is taken down."

"Amen, Mama," Harry said, in an uncharacteristic moment of solemnity.

* * *

---

[*] "*Union Maid*," lyrics by Woody Guthrie, 1960

JUMPING AHEAD

A nd go about their regular business they did. Franklin and Holly got back to their class schedules and progressed toward the degrees they would each earn 1-1/2 years later. Franklin would go on to become a highly-respected and successful physical therapist, known throughout New England for his abilities to motivate previously unmotivatable patients. Patients with virtually no hope of lower and/or upper body mobility. Patients who would constantly do their best to impress Franklin with their unwillingness to give up.

Within five years, spinal cord-injured patients from all across the U.S.A. and even Great Britain would travel thousands of miles for treatments at his private clinic – where patients __never__ were turned away for inability to pay and where almost all patients (those with family incomes under $150,000 a year) paid *nothing at all.*

$$* \quad * \quad *$$

BACK TO JUNE 2016: A
NEUROLOGICAL DEVELOPMENT

O n June 5, 2016, about six weeks after the Whittmyer Building candidate sessions with Fennie Rupphauser, the Poughkeepsians were gathered in Phil's basement on a Sunday evening (he'd had a top of the line security system upgrade installed by then with tamperproof 24-hour security video cameras monitored by a top personal security firm).

They were watching a televised campaign speech by Hillary at the Dolby Theater in Los Angeles less than 48 hours before she was set to go "over the top" with enough primary delegates from the California Primary to secure the Democratic nomination for President. The speech had been promoted as her key, definitive issues positions presentation for the remainder of the campaign.

She began the speech by asking for a moment of silence for all victims of gun violence from earlier in the year, especially the four New York subway shooting victims and law enforcement victims from around the country, not to mention the almost-impossible-to-count numbers of victims of public school shootings over recent years, going back to Newtown, Connecticut.

As she progressed through her speech, she first went after her traditional 'low-hanging fruit,' repeating her stump speech promises to support equal rights for all women (though, pointedly, not advocating for a constitutional amendment).

As she ventured into her support for same-sex marriage, the Poughkeepsians noticed there were late-arrivers being ushered into their front row seats. Shortly after they'd been seated, she began expressing praise for their valiant service in Afghanistan, Iraq and as Special Forces advisers in Syria. As the TV cameras zoomed in on them, Franklin was the first to notice each of them had bandaged heads, some of the bandages lightly stained as though their head wounds weren't completely healed yet.

Less than a minute later, as the cameras were panning for smiling and otherwise supportive reaction images of Hillary supporters – including husband Bill – the facial expressions from those sitting on the dais suddenly appeared to change from supportive smiles to worried frowns and gasps.

At that same moment, the sound of Hillary's speaking voice became halting and stuttery and then, suddenly, it stopped altogether.

Then the camera panned away from the reaction shots of Bill and the others on the dais to Hillary herself. There not only were audible gasps from the Dolby Theater audience, but from everyone in Phil's basement as well.

Hillary's body had suddenly frozen up in a stiff vertical position as she appeared simultaneously to be shaking like not just a bobble head, but a bobble body. If it had been in a comedy club, it would've drawn howls of laughter. Before anyone on the dais had time to react, the shaking stopped and a kind of a glaze appeared to come over Hillary's eyes.

The next thing everyone saw caused muffled screams in the crowd and even a few in Phil's basement (from Marcia, especially).

Hillary lifted her legs up onto the dais table which touched against the side of the podium and began climbing over it. As she climbed in the direction of the audience, strands of drool appeared to be coming out of each of the corners of her mouth as she bared her teeth, which were clenched together.

Her climbing was so rapid that even her long-armed husband couldn't reach her in time to prevent her from hopping over the table, onto the stage in front of the table and then into the narrow orchestra pit below the stage.

There was a loud gasp from the crowd as she disappeared into the orchestra pit. The Poughkeepsians assumed she must have been stunned by the fall because she was out of sight for perhaps five seconds or more.

But then, suddenly, she sprang up from the orchestra pit and quickly was tearing at the bandages on the soldiers' head wounds before anyone could reach her. (Phil thought her flailing hands resembled an old Three Stooges routine – but he held his tongue. This occurrence did NOT call for levity.)

Hillary's eyes seemed as big as saucers – like Franklin had looked during his previous decompensation episodes, she appeared to be terrified by what she was doing, as though she had no control over her actions (she didn't). By the time security staff and her currently not-so-randy husband caught up to her, she'd completely torn all bandages off of two soldiers' heads and had grabbed an extra-long stiletto-heeled shoe off the foot of a woman in the front row and was holding it high in the air, about to bring it down like a roofing hammer onto the head wound of a 30-something male soldier who must've weighed twice Hillary's weight.

Once the security staff and Bill grabbed her, they couldn't maintain their grips. Her strength was off the charts. She almost got in one good hammer swing of the stiletto heel just as six security officers plus Slick Willie took her to the ground. Three of the security officers were so terrified at what they'd seen that they **each** actually tasered her. One of them even tasered her a second time.

"Oh. My. Sweet. Jesus!" Cherisse exclaimed. "I fucked up."

"Dear God, Cherisse – while Franklin was seizing up at the Whittmyer, you must've put that micro needle he'd just licked clean back into Hillary's head," Bianca said.

"No shit, Sherlock," Cherisse said snidely. "Like you couldn't have waited ten minutes to give it to him."

"Christ, let's stop assigning blame and watch what's going on on the telly, you guys," Harry pleaded.

And watch they did. It was a new generation's equivalent of O.J.'s slow speed freeway chase. Must-watch live drama.

Within about three minutes, though, there was one of those impromptu "Breaking News" news breaks from the network's New York headquarters. So the New York anchor could tell the rest of the country what they'd just seen – and, more importantly, so they'd have an excuse to get the live camera feed away from the shocking behavior of the previously-likely next leader of the free world.

The entire country was relieved to not have to watch Hillary go through her – for lack of a better word – zombie mental breakdown. But viewers were actually thoroughly entertained by the efforts of the newsreader – former Iraq War cheerleader/anchor Lester Holt – to come up with different euphemisms for wack-job. His hilarious fumbling efforts to find non-offensive ways to describe Hillary's bizarre episode would go on to become a legendary moment in live television broadcasting. And definitely _**not**_ in the Edward R. Murrow Battle of Britain calm-under-fire way.

Oh, well.

* * *

As Jon Stewart was watching at home, he was waxing nostalgic over how much fun it would've been to have _**that**_ campaign speech to dissect on a Monday "_Daily Show._" Not to mention the classic Lester Holt performance. "_Shit, shoulda stayed another year,_" he thought to himself. Maybe, he thought, he could convince his successor to bring him on the following night for a guest appearance.

Oh, well.

* * *

The following day, it was announced that Hillary would be making a momentous announcement in a live televised speech the night of the California Primary.

It would become the most-watched televised political speech since Nixon's resignation speech almost 42 years earlier.

* * *

COMPULSIVE HONESTY

Hillary began her speech contritely. (As though she had any other choice.) "Two nights ago, much of the nation witnessed on live television some sort of seizure attack I suffered while making a speech at the Dolby Theater here in Los Angeles. I am here tonight to offer my deepest apologies and requests for forgiveness to every person who was affected by that attack.

"I have no idea why the attack happened. I have been undergoing diagnostic examinations during the past day and a half. My physicians also have no idea why the attack happened.

"So it is with great grief that I must express to you that, if my party does, in fact, go forward with my nomination to be your next President, you need to understand that those kinds of attacks apparently could happen again, at any time, without any warning.

"Please rest assured, though: on the remote chance that the attacks are somehow related to exposure to people with open head wounds, such as those kind souls I assaulted, I will make it my top priority as a candidate and as an elected officeholder to avoid whenever possible being within a football field's length of anyone who has such an injury.

"So, much to my regret, you won't be seeing any pictures of me visiting armed services veterans recovering from their wounds.

"Also, in the spirit of full disclosure, I am compelled to owe up to the following facts:

"First, I enjoy the company of persons blessed with massive wealth. No matter how they accrued that wealth. Well, I suppose if they made their billions by murdering babies for their organs and blood, **_that_** probably would be over the line. For a while, anyway. But, normally, the bigger the billions, the better. I make no apologies for that. It's part of who I am.

"It's not that I'm not fond of those who are not billionaires. It's just that I would prefer not to have to be around them for very long at any given time. Well, actually, I'm **_not_** fond of them anyway. Unless they're middle aged women like myself who've had lying, cheating husbands who screw just about anything with tits.

(Gasps in every living room all over the country.)

"And even then, I get tired of hearing most of **them** whine. If you're going to stay with a lying, cheating, fornicating pussy chaser, you should be getting **something** out of it. Take it from me, there's no fucking way on earth I'd still be with Slick-o there (pointing off camera to stage left) if it didn't give me a greater opportunity to achieve my goals. Or goal, that is: becoming the first woman to hold the Presidency.

"Now surely you've heard the allegations that Slick-o and I took money from foreign governments and foreign businesses for our Clinton Foundation while I was Secretary of State. Some have suggested that there was a quid pro quo – something in exchange for something else – involved in those eleven-hundred-plus donations.

"Well, *shit*! Is there anyone out there *fucking stupid enough* to believe that our donors didn't expect **something** in exchange for those donations? By the way, here's a true shout out from all The Blue Wellesley girls to Frank Giustra! Thanks for the jazillions, Canuck-Buddy! *No, Bill, I did NOT say Fuck-Buddy!* Shit, he's *your* fucking friend. (She looked off camera to stage left as she said that.) No problem with the Colombian trade clearance thing, Frank – everyone needs oil, right?

"Also, in the spirit of full disclosure: I absolutely fucking *adore* Wall Street. I would give every last Wall Street CEO a blow job if I thought it might mean they'd trickle down a little more on all you little people out there. Shit, I think I just might do that. Don't know why I haven't thought of that sooner. All of you Occupy Wall Street losers out there: feel free to sit and shit in the city parks all you like. I'm still gonna give as many financial handjobs to the Koch boys as it takes to bring them around. Shit, remember what I **just said**? They're fucking *billionaires*, times a jazillion!

"I took $3,500 in donations from them and I'm ready to take more.* I am going to make it my goal to demonstrate that their plans to spend $900 million to defeat me if I'm nominated – *Ha!* **IF**!! – that those $900 million would be better spent juicing individual members of Congress and members of state legislatures. Fuck, I am *ON BOARD* for the Keystone XL. Haven't you dipsticks read what I said when I was Secretary of State?

"Who fucking needs boreal forests in the middle of nowhere in Canada anyway? *You* already know I'm right, Frank, wherever you are.

"Anyway, enough full disclosure: just send my campaign all the money you fucking can. No amount is too much. Many amounts are too small, though. All of you deluded little wage serfs out there, if you think your little $5 and $10 donations mean shit to me, then just keep sending 'em in. By all means. We'll cash 'em. We'll even keep your street address for direct mailings and your E-Mail address for lots of junk E-Mails. But if you think I give a flying fuck about what you

_____
* *Truth Revolt*, 4/14/14

and your tiny bank balances mean in the great scheme of the cosmos, you can eat shit and die for all I care.

"Don't send cash, though. Bill might be too tempted to pilfer it to tip his latest big-breasted bimbo.

"Now, please accept my thanks for taking time out of your little evenings to hear my explanation for what happened the other night.

"My hope is that you'll never have to see that kind of display again. Please be kind to your children and grandchildren. They deserve better than what we've given them. You already **_know_** what we've given them: a planet that will be hotter than fucking Venus by the time their great-grandchildren are born. *IF* they're born.

"Happy trails to all of you oblivious pathetic morons!" Then, under her breath in the direction of stage left off camera just as the video was fading out, "*Get your hands off of your fuckin' willy, Willie!*"

✳ ✳ ✳

Many, but not most, of the television stations carrying Hillary's speech cut away from it as she uttered the second obscenity. All of the stations carrying it had a three-second delay which allowed each obscenity to be bleeped (one network, Fox, goofed and let the first three obscenities through un-bleeped, though). Those who chose to carry the entire speech quickly followed it with stunned pundits who observed that she simply must've been under the influence of heavy medication.

Millions of stoners scattered all over the country who were watching the speech while high were convinced it was just an excellent live-action, Saturday Night Live-style parody of a Comedy Central "*Drunk History*" episode. Just something designed to ingratiate Hillary to the slacker-stoner community.

The corporatists at the helm of the Democratic National Party were torn: she actually had said all the things they'd hoped to hear. *Except those were things they'd hoped to hear **behind closed doors in secret**, they way the <u>usually</u> got their candidates' true positions.*

What to do. What to do.

Here's what they did: they pretended, more or less, that her speech never happened. Of course, when asked about it, they blamed it on medications. What they didn't know was: this was the **_new Hillary_**. Thanks to an infusion of Franklin's bodily fluids and reconstituted DNA directly into her brain (bypassing the blood-brain barrier), she now had no way to prevent herself from being anything other than completely candid about what she was thinking and what she was planning.

So, they allowed her nomination to go forward. It would take a complete and unprecedented grass roots rebellion by the delegates to *prevent* her nomination from proceeding. And that wasn't in the cards.

Fortunately for Hillary, the vast majority (literally 96 percent) of her delegates were middle-aged to elderly women who were completely invested in seeing that she was elected the first woman President. They simply couldn't accept that this 'new Hillary' was real. Many of them were convinced *beyond even the remotest doubt* that her new personality had to be part of some sort of Republican conspiracy to infuse her with some new GMO. Some sort of GMO which mutated her personality in such a way as to __prevent__ her from expressing her true feelings, rather than forcing her to express them with uncontrollable candor.

* * *

B ack in Poughkeepsie, Franklin felt nothing but remorse for Hillary.

"**No one** *should have their innermost thoughts belched forth from a loose mental sphincter under the unforgiving eye of a television lens,*" he thought to himself. "*Not even someone who owes would-be constituents far more candor that she's ever provided. There but for the whims of providence go I.*"

* * *

MOVING ON

A s far as Franklin and the rest of the Poughkeepsians were concerned, though, the rest of the Presidential campaign was virtually meaningless. Until they could excise the cancers of greed and bigotry from the Congress by replacing members of both chambers who stood foursquare against the USA-SBR, whoever held the Presidency would be hamstrung and – for lack of a better term – emasculated when it came to accomplishing almost all politically liberal or progressive goals.

Almost every one of the Poughkeepsians asked Franklin if he would cast a vote for the Democratic Presidential candidate if it were Hillary.

His answer was the best any contemporary political ethicist has ever given:

"You vote for the *person* and what she or he **stands for**. You **don't** vote for the person *because of the party they're in*. There are many Democrats who are Democrats *in name only*, especially in the South. Their ilk would sell their own mothers' souls for the right price. That said, if you're voting for a *Republican* **OR** a *closet Republican* in 2016, you must either be mentally defective or striving to *evolve* merely to the level of a completely and unredeemably ignorant ambulatory anal orifice."

* * *

A s it turned out, the 2016 Democratic National Convention in Philadelphia was definitely _not_ always sunny. It turned out to be the most divided convention since the 1968 fiasco in Chicago when Chicago Mayor Richard J. Daley made it his mission to have anti-war protestors beaten to a pulp by police both outside and, occasionally, inside the International Amphitheater convention hall (even television news reporters were roughed up by police and security staff in '68). Thankfully, no network television reporters were beaten during the 2016 convention (at least, not any _white_ reporters) – but despite Hillary's **image** taking a severe beating at the convention following her televised attempted brain harvesting, she simply would **NOT** voluntarily relinquish her claim at political dynasty.

Not even when polls showed she was likely to lose to the Republican nominee by at least 10 percentage points.

Delegates for Sen. Sanders and ex-Gov. O'Malley split Hillary's opposition so severely that Hillary was able to manipulate the process to guarantee her nomination. *Despite*, on two separate occasions, security staff manhandling and battering Sanders' and O'Malley's operatives when they tried to bring into Wells Fargo Arena recently-returned Army veterans from Afghanistan with completely-bandaged (but serious) head wounds.

Meanwhile, Democratic National Party bosses remained completely tone-deaf over the choice of *Wells Fargo Arena* as the site where delegates would vote on the nominee: Wells Fargo was involved in cheating 34,000 minority home loan applicants during the 2004-2008 housing boom by charging them higher fees than non-minority applicants and unnecessarily steering them into more risky loans than non-minority applicants. Wells Fargo's consequence for its racism: a $175 million fine with no criminal charges whatsoever.[*] In addition, the "too big to fail" Wells Fargo earlier had to accept $25 billion in 2008 Federal bailout funds to keep from going under due to its involvement in toxic subprime loans.

The Poughkeepsians viewed the election as a lost cause until Hillary was caught on a security video recording at a neurological hospital nine weeks before election day forcing her way into a lab with brain tissue awaiting biopsies after sneaking away from her Secret Service escorts. The video showed her actually forcing open biopsy cassettes and slurping out the contents. Although the experience did wonders for her complexion – she looked 30 years old again literally overnight – it finally forced her to withdraw from the race. Barely in time for ballots across the nation to be printed with a new standard-bearer.

The new standard-bearer? None other than U.S. Sen. Elizabeth Warren, who, literally against her will, was drafted as the candidate by unanimous acclamation during an impromptu weekend gathering of all 50 states' Democratic Party chairpersons.

When, in private, she objected testily to being *forced* to run, the national party chairperson responded, "Tough shit. You're needed. You can win. Even though our Wall Street financiers are going batshit crazy, we've got no other choice.

---

[*] *AllGov*, 7/16/12; *The Week*, 7/13/12

"My advice would be to pick your running mate carefully, because all those semi-literate gun-totin' Tea Partiers are going to have you in their crosshairs."

Without missing a beat, right then and there she named Sen. Sanders as her running mate.

Despite almost **$2 billion** worth of negative ads funded by the Koch brothers and various undisclosed Wall Street interests – plus predictions by 'inside the beltway' pundits that she'd get creamed by big money media manipulators - Sen. Warren "eked out" a win.

By 25 percentage points.

Voters of all stripes – except Tea Partiers - simply adored her.

And her coattails brought in dozens of new progressive candidates into the U.S. House and U.S. Senate, not to mention into state legislatures nationwide.

It was the first of several significant steps which, a few years later, would lead to passage of the USA-SBR in both Congressional chambers. After overcoming a number of unanticipated hurdles, that is - a few of those hurdles, figuratively speaking, approaching the size of Mount Everest.

* * *

Following that 'wave' election and completion of his physical therapy doctorate the following year, Franklin intended to devote most of his energies for the rest of his healthful life to his physical therapy practice in the Hyde Park-Poughkeepsie area. He would still occasionally make himself available for USA-SBR activities, but his *main* focus was to help improve the lives of spinal injury victims and Third World polio victims, one person at a time.

As in his earlier life, that focus was sharp. And productive.

The stellar reputation of his practice soon spread like an uncontrolled virus. A virus for which no Salk vaccine was needed.

* * *

EPILOGUE

On a hot late summer evening on Aug. 16, 2017, seven years to the day after Franklin's revival, there was a meteorological event of some note in Southern California. In the area along Presidential Drive near Simi Valley, California, there was an unusually strong lightning storm with record rainfall totals for the date. Meteorologists on the late local news that evening referred to witnesses seeing a rare occurrence of "sprite lightning," with a bright red explosive-looking bolt of energy reaching far into the evening sky, even into space.

Witnesses in the area reported seeing the bottom end of that colorful bolt strike at the Ronald Reagan Presidential Library, about four and a half hours after its 5 p.m. closing time, in the area where Reagan and others were interred.

An extended power outage at the facility prevented direct contact by authorities with staff there. However, there were a couple of 9-1-1 calls received from what sounded like staff personnel at the site, but each of the calls was cut off in mid-sentence by disconnection on the callers' end of the signals.

The 9-1-1 operator later reported each of the callers sounded a little panicked. The 9-1-1 operator was brought up on disciplinary proceedings weeks later for not sending emergency personnel to investigate. She explained that she'd already dispatched all available police cruisers, EMT's and fire trucks to other seemingly more serious calls where the callers were able to stay on the line. There were no additional law enforcement or emergency personnel to send to the site, she insisted. Which was truthful.

The disciplinary action against her was soon after dropped. The reason her managers chose to bring the disciplinary proceedings in the first place wasn't disclosed.

That is, not until six full months after a Freedom of Information Act (FOIA) request was submitted the following January. The San Jose Mercury News reporter who received the response to the FOIA request went missing the day after he got it, **_along with_** that FOIA response, which he hadn't had time to enter into his work computer.

But his description of its details over the phone with his co-worker-slash-best friend the night that he disappeared left her unable to sleep and constantly looking over her shoulder for _days_ afterward.

AFTERWORD

This effort at a blend of historical fiction, science fiction and social commentary could not have happened but for the shockingly sobering hypocrisies exemplified through the public political life and, to a lesser extent, the publicly aired details of the private life of Hillary Rodham Clinton and her unestranged-slash-estranged-slash-unestranged husband Bill, a man with unequaled oratorical gifts – and, apparently, unequaled sex appeal. As a confirmed heterosexual, I honestly wouldn't know about that last part. I only know what I read.

Described by Michael Moore as our finest Republican President, Mr. Clinton – nominally, a Democrat - has maintained for the most part a fairly admirable and respectable public persona since his presidency, especially after the 2004 Thailand tsunami. That is, if all you do is watch TV, anyway (except for Saturday Night Live, Fox News, MSNBC and Comedy Central).

But his and Hillary's real-life *private* lives probably have sold more tabloid newspapers than all of the phony "Aliens Probed My Anus" stories combined over the last 25 years.

Of course, it's *possible* that real-life Hillary – *unlike* in this book's parallel universe - never has uttered a single expletive in her private life, whether about her husband, her career or anything else. And it's entirely *possible* that it could *never even enter her mind* to express in public anything remotely resembling the language she uses in this book's parallel universe. But accounts from the likes of Ronald Kessler, who had access to Secret Service agents on the Clintons' protective details, would suggest she has no qualms using strong language when it suits her.

Nevertheless, dear reader, this author must implore you to remember: the **_fictional_** Hillary in the parallel universe of this book who goes on a televised expletive-laced rant has a **_pretty good_** _excuse_ – her own brain has been involuntarily invaded by the candor-inducing bodily fluids of a back-from-the-dead President.

All of that said, the focus of this book never was intended to be Hillary's dysfunctional marriage, except to the extent that her **remaining _in_** that marriage – despite documented husbandly _infidelity after infidelity after infidelity, ad infinitum_ – constitutes a massive cognitively-dissonant 500-pound gorilla-in-the-room-sized hypocrisy for every last thinking feminist still drawing a breath in this nation.

Poor, poor woman **whose man done her wrong** but still underneath underline endures, **still** puts her heart out there day after day, hope against hope, to be the glue which keeps her marriage thriving, that golden example of making a marriage work when a lesser person would give up and abandon the cheater, a cheater who's actually a loving father and grandfather.

Such.   Radioactive.   Bullshit.

As in: anyone with half of an (un-slurped) brain surely has to infer that she's stayed with that horndog primarily to improve her prospects for winning the Presidency. _No woman of independent means who's **not** brain dead_ puts up with a serial adulterer whose reputation for cheating is known not just up and down the block where they live, but in virtually every home from sea to shining sea and beyond. Not since the 1950's anyway.

And, yet, every time HRC makes a publicity stop on a book tour or on her nascent campaign, **seemingly conscious and sentient women** in their 40's and older queue up by the carload to express their admiration for the oppressed fair maiden (formerly) of the Ozarks.

If nothing else, Hillary has strengthened the gagging reflex of every single American who's followed the dramatic saga of her public and private lives over the years. (You may insert your favorite gagging reflex joke here, America.)

Oh, well.

My hope is that this book will compel Hillary, U.S. Sen. Elizabeth Warren and every last progressive-slash-liberal voter who reads it to embrace the possibility of lasting positive change through a government **forced** in non-violent ways by its own people to be accountable to the least of its citizens rather than to the wealthiest of them.

As that long-haired dude in those books the Gideons leave in motels all over the land is rumored to have said, "Inasmuch as ye have done it unto one of the **least** of these my brethren, ye have done it unto **me.**"*

Translation: when Republicans and closeted Republicans self-identifying as Democrats defecate all over the poor, the working poor and the disintegrating middle class, they're really shitting all over Jesus - unless I'm not up to date on my English language proficiency.

Not a pretty picture.

My thanks go out for help with this book painting whatever picture it paints to the Franklin Delano Roosevelt Presidential Library and Museum staff, even if they're not crazy about the picture painted here. Especially their archives staff, including archivists Virginia Lewick and Sarah Malcolm.

---

* KJV, _Matthew_ 25:40

In addition, Museum Curator Anne Jordan and Museum Technician Tara McGill were of assistance in trying to solve a technical mystery related to FDR's first exposure to television. The mystery remains unsolved, but they did their best to help. Likewise, Mr. Barry Mishkind helped point me to a possible source to solve that little mystery. Not so many thanks to the Library of American Broadcasting at the University of Maryland in College Park, MD, which ignored my plea for help with that mystery – same for a request to NBC's archives. Sometimes, certain details apparently are simply lost to time, or to people who claim they don't *have* time to help.

Massive appreciation also is extended to Dr. Alexander R. MacKay, a Spokane, Washington neurosurgeon who took pity on me and shared vital basic details about procedures for obtaining brain biopsies after College of Medicine reference librarians at both the University of Washington and the University of Arizona (my alma mater!) flatly declined to help. I'm hopeful Dr. MacKay will forgive me for abbreviating the time for recovery from those procedures. Likewise, I must emphasize that the idea of using nitrous oxide on the candidates undergoing those biopsies was entirely mine. Dr. MacKay made it clear that, due to there being no nerve endings within the brain, the procedures could be done quite nicely just with a local anesthetic.

I've done my best to notate where I obtained the facts for the historical parts of this fiction. Where there are no notations about sources for facts, the facts came from *well-sourced* Wikipedia entries or other similar resources.

By the way, according to U.S. National Weather Service records, there really **was** a strong thunderstorm in the Hyde Park area on Aug. 16, 2010 – but, no, to the best of my knowledge there was no sprite lightning then, certainly none which blew open a hole into a President's - or anyone else's - burial vault six feet underground.

Likewise, there really was a person who asked Jon Stewart the question at his Oct. 9, 2012 Daily Show episode taping about trying to use on-air pressure to compel the Koch brothers to appear on his show. That was yours truly.

In addition, there really was someone who tried to find out why the Spokane International Airport wrote a contract for its food service provider (Host International) which allows the provider to severely limit the brands of soft drinks sold at the facility for no additional benefit to the airport or its customers. Again, that was yours truly. The politically-appointed airport director really did tell me, essentially, to stuff it because he only has to answer to the State Auditor (yes, I have that in writing).

Much of the inspiration for details in the book came from the exceptional biography, "*Traitor to His Class: The Privileged Life and Radical Presidency of Franklin Delano Roosevelt*," by H. W. Brands (2008, Doubleday). I'm hopeful Mr. Brands will forgive me for making FDR a much more accomplished secondary education pupil and college student during his second go-round in life than he was during his actual life. Like most of us, I suspect that, as a more mature student, FDR would've excelled scholastically, especially with all that resume-enhancing on-the-job education he had while serving as 'leader of the free world.' Besides, even if he still were a quasi-slacker student in his second go-round, it's completely plausible that modern-day grade inflation would show, superficially at least, a superb scholastic performance by the man who defeated Hitler. I'd like to think as well that Mr. Brands would agree it's plausible that a resurrected FDR would, literally, jump at the chance to make good use of his polio-free legs to become an accomplished hiker and outdoorsman. It seems much easier for me to imagine that scenario, given that he's sharing his day-to-day life in this book with a real middle class family, than imagining him gravitating back to a rich man's leisurely pursuits, like sailing and deep-sea fishing.

Most of the inspiration for additional historical details came from Howard Zinn's "*A People's History of the United States*" (2003, Harper & Row), a book which should be required reading for *every single high school senior* in the U.S.A. If I'd been required to read it as a 17-year-old, it just might've inspired me to an entirely different life path. And I most certainly would've sought out an opportunity to meet Mr. Zinn, a World War II Army Air Force bombardier who flew on multiple combat missions in Europe. His experiences being ordered to drop conventional bombs and napalm explosives on civilian targets shaped his anti-war perspectives for the rest of his life. He died in 2010, before I'd even realized his seminal work existed.

Oh, well.

Bill Moyers' April 12, 2013 "Moyers & Company" interview with Sherman Alexie also was a wonderful resource, providing keen insights into the beautiful mind of Mr. Alexie and the Native American experience, not to mention reaffirming Mr. Moyers' unsurpassed compassion and insight as an interviewer.

Some additional tidbits of Roosevelt lore were culled from "A White House Christmas," Alvin Rosembaum, 1992, Preservation Press, courtesy of a suggestion by Ms. Malcolm of the FDR Library.

And I would be remiss if I didn't credit the movie versions of Jack Finney's 1955 book, "The Body Snatchers" (Dell Publishing), for the inspiration leading to the back cover art for the print version of this book (and the brief passage about Sen. Franken's unanticpated endorsement of Hillary Clinton's campaign).

For those who fault this book for making FDR's updated Second Bill of Rights so comprehensive that it might be tough for the so-called 'average' voter to comprehend, well, please ask yourselves when the last time was that you looked at general election ballots in any of the states which have the ballot initiative process. A bullet-pointed summary of the 38-page Un-Screwing of America Second Bill of Rights (USA-SBR) would look right at home on the average general election ballot in those states.

But that misses the point, because our process for amending the Constitution as it now stands doesn't even go to the ballot for approval by citizens themselves. The current process is unwieldy and designed to be next-to-impossible to complete when initiated through the Congress. And it's designed to be dangerously wide-ranging and even less likely to culminate in enactment when attempted through a constitutional convention.

Simply put, the Constitution is de facto-designed to be nearly impossible to change under modern-day circumstances. Despite the fact that it is entirely conceivable that amending it could be the only way to stave off a complete collapse of credibility for the main institutions of governance.

When the only choices for a frustrated, nickeled-and-dimed to death sea of poor, working poor and middle class citizens is between (1) attempting a next-to-impossible constitutional amendment process or (2) allowing social and economic injustices to remain unaddressed by a corporatized system stacked against them or (3) initiating a revolution – well, that's like getting to choose for one's dinner between sugar-frosted baked shit, chocolate-glazed microwaved shit and deep-fried shit with sprinkles on top.

Not a recipe for hope, much less success.

We.   Have.   To.   Do.   Better.

Aug. 15, 2014-July 18, 2015
Spokane, WA

ABOUT THE AUTHOR

R ob Ethington graduated from the University of Arizona with a degree in journalism, working more than five years for daily newspapers – including one owned by former Vice President Dan ("potatoe") Quayle's grandfather – before eventually choosing a career in social services, in which he has worked almost continuously since 1984. He and his late father both were born and raised in the god-forsaken searingly hot deserts of central Arizona – a good place to visit for about three months out of each year, but not much else. Unless you have plenty of H2O.

Father of a son, 32, and daughter, 28, by two failed marriages to different women, he has resided in Spokane, Washington from Dec. 31, 2000 through the present, currently living alone but blessed with wonderful neighbors on all sides. A formerly prolific letters-to-the-editor contributor, this is his first foray into novel writing.

His main literary influences are Edward Abbey, Matt Taibbi, Howard Zinn, Jim Hightower, John Steinbeck, Michael Moore, William Greider, Alan Weisman, Mary Roach, Thomas Frank, Stephen King, Thom Hartmann, Garrison Keillor and Molly Ivins...to name a few.

Detachable Copy of USA-SBR (For Reproduction and Sharing)

_I._ _PROTECTION FROM MANIPULATION BY WEALTHY CAPITALISTS_

Recognizing once and for all that **the influence of wealth on the political system is directly associated with the likelihood of corruption**, this Second Bill of Rights establishes, among other rights, **the right to be protected from manipulation of the political process by monied interests**, including:

> # **A permanent ban on corporate personhood**, forever undoing the Supreme Court's Citizen United ruling that the use of unlimited amounts of campaign contributions is free speech protected by the First Amendment and forever banning the legal fiction that corporations have the same rights as human beings. In addition, businesses (incorporated or otherwise) now have the same criminal law accountability and civil damage liabilities for negligence and intentional harm as human beings; likewise, business owners, corporate officers and CEOs shall **not** be immune from liability for actions or inactions which cause harm to any person, business or other entity.

> # **A permanent ban on at-large elections** involving commissions, councils and other government entities with two or more voting members where the population being represented is 1,000 or more based on the latest U.S. Census data. Recognizing that at-large elections for such entities are designed to protect the influence of monied interests and non-ethnic minority voters, the ban requires that those entities be divided into equally-proportional districts (if not already so divided) and requires election-by-district voting and representation for **both** primaries **_and_** general elections.

A permanent ban on the use of caucuses to determine parties' candidates for general elections, recognizing that caucuses are subject to disproportionate influences of the wealthiest individuals and organizations able to hire organizers to pay persons to show up at caucus meetings and to pay those same persons to promise to cast their non-secret votes as instructed by the organizers. The permanent ban is enacted recognizing that caucus gatherings to nominate candidates involve only a tiny fraction of all eligible voters and, as such, by definition are an undemocratic and ineffective method of determining the will of the majority of voters. All political parties now are required to nominate all candidates for all elections through primary elections conducted by election officials of counties and states throughout the nation. In addition, recognizing that states' individual Presidential primaries serve primarily to allow candidates to dupe residents of each state into believing that their needs somehow supersede the needs of residents of other regions, all individual states' primary elections now are replaced with a single nationwide primary election conducted every Presidential election year on the Tuesday closest to 100 days in advance of Election Day. Barring the death or voluntary withdrawal of a candidate or a lawful court order, political parties now are bound by results of all primary elections.

Recognizing that monied interests have a history of paying witnesses, expert or otherwise, to mislead congressional panels, legislative committees, county boards, city councils, etc. in order to achieve their lawmaking goals, there is a permanent ban on testimony and other remarks _not_ taken under oath before all levels of government – Federal, states, counties, cities, towns, etc. Persons participating in any and all such gatherings before any and all levels of government who are alleged to have knowingly spoken untruths during their participation shall be subject to Class C Federal felony perjury charges.

Recognizing that political parties holding majorities have a history of gerrymandering districts to gain ballot advantages, there is a permanent ban on gerrymandered districts of _all_ political entities; the ban would require districts to have regular rectangular shapes with 1x1, 1x2, 2x3, 3x5, 4x6, 5x7, 8x10 & 11x13 proportions, with voters in any overlapping areas getting to choose on their own the district in which they would be voting. Overlapping areas shall be the smallest possible size.

Expanded representation by elected officials: Recognizing that continued population growth without matching expansion of representational membership both dilutes the power of voters and increases the likelihood of manipulation by monied interests, membership of the

U.S. Supreme Court, U.S. Senate and U.S. House of Representatives shall immediately be expanded proportionally based on the increase in U.S. population since 1911 (93.9 million to current 308.7 million), when Federal law set U.S. House membership at 435; future membership adjustments shall be based on population changes every 10 years using U.S. Census data. The same expansions of representation shall be required immediately of all state legislatures, county commissions, city councils, school boards and all other government entities with voting members nationwide in jurisdictions with populations of at least 1,000 persons, with subsequent adjustments every 10 years based on the latest U.S. Census data. Should U.S. population ever shrink (for example, due to catastrophic events related to disease epidemics or natural disasters or dramatic declines in birth rates), representation shall be adjusted downward on the same proportional basis using data from the U.S. Census.

Recognizing that the current system of Supreme Court justice selection traditionally results in disproportional representation by corporate-biased justices, **there shall be national popular-vote elections of no more than one-half of the justices of the newly-expanded U.S. Supreme Court**, with the remaining half selected by U.S. President under the previously-existing system; under this new Bill of Rights, **all** U.S. Supreme Court justices are subject to *national retention votes* every four years, running against jurist candidates who collect signatures of at least 1 percent of the voting-age population in each and every state.

A more representational U.S. Senate. By reducing the mandated number of U.S. Senators guaranteed for each state from two to one, representation of voters in more populous states will be less diluted. The remaining U.S. Senators shall be apportioned among the states by districts according to the most recent U.S. Census in the same manner as membership of the U.S. House of Representatives.

A guarantee that the majority of voters shall always be the deciding factor in Presidential elections. Recognizing that the Electoral College is an anachronism long overdue for elimination, an outmoded vestige from the time when the only a small handful of states in the eastern half of the country were densely settled, it now is immediately and permanently dropped. All Presidential elections shall be decided based on the votes of the majority of persons casting ballots. When the top Presidential vote-getter receives only a plurality of votes, a national runoff election shall be held on the Tuesday before Thanksgiving featuring the top two vote-getters.

Publicly financed Federal, state and local elections. This new Bill of Rights shall implement a hybrid of the public election financing systems set forth by Maine and Arizona, but using Arizona's original

system for permanent removal of elected lawmakers and judges who knowingly violate rules of the financing system. In addition, there shall be a $10 Federal income tax credit for each tax filer ($20 for jointly filing parties) who provides proof that she or he voted in the most recent general (even-numbered-year) election to stimulate voter participation. Each county in each state shall issue by U.S. Mail a Federal uniformly-designed numbered national proof of voting card to each voter within 30 days after each of those general elections.

A national right to vote for all persons 18 and older, including even ex-felons who have completed their sentences and have been complying with court-ordered restitution and fine payment plans. As with Canada and some European countries, national right-to-vote cards shall be issued to each voter just prior to their 18th birthdays. Only those convicted of voter fraud shall be permanently barred from voting. The definition of voter fraud shall include actions to intimidate and otherwise suppress lawful voting, including conspiracy to suppress and attempted suppression. No voter photo identification shall EVER be required - just the voter's signature. Persons convicted of felonies shall have their voting rights restored once they are released from prison and have started making regular installment payments on fines and restitution. Voters shall be entitled to vote up to 21 days early in person or by mail and at *any* in-county polling site (*regardless* of the voter's residential voting precinct) on election days. Election days shall be defined as a 25-hour period for in-person voting starting at noon on the first Tuesday of November and ending at 1 p.m. the following day; mailed ballots postmarked by the second day of voting shall be honored. Recognizing that electronically-tallied ballots are subject to computer programming manipulation, voters now have the right to cast secret paper ballots on which simple "X" marks designate the voters' choices; photocopies shall be made of each ballot for purposes of quality control during the tabulation process. Citizens also have the right to register to vote as late as election day at **any** polling site **regardless** of the location of their residential voting precinct. The voter registration process also shall include a declaration on registration forms specifying that voters have the right not to participate in exit polls and discouraging participation in exit polls unless the Congressionally- or court-authorized organization conducting the exit poll is attempting to document whether there is fraud in the vote tallying process. In addition, all registered voters now are entitled to at least four hours of paid leave time from employers during the 25-hour voting period.

Strict limits on campaign contributions: $200 per person, per union and per business (incorporated or otherwise) for national

campaigns; $100 per person, per union and per business (incorpo-
rated or otherwise) for statewide campaigns and $50 per person, per
union and per business (incorporated or otherwise) for countywide
and citywide elections; those limits shall be inflation-adjusted annually.
Contributions by political action committees and their equivalents are
permanently banned. Those convicted of intentionally violating contribution limits and/or conspiring to violate those limits shall have their
voting rights permanently forfeited. In addition, campaign contributions at all levels shall be banned during the 31 days immediately prior
to each election. Each candidate and ballot initiative organization shall
be required to disclose to the Attorney General of the appropriate juris-
diction no later than 24 days prior to each election reports which fully
detail total amounts received from each, separate campaign donor during the entire campaign period. Failure to timely submit those reports
disqualifies the candidate/initiative from the election (whether or not
the candidate's name or initiative can be physically removed from ballots before the election). Failure to submit any such reports at all, even
untimely, shall result in the candidate/initiative organization director
being subject to Class C Federal felony charges.

 # There is **the right of all citizens to be exposed to print and
broadcast media which are _not_ the products of concentrated ownership**.
Therefore, the same individual or business (incorporated or otherwise)
is permanently banned from having an ownership interest in more
than one newspaper plus one broadcast station or pay-television station
(radio or television) anywhere in the U.S.A. Individuals or businesses
which own both a newspaper **and** a broadcast station or pay-television
station are permanently prohibited from owning both the newspaper
and the broadcast station based within the same state. In addition,
all broadcast stations **and** pay-television stations are subject to Federal
Communications Commission (FCC) licensing requirements. Once
each station's seven-year license is due to expire or be renewed, the
license shall be rewarded to the applicant for the license who has the
most investors who have invested at least $50 apiece; the total amount
of money invested shall be irrelevant. Any license applicants who knowingly submit applications listing fraudulent or sham investors shall be
subject to Class B Federal felony charges. Likewise, pay-television service providers also shall be subject to FCC licensing rules. Those service
providers also shall have seven-year licenses. Once each pay-television
service provider's seven-year license is due to expire or be renewed, the
license shall be rewarded to the applicant for the license who has **the
most investors** who have invested at least $50 apiece; the total amount of
money invested shall be irrelevant. Any pay-television license applicants
who knowingly submit applications listing fraudulent or sham investors

shall be subject to Class B Federal felony charges. Investor groups shall be permanently prohibited from holding more than one pay-television service provider license per county at a time. The number of pay-television service provider licenses shall be limited to seven per county (there are 3,144 counties or county-equivalents in the U.S.A.); no service provider shall have more than one license per county. A primary condition to qualify for a license is an indemnified agreement to make dependable services available to each and every home in the county covered by each license. The FCC shall be responsible for setting new license, re-licensing and annual operation fees county by county based on fixed percentages of full market value as determined by the FCC. The total annual fees assessed by the FCC against each license holder shall not exceed 5 percent of each broadcast station's/pay-television provider's full market value. One-fifth of all FCC-collected fees shall go to a fund dedicated to providing free general election campaign advertising for candidates who win their parties' primaries and who have signed a binding contract to abide by clean election rules set forth under the USA-SBR's provisions.

Recognizing that existing sales taxes, property taxes and small business fees and taxes inflict a disproportionately unfair economic burden on the non-wealthy **and** recognizing that the nation's most prosperous economy occurred when Federal income tax rates on the wealthy were as high as 90 percent (thus providing sufficient revenues for massive infrastructure projects including the interstate freeway system), this new Bill of Rights **permanently bans _all_ sales, property and non-income-related taxes nationwide and requires that they be replaced within 90 days after ratification with truly progressive income taxes** on individuals and business entities (whether incorporated or not), with the exception of the temporary stock purchase transaction tax (see Section L. below). So-called "sin taxes" designed to discourage otherwise legal activities or consumption of items determined to be less than healthful also are exempt from that requirement. Likewise, tax cuts for wealthy individuals and corporations are permanently banned for as long as government entities at **any** level have a deficit balance.

All tax loopholes for wealthy individuals and for-profit businesses (incorporated or otherwise) are permanently banned, while existing mortgage interest deductions for each homeowner's primary residence (including deductions for points fees) are permanently protected; never again shall a wealthy person or wealthy family or for-profit corporation end up paying zero taxes or end up with an effective tax rate of less than 39 percent on gross income or, for businesses, on net profits. The sole exception to the ban on loopholes is a 5 percent tax credit for businesses with 50 or more employees which can prove beyond a

reasonable doubt that the tax credit caused them to schedule at least 98 percent of their workforce for 40-hour work weeks. Wealthy individuals are defined as anyone whose gross income is more than $150,000 per year; wealthy families are defined as any family with gross income of more than $200,000 per year. Wealthy corporations are defined as any corporation with more than $250,000 per year pre-tax net profits. Those graduated amounts shall be inflation-adjusted annually.

High-income limits on F.I.C.A. Social Security payroll taxes (which prevent the wealthy individuals, unlike non-wealthy individuals, from having to pay a progressively increased share of their incomes) are permanently removed.

Recognizing that employers are motivated to pressure Congress to make as many employees as possible exempt from wage laws requiring overtime pay, **there are now no employees whatsoever** – regardless of pay rate, pay scale, pay frequency or job description – **who are ineligible for at least time-and-a-half overtime pay** once their work hours exceed 40 hours during any seven-day period. Likewise, there is **no right for employers to implement mandatory overtime** hours. In addition, **all employees now have the right to at least double-time overtime pay** once their work hours exceed 50 hours during any seven-day period – and **all employees now have the right to at least triple-time overtime pay** once their work hours exceed 60 hours during any seven-day period. All employees also have the right to at least two full unpaid days off consecutively every week in addition to all other forms of paid and unpaid leave time; employees on five-day weekly work schedules have the right to overtime pay on each day they work more than eight hours. **All employees have the right to decline compensatory time in favor of overtime pay; all employees also have the right to decline overtime work, with employers permanently banned from implementing both direct and indirect sanctions, penalties and other punishments against employees who assert any and all rights under this and other provisions of the USA-SBR.** Employers formally alleged to have violated any of *these* provisions of the USA-SBR are subject to Class C Federal felony charges.

Recognizing that the **General Mining Act of 1872** constitutes nothing less than government welfare for the mining industry, that act **is permanently repealed. U.S.A. taxpayers have the right to be properly compensated for private mining companies' activity on public lands** through royalties based on **FULL actual market value** of the minerals, gases and oils extracted from those public lands as determined by the Secretary of the Interior. Failure to accurately set actual market values of such items shall result in the Secretary of Interior being charged with a Class B Federal felony. Whenever practicable, extraction of minerals, oil and gases from **public lands** shall be conducted

by **Federally-employed resource extractors (including miners, oil drillers, etc.) and resource extraction administrators** through a new branch of the Department of the Interior known as the **Federal and Private Lands Mining Administration (FPLMA)**, *recognizing that privatized mining results in lower profits for the Federal government, less safety, fewer benefits for employees and less accountability for environmental damages*. **Mining on private lands** is subject to strict safety and environmental inspections conducted on a surprise basis at least weekly by the FPLMA. Failure to comply with Federal safety and environmental regulations shall result in Class B Federal felony charges against mining managers and owners, as appropriate. Managers and owners of mines in which fatal incidents have occurred are subject to Class A Federal felony charges if there is evidence of gross or willful negligence and to Class B felony charges for simple negligence. Those same managers and owners of mines are subject to Class B Federal felony charges for each formally alleged instance of environmental contamination.

Recognizing that for-profit utilities and for-profit energy extraction companies have built vast empires upon huge profits as the result of extracting natural resources from public lands for more than a century at artificially low prices **and** as the result of being able to expel invisible pollutants (including CO_2) into the air without paying for the damage caused to the atmosphere (primarily due to those exhausts being invisible), all due to the influence of their paid lobbyists, **there shall be a national binding referendum vote** in the first Presidential general election after passage and ratification of the USA-SBR. That referendum shall determine whether those for-profit utilities and energy extraction businesses shall be permanently nationalized as promptly as possible for conversion to not-for-profit entities operated by the Federal government, never again to be privatized.

Recognizing that contracting out not-for-profit government services to for-profit business entities (incorporated or otherwise) means profits can be achieved only through private entities cutting types of services and hours of services, hiring persons who are less-than-fully qualified, cutting staff pay and benefits (leading to low morale and reduced employee retention), using cheap infrastructure and amenities (often designed to last only for the duration of the contract), cutting corners on safety and lobbying for more mandatory prison sentences as well as mandatory lengthened prison terms, there is the **right of all citizens to not-for-profit government services which are untainted by private sector profit motive.** Thus, _all_ for-profit contracts for not-for-profit government services through private corporations are banned, including – **but not limited to** - for-profit prisons, for-profit government hospitals, for-profit toll roads and highways, for-profit waste collection,

for-profit parks management, for-profit law enforcement services for both criminal *and* civil laws, for-profit child support enforcement services, for-profit welfare eligibility determination services, for-profit fire departments, for-profit security services, and all other for-profit public safety services. Likewise, recognizing that monied interests from Wall Street and elsewhere will attempt to find ways for the Congress and Legislatures to privatize institutions which provide government services by taking steps *causing those institutions to fail,* **such backdoor privatization** – including, but not limited to, requiring retirement accounts of future employees to be funded far into the future (causing agencies to be unable to perform their statutorily prescribed responsibilities by underfunding them or by refusing to fund them altogether) and agencies' management failing to require enforcement of agencies' laws, rules and regulations – **is permanently banned.** Therefore, existing such laws - like the Orwellian-named *Postal Accountability and Enhancement Act of 2006,* which was designed to cause the U.S. Postal Service *to fail* by requiring pre-funding of employee retirement accounts 75 years in advance – are immediately rendered unconstitutional and unenforceable. In addition, direct privatization of government-provided services – including, but not limited to, public schools, the U.S. Postal Service, welfare services, food and safety inspection services, law enforcement, military services and so forth – is permanently banned. Recognizing that they deplete funding for conventional public schools and "cherry pick" students, charter schools shall be disbanded or converted into conventional public schools effective with the upcoming school year.

There is the **right of all citizens and permanent residents to protection from all types of fraud**, including but not limited to schemes such as the credit default swap scams which led to the 2008 national financial meltdown. Financial institutions which perpetrate such frauds are subject to immediate and permanent nationalization by the executive branch.

Recognizing that Federal, State and local governments may at times be tempted or pressured by monied interests to sell off or lease off government-owned infrastructure – including, but not limited to, parks, wilderness areas, senate and house buildings, historical landmarks, school and university buildings, bridges, airports, railway stations, scientific research facilities, etc. - for short-term profit at long-term loss to taxpayers simply to balance a short-term budget, **citizens have the right for all government commons to be protected from liquidation and/or leasing.** Therefore, all levels of government **are forever banned** from selling off and/or leasing off government commons unless a ¾ majority of the legislative body votes to place a referendum on the sale of such an item on a Presidential election ballot and voters approve

each such proposed sale by a ¾ majority. Previous agreements to sell off or lease off such commons are immediately rendered retroactively null and void and unconstitutional. Buyers and lessees are entitled to reasonably negotiated compensation for returning the purchased and/or leased properties to the government under the doctrine of estoppel.

Recognizing that the financial influence of the military-industrial complex has led the U.S.A. into unnecessary wars and prevented the U.S.A. from entering into treaties which would deter armed conflicts and improve other international relationships, Congressional *rejections* of Executive Branch-negotiated treaties with foreign nations for peace and other armed conflict prevention issues now require a ¾-majority in both chambers of Congress, while declarations of war and other authorizations of armed conflicts in foreign lands now require approval of a ¾-majority in both chambers of Congress.

Recognizing that wealthy individuals, sole proprietorships and corporations have used their lobbying prowess to limit access to the courts by parties alleged to have been damaged, injured or harmed by their abuses and/or negligence, those who seek to pursue class action lawsuits against individuals, sole proprietorships and corporations now have **the right to pursue such lawsuits in any state in which any plaintiff has resided, in any state where the defendant does business and/or in any state in which any plaintiff is alleged to have been damaged, injured or harmed** by abuses and/or negligence of the defendant individual(s), sole proprietorships, corporations or any other business entities.

Economic treason: There is the right of consumers, taxpayers and other members of the general public to know which corporations and sole proprietorships are undermining national, regional and local economies by outsourcing jobs to foreign nations where employees will earn less than U.S.A. residents who had been filling those positions: those businesses which outsource 5 percent or more of their full-time equivalent positions to other nations are deemed to have committed economic treason and are required to label all items they produce in the U.S.A. as "Made By Economically Traitorous Company"; likewise, they are required to include in all business logotypes for their U.S.A. operations the designation "Economically Traitorous Company" in bold-faced type visible to anyone with 20/20 vision from 100 feet away when placed on outdoor signage and in at least a 16-point bold typeface on pre-printed materials. Such businesses shall be removed from that designation once they prove beyond reasonable doubt that at least 99 percent of their full-time equivalent staff positions are located in the U.S.A. The U.S. Department of Labor is responsible for enforcing these provisions. Corporate and/or sole proprietorship officials

formally alleged to have evaded or attempted to evade responsibility for such outsourcing shall be prosecuted for Class B Federal felonies.

Commissioner of the Food and Drug Administration (FDA) shall be selected by popular vote in national elections held at the same time as Presidential elections. That commissioner has the authority to permanently ban all food additives and medicines which have been demonstrated to have harmful side-effects. Producers of food additives and medicines with harmful side-effects are no longer permitted to escape liability for damage caused by their products and by consumer items containing their products simply by listing side effects on those products. FDA requirements for listing harmful side effects of products shall continue, however. Persons formally alleged to have suppressed or omitted such information shall be charged with Class B Federal felonies. That commissioner has the authority to enforce all FDA laws, including the authority to charge individuals, businesses (incorporated or otherwise) and business officials with felony crimes.

Administrator of the Environmental Protection Agency shall be selected by popular vote in national elections held at the same time as Presidential elections. That administrator has the authority to enforce all environmental laws, including the authority to charge individuals, businesses (incorporated or otherwise) and business officials with felony crimes.

Secretary of the Treasury shall be selected by popular vote in national elections held at the same time as Presidential elections. The Secretary is barred from declaring any financial institution as "too big to fail." A declaration of failure of any financial institution shall be followed immediately by the institution being permanently nationalized by the Federal government to function as a not-for-profit Federal government-operated entity.

Secretary of Transportation shall be selected by popular vote in national elections at the same time as Presidential elections. The Secretary's title is changed to **Secretary of Transportation Safety and Efficiency.** In addition to existing responsibilities, the Secretary's primary priority is to facilitate the public's transition off of using fossil fuels in favor of renewable energy not related to food production and promoting use of mass transit and other alternatives to freeways such as one-way surface streets and Commute Trip Reduction (CTR) program incentives (such as reimbursing employees for 100 percent of the cost of monthly bus passes). Recognizing that *freeway systems* _within_ *metropolitan areas contribute to urban sprawl, traffic fatalities and gridlock during heavy volume commuting periods (failing at the most crucial times),* contrary to what freeway promoters claim, the Secretary

is required to enforce a ban on Federally-funded new projects which facilitate continued use of single-occupancy vehicles by commuters (such as new freeways) _within_ metropolitan areas. Completion of such projects which are already approved and already fully-funded shall be allowed; however, expansion of those in-progress roadways and already-existing freeways in the future shall be funded only to the extent that the expansion encourages use of mass transportation and high-occupancy vehicles (HOV's); for example, widening of freeways is allowed only for lanes permanently designated as HOV lanes, with HOV usage defined as three or more occupants during high-traffic hours and two or more occupants at all other times. Funding for new non-HOV freeway construction is restricted only to interstates between metropolitan areas, not within metropolitan areas, recognizing that the interstate highway system originally was intended to facilitate transportation between metropolitan areas rather than within metropolitan areas as a strategy to facilitate evacuations of metropolitan areas during emergencies. Highest funding priority is granted to construction of subway systems within metropolitan areas.

Secretary of Agriculture shall be selected by popular vote in national elections held at the same time as Presidential elections. The Secretary is responsible for enforcing mandatory nationwide labeling of all items for sale containing laboratory-produced genetically modified organisms (GMOs), as well as all items for sale which were produced from animals fed with products containing GMOs. Likewise, the Secretary is responsible for ensuring animals used for agricultural purposes are raised under cruelty-free conditions. In addition, the Secretary is responsible for ensuring that all animal processing facilities are subject to surprise safety and health inspections conducted at least weekly by inspectors who are fully funded by the Federal government and unlinked in any way to the facilities they are inspecting.

Secretary of Energy shall be selected by popular vote in national elections held at the same time as Presidential elections. The Secretary's title is changed to **Secretary of Renewable Energy**. The Secretary's top priority is to transition all energy uses from fossil fuels and food-related renewable energy to solar energy, wind energy, hydropower which doesn't interfere with or endanger fish migration/spawning and non-food-related renewable energy (such as from sawgrass and waste biomass), provided the non-food renewable energy isn't derived from acreage historically used for food production. The Secretary is required to enforce a ban on all taxes and fees against solar energy and wind energy generated by private homeowners. Entities (and their agents) attempting to create and/or collect such taxes and fees from private homeowners shall be charged with a Class B Federal felony.

Chairperson of the Consumer Product Safety Commission shall be selected by popular vote in national elections held at the same time as Presidential elections. That chairperson is responsible for enforcing all consumer protection laws, including the authority to charge individuals, businesses (incorporated or otherwise) and business officials with felony crimes.

Secretary of the Department of the Interior shall be selected by popular vote in national elections held at the same time as Presidential elections. The Secretary's title is changed to Secretary of Interior Lands Protection. The Secretary is responsible for enforcing all laws related to lands administered by the Federal government, including the authority to charge individuals, businesses (incorporated or otherwise) and business officials with felony crimes. The Secretary has a fiduciary duty to bring all accounts receivable collections for the Department – including but not limited to lease payments, grazing fee payments, etc. – up to date and is responsible for ensuring that lease fees are set at full market value; formal allegations of willful failure to perform due diligence on collections and fee-setting shall result in Class B Federal felony charges against the Secretary followed by automatic removal if found guilty.

Secretary of Labor shall be selected by popular vote in national elections held at the same time as Presidential elections. A primary responsibility of the Secretary of Labor is to remove barriers to union representation elections in the workplace and to enforce penalties for employer retaliation against pro-union employees.

Secretary of Health and Human Services shall be selected by popular vote in national elections held at the same time as Presidential elections. Primary responsibilities for the Secretary of Health and Human Services are enforcement of requirements for food safety, requirements for out-of-pocket cost-free health care services and requirements for accessibility to low-cost prescription medicines from the least expensive FDA-certified-safe sources worldwide.

Consumer Financial Protection Bureau Director shall be selected by popular vote in national elections held at the same time as Presidential elections. That director has the responsibility to enforce all laws related to protection of consumers' financial interests, including the authority to charge individuals, businesses (incorporated or otherwise) and business officials with felony crimes.

U.S. Attorney General shall be selected by popular vote in national elections held at the same time as Presidential elections. The Attorney General, in addition to historical law enforcement responsibilities, shall make as his top priority enforcement of anti-trust laws and anti-corruption laws related to Wall Street and banking interests;

691

the Attorney General is permanently banned from substituting civil sanctions for criminal charges. The Attorney General's office shall review all corporate mergers approved during the previous 30 years for possible rescissions. Future mergers shall not be approved if it can be proved in court by a preponderance of evidence that the merger would result in more than five persons being laid off. Another top priority for the Attorney General is prosecution of any individual and/or business entity (incorporated or otherwise) charged with fixing prices or conspiring to fix prices; those formally alleged to be involved with price fixing are subject to Class B Federal felony charges. De facto evidence of price fixing sufficient to constitute probable cause for search warrants, criminal charges and/or criminal indictments shall include print or broadcast advertising from the same day by multiple (more than two) competing businesses showing the exact same prices for the exact same products and/or services.

Recognizing a long history of political manipulations of grand juries by both elected and appointed prosecutors, **all citizens have the right to present to grand juries at all levels of government – including, but not limited to, Federal, state, county and city – true bills of indictment.** This provision enables citizens to pursue prosecutions of persons and corporations often considered "too powerful to prosecute," such as when prosecutors declined to charge President George W. Bush with felonies after he admitted in 2005 to violating the Foreign Intelligence Surveillance Act prohibiting warrantless wiretaps. Likewise, all prosecutors – whether elected or appointed – at all levels of government are permanently barred from dismissing grand juries before their terms expire because grand jury jurors aren't voting as the prosecutor prefers or because grand jury jurors are presenting questions not endorsed by the prosecutor to grand jury witnesses. Any prosecutor formally alleged to have impeded or refused any citizen's right to present a true bill of indictment or to have improperly dismissed any grand jury before its term was to expire is subject to Class B Federal felony charges. In addition, all grand jury jurors (as well as all other juries' jurors) shall be selected truly at random from databases including all registered voters. To encourage the best work by jurors, all jurors are guaranteed full-time daily pay equivalent to at least the median net income (converted to gross income) for their age group based on U.S. Bureau of the Census data. Jurors whose incomes are greater than the median net income (converted to gross income) shall be compensated based on their verified actual gross income from current employment.

#Recognizing that powerful corporations and sole proprietorships have demonstrated a history of infringing upon patents of private party inventors, any plaintiff inventor(s) alleging patent infringement by a corporation or sole proprietorship is (are) entitled at government expense to representation in litigation by a well-qualified attorney specializing in patent law. If the plaintiff's/plaintiffs' litigation is successful, the defendant is responsible for paying attorney fees incurred by the government on the behalf of the plaintiff(s). This shall be known as the **Robert W. Kearns/Philo T. Farnsworth Provision** of the USA-SBR.

Recognizing that all citizens of the United States are entitled to reasonably equal physical access to the halls of government to minimize disproportionate accessibility by corporate interests based on the east coast, **the national U.S. Capital - including the Congress, U.S. Supreme Court, Presidential and Vice Presidential residences, Executive Branch agencies, etc. – shall be re-located to the demographic center of the 50 states**, which is near Plato, Missouri, approximately a 1,000-mile drive west from Washington, D.C. (Plato, Missouri is approximately 782 miles southeast of the geographic center of the 50 states at Belle Fourche, South Dakota.) The re-location of the U.S. Capitol shall begin the month after ratification of the USA-SBR and shall be completed within 10 years after ratification. The re-location shall not affect the continued operation of government museums and other tourist facilities in Washington, D.C.

II. *PROTECTED RIGHT TO PRIVACY*

Recognizing that all levels of government in the U.S.A. at times have violated private citizens' right to privacy - also known as the right of protection against unlawful search and seizure - there is a sacred right to privacy for all U.S. citizens and lawful resident aliens for whom there is neither probable cause nor reasonable suspicion for government authorities to believe they are involved in a criminal offense. Bulk collection of private citizens' phone, E-Mail and other electronic data by government is forever banned. Government authorities are required in all instances to obtain search warrants from a judge sitting on a newly-established Federal Civil Liberties Court in advance of any surveillance or search activity – except for expedited instances when a F.I.S.A. court judge rules *on the record* that there is, in fact, probable cause to believe a terrorist act or act of mass murder would occur if a warrant had to be sought in open court. Government employees at all levels of government – including all elected and appointed officeholders – formally alleged to have knowingly violated this right of privacy are subject to Class B Federal felony charges.

III. *RIGHT TO PROTECTION FROM TOXINS AND CARCINOGENS*

Recognizing the proliferation of toxic and/or carcinogenic substances (such as butylated hydroxyanisole (BHA) and butylated hydroxytoluene (BHT), which are found in almost all U.S. packaged foods despite being banned for human consumption in more than 160 countries[*]) used by various domestic and international industries and the tendency of those substances to find their way into persons' bodies, there is the right of all persons not to be subjected to either intentional or negligent exposure by individuals, businesses and governments to toxins and carcinogens in air, water, food, clothing, building materials, bedding, furniture and any other potential source of consumer exposure to those harmful materials. Members of Boards of Directors, CEO's and owners of corporations, sole proprietorships and partnerships and any other business entities which continue to include those substances in the items they sell, grow or otherwise produce shall be subject to Class B Federal felony charges as well as Federal felony charges for violations of civil rights.

IV. *RIGHT TO PROTECTION FROM BIOLOGICAL CONTAMINANTS IN FOODS*

There is a right of all persons to be protected from biological contaminants in foods presented for sale throughout the country. The U.S. Department of Health and Human Services (DHHS) and its Centers for Disease Control and Prevention (CDC) shall take over operations of the U.S. Department of Agriculture's (USDA's) Food Safety and Inspection Service (FSIS). Under that new management, the FSIS, in co-operation with states' food safety agencies, is obligated to promptly identify potentially deadly strains of foodborne bacteria and viruses (including, but not limited to, E Coli O157:H7 and Heidelberg salmonella) and declaring each of those potentially deadly strains to be adulterants, effectively banning the sale of all foods containing those potentially deadly bacteria and viruses. The DHHS, CDC, FSIS and USDA shall immediately implement the farm to market protocols used by Denmark to rid the food chain of salmonella; those protocols include compensation to farmers for destruction of their flocks when salmonella (such as Heidelberg salmonella) is found to contaminate their flocks (Denmark has had no salmonella outbreaks since 2011 under its new protocols[**]). The Congress also is obligated to adequately budgeting the DHHS, CDC and FSIS so that at least 1 percent of foods potentially carrying foodborne bacteria and viruses implicated in serious health risks are inspected daily by FSIS inspectors using the most advanced microbiology testing kits available; testing by merely visually examining, smelling and touching food products shall be immediately discontinued. Furthermore, DHHS, CDC and FSIS have the obligation to issue mandatory immediate recalls against food producers whose products, based upon a preponderance of evidence (potentially including DNA evidence), have been determined to be probable carriers of such deadly adulterants. Persons working for the DHHS, CDC and FSIS who are formally alleged to have failed to meet their obligations under this provision of the USA-SBR are subject to Class B

---

[*] Microsoft News 5/8/15
[**] PBS Frontline, "The Trouble with Chicken," 5/12/15

Federal felony charges. Businesses and individuals formally alleged to have failed to comply with immediate recalls of suspected contaminated food products are subject to Class B Federal felony charges.

V. RIGHT TO LIVABLE WAGE EMPLOYMENT

There is the right for all persons who have reached their majority to a useful and good-paying job, paying enough to provide adequate food, clothing and recreation; that pay rate is defined as $15 per hour in 2012 dollars or 275 percent of the latest Federal poverty guideline income level for a single-person household, whichever is greater; that minimum hourly wage shall automatically be indexed to the rate of inflation annually. There shall be **no exceptions**, including businesses with employees who receive tips, to that minimum wage. In addition, governments at all levels are banned from reducing wages (with the exception shown below) paid through prevailing wage requirements, requirements which shall be adjusted annually based on the rate of inflation. Those prevailing wage requirements shall remain the law of the land, except during times of deflation, when they may be adjusted downward annually based on the rate of deflation.

VI. RIGHT TO PROTECTION FROM EXTREME INCOME INEQUALITY

Recognizing that income disparity among working persons is a primary cause of poverty, bankruptcies, homelessness, ill health, family separations and divorces, foreclosures, child abandonment, unfulfilled education goals, etc., **all workers have the right to be paid no less than 1/25th of the earnings of the highest-paid persons** affiliated with their employer regardless of whether the employer is a corporation, a sole proprietorship or any other entity; calculations of the highest paid persons' incomes shall include all forms of compensation including – but not limited to – deferred compensation, stock options, vehicle allowances, retirement contributions, etc. Likewise, **all employers** – whether those are corporations, sole proprietorships or other entities – are permanently barred from paying the highest-earning persons affiliated with their organization more than 25 times the earnings of the lowest-paid persons affiliated with their organization. Due to the nature of employment in the entertainment and professional sports fields, where career durations are unpredictable and often short, pay for those employed in those areas are exempt from the 25 times lowest pay rate cap.

VII. RIGHT TO EFFECTIVE INVESTIGATIVE JOURNALISM FROM INDEPENDENT ENTITIES NOT PART OF MULTI-STATE CORPORATE MEDIA EMPIRES

Recognizing that predatory capitalists have rendered print, broadcast and on-line journalism virtually toothless in its traditional role of 'afflicting the comfortable and comforting the afflicted,' there shall be created upon USA-SBR ratification a permanent investigative journalism subsidy account funded out of general Federal tax revenues which shall be distributed proportionately – based on certified circulation and viewership data – among all daily and weekly newspapers, weekly, monthly and semi-monthly magazines, radio stations and television stations throughout the nation which are *NOT* part of multi-state corporate media empires. The fund balance shall be no less than .005 percent of the nation's gross domestic product annual equivalent at the beginning of each year and the entire amount of the fund shall be distributed each year. Any formal allegations by prosecutors or grand juries of misuse of the fund's proceeds shall result in Class C Federal felony charges. There shall be a permanent firewall created to protect those news outlets receiving the subsidies from interference by elected officeholders. It is the responsibility of Congress to authorize any additional funding for the account if the required set-aside from general tax revenues proves to be insufficient.

VIII. *RIGHT TO PROTECTION FROM UNFAIR PROPERTY SEIZURES OF PERSONS ONLY PERIPHERALLY INVOLVED WITH CRIMINAL PERPETRATORS*

Recognizing that asset forfeiture laws allowing seizure of property belonging to persons accused of and/or convicted of crimes have resulted in widespread abuses of authority and evasion of due process by prosecutors seeking to augment government budgets, such asset forfeiture proceedings are banned except in instances where law enforcement officers recover monies proved to have been received by the perpetrators convicted of sales of illegal substances. Even then, however, the asset forfeitures are limited only to the actual recovered monies and property proved to have been purchased with such monetary proceeds from the sale of illegal substances. Asset forfeiture laws banned include, but are not limited to, those laws allowing seizure of vehicles driven by intoxicated drivers and laws allowing seizure of long-held family farms on which relatively small tracts of illegal substances were being cultivated with or without the knowledge of the landowner.

IX. *RIGHT TO VIEW UNEDITED VIDEO-RECORDED ACTIONS OF LAW ENFORCEMENT OFFICERS*

Recognizing that disputes over interactions between law enforcement officers and the general public can often be resolved through video evidence, all government officers involved in enforcement of criminal laws are required to wear digital forward-facing head-mounted cameras at all times while they are on duty effective 30 days after ratification of the USA-SBR. Persons who are arrested and/or charged with criminal offenses have the right to have suppressed any of their remarks which are video-recorded before an arresting officer explains their Miranda rights to them. Copies of video recordings of persons suspected and/

or arrested and/or charged with criminal offenses shall be made available to the attorney representing the person as promptly as possible. Any law enforcement officer formally alleged to have tampered with such video recordings shall be subject to Class C Federal felony charges.

X. *RIGHT TO GOVERNMENT NOT ENGAGING IN DEADLY ACTIONS AGAINST NON-COMBATANTS IN LOCALES NOT INCLUDED IN ANY DECLARATION OF WAR*

Recognizing the hatred toward the U.S.A. generated by killings of non-combatants through the use of drone aircraft and other deadly methods of assault used by the U.S.A., any non-combatant deaths stemming from drone use or other methods of assault **in locales for which there is no lawful declaration of war by the U.S.A.** shall result in Class B Federal voluntary manslaughter charges against *each and every person involved in such authorizations and executions of deadly force,* including even the President of the United States if the President's specific authorization was required for that drone action.

XI. *RIGHT TO EFFECTIVE ENFORCEMENT OF WORKPLACE SAFETY VIOLATIONS*

Recognizing the widely understood ineffectiveness of misdemeanor charges and negligible fine levels for enforcement currently in place with the Occupational Safety and Health Administration (OSHA), the right of employees to a safe workplace shall be enforced through minimum charges of Class C Federal felonies for simple negligence, Class B Federal felonies for gross negligence and Class A Federal felonies for willful negligence. Minimum OSHA fines shall be $500,000 for each partial loss of a limb or other body part, $1 million for each complete loss of limb or other body part and $10 million for each loss of life resulting from an employer's negligence. Fines for gross negligence shall be at least five times those amounts. Fines for willful negligence shall be at least ten times those amounts. Minimum fine amounts shall be adjusted annually for inflation.

XII. *RIGHT TO LAW ENFORCEMENT BY HUMAN BEINGS*

Recognizing that corporations such as Lockheed Martin have entered into for-profit contracts with local governments around the nation to provide technology for traffic and transportation enforcement which does not involve actual human beings issuing citations and recognizing that local governments often have implemented such technology without regard to actual risks involved with the such enforcement (using augmented revenues as their primary motivator), all motorists and other potential defendants have the right to be free from prosecution and persecution involving automated ticketing/citation systems such as red light cameras. Elected and appointed officeholders of such governments which continue to use that technology for ticketing and citations involving traffic and transportation enforcement are subject to Class C Federal felony charges.

XIII. *RIGHT TO NATIONWIDE UNIFORM FAIR COMPENSATION FOR ON-THE-JOB INJURIES*

There is the right to fair compensation for on-the-job injuries and illnesses including the right to compensation without discrimination based on the state in which the on-the-job injury or illness occurred. Never again shall the on-the-job loss of one person's body part(s) in one state result in compensation which is different from what is provided in a different state. There shall be a uniform system of compensation nationwide for on-the-job injuries and illnesses administered through the new Federal agency known as the Workers Compensation Administration (WCA), led by the Secretary of Workers Compensation, a Presidential Cabinet-level position. The Secretary of Workers Compensation shall be elected in national elections at the same time as Presidential elections. The Workers Compensation Administration shall be funded from general tax funds rather than employers' workers' compensation insurance fees; fees which employers previously paid for such coverage shall be incorporated into progressive income taxes levied against corporations. Federal lawmakers, Congressional staff, the Secretary of Workers' Compensation, lobbyists and immediate family members of all those previously-mentioned persons are barred from purchasing supplemental Workers Compensation coverage, as motivation for coverage through the WCA to be as generous as possible.

XIV. *RIGHT TO DECENT HOMES AND IN-HOME CARE*

There is the right of every family to a decent home, including residential care for the aged and terminally ill. Within 90 days after ratification, there shall be created a permanent family housing/terminally ill and aged residential care subsidy account funded out of general Federal tax revenues which shall be distributed proportionately among all states based on annually adjusted U.S. Bureau of the Census data. The fund balance shall be no less than .01 percent of the nation's gross domestic product annual equivalent at the beginning of each year and the entire amount of the fund shall be distributed each year. Any alleged misuse of the fund's proceeds shall result in Class C Federal felony charges. It is the responsibility of Congress to authorize any additional funding for that account if the required set-aside amount from general tax revenues proves to be insufficient.

XV. *RIGHT TO SINGLE-PAYER HEALTH CARE WITH NO OUT-OF-POCKET COSTS WHATSOEVER; BAN ON TOBACCO PRODUCTS*

There is the right to adequate medical, dental, vision and pharmaceutical care and to achieve and enjoy good health, including the right to single-payer

Medicare For All with **no** out-of-pocket expenses for all medical, dental and vision care, as well as for all prescription drugs. There shall be a major emphasis on preventive health care due to the documented costs savings of prevention. Based on the philosophy of prevention, therefore, all tobacco and nicotine-containing products are permanently banned effective 30 days after ratification of the USA-SBR.

XVI. _RIGHT TO STABILIZED POPULATION GROWTH AND ASSOCIATED INCENTIVES_

Recognizing that continued unlimited population growth in the U.S.A. and the remainder of the world constitutes an existential threat to finite supplies of potable water and acreage on which crops can be farmed and homes can be built, the tax codes for all levels of government (Federal, State, County, City, etc.) shall no longer provide as a deduction from taxes the same amount for the 20th child in a family as for the first child. Effective for the tax year at the time of ratification, tax deductions for the third child in a family as well as each subsequent child shall be eliminated. Persons having more than three children are required to pay an annual surtax for the fourth and each additional minor child; the surtax for each of those children shall be the equivalent of 1 percent of the filer's adjusted gross income.

XVII. _RIGHT TO PAID TIME OFF FOR RECOVERY FROM HEALTH PROBLEMS AND FOR LEISURE ENJOYMENT_

Recognizing that virtually all industrialized nations guarantee rights of employees to paid vacation leave time, it is now the right of all employed persons upon completion of a full year of employment to at least four weeks of paid leave time (part-time workers are entitled to paid leave based on their average hours worked per week); upon completion of five years of employment, there is a right to at least six weeks of paid leave; upon completion of ten years of employment, there is a right to at least eight weeks of paid leave; upon completion of fifteen years of employment, there is a right to at least 12 weeks of paid leave. Likewise, recognizing that virtually all industrialized nations guarantee rights of employees to paid maternity leave and paid paternity leave as well as paid non-maternity/non-paternity sick leave, upon completion of one full year of employment, all employed women have the right to at least nine months of paid maternity leave and all employed men have the right to at least three months of paid paternity leave. Likewise, at least 90 days per year of non-maternity/non-paternity paid sick leave is guaranteed once the employee has completed a full year of employment (see above). Maternity, paternity and non-maternity/non-paternity paid sick leave times each shall be _in addition_ to other earned paid leave times **and** _in addition_ to any rights to paid and unpaid leave already required under the Family and Medical Leave Act. Employees have the right to use their non-maternity/non-paternity paid sick leave to care for members of their immediate families and extended families. Employers have the right to request documentation of the conditions prompting extended sick leave requests. Employers shall **not** have the right to discharge any employees who have documented personal health-related reasons or family/extended-family member health-related reasons for taking extended leave, whether paid leave or unpaid leave.

XVIII.   *RIGHT TO DEPENDABLE RETIREMENT BENEFITS AND ECONOMIC SAFETY NET BENEFITS*

There is a right to adequate protection from the economic fears of old age, sickness, non-work-related accidents, on-the-job injuries, illnesses and unemployment: Workers' Compensation, Unemployment Compensation benefits, TANF benefits and Food Stamps/SNAP benefits nationwide shall be **indexed annually to inflation.** Likewise, private businesses and all levels of government which offer retirement plans for their employees are banned from offering anything other than defined retirement benefits plans which shall be **adjusted annually for inflation**; 401K accounts shall no longer be offered in place of defined retirement benefits. Furthermore, businesses and all levels of government are barred from reducing those promised retirement benefits – except that, in the event of deflation, they are allowed to adjust those benefits based on the Federal government-certified rate of deflation.

XIX. *RIGHT TO TUITION-FREE AND FEE-FREE PUBLIC EDUCATION THROUGH COMPLETION OF COLLEGE UNDERGRADUATE DEGREE*

There is the right for all to a good tuition-free and fee-free public education, including up to four years of undergraduate enrollment at any government-operated university or college or trade school, as well as completely free public education at government-operated schools from full-time pre-school and kindergarten through 12th grade. There shall be no use of government funds for privately-operated schools (including church-operated schools), either non-profit or for-profit.

XX.   *RIGHT TO PROTECTION FOR BUSINESSES FROM UNFAIR COMPETITION AT HOME AND ABROAD AND RIGHT TO TRADE WITH OTHER COUNTRIES NOT INVOLVED IN OR PLANNING ARMED CONFLICTS*

There is the right of every businessman, large and small, to trade in an atmosphere of freedom from unfair competition with monopolies at home and abroad, including the right to trade with any and all nations who aren't involved in armed conflict with the U.S.A. or its allies, who aren't actively supporting armed conflict in other countries and who aren't actively planning an armed conflict with the U.S.A.

XXI. *RIGHT TO PRACTICE RELIGION AS LONG AS PRACTICE OF RELIGION DOESN'T IMPOSE ON OTHERS' RIGHTS AND RIGHT TO MAKE ONE'S OWN CHOICES ABOUT ONE'S OWN MEDICAL PROCEDURES*

There is the right of all persons to participate in the religion of their choice, provided that such religions comply with all civil and criminal laws. Likewise, those who don't wish to participate in a religion shall have the right to be free from proselytizing by persons outside their immediate families after an initial contact from the proselytizing organization. Religious organizations shall have the right to attract new members the traditional American way: by using their own revenues to do unconditional good works of charity and kindness for the needy in their local communities. In addition, there is the right of persons to be free from interference by any other persons or groups claiming to be acting on the basis of religious belief with their choice of any and all medical procedures done upon their own bodies or on the bodies of persons for whom they are the lawful guardians.

XXII. *SPECIFICALLY CIRCUMSRIBED LIMITED RIGHT TO BEAR ARMS*

To clarify ambiguity within the 2nd Amendment of the original Constitution, it shall be clear that prohibiting infringement of the rights of the people to keep and bear arms shall involve only those rights associated with being an officially-appointed member of a government-organized militia which is well-regulated, including (but not limited to) members of police departments, sheriff's departments and sheriff's posses, state police agencies and militias such as the National Guard, federal armed services, executive branch law enforcement, etc. Non-law enforcement and non-military/militia firearm users shall have a qualified right to purchase, own and use firearms provided that those persons:

> # have no record whatsoever of any violence-related criminal convictions.
>
> # pass a formal Federal background check for such criminal convictions and for mental health issues.
>
> # pass a mental health screening by a mental health professional; in lieu of such a screening, the would-be purchaser may provide affidavits from three persons familiar with the person's personal history. However, persons providing false information on such affidavits are subject to Class B Federal felony charges.

These requirements apply to all sales and purchases, including licensed dealers, gun show participants and private parties. In addition, mechanisms of firearms manufactured for non-military/militia and non-law enforcement use are limited to bolt-action and lever action functions with tubular/cylindrical/magazine capacities of no more than six cartridges/shells. Within six months of ratification of the

USA-SBR, there shall be ongoing Federally-funded gun buy-back programs administered through local criminal law enforcement agencies throughout the country focused primarily on incentivizing owners of semi-automatic weaponry to give up those guns, which are the weapons of choice of mass murderers. Recognizing that state and local governments around the country have a hodgepodge of rules and regulations governing where a person may lawfully carry a firearm openly - with the exception of certified law enforcement, military and state-sanctioned militia personnel - there is no right to openly carry firearms or to carry concealed firearms in any public gathering place (except licensed shooting ranges and designated hunting areas) or in any public park, including within storage areas in vehicles.

XXIII.   *RIGHT TO RESIDE IN THE COMMUNITY OF ONE'S OWN CHOICE IN THE
          COUNTRY OF ONE'S OWN CHOICE*

There is the right of every human being to freely immigrate from a foreign country to the U.S.A. if that foreign country formally recognizes the right of every U.S.A. citizen without felony criminal convictions (including persons whose felony convictions were expunged and/or pardoned) to immigrate without restrictions into that country (regardless of whether the Congress formally recognizes reciprocal such rights in the U.S.A.). It is a primary duty of the Secretary of State to negotiate treaties with all other countries providing for a right to unrestricted immigration into those countries by U.S.A. citizens without felony criminal convictions (including persons whose felony convictions were expunged and/or pardoned). Likewise, there is the right of every human being without felony criminal convictions (including persons whose felony convictions were expunged and/or pardoned) to freely immigrate at any time from the U.S.A. to any other country with which the U.S.A. has a treaty recognizing the right of mutual immigration for citizens of the countries which are parties to the treaty. In addition, there is the right of every human being without felony criminal convictions (including persons whose convictions were expunged and/or pardoned) to freely immigrate at any time from the U.S.A. to any other English-speaking country and from any other English-speaking country to the U.S.A. provided both the U.S.A. and the other country(ies) have signed a treaty recognizing that right of mutual immigration for citizens of the country(ies) which are parties to the treaty. English-speaking countries are defined to include all countries in which a *plurality* of residents *speak English as a second language.* There also is the right of every human being brought into the U.S.A. by her or his parents, *legally or illegally,* when that human being was under the age of 16 to remain in the U.S.A. as a permanent legal resident, provided that person has no felony criminal convictions in that person's previous country of residence.

XXIV.   *RIGHT OF CHILDREN TO BE TRIED AS MINORS*

There is the right of children under the age of 16 to be tried in all U.S.A. courts as minors.

XXV. *RIGHT TO A FRESH START*

Recognizing this country's tradition of providing persons with challenging back-grounds a fresh start, all persons whose criminal records include **only** non-violent felony and/or non-violent misdemeanor convictions who have completed twenty-four consecutive months without any offenses of any kind (including misdemeanors) and have maintained the obligation to make payments toward restitution and fines have a right to have their criminal records expunged by petitioning the county-level court in which their most recent felony conviction occurred. The records expungement for those non-violent offenders shall be automatic once the court has certified that the petitioner has met the minimum required offense-free and payment maintenance period. There shall be only two such opportunities for fresh starts during those persons' lifetimes. All persons with felony and/or misdemeanor convictions *involving violence* shall have the right to *petition* the court of their most recent conviction for expungement of their criminal records once they have completed a thirty-six month period *without* any offenses of any kind (including misdemeanors) and *with* required payments for restitution and fees, but expungement for persons with violence-related convictions – unlike for persons with non-violence-related convictions – shall not be automatic upon certification of completion of the required offense-free period. There shall be only one such opportunity for an offender with one or more violence-related convictions to successfully petition the court for a fresh start. If and when expungement is approved by the court, all of the petitioners' rights shall be restored, without exception, including voting rights. However, if the petitioner fails to maintain her or his obligations to make payments toward restitution and/or fines, those rights shall be suspended until the court certifies that the petitioner has resumed maintaining those payment obligations.

XXVI. *JEAN VALJEAN/SCOTT SISTERS RIGHT TO REASONABLE PROSECUTION AND SENTENCING*

Recognizing that many states have sentencing provisions which fail to take into account certain key factors about offenders, this provision of the USA-SBR, which shall be known as the **Jean Valjean/Scott Sisters Provision**, requires that persons convicted of their first offense for any crime in which the victim(s) was (were) neither physically harmed nor both intentionally and severely psychologically tortured shall be automatically diverted into a first-offender program (involving **no** prison time) aimed at discouraging recidivism. Offenders who complete the diversion program and don't re-offend within 24 months after their conviction shall automatically have their conviction expunged and all their rights restored, provided they maintain any required restitution and fee payments once they are employed. In conjunction with this amendment, there shall be established a Sentencing Consistency Commission which shall keep statistics on sentences handed down against affluent offenders. When non-affluent offenders are being sentenced, they shall receive sentences which are no more severe than the average sentence handed down for the same offense committed by an affluent person. All courts throughout the U.S.A. and its territories are required to comply with statistics collection requests from that Commission. Judges or justices of any individual courts failing to comply shall be notified of intent for removal; if they still haven't complied within 60 days after receiving that notification, they shall be removed from office permanently. Offenders are considered affluent if their Federal adjusted gross income on their latest Form 1040 is $100,000 or greater on a person filing an individual return or $200,000 or greater on persons filing a joint return. Those amounts shall be adjusted annually for inflation once the USA-SBR is ratified. Judges or justices in individual courts found through the Sentencing Consistency Commission's statistical studies to have discriminated negatively against non-affluent offenders shall be permanently removed from the bench within 20 days of such a statistical determination. A judge's or justice's only basis for appeal of removal shall be a finding of tallying errors in the statistical study(ies) involved.

XXVII.   *RIGHTS OF CONVICTED NON-VIOLENT SUBSTANCE ABUSERS*

All persons currently imprisoned or incarcerated only for non-violent substance abuse offenses with records of good behavior shall be reviewed for eligibility for early release into drug rehabilitation programs within 90 days of ratification of the USA-SBR. There is a presumption of qualification for release unless there are issues which overcome that presumption. Those who fail to comply with drug rehabilitation requirements after their release are subject to prompt re-imprisonment or re-incarceration.

XXVIII.   *RIGHT TO CLEAN WATER AND AIR PLUS RIGHT TO PROTECTION FROM HUMAN-CAUSED EXACERBATION OF GLOBAL WARMING*

Recognizing the right to a clean environment without exacerbating global warming, including the right to clean water and air, activities known to contaminate water, including hydraulic fracturing (i.e., "fracking"), are permanently banned. Except for aircraft, watercraft and railway engines, combustion is allowed only for heating and for production of electricity by utilities, provided that all combustion wastes are neutralized or scrubbed. Purchases of **new** internal combustion engines are prospectively banned forever, except for aircraft, watercraft and railway engines – but purchases of new internal combustion aircraft, watercraft and railway engines also shall be permanently banned as soon as new technology enables reliable use of electric- or solar-powered aircraft, watercraft and railway propulsion. Meanwhile, conversions of existing aircraft, watercraft and railway internal combustion engines to non-food renewable biomass fuels such as sawgrass and waste product fuels such as used cooking oils and logging/sawmill wastes are required within four years of ratification of this Second Bill of Rights. In addition, all direct and indirect government subsidies for fossil fuels industries are forever banned. Likewise, **industries** which caused pollution at existing and future congressionally-designated Superfund sites are required to pay for clean-up of all such sites; the government is banned from using taxpayer dollars to clean up such sites except when the business responsible for the pollution is completely defunct. Furthermore, recognizing that wastes from nuclear power plants are the most long-lastingly toxic substances in the universe (deadly toxic for hundreds of thousands of years), construction of new nuclear power plants are permanently banned; existing nuclear power plants shall be decommissioned and permanently shuttered as soon as their current licenses to operate expire, with the exceptions of nuclear plants located within 10 miles of seacoasts to prevent risks of tsunami damage and nuclear plants located within 50 miles of fault lines with risks of 5.0 Richter Scale or higher quakes as designated by the U.S. Geological Survey. Coastal area and fault line area nuclear plants shall be decommissioned and permanently shuttered immediately. In addition, *all restrictions*, including aesthetic restrictions, on residential uses of rooftop and other solar energy generation devices are immediately and permanently banned. Likewise, sales of non-white colored roofing materials are immediately banned to improve solar heating reflectivity of rooftops. Finally, all new power transmission lines shall be buried at a safe depth (determined by the Secretary of Renewable Energy) and all existing above-ground power transmission lines shall be buried within 10 years from the date the USA-SBR is ratified. New above-ground power transmission lines are immediately banned forever. Utilities refusing to comply or failing to comply with USA-SBR requirements shall be permanently nationalized, to be owned and operated not-for-profit by the Federal government. Furthermore, all for-profit utilities are required to convert to hydropower (which is certified as not interfering with fish migrations and spawning), solar and wind energy technologies for 90 percent of energy generation and to non-food-related waste biomass technology for the remaining 10 percent of energy generation within 10 years of the passage and ratification of the USA-SBR. Those utilities are required to convert to hydropower (which is certified as not interfering with fish migrations and spawning), solar and wind energy technologies for 100 percent of energy generation within 15 years of passage and ratification of the USA-SBR. Any utilities which fail to comply with those requirements shall be immediately nationalized by the Federal government and operated by the Federal government as not-for-profit entities, never again to be privatized.

XXIX. *RIGHT TO EQUAL COMPENSATION*

There is the right to equal pay for equal work, regardless of gender, gender preference, age or physical/mental barriers.

XXX.   *RIGHT TO PROTECTION FROM DISCRIMINATION*

There is the right to be free from discrimination based on gender, same-sex orientation, trans-gender orientation, physical disability, mental disability, age and race. There is no right for government or businesses of any kind to discriminate against any person on any such basis. There is no right to refuse to marry **any two persons, including persons of the same gender,** who have reached the age of majority and are no more closely related than 2nd cousins, provided neither party isn't already married to someone else. Persons formally alleged to have committed acts of discrimination are subject to Class D Federal felony charges, one charge for each act of discrimination.

XXXI.   *RIGHT TO PROTECTION FROM WRONGFUL EXECUTION*

Recognizing that the criminal justice system in the U.S.A. has a long history of imposing wrongful convictions, *unless* a method is developed (with complete success and without permanent harm) to reverse the death penalty once it is imposed **and** *unless* the governor, judge, jury and prosecutor who authorize the death penalty on a *convicted serial/mass murderer* are willing to promise to accept the imposition of that same death penalty on themselves were it to be demonstrated at a later date that the conviction was wrongful, there is the right of persons convicted of any crime **not** to be put to death. All juries have the right to sentence persons convicted of multiple pre-meditated murders to life in prison without the possibility of parole. Persons convicted of any crimes have the right to have their convictions reversed at any time post-conviction upon a hearing in which new evidence establishes to the court's satisfaction that the previous conviction was wrongful and/or unjust. Criminal law enforcers formally alleged to have knowingly used false or unsubstantiated evidence which led to a conviction are subject to Class A Federal felony charges.

XXXII.   *RIGHT OF PRISONERS TO HUMANE TREATMENT AND EFFECTIVE REHABILITATION*

There are the following rights for prisoners: the right of incarcerated and imprisoned persons to humane treatment, including the right **not** to be placed in solitary confinement for more than one 48-hour period per month (with two hours per day spent outside during solitary confinement), the right to healthfully nutritious meals and hydration; the right to adequate clothing and bedding (including blankets during winter); the right to a quiet environment during rest periods; the right to competent medical, dental and psychiatric care; the right not to be subjected to involuntary labor without reasonable compensation (defined as at least minimum wage less no more than 50 percent deductions to offset costs of income taxes, FICA, food, shelter, child support, restitution and fines), the right to be sheltered indoors at a reasonable temperature no greater than 76F and no less than 68F plus the right to be protected from extreme outdoor weather elements, including outdoor temperatures above 86F and below 50F, with seasonally-appropriate clothing provided. Likewise, recognizing that the vast majority of prisoners eventually are released back into the general population, there is a right of incarcerated and imprisoned persons to participation in reasonable rehabilitation programs, including education programs, provided the inmate does not commit successive acts of violence during such rehabilitation programs.

XXXIII. *RIGHT OF THE PUBLIC NOT TO BE REPRESENTED BY PERSONS WITH HISTORIES OF RACIAL BIGOTRY*

Recognizing the especially long-lasting corrosive effects of racial bigotry, **persons determined, from the age of 21 forward, to have participated in or publicly encouraged any actions – either overt and implied – involving racial bigotry shall have no right whatsoever to hold any and all elective AND appointive offices at all levels of government, including – but not limited to – federal, state, county and city.** Such actions shall include actions which were previously legal but have since been made to be illegal, as well as actions which, while not considered illegal due to First Amendment free speech protections, are nonetheless racially bigoted. For example, U.S. Supreme Court Chief Justice William Rehnquist's aggressive participation during his late 30's in then-legal voter literacy testing in Phoenix, AZ African-American and Hispanic neighborhoods (as part of a co-ordinated Republican Party effort to disenfranchise minorities during the 1960s) would've precluded his nomination to the Supreme Court had this provision of the USA-SBR been in effect at the time of his original 1971 nomination by President Richard M. Nixon. Persons involved in such racial bigotry who already are in office at the time of the USA-SBR's ratification are allowed to complete their current terms – but they are barred from seeking re-election **or** being re-appointed.

XXXIV. *ROY S. MOORE RIGHT TO PROTECTION FROM JUDGES WHO REFUSE TO ACCEPT ARTICLE 6, CLAUSE 2 (SUPREMACY CLAUSE) OF U.S. CONSTITUTION*

Judges in state courts who refuse to comply in a timely fashion with orders from Federal courts shall be immediately and permanently disbarred from the practice of law nationwide and permanently removed from all judicial offices and permanently ineligible to hold such offices throughout the country – once they have exhausted their due process rights. This is referred to as the Roy S. Moore Provision of the USA-SBR.

XXXV.   RAY BRADBURY RIGHT TO PROTECTION FROM THOSE WHO WOULD BAN TEXTBOOKS AND OTHER LITERATURE DESPITE THE ACCURACY AND EMPIRICAL REALITY OF THEIR CONTENTS

There is the national right to a free public education based on **empirical reality**. School boards for both public and private schools nationwide are prohibited from banning any textbook contents or other forms of literature unless those items don't comport with empirical reality or they contain material **intended** to be pruriently pornographic. Both public and private schools, likewise, shall have no right to discipline their students for making use of any forms of literature which comport with empirical reality and aren't **intended** to be pruriently pornographic, whether those sources are on "approved" reading lists or not.

XXXVI.   RIGHT TO PEACEABLY GATHER IN ALL PUBLIC COMMONS INCLUDING DE FACTO PUBLIC COMMONS

There is the right to *non-violent assembly* in **any** government-owned or government-leased commons area, as well as in any *de facto* public commons, such as shopping malls open to the general public. Only privately-owned areas with lawfully-restricted access would be exempt from that right. Law enforcement officers formally alleged to have violated this right or to have conspired to violate this right are subject to Class D Federal felony charges followed by prompt dismissal proceedings and a permanent ban nationwide from the law enforcement profession if convicted.

XXXVII.   RIGHT TO PEACEFUL RESIDENCES

There is the right to peaceful residential neighborhoods, free of noise which disturbs or prevents sleep (except for use of emergency vehicles during actual emergencies). Commercial aircraft, general aviation airplanes, private business airplanes and military aircraft (except during declared wars or propulsion difficulties) are banned from flying lower than 5,000 feet above ground level over all residential neighborhoods. Neighborhoods already established within two miles of airports beneath lower-level takeoff and landing flight paths are exempt from this requirement; however, those neighborhoods shall be given highest preference for rezoning conversion to industrial uses.

XXXVIII.   RIGHT TO LEGISLATIVE INITIATIVE PROCESS AT ALL LEVELS OF GOVERNMENT, INCLUDING FEDERAL; PAID SIGNATURE GATHERERS BANNED

There is the national right of legislative initiative for *all levels* of government, enabling citizens to circulate petitions nationwide, statewide, countywide and citywide in all jurisdictions to place national, state, county and city legislation on Federal, state and local election ballots every two years (odd-numbered years for many local elections) for approval or rejection by voters at all levels of government. There is no veto right for initiatives approved by voters. The minimum number of required signatures is the equivalent of 10 percent of the national voting-age population for national initiatives (including 10 percent in each state), 10 percent of state voting age population for statewide initiatives, 10 percent of county voting age population for countywide initiatives and 10 percent of municipal voting age population for citywide initiatives, based on the latest U.S. Bureau of the Census data; signatures shall be verified by each state's Secretary of State. The U.S. Attorney General is responsible for determining the constitutionality of each proposed national legislative initiative before petitions could be circulated; states' attorneys general shall determine the constitutionality of non-Federal initiatives. Gathering of signatures by paid signature gatherers is permanently banned, recognizing that the absence of such a ban would result in wealthy corporations and wealthy individuals dominating the initiative process. There also is a right of citizens to use the initiative process to amend both state and Federal constitutions using the same process described for legislative initiatives; no Attorney General vetting is required for the constitutional amendment initiative process.

XXXIX. _VOTERS' RIGHT TO ENDORSE OR RESCIND DECLARATIONS OF WAR OR OTHER ARMED CONFLICTS WITH FOREIGN COUNTRIES OR ORGANIZED ENTITIES_

There is the right of voters to participate in a binding national ballot referendum on whether or not to declare war or to authorize any other armed conflict against another country or organized entity. The referendum shall be conducted as promptly as is practicable. The right of voters to that prompt referendum shall not prevent the President from taking prompt action in response to military threats during emergency situations, provided the President obtains Congressional authorization for such actions as promptly as possible.

XL. _RIGHT TO OPEN GOVERNMENT AT ALL LEVELS_

Recognizing that secrecy in government is like a cancer which discourages and eventually kills effective grassroots participation in the legislative process, **all government proceedings** – including whenever **two or more** voting members of a government entity _meet or communicate_ with each other – **shall be open to the public** – including all print and broadcast media, with no restrictions on pooled video and radio coverage – at all stages of the legislative and deliberative processes, including the executive, legislative and judicial branches of _all levels_ of government from the smallest community and school district to the Federal government. This requirement includes, but is not limited to, all proceedings involving direct and indirect expenditures of government resources. The only exemptions for required open proceedings are for court juries and for when there has been a documented finding – through open government deliberations and proceedings –

by an open vote of Congress that a foreign government is planning to wage war or already has recently (within the previous 12 months) committed acts of war against the U.S.A. Members of government entities who are determined through due process to have violated this provision of the USA-SBR shall be immediately and permanently removed from the entity on which they were a voting member and they shall not be eligible to be a voting member of that or any other government entity ever again.

XLI. *RIGHT TO PROTECTION FROM ALL FORMS OF TORTURE*

There is the right of **all parties** within and outside of our country to be protected from all forms of torture (including so-called "enhanced" or "harsh" interrogation techniques) committed by persons employed by the U.S. government or acting on behalf of the U.S. government. Persons formally alleged to have committed such acts or to have conspired to commit such acts are subject to Class A Federal felony charges. There shall be no Statute of Limitations on the crime of torture.

XLII. *RIGHT OF ALL WORKERS TO ORGANIZE FOR COLLECTIVE BARGAINING*

There is the right of all employees working for any employer with 10 or more employees to automatically be certified for labor union representation whenever more than 50 percent of employees sign National Labor Relations Board (NLRB) union authorization cards designating the union. The cards shall be available online through the NLRB website. When less than 50 percent but more than 30 percent of employees sign such cards the NLRB shall conduct a union representation election by secret ballot. Persons formally accused of intimidating, attempting to intimidate or conspiring to intimidate employees trying to organize a union during a unionization campaign are subject to Federal Class C felony charges. Employers found by the NLRB to have demoted or fired an employee for trying to organize a union are subject to Federal Class B felony charges. Once union representation is certified by the NLRB, the union has the right to collect union dues from all employees (because the union is required to represent all employees); there is no right for employees represented by NLRB-certified unions to opt out of representation or opt out of paying union dues, because all such employees benefit from union representation whether or not they support union organizing efforts.

XLIII. *RIGHT TO GROW, PRODUCE, POSSESS AND USE ANY NATURAL SUBSTANCE UNLESS THE FOOD AND DRUG ADMINISTRATION HAS DECLARED THE SUBSTANCE TO BE TOXIC AND/OR CARCINOGENIC*

There is a right of all adult citizens at least 21 years old to grow and/or produce at home, possess and use – without being subject to either criminal or civil charges – any natural substances unless the Food and Drug Administration has declared the substance in question to be toxic and/or carcinogenic when used in moderation.

XLIV.   *RIGHT TO UNIFORM FEDERALIZED CHILD SUPPORT ENFORCEMENT ADMINISTRATION THROUGHOUT THE U.S.A. AND ITS TERRITORIAL POSSESSIONS*

Recognizing that varied state-by-state laws governing child support enforcement have erected significant barriers to effective support collections, there shall be a nationalized Federal child support enforcement system which shall within nine months of ratification of the USA-SBR replace the hodgepodge of state and county child support enforcement agencies and their widely varying enforcement standards and limitations. Employees of existing non-privatized child support enforcement agencies shall have hiring preference for the new Federalized agency; all privatized support child support enforcement agencies shall be permanently closed. Establishment and enforcement provisions shall include:

#Federal administrative establishment of orders of enforcement (which would be superseded by orders established through county-level courts during divorce or other proceedings).

#Bi-annual reviewability for order modification of both administrative and court orders, with a right to a free modification action if the proposed support amount is at least $100 per month greater or less than the existing monthly order amount.

#Free paternity testing at each child's birth hospital within a month after birth.

#Obligations to pay appropriate portions of out-of-pocket health care and child care expenses.

#Automatic seizure of both state and federal income tax refunds up to the full amount owed once debt is at least $250 past due as of Dec. 1st each year.

#Automatic suspension actions against **all** of a non-custodial parent's government-issued licenses once debt is the equivalent of six months past due.

#Automatic statewide liens in state of latest residence on both real estate and vehicles once debt is at least $250 past due.

#Automatic passport revocation once debt is at least $250 past due.

#Automatic referrals for Civil Contempt through local county-level courts once debt is at least $1,000 past due (with Federal Class C Felony prosecution against any county prosecutor who fails to pursue such actions).

#Enforcement officers' option to seize financial accounts balances if a parent goes more than 31 days without making a payment, with *ALL*

U.S. city-, county-, state- and federally-chartered financial institutions required to honor administrative Orders to Withhold and Deliver.

#Enforcement officers' option to have non-custodial parents' vehicle(s) seized by the appropriate county prosecutor and auctioned once debt is at least $2,500 past due.

#Enforcement officers' option to withhold up to 50 percent from **any and all** monthly net earnings and benefits from Federal sources [including but not limited to all Department of Veterans' Affairs retirement _**AND**_ disability benefits, Department of Defense net earnings, Social Security retirement _**AND**_ disability benefits (but not SSI, except for 50 percent of lump-sum payments) **and** Federal payments to contractors].

#Requirement that employer payments to **all** employees on their regular payroll, contract workers, subcontractors and private parties are subject to withholding of up to 50 percent of net pay (net defined as gross pay less withholding which is **not** optional to the payee).

#Immediate wage withholding is _**ALWAYS**_ required in both administrative and court orders.

#Paying parents are **always** required to make payments _**ONLY**_ through the new Federal Support Registry (FRS) (with _**each state**_ having a registry processing center to speed up payment processing). Paying parents **shall not** receive credits for payments not made through the Federal Support Registry because parents receiving child support _**and**_ parents paying child support have the right to a permanent and indisputable record of all payments and the requirement to pay through the FRS shall be made clear in EVERY child support order, whether the order is administrative or filed through a court.

#After the paying parent is served with an order of support or a support order is signed by a county-level court judge, non-custodial parents have financial liability for cost of process service when an enforcement officer determines the paying parent has been avoiding service of process.

#Custodial parents have the right to have administrative and/or court orders established for the support of children under age 23 during periods of post-secondary education.

#There is the right to have _**all**_ employers comply with child support wage-withholding requirements. Employers are required to begin and continue compliance with wage-withholding within 20 days of receiving a wage-withnolding notice. Employers which fail to comply shall be fined $250 for each violation and shall be subject to having funds seized from their financial accounts for both the fines and the unpaid child support (subject to the results of any due process appeals requested). Employers which pay any worker "off the books" to avoid having to comply with wage-withholding requirements are considered in violation and their fines shall be doubled.

#There is the right to have **all** employers comply with the mandatory Federal New Hire Reporting system, through which employers must electronically report all new hires within 24 hours (one business day) of each new employee formally accepting a job offer (whether in writing, in person, by phone or via electronic media). Employers which fail to comply are subject to a $1,000 fine for each violation; employers which pay workers "off the books" to avoid reporting are considered in violation and their fines shall be doubled.

#**All commercial trade is suspended** between all entities in the U.S.A. and all entities of all foreign nations the governments of which have not signed **and** complied with reciprocal treaties promising to honor all lawful child support enforcement orders created through government administrative agencies and/or government courts of each treaty signatory. Those trade suspensions shall be lifted country by country once each country has signed the reciprocal treaty with the U.S.A. and had begun complying with all treaty provisions, as certified by the U.S. Secretary of Health and Human Services.

XLV. *RIGHT TO FACILITATION OF PARENTING PLAN WITH DETAILED SPECIFIED VISITATION RIGHTS*

Recognizing that non-custodial parents who have regular visitation are more likely to co-operate with the financial support of their children, there shall be established within nine months after ratification a Federal system for administratively-determined Parenting Plans administered through administrative law judges in each county of each state. The parents of each child shall have a right for an administrative law judge to set forth specific rights to weekly visitation and visitation during holidays and school break periods, unless an administrative law judge determines visitation is inappropriate due to a non-custodial parent's personal circumstances, including (but not limited to) substance abuse, psychological and/or psychiatric disorders, records of criminal law violations, abusive behaviors and lack of a suitable residence. Non-custodial parents have the right to appeal administrative law judges' determinations to the county-level trial court in the county of the child's primary residence. Non-custodial parents are responsible for transportation costs associated with visitation when the non-custodial parent chooses to reside in a county which is different from the child's primary residence. Otherwise, such transportation costs shall be shared equally between the two parents. The non-custodial parent's share of costs associated with visitation is collectable through the Federal child support enforcement system if the custodial parent alleges non-payment.

XLVI. _RIGHT TO SIMPLE MAJORITY APPROVALS FOR REVENUE INCREASES_

Recognizing that adequate funding of government is crucial to providing essential government services, it is now unconstitutional to require more than a majority of voters (50 percent plus one vote) to approve any increases in taxes at all levels of government nationwide.

XLVII. _RIGHT TO GOVERNMENT WITHOUT GRIDLOCK_

Recognizing that government gridlock often prevents passage of crucial legislation, the U.S. Senate is permanently prohibited from requiring the votes of more than 55 percent of senators to cut off filibusters and is permanently required to allow filibusters only when senators participate in filibusters **in person** on the floor of the Senate; likewise the U.S. Senate is permanently prohibited from allowing a single senator to block any Executive Branch nomination or other action.

XLVIII. _RIGHT TO PROTECTION FOR NATIONAL PARK SERVICE-ADMINISTERED LANDS, WILDERNESS AREAS, NATIONAL MONUMENTS, NATIONAL RECREATIONAL AREAS, NATIONAL WILDLIFE REFUGES, NATIONAL FORESTS, ETC._

Resource extraction projects – including, but not limited to, oil, natural gas, precious metals, etc. – within 60 miles of any U.S. National Park Service facility and/or Federal wilderness area and/or Federal national monument and/or Federal wildlife refuge area are permanently banned prospectively; existing such projects shall be permanently closed no later than one year after this Second Bill of Rights takes effect. In addition, National Monuments and National Parks created through Executive Branch actions shall require a ¾-majority vote of both chambers of Congress to override those designations. The Congress shall have only a three-month period during which to override such designations; once that three-month period has passed, the designations are permanent and cannot be overridden, ever.

XLIX. _RIGHT TO PURSUE AND COLLECT CIVIL CLAIMS FOR DAMAGES AGAINST GOVERNMENT AT ALL LEVELS; BANNING ALL REMAINING VESTIGES OF THE LEGAL DOCTRINE OF REX NON POTEST PECCARE (THE KING CAN DO NO WRONG)_

There is an absolute right to submit civil claims for damages and to recover such claims for damages through due process actions against all levels of government throughout the U.S.A., including the Federal government. All remaining vestiges of the legal doctrine of "_rex non potest peccare_" (the king can do no wrong), also known as sovereign immunity, are forever considered null and void. In fact, all civil claims previously denied by any court in the U.S.A. under that doctrine for which the Statute of Limitations has not expired, may be filed or re-filed against all levels of governments. The principle in law that any level of government must give its consent to be sued on issues of liability under the doctrine of sovereign immunity is forever considered null and void. Surviving justices and judges who in the past voted to uphold that archaic legal doctrine are required within 30 days of ratification to issue formal apologies to plaintiffs whose claims were denied as the result of such actions by those officers of the court. Their apologies shall acknowledge that the archaic legal doctrine they voted to uphold is an un-American vestige of historical monarchies which never should have held sway since the success of the American Revolution, a doctrine designed to allow governments at all levels to avoid responsibility for incompetence, negligence, intentional wrongdoing and unwillingness to properly fund government oversight activity through increases in tax revenues, especially tax revenues against the wealthy. Officers of the court formally alleged to have failed to comply with that obligation to apologize are subject to Class D Federal felony charges.

L. *NATIVE AMERICANS' AND AFRICAN-AMERICANS' RIGHT TO REPARATIONS*

Recognizing that all Native American tribes suffered inestimable losses of their inalienable rights to life, liberty and pursuit of happiness, as well as inestimable losses of property rights, during centuries of forced colonization with multiple deadly assaults and massacres of non-combatant men, women, children and the elderly by the armed forces of the United States of America – including an 1862 mass execution in Mankato, Minnesota ordered by none other than President Lincoln – each and every Native American who was born in the U.S.A., who still resides in the U.S.A., who can prove at least ½-blood Native American ancestry and who is at least 18 years old at the time of ratification shall receive a one-time reparations payment from the U.S. Treasury of $1 million within 120 days after ratification. Likewise, there shall be $1 million reparations payments set aside for each African-American who had been enslaved at any time during the Civil War. Those reparations payments shall be made to the surviving descendants who provide documentation proving they are, in fact, descended from at least one person who was a slave during the Civil War. The first descendant to make such a successfully-documented claim for each such slave ancestor shall be paid the $1 million for that ancestor, with the condition that the $1 million be paid into each claimant's account with the newly-created Federal Slave Descendants' Trust Administration pending claims from other possible descendant claimants (for the same enslaved person) whose claims, if approved, would result in proportional shares of each original claimant's $1 million. Those additional claimants shall have one year to submit their documentation of ancestry to the Federal Slave Descendants' Trust Administrator (appointed by the President with consent of the U.S. Senate). At the end of that year, the administrator shall have 120 days to determine the validity of claimants' claims on those reparations payments and to disburse proportional payments among claimants of each slave's descendants (claimants may make multiple claims if more than one ancestor was enslaved). The costs of all those reparations payments shall be funded through a 5 percent Federal transactions tax on all stock purchases. That transactions tax shall expire once the costs of all reparations payments are recovered, unless a simple majority of each chamber of Congress approves its extension. Those reparations payments are permanently exempt from taxation by Federal, state and local governments.

Candidates' Contract of Support *for* the Un-Screwing of America Second Bill of Rights (USA-SBR) in Exchange for Support *by* USA-SBR Advocates

The undersigned promises to use all opportunities to advocate for and to vote for passage of the amendment of the U.S. Constitution known as the Un-Screwing of America Second Bill of Rights (USA-SBR). Likewise, the undersigned promises to actively advocate for ratification of that constitutional amendment once it is passed by the U.S. Congress. In exchange for that active support of the USA-SBR, the undersigned shall receive advocacy and votes of other USA-SBR backers during any campaign for elected office. If the undersigned breaks this promise of advocacy and support for the USA-SBR, then supporters of the USA-SBR shall campaign against and advocate against the promise-breaker.

Signed on this _____ day of _____, 2_____,

_____
Signature
State of _____
County of _____

The foregoing instrument was acknowledged before me this _____day of _____,
2_____, at
_____(city), _____(state), by _____ to be his/her voluntary act and deed.

_____
Signature of Notary Public

_____
Printed Name of Notary Public   SEAL

Notary Public, State of _____
My commission expires: _____

www.ingramcontent.com/pod-product-compliance
Lightning Source LLC
Chambersburg PA
CBHW030837030726
47495CB00005B/1257